KU-081-669

WITCHSIGN

DEN
PATRICK

HARPER
Voyager

Newport Community Learning & Libraries	
X060575	
PETERS	06-Sep-2018
JF	£12.99

Harper*Voyager*
An imprint of
HarperCollins*Publishers* Ltd
1 London Bridge Street
London SE1 9GF

www.harpercollins.co.uk

First published by HarperCollins*Publishers* 2018
1

Copyright © Den Patrick 2018
Map copyright © Nicolette Caven

Den Patrick asserts the moral right to
be identified as the author of this work

A catalogue record for this book is available from the British Library

ISBN: 978-0-00-822813-2 (HB)
ISBN: 978-0-00-822814-9 (TPB)

This novel is entirely a work of fiction.
The names, characters and incidents portrayed in it are
the work of the author's imagination. Any resemblance to
actual persons, living or dead, events or localities is
entirely coincidental.

Set in Meridien by Palimpsest Book Production Ltd, Falkirk, Stirlingshire

Printed and bound in the UK by CPI Group (UK) Ltd, Croydon CR0 4YY

All rights reserved. No part of this publication may be
reproduced, stored in a retrieval system, or transmitted,
in any form or by any means, electronic, mechanical,
photocopying, recording or otherwise, without the prior
permission of the publishers.

MIX
Paper from
responsible sources
FSC
www.fsc.org
FSC™ C007454

This book is produced from independently certified FSC™ paper
to ensure responsible forest management.

For more information visit: www.harpercollins.co.uk/green

For Kevin

THE CONTINENT OF
VINTERKVELD

CHAPTER ONE

Steiner

The Holy Synod has done much in the last decade to expunge all mention of the goddesses Frøya and Frejna. We have had less success in the Scorched Republics, whose people still hold affection for the old ways. It is the Synod's hope that veneration of these goddesses passes into history as our grip tightens on Vinterkveld.

— From the field notes of Hierarch Khigir,
Vigilant of the Imperial Synod.

The furnace burned bright in the darkness. The old timbers of the smithy were edged in orange light, tools hung from iron hooks, gleaming. Steiner loved it here, the smell of hot metal and coal dust, the pleasant ache of muscles hardened from work, jobs in need of doing and jobs well done. The product of his labour lined the walls: small knives; pots and pans; hammers; scythes and the odd sickle.

The anvil chimed as Steiner brought the hammer down on the white-hot metal. Sweat dampened his brow and ran down his back with each breath. A deep contentment settled upon him; something was being made, something was being created.

'That's enough of that,' said his father. 'Looks like you're making a sword. And you know how the Empire feels about that.'

Steiner grinned. 'Could I at least finish it? I'll melt it down afterwards.'

Marek allowed himself a smile, caught up in Steiner's enthusiasm. 'A sword does a strange thing to a man's mind—'

'Being beaten over the head with one thing is much like another, I reckon.' Steiner shrugged and gave a chuckle.

'I mean wielding a sword, you oaf.' Marek returned Steiner's chuckle with one of his own. 'It makes a man think he has some destiny or privilege.' Marek's tone made it clear exactly how he felt about the latter.

'Not much destiny or privilege in Cinderfell,' said Steiner, feeling the joy of creation grow cold despite the searing heat of the smithy.

'No, there isn't. It's why I moved here.' Marek rolled his heavy shoulders and rubbed one scarred forearm with an equally scarred hand. 'Come on, we're done for the day.'

They stepped out beneath overcast skies. Every day was overcast in Cinderfell. The Empire said it was a legacy of the war with the dragons, that the terrible creatures had scorched the skies above the continent for decades to come.

'Must it always be so grey?' muttered Steiner, as the wind chilled the sweat on his skin.

'It's not like this in the south,' said Marek. 'They can see the sun in Shanisrond.'

Steiner gave an incredulous snort. 'Next you'll be telling me the dragons still live.'

Marek shook his head. 'No, the Empire saw to that. And you know that when the Empire take an interest in something—'

'It usually ends up dead.' Steiner ran a hand over his jaw, the feel of stubble beneath his callused fingers still a novelty. The downy fuzz of his early teens had given way to something

rougher. 'So why don't we buy a cart, pack up, and head off
to Shanisrond?'

Steiner followed Marek's gaze as he looked over the town
and the cottages that nestled against the steep incline rising
up from the coast. The small windows bore heavy wooden
shutters stained with salt, and verdant moss clung to thatched
rooftops. The dour atmosphere was well matched by the cruel
temperature.

'Not much of a home, is it,' admitted Marek.

'So why stay?'

Steiner regretted the question as soon as he saw the pained
expression cross his father's face. For a moment they stood
in silence beneath the flat grey sky. Marek lifted his eyes to
the sea and Steiner wasn't sure if he was searching or pleading
with the choppy waves that danced against the stone pier.

'You still hope she'll come back.'

Marek nodded, opened his mouth to speak, then decided
against it and headed back into the smithy.

'Did you sell the sickle we made last week?' asked Steiner,
keen to change the subject from an absent mother, an
absent wife.

Marek nodded but said nothing. Steiner was well used to
his father's silences.

'Strange time of year to harvest herbs. Who bought it?'

'One of the fishermen.' Marek cleared his throat. 'I don't
remember now.'

Steiner frowned and pulled off his thick leather gloves. In
a town this small they knew every customer by name. The
sale of a sickle was no small matter and would bring some
much needed coin. He opened his mouth to press for an
answer but the latch on the door rattled and his father nodded
towards it.

'I wondered where Kjell had got to,' said Marek.

The door to the smithy creaked as Kjellrunn pushed the

heavy wood aside. She stepped forward into the furnace's glow. Small for her age, she looked closer to twelve than her sixteen years. Her tunic was overlong, reaching her knees, while her britches were patched many times; Steiner's hand-me-downs. All their coin was spent on food and supplies for the smithy; money for clothes was scarce.

'Would it kill you to pull a brush through your hair before you go to school?' said their father with a slow smile.

'She does a fine impression of a rusalka,' said Steiner, noting the driftwood and black feathers she clutched; treasures from the beach no doubt.

'You said you don't believe in the old tales,' replied Kjellrunn.

Steiner shrugged. 'That may be, but I'm still halfway convinced you're one of them.'

'There are worse things than rusalka,' replied Kjellrunn. 'A ship has just arrived in the bay.'

'We were out there not more than a minute ago,' replied Steiner.

'See for yourself if you think I'm a liar,' she replied, jutting her chin with an obstinate look in her eye.

'I'd rather start preparing dinner if it's all the same to you,' said their father. He looked away, unwilling to meet their eyes. 'A ship in the bay means the Empire.'

'And that means a troika of Vigilants,' said Steiner, feeling the familiar fear the Holy Synod evoked.

'Perhaps not.' Kjell eyed both of them. 'Not this time. You'll want to see this.'

'Did Uncle Verner bet you could lure us down to the bay?' Steiner asked as they followed the rutted track that led to the coastal road.

'I haven't seen him in days,' replied Kjellrunn, her eyes fixed on the blue-grey swell of the sea. Something between mist and rain dampened their spirits even as curiosity kindled inside them.

'There it is,' said Marek, pointing a finger. The bay rarely saw anything larger than fishing boats; no one put in at Cinderfell to trade. Only when the Sommerende Ocean sent vicious storms did captains seek the safe haven of the drab town.

'A ship,' said Steiner. 'A frigate, I reckon. Though why you'd care to paint it red is anyone's guess.'

'You reckon right,' said their father. 'It's a frigate, but not like I've seen before.'

They continued to walk down to the bay, past cottages arranged in curving rows, down the narrow cobbled road that wended its way to the shore. The Spøkelsea rushed over the shingle beach in a hushed roar, leaving trails of foam and seaweed as the water retreated once again. Steiner studied the sleek ship as it lay at anchor, sails stowed like folded wings. The sailors aboard were ant-sized at this distance and just as busy. The whole vessel was dark red from prow to stern while the figurehead jutted from the front in forbidding black, wings outstretched along the hull.

'What is that? muttered Steiner.

'It's a crow,' replied Kjellrunn. 'After Se or Venter, I expect.'

Steiner frowned. 'More of your folk tales, I suppose?'

'Se and Venter belong to Frejna, they're her crows.'

'It's not an Imperial ship then,' said Marek.

'You know how they feel about the old gods,' added Steiner.

'Goddess. Not god. Frejna is a *goddess*.' Kjellrunn rolled her eyes. 'Of winter, wisdom and death.'

Other families had appeared at the doorways of cottages or emerged from the few shops to see the dark red ship. Parents held their children close and anxious glances were traded.

'All the Imperial ships are in the south,' said Marek, 'harassing Shanisrond or escorting cargo ships up the Ashen Gulf.'

'Perhaps they're pirates,' said Steiner with a smile, nudging his sister.

Kjellrunn looked over the town and wrinkled her nose. 'How much do you think they'd give me for a half-trained, half-wit blacksmith?'

'Just because I can't read doesn't make me a half-wit,' said Steiner through gritted teeth.

'If they are pirates they're not trying very hard,' said Marek. 'Perhaps they stopped in for repairs,' he added, before turning to walk back up the hill.

'What do you think it is?' Steiner called after him. The frigate's arrival would be the talk of the town for weeks to come.

'I don't know.' Marek frowned and cleared his throat, as if it troubled him. Kjellrunn stopped and looked over her shoulder. There was a faraway look in her eye, as if she could see something Steiner could not. It was the same look she had after she'd been in the woods, or when she spoke of folk tales.

'No good will come of it,' she said, 'whatever it is.' Her words were as cold and grey as the skies overhead. Steiner struggled to suppress a shiver as she turned her eyes on him. There was something not right in his sister, nothing he could put a name to, yet he feared they would find out what it was all too soon.

'Hoy there, Steiner.' Kristofine stood outside the tavern's doorway with a playful smile, arms folded across her chest. She was of a similar age to the blacksmith's son, always top of the class and always polite to her teachers, though their school days had ended two years previously.

The meagre daylight had dimmed and a stillness had descended on the bay, as if the four winds themselves held their breath in anticipation.

'Hoy there,' said Steiner. 'Working tonight?'

'And every night, my curse for having a father who owns a tavern.'

'Is my uncle here?'

Kristofine nodded. 'Was it only your uncle who you came to see?'

Steiner shrugged. 'Well, you never know who you might run into at a place like this.'

They smiled at each other and Steiner wondered what to say next. Kristofine watched him for a moment and looked away.

'What's got you hanging around the doorstep on a cold night like this?'

Kristofine nodded to the bay, where the ship's lanterns looked like stars fallen to the sea. 'Our new friend there, not that you can really see it now.'

'What news?' asked Steiner.

'The worst kind,' she replied. 'It seems the ship brought a score of soldiers ashore. They're staying at the Smouldering Standard, booked out every room.'

'Imperial soldiers?'

'It has to be the Synod,' said Kristofine. 'Though they're late this year.'

'An Invigilation then?' said Steiner, thinking of Kjellrunn. This would be the last year she'd have to face it, but the fact offered small comfort. 'You going to let me in before I die of cold?' he asked, forcing a smile.

'Maybe I'll charge you a kiss to step over the threshold.' She cocked her head to one side and Steiner wondered at this new-found playfulness. He'd be lying if he said he hadn't noticed her. Everyone in Cinderfell had noticed Kristofine.

'A kiss is about all I've got,' he replied.

'Then how will you pay for the beer?'

Steiner rattled the coins in his pocket. 'Maybe I have more than just kisses.'

Kristofine pushed back against the door and Steiner felt the faint sting of disappointment as he realized there'd be no kiss after all.

The tavern was full of old salts, fresh-faced youngsters and all ages in between. Bright lanterns hung from the beams and the smells of stale beer and pipe smoke teased Steiner's senses, not unkindly.

'He's over here,' said Kristofine, beckoning to him. They emerged through a knot of fishermen to find his Uncle Verner sitting alone in a corner, away from the hustle of the main bar.

'Hoy there, young Steiner!' Verner had his boots up on the table and was cleaning his nails with a short knife. He was a blond man with a face lined deep by wind and rain, and he wore his beard short, unlike many of the Cinderfell men.

'The wanderer returns,' replied Steiner.

'You going to sit down or fall down? You look shattered. Isn't Marek feeding you?'

'Money is tight, there's not much food. You know how it is.'

Verner rose from his seat and caught him in a rough embrace. 'Kristofine, a beer for my nephew and a bowl of stew with some bread to go with it. We need to get some meat on these bones.'

Kristofine paused to look Steiner over. 'That we do.' She slipped away through the crowd, Steiner's eyes searching for her even as she was lost from view.

'Frøya's tits!' said Verner. 'I'm out of town for a week and you're all but courting Kristofine there. Not that I blame you.'

'Keep your voice down. We're *not* courting,' said Steiner. He leaned in closer. 'We've missed you, I've missed you. Where have you been?'

'Ah, it was nothing.' Verner took a sip from his tankard. 'Nothing important. I just took some smoked fish to market in Helwick.'

'Helwick? The local market not good enough for you any more?'

Verner smiled but said nothing. The chance to ask further questions slipped away as Kristofine arrived at the table with a battered wooden tray bearing equally battered tankards.

'Thanks,' said Steiner.

'Your stew will be over shortly.' And then she was gone again.

'You look like you've all the world on your shoulders,' said Verner.

'Just worried about Kjellrunn is all. There'll be an Invigilation any day now. I know she doesn't have any of the arcane about her, but the way she talks about goddesses and portents . . . It makes people uneasy.' Steiner stared into his tankard. 'It makes me uneasy.'

'Be nice if they could let us alone for just one year,' said Verner, voice close to a growl. 'It's not as if Nordvlast is part of the Empire, is it?'

'And when has that stopped them?'

The Synod scoured every town and village on the continent of Vinterkveld, and even the neighbouring Scorched Republics were not spared: Svingettevei, Vannerånd, Drakefjord and Nordvlast all acquiesced, yet all resented surrendering their children to the belligerent Empire.

'Why do we let them come here?' said Steiner. 'Why do we let them take our children year after year? Couldn't we stand up to them? I've asked Marek but he refuses to speak of it. I'm a man now, don't I deserve a few straight answers?'

'Straight answers, is it?' said Verner. 'The Scorched Republics may not be part of the Empire, but this is the price they pay so the Empire remains on their side of the border. None of the Scorched Republics would last longer than a month or two if the Empire invaded.'

They sipped their pints and stared at the dancing flames of the hearth, each imagining the terror of war and sack of every

town and farmstead. Steiner's thoughts found their way back
to Kjellrunn.

'She's so . . . strange, with her driftwood charms and crow
feathers. I think she looks like a witch, and I'm her own kin.'

'Her own kin might want to keep his voice down when
using the word "witch".'

'Sorry.' Steiner glanced about the room but the many fishermen and townsfolk were intent on their own conversations.

'It will turn out fine,' said Verner, and Steiner wanted to
believe him.

'We've not had witchsign here for two decades,' said Steiner,
but even as he said the words he thought of Kjellrunn, the
tousle-haired girl with a faraway look in her eye. He thought
of how subdued she'd been watching the red ship in the bay.
The dire feeling she'd fail the Synod's inspection plucked at
him like icy fingers. The Vigilant would sniff around her,
declare her corrupted by the power of dragons, and they'd
never see her again.

'It's the same every year,' said Verner. 'Cinderfell is the last
stop on the Synod's route to Vladibogdan'.

'Vladibogdan?' Steiner frowned. 'Where is Vladibogdan?'

'Ah, Frejna.' Verner squeezed his eyes shut, then released
a sigh. 'Keep it to yourself. I know you will.' He leaned in
closer and looked over his shoulder to check none of the
fishermen were listening.

'The island of Vladibogdan lies twenty miles off the coast
of Nordvlast, to the north-west.'

'I've never heard of it.' Steiner leaned closer, his voice a
whisper.

'Of course you haven't. It's the largest of the Nordscale
islands and the Solmindre Empire's dirty secret. It's where
they take children with witchsign for cleansing.' Verner's face
creased with torment and Steiner thought he saw the glimmer
of tears at the corners of his uncle's eyes.

Steiner didn't need to ask what cleansing entailed. Witchsign wasn't tolerated in Vinterkveld, and those with witchsign were expunged, though none truly knew how. Some said fire, some said beheading.

'How is it you know of this mystery island then?' whispered Steiner.

'I'm a fisherman.' Verner didn't meet his eyes. 'Sometimes we go out to sea further than we intend.'

'Twenty miles out?'

Verner forced a grin. 'Perhaps I used to raid Imperial vessels. Perhaps I used to be a pirate?' He downed the last of his beer and stood up, fetching his coat.

'And they take the children to Vladibogdan?' asked Steiner, keen to know more, but Verner held a finger up to his lips. 'I have business elsewhere.'

'At this time of night?'

'Aye, no rest for the wicked and all that. Keep your sister safe. I'll see you tomorrow.' The blond man crossed the room, exchanging handshakes and slapping shoulders in farewell as he left.

'You look as if you lost an axe and found a knife,' said Kristofine.

'I'm not sure I even found the knife to be honest.'

Kristofine set down two bowls of stew and a plate of bread, then to Steiner's surprise sat down and began to eat.'

'I don't have long,' she said, 'but I'm famished and you looked like you needed a dining companion.'

Steiner laughed. 'Dining companion? You make me sound like a merchant.'

'You're a blacksmith, aren't you?'

Steiner smiled and began to eat. 'What's got into Verner tonight? He's not himself.'

'Worried for Kjellrunn, I expect,' replied Kristofine. 'They're close, aren't they?'

'She's always pressing him for stories of Frøya and Frejna, mysterious crows and the old wars. Children's tales really. You wouldn't guess she's sixteen summers.'

'No, you wouldn't,' agreed Kristofine. 'You keep a close eye on her while that ship is in the bay, won't you?'

Steiner nodded, struck by the seriousness of Kristofine's tone.

'Anyway, I didn't come here to talk about your sister.'

'What did you come here to talk about then?' replied Steiner, feeling out of his depth and not knowing in which direction to swim.

'You don't speak to many girls, do you?' said Kristofine.

'I don't speak to many people. Mainly just hammer metal on an anvil.'

'Maybe another mead will loosen your tongue.'

Steiner watched the woman cross the tavern as excitement and confusion vied for the upper hand. It had been a curious day; it looked to be a curious night.

CHAPTER TWO

Kjellrunn

The compact made between the Solmindre Empire and the Scorched Republics allows a member of the Synod to enter all dwellings across Vinterkveld in order to carry out an Invigilation. Taking children from their parents is no small matter but the children are dangerous. The threat of open rebellion weighs heavily during times such as these and a Vigilant should take as many soldiers as they can gather. You must meet resistance with intimidation, and match violence with brutality.

– From the field notes of Hierarch Khigir,
Vigilant of the Imperial Synod.

Kjellrunn hated the kitchen. The ceiling was too low, the chimney never seemed to spirit away the smoke as best it could, and the table at the centre was too large. She had spent a lifetime shuffling and side-stepping around the vast slab of timber. Such a large table and rarely anything good to eat, a bitter irony. She belonged in the forest and lived only for the summer months when she could wander through the trees for hours, alone and at peace.

Steiner served a dollop of porridge into a bowl from a

wooden spoon. He hummed quietly as he circled the table, serving more porridge into his bowl, then sat down and began to eat, barely noticing her. Marek was already in the smithy, tinkering with some half-finished project.

'Why are you smiling?' said Kjellrunn, her porridge untouched. 'You never smile.'

Steiner looked up, spoon halfway to his mouth, eyebrows raised in surprise. 'What?'

'And you're humming. You hate music.'

'I don't hate music, I just can't sing. You have the greater share of that talent, always singing folk songs and laments and Frøya knows what else.'

'You hate music,' said Kjellrunn once more, hearing how petty she sounded. Steiner shrugged and continued his repast.

They sat in silence for a moment and Kjellrunn began to eat.

'No singing today, Kjell,' said Steiner. 'There's Imperial soldiers in town, perhaps a Vigilant too. You know how they feel about the old gods—'

'*Goddesses.*'

'Fine, goddesses.' Steiner rolled his eyes. 'Just keep your songs for the forest, eh? And pull a comb through that briar patch you call hair. You look like a vagrant.'

Kjellrunn showed him the back of her hand, raising four fingers to him, one each for water, fire, earth and wind. In older times it had meant good luck, but these days it insinuated something else entirely.

'And don't let anyone catch you flipping the four powers in the street. The soldiers will hack your fingers off to teach you a lesson.'

Kjellrunn stood up, feeling as restless as the ocean, her pique like jagged snarls of lightning.

'Why are you so happy today, with all these soldiers here and a Vigilant too? What cause have you to be happy when you've a witch for a sister?'

Steiner dropped his spoon and his eyes went very wide. The fragile autumn light leeched the colour from his face.

'Kjell . . .'

'I'm sorry.' Her voice was so low she could barely hear herself over the crackling fire in the hearth. 'I didn't mean it. Of course I'm not a witch.'

Steiner rubbed his forehead a moment, picked up his spoon and then put it down again, his appetite fled.

'I *was* in a good mood because Kristofine and I started talking last night and, well, it was nice. I don't know if she likes me or what I'm supposed to do, but it was . . .' He floundered for the word, then shrugged. 'Well, it was nice. And there's precious little of that in Cinderfell.'

'Oh,' was all Kjellrunn could manage in the cavernous silence that followed. The kitchen suddenly felt very large.

'Father needs me,' said Steiner, not meeting her eyes as he stood. A moment later he was gone.

The dishes didn't take long but sweeping the kitchen was always a chore on account of the huge table. Kjellrunn put off leaving the cottage for as long as she could but the shops would only stay open for so long. She entered the smithy with downcast eyes. She disliked the smithy more than the kitchen, all darkness and fire; the smell of ashes and sweat.

'I need money for food,' was all she said as Marek looked up from his work. Steiner was filing off a sickle blade, pausing only to spare her a brief glance. She imagined she saw annoyance in the set of his brow. He turned away and continued his work.

'Business has been slow and I've not got the coin for meat,' said Marek. 'Unless it's cheap.'

Kjellrunn nodded and noted just how few coins he'd given her.

'Sorry,' he said, and Kjellrunn felt his shame in the single word. Not enough money to feed his children right, that was hard to take for a man like Marek.

'I'd best go with her,' said Steiner quietly. 'What with the Empire and all.'

Marek opened his mouth to object but said nothing and nodded before turning back to his work.

They had no sooner slipped through a gap in the double doors to the smithy when Kjellrunn spoke first.

'I'm sorry about this morning. You do smile, of course you do. I'm just not myself today is all.'

Steiner put an arm around her shoulders and squeezed her close, pressing his face into her tangled hair to kiss her on the crown.

'Of course you're yourself today. Who else would you be?'

'That's not what I meant.'

'You're difficult and sullen and uncombed and lovely and my sister. That's the only Kjell I'm ever going to know, I reckon.'

Kjellrunn smiled before she could stop herself. 'You say I'm "difficult and sullen" when I apologize to you?'

'What would you prefer?' said Steiner, his arm now performing more of a headlock than a hug.

'I'd prefer you to get off me, you great oaf. I may need to comb my hair but you need to wash.'

Brother and sister picked their way along the cobbled streets, past the winding rows of squat cottages and the few townsfolk brave enough to set foot outside.

'Quiet today,' said Steiner. 'People are staying out of sight what with the soldiers here.'

'Maybe you should go into town alone,' replied Kjellrunn, mouth dry and a terrible feeling like seasickness rising in her gut.

'We can't let them push us around, Kjell. This is Nordvlast, the power of the north! Not very powerful if we can't even buy food in our own town.'

'It's not the soldiers I'm scared of, it's the Vigilants.'

'If you've not got the witchsign you've nothing to fear,' replied Steiner, but Kjellrunn had heard it a hundred times before. It was one of those mindless platitudes so popular with the dull and uninteresting people of Cinderfell.

Steiner slowed down and Kjellrunn felt his gaze on her, a glance from the side of his eye.

'What you said this morning—'

'I was angry. Of course I'm not a witch. I'm not scared of the Vigilants because I'm a witch, I'm scared of them because they're decrepit old men. Men like that usually only have a couple of uses for a girl my age.'

Steiner winced. She knew only too well he thought of her much as he'd done when she was ten or eleven. Her body hadn't begun to make the changes most sixteen-year-old girls took for granted; she felt frozen somehow, trapped in her girlhood.

'Why don't you go on in to Håkon's and see if you can buy us some lamb neck or beef shin?' Steiner shrugged. 'I don't know, something cheap.' He pushed a few coins into her hand and pressed a finger to his lips so she wouldn't tell Marek.

The shop was a single room, lined on three sides with dark wooden tables. Small panes of cloudy, uneven glass sat in a wooden lattice at the front, allowing dreary light to wash over the meat. Two lanterns at the rear of the store held back the gloom.

Kjellrunn told the butcher what she was after and endured the sour look she received. Håkon was a slab of a man, bald and compensating with a beard long enough to house hibernating animals. His eyes were small, overshadowed by a heavy brow that gave him a permanent frown.

Håkon named his price and Kjellrunn stopped a moment and regarded the selection of coins in her hand. The words were out of her mouth before she'd even thought to answer.

'I've bought beef shin from you before and it never cost so much.'

Håkon shrugged and wiped a greasy hand down the front of his apron, then folded his arms.

'Could you not the lower the price just a small amount?'

'Yours isn't the only family that needs to eat,' said the butcher.

'What's keeping you so long, Kjell?' Steiner had slipped into the butcher's; despite his size he was quiet on his feet and often caught Kjellrunn unawares.

'I . . .' Kjellrunn glanced from Steiner to the butcher and down to the coins in her hand.

'Some issue with the price, is there?' said Steiner, a note of warning in his voice.

'This your wife, is it?' said Håkon.

'She, not it,' said Steiner, 'and *she* is my sister.'

Håkon pulled on a grin as greasy as the apron he wore and held up his hands. 'Why didn't you say, little one?'

Kjellrunn looked at Steiner and sighed. 'You know exactly who I am,' she said. 'And you always find a way to make things difficult.'

'Is that so?' said Steiner, his eyes fixed on the butcher, sharp and hard as flints.

'I'm just gaming with the girl is all,' said Håkon. 'You know these young ones, they can't take a joke.'

'Maybe we'll have some jokes next time you come to the smithy to buy new knives,' said Kjellrunn. She took the bundle from the counter and slammed down a few coins, before taking her leave of the dingy shop.

'I meant no harm,' said Håkon.

'I'm sure,' replied Steiner in a tone that said anything but.

The butcher's expression hardened and his eyes settled on Kjellrunn, now waiting in the street outside.

'You watch yourself, Steiner.' Håkon leaned across the

counter, his voice rough and low. 'She's not right, always sneaking off to the woods and gathering herbs and mushrooms and crow feathers. Sister or no, she's not right.'

Kjellrunn heard all of this and stood in street, rigid with fear. Her eyes darted to the townsfolk nearby to see if they'd heard the outburst, but none met her eye, scurrying away, keen to avoid any trouble. Steiner emerged a few seconds later, red-faced, jaw clenched in fury and hands closed into fists.

'I'm sorry,' said Kjellrunn in small voice.

'You did nothing wrong, Kjell,' replied Steiner, though she had the awful feeling he didn't really mean it.

'He's always the same, always making things awkward.'

Steiner gave a curt nod but didn't speak. They marched down the street and Kjellrunn struggled to keep up, almost slipping in the grey slush that coated the cobbles.

'There's Kristofine,' she said, pointing ahead to where the tavern-keeper's daughter stood outside the baker's, chatting with another woman.

Steiner looked up and his eyes widened. 'Who is that?'

The woman Kristofine was talking to was unlike anyone Kjellrunn had seen before, and the wry smile she wore was evidence she knew it. All of Cinderfell were acquainted with the occasional sailor from Shanisrond, but there was something truly different about the stranger, not simply the tone of her skin. She was lighter than the dark-skinned sailors of Dos Fesh, and the cast of her eyes marked her as a descendant of Dos Kara; the hair that hung to her waist was raven black. Kjellrunn found it impossible to guess her age. She wore a deerskin jerkin with matching knee-length boots and her shirt sleeves were rolled back to the elbow, revealing wrists encircled by copper hoops, bright with verdigris, bangles of shining jet and polished ivory. A sabre hung from one hip and the scars on her forearms proved it wasn't for show.

'Hoy there,' said Steiner, a touch of uncertainty in his tone.

Kristofine grinned and the woman beside her rolled her eyes.

'I don't bite. I was just asking your friend here if there's a room I can take for the night.'

'Ignore my brother,' said Kjellrunn. 'Unusual women make him nervous.' Kristofine and the stranger burst out laughing and Kjellrunn found herself laughing along with them. Steiner scratched the back of his head.

'I was just surprised to see Kristofine is all,' he replied and looked away.

'How are you, Kjell?' asked Kristofine. 'Been to Håkon's? Make sure you wash that meat. You never know where his hands have been.'

Steiner pulled a face. 'I think I've just lost my appetite. Possibly for the whole week.'

'The man is a pig,' said Kjellrunn, 'A dirty great pig. Imagine a pig running a butcher's, how absurd.'

Steiner and Kristofine frowned at her observation, but the stranger smiled and held out her hand.

'I'm Romola. I like the way your mind works. Like a poet or a madman.'

'Uh, thanks,' replied Kjellrunn. 'I'm not sure I'm so keen on being mad.'

Romola pouted. 'In a world this strange, madness seems like a good option, right?'

Kjellrunn wasn't sure what the woman meant, but drank in every detail of her. 'Are you a pirate?' she asked.

'Kjell!' Steiner stared at his sister and glanced at Romola. 'Forgive my sister, she, uh, well . . .'

'Some days,' replied Romola.

'Some days what?' said Steiner.

'Some days I'm a pirate.' Romola turned a smile on Kristofine. 'But not today and not recently.'

I was right, mouthed Kjellrunn to Steiner, and smiled.

Steiner began to laugh and stifled it with a cough behind his hand.

'Why don't you two come to the tavern,' said Kristofine. 'I was going to show Romola around and we could have something to eat.'

Kjellrunn caught the way Kristofine looked her brother and felt some unknown feeling course through her, swirling dangerously.

'I should get back,' said Kjellrunn. 'Father will be waiting.' These last words were pointed at Steiner, but he was too busy smiling at Kristofine to notice.

'It was nice to meet you,' said Romola. 'You take care of yourself now.'

Kjellrunn nodded and stalked away, angry with Kristofine but unsure why.

'Tell Father I'll be home in a while,' Steiner called after her, but Kjellrunn pretended not to hear and bowed her head.

'Not sure I care for a half-wit brother who abandons me halfway through a trip to town,' she muttered to herself. 'And I'm not sure I care for being called mad by an ex-pirate.' A passerby on the street glanced at her and crossed to the other side. 'And I certainly don't care for the way Kristofine stares at my brother. What is going on between those two?'

Steiner didn't reappear for the rest of the afternoon and if Marek minded he didn't show it. Kjellrunn stayed up after dinner and fussed with this and that in the kitchen. Finally the latch rattled on the kitchen door and Steiner shouldered his way into the room, a little unsteady on his feet.

'Did you see a ghost on the walk home?' Kjellrunn was sitting at the table in her nightshirt, hands clasped around a mug of hot milk.

'Not a ghost, but it turns out Romola is a storyweaver as a well as a pirate. She told a story that was unsettling.'

'Which story?'

'Bittervinge and the Mama Qara.'

'That's not a scary story. Not really.'

'It depends who's telling it, I suppose,' said Steiner quietly.

'What else did she say?' Kjellrunn's eyes were bright with curiosity.

'No stories, only that Imperial soldiers are in town, and there'll be an Invigilation tomorrow.'

Kjellrunn sat up straighter in her chair, then set her eyes on her mug.

'I hate it,' was all she said.

'So did I,' replied Steiner.

She remembered being inspected by the Synod, how her palms had sweated and her stomach knotted like old rope, wondering if she would be taken away for bearing the taint of dragons.

'But this is the last time you have to do it,' said Steiner. 'You'll be fine, Kjell.'

She struggled not to tremble and said nothing.

'There's been no witchsign in Cinderfell for twenty years,' said Steiner. 'And you've always passed without a problem before. This year won't be any different.'

'I hope you're right,' she said, her mouth a bitter curve of worry.

'Kjell, is there anything, any reason . . . Do you doubt you'll pass this year? If there's anything you wanted to tell me . . .'

'Of course not!' She stood up and marched past him, climbing the stairs without a backward glance.

'Good night then,' he called after her, but there was little good about it.

CHAPTER THREE

Steiner

Though many Imperial scholars argue there is no proof linking the emergence of the arcane with our former draconic masters, the Holy Synod takes it as a matter of faith. Ours is a double poisoning; ash and smoke have tainted the sky just as young children manifest unearthly powers. How else to explain the unexplainable?

– From the field notes of Hierarch Khigir,
Vigilant of the Imperial Synod.

Steiner looked up into the skies from the porch and watched the grey snow drifting down, obscuring roof and road. It lay along lintels and windowsills, a hushed drabness for the gloomy town. The chill wind, so often a feature in Cinderfell, was absent that day.

'The snow will cover everything if it keeps up like this,' whispered Kjellrunn, joining him in the porch, a shawl wrapped about her shoulders. Her breath misted on the air and for a moment Steiner's mind wandered to Romola's tale of dragons from the previous night. 'Perhaps the Vigilants will forget we're here,' added Kjellrunn.

'Small chance of that.' Steiner forced a smile at his sister.

'Still, they might catch a cold and go home.' He knew exactly how she felt; he had stood for six Invigilations and was glad he'd not have to do so again. Each time he'd wondered if some glimmer of the arcane would see him taken by the Synod.

'Last night, you said you hoped you'd pass the Invigilation. You haven't . . .' Steiner struggled for the words.

'Started casting spells that summon the winds and make people burst into flames?' said Kjellrunn.

'I think I would have noticed that,' replied Steiner with a smile, but Kjellrunn didn't return it, looking away to the falling snow. 'You and Father are all I have. I don't know what I'd do if they took you, Kjell. I don't know what Father would do.'

'No one is going take me,' replied Kjell, but Steiner couldn't miss the way she looked off to the horizon as she said it, not meeting his eyes.

'You'll walk your sister to school today?' said Marek from the kitchen, as if Steiner would refuse.

'Of course.'

'And wait until she can come home.' Steiner couldn't miss the guarded tone in his father's voice. There would be no lessons today. There would be no teachers. It was impossible to spare a thought for anything else at times like these.

'We'd best get to it,' said Steiner, slipping an arm around Kjellrunn's shoulders.

'Wait now.' Their father's voice was soft, softer than the snow falling outside. Marek pulled a brooch from a pocket. He took a step towards Kjellrunn with a sad smile on his lips. 'This was your mother's. You should have it.'

Kjellrunn blinked, then her expression fell as she saw the brooch, styled in the shape of a sledgehammer. It had been cast in black iron; hardly the jewellery a young woman yearned for.

'Wear it today.' Marek pulled open her shawl and reached for the tunic beneath, pinning the brooch in place. 'If you get scared at the Invigilation, remember your mother.'

'But . . . but I *don't* remember my mother,' said Kjellrunn in a whisper. 'I don't remember her at all.' The pain of that absence was written across her slender face in that moment, as tears blossomed at the corners of her eyes. Steiner did not share her pain, only nursed a resentment that the woman who'd birthed him had fled to gods knew where.

'She loved you,' said their father. 'Be brave.' Marek waved them off and closed the door, leaving Kjellrunn and Steiner with the long walk ahead, surrounded by drifting grey motes of snow.

'Do you have one?' asked Kjellrunn, when they were a few streets away. Steiner was glad of the question, for the distraction. Anything was preferable to the endless din of anxiety in his mind, like a smithy consumed with work.

'No,' he replied, glancing at the hammer brooch. 'But I'd rather have the real thing anyway. I couldn't do much in the smithy with a hammer that small.' He nudged her with an elbow and was rewarded with a smile which faded as they drew closer to the bay. The menace of the red ship was not lessened by the cheerless weather. Three soldiers idled on the pier, waiting for a smaller boat that ferried indistinct figures across the water.

'That's the ship.' Kjellrunn's voice was a whisper. 'That's the ship that will take all those poor children away for cleansing.'

Every year the Synod arrived in Cinderfell with around two score of children, gathered up from across Vinterkveld. Every year those children were piled on a ship and never seen again. Cinderfell was the last stop on their unholy tour of the continent.

'Perhaps they take them to Khlystburg?' said Kjellrunn. It

was an age-old pastime, wondering where the ships took children tainted with witchsign.

'Khlystburg.' Capital of the Solmindre Empire and final destination of dissenters and traitors. 'No, they're not taken to Khlystburg,' said Steiner.

'Then where?' She eyed him and frowned. 'Do you know?'

Steiner's eyes strayed to the sea even as his thoughts turned to Vladibogdan, the mysterious island Verner had mentioned. The waters were a flat green expanse that swallowed each snowflake and Steiner reached for Kjellrunn's hand and held it tight. Together they watched parents walking their children to the Invigilation with heavy hearts. The chill in their bones had nothing to do with the weather.

'I wish Mother was here,' said Kjellrunn, her grip tightening on his hand as the words slipped free. 'I'd like to see her just once in my life.'

'Your life isn't over, Kjell. They'll not take you today. Look them in the eye when they come close, don't let them see you're afraid.'

'That's easier said than done,' grumbled Kjell.

'Don't look down at your boots, it makes them think you have something to hide. And don't sing, even to comfort yourself. Don't breathe a word about the old gods either.'

'*Goddesses*. And I'm not a fool. You really think I'd bring up Frøya and Frejna on a day like this?'

Steiner didn't answer, but watched Kjellrunn's expression darken.

'Of course not,' he replied after they'd trudged on a dozen feet. 'I'm just worried is all. There's been no witchsign in Cinderfell for decades and I don't want that to change today.'

'Nor will it,' said Kjellrunn, her hand straying to the hammer brooch Marek had given her.

Steiner considered another truth, one the fishermen spoke of when they were in dark moods and well into their cups.

Was it possible that the Vigilants had darker motives for taking the children away? Kjellrunn marched beside him, all tangled hair, built like a sparrow with a watchful cast to her eye. She was more urchin than woman, and Steiner hoped it would provide some measure of protection.

Kjellrunn scowled over her shoulder at the blood-red ship. The clouds overhead had darkened and a cold breeze carried the scent of fresh snow. 'What if I refused to go? I doubt the Vigilant will notice the absence of one child. We could go home right now.'

They'd played this game before, two children teasing at 'what if' and 'if only'. The outcome was always the same: bleak as the Cinderfell weather.

'It's their job to notice,' replied Steiner. 'They're called Vigilants and they have the school register. If you don't attend then they'll come to the house for you.'

'I'll hide in the woods all day,' she replied, daring to look pleased with herself.

'And then they'll search the whole town and the soldiers won't be gentle or shy about letting people know how much they dislike being defied.'

'I won't go!' She stopped walking and folded her arms, a scowl on her face. All traces of the Kjellrunn fascinated by Spriggani and rusalka had disappeared, only a stony-eyed blonde girl remained. Steiner looked down the slope to where the track met the coastal road. The three soldiers he'd seen on the pier were headed for the school, coming closer with every heartbeat.

'Come on,' he whispered, but Kjellrunn shook her head. 'Come on, Kjell. I never wanted to go either but . . .'

'Maybe our mother didn't leave at all,' hissed Kjellrunn. 'Maybe she was taken, taken by the same soldiers who are here today.'

'Kjell, you're just telling stories now. Come on, please.' The soldiers were coming closer, less than a stone's throw from where they argued.

'You'd hand me over to the same Empire that took our mother?'

'Kjell, you don't know that's true, Father never mentioned anything like this—'

'He's barely mentioned her at all.' Kjellrunn turned and walked into the chest of the nearest soldier with a grunt. They were all taller than her by a head and a half at least, mail gleaming in the gaps between their black enamelled armour. Their matching helms bore the red star of the Solmindre Empire while the narrow eye slots revealed nothing of the men inside. The same red star was embossed on each arm and heavy maces hung from loops at their leather belts. Their cloaks, boots and gloves were as black as tar. Steiner held his breath; he'd seen soldiers before but never this close.

'You'd best be moving on,' said the nearest soldier in heavily accented Nordspråk. 'You wouldn't want to be late now, would you?'

Steiner watched as Kjell's anger was eclipsed by the sheer size of the three men. Her head bowed, shoulders slumped with resignation.

'N-no,' was all she managed.

Cinderfell's only school had started as a lone classroom, a log cabin with a stone chimney and a thatched roof that had gone green with moss. Some said the chimney had stood since before the uprising against the dragons. Other classrooms had been added, and one had famously burned down, though not from dragon fire despite many a tall tale. The cabins were arranged around two wide squares, rebuilt in stone as the decades passed. New storeys had been added, a bell tower and then a cloister. Columns supported covered walkways inside each square, keeping the students dry from grimy rain during the wet months and free from the dirty snow during the cold ones. A fine layer of soot settled on everything during summer, adding to the misery. The lawns of the school were kept neat and a lone spruce pointed towards the overcast skies.

The children filed into the square, swapping fearful gazes as if eye contact alone might save them. Row by row they formed an anxious mass, boots crunching in the gritty slush. Steiner took up a spot by the archway, reluctant to head into the school. The snow had stopped but an unrelenting chill persisted.

'Steiner, I'm scared,' said Kjellrunn in a harsh whisper.

He nodded. 'Everyone is,' he said softly. 'Go and stand with the others. It will be over quick enough.'

Kjellrunn picked her way through the rows and found a space to stand with her classmates. None spoke to her, none offered so much as a look. She was a strangeling among the townsfolk, a curious girl with a head full of old gods and things that were no longer fashionable to speak of in Nordvlast. Soon all talk of Frøya and Frejna would be forbidden, just as it was in the Empire, and in Drakefjord, so it was said.

The soldiers entered first, their spiked maces clasped in gloved fists. The armoured men took up positions at each corner of the cloister, figures of deeper darkness on an over-cast day. Steiner felt a terrible dread settle upon him, a compulsion to look over his shoulder. Not one but two members of the Synod approached. They wore padded cream jackets that reached their knees with long sleeveless leather coats over the top. The leather was embossed with the geometric designs of the Holy Synod and dyed the colour of dried blood. Only their masks were different. The first wore a mask of polished silver with a gentle smile whereas the second had opted for an almost featureless mask, save for the frowning brow above the eye holes. Crafted from pitted bronze, the mask made the Vigilant appear like some ancient horror. The first announced himself in a voice so loud that several children flinched.

'I am Hierarch Shirinov of the Holy Synod of the Solmindre Empire, and my colleague is Hierarch Khigir.' The heavy Solska accent made each word more severe. Shirinov had the stoop of an old man and his steps were aided by a stout walking stick, yet his frailty did not extend to his voice.

'Fear not, children of Cinderfell,' said Khigir, in a deep and mournful tone. 'The pitiful Scorched Republics only produce witchsign but rarely.'

Steiner frowned. Vigilants operated in groups of three, known as Troika, when they were about the Emperor's business. That two Vigilants should visit Cinderfell was most unusual and Steiner feared some deeper problem.

'Know that I will spirit away the unclean souls bearing the taint of witchsign,' said Shirinov. 'Think of me not as a persecutor, but a cure for the sickness of draconic sorcery.' The Vigilant stopped before Kjellrunn, the smiling silver mask so close their noses almost touched.

'And what is your name, girl?'

'Kjellrunn Vartiainen,' she replied. Steiner's hands became slick with sweat. Surely it could be no accident that the Hierarch had gone straight to her? Wouldn't a brother know if his own sister had been corrupted by the taint of dragons? Rumours spoke of bodies rebelling against the strangeness: discolouring, twisting, wasting away, yet Kjellrunn remained whole. Other tales mentioned strange dreams, or being able to able to pluck thoughts from people's minds. Nothing of the sort had befallen Kjellrunn, and yet in that moment Steiner was sure she would be shipped away to Vladibogdan, never to be seen again. Steiner promised himself he'd be a better brother if Hierarch Shirinov turned away, promised himself he'd look after his sister until the end of days if she walked free from the Invigilation.

'Now,' said Shirinov, voice booming across the square. 'Let us see what we shall see.' A few of the children began crying. Others stared into space and trembled. Steiner watched as Kjellrunn bunched her hands into fists and stared straight ahead, just as he'd told her.

'That's it, Kjell,' he breathed. 'Show them no fear.'

Shirinov pressed his face up close to her once more and Steiner realized he was holding his breath. The Hierarch's gaze shifted to another child and he hobbled away, Kjellrunn instantly forgotten.

Every Invigilation was different. Some Vigilants would prowl the rows of children, dismissing each in turn once satisfied the taint of witchsign was not present. All fine and good if you were the first child inspected, not so much if you were the last, kept waiting in terrible anxiety to the bitter end.

'Hel is all waiting,' Verner often said and Steiner couldn't help but agree as he stared at Kjellrunn, hoping she would pass.

Some said witchsign had a scent, a scent only a Vigilant could detect. Others told of a ghostly aura or shadows that writhed in the cold. Steiner didn't know the truth of it, simply glad to have passed his own Invigilations.

Shirinov did not inspect them one by one, nor did he work through the rows in an orderly fashion: he circled, he wandered, he dawdled. Hierarch Khigir stood to one side, unable or unwilling to move among the children, observing them from afar.

Three times Hierarch Shirinov returned to Ditlef, sniffing at the boy until he was pale as milk, hair slicked to his forehead with nervous sweat. It would not do to wail for one's parents at times like this. Those children who fainted, or worse yet lost control of their bladders, were not given an easy time in the months following an Invigilation. Steiner wondered if the Vigilants didn't pass on some measure of their cruelty to the children during their yearly visit.

Moment after anxious moment crawled by. No one wanted
to be marked out for bearing the draconic taint, no one wanted
to be cursed with arcane powers. The Empire had spent the
last seventy-five years erasing all trace of the dragons, and
exterminating anyone who evinced their powers.

The Hierarch wound his way through the rows, feet
crunching in the gritty slush, his cane stabbing the ground
hatefully. Steiner watched as Shirinov drew close to Kjellrunn
and felt powerless to stop what he felt sure would come next.

'You are all free to go, children of Cinderfell,' barked the
old man. He slumped against his cane as if weary, and Steiner
thought he heard disappointment in Shirinov's voice. Several
of the children cried out with relief, while others merely
clutched themselves and fled the cloister. Kjellrunn approached
him in a daze, walking slowly as if recently woken.

'I can't believe it,' whispered Kjellrunn. 'When he came
straight to me at the beginning . . .' Brother and sister clung
to each other, and Steiner suppressed a sob which Kjellrunn
answered with one of her own.

'Come on,' said Steiner, eying the two Hierarchs. 'Let's tell
Father you're safe.'

They slunk from the cloister together, emerging from the
school with relieved smiles on weary faces. Steiner couldn't
wait to get back home and put the ordeal behind them once
and for all.

'You made it, Kjell. That's the last time you have to go
through that.'

Kjell nodded and smiled through tears that gleamed silver
as they tumbled from her cheeks.

'I'll make a fish stew tonight,' said Steiner.

'And boiled potatoes served in butter and herbs?' asked
Kjellrunn.

Steiner nodded. Not much of a celebration meal, but it was

important to remember the small victories. Small victories were all you had in Cinderfell.

'Wait.' Kjellrunn stopped.

'What's wrong?'

'The brooch. It just came loose. I felt it fall but I can't see it.'

The pair of them looked at the muddy ground, casting about for Marek's hammer brooch, while all around them children were held close by their parents.

'It can't be far,' said Steiner, as his eyes scoured the gritty slush at their feet.

'It's important, Steiner,' said Kjellrunn. 'It was Mother's.'

'I know,' he replied. While he didn't believe in superstition there was something about the crude lump of metal, some luck that had seen his sister walk free of the Vigilant's grasp.

'You there! Stop!' Steiner froze as the few children and parents who remained looked on with sickened expressions. Shirinov and Khigir passed under the arch, smiling silver face and frowning bronze mask fixed on them.

'Steiner, run,' whispered Kjellrunn, as two soldiers emerged from the school, flanking the Hierarchs. A look over his shoulder revealed two more soldiers waiting down the street.

'There's no running,' said Steiner. 'Not from the Empire.'

Shirinov hobbled forward, his cane dragging a furrow through the grey slush. Khigir loomed at his shoulder, ever frowning.

'The brooch!' whispered Kjellrunn, her eyes staring wildly at the ground.

'Never mind that now, it's gone,' said Steiner, pulling her close as the Hierarchs approached. 'Get behind me, Kjell.'

CHAPTER FOUR

Steiner

Though such distinctions escape the majority of the population, it should be noted the ranks within the Holy Synod ascend accordingly: Initiate, Brother/Sister, Holy Mother/Holy Father, Ordinary, Hierarch, Exarch, Patriarch/Matriarch. Our devoted Mothers and Fathers are entrusted with the work of Invigilation, though sometimes more experienced minds are called on.

– From the field notes of Hierarch Khigir,
Vigilant of the Imperial Synod.

'You!' shouted Shirinov, louder than was necessary. 'What is your name?'

'I'm not deaf,' said Steiner, scowling.

'This one has spirit,' said Khigir to Shirinov as they approached. The Hierarch steepled his fingers. 'He asked your name, boy.'

'Steiner. Steiner Erdahl Vartiainen.'

'Steiner. Like stone,' said Shirinov. 'Perhaps you have rocks for brains?'

'Better a stony brain than a stony heart,' replied Steiner.

'Why are you here?' asked the Hierarch, leaning on his cane.

'I brought my sister here.' Steiner looked down his nose at the Hierarch. The old man was a handspan shorter though that didn't stop Steiner's hands shaking with fear and fury; he clenched them into fists so that the Hierarch wouldn't see his nervousness. 'And now I'm taking her back.'

'And you have passed your testings?'

Steiner swallowed but didn't look away, dared not look away. He had nothing to be guilty of. 'I passed every one, from ten summers until my sixteenth, when I left the school.'

'We should return,' said Khigir.

'Wait a moment, brother,' replied Shirinov. He stepped closer to Steiner and the sound behind the smiling mask was unmistakable. Shirinov sniffed, like a wolfhound scenting a hare or fox.

'And how old are you?'

'Eighteen,' said Steiner. 'I just told you, I've stood through six Invigilations, and so has my sister. We'll take our leave now.'

'No. You will not.' Shirinov leaned close and cocked his head to one side. 'I deem you corrupted.' He sniffed again. 'You have the taint of witchsign about you.'

'That's ridiculous,' grunted Steiner. 'You're lying.' Kjellrunn squeezed his hand.

'I sense the power of the earth,' said Shirinov. 'And of the sea. I sense much power within you. I don't know how you passed through earlier Invigilations undetected, but we have you now.'

Steiner opened his mouth to speak but couldn't find the words. The power of the sea? Of the earth? He'd expected Kjellrunn to be found with witchsign, but never himself. Kjellrunn squeezed his hand again but Steiner barely felt it, his eyes locked on the smiling mask of Hierarch Shirinov.

'You're lying,' he repeated, though his voice was distant, as if hearing himself in a dream. Wouldn't he know? Wouldn't he have experienced something, some unearthly event or strange turn?

'I am many things, Steiner Erdahl Vartiainen,' said Shirinov, 'but a liar is not one of them.'

'All because I spoke back to you, is that it?'

'No, that is not it. I sense the power of the earth upon you, and of the sea. What violence might you visit upon the Empire if left unchecked? What terrors might you summon?'

'Summon? I have no powers, old man.' But the words were carried off on the wind, frail as smoke, like embers dying. Steiner's world dimmed and a terrible uncertainty stole both his breath and his resolve.

'You will present yourself at the pier tomorrow morning,' said Shirinov, 'or I will send the soldiers to find you.'

'You're wrong,' said Steiner, hearing the disbelief in his voice. 'This is all wrong.'

'Do not try to run, Master Vartiainen.' Khigir's voice was mockery dressed as concern. 'If we fail to find you by noon tomorrow you will leave us no choice but to sack the entire town.' Khigir leaned closer. 'It would be unfortunate. Many deaths occur when a search is conducted, accidentally of course.'

'You're mistaken.' Steiner shook his head. 'I've passed every Invigilation since I was ten.'

'Not this time,' said Shirinov, and Steiner was certain the Vigilant grinned behind the mask.

The Hierarchs turned away and disappeared beneath the school's archway, leaving Steiner to stare after them. He remained statue-still and mute with shock until the heavy fist of a soldier caught him under the ribs, forcing the air from his lungs.

'Be at the pier tomorrow, and keep that smart mouth of yours shut.'

Steiner was about to answer when another soldier struck

him across the face, hard enough that his head whipped to one side. Suddenly he was kneeling in the snow, staring at flecks of soot and spatters of crimson. Blood, he realized.

'Steiner.' Kjellrunn fell to her knees and hugged him, shoulders shaking with fierce sobs. 'Oh, Steiner.' He reached into the snow with numbed fingers and produced the sledgehammer brooch.

At least I found this, he wanted to say, but his bruised jaw refused him, unwilling to shape the words.

They sat at the kitchen table and Steiner could only blink and try to wonder how such a thing had happened. His father had transitioned from silent shock to whispered denial and then roaring anger. He'd spent long minutes hatching plans for Steiner's escape.

'You know we can't risk such a thing,' said Verner.

'The Vigilant, Khigir, he told me they'd tear the town apart if I didn't turn myself in tomorrow.' Steiner pressed a rag to the cut on his cheekbone.

'Better the whole town than my brother,' said Kjellrunn.

'You told me we'd escape Invigilation this year,' said Marek, hard eyes set on Verner. 'You told me—'

'I told you I *hoped* that we'd avoid a visit from the Synod this year. I made no promises.'

'Why were there two Vigilants?' said Kjellrunn in a distant, faraway tone. 'Why not the usual Troika?'

'And why were they both Hierarchs?' added Steiner.

'We've never had such high-ranking members of the Synod here before.' Kjellrunn shook her head. 'Nothing above a Holy Mother anyway.'

'Two Vigilants turned up dead in Helwick, and the third went missing,' explained Verner. 'None of the soldiers could explain why. It seems the Synod sent two more Vigilants to investigate.'

'And they just happened to stop in Cinderfell to conduct the Invigilation,' added Marek, glaring at the fisherman.

'No one could have predicted they'd come so soon,' said Verner.

'Two Vigilants dead and a third missing?' said Steiner.

Verner nodded.

'You didn't mention anything in the tavern last night?'

Verner shrugged and glanced across the table at Marek, who refused to meet his gaze. 'Steiner, I'm so sorry.'

'Why are you apologizing to me?' He turned the sledge-hammer brooch over in his hands. 'You didn't find witchsign on me. Real or not. It's not you forcing me to take the ship to Frøya knows where.'

'Of course not,' said Verner. 'I just wish . . .'

'I can't believe it,' said Marek. 'All this time. If it had been Kjell I might have understood.'

'Hoy! Don't speak of me as if I'm not sat here.' Kjellrunn glanced at Steiner before looking away to the roaring flames in the fireplace.

'And I was just beginning to find my way around the smithy,' said Steiner with a bitter smile. 'I might have made a good smith in time.'

'The finest,' said Verner, laying a hand upon his shoulder.

Marek cleared his throat and stood up, his chair grating on the flagstones. 'I have something for you.'

'I'm going to be shipped off and killed, I doubt there's anything that will help with that.'

Marek looked to Verner and the fisherman nodded. 'We don't truly know that the children who are taken are killed.' Marek sighed. 'We don't know what happens to them.'

'What are you talking about?' whispered Kjellrunn. 'Every child from Svingettevei to Nordvlast knows the Empire kills anyone with witchsign.'

'I'm already dead,' said Steiner. 'Everything else is just waiting.'

'Come on,' said their father, 'I've something to show you.'

The smithy welcomed Steiner into its darkness, the usual ruddy light escaping the edges of the furnace, the familiar smell of coal dust and hot metal. There was a tang of iron on the air like the promise of violence, like the taste of blood.

'How do you know so much about Vladibogdan?' said Steiner when Verner had shut the door behind them. 'And don't tell me it's because you're a fisherman. What else do you know about the Empire that you're not telling me?'

Verner looked guilty for a moment. 'We keep an eye on Imperial movements and pass the information on to certain people,' he explained. 'Your father does less these days on account of looking after you two. We both agreed a long time ago that we didn't care for the way the Solmindre Empire does as it wishes.'

'You're spies,' said Kjellrunn, frowning.

'I'm a blacksmith, not a spy,' said Marek. 'And if you knew what I knew about the Empire then there's nothing you wouldn't do to keep your loved ones safe.'

'But that's the problem, isn't it?' Steiner glowered at his father. 'You've never told us what you know about the Empire, you barely speak of our mother, you barely speak at all.'

'Steiner!' Marek walked around the anvil and grasped his son's shoulders, but Steiner shoved the man back.

'It was you!' Steiner hissed at Verner. 'You went to Helwick.' He scowled at Verner in the darkness of the smithy. 'It was you who killed the two Vigilants. You promised my father we'd be spared an Invigilation so Kjellrunn might go unchecked this year.'

'I didn't kill anyone,' said Verner, though the lie fooled no one.

'For Frejna's sake, Steiner.' Marek shook his head. 'Listen to yourself!'

'No,' said Kjellrunn. 'You all listen to me.' The monotone hardness had edged into her voice again and the furnace cast her in a dire light. 'Steiner may not be able to read but he's not stupid. And neither am I.' She turned to their father. 'You sent Verner to kill the Troika because you feared I'd fail the Invigilation.'

'Wouldn't that just bring more Vigilants?' said Steiner.

'Yes, but it would bring them to Helwick, not Cinderfell, and we might be forgotten about as the Empire searched for the killer.' Marek held out supplicating hands and shook his head. 'I was merely trying to protect you.'

'That brooch you gave me.' She gestured to the glint of metal in Steiner's hand. 'It was meant to disguise the witchsign, your last desperate attempt to keep me safe during the Invigilation.'

'So it's true then?' said Steiner. 'You have the taint?'

'I prefer to call it witchsign,' replied Kjellrunn, holding his gaze.

'You both knew? And you never told me?' said Steiner, looking from father to sister.

'I suspected,' said Marek, eyes fixed on the floor. 'I've always suspected. She has too much of her mother in her for it to be otherwise.'

'Kjell?' Steiner's voice was a whisper, his expression stricken.

'I've always known,' said Kjellrunn. 'I'm sorry, Steiner. I wanted to tell you but I was afraid. I don't even know what my powers are.'

'Why didn't you tell me?' Steiner slumped against the anvil. 'Your own brother. You distrust me that much?'

'To hear you talk of folk tales and goddesses, it's as if you can't bear the thought of anything but hard steel and driving rain. I was afraid, Steiner, afraid you might be so disgusted that you'd do something rash.'

'I'd never sell you out to the Empire. Do you think so little of me?'

'Steiner, I'm sorry. I didn't know what to do.' Kjellrunn hugged herself and dipped her head, tousled tresses falling forward to cover her face. 'I was too scared to trust anyone.'

'It was you the Hierarchs detected today,' said Steiner. 'You were stood right behind me. The moment the brooch slipped free they scented trouble.'

'I'm not trouble,' replied Kjellrunn. Her chin came up and there was anger in her eyes. 'I've not hurt anyone. I've done nothing wrong.'

'The thing is,' said Marek after a pause, 'the children sent to the island aren't executed.'

'At least we don't think so,' said Verner.

'I can't go to the island,' said Steiner. 'What will happen to me once I get there?'

Marek looked to Verner and the fisherman shrugged. 'We don't know.'

'We've been trying to get someone sympathetic to the Scorched Republics on the island for years,' said Verner.

'So you are spies then,' said Steiner.

'Steiner.' Verner said his name so softly it had the tone of apology. 'This is terrible, but it's also an opportunity. You could be the person we need to infiltrate the island.'

Steiner stared at his uncle and shook his head. 'All this time I thought I knew you, and now you'd send me off to Vladibogdan without a second thought.'

He turned on his father and stabbed out an accusing finger. 'And you're supposed to protect me. Aren't parents meant to protect their children? Some father you are.'

'I never wanted this for you,' said Marek, but his voice broke and he looked away.

'Steiner,' said Kjellrunn, 'just hear them out.'

'Because that would suit you perfectly, wouldn't it? Sacrifice me so you're spared whatever happens on the island.'

'She can't go to the island,' said Marek. 'If she's forced to use her power for the Empire . . .'

'What? What is it you know?' asked Steiner, stepping closer.

'Using the arcane burns people up,' said Verner. 'It hollows them out, renders them sick and useless. It's like fire with coal and wood.'

'Kjell will die,' said Marek, though it barely needed saying.

'And you think they won't kill me the moment I fail to . . .' Steiner waved a hand, unsure what he was gesturing. They all knew he meant displaying the arcane.

'You can't go to the island, Kjell,' said Marek. 'No good will come of it.'

'Even if we did tell the Vigilants about Kjell–' Verner shook his head. 'They'd likely take both of you. A Vigilant can't be seen to make a mistake.'

'I'm glad you three are in agreement then,' said Steiner bitterly. 'Now if you don't mind, I'm going to make the most of my last few hours of freedom.'

Kristofine stood on the front step of the tavern, and once again she favoured Steiner with a smile, though the sadness in her eyes could not be missed.

'Hoy there, Steiner.'

'Hoy yourself. I suppose you've heard the news?'

She nodded and sighed.

'Will you let me in? I fancy drinking my cares away, though I fear they'll still be here come morning.'

'I can't. Father said the other patrons would leave.'

'I don't have witchsign,' he grunted. 'There's been a mistake.'

Kristofine nodded again but she didn't move. 'He said you might say that. Why not stay home with your family?'

'We had a fight.' Steiner looked away, and for a moment he couldn't think, couldn't breathe, couldn't find the words for the way he felt about Kjellrunn, Verner and Marek.

Kristofine stepped forward and laid one hand against his arm. 'Why don't you get comfortable in the stable?' she said, breaking his introspection. 'I'll bring a jug of mead out to you?'

'I'm not going to drink in the stable. I don't have the witchsign and I'm not a horse.'

'It's drinking in the stable or no drinking at all. Now get in there and don't let anyone see you.'

Steiner gave a reluctant nod. He slunk around the outside of tavern in a daze; the stable was a ramshackle wooden building that squatted like a beggar at the rear of the building. The raucous voices from inside drew Steiner's attention; for a moment he fancied he could hear his name. His eyes lingered on the light that glowed from beneath a shuttered window. He savoured the smells of old beer and the straw strewn on the ground, listened keenly for the rise and swell of laughter and the low din of conversation. Small chance there'd be any such comforts on the island.

Steiner slipped through the stable door and found an empty stall. Kristofine had prepared in advance; two stools with a lantern and two tankards awaited them. An old horse blanket had been laid over the straw. She snuck into the stall behind him with a clay jug of mead and a mischievous smile.

'I notice there are two tankards,' said Steiner.

'It's a bad habit to drink alone,' she replied, nestling on the blanket.

Steiner looked at her. 'Why do you care? Why do all this for me?'

'All that time we had at school and I was too shy to talk to you. As we got older I worried about what the other girls would say.'

'Because I can't read,' said Steiner, feeling the old shame.

Kristofine shook her head and ignored his interruption. 'Now you're going, and I realize I should never have let shyness or people or anything else stop me from talking to you.'

'But tonight? And me with witchsign and all.'

'What's it like?'

'What is what like?' Steiner frowned.

'The witchsign, of course. What powers do you have?'

Steiner gave a resigned chuckle and pressed a callused palm to his forehead. For a moment he thought he might give in to despairing tears. He closed his eyes tight to spare himself crying in front of Kristofine. He felt her warm hand on his, slowly prising his fingers away from his face.

'Fewer questions, more drinking,' she said and began to pour.

'I don't have the witchsign, I promise you. It's that damned Hierarch and—' But anything else he wanted to say was silenced as she pressed her lips to his.

'I believe you,' she said when the kiss was done. Steiner put aside all thoughts of Vladibogdan, the Synod and the Empire, determined he should have this last night for himself.

CHAPTER FIVE

Kjellrunn

Though there is still much we do not understand, it has been documented that witchsign results in powers belonging to four schools, each with a ruling element. Telepathy and prescience are derived from those born with the element of wind, for example.

— From the field notes of Hierarch Khigir, Vigilant of the Imperial Synod.

Steiner's departure marked the beginning of yet another long silence, a silence that Kjellrunn longed to shatter. She stood at the double doors to the smithy wanting to scream. She wanted the whole town to know of her frustration. She wanted to scream loud enough so the dead might hear her in Hel. She wanted to scream that Steiner come back and scream for the witchsign be taken away.

Her eye rested on the few lanterns in the harbour, bobbing gently with the tide, revealing the location of the frigate, but not the form. She could feel the way sea swirled against the hull, just as she could feel the cold wind on her skin. Come the morning the blood-red ship would spirit Steiner away and there was nothing she could do about it.

'Come in from the cold,' said Marek, laying a hand on her shoulder and pulling her into a rough embrace. She let his arms enfold her with reluctance, feeling an icy fury for the man who had suspected her of witchsign and said nothing.

'I take after her, do I?' There was no wistfulness in her voice, only a resentment that he'd not told her sooner. Discovering tiny truths about her mother should have been a happy event tinged with tears, not a revelation on Steiner's last night in Cinderfell.

'You have her eyes, and her hair too if you'd ever care to pull a brush through it.'

'And where is she now?'

'The Empire took her,' said Marek. He stepped away, not meeting her eyes, gazing into the darkness outside their door. 'We had a handful of happy years together, and two beautiful children, but she was always looking over her shoulder, waiting, waiting.'

'Waiting for the Vigilants to find her,' said Kjellrunn.

'They can track anyone down given enough time.' Marek prodded the anvil with his boot. 'In the end she went of her own accord. Better that way.'

'The Empire doesn't know she had children?'

'Of course not.' He pushed the door closed and set the latch in place, locking the night outside. 'They'd have killed you to make an example to the others.'

'What others?'

He ignored that question and provided one of his own. 'How are you . . .' He frowned and tried again. 'How are your powers?'

'Powers?' She gave a lop-sided smile, filling the word with disdain. 'I don't feel very powerful. I don't feel powerful at all. They're just sensations really. I know when it will rain, and what tide it is.'

'That's it?' said Marek, and Kjellrunn felt a sting of shame.

'Were you expecting some great sorcerer?'

'Sorry, Kjell. I don't know how it works and I forgot that you've not been trained.'

'And that I'm just sixteen. You forgot that too.'

'Yes, sorry, Kjell.' Marek pressed his fingertips into the corners of his eyes and she could almost see the wave of tiredness wash over him. 'So just senses then?'

'I'm happiest when I'm in the forest; it feels more natural there. I imagine I can feel the animals moving around in their lairs and sets under the earth.'

'You may not be imagining that so much as feeling it.' He fixed her with a long appraising look, then gestured that she follow him into the kitchen.

Verner sat at the table, cleaning his nails with a small knife. He looked up at Kjellrunn but no expression crossed his face. The way Steiner told it, Kjellrunn was Verner's favourite out of the two of them. She didn't care. To her mind Steiner had long been their father's favourite so it was almost fair, inasmuch as families are ever fair.

'Don't worry, Uncle, I'll not call a storm down on your little boat next time you sail.'

Verner didn't smile, simply put away his knife and stared into the fireplace where the embers glowed orange.

'You shouldn't joke about such things. People have died for the power you hold, died and suffered for it.'

'You think I'm not suffering?' she replied, her tone as cold and unforgiving as the Sommerende Ocean. 'My only brother has no choice but to go to the island to be killed.'

'We don't know for sure he'll be killed,' replied Verner, getting to his feet. 'And he may learn something useful if he keeps his wits about him.'

'You can't send him to the island.' She gazed up into the fisherman's eyes. 'I won't let you.'

Marek and Verner exchanged a glance and both turned to her with wary expressions on their faces.

'Kjell, it's not up to us. If there was a way to stop the Empire I would, but . . .' Marek held out a placating hand to her but she had no mind to take it, no mind to be held by him when he had held back so much. The urge to scream came again, to howl like a trapped animal. Her hands closed into fists and the room took on a dreamlike sheen; she was suddenly light-headed and took a deep breath to steady herself.

The Empire mean to take my brother.

The kitchen door rattled on its hinges and blew open, smashing into the kitchen counter behind it. The fire in the grate was swept up and cinders and ashes swirled about the dim chamber, an angry blizzard of grey and radiant embers. An old rag was blown about like a discarded flag of surrender. Marek and Verner stumbled backwards, one of them calling out in alarm. Kjellrunn fled the kitchen, her eyes shut tight, almost tumbling through the door and out into the street.

Marek was at the door coughing, reaching after her, but she retreated from the man who used the truth so sparingly when it meant so much.

'Kjell, please. You don't know what it does to a person.' His voice was a harsh whisper, afraid of being overheard on the quiet street. 'Over time the body rejects the arcane, or is burned up by it. I've seen people turned to stone, petrified for all time.'

'I won't let them take him,' she said, loud enough that a few curtains twitched in the neighbouring windows.

She sprinted down the street, glad to be away from the smithy and the smell of metal and fire, glad to be away from the low-ceilinged kitchen and the over-large table. And though she was loath to admit it, she was glad to be away from people, even her own father, her own uncle. People. She'd rather have the company of trees and her own restful solitude.

The wind howled, given voice by the jagged cliffs. It wailed and sang, filling Kjellrunn's senses with a deep unease. She

squinted through a flurry of grey snow, finding her way
through the drab town, slinking through side streets and
shadows so she might avoid the patrols of Imperial soldiers.

The winding roads were almost completely dark at this time
of night and she'd fled without torch or lantern to light her
way. Slivers of illumination spilled from windows, ribbons of
glowing gold shining from the cobbles or glittering on the
snows. How many families lived in Cinderfell, she wondered?
How many families lived in these shuttered cottages? How
many people with nothing to consume their thoughts but the
simple pressure of existence? Where to work? Where to find
food, find comfort, find peace? Here they slept, these simple
families, beneath thatched roofs, untroubled by old secrets
and unearthly powers. Only the howling wind and the ever-
present cold troubled them, and Kjellrunn felt a deep
wellspring of envy.

Bjørner's tavern was a beacon in the darkness, light
streaming from windows, declaring a welcome to any who
might climb the steep street leading to its door. Kjellrunn's
teeth chattered as she pushed herself onward. She had no
desire to be here, but it was the only place she could think
of where Steiner might seek refuge. A burst of laughter
sounded from inside, though it sounded coarse and unfriendly,
and the smells that greeted her were no different. She wrinkled her nose as she lifted the latch on the door, pressing her
shoulder against it.

'Everything seems coarse and unfriendly tonight,' she
muttered to herself, willing the courage to look for Steiner
and find him and bring him home.

She had no sooner placed one tentative foot across the
threshold of the tavern when the wind gusted in behind her,
blowing the door wide open. All eyes in the tavern turned
to her and chagrin made her small as she struggled to close
the door. No one moved to help her, no one spoke.

Bjørner came out from behind the bar, hands fussing with a cloth, struggling for a serious expression if Kjellrunn had to guess, though she hadn't missed the shock in his eyes as she'd entered.

'Kjellrunn Vartiainen,' was all he said, and still no one spoke. Håkon the butcher stood behind the tavern owner and two dozen faces all gawped, mouths open, like fish caught up in nets and just as stuck.

'I'm looking for my brother,' she said, though the silence of the room made her words sound frail and weak.

'He's not welcome here,' said Bjørner. 'And neither are you, Kjellrunn.'

'Has anyone seen him?' She turned to the room, trying to make eye contact with any one of them, but they all turned to their drinks or cast guilty glances at their boots. 'Has anyone seen Steiner?' she said, and now her voice was loud, too loud in the strangling quiet of the tavern.

'Best you head home now, girl,' said Håkon, rubbing one hand over his huge beard.

Kjellrunn looked around desperately. 'Someone must have seen him.'

'You need to go now,' repeated Bjørner. He stood a little taller now with Håkon beside him.

Kjellrunn glared at them, then held up four fingers. 'Go to Hel, all of you can go to Hel for all I care.' The door slammed after her and she stalked down the street trailing curses.

Marek and Verner were waiting for her when she returned. They had built up the fire and swept out the ashes, but made a bad job of it as men are wont to do. A lantern had been lit and the room had a cosy glow to it after the bright light and stark truth of the tavern.

He's not welcome here, and neither are you, Kjellrunn. Had Bjørner meant the tavern, or all of Cinderfell?

'You didn't find him then,' said Verner. He looked strange,

with his beard fringed in milk. A steaming mug sat before him and another before Marek.

'Why are you drinking hot milk like old women?' she replied. 'I would have thought you'd be well into the mead by now.'

'Mind your mouth,' growled Marek. 'No good comes of getting drunk at a time like this. It's a cold night is all. Perhaps if you keep a civil tongue in your head you can have some too.'

Kjellrunn dragged a chair out and slumped into it, crossed her arms on the table and rested her head on her forearms.

'Where did you go?' asked Verner softly.

'To Bjørner's, of course,' replied Kjellrunn, not looking up. 'Where else?'

'Not much of a welcome there, I suspect,' said Verner.

'There won't be much of a welcome anywhere after this,' said Marek. 'We'll be lucky not to be run out of town.'

'Why is the witchsign regarded as a bad thing?' asked Kjellrunn. 'I'm hardly a great danger, am I? A girl of sixteen who can predict the weather.'

'You've heard the tales, Kjell,' said Verner. 'You've been asking me for stories of dragons and the arcane for as long as I can recall.'

'But surely that's all they are. Stories. The dragons have been dead for nearly a hundred years—'

'Seventy-five,' said Marek, pouring hot milk from the pan into a mug.

'Longer than living memory,' replied Kjellrunn, determined to make her point.

'There are those who remember the war, Kjell,' said Marek. 'And those whose fathers fought in it passed their memories to their sons.'

'But the witchsign as something dangerous?' Kjellrunn frowned. 'That's just old tales, embellished by time.'

'Embellished,' said Verner, and grinned. 'She even speaks like her mother.'

'She certainly doesn't get her vocabulary from me,' said Marek. Kjellrunn slipped her chilled fingers around the mug and felt the warmth.

'The Empire blames the emergence of the arcane on the dragons,' said Marek. 'And for that they will not rest until all trace of it is scoured from the world.'

'Even if it means murdering children?' asked Kjellrunn, her thoughts straying to Steiner, though he could hardly be mistaken for a child these days.

'Even if it means murdering children,' replied Marek. 'There is nothing they will not do to keep the arcane out of the hands of commoners and serfs.'

Kjellrunn drank and drank deep, but there was a bitter note to the milk that caused her to hesitate. Marek and Verner continued to sup and stare at the fire, as if the answers to Steiner's predicament might be found there.

'Drink up now,' said Marek, and she did. The stairs to the loft seemed many, and harder to climb than ever before. How had she become so tired? It had been a long day, true enough, but she fell into bed still dressed, too exhausted to rise again. She shucked off her boots, and curled into a ball.

'Where are you, Steiner?' she whispered to the darkness, but no answer came.

CHAPTER SIX

Steiner

Cinderfell holds especial importance, lying as it does on the North-western coast of Nordvlast. It is the last stop before taking ship to Vladibogdan, and the last town that many of the taken children will ever see. The people of Cinderfell have watched us take scores of children year after year. I fear that if there is some uprising then it must surely occur in Cinderfell, or close by. We must be watchful.

— From the field notes of Hierarch Khigir,
Vigilant of the Imperial Synod.

Steiner had not meant to be late. It seemed as if all the people of Cinderfell had crowded around the lonely stone pier to witness his leaving. He descended the rutted track leading to the coastal road, not bothering to call in at home. He had no wish to speak with those who had cast him to the fate awaiting him on the island. The crimson frigate lay at anchor and rowing boats headed back and forth, ferrying cargoes of children with witchsign from all across the Empire and Scorched Republics. The sky resembled a vast quarry, inverted, the clouds all arrayed in shades of brutal grey, jagged and dangerous.

'There he is!' shouted a voice from the back of the crowd. Heads turned and the crowd parted. Steiner's head was a dull throb of pain and his guts fared no better. Pieces of straw clung to his tunic, evidence that he'd spent the night in a stable. Better that people not know which one.

'Took your sweet time,' said a gruff voice.

'They've almost got all the children aboard,' chided another.

'Thought you'd try to run,' said another voice.

'Don't mind me,' replied Steiner, senses too dull to form a more biting response. He walked and glowered and walked some more.

'Not such a smart-arse today, eh?' said Håkon, the butcher.

The crowd withdrew from Steiner as if the taint of the arcane was contagious. Men and women and dozens of children watched; a few kissed their fingertips as he passed – the old sign for warding off evil. Steiner struggled not to curse at them. At least Kristofine was not among the townsfolk, he was glad of that. She was the last person in Vinterkveld he trusted; he'd rather she'd be spared witnessing his departure.

The pier was clear of everyone but soldiers, six of them forming a cordon to keep back any desperate parents, though none had followed their offspring north from the other Scorched Republics. Hierarchs Khigir and Shirinov lurked together, all folded arms and stooped shoulders.

'I told you the boy had spirit,' said Khigir in his deep drone. The frown on the plain bronze mask was no less strange.

'I was about to order the sacking of the blacksmith's cottage,' said Shirinov from behind the silver smile.

'Sorry to have made you wait in the cold so long,' said Steiner. 'Must be hard when a chill gets into old bones.'

Shirinov slunk forward, then raised his hand.

'Steiner!' The shout came from the crowd.

The Hierarch stopped and looked at the newcomer but Steiner had no need to turn. He knew the voice well enough.

'Steiner, I have something for you.' Marek's statement was a plea, but Steiner had no care to answer it. 'Steiner, please?'

He flashed an angry glance over his shoulder and saw the blacksmith and fisherman side by side, held back by soldiers. Kjellrunn was nowhere to be seen, probably for the best with Vigilants so close at hand. Marek held a rough sack and offered it towards him.

Steiner walked to the cordon of soldiers and eyed the sack. 'What am supposed to do with this?'

'It's for the journey,' replied Marek, his expression pained.

'Keep it,' replied Steiner. 'I want nothing from you.'

'Steiner, I'm sorry.' Marek's voice cracked.

'Just remember I'm not doing this for you, I'm doing it for Kjell.'

'Steiner.' Marek looked crushed but Steiner couldn't find it within himself to feel much pity. He turned on his heel and walked the length of the pier, away from the cordon of soldiers, away from the despairing eyes of his father. The sound of the Spøkelsea washed over him and several gulls pierced the quiet with mocking calls, setting his nerves on edge.

'You turn your back on family?' It was Khigir, the frown of the pitted bronze mask no less intimidating up close.

'What do you care?'

'There are some who are taken and never truly let go of their previous lives.' Khigir looked back towards the crowd. 'Yet you are not one of them.'

Steiner shrugged and watched the rowing boat leave the ship.

'You are a contradiction, yes?' added Khigir.

'I'd say I'm straightforward if you've a care to know me.'

'Straightforward how?'

Steiner took a step towards the Vigilant. 'When I'm happy I smile and when I'm angry I frown. I don't need a mask to hide behind.'

'You will change in time. You will have a mask soon, I think.' Steiner thought he heard a mocking tone in Khigir's words.

'Why would I need a mask?'

'Come now, boy,' said Khigir. 'It is time to depart.'

'I'm not your boy,' he replied through gritted teeth. 'My name is Steiner.'

The wind gusted across the bay and the townsfolk drifted along the coastal road in threes and fours, like frail autumn leaves. Steiner glanced down the pier one last time and saw the crowd part around Marek as Verner led him away. Anger burned brightly even as a stony desolation filled his chest. A light rain began to fall, making a susurrus on the surrounding sea.

Shirinov was elsewhere as Steiner descended from pier to boat, shouldering his way between surly children who scowled as he sat down. Steiner struggled to keep his composure and he bowed his head, clenching his hands into tight fists.

The last words he'd said to his father rang in his ears, *Just remember I'm not doing this for you, I'm doing it for Kjell.* Anything to keep her out of the hands of the Empire and its Vigilants. Rain dripped from his nose and down his temples.

At least no one will notice if I shed any tears, he thought.

The Hierarchs struggled to take their seats, aided by the arms of four stronger, younger soldiers, who joined them. The effort of embarking ushered a coughing fit from Shirinov, who slumped into a doze when the wracking passed.

They were halfway to the frigate, bobbing across the dark green waters, when another rowing boat passed them. Romola was aboard, stood at the front without a care, heading towards the stone pier. A few crew manned the oars and shot sour glances at the Hierarchs and darker looks at Steiner himself.

'Romola?' said Steiner.

'You have seen her before?' intoned Khigir.

Steiner nodded. 'Does she work for the Empire?' he asked, annoyed he'd let the Vigilant goad him into conversation.

'In a manner of speaking.'

'Is that the same manner that murders children?' asked Steiner.

'Such spirit,' Khigir leaned forward, 'will not last for long. Vladibogdan changes everyone.'

Any romantic notions of sailing Steiner entertained were quickly drowned. He'd not had a chance to take in his surroundings before being forced into the hold. There were no seats, only old crates, the smell of salt water and darkness. The sole chance to fend off the spiteful chill was to choose from a selection of mangy blankets, though lice roamed the folds of the fabric causing children to squeal as they shook them loose. It was difficult to count just how many captives were confined in the gloomy hold. Steiner had not expected the ship to groan and creak and struggled to keep the alarm from his face. The motion of the sea did nothing for his hangover and he settled down between two crates and closed his eyes.

Invigilation began at age ten and continued once a year until a child left school at sixteen. Many children dropped out of school long before then, required to attend the Invigilations all the same. Steiner had heard tell of cunning parents who sought to keep their children off the school registers in remote villages, far from the prying eyes of the Synod. None of their efforts mattered in the end. A vast network of the Synod's clergy scoured the continent, sending their finds north and west until the children fetched up in Cinderfell, escorted by soldiers.

Steiner recalled his father's words from the previous night. *The thing is, the children sent to the island aren't executed.*

At least we don't think so.

'I'm not dead yet,' said Steiner to no one in particular.

He was answered by a whimper and opened his eyes to find a boy of ten squatting down and clutching himself. He had a hint of Shanisrond blood in him; his delicate eyes were at odds with his plump, olive-skinned cheeks.

'Hoy,' said Steiner. 'Get yourself a blanket.'

The boy shook his head.

'What's your name?'

'M-Maxim.'

'Why don't you get a blanket?'

Maxim raised a hand towards a pile of crates where a blond-haired boy sat atop an improvized throne. 'He won't let me.'

Steiner pushed himself to his feet and rolled his shoulders. He felt scores of eyes upon him and realized he was the eldest by a couple of years, and certainly he was the largest.

'Wait here,' he said to Maxim. The boy nodded and his bottom lip quivered with misery. Steiner crossed the hold, stepping over huddles of children until he stood before the pile of crates. The boy who sat at the summit had nestled among a dozen blankets, looking impossibly smug.

'And who might you be?' Steiner asked with arched eyebrow.

'I am Aurelian Brevik; my father is the richest man in Helwick. I won't be staying long.' He smiled. 'Once my father has paid off the Empire I will return home.'

'Is that so, son of the richest man in Helwick?'

'Of course.' Aurelian pouted. 'There's been a mistake. I can't possibly have witchsign, not like these disgusting creatures. Not like you.'

Steiner guessed Aurelian was around sixteen years old. He had eyes as cold as the north wind and was dressed in sheepskins dyed red, splendid and expensive. His heavy boots were fine and new.

'How about you hand over some of the blankets?' suggested Steiner.

'I think not,' replied Aurelian.

'Listen to me,' said Steiner, voice low. 'I'm hungover, I've just lost everyone I've ever cared about, and I didn't pack much in the way of patience.'

'Am I supposed to be intimidated?' sneered Aurelian. He stood up but the smile slipped from his face. The throne had given him the impression he was taller than Steiner. They stood face to face and Steiner knew Aurelian wouldn't back down. Money never did.

'Why don't you crawl back to your side of the ship like the peasant you are and I'll forget—' Aurelian got no further as Steiner's fist took him on his left eye and nose. He fell back against his improvized throne and released a whimper, holding a hand to the source of his pain.

'You dare strike me?'

'I dare just fine,' replied Steiner. 'And I'll dare again if you don't shut your stupid face.'

Steiner took the bundle of blankets from the throne of crates and began handing them out to the children that lacked them.

'Shake it out. Get rid of the lice,' he said to one child. 'Calm yourself and dry your eyes,' he said to another. 'Here you go.' He passed a blanket to Maxim and before long he'd drawn an audience of fifteen imploring faces, all sensing protection was at hand and drifting towards it.

'Ugh,' managed Aurelian from across the hold, but he held his tongue.

Steiner settled down among his adopted charges, massaging his aching knuckles, then cleared his throat.

'All right, stop crying. I know it's a sad business being taken from your families and all. And I know you're scared. Hel, I'm scared too.' More faces appeared at the huddle.

'How will they kill us?' asked a painfully thin girl, perhaps eleven summers old.

'I don't know,' replied Steiner. He wanted to promise them they wouldn't be killed at all, but it was a promise he couldn't give in good faith. 'All I know is that we're being sent to an island called Vladibogdan. Stay together, work together, you'll need each other if we're to survive this.'

It was strange to have such a rapt audience. He'd spent his life being the son of the blacksmith, or the brother of the strange girl. He'd largely been ignored by the teachers at school. No one had paid him much mind before Kristofine. His face contorted as he thought of her, thought of never seeing her again. He shook his head and cleared his throat.

'And I don't want to see any more of this kind of foolishness.' He gestured towards Aurelian. 'All we've got is each other now.'

The younger children settled down and the older children spread word through the hold to other pockets of children. Maxim wriggled beside Steiner and fell asleep in his lap. Kjellrunn had been much the same when she'd been five and six. The memory of it brought tears to Steiner's eyes, tears of frustration and tears of loss.

'Why didn't you tell me, Kjell?' he whispered. For long moments he sat, head slumped, resigned to his misery. The feeling of being watched pressed against his awareness and he raised his head to find Romola peeking over the edge of the hold. She was not smiling as she had done in Cinderfell, nor did she give any indication she recognized him.

The Spøkelsea was not the serene expanse of water Steiner had hoped for. The ship lurched and rocked with each wave that broke against the hull. A few of the children began retching and the hold filled with the unmistakable scent of vomit.

'Frøya save me.' Steiner covered his nose. 'I had to choose today for a hangover.'

Maxim looked up with sleepy eyes. 'Wha?'

'Nothing, but if you throw up on me I'll toss you overboard.'

Maxim nodded with a solemn expression that said he would do the same if their places were reversed. The boy wriggled closer and went back to sleep.

'How long does it take for a frigate to travel twenty miles anyway?' muttered Steiner, just as a member of the crew climbed down from the deck above. She was a hard-looking woman with a black headscarf and a faded tunic the colour of mud. It was her britches Steiner liked the most: broad stripes in black and white.

'I like your britches.'

'Thanks. You Steiner?'

'Am I in trouble?'

'You tell me.' The sailor shrugged. 'Captain wants to see you. Follow me, and don't get any fancy ideas. We're already a good five miles from Cinderfell and I doubt you can swim that far.'

Steiner cocked his head to one side and considered it.

'Trust me,' said the sailor. 'The current is strong and you'd likely fetch up in Shanisrond. In a few months after the fishes had nibbled on your corpse.'

Steiner dislodged the sleeping Maxim as gently as he could. 'I'll be back before you know it,' he said when the boy whimpered.

'Didn't realize you had a little brother,' said the sailor.

'Neither did I.' Steiner followed the sailor onto deck and was certain Romola had overheard him speaking to the children, just as he was certain she would have informed the Hierarchs. He didn't relish another conversation with Khigir and Shirinov; they might suddenly realize the witchsign was mysteriously absent and throw him overboard. All these thoughts weighed on him like the coils of rope on deck, damp with mist and sea spray.

'Here you are,' said the sailor. She jerked her thumb at a door and then reached out a hand to steady herself as the ship lurched.

'How much longer until we get there?' asked Steiner.

'The wind's not on our side, so we're not able to sail as the crow flies.'

'What's he like?' asked Steiner.

'Who?'

'The captain. What's he like?

The sailor smiled. 'Best you see for yourself.' And with that she opened the door and ushered him into the gloomy cabin.

CHAPTER SEVEN

Steiner

*The uprising against our draconic masters cost Vinterkveld dearly.
Many men and women lost their lives. It should be noted that the
various pockets of Spriggani, who infest the forests like fungus, did
not answer the call of revolution against the dragons. It is for this
reason they are not, nor will they ever be, members of the Empire.*

– From the field notes of Hierarch Khigir,
Vigilant of the Imperial Synod.

The cabin was full of curios and oddments from across Vinterkveld. Here a tankard with the embossed crest of Vannerånd,
there a bone dagger with a hilt bound in lizard skin, while
the floor was home to a yak-skin rug. The cabin's two lanterns
contained coloured glass, shedding red and blue light over
everything, yet it was the music that entranced Steiner most
of all.

Romola sat with her back to him, one hand strumming the
strings of a long-necked instrument with a rounded body. The
tune was restful yet carried an undertow of melancholy. Each
note was a tiny miracle, each chord a sound from dreaming.
No one in Cinderfell had ever had the money for such things;

there had barely been money for food when the winters were
bad. Music had remained as rousing song and hearty claps to
keep time, the stamp of boots and hollered choruses.
Instruments belonged to another world somehow.

'Where did you get such a thing?' Steiner asked in a reverent
whisper.

Romola looked up from her playing and regarded Steiner
from the corner of her eye. 'I took it from an old lover. It's
called a domra.' A sad smile touched her lips and she sighed.
'He and I had a parting of the ways when I discovered he'd
kept certain truths from me.'

Sadness weighed on Steiner, recalling his father's admission
in the smithy and Kjellrunn's revelation. That Verner too had
kept his own secrets had only salted the wound.

'Keeping certain truths,' he said.

'I never really said goodbye,' added Romola, her eyes
looking away to a corner of the cabin deep in shadow. 'Just
took his coin purse and the domra. And never looked back.'

'I'm sorry,' said Steiner. 'It's hard when—'

'All of life is a game of cards. You bet big and you bet small.'
Romola cocked her head on one side. 'You'll never really
know how things will play out until they play out.'

Steiner nodded. He'd not been one for cards, but he understood the sentiment.

'When will I meet the captain?' His mind lingered on stone
piers and the last angry glares he'd favoured his family with.

Romola couldn't hide her amusement. 'The captain? You
were expecting a burly man with a long beard and parrot,
right?' She stood and performed a bow.

'You?'

'No wooden legs here I'm afraid.' Another smile, halfway
mocking.

'But you're a storyteller?'

'I tell stories on my nights off.' She placed the domra on

her bed with care. 'It's good to get off the ship, and I make it my business to sleep one night in every town we put in at. No point sailing the world if you're not going to see it.'

'There's not much to see in Cinderfell.'

'Something we agree on.' She sat down and reclined, one ankle resting on the opposite knee, then narrowed her eyes.

'You might have mentioned you were the ship's captain when I saw you in Cinderfell.' Steiner narrowed his eyes; he had the feeling he'd been made a fool of and didn't care for it much.

'And what would that have achieved? People are hardly going to thank me for bringing the Empire to their shores, are they?'

'So why do it? Why bring Shirinov and Khigir to Cinderfell?'

'Why does anyone do anything?' Romola shrugged. 'Money. And it keeps me in the good graces of the Empire.'

Steiner clenched his fists and tried to think of something to say.

'That was a good thing you did for the children in the hold,' she said.

'And I suppose you told Shirinov and Khigir.'

'No. I don't make trouble when I can help it.' Romola poured herself a tumbler of wine. 'But you need to be more careful when speaking out against the Empire. Men have been killed for less.'

Steiner nodded. Difficult to argue with reason that sound.

'And how does a storyweaver find herself working for the Solmindre Empire? If Shirinov caught you telling folk tales about dragons and—'

'It's forbidden to tell such stories in the Empire, but the same rules don't apply in the Scorched Republics, part of the reason I gave up the Ashen Gulf for the Sommerende Ocean.'

'So you gave up the life of a pirate so you could be a mercenary for the Empire?'

'You're so young.' Romola smiled. 'Everything is so black and white when you're young. Wait a few years, then you might start to understand.'

Steiner looked around the room, noting a framed illustration of a dark bird.

'Your figurehead. It's a crow?' Steiner asked, keen to change the subject.

Romola nodded. 'The ship is called the *Watcher's Wait*. I'm hoping we appeal to Frejna so that she spares us misfortune.' Romola reached under the chair and brought forth a weighted sack, the fabric straining with the load.

'This is for you. An old acquaintance of mine insisted I bring it on board.'

Steiner approached knowing it must be the sack his father had offered back at Cinderfell. There was a wave of relief, but also of regret that he'd refused it, and beneath both feelings the undertow of betrayal remained. Had they thought him too stupid to be a spy, or too weak? He wasn't a child any more.

'You can take it, it's yours,' said Romola, noting his hesitation.

The lurching motion of the ship tipped him towards Romola and the bundle she offered. The rough cloth parted to reveal a wooden handle. He drew it out of the sack and eyed the stout metal head at the opposite end.

'Verner gave it to me,' said Romola. 'Apparently this is your great-grandfather's.' Steiner blinked and held up the sledge-hammer, the wood filigreed with dust, while the metal was dull. It was not beautiful in any way, a simple tool for a simple task. The sack was not empty. Further investigation revealed a pair of heavy boots.

'Those belonged to your mother,' offered Romola. 'She must have been a half ogre judging by the size of them, right?'

'Ogres don't exist,' scoffed Steiner.

'No, you're right,' said Romola, looking away. 'Not any more.'

Steiner ignored the comment, thinking she was gaming him, more interested in the boots. His own mother had laced these boots and worn them on cold days and long walks. He'd never seen such fine craftsmanship and the boots reached to his calves when he tried them on.

'We have the same size feet,' he mumbled.

'Maybe you're a half ogre too.' Romola smiled.

'Hardly.'

'You're still young. There's plenty of growing to be had.'

'What in Frejna's name am I supposed to do with this?' He gestured to the sledgehammer.

Romola waved off his question. 'I'm just the messenger, right?'

'Am I supposed to use it on the island? What will happen when we get there?'

'I don't know, and if I did know I could be killed for telling you.'

'Please, will we be executed, or drowned, or—'

'I don't know. I've been no further than the gatehouse at the top of the steps—'

'What steps?'

'You'll see.' Romola cocked her head on one side and smiled. 'Why don't you come up on deck to get some fresh air?'

'What about the Vigilants?'

'They're asleep, or throwing up everything they've ever eaten.'

'Don't even speak of it.' Steiner held a hand to his mouth.

'You think you've got it bad, you should see Shirinov,' said Romola, stifling a laugh.

Steiner followed the captain out of the hold and emerged on deck to see a touch of gold along the horizon. The sun was brightest at dawn. Only as the day progressed was it subdued by the endless grey of Nordvlast's skies.

'I don't think much of your ship,' said Steiner. 'It's taken all night to sail twenty miles.'

'It's not been the crossing I'd hoped for,' admitted Romola. 'Come up on the quarter deck with me.' She took the ship's wheel from a sour-looking sailor with a scar that had healed badly and left him with a permanent sneer. The sailor ignored him and slunk away.

'He must be related to Håkon,' said Steiner.

'The infamous butcher of Cinderfell.' Romola smiled. 'That Kristofine is a fine-looking girl. Were you two . . .' The pirate arched an eyebrow and Steiner felt himself blush at the implication.

'Looks like it ended before it began,' said Steiner. He realized he'd lost more than just his family, and a swell of bitterness rose within him.

'If I can get word back to her I will, let her know you're safe and all.'

'And will I?' Steiner shook his head. 'Will I be safe?'

Romola shrugged. 'That's up to you.'

'And my father, will you get word to him?'

Romola nodded. 'Your father and I go back a way, and you'll keep that bit of information to yourself.' She gave him a stern look at odds with her usual wry demeanour. Steiner felt a dozen more questions beg to be answered, but the look on Romola's face said he'd get no answers from her.

They stood on the deck in silence as the ship heaved itself over rising waves, Steiner clinging on to a railing and trying not to shiver. This might be the last bit of freedom he'd have, and he was keen to grasp it with both hands.

Romola shook her head, then pointed out to sea. 'Those are the Nordscale islands. They keep the worst storms from battering Cinderfell.'

Steiner squinted into the distance and sighted near two dozen pinnacles of dark rock emerging from the sea. Some were slender, like huge fangs, others were squat, cracked things. The largest formed an imposing mass that dominated the sea ahead, the stone reached far into the sky and a steady plume of smoke emerged from hidden places.

'Is it a volcano?' asked Steiner.

'It's no volcano,' said Romola. The smoke formed a dark halo about the island, fading to dark grey as it rose higher, staining the sky in all directions.

'Vladibogdan,' whispered Steiner.

'Right.' None of Romola's wry amusement remained in the shadow of the island. 'Your new home, I'm afraid.'

The vastness of the dark rock gave no clue of habitation, there seemed no way to live there at all. Romola barked some orders and the ship began to circle the island.

'I don't suppose you're looking for a new deck hand, are you?' said Steiner. 'I'm a hard worker.'

'Nice try, and I like you and all, but our paths don't lie along the same route.' She turned the wheel until the *Watcher's Wait* sailed in a channel between Vladibogdan and the smaller Nordscales. The ashen pall was darker here, an ominous presence lingering in the sky.

'It would be no bad thing if this whole island slipped beneath the waves,' said Romola.

'Before I disembark would be preferable,' said Steiner.

The cliffs grew ever higher as they approached, sweeping down at the rear of the island until a wide cove revealed black sands and dark-eyed watchtowers. Gulls drifted on the morning air, calling out to them with mournful cries as the *Watcher's Wait* cut through the water.

'What happens now?' said Steiner.

Romola shrugged. 'Can't say. I've never set foot in the Dragemakt Academy.'

Steiner raised a questioning eyebrow. 'I've never heard of any academy before.'

'You'll see when you get there.' Romola frowned, annoyed that she'd said too much.

'An academy. That's just what I need.' Steiner shook his head and drew an anxious breath.

'Something to do with the Vigilants,' added Romola. 'I tried to find out once, but I never got further than the gatehouse. They don't like prying eyes around these parts.'

'An academy,' said Steiner, with a tiny suspicion of what was to come.

'You had better get below,' said Romola. The island had cast a shadow over the *Watcher's Wait*, crowding out the sky as they passed into the cove. 'I can't risk you being seen up here. Go on now.'

Steiner headed back to the hold and tried to slip in unnoticed, but there was small chance of that. The other children were wide-eyed and full of questions. There were a few pointed comments about being 'the captain's favourite', but the conversation focused on what he'd seen. Steiner answered their questions as best he could, close-mouthed for the main, until he felt the ship slow and the Spøkelsea's constant motion troubled them no more. All eyes turned upward, staring at the rectangle of grey sky above the hold where soldier's faces would appear, summoning them on deck, leading them to Vladibogdan.

The cove was not large and the ship rested in sombre waters, a scarlet shadow beneath granite cliffs. The children were ferried to a stone pier and told to wait by looming soldiers, as if any might be inclined to venture to the black sands and the many steps that rose beyond.

'May Frejna's eye not find you,' said Romola.

'And may Frøya keep you close,' replied Steiner. It was strange to speak of the old goddesses with a person from Shanisrond, but he felt in his bones that she meant every word.

'I didn't have you as one believing in the old ways,' said Romola.

'I don't, but I'll need all the good fortune I can get, divine and otherwise.'

'You'd best not mention the goddesses on the island,' warned Romola, 'or you'll be severely punished.'

The Hierarchs Khigir and Shirinov were the last to leave the ship. If either of them was a natural sailor he hid it well. The old men moved slowly to the boats below and were hoisted onto the pier by struggling soldiers. The children watched with wide eyes, barely daring to breathe as the masked men pushed through the press.

'What happens now?' whispered Maxim.

'A steep climb,' muttered Steiner, nodding towards count-less steps etched in the steep rise. Maxim's eyes widened but not for the reason Steiner supposed. Shirinov's gloved hand caught him across the mouth and he felt his lip split in a bright pinprick of pain.

'Silence! You will learn discipline!' Shirinov's smiling mask turned to the other children. 'You will learn obedience. And you will learn that the Empire's needs come before your own. Always.'

Steiner's head swam from the force of the blow, but he did not stagger. He licked his lip and tasted coppery blood, not taking his eyes from the Vigilant for a moment.

'You'd do well to tame that dark look you're so fond of giving me, boy.'

'The look will be the least of your problems,' replied Steiner, though he struggled to form the words. 'And I'm not your boy.' Shirinov raised his fist again but Khigir caught his arm.

'Plenty of time for that in due course, brother,' said the Vigilant from behind the frowning mask. Shirinov shrugged him off.

'Thank the Emperor we are finally back,' added Khigir, then

released a sigh. A dozen tongues of fire grew on the stone around his feet. The children squealed but for a few who looked aghast and perhaps guilty. The soldiers ushered them up the stairs with a few well-placed shoves, barking commands in Solska. Many of the children stumbled with the effort of looking at Khigir's raw manifestation of the arcane as much as from the punishing climb. Shirinov led the procession, while his colleague joined Steiner at the back, the dancing flames at his feet following with every step.

'My sister used to tell tales of such flames,' said Steiner. 'She called them corpsecandles.'

The frowning mask nodded. 'There is an old tale that on nights of full moon you can see Spriggani venture from the forests. Spiteful people in the dark going about their wicked business.'

'And what business would that be?' Steiner was already beginning to tire as he climbed the granite steps.

'It's said that Spriggani enter graveyards, perching on tombstones or cairns.' Khigir was wheezing behind the mask. 'The Spriggani sing horrible rhymes and draw out the last vestiges of life from those who have died. Tiny flames emerge and Spriggani capture them under glass, use them to light lanterns.'

'Corpsecandles.'

'This is so.'

Steiner looked at the Vigilant's robes and noted they did not singe or blacken.

'And you can make them disappear?'

'Yes,' replied Khigir, 'though it pains me to do so.'

They climbed higher. The cliffs were dead and lifeless crags; no sign of nesting birds or lichen clung to the cracks. Steiner watched Maxim struggling to put one foot in front of the other until one stone step, worn smooth by time, betrayed him. Steiner caught the boy by the shoulder, preventing a long and likely fatal fall. The two boys looked beneath them to the base of the stairs and the black sands of the cove. Khigir took the opportunity to catch his breath, each exhalation amplified by the stifling mask.

'T-thanks,' muttered Maxim. The Shanisrond boy stared down at the *Watcher's Wait*.

'Do not delay,' said Khigir, gesturing the boys onward. Maxim closed his mouth and bowed his head. They passed beneath a stone arch wide enough to admit four men abreast and struggled to make it much further. Those children who were not exhausted from the climb were mute with shock. The island had been hollowed out around a vast square, steps at every side leading to towering stone buildings carved into the very rock. Steiner noticed none of this, transfixed by the dragon standing before the rabble of children. He did not know it was a dragon, how could he? The Solmindre Empire had banned all icons and images of those terrible creatures. Yet there was nothing else in all of Vinterkveld that the creature could possibly be. Scores of feet high with a serpentine body perched atop powerful hind legs, the creature made a mockery of even the tallest soldiers. The muzzle was split wide to reveal teeth like short swords, the mouth seemingly frozen in a tortured, silent howl. Steiner shivered as he looked into one heavy-lidded onyx eye, where there was a maddened gleam that spoke of hunger and fury. Sheets of flame danced over the dragon's numberless scales, while the wings rivalled the mainsails of the *Watcher's Wait*.

'And may Frøya keep me close,' breathed Steiner.

CHAPTER EIGHT

Kjellrunn

It is easy to assume that the Emperor trusted his power to the Vigilants and the Synod alone, but all organisations are capable of corruption. To Hierarchs tempted to flee the Empire, I say steel yourselves. To Ordinaries turning a blind eye to those with witchsign, I say look to your duty. And to those who resort to assassination, I say abandon your schemes. To err is to invite the attention of the Okhrana, to err is to be hunted by the riders in black.

– From the field notes of Hierarch Khigir,
Vigilant of the Imperial Synod.

The day let itself be known to Kjellrunn in glimpses and flashes, like sunlight reaching far into the depths of the ocean. Here the sound of a voice in the street outside, elsewhere a maddened dog barking in the distance. She was warm and heavy with darkness, wrapped in blankets and yesterday's clothes. Her eyes were comfortably heavy-lidded and she'd no wish to rouse herself. Let Marek fetch the water from the well. Steiner could make his own breakfast. It wouldn't hurt him to sweep the kitchen and stoke up the fire.

Steiner.

Something was wrong, something nameless and sour.

'Steiner?' she mumbled, but no answer came.

Kjellrunn rolled onto her side and forced herself to stand. She'd been disorientated before, blindly stumbling through mornings, but never anything like this.

'Steiner, I think I'm ill.' Still no answer.

Her thoughts were like dandelion seeds drifting on the wind.

'Steiner?'

No need to dress, her rumpled clothes were testament to her collapsing into bed late last night. It must have been a long day. She became very still in the darkness of the loft.

The Invigilation.

To call it running would have been inaccurate, but her body did its best to obey her wishes, her feet slipping and catching on the staircase down. No need to search the smithy or the kitchen. She was out into the street and loping towards the bay with her heart beating fierce and insistent. The sun was well up past the horizon, up behind the blanket of frail grey cloud that hung over Cinderfell day in and day out.

How could I have slept in on a day like this?

She ran on, her senses becoming clearer, the cold air jagged in her lungs and throat. Her fingers burned with cold. She hadn't even noticed the light rain until she almost slipped on the slick cobbles.

How could I have forgotten what happened yesterday?

Through the town and past cottages with plumes of grey smoke drifting from their grey stone chimneys, down the street with dark grey cobbles shining wetly in the rain. So much grey she could almost feel it, leaching the life out of her, leaching hope.

Steiner. He was all she could think of, and though her calves burned with pain she ran onward. Pinpricks of agony stabbed at her lungs, and still she ran.

Steiner. Kjellrunn knew he'd gone before she'd reached the pier. The dark red frigate was nowhere in sight, only a flat expanse of the Spøkelsea. Kristofine stood on the pier, a lonely watcher, head covered with a shawl. Gulls keened above them and the wind gusted into land, bringing showers like formless spirits trying to return home from the sea.

'He's gone,' said Kjellrunn, unable to think clearly, tears tracking down her cheeks.

Kristofine turned and opened her mouth, closing it quickly to still her quivering lip, then answered with tears of her own.

'Where is everyone?' asked Kjellrunn. A deathly stillness had come to Cinderfell, and not a soul could be seen except for the woman beside her.

'They've all retired home,' replied Kristofine, her voice flat and tired. 'They came to watch him leave.' She paused a moment, a shadow of frown crossing her face, a fleeting sneer on her pretty lips. 'They came to make sure he was taken. A few even watched the ship sail away, but they've all slunk home now like whipped dogs.' She took Kjellrunn's arm in hers and led her back to the town, beginning the incline up to the tavern.

Kjellrunn wanted to speak, but her mind remained blank and the words wouldn't come. No sobs wracked her slight frame, but new tears appeared every few heartbeats, new tears that burned with cold as they dried on her face.

'There are a few dozen old sots at the Smouldering Standard and half that at my father's,' said Kristofine. 'Most people are home with their loved ones, I expect.'

'Grateful their own weren't taken,' replied Kjellrunn, gazing ahead and holding tight to woman beside her.

'Yes, I suppose they are. Nothing like this has happened in Cinderfell for decades.' Kristofine sighed. 'I see them take the children away every year, but somehow witchsign was always something that happened to other towns, other countries, other people.'

'Like an accident,' said Kjellrunn. 'Like a cart that overturns and kills the driver.'

Kristofine stopped and looked into her eyes.

'Are you unwell, Kjellrunn? You seem, I mean I know what's happened to Steiner is awful, but you seem drowsy—'

'Or drugged,' said Kjellrunn, remembering the bitter tang of the hot milk that Marek had given her. 'My father drugged my milk so I wouldn't wake this morning and cause a fuss, wouldn't tell them . . .'

'Tell them what?'

Tell them not to take Steiner, tell them that's it's me with the witchsign, it's me they should be taking to the island. This is all my fault and—

'Tell them what, Kjell?' Kristofine's words silenced the deep ocean of guilt and the undertow of shame. Kjellrunn swallowed and stared into her eyes.

'Tell them not to take Steiner, of course.' For a second she wasn't sure if Kristofine believed her. Kjellrunn dropped her gaze.

'My own father drugged me so I wouldn't wake. I didn't even get to say goodbye.' More tears tracked down her cheeks, though it made small difference in the rain. Kristofine pulled her close and woman and girl resumed their walk up the hill to Bjørner's tavern.

'I can't come in with you,' said Kjellrunn, remembering the flat, unfriendly stares she'd received yesterday and Håkon's looming presence.

Kristofine inclined her head and circled the building, leading Kjellrunn through a side door. A small sitting room waited for them, shrouded in darkness. Kristofine lit an expensive-looking brass lantern.

'Wait here, build up the fire if you like. I'll make you some tea to warm you up. And I'll bring a blanket. We should try and dry your clothes or you'll catch a chill.'

Kjellrunn could only nod, too stunned to smile. No one had ever fussed over her so tenderly. Marek was a good father, but his was a functional mind, only affectionate when he remembered to make the effort.

'Thank you,' said Kjellrunn, an uncertain smile on her slender face.

'I'll be right back.' Kristofine left the room and her footsteps sounded on the stairs in a series of creaks.

The sitting room had three armchairs, all draped with blankets and cosy with cushions. Kjellrunn wondered what it must be like to have another room besides the kitchen and a place to sleep. Another door led from the sitting room; the rumble of men's voices could be heard through timber. She guessed the door must lead to the tavern itself.

'Bad enough he was a half-wit that couldn't read, but to have the taint too,' said one voice.

'He was no half-wit, and there's no shame in not reading,' replied another. 'There's plenty of us that get by without words.'

There were a few sullen grunts at this admission.

'They say it runs in families,' said Håkon; Kjellrunn would know his gruff tone anywhere. 'We need to keep an eye on that girl.'

'She passed the Invigilation,' protested a woman's voice. 'Let her be. She's just lost her brother.'

'Mark my words,' replied Håkon. 'There's something unseemly about her.'

'You mean unearthly, you dimwit,' said another voice, and the room filled with mocking laughter.

'Kjellrunn, you're white as a ghost.' Kristofine had returned, a blanket slung over one arm. 'What's wrong?'

'I shouldn't be here. It's not safe for me. I don't know what I was thinking. Your father told me I wasn't welcome here.'

'I brought you here,' said Kristofine, quiet yet defiant. 'You've just lost your brother and you're wet to the skin. Now come on, off with those clothes and get this blanket around your shoulders.'

Kjellrunn stared at the woman, just two years between them but worlds apart. She felt tears fill the corners of her eyes once more and stony grief weighed on her chest.

'Come on now,' whispered Kristofine. Kjellrunn shucked off the wet clothes and pulled the blanket around her quickly. Slipping into an armchair and pulling her knees up to her chest.

'I was sorry to hear about your mother's passing,' said Kjellrunn.

'Oh, that.' Kristofine shook her head. 'It was a year ago.'

'I didn't know you a year ago.' Kjellrunn paused, watching the woman hang her clothes out by the fireplace. Kristofine knelt down and stoked the fire, adding a few logs.

Why are you being so nice to me? she wanted to ask.

Kristofine smiled and took a seat in the armchair opposite.

'Strange you mention my mother. I was just thinking about Steiner, he told me that you never knew yours. He said he can barely remember her. That must be hard.'

Kjellrunn nodded but didn't trust herself to speak. Hadn't Verner said that she took after her mother? Hadn't Marek said the arcane burned people up and hollowed them out? Her mother might well have passed on to Frejna's realm.

'Why are you being so nice to me?' said Kjellrunn, so quietly the words were almost lost as the fire crackled and popped.

'I suppose I know what it is to miss someone,' replied Kristofine. 'I didn't always see eye to eye with my mother, but I'd give anything to have her back.' She leaned forward in her chair, rested her elbows on her knees and laced her fingers together. 'I imagine you feel like that right now about Steiner. And your mother too.'

The rumble of voices in the tavern fell quiet and Kjellrunn

turned her head, ears straining for a snatch of sound or some clue.

'Come here,' said Kristofine, and led her to the wall where the timber's grain formed a whorl, a knot of wood. Kristofine picked at the knot until something came free.

'It's a cork from a wine bottle,' said Kjellrunn.

Kristofine nodded and held a finger to her lips, then gestured to Kjellrunn to peek through the hole in the wall. The view of the tavern was a good one, though Kjellrunn had to go up on her toes to see through the hole.

Bjørner stood behind the bar, one brawny hand resting on the polished surface. It was the only thing polished about the tavern; Steiner used to joke that Bjørner spent more time caring for the bar than he did himself. Håkon leaned against the wall nursing a pint and fixing an unfriendly stare across the room. Two men in black stood beside the door, cowing the room into silence. Kjellrunn pulled back and gestured that Kristofine look.

'What will you drink?' said Bjørner, his words too loud and too forced in the sullen quiet.

'They're Okhrana,' whispered Kristofine, pulling back from the spy hole.

'Imperial?' replied Kjellrunn.

Kristofine nodded. 'Has your father never told you of the Okhrana?'

Kjellrunn pressed her eye to the hole again. 'My father never told us lots of things.'

The men in black had moved out of sight, but the sidelong looks of the townsfolk told Kjellrunn the Okhrana hadn't left. She saw the furtive glances and faces lined with worry. Hands grasped at pints and even the most bellicose of the townsfolk became as field mice.

'They are the Emperor's watchmen, his bloody left hand,' said Kristofine.

'And the soldiers?'

'The soldiers are his bloody right hand,' replied Kristofine. 'The mailed fist used to ensure obedience.'

'And where does that leave the Synod and the Vigilants?'

'They are the Emperor's heart. The Emperor is one of them, after all.'

'The Emperor is a Vigilant?' Kjellrunn frowned.

'Does your father tell you nothing?'

'He tells me to brush my hair and wash dishes. He only scowls when we mention the Empire, and the meisters at school refuse to acknowledge anything east of the border.'

Kristofine peeked through the spy hole once more and then stoppered it with the cork.

'We've never had Okhrana here before. In Cinderfell perhaps, but they usually stay at the Smouldering Standard. They never darken our door. Why are they here?'

'Because of what happened at Helwick,' said Kjellrunn, her eyes straying to the sitting room door, expecting the Okhrana to enter at any moment.

'What happened at Helwick?'

'I have to go,' said Kjellrunn, and began pulling on her damp clothes.

Kristofine folded her arms and watched the girl dress from the corner of her eye, disapproval written clearly on her sullen pout.

'What happened in Helwick?' she repeated, and all trace of the kindly elder sister she'd pretended to be disappeared.

'A Troika of Vigilants were killed. Or went missing. Something like that.'

'A whole Troika?'

'All three. A traveller told us just yesterday morning as he was leaving town.' Kjellrunn hated lying but how else would she know if not for the fact she knew the killer?

'So why don't the Okhrana search Helwick? Why are they in Cinderfell? Why are they here?'

Kjellrunn pulled on her boots and shrugged, then looked away, unwilling to add to the tangle of deceit.

'I have to go,' was all she said.

'Fine,' replied Kristofine, 'I need to get to work, my father will be wondering where I've fetched up.'

'Thank you,' said Kjellrunn awkwardly as she fumbled with the door handle. Kristofine didn't move from the fireplace, watching her leave with an accusing gaze.

The sky was full of keening wind and cold rain as Kjellrunn trudged home, and remained so for many hours to come.

CHAPTER NINE

Steiner

There can only be true peace when the Scorched Republics give up their foolish notions of autonomy and join the glory of the Empire. Once we are united we will crush the city states of Shanisrond in the south. Until then, the Empire waits for war and all its chances for glory.

> – From the field notes of Hierarch Khigir,
> Vigilant of the Imperial Synod.

The creature remained unflinching, unmoving beneath writhing fire. Steiner dared himself to look away. The newcomers were not alone; other girls and boys lined the edges of the square, ranging from ten to twenty years old. All were pale with tiredness and sullen-eyed. They wore quilted coats in mottled scarlet that reached their knees, while heavy boots and mittens completed the attire. Steiner guessed them to be novices, cargoes from previous years, other lives separated from their loved ones. Here was the living proof they would not be executed after all. The children hunkered in the doorways of buildings many storeys tall, others hid in shadows beneath brightly coloured awnings.

The soldiers filed into the square behind the new arrivals, blocking the archway beneath the gatehouse. There would be no frantic dash down the steps to Romola, no desperate begging to escape. The soldiers unslung their maces and held them close to their sides, hidden along the line of their cloaks. The dragon remained still, even as the fire continued to roil about it.

'It's a statue,' said Steiner after a moment. He stepped forward and held his hands up. The fire at least was real, he could feel the warmth even at a distance of several feet.

'This one has a brain,' said Shirinov. He moved through the throng of children, leaning heavily on his walking stick as he went.

'You are almost right about the statue,' said Khigir, but was prevented from explaining further as Shirinov bellowed at the new arrivals to form three rows directly beneath the maddened gaze of the dragon.

'There's been some mistake,' muttered Aurelian. 'If you could just get word to my father he'll see you're handsomely rewarded.' The blond-haired boy preened. 'I don't have witchsign, I can assure you.' He was duly cuffed by Shirinov for not standing to attention.

'For years you have been told that children with witchsign are cleansed.' Shirinov let the last word hang in the air. That the far side of the square was crowded with children undermined the threat of any cleansing, whatever the term had implied.

'You are not to be killed or cremated. You will in fact be quite safe. At first.' Shirinov's silver smile was, as ever, at odds with the words emanating from behind it. 'You are to become the next generation of Vigilants in the service of the Solmindre Empire, new blood for the Synod.'

The novices at the far side automatically stood straighter at the mention of the Empire, a few standing to attention, almost snapping out salutes.

'You can do this willingly, or you can serve the Empire in a less pleasing but infinitely longer fashion.' Shirinov lifted his gaze to the dragon, regarding the massive form as if it were some great work of art. 'There will be some of you who are reluctant to use your powers, and some of you,' the Vigilant paused, clamping one hand on Steiner's shoulder, 'remain unknowing.' Shirinov hobbled a few paces and thrust his face towards Maxim. 'But there is witchsign upon you, within you, and we will draw it out. If you must be tainted with the arcane then you will use your powers in service to the Empire.'

'I'm sure if you test me again you'll see—' Aurelian's protest was cut short as Shirinov knocked him to the ground with a gesture from several feet away. The boy yelped and several children flinched on instinct. All stared, mouths slack with shock, faces frozen with disbelief that Shirinov could mete out punishment from afar.

'You will demonstrate your abilities,' continued Shirinov, 'just as I have demonstrated mine.' He paced along the row to where Aurelian had fallen. 'You can demonstrate them willingly.' He leaned low over the blond-haired boy, his silver mask falling into shadow. 'Or under duress. The choice is yours. I suggest you make the most of it; you'll have few choices available in the years ahead.'

'You don't have it, do you?' said Maxim under his breath.

'Have what?' replied Steiner.

'The witchsign. I can tell, I could sense it on everyone in the hold, but not you.'

'Don't say anything,' growled Steiner. Shirinov was shouting at a rake-thin girl who looked ready to collapse.

Maxim frowned at Steiner again and muttered, 'Tell them. They'll let you go home.'

'No, they won't,' replied Steiner. 'Now that I've seen the island there's no going back.'

'Tell them,' urged Maxim.

'Tell us what?' grunted Khigir. Whereas Shirinov had been visible and loud, Khigir remained silent, haunting the back of the crowd like a lost soul. Somehow Maxim had missed the Vigilant standing nearby, despite the many tongues of fire that danced around his boots and the hem of his coat. 'Tell us what?' repeated Khigir.

'Nothing,' replied Steiner, though he knew the ruse would be over shortly. They'd ask him to demonstrate witchsign in some form and nothing would happen. Then would come the consequences; what would happen to him? Would the Vigilants return to Cinderfell? Would they return for Kjellrunn?

Shirinov strode across the square until the two Vigilants stood shoulder to shoulder, looming over Steiner, who remained unbowed by the smiling and frowning faces that crowded his vision in silver and bronze.

'Tell them what?' shouted Shirinov so loud the child beside Steiner began snivelling.

'Nothing. There's nothing to tell. The boy misunderstood me is all.'

Shirinov turned to Maxim and levitated him with a gentle motion from an open palm. The children around them gasped and Maxim could only stare at the ground in sickened awe.

'Tell. Them. What?' repeated Shirinov.

'Steiner doesn't have witchsign! You chose him wrongly! He shouldn't be here. Let him go home.' Maxim had squeezed his eyes shut but none failed to notice the tears at the corners. He was seven feet from the ground and trembling with fear.

'You think I don't know how to conduct an Invigilation?' seethed Shirinov.

'He means no harm,' said Steiner. 'He's just mistaken is all.'

'Mistake? I do not make mistakes.' The Vigilant crooked his fingers until they were claw-like, grasping at something unseen. Maxim began wailing, and held hands up to his face and curled into a ball.

'That's enough!' shouted Steiner. Khigir remained silent, but edged away from Shirinov, who continued to tighten his arcane grip on Maxim.

'It will be enough when I say it's enough,' replied the Vigilant. 'Is it not like the grip of the Empire? Absolute in every way.'

'I said that's enough,' bellowed Steiner. He pulled the sledgehammer free of the bag and swung it in a broad arc. Steiner felt the heat of all his anger, his frustration, his disappointment, all joined in the surging motion of the attack. The sledgehammer caught the Vigilant in the side of his chest, but not before Shirinov raised a hand to ward off the blow. Steiner felt the resistance, noticed the hammer slow before it took Shirinov from his feet, lifting him into the air. The hunched Vigilant staggered and collapsed amid the newcomers, who scattered to all corners of the square. The walking stick clattered on the flagstones as Maxim landed face down on the cobbles with a grunt. The boy did not move and a terrible hush settled over everyone, all eyes turning to Steiner, Shirinov, and the crumpled form of Maxim.

For a moment the only motion in the square was the flickering of flames. It seemed to Steiner that the dragon who stood above them was not wreathed in flames, but contained by them instead. Smaller flames continued to dance around Khigir's feet and the frowning mask moved side to side in a slow shake.

'Steiner. What have you done?'

The soldiers burst forward, raising their maces. Steiner stood his ground, grasping the hammer defiantly, but it was not the soldiers with their helms and red stars that concerned him. Shirinov dragged himself to his feet, hands pressed to his ribs. The silver mask lifted and the smile on its lips had never been crueller, a trickle of blood leaking from one corner.

'I'm going to enjoy destroying you,' said the Vigilant. He reached out again, a tender gesture at odds with the intended result. Steiner glanced down, rewarded with the sight of solid ground beneath his boots.

'What is this?' The Vigilant reached forth with both hands, fingers splayed, shaking with effort. Steiner felt the power brush against him, no more than a harsh breeze. He was unsure why he resisted Shirinov's power but was grateful all the same. The Vigilant stumbled, as if buffeted by the wind. Shirinov took a moment to retrieve his walking stick before lifting his hand once more. This time the gesture was a command, not a summoning of power.

'Take him,' he said. The soldiers behind Steiner drew close and raised their maces. Steiner hefted the sledgehammer in response, knowing he'd be lucky to take just one of them before they beat him to the ground.

'*Stand down!*' The words were a thunderclap across the square and the soldiers fell back two steps and stood to attention. Steiner turned to find another Vigilant descending the steps of one the larger buildings. Other Vigilants followed in her wake, including one wearing a mask like a wolf's face, but it was clear who was in charge. The many novices bowed their heads and Khigir and Shirinov stood to attention. A single word rushed around the square, an awed susurrus:

Felgenhauer.

The Vigilant wore a mask the colour of drab stone, all features angular, neither masculine nor feminine. The mouth was a displeased slash and the eyes that stared through the holes bore many questions.

'What is going on here?' said the Vigilant.

'The boy struck me with the hammer,' muttered Shirinov.

'I wasn't talking to you.' There was a softness to the voice despite the anger. The person behind the angular mask was a woman. She was perhaps an inch or two taller than Steiner, with a long-limbed, rangy physique. 'I asked you a question, boy.'

'The Vigilant was crushing that boy to death.' He pointed at Maxim, still splayed across the cobbles. 'I tried to stop him.'

The woman crossed to the unmoving boy and removed a thick leather glove before feeling for a pulse. Her shoulders slumped and Steiner could hear her sigh even with the mask on.

'Is he dead?' asked Steiner, but the Vigilant didn't answer. She stood slowly, collecting herself, then raised her voice.

'I am Matriarch-Commissar Felgenhauer. While you are on this island you will obey my commands. You will anticipate my commands. You will comport yourselves in a manner befitting an Imperial Vigilant.' She crossed a few steps to Shirinov and looked over his shoulder at the novices behind him.

'From the lowliest newcomer, to the thorniest Ordinary or most hallowed Exarch.' She leaned closer to Shirinov. 'You will behave like servants of the Empire. Do you understand?'

All present in the square nodded except Shirinov.

'Do you understand?' said Felgenhauer, her voice quiet, but no less threatening for the lack of volume.

Shirinov bowed his head. 'Of course, Matriarch-Commissar.'

Felgenhauer turned her attention back to Maxim.

'And what exactly did this child do to threaten our continued existence?' Maxim had never looked smaller as Felgenhauer stood over him. Steiner wanted to rush to the boy's side and see if he still breathed.

'He spoke out,' mumbled Shirinov. 'He accused me of being wrong.'

'Wrong?' said Felgenhauer 'Wrong how, exactly?'

'He said the hammer-wielder doesn't have witchsign.'

'Is it true?' asked Felgenhauer, her voice loaded with indignation.

'Of course it's not true.' Shirinov's chin lifted and his hands clenched into fists. 'I've conducted scores of Invigilations and never been wrong.'

Felgenhauer turned her back to him, her angular mask intimidating as the firelight gleamed and shone from its edges.

'Do you have a name, boy?'

'Steiner.'

Felgenhauer paused, as if her line of thought had been broken by that single word.

'And where do you hail from, Steiner?'

'Cinderfell,' he replied. The Matriarch-Commissar took a moment to compose her next question, then cleared her throat instead. Steiner felt the intensity of her gaze and set his eyes straight ahead. The Matriarch-Commissar circled him, much as Shirinov had done in the school square.

'The Solmindre Empire preach that witchsign is a taint, something to be feared, something to be despised.' Her voice was loud enough to carry to every corner of the square and all the novices and students listened intently, wearing expressions of awe.

'We do this so the people will gladly give over their children, we do this so people are glad to be rid of them. To be rid of you. In truth the Empire would be nothing without witchsign.'

She had circled behind Steiner now, yet he could feel the weight of her regard upon him, a tangible force upon his shoulders.

'Witchsign is power, but all power comes at a cost, as you will find out in the days, months and years ahead. Those who wield the greatest power know little peace.' She continued pacing, coming full circle until she faced Steiner and pressed her masked face close to his. 'There is witchsign here!'

'As I always said,' replied Shirinov, wiping the blood from his mask with the back of a gloved hand.

'This is so,' added Khigir.

Steiner swallowed in a dry throat, then shook his head, confused.

Felgenhauer turned to the two Vigilants, and Steiner saw them for what they were: two old men, attired in frayed finery, dressed up with self-importance.

'Put down the sledgehammer and remove your boots,' said Felgenhauer without turning.

'W-what?' replied Steiner.

'I said, "Put down the sledgehammer and remove your boots,"' she bellowed.

'I'm not deaf,' mumbled Steiner.

'You're not stupid either,' said the Matriarch-Commissar. 'So don't ever dream of speaking back to me again.'

Steiner relinquished the gifts Romola had given him just a few hours before. The sledgehammer made a dull scrape on the flagstones as he set it down. One boot followed another and the cold crept into the soles of his feet through the worn wool of his socks. Felgenhauer drew close and Steiner forced himself to look at the dragon, wreathed in terrible flames, anything to be spared the piercing eyes of the Matriarch-Commissar. She picked up one of the boots and spent a few seconds inspecting it as if it were a precious jewel or sacred relic.

'Nice boots,' she said quietly.

'Thanks,' mumbled Steiner on instinct. 'My mother gave them to me,' he added, without really knowing why.

Felgenhauer turned to Shirinov and shook her head.

'You fool! Can you not tell the difference between witchsign and enchanted boots? How many years have you served, how many decades?'

'Boots?' replied Shirinov. 'What enchanted boots?'

'What?' moaned Khigir.

'I've more arcane power in my smallest finger than this boy does in his whole body,' said Felgenhauer. 'How could you make such a mistake?'

Khigir shook his head and Shirinov could only hold out placating hands.

'This is most irregular.'

'What am I supposed to do with a boy without witchsign?' said the Matriarch-Commissar.

'I'm a man really,' said Steiner. 'I turned eighteen last—'

'Shut up,' said Felgenhauer quietly.

'How could I know the boy wore enchanted boots?' replied Shirinov. 'Peasants don't possess such items. I'm sure he wasn't wearing—'

'Be quiet,' said Felgenhauer.

Khigir stepped forward. 'Only the very highest-ranking—'

'I said be quiet!' growled Felgenhauer.

Shirinov's shoulder's slumped and he clutched his walking stick with both hands. Khigir all but cowered behind him.

'This is unprecedented,' stated Felgenhauer. The other Vigilants conferred among themselves, the snarling wolf face turning to a Vigilant wearing a silver oval, blank of any feature including eyes. Steiner felt sure he was being watched despite the omission. There was a faint haze around the Vigilant, and motes of grit flared silver before burning up.

The Matriarch-Commissar turned to the Vigilant with the blank silver face.

'Silverdust, take these soldiers and escort the boy to my office. Don't take your eyes off him.' Felgenhauer's eyes glittered behind the angular mask.

'What will happen to me?' asked Steiner.

'You raised a weapon against a member of the Holy Synod.

Such crimes do not go unpunished, and on Vladibogdan the punishments are severe.'

The Vigilant called Silverdust drew close, raised one hand and gestured for Steiner to follow.

CHAPTER TEN

Kjellrunn

Vladibogdan was originally the lair of the grandfather of all dragons, Bittervinge. It was here that the final battle was fought during the Age of Tears, bringing an end to draconic tyranny and ushering in the Age of Steel. The events of that final battle were wreathed in secrecy, and to this day, few know what happened between the Emperor, Bittervinge, and the Emperor's most trusted bodyguard.

– From the field notes of Hierarch Khigir,
Vigilant of the Imperial Synod.

Kjellrunn stood in the kitchen, arms crossed over her stomach, shoulders hunched. She had fled from Kristofine's stern gaze and found the cottage empty. Only when Marek coughed and spluttered from upstairs did she realize he had gone to bed.

Kjellrunn stood before the fire but it seemed as if Steiner had taken some measure of the warmth with him. Her gaze was locked on a point neither near nor far, her attention equally unfocused. The low grumble of her brother's waking was gone. The way he cleared his throat first thing in the morning – a habit that infuriated her – was also absent. His face, always so serious in repose, would not be seen again, nor the way he stretched in front of the fire before heading to bed each night.

She remained lost to reverie when Marek found her. Her father had aged overnight. It was apparent in his red-rimmed eyes and ashen complexion, revealed in the faltering steps he took across the room, manifested in the stoop and curve of shoulders once wide and strong.

'You put something in my milk.'

Marek didn't attempt the lie, merely nodded wearily, not meeting her eyes.

'We had to keep you safe, the things we have done to keep you safe . . .'

Her father shuffled forward until they opened their arms to each other. Marek's was a sombre hug, and Kjellrunn returned it with reluctance. The embrace consumed long seconds of stillness until Marek took a sharp intake of breath. Her first thought was that he was hurt in some way, but then he began to sob. It was a silent shaking grief that escaped him; making a sound would be the final admission he was grieving. Better to cling to the quiet, better to cling to words unsaid.

'Build up the fire, Kjell.' The words were a rough whisper on the air, so faint she nearly missed them. Marek turned, no sign of his usual vigour, no certainty in his steps save for the fact they would lead him back to bed. She didn't doubt he would remain there for the rest of the day. So unlike the man she knew, so unlike Marek the blacksmith that the townsfolk admired and respected. But what did she really know of Marek Vartiainen? Not much, she decided. Steiner had called Marek a spy, and Verner had admitted as much. What other secrets did they keep?

Kjellrunn knelt at the hearth and picked up the firewood. She would not stay prisoner to the drabness of the cottage, could not stay in a place so drowned in sadness. The fire curled into life, from a dull wisp of smoke to a single tongue of fire. Minutes passed until a choir of flames danced beneath the mantelpiece.

'I will not stay here,' she breathed. 'I will not stay with spies and sadness and sleeping drafts.'

Cinderfell's skies offered no reprieve from Steiner's absence. The sea continued its ebb and swell, miles of mindless waves throwing themselves against the shingle without enthusiasm. Kjellrunn closed her eyes, aware of the water's motion and mood, even at this distance. Somehow she could feel the wake of the ship's departure, as if this event were cut into the Spøkelsea like a scar.

'Kjell?' Verner stood a half-dozen feet away with a wary look in his eye. How long had she been standing there, lost to the hushed rapture of the sea?

'I . . .' No explanation would suffice, no reason a supposedly sane girl was standing in the street on a winter's day with her eyes closed. 'I was just thinking about Steiner, is all.'

'You should be behind doors,' said Verner. 'If anyone sees you like this—'

'What will they do, Verner? Accuse me of witchsign? As if such things haven't been thrown in my face my entire life. And now Steiner's paying the price, paying *my* price, for whatever it is I am.'

'Don't speak of such things in the street!' said Verner, mouth twisting at the corners. 'He won't be killed.'

'If he lives or dies is beside the point,' said Kjellrunn. 'This is all wrong, and don't think I didn't realize your trick with the milk.'

'Kjell, I'm sorry. We were worried the Vigilants would take you too, or you'd do something rash—'

'Like tell them the truth?'

'It's for the best, Kjell. If they take you then there's no telling what they'll do to you. The arcane demands a high price from those who use it.'

'For the best? This is the best of things, is it? I'm left here with the shadow of the man who used to be my father and an uncle who fancies himself an assassin.'

Verner's face became dark, and he stepped closer, shooting wary glances over his shoulder. The street remained empty. 'Why don't you tell the whole town? Perhaps you could perform it in song.'

'Perhaps I will,' said Kjellrunn.

'Your father wanted to tell you things when the time was right.'

'My father is a stranger to me. And so are you. The only person I really knew is Steiner, and he's gone.' She clutched her shawl tighter, bending against the cold wind that swept down from the north and gusted through Cinderfell's lonely streets. 'The Verner I grew up knowing would never have hurt anyone, much less killed them.'

'Kjell, I didn't . . .' He shook his head and looked away. 'Where are you going?' he asked after a harsh gust of wind buffeted them.

'I don't know,' she replied. 'Anywhere.' She gestured at the cottage before them. 'Anywhere but here with all its sadness.'

She had no desire to wend her way through Cinderfell's streets. Steiner had always loved the town, drawn comfort from the squat cottages and thatched roofs. He was never happier than when he had cobbles beneath his feet and a few coins to spend at the tavern. Kjellrunn blinked away tears.

'Why didn't I go? Why didn't I speak up? Why did I let them take him?' The questions were mangy hounds following at her heels, thick with fleas and rabid in their intensity. 'I'm a coward,' she muttered. The words, louder than she intended, carried on the breeze, raising a look from a fisherman on his way to work. His was a wary expression and Kjellrunn frowned in return.

'I'm not going to turn you into a toad, you fool.' She regretted the words the moment they left her lips. The fisherman looked away, hurrying in to town. No doubt there'd been a good deal of talk about the blacksmith's son, and hadn't everyone always assumed it would be his daughter that would fail the Invigilation? Hadn't she always been the strange one? Not Steiner, so strong and dutiful. Not Steiner, who dreamed of hammered metal in his sleep. Not Steiner, though he struggled to read and had no head for numbers.

Her strides became longer, quicker. Dark clouds hung low in the sky, and Kjellrunn felt them keenly, as if they meant to suffocate her. The cobbles gave way to a road of hard-packed earth, the cottages replaced by hedgerows and sickly evergreens. She hadn't intended to head north and the wind admonished her with every step. Each breeze and gust was light but the chill it carried was bitter. Kjellrunn shivered and clutched her shawl tighter, glad when she reached the edge of the woods.

'Hello, my friends,' she whispered. 'I've much need of you today.'

The trees did not whisper back. The stark bare branches of the oaks had no welcome for her, while the pines stood dark and silent. Gone was the ecstatic susurrus of summer, trees whispering in a joyous hush. Gone were the many sounds of life, bird song and the commotion of woodpeckers. The ground was a sea of fallen leaves, consumed with the gentle business of decay. The ferns, so abundant in summer, so vibrant and green, were now an unlovely brown signalling their intent to rot. They would return to the very earth that had nurtured them.

'How nice it would be to simply slip to the floor and do

nothing but dream of spring, speak to no one, see no one, be spared Cinderfell and Nordvlast and the Empire.' She brushed fingers against an oak tree's rough bark. The tree was a marker, the tiny clearing a spot she retreated to, an enclave away from the town. 'But not today,' she whispered, pressing deeper in to the woods. Marek had warned her it was unwise to wander so far from home, but she refused to turn back. Chilled fingers gathered the odd stick of wood; the idea of going home empty-handed was not a welcome one. Her father may not notice, lost to grief as he was, but they'd need firewood soon enough.

She journeyed deeper into the forest, lost to her thoughts and picking out sticks of firewood when she remembered. The chalet was as unexpected as it was unremarkable. A single storey with the thatched roof and short chimney so common to Cinderfell. Moss grew in a rich blanket across one wall, finding purchase on the slope of old thatch above. Windows remained shuttered against the day, yet the door was ajar, though only to the keenest eyes.

'It can't hurt to take a look,' she reassured herself.

A wide stump of wood emerged from the earth between Kjellrunn and the chalet door, marked with cuts now dark from rain and moss. A woodcutter's chalet then. Her father had mentioned it before, but she'd never given much thought to where it was.

She drew closer, curiosity making her bold. No light flickered from the gap in the door. No golden glow escaped the shutters' edges. A trio of sensations gave her pause: unease at being alone in such a secluded place, cold at the dictates of the wind that found a way to her, even here deep in the woodland. And of being watched, yet that was the work of a foolish mind, she chided herself.

'I'm not scared,' she whispered to herself. 'I'll not jump at shadows,' she said, keen to reassure herself.

The snap of a branch beneath her foot made her flinch so hard she slipped and fell amid the dead leaves. The firewood she had gathered lay all around her. No sooner had she recovered herself than two crows called out, strident at first then settling into a brooding silence.

'You might have warned me about the branch.' Kjellrunn favoured the crows with a dark look. The first hid its head under a wing, while the other raised tail feathers and released a jet of watery droppings.

'Would it kill you to show some manners?' Kjellrunn turned her back on the birds and regarded the chalet. It was less imposing now she'd scared herself insensible. She reached for the door and once again the crows called out. Kjellrunn froze; a wary look over her shoulder confirmed the raucous birds were agitated. They flapped wings and fussed until one knocked the other from their perch, causing Kjellrunn to smirk.

Steiner wouldn't be deterred by a couple of noisy old crows.

One of the birds stared after her, the other flapped about on the ground, aggrieved.

Her chilled fingers pushed the door open and Kjellrunn blinked in the gloom. She remained in the doorway, unwilling to cross the threshold, hoping the meagre daylight would reveal some clue about the derelict dwelling. Nothing stirred in the darkness yet Kjellrunn's curiosity burned brightly. She crossed to the hearth, hands held out to ashes, palms rewarded with the faintest warmth. Someone had been here, just last night perhaps. A puddle of water had collected in the dust nearby. Kjellrunn traced the source to a cloak hanging from an iron peg. She had a vivid impression of stumbling through the woods late at night, wet to the skin and desperate for shelter.

The chalet was not so different to her own home. Three chairs attended a table standing in the centre of the room.

An unlit lantern hung from a hook by the door, soot-black and rust-red. Leaves lay strewn about the flagstones, collected in drifts at the corners, the alcove beside the fire deep with them. Dead ferns and twigs added to the debris. Rustling sounded and Kjellrunn stared with widening eyes. A breeze gusted through the doorway, making her shiver. Wild thoughts summoned the spirit of a long-dead woodcutter, appearing to defend the home he had loved so much in life. The leaves in the alcove continued to shake. Kjellrunn lurched towards the door as a bleary-eyed winter fox appeared, snuffling about the cold flagstones.

Kjellrunn released a long sigh. 'Sorry to wake you.'

The winter fox blinked at her, white fur spectral in the darkness.

'It's fine,' said a voice from the back room, rusty with sleep.

Kjellrunn's heart kicked in her chest and she was running before the thought had occurred. Her elbow glanced painfully off the doorway as she fled through it and she was under the grey sky again, panic gripping lungs that sought air to speed her on. Feet slipped and skidded on mud, tree branches reached for frantic eyes and all was blind panic. Only when she reached the opposite side of the clearing did she stop, listening to her ragged breathing, eyes fixed on the chalet door.

No one emerged, living or dead. Not the phantom wood-cutter of her imagination or the slumbering winter fox. No one chased after her, nor did they peer from the doorway with a frown. The crows called out, mocking this foolish frightened girl, she imagined.

'Shut your beaks,' said Kjellrunn, not taking her eye from the lonely chalet. The occupant did not sate her curiosity by stepping outside.

'I was more frightened than the fox was,' she muttered. Still nothing. No sign of the voice in the darkness.

Kjellrunn gathered the scattered firewood as she departed. *Perhaps I imagined the voice. A figment of a scared girl in the woods alone.* She knew full well her imagination needed no provocation.

The chalet was almost lost from sight when she stole a glance over her shoulder. A curl of smoke drifted from the chimney, faint grey but unmistakable. Someone had lit a fire, but who?

CHAPTER ELEVEN

Steiner

The Solmindre Empire is ruled from the capital at Khlystburg, where our most benevolent Emperor receives counsel from trusted advisers. There is, however, another locus of influence. Arkiv Island is a vast library where Vigilants are invited to meditate and research. Rumours persist that Arkiv is home to moderates within the Synod, those uncomfortable with the Emperor's more direct approach.

– From the field notes of Hierarch Khigir,
Vigilant of the Imperial Synod.

Steiner was marched up to the fifth floor of the academy building, past circular portals large enough to admit men three abreast. Everywhere they went novices mopped floors or polished banisters. Patched britches and simple smocks for the boys, shawls, blouses and peasant skirts for the girls. Steiner regarded their naked dirty feet and shivered. None of the children looked up from their work as the soldiers stamped by. They were ten or eleven at most, heads bowed in obedience or fear. Steiner wondered if Maxim had survived, or if he had been maimed by Shirinov's power.

Silverdust remained silent on the short journey. Grit floated into the air with each step the Vigilant took, combusting into brief flares of silvery light every few heartbeats. It was difficult not to be awed by such a vision, and the heat caused Steiner to sweat.

'Does it hurt?' he asked, unable to keep the question to himself any longer. 'The heat, I mean.'

The Vigilant turned to him and Steiner saw his face reflected back, warped and foolish in the blank silver mask.

I have long been used to the heat. The words crawled on the air, not quite a whisper. Steiner wondered if he'd imagined them, or if the Vigilant had spoken at all.

The waiting room outside the Matriarch-Commissar's office was a windowless chamber devoid of decoration. A lantern stood in each corner of the room on a mahogany stand. Red glass bore the geometric symbols of the Empire, making the walls seem doused in blood. Steiner swallowed in a dry throat and clenched his fists, more to keep his fingers warm than from fear or frustration. The soldiers flanked the door, maces in hand, feet spread apart. There would be no warning. If he tried anything he'd been bludgeoned to death. Silverdust turned to leave and Steiner called out.

'Surely that can't be your real name.'

More of Silverdust's words appeared in his head.

A moniker given to me by the children many years ago. I gave up my real name, just as I gave up my old life.

'And the other Vigilants? Do they have such names?'

Shirinov is called Shatterspine, but never to his face. Felgenhauer is Flintgaze and Khigir is known as—

'Corpsecandle,' said Steiner.

You are not as foolish as you look. Silverdust inclined his head. *Wait here.*

The mirror-masked Vigilant departed, leaving Steiner in the company of four soldiers but not for long. The Matriarch-Commissar swept into the room, closely followed by Shirinov, who hobbled to keep up, his stick clattering on the flagstones. Khigir waited in the corridor beyond, the tongues of flames around his boots pale and yellow.

'This is an outrage!' seethed Shirinov as the Matriarch-Commissar entered her office. 'How was I to know the peasants have access to those sorts of artefacts?'

'Because you're a Vigilant,' said Felgenhauer. 'And you're supposed to be vigilant. The aura an enchanted item emits is quite a different signature to witchsign.' She slammed the door to her office, leaving Steiner in the waiting room with four soldiers and Khigir haunting the corridor beyond. The closed door made no difference; the Hierarch gave free reign to his anger, voice clear despite the heavy wood. The Matriarch-Commissar could barely be heard by contrast.

Steiner regarded the soldiers, ruddy in the lantern light. Only Khigir offered any reprieve from the endless red gloaming.

'Why aren't you in there?'

'I do not have the sight for such things,' replied Khigir.

'The sight?'

'I cannot detect witchsign,' explained Khigir. 'I have worked hard to serve the Empire in different ways, but in this respect I am flawed.' The pitted bronze mask dipped forward, looking melancholy, lit from beneath as it was by the spectral flames.

'So why were you sent to Cinderfell if you can't detect witchsign?'

'Cinderfell held no interest for me. My business was elsewhere.'

Sent to investigate the murdered Vigilants in Helwick, Steiner decided.

Khigir made to speak but paused as more shouting issued from behind the Matriarch-Commissar's door.

'I say we throw him in the sea!' shouted Shirinov. Steiner straightened and glanced anxiously at Khigir.

'This is *your* mistake,' countered the Matriarch-Commissar

as she opened the door. 'I should throw *you* in the harbour for being so inept.'

'What will happen to me?' whispered Steiner.

'There will be plenty of time to decide what to do with you,' said Khigir. 'There is always time on Vladibogdan.'

'Get out of my sight,' yelled the Matriarch-Commissar.

'The boy is trouble, mark my words!' Shirinov exited the office with as much dignity as he could, his limp pronounced, one hand pressed to his ribs where Steiner had struck him. Shirinov leaned forward until the smiling silver face forced Steiner to take a step back.

'He's just a scruffy boy from Cinderfell. Who cares if he lives or dies?'

'What did you do in Cinderfell, boy?' said Felgenhauer, framed by the circular doorframe.

'I was training to be a blacksmith.'

'There's our answer.' The Matriarch-Commissar crossed her arms. 'We're short of workers. He can tend the furnaces with Enkhtuya.'

'This is most unusual,' spluttered Shirinov. 'I will be filing a report to the High Patriarch at Khlystburg. Even your friends at Arkiv will have trouble helping you this time.'

'You must do what you must, Shirinov,' said Felgenhauer in a level voice. 'The failure was yours, I am merely dealing with the consequences. Something you have yet to learn about.'

The stooped Hierarch muttered something, lost behind the smiling silver mask, then shuffled away, one foot all but dragging behind him. Steiner watched as Khigir fell in beside him and conferred in a low voice.

'Boy.' Felgenhauer's voice was quiet. 'Step into my office.'

The soldiers took a step forward but were stilled by the Matriarch-Commissar's outstretched hand.

'I think I can handle one boy, don't you? Without his boots and his hammer he's not so fearsome.'

The soldiers took a step back yet none released his mace. Steiner slunk into the office and the Matriarch-Commissar pointed to a seat. The heavy wooden frame was covered with smooth leather and he sank into the chair. A wave of tiredness swept over him as the tension abated.

The office comprised shelves all lined with neatly ordered leather-bound tomes. More books than the school at Cinderfell owned, though Steiner had never had much use for them. The desk was wide and imposing, made from dark wood. There was nothing in the room to indicate even a mote of character or personal preference. The floorboards lacked a rug, so popular with the people of Solmindre and Nordvlast. The walls were plastered and whitewashed yet no pictures adorned them. The room's focal point was the Matriarch-Commissar herself, looming behind her desk. Steiner bowed his head to be spared her weighty gaze.

'You make quite the entrance, Steiner Erdahl Vartiainen. A peasant arriving on the island with these.' She held up the boots. 'Not to mention striking a Vigilant on the first day.' She placed the sledgehammer on the table with a reverence, the way his father would hold a newly finished piece of work. Nothing remained of the imperious Felgenhauer he'd seen in Academy Square. 'It usually takes a student a year or two before they attempt rebellion.'

'He was hurting Maxim. Is he . . . ?'

'Alive?' Felgenhauer sighed. 'Yes, the boy is alive. For the moment anyway.'

Steiner relaxed into the chair a little more.

'It seems to me you might be useful,' said the Matriarch-Commissar. 'And only a fool kills useful people. Can you promise to stay useful?'

Steiner nodded and clasped the arms of the chair, his breathing quick and shallow.

'Good.' Felgenhauer nodded slowly and folded herself into

her chair. 'I'm putting you to work in the deepest, darkest part of Vladibogdan. It will keep you out of Shirinov's reach if nothing else. I suggest you stay there.'

'What's down there?' said Steiner. Whatever waited below the island was preferable to being cast into the frigid Spøkelsea.

'A smithy, of sorts. Work hard and you'll stay alive. There's no room for weakness down there.'

'Stay useful,' said Steiner, wondering how dreadful the underworld of Vladibogdan could be. 'Stay alive.'

'Go now,' replied Felgenhauer. 'Tell the guards to deliver you to Tief, and pay no mind to Enkhtuya.' The angular features of the mask were at odds with the soft, almost wistful sound of her voice.

'Who is Enkhtuya?'

'Go now.'

Steiner rose from the seat, still unable to make eye contact with the Matriarch-Commissar.

'You don't have to worry, Steiner, I won't turn you to stone.'

'Y-you can do that?'

Felgenhauer nodded. 'With nothing more than a look.'

Steiner performed an awkward half-bow and stumbled against the chair as he left the room and was almost through the door when she spoke again.

'You'll need these if you're to work in the furnaces. Stockinged feet have no business around hot coals.' She rose from her chair and passed him the boots and the sledge-hammer. 'Now get out of my office and don't strike any of my Vigilants. I have an island to run.' Steiner backed into the waiting room as the circular door slammed in his face.

'Stay useful, stay alive,' he muttered before releasing a breath of relief. He took a moment to lace up his boots and the soldiers shifted. He could feel their questions, keen on their lips.

'Can you take me to Tief? In the furnaces?' he said, rising from the bench.

'We are soldiers,' said the tallest of the four. 'We are not here to escort the likes of peasants—' The soldier fell silent as Steiner crossed the wide door of Felgenhauer's office and raised a hand to knock.

'Wait,' said the soldier, the word heavy with the Solska accent.

'Reckon I should have phrased it better,' said Steiner. 'The Matriarch-Commissar wants you to take me to the furnaces and deliver me to Tief.' He hefted the sledgehammer; it was nice to have power, even if he was only borrowing it from Felgenhauer.

'Follow,' said the soldier, and exited to the corridor beyond, descending the first of many steps leading them ever downward.

Only two of the soldiers escorted him, grunting and pointing, shoving him in the desired direction when he moved too slowly.

'How much further?' Steiner asked, keen to fill the stifling silence with something. None of the buildings in Cinderfell rose above two storeys and Steiner marvelled at the winding staircase. The soldiers said nothing, still smarting from the prospect of escorting the troublemaker to the furnaces, wher-ever they were.

'It's a wonder I can get a word in edgeways with you two,' said Steiner over his shoulder, and still nothing.

Neither of the soldiers took the bait, silently ushering him outside to Academy Square, now empty with only the flicker-ing flames of the stone dragon to light the rain-slicked cobbles. Steiner craned his neck to see a patch of grey sky, framed on all sides by the jagged peaks of the island on every side. It was as if he'd fallen into a chasm or a deep crater.

'This way.' The soldiers were identical in the gloom. The outstretched hand pointed to a narrow lane that led away from the square, nestled between two of the academy buildings, towering above.

'But I can't see,' mumbled Steiner, his earlier confidence fled now Felgenhauer was out of sight.

The soldiers shoved him, leaving him no choice but to take step after anxious step along the alleyway. The smell of rotting food was strong here and Steiner gagged behind his sleeve. There was another more familiar smell: smoke and ashes.

'Wait a moment,' said one of the soldiers. 'You stop here.' Steiner waited, squinting into the darkness where the soldiers remained as shadows, only the red stars on their helms hinted that colour had not been leached from the world. One of the soldiers hefted his mace and Steiner felt a surge of fear, felt the cold sweat across his back as his mouth went dry. Surely they wouldn't dream of murdering him in this dank place? Wasn't he under Felgenhauer's protection?

The other soldier busied himself in an alcove and a series of strikes and sparks sounded and shone in the darkness. A torch flared to life and then another. The soldier handed one over.

'You will need this to see way down. Otherwise you break neck.'

Steiner grasped the torch, the smell of pitch overwhelming the other odours of the alley.

'Do not use as weapon,' said the soldier.

Steiner hefted the sledgehammer in his other hand. 'I'm not sure the torch would be my first choice. Where are we going now?'

'Behind you,' said the soldier. Steiner turned and saw what the darkness had concealed. A ragged hole had been punched through the rock at the alley's end. The cobbles stopped and turned up like the blunt teeth of some colossal creature.

'That is where you go,' said the second soldier. He made no move to follow.

'She did say the deepest darkest place,' said Steiner, surprised at the steps, carved into the island itself. The walls pressed in overhead, meeting in a rough arch, twice his height.

'You were supposed to deliver me to Tief,' he said. The soldiers said nothing and turned away, the clink and jingle of armour sounding with each step.

'You can't just leave me here. I don't know my way around.' Steiner couldn't know the expressions they bore beneath the helms but he guessed they might be of relief. 'Some escort you were.' Steiner frowned into the darkness and fought off a wave of panic that rooted him to the spot. The stairwell curved in a gentle arc, the end always just out of sight. Each step was worn smooth and water trickled along channels carved at each side.

'Frejna's teeth. How deep does this go?' he muttered under his breath, pressing deeper along the endless stairs. The torch-light was dwindling. No matter how he twisted the wood the flame would not take, and soon he would be plunged into darkness and lost beneath Vladibogdan.

Deeper and ever downward. If the abandoned square had felt like a chasm then surely this was an abyss. A pause to rest his aching legs and a glance over his shoulder confirmed what he'd known; the oppressive gloom crowded in, held back by the guttering torch. Steiner held up his hand, shielding the torch from the gusts of wind that howled after him in the tunnel, the glow no more than a candle flame.

Steiner hurried onward, downward, wondering if he were beneath the level of the sea. A ruddy light signalled the passage's end, and with the red glow came a terrible heat. The scent of hot metal and coal dust welcomed him, just like in his father's smithy. His feet led him onto a stone balcony above a cavern hundreds of feet wide, lit at intervals by great furnaces. The air was thick with smoke and the sound of hammered metal yet Steiner failed to see a single soul in the ruddy half-light. Leaning from the balcony's edge offered no clue where the noise came from but revealed gleaming metal rungs hammered into the rock. Steiner climbed from rung to rung, cursing his sweating palms, the spent torch discarded.

The air was warm enough to make his skin tight and the smoke forced him to hold a sleeve to his face so he might breathe. He stumbled on, blinking away tears brought on by scorched air and the fine ashes that drifted on it. Never had he seen such a vast scene of industry.

A dark spectre of swirling cinders emerged from a nearby shadow, its eyes the orange of stirred embers, face a shapeless, unknowable darkness. Steiner raised the sledgehammer with shaking hands, hoping the weapon might prove a deterrent. The apparition edged closer, eyes bright with malice.

'May Frejna's eye not find you,' said Steiner, stumbling backwards, voice small in the darkness, 'and may Frøya keep you close.' The apparition reached forth and Steiner called out.

'Stay back now,' he shouted, but the wraith drifted closer still.

CHAPTER TWELVE

Steiner

Perhaps the most troubling discovery of my travels across Vinterkveld is that Spriggani have knowledge of arcane power. It is rooted in the earth and water schools and these schools alone, yet it does not corrupt their bodies in the way that Vigilants become twisted, blackened things.

– From the field notes of Hierarch Khigir,
Vigilant of the Imperial Synod.

Steiner brandished the sledgehammer and still the apparition closed on him, orange eyes bright in the ruddy cavern's gloom.

'Get away from me!' he bellowed and still it came. Steiner swung and the creature came apart like smoke and fine ashes, tendrils of darkness dispersing on the air. The eyes, burning with intent, blinked out, lost to darkness. Steiner took a step back, chest rising and falling with shock.

You never told me stories about these, Kjell.

His eyes remained transfixed on the floor where he'd sundered the spirit. The smoke coalesced and the apparition formed anew, the orange embers of its eyes coming to life as the spirit resumed its shape.

'Just die, will you?' growled Steiner. He desperately wanted to run, but where?

'What foolishness is this?' said a heavily accented voice. 'Get away from him! He'll soil his britches if you keep on so.'

Escorted by three dark apparitions was a man. He stood about a hand's width shorter than Steiner, and wore patched trousers with a grubby smock. The outfit was completed with a thick strap of leather worn across his body from shoulder to hip, festooned with tools. The man held up a lantern and peered into the gloom at Steiner.

'And what might you be doing in this Frøya-forsaken place?' The lantern light revealed high cheekbones, dark eyes and olive skin. Steiner struggled to guess how old he was, at least twenty-five if he had to say.

'You're a Spriggani.'

'And you're not as stupid as you look, which is plenty I might add.'

'What?'

'Never mind. What are you doing down here?'

'My sister would be beside herself, if she were here.'

'It would seem you're fairly beside yourself too. And you still haven't answered my question.'

'My sister said the Spriggani can use the arcane, but the Empire had mostly driven you south, to Shanisrond.'

The man nodded with a grim expression on his face. 'Those Spriggani who could run, fled. And those foolish enough, or stubborn enough, to stay have been killed and captured.'

'Stubborn like you?' asked Steiner.

'Stubborn like me,' agreed the Spriggani. 'Now, are you going to tell me why you're down here?'

'Felgenhauer sent me down here to find someone called Tief. She said I had to help out in the forges.'

'Well, the goddess is with you. I'm Tief and this is the forge.

We're not used to outsiders down here. It usually means trouble.'

The Spriggani pulled out a pipe and set to making himself a smoke as more and more apparitions gathered around them, forming a circle of ashes and shadows. The glowing coals of their eyes were fixed on Steiner and he cast fearful glances over his shoulders.

'Pah!' said the Spriggani. 'You've no need to worry yourself about these lost souls. They'll not harm you. You're one of us now.'

'What are they?'

'Cinderwraiths, forgotten slaves to the Empire, out of sight and out of mind.' The Spriggani blew a jet of smoke that mingled with the wraith Steiner had dissipated with his hammer just moments before.

'Did I hurt it?'

'Hurt isn't the right word,' replied Tief. He added another jet of pipe smoke to the creature. 'Though I've never seen that happen before, truth be told. Still he seems to have got himself together again. If it is indeed a him. I'd say you're more shaken than he is.'

Steiner nodded. That he was talking to a living, breathing, pipe-smoking Spriggani was unbelievable enough, but the cinderwraiths were like something from a nightmare. How many times had he laughed at Kjellrunn for wanting to meet the forest kin?

'So do you have a name, or shall we call you Hammersmith, on account of that great sledge you're so keen on waving about?'

'Steiner. I was brought to the island by mistake. I don't have witchsign.'

'Ah, there's no telling the deaf or the foolish. I said they'd make a hash of things one day. Shame you have to pay the price for their incompetence. Still, at least you'll never be cold again.' Tief had found the silver lining, the furnaces were beyond warm and perspiration dotted Steiner's forehead.

'Felgenhauer said something about Enkhtuya,' said Steiner. 'Does this Enkhtuya run the forge?'

The cinderwraiths drifted away, returning to their furnaces and resuming their tasks.

'Aye, something like that,' said Tief, clamping his teeth on the pipe stem. 'But Enkhtuya doesn't care much for Northmen, so watch your step.' Tief cleared his throat and dipped his chin before muttering, 'Felgenhauer should know better.' The Spriggani toked on his pipe and beckoned with his other hand. 'Come on, now. There's work to be done.'

Tief led him through an underworld of furnaces and fires; barrels of brackish water waited to quench burning hot metal. Cinderwraiths worked in teams; they looked up from their work with burning gazes as Steiner passed.

'They can't speak?'

'No,' said Tief. 'At least no sound I've ever heard. They can converse among themselves, but I've never ascertained how. Only Frejna would know.'

Tief led him on through the cavern and stout crates greeted them at every juncture and turn. Steiner couldn't help but peer into one as they passed by, seeing swords sleeping on beds of canvas and straw.

'I thought the Empire's treaty with the Scorched Republics forbids the forging of weapons.'

'Did you now?' said Tief.

'It was one of the few concessions the Republics won after the destruction of the dragons.' Steiner was less sure of himself. 'A concession meant to stop Imperial expansion.'

'Pah! Expansion. The Hammersmith has all the long words.' Tief toked on his pipe. 'And who told you all of this?'

'My uncle Verner,' said Steiner with a frown, 'in Cinderfell.'

'And where are you now?'

'On an island of crazed Vigilants?'

'True enough, but try again.'

'Trapped in a huge forge with a workforce of lost souls?'

'You were closer the first time.'

'On an island?' ventured Steiner.

'Yes, the island of Vladibogdan.'

'And Vladibogdan . . . isn't part of the Empire?'

'Precisely.' Tief nodded with a solemn look on his face. 'Vladibogdan doesn't exist; it doesn't fall within the borders of Solmindre.'

Steiner regarded the cavern of cinderwraiths working tirelessly. Swords and shields, vambraces and breastplates, knives and spearheads.

'Which means they can make all of this and not break the terms of the treaty.'

'Clever bastards, aren't they?' Tief cleared his throat. 'When the world ends it will be due to a technicality. The Empire will use the swords to fight their war in the south and they'll use the spears to arm their garrisons in the Scorched Republics.' Tief took a step closer and beckoned with a finger. Steiner leaned closer so he might hear better over the din of the forge. 'They'll use the knives to slit the throats of those who speak out against them. And when the city states of Shanisrond are defeated, and when Svingettevei, Vannerånd, Drakefjord and Nordvlast bend their knee to the Empire, there'll just be one last thing to do.'

'What?' asked Steiner.

'Exterminate everyone without pale skin.' Tief leaned close. 'Cheery thought, is it? As I said, they're complete bastards.'

'But what have the Spriggani, the Shanish and the Yamal ever done to the Empire?'

'Dared to be different. Dared to use the arcane. Dared to stand our ground.'

'But you can't exterminate an entire people.'

'Tell that to the Emperor.' Tief shook his head, then turned his back and stamped off into the gloom. Steiner followed him towards the cavern's centre, watching the smoke emitted by the countless fires; it did not settle as a fog but drifted to a dark corner. Tief caught his gaze and nodded.

'So you've spotted the breeze. There are a few cracks here and there that let the wind in. And out. If it wasn't for those we'd all choke to death.'

They were near the centre now and Steiner spotted more and more Spriggani among the cinderwraiths. Around a dozen of them looked up from their work; some scowled, but most appeared uninterested.

'You're slaves,' he whispered as they neared the journey's end.

'We are all slaves, Hammersmith. Some wear chains and some don't, but dry your eyes, it's not so bad. There are far worse things in Vinterkveld than slavery.'

The cavern's centre was home to a stone dais dozens of feet across, and pitted with age. At its centre was the largest furnace Steiner had ever seen, flanked by two anvils, and a rack of tools. Sacks of coal lay at the edge of the dais, well away from stray cinders or burning embers.

Enkhtuya hammered at brightly glowing metal with a grim expression on her face.

'Frøya's tits,' whispered Steiner.

'Mind your language,' grumbled Tief.

'I've never seen anyone from Yamal before.'

'Don't say anything stupid,' warned Tief.

'Her skin is so dark, are they all like that?'

'Yes, they are. And that's the one stupid question you're allowed.'

Enkhtuya wore a heavy leather apron. The light brown material had been fashioned from broad chevrons stitched together, all pointing up to the broad shoulders and stern visage of the Yamal woman. Her hands were bound up in thick gloves and a heavy amulet hung from a cord around her neck.

'Kimi! Stop fooling about with hot metal.' Tief pulled himself up onto the dais. 'We've got company.'

Enkhtuya turned to them. She had a wide mouth and serious eyes. Plaits of dark hair ran in neat rows along her scalp, terminating in metal thimbles near her neck.

'Why is there a Northman in my forge?' said Enkhtuya, her Nordspråk perfect.

'Felgenhauer sent him down,' said Tief. 'It wasn't my idea,' he added as Enkhtuya's expression hardened. She kicked a bucket, a curse word escaping her lips. The bucket upended, splashing the water over a cinderwraith who hissed and disappeared, the orange eyes extinguished in a heartbeat.

Tief knelt down at the spot the cinderwraith had disappeared, the knees of his breaches stained with wet ashes.

'What did you do?' he hollered. 'I'm going to need some coal and kindling. Be quick about it!' A handful of wraiths hurried to fetch the materials and the Spriggani set about making a fire. Steiner watched in horror, trying to ignore the glowering presence of Enkhtuya while avoiding the many wraiths as they dashed about. The phantom workers were insubstantial, but somehow carried items that were not.

'What are you doing?' Steiner whispered, kneeling beside Tief.

'Resurrection,' he replied. 'The spirit will fade unless I start a fire to give it a new form. It needs smoke.'

Steiner watched in fascination as tongues of flame gave off tendrils of grey and black, curling around Tief's fingers.

'That's it, my friend,' soothed Tief. 'Come back to the land of the living.' He frowned. 'Well, almost living.'

The pall grew around Tief's fingers and two motes of orange light appeared and began to swell. They waited for long minutes, Enkhtuya and Steiner watching Tief coax the spark of unlife back into the cinderwraith.

Finally Tief stood up with a grunt and turned to Enkhtuya, frowning hard. 'You nearly invented a new meaning for "kicked the bucket", your highness.'

Enkhtuya gave a half-shrug and rolled her eyes. 'I'm not having a Northman in my forge.' Her voice was quiet, and Steiner was reminded of Felgenhauer, and the aura of command she attired herself in.

'I'm a blacksmith's son. I can help,' said Steiner. 'I want to help.'

'See,' said Tief. 'He wants to help. He's not one of them. I daresay he hates the Empire.'

'I'm not having a Northman in my furnace. Regardless of his hatred for the Empire.' Enkhtuya stepped down from the dais and Steiner's eyes widened as he realized she was squaring up to him. He'd seen it before plenty of times, in the school yard and the tavern.

'I don't want to be here either,' replied Steiner. 'But it's not like I have a choice.'

'Out,' said Enkhtuya, jutting her head towards the balcony where Steiner had entered. 'Get out. Tell Felgenhauer to set you to work in the kitchens. It's probably all you're good for.'

'My father was a blacksmith.' Steiner took a step forward, raising his chin. 'I'm a blacksmith.' He was aware that Enkhtuya was the same height as him, and almost as broad. 'You don't get to send me to the kitchens. Who in Hel do you think you are?'

The first blow collided with his chest, sending the air out of him in a heartbeat. Steiner stumbled back a few steps but didn't fall. He tried to suck down air into his lungs without success. The fact that he remained standing only seemed to annoy her more.

'Stop this!' said Tief, but Enkhtuya unleashed another fist and Steiner staggered back a step, turning the blow aside on a forearm; it missed his chin, but only just.

Enkhtuya said something in a tongue he didn't recognize, though Steiner knew from the tone and volume the word had no place in polite conversation.

'Will you knock it off?' he said.

This time she swung with the other arm, an outflung back-hander. The heavy blacksmith's glove caught Steiner in the face and his vision exploded into white light before going dark. The panic that he couldn't see was matched only by the profound confusion he remained standing. He blinked furiously and his sight swam into focus just as Enkhtuya closed on him once more. She swung again, catching him on the shoulder as he twisted away.

'I don't want to hurt you,' he growled, but she jabbed a fist at him, catching him in the mouth. Steiner ran his tongue over numb lips and tasted blood, then pressed fingers to his nose. Hard to see in this light but no question his fingers were wet. He'd not taken a beating like this in a long time, not since a few boys at school had outnumbered him.

'So it's blood then?'

'Get out of my forge, Northman.'

Steiner's anger lit within him, a roaring furnace flame. He hadn't asked to be brought here; hadn't asked to be a slave in the forge; and now this sour-faced woman from Yamal was determined to beat him unconscious.

He bent his knees and delivered an uppercut, not to the face but the sternum. The air went out of her and Steiner circled to the side, then kicked her legs out from under her. Silence overtook the ruddy scene.

Enkhtuya stared up at him, hatred etched onto her face, the red light of the forge making her look like some creature of legend.

'Will you stop hitting me now?' said Steiner, looming over her with clenched fists.

Enkhtuya glowered at him and scrabbled away on hands, feet and arse, then got to her feet when she was out of range of his fists.

'If you won't leave the forge at least get out of my sight.'

'Not like I have much of a choice, is it?' said Steiner. He wiped his bleeding nose along his arm and clutched his ribs. It was a long walk to the outer reaches of the forge, struggling to ignore the pain. He slumped to his knees in the deep shadow beneath a series of crates. His bed was old sackcloth, gritty with coal. Tief crouched nearby, concern writ plainly on his face.

'She really doesn't like Northmen.'

'Thanks,' replied Steiner. 'She made that painfully obvious.' He could already feel his lip swelling as the blood in his nose started to dry.

'I'm surprised she didn't put you down.' Tief stared at him. 'She's faster than you, stronger too if I guess right.'

'I'm surprised she didn't put me down too. We don't usually fight women in Cinderfell.' Steiner took a ragged breath. 'Are they all like that in Yamal? All tall and strong as oxen and pissed off?'

Tief shrugged. 'They're pissed off, no question about that. And they make no distinction between the Empire and the Scorched Republics.'

Steiner turned on his side and closed his eyes. 'Well, one thing's for sure.'

'What's that?' said Tief.

'I'll never tell anyone they hit like a girl again.'

CHAPTER THIRTEEN

Steiner

The Spriggani do not have an organised religion as we understand it, nor do they have temples or churches. One can commune with Frøya whenever one is in the presence of nature, particularly lakes, rivers or sea. Frejna is both feared and respected, being the goddess of winter, wisdom and death.

– From the field notes of Hierarch Khigir,
Vigilant of the Imperial Synod.

Steiner woke in dull increments. First there was sound, hammers beating steel. He refused to open his eyes, wishing himself back to a sleep that would not return. Next came sensation, aching ribs hard to ignore. A profusion of bruises awaited him should he find somewhere to wash. His nose was thick and crisp with dried blood and he rubbed at his nostrils with a knuckle, eyes still closed. Still the sound of hammers assailed him, ringing from anvils close by. He wanted to believe he was back in Cinderfell, back at his father's smithy, though he struggled to think what he would say to Marek and Verner. He wondered how Kjellrunn would fare without him.

Steiner opened his eyes to the scarlet twilight of the forge, the oppressive weight of Vladibogdan above him, with all the dangers and mysteries of the Solmindre Empire.

'I was beginning to think you'd never wake up,' said Tief. He was sitting on a crate, playing cards by himself.

'I take it the cinderwraiths don't play cards?'

'What have they got left to bet?' said Tief bitterly. 'The Empire took everything from them, including their lives.'

Steiner sat up and discovered someone had laid empty coal sacks over his body in the approximation of a blanket. Two or three rolled sacks had been pressed under his head as a pillow. He was coated in coal dust but had slept well all the same.

'Who did all this?'

Tief gestured to the cinderwraiths. 'They did.'

Steiner looked down at the sacks feeling gratitude, but it was quickly swallowed by dread as he remembered the previous day's events.

'You said they were slaves,' said Steiner, nodding at a cinderwraith as it drifted to a nearby furnace carrying a set of chisels. He shivered despite the heat. Though the phantasms had shown him kindness they were no less unsettling, reminders that death was close at hand.

'Slaves,' repeated Tief. He gathered the cards and shuffled them. 'The Empire never turned away cheap labour, even after death.'

'Why this?' Steiner held up his sackcloth blanket.

'They seem to have taken a shine to you.' Tief shrugged. 'Probably because you're about the same age as they were when they died.'

'The same age?' Steiner looked at the cinderwraith.

'Give or take a few years. Most of them would have been younger than you when they passed on.' Tief frowned and slid off the crate, then offered a hand. Steiner took it and got to his feet, wincing as his body complained bitterly.

'This is monstrous,' he breathed, staring around the forge with new eyes.

'Each of these lost souls is a young boy or girl,' said Tief. 'Brought to Vladibogdan.'

'Brought here to become a Vigilant, like me,' whispered Steiner.

Tief nodded. 'Each cinderwraith is some poor fool who failed at the academy and paid the highest price.'

Steiner glanced from one shade to another, wondering who they might have been in life, too shocked to speak.

'To die on Vladibogdan is the cruellest of fates.' Tief gestured to the many cinderwraiths working in teams at anvils, pairs of cinderwraiths hauling crates of weapons. 'This is the Ashen Torment, an eternal punishment.' Tief pulled out his pipe and beat the bowl against the back of his palm.

'Where do they come from?' Steiner asked after a moment.

'I told you. Anyone who dies on the island becomes a cinderwraith.'

'But what causes it?'

Tief tugged at his bottom lip, then shrugged. 'They say Bittervinge set down the enchantment, though I'm not clear how it works. Only a dragon could do something so cruel.'

For a while they stared at the cinderwraiths, lost in their thoughts, until a Spriggani emerged from the gloom with bread and cheese wrapped in coarse brown paper. A steaming jug of black tea followed and Steiner wolfed the food down.

'Thanks,' he mumbled between bites, but the Spriggani simply frowned and slipped away into the darkness. Tief said nothing as Steiner ate, only loaded his pipe with evil-smelling weed, waiting for the boy to finish his repast.

'Have you seen Enkhtuya?'

Tief shook his head. 'Kimi's not talking to anyone today.'

'Kimi?' Steiner forced a smile.

Tief looked at Steiner and shook his head and sighed. 'Kimi is her first name, halfhead. Kimi Enkhtuya of the Red Hand Tribe, currently the ruling tribe of Yamal.'

'She's like a princess?' asked Steiner.

'She's not *like* a princess, she *is* a princess. And you picked a fight with her.'

'She picked a fight with me,' protested Steiner.

'Eh, maybe she did,' conceded Tief, breathing a plume of smoke from his nose. 'Wouldn't be the first time.'

'Frøya's tits.' Steiner pressed a finger to his nose and winced. His bottom lip was crusted with dried blood.

'Frøya is the name of my goddess, you damn fool.' Tief dispensed a light cuff to the head. 'Just because you cowards in the Scorched Republics have given up the old ways doesn't mean you can take her name in vain.'

'Not everyone in Nordvlast has turned their backs on the old ways,' replied Steiner, thinking of Kjellrunn. 'Is there anything else I should know?'

'Kimi is third in line to her father's throne,' said Tief as he toked on the pipe.

'Who keeps a member of the Yamal royal family on a distant island making weapons all day?'

'The sort of people who know a father will do anything to keep his daughter safe.'

Steiner thought back to his father, of Marek's admission that he'd always suspected Kjellrunn of bearing witchsign, the lengths he'd gone to in order to spare her the Invigilation.

'Why doesn't Kimi's father raise an army to rescue her?'

'This isn't some children's tale.' Tief frowned. 'Yamal is on the opposite side of the Empire. The Vigilants will execute Kimi the moment the Yamal move against Solmindre. That's why she hates Northmen so much.'

'I didn't capture her. I don't care for the Empire any more than she does.'

'I know that, and you know that but . . .' Tief shrugged. 'I need to get to work.' He tucked his pipe away. 'If I were you I'd think of a way to get on her good side. This cavern is only so large and it's not big enough for another bout between you two.'

'I know,' replied Steiner. 'At least my ribs know. I think she cracked one.'

Tief squinted at the young man and shook his head. 'Frøya only knows how you remained standing during the fight.'

'Where did this come from?' He held up the jug of black tea. Tief frowned and cast a look at the ceiling.

'The academy, of course. They send down food each day, as long as we behave ourselves.'

'Can you show me?'

'I'm going to regret this, aren't I?'

'Not as much as I'm regretting what happened yesterday with Kimi.'

Tief shook his head. 'We'll see about that.'

An idea was forming in Steiner's mind. It wasn't much, but it was all he had.

'Come on,' said Steiner. 'Just a little further.' Tief lingered at the mouth of the tunnel and scowled.

'This was your grand idea? Getting us killed?'

'We're not dead yet,' replied Steiner, his irritation with Tief was almost as bad as the anxiety he felt.

'Not yet. Hardly reassuring,' replied the Spriggani.

The climb had been arduous and much too long. Steiner's heart sank as he gazed upward between the narrow strip of sky above Academy Square. He'd hoped for a hint of blue, even a ray of light, knowing it was ridiculous. The firmament remained an unrelenting black; Steiner couldn't be sure if it was stars that were twinkling or flecks of coal dust in the poisonous air.

'Where are the kitchens? You must know,' pressed Steiner.

'Of course I know, halfhead. Follow me.'

Steiner set down his torch in a sconce inside the tunnel mouth where it flickered in the breeze but remained alight.

'Keep an eye out for the guards,' whispered Steiner.

'I'm already keeping an eye out. How about you stop stating the bloody obvious.'

Around the edge of Academy Square they went, avoiding the inferno at the centre, the roiling flames that continued to flicker around the stone dragon. It was a small relief as they passed behind it, as Steiner expected the creature to turn an accusing gaze upon them at any moment. The statue remained still, only the shadows writhed, dancing upon the academy buildings that towered over them. Far above them, Steiner could see window ledges and shutters picked out in faint golden light.

'I hope no one's awake,' whispered Steiner.

'There's always someone awake,' replied Tief. 'And they're always armed.'

Steiner glanced around Academy Square, eyeing windows set between alcoves. Not alcoves, he realized, but buttresses to support the great weight of stone pressing down. Each building was many storeys tall with neat rows of windows bearing curving arches, glass grimy from the ever-present soot and dust. The buildings were far removed from the crude wood and stone cottages of Cinderfell.

Tief tugged at his elbow. 'Come on, we can discuss architecture later.'

Gruff voices sounded in the darkness ahead. Steiner and Tief slunk to the nearest buttress and clung to the cold stone. Footsteps now, coming closer, the light jingle of armoured men. They were muttering in their mother tongue, one sounding bored, the other sour. Steiner didn't need to understand Solska to know they were discontent with their duty. Torchlight slid over the cobbles, etched the soldiers in wavering light, a nimbus in the deep darkness. Steiner slid to his haunches in the shadow of the academy building and Tief did likewise. The soldiers were all but standing over them and Steiner hoped to whatever gods still listened that he wouldn't be dragged before Felgenhauer or, worse, Shirinov.

Tief made a gesture and the din of rock on cobbles sounded from the far side of Academy Square. The soldiers both turned to the source of the sound, took a moment to confer with each other, then departed. 'You have witchsign!' Steiner whispered when the armoured men had crossed the square.

'Of course I do,' said Tief. 'Any Spriggani worth a damn has a few tricks up his sleeve.' He hurried onward and Steiner scurried after him. They were almost through the double doors of an academy building when someone called out from high above.

'You there! Identify yourself!'

Tief grabbed Steiner by the neck and forced him through the doorway without looking back. Angry voices in harsh Solska called out in the night and Steiner's heart pounded fearfully.

'Where are they?' called someone in Nordspråk.

'Two boys. One tall, one short,' said another.

'Now we're for it, halfhead,' said Tief. He pressed himself to the wall and took silent steps in the darkness. Steiner followed into the vestibule. Light glinted from a narrow rickety door leading to an equally rickety wooden staircase. Steiner struggled downward and his foot slipped from the bottom step. For a second he was sure he would fall, but he slammed into a rack of saucepans and ladles, all chiming in the dark like demented bells.

'Why not just hang a sign up saying "We're here, arseholes!"'

whispered Tief, a furious look on his face. Steiner looked around and realized there was nowhere else to go.

Heavy footfalls followed. Torchlight illuminated the top of the staircase and two soldiers clattered down each step, armour banging from the walls. Tief shifted a sack of potatoes and pulled up a trapdoor.

'What the Hel are you doing?' asked Steiner.

'Hiding, you damn fool boy,' replied Tief, then disappeared into the hole.

Steiner was about to follow when a heavy hand slammed down on his shoulder, spinning him about.

'And what have we here?' said a soldier, his black helm pressed close to Steiner's face. The soldier was so close Steiner could see the red star on the soldier's helmet was dented and the paint had flaked off.

'Creeping around after lights out?' said the soldier. 'Thought you'd get yourself extra portions?'

Steiner opened his mouth to speak but nothing came out.

'He's come to take over,' said a tired voice from the far end of the cellar.

Maxim stood up from his place of concealment, surrounded by buckets of potatoes bobbing in water, all pale and peeled. His hands were wrinkled and red and a short stubby knife hung from his hand. The boy's face was a riot of purple bruises.

'Right,' blurted Steiner. 'Take over. That's right.'

'And you're late,' said Maxim with a frown. He was so convincing even Steiner believed him for a second. Maxim kicked the trapdoor closed and folded his arms, then scowled at Steiner.

'You're late,' repeated the soldier, who gave Steiner a shove for good measure. 'And in future, don't sneak around without a torch. We might have killed you for spying.'

The soldiers clattered back up the stairs muttering to each

other in Solska. Steiner wondered if the wood would collapse under the combined weight of their armour.

'Thanks,' he whispered to Maxim when they gone. 'I didn't expect to see you up and about.'

'They let me spend the day in the hospital,' said the smaller boy. 'Said I had to perform "light duties" for the rest of the week.' Maxim took an uneasy breath. 'Shirinov would have broken me if you hadn't stepped in.'

Steiner shrugged. 'I lost my temper. Not the smartest thing I've ever done, probably won't be the last time either.'

Maxim crossed to the stairs, making sure the soldiers were well on their way. 'They'll skin you alive if they catch you.'

Steiner nodded. The plan had seemed more straightforward when it was just a plan, but plans had a habit of turning on you like that.

'And they'll skin me alive just for talking to you,' added Maxim.

Steiner and rubbed his forehead. 'This isn't going well at all.'

The trapdoor jolted under Steiner's foot and a sliver of darkness appeared between the door and the flagstones.

'Have they gone yet?'

Steiner opened the door and extended a hand, helping Tief up out of the hole.

'Good thing your friend here stepped in, halfhead,' said Tief, jerking a thumb at Maxim.

'What's it like? Down in the forges?' asked Maxim.

'How do you know about that?' demanded Steiner.

'Silverdust told me,' replied the boy. 'He watched over me in hospital and I asked after you.'

'It's terrible,' admitted Steiner. 'A vast cavern of furnaces making weapons, all attended by ghosts.'

'What?' Maxim stared at him. 'There's no such things as ghosts.'

'They're the spirits of all the children who died during their training on Vladibogdan,' said Steiner.

'It's true,' added Tief. 'An enchantment binds the souls of the dead to the island, they're forced to work below.'

'They call them cinderwraiths,' said Steiner.

'That's impossible,' replied Maxim. He shook his head and looked at the knife in his hand; such a simple implement could damn him to an eternity of toil.

'Best you keep this little secret to yourself,' said Tief.

'We can't stay in this place,' said Maxim after a moment. 'How are we going to escape?'

'I don't know. Yet.' Steiner looked around the pantry. 'But I do know I'm going to need to make some friends downstairs if I'm going to survive.'

'That's the first sensible thing you've said all night,' said Tief.

'What do you need?' whispered Maxim. 'It must be pretty important if you're willing to risk coming up here in the dead of night.'

'Well.' Steiner smiled; things might work out rather well after all. 'I need access to the kitchens.'

'Kitchens?' Maxim nodded, sombre and serious. 'I'm your man when it comes to kitchens.'

Steiner smiled at the bruised and rangy ten-year-old before him. 'Thank you.'

Maxim headed deeper into the kitchens, past sacks of flour and battered barrels, towards what Steiner hoped was the pantry door.

'He's our man, is he?' said Tief, with a mocking smile and shake of his head.

'Men come in all shapes and sizes,' replied Steiner. 'He's risking his neck for us, so you could at least act like you're grateful.'

'I didn't mean anything by it.' Tief looked away and shrugged. 'He's just so small is all.'

'Let's just get the food and get back to the forges in one piece.'

CHAPTER FOURTEEN

Steiner

A Vigilant draws his power from the schools of fire, air and earth, power that flows from dragons. It is possible for some students to draw on the power of earth from another source, Frejna. This is to be discouraged. Students stumbling across the school of water invariably start asking questions leading to doubt. Water is the sole province of Frøya. It will not do for the Synod to suffer a schism of orthodoxy, any more than it suits us to have a schism of politics.

– From the field notes of Hierarch Khigir,
Vigilant of the Imperial Synod.

A hush descended on the cavern; the absence of sound a wondrous luxury. The cinderwraiths needed no sleep, and having no need to eat or make ablutions, they rarely paused in their tasks, yet no hammers fell on iron or steel. No anvils chimed with the sound of indentured industry, no echoes of artifice sounded in the dismal cavern. The clatter of weapons in crates was silenced and only the dull scrape of a wooden spatula on a frying pan could be heard. Sound had given way to smell, and it was the smell of meatballs emanating from the pan that Steiner worked at. An old shield had been pressed into service as a griddle, and a score of herring sizzled in a mustard marinade.

'How in Frejna and Frøya's name did you steal all this?' said a Spriggani woman with long black hair. She bore a stern cast to her delicate features and Steiner took a moment before answering her.

'I know people. Good people.' Steiner turned his attention back to the task at hand. 'Who's your friend?' he asked Tief, casting a glance to the Spriggani who had questioned him.

'This is Sundra. And she's not a friend, she's family.'

The woman stepped closer, into the light of the furnace and few lanterns. She wasn't coated in soot as Tief was, but wore black robes. Bird skeletons had been sewn onto her sleeves near the shoulder, wings splayed wide and stark against the dark fabric. Another bird skull adorned her breast, framed in a diamond shape made from other bones.

'Are those crow skulls?'

Sundra gave a curt nod, her expression disapproving.

Steiner pushed the meatballs around the pan with the spatula. 'Is she always this cheerful?' he whispered to Tief.

'I thought this business was an attempt to make friends?' replied Tief, gesturing at the food.

Steiner lifted the shield from the furnace he'd commandeered and set it down on an anvil. A vast audience of cinderwraiths had come to watch him cook, which Steiner found mildly disconcerting. Sundra continued to regard him with a baleful look.

'I foresaw your coming,' whispered the black-clad woman. 'The bones whisper your name.'

'Not now, Sundra,' said Tief, under his breath.

'The bones?' Steiner frowned in confusion.

'Tokens and charms,' explained Tief. 'It's all interpretation and nonsense if you ask me.'

'No one asked you,' replied Sundra.

'Did these bones of yours whisper anything about meatballs,' asked Steiner with a wry smile. 'Or creamy potatoes and grilled herring?' He plucked a side of fish from the griddle and held it out to her. 'Did they mention cheese or fresh bread?'

'It's not often a Northman comes bearing food,' admitted Sundra. She extended a hand slowly and accepted the morsel.

'Are you . . . ?' Steiner eyed Tief warily, keen not to show his ignorance again. 'Are you a priestess of Frejna?'

Sundra drew herself up to her full height, which was not much at all, and raised her chin. 'I was before I was brought here.'

'Now we're just slaves,' said another Spriggani.

'My other sister,' supplied Tief, eyeing the frying pan with a ravenous look. The second woman was attired in green robes, grimy and patched in grubby grey. 'I'm Taiga,' she replied. 'The youngest.'

'You want to help me and cut that bread, Taiga the youngest?'

Taiga cocked her head on one side as if considering some great decision, then nodded and picked up a knife.

'What's this?' The words were loud enough to turn heads, with enough steel in them that cinderwraiths shrank back, parting to let Kimi Enkhtuya through.

'Just some food is all.' Steiner forced a smile he didn't feel. His ribs had ached with every step down the stairs from Academy Square. He had no wish to earn more injury. 'This is for you.' He held up two thick slices of dark bread, meatballs gleaming and sizzling between them.

'I'll not take food from a Northman.' Enkhtuya's face was hard as stone. 'What is this meagre offering?'

'We call it housman's fare. Peasant food made by workers for workers.'

Tief cleared his throat. 'The boy risked his life getting this for us, Kimi. And if you don't want it . . . Well, there's no need to waste good food. That would be foolish. And it will only stretch so far between this many.'

Steiner eyed the thirty or so Spriggani and winced. The portions would be small indeed. Enkhtuya waved away Steiner's offering and turned her head in disgust. It wasn't long before Tief, Sundra, Taiga and the other Spriggani were sitting in a loose circle. Their lips were bright with grease and the sound of smacking lips and contented mumbles could be heard over the sizzling pan. Steiner served up more of the bread and herring, placed it on a chopping board and set the offering at Enkhtuya's feet.

'In case you change your mind,' he said, backing away from the stern-faced Yamal princess.

'Fish? All we ever have on this island is fish,' she said, though she didn't take her eyes from the food. There had to be half a loaf on the chopping board, not too soft, not too crispy, just as how Marek loved it, Steiner realized.

'You've not had it like this before. It's a marinade my father taught me.'

'Turns out the boy is a cook *and* a blacksmith,' said Tief contentedly.

'Do you have any salt?' rumbled Enkhtuya after a moment's consideration.

Steiner's eyes widened. He had fetched a pan and kettle, tea leaves, meat and fish, cheese and bread. He'd even managed to swipe two dozen withered apples but salt had not been a priority as he'd raided the kitchens with Maxim.

'Salt?'

'I need salt,' said Enkhtuya.

'I . . .' Steiner froze. All of his good work was about to unravel for the want of a pinch of salt.

'I marinaded it for about an hour. I'm not sure it needs more—'

'I have salt!' Tief wiped his hands on a kerchief. He tucked the scrap of fabric away and produced a small pouch. 'For soups and so on,' he said by way of explanation. 'We're slaves, not feral beasts,' he added indignantly.

Enkhtuya sat cross-legged by the chopping board, took one pinch, and threw the powder over her shoulder.

'Now we can eat,' she said, though she refused to look at Steiner, biting and chewing, slow and methodical. Steiner tried not to stare, mindful of causing further insult. The Spriggani watched with fascination though Steiner guessed they hoped for leftovers. It was a faint hope as it turned out.

'It's good, no?' said Tief, sidling up to the Yamal princess.

'Better than the slop you call food.' Kimi allowed herself a brief smile before she stood, brushed the crumbs from her palms and rinsed her hands in a nearby barrel of water. She glanced at Steiner.

'I still don't like Northmen.'

'You made that much clear,' replied Steiner, one hand straying to his ribs.

'You're too puny to be of any use,' said Enkhtuya. 'No better than the cinderwraiths. Stay out of my way.' She slunk off, sending the odd cinderwraith flitting from her path.

'For frigg's sake.' Steiner's shoulders slumped and he released a long breath of disappointment. 'That didn't go anywhere near as well as I'd hoped.'

'Don't be so damn foolish,' said Tief, grinning. 'She threw salt.'

Steiner shrugged. 'And what does that mean?'

'Frøya save us but the boy is stupid.'

'It means,' said Taiga, 'that she'll be civil with you. The Yamal put great store in flinging a pinch of salt over their shoulder. They say it discourages evil spirits and wards off unfavourable destiny.'

Steiner looked around at the host of cinderwraiths and

opened his mouth to comment on spirits and unfavourable destinies but thought better of it.

'The fact she honoured your meal with salt, well . . .' Tief shook his head. 'You've got some stones, sneaking up to the kitchens like that.'

'What stones?'

'Never mind about stones,' replied Tief. 'We need to get you strong. It's all to the good you're brave and all, and it would be better if you had some brains, but what you really need is strength. Fortunately, we have just the thing.' Tief kicked the nearest sack of coal.

'And what am I supposed to do with that?'

'Carry it to the furnaces. And there'll be plenty more so don't dawdle.'

'Can I have my food first?' said Steiner with a scowl.

'I reckon you've earned it,' said Tief.

Steiner was no stranger to hard work. His father's forge was not a place for the weak or the idle, but there was at least the odd snatch of friendly conversation. People would knock politely and stop in for the occasional repair, perhaps buying a pan or knife, or less commonly a horseshoe. And when the day was done there was the tavern with all its good cheer and Verner's tall stories.

The cavern was devoid of such things, as if scorched by the heat or occluded by the ever-present coal dust. Steiner carried sacks along avenues between the workstations, each step rewarding him with pain from his fractured rib. Every time he set down a burden his bruises rumbled and moaned. The only words he whispered were curses, words said aloud were spare and sparse. A dozen or so of the workstations featured Spriggani overseers, but none had much to say, eyes dull with tiredness.

At first the place had simply been a sprawl in the darkness.

Hundreds of cinderwraiths drifted over the packed earth of the cavern's floor. The spirits of doomed children attending the fires, the hammering of iron and steel. When the air wasn't filled with the sound of beaten metal it was the harsh hiss of quenched steel, slipped into barrels of grimy water. In truth the cavern was arranged like a vast cartwheel, the many spokes leading to the great furnace at the centre where Enkhtuya worked alone. Sometimes the Yamal princess would step off the dais and give instruction to a crew of wraiths but for the most part she made an ally of solitude.

'There you are.' Sundra emerged from the darkness.

Steiner nodded. 'Of course I'm here. Where else would I be? And where is Tief?'

'Tief is our unofficial foreman,' replied Sundra. 'And is currently busy. He asked that I speak to you, though the bones do not speak favourably of you, Northman.'

Steiner set down the sack of coal that he carried across his shoulders and glared.

'Were you going to get to the point any time soon, because more coal came in this morning and I need to get it to Enkhtuya before . . .' He opened his mouth but the words turned into a sigh. Time was meaningless down here with no day and no night to mark the passing of the hours. There were no clocks to be read, certainly none that announced the hour in muted chimes, even if such things could be heard down here.

'Come with me,' said the sullen priestess. 'We have found something for you.'

Steiner followed, more concerned with putting one foot in front of the other than the where or the why of it. Sundra glided past the furnaces in her black robes, to the edges of the vast cavern, where the workstations were less crowded. Pallets of coal loomed in the darkness, some as tall as Steiner himself.

It was darker here, away from the constant sunset glow of the furnaces and the cinderwraiths' coal-ember eyes.

Sundra bowed her head and mumbled a few words and a ring of flames danced up from the ground at her feet.

'Corpsecandles,' whispered Steiner. Sundra arched an eyebrow.

'They are not corpsecandles, just a minor spell. The Spriggani rarely summon fire, but there are precious few spells of illumination in the earth or water schools, so fire it is.'

Steiner blinked. He never heard anyone speak so casually of something so wondrous, so unknowable. So illegal.

'Is it true that Spriggani take the last spark of a person's spirit and make it a light for their lanterns?'

Sundra turned to him slowly, crossed her arms and frowned.

'Sorry. I was told . . .'

'You were told wrong.' Sundra sighed and shook her head. 'Imperial soldiers have been telling that story to each other for decades, centuries even. It is stories like those that mean my people are distrusted, or killed when Northmen think they can get away with it.'

Steiner looked down at the tongues of flame as they danced around Sundra's feet. Suddenly he was jealous of Sundra and Kjellrunn. What might he be able to do if he had witchsign? How might his life have turned out differently but for this small quirk of fate.

'Do you think you can teach me to do that?'

Sundra shook her head. 'It's not something you can teach. You cannot name it. You cannot categorize it or pin it down. You cannot write it in books neatly. The arcane is more like . . .' Sundra smiled then. 'It's more like a feeling.'

'I'd give anything to be able to do that.' Steiner gestured at the dancing flames.

'The arcane demands a high price. It poisons people and makes them sick. Why do you think Shirinov is so twisted? Why do you think he suffers that wracking cough?'

'And Khigir? Felgenhauer?'

'Their time will come,' said Sundra.

'And what about you?'

'The Spriggani draw their powers from the goddess, water and earth are our birthright. Fire and wind are the province of dragons.'

'Aren't you afraid it will make you sick, or kill you?' asked Steiner.

'Do you think I will leave this place alive, Steiner Vartiainen?' Sundra gestured to the cavern. 'Do not worry for me, I have my goddess.' The priestess turned on her heel and disappeared into the rock wall at the cavern's edge.

'Sundra!' Steiner stumbled back in shock. Only when the priestess' head reappeared did he start breathing again.

'There is a cave here, a fissure in the side of the cavern. Did you think I could pass through solid rock?'

'I've seen a lot of things in the last few days. Nothing's impossible on Vladibogdan.'

The cavern wall parted in a cruel jag, an opening in the rock, almost invisible in the darkness. Sundra's circle of flames illuminated the inside of the fissure, throwing flickering light across dark stone.

'Come on, now,' said the priestess. 'I want to show you this.'

Steiner bowed his head to enter the split rock and found himself in a small cave, perhaps the size of his kitchen back at Cinderfell. How he wished he were back there now.

'I brought some sackcloth for you to sleep on,' said Sundra, gesturing to one corner. 'And there are two barrels in the corner there. One for your ablutions and the other for . . .'

'You found me a bedroom?'

'We thought you should have some privacy.' She narrowed her eyes and looked over her shoulder, back towards the furnaces. 'That infernal racket will still get in but it is quieter in here.'

Steiner looked around. The stony nook wasn't much but it was his.

'You had best get some sleep,' said Sundra. 'Your rib will not heal if you continue working like this.'

Steiner sat down on his sackcloth bed and looked up at the priestess. He couldn't guess how old she was, perhaps forty years or more.

'You have a question,' said Sundra.

'I was curious is all,' grunted Steiner.

'The bones.' Sundra frowned, picked up one of the corpse-candles in her hands. 'Take this.' The other tongues of fire winked out and Steiner stared her, incredulous.

'What?'

'Hold out your hand,' said Sundra. Steiner did as he was asked and the priestess passed the corpsecandle to him. The sliver of flame emanated just above his outstretched palm. It burned without heat, a ghostly white light, pale blue at the tip.

'Good,' was all she said, then knelt down and fussed at a pouch of black velvet on her hip. She laid the square of fabric on the ground and smoothed out the creases.

'The bones are a form of divination, and no two sets are the same.' Sundra took a deep breath and held up two fists, then splayed her fingers, revealing the contents. There were small fragile bones, a tiny copper leaf, an old rusty coin and thimble.

'Not all of them are bones,' said Steiner.

'Just like a Northman to be so literal,' replied Sundra. 'For hundreds of years we used bones and bones alone, but more recently we use other items, anything that may hold significance.'

'Right,' said Steiner, finding himself remembering Tief's opinion. It did seem to be mainly interpretation and nonsense.

'Now think. Think hard. Think of a question you want the answer to.'

Steiner's first thought was his father, then Kristofine came to mind, but he settled on Kjellrunn. Would he ever see his sister again?

Sundra cupped her hands together and shook the tokens and charms, then flung them onto the velvet fabric, scattering them.

Steiner raised his eyebrows and held his breath. 'And?'

'The bird skull is facing away from the other tokens, meaning the way ahead is unclear.' Sundra took a deep breath and frowned at the scattered tokens. 'The thimble has landed tip facing up, meaning something is trapped inside, perhaps.'

'Trapped inside?' Steiner rolled his eyes. 'I hardly need a divination to tell me that.'

Sundra shook her head and continued. 'The coin has landed far from the other tokens—'

'My family never did have much money,' said Steiner.

'And the copper leaf is underneath the crow's wing bone.'

'Kjellrunn always preferred the forest, perhaps she's the leaf.'

'She may well have protection from an unknown source,' said Sundra, as if this were a profound truth. Steiner couldn't shake his incredulity and supposed the priestess caught his disbelieving look. She gathered her bones and made to leave. Steiner felt the whole ceremony had been disappointing, and was no closer to an answer than when he started.

Sundra summoned the corpsecandle from his hand with a deft motion, then withdrew to the split in the cavern wall. Kjellrunn would be beyond excited to witness the many things he'd seen, yet all he felt was exhaustion.

'Sundra?' said Steiner, lying down on his sackcloth bed.

'Yes?' said the priestess, her grim face lit by the corpsecandle as she passed through the fissure in the rock.

'Thanks for my room. And for the reading. I'm not sure it really answered my question, but thanks all the same.'

The priestess nodded. 'Your way ahead is unclear, but it will be hard, and there will be a high cost. Sleep now.' And with that the corpsecandle extinguished, leaving Steiner in the darkness of his sanctuary.

CHAPTER FIFTEEN

Kjellrunn

The Emperor does not tolerate loose ends unless he can use them as a noose to hang the incompetent. Those who find themselves losing faith in his grand vision for a united Vinterkveld are often stationed at Vladibogdan until they are brought back into the fold. Those who do not espouse appropriate loyalty find themselves staying on the island indefinitely.

– From the field notes of Hierarch Khigir,
Vigilant of the Imperial Synod.

Life in Cinderfell returned to its usual rhythm. An Invigilation was much like the turning of the seasons; there was a certain grim inevitability to it, like the shortening of the days in autumn, or the terrible midwinter cold. And while the townsfolk settled back into the comfortable rut of familiarity Kjellrunn found her life much changed. Her school days were done and all that remained was the cottage and its myriad tasks: she scrubbed flagstones, stacked firewood, cooked and cleaned and sewed. Her chores were carried out in silence while her father slept late or did a good deal of nothing in the smithy, only to retire to bed with a jug of ale or mead each night.

'We're low on firewood,' said Marek as they ate that night. The lines on his face had put another five years on him. His beard was unkempt and his clothes rumpled. Money, which had never been abundant, had been in shorter supply since Steiner's departure. Kjellrunn eyed the jugs in the corner of the room, now divested of their contents.

'I know,' said Marek, rubbing his forehead with the back of one fist. 'I'll put a stop to that.'

'A stop? To what?' Kjellrunn looked at her father, though his gaze was fixed firmly on his empty bowl. Fingers fussed with breadcrumbs where they lay in the grooves of the table.

'The mead. The drinking.' He fell silent, and the wind outside moaned and wailed, gusting over the rooftops of the lonely town.

'I don't mind you drinking,' said Kjellrunn after a moment. 'I just wish you'd do it at the tavern with Verner. You should be with people, not hidden away in your bed like an old man.'

Marek considered this for a moment, nodding like a mule. His eyes flicked up, found her face. He leaned forward. 'And you?'

'It's always been different for me. You know what the children at school said. Now we know it's true.'

'Have you seen Kristofine lately?' said Marek, clearly keen to speak of anything but witchsign.

'No.' Kjellrunn thought back to the day Steiner had been taken; the fleeting moment of tenderness she'd been shown. 'No I haven't.' She'd not spoken to a soul and found herself desperate to share a word with anyone but Marek. 'I'll head up to the woods tomorrow to fetch some firewood,' she added.

Marek nodded. 'A good idea. We're low and I've a busy day ahead of me.'

'I thought I'd venture up to the old woodcutter's chalet.' She waited for Marek's reaction, but none came. She'd thought of nothing else all week. Her fright had receded enough for her curiosity to be near-irresistible. 'Does anyone live there these days?'

'Live there?' Marek shook his head. 'Not for thirty years. I'm surprised the chalet is still standing.'

'What happened?'

'They say he was a kind man, quiet but kind. His wife passed one winter. Something got into her lungs and wouldn't let go. The fever was fierce. He had two years to grieve her before the Empire took his daughter.'

'His daughter had witchsign?'

Marek nodded. 'After that he gave up. Lasted about six months, then sold what he owned and moved to Vannerånd. Can't say I blame him.'

'And no one moved to the chalet?'

'No one would buy it from him on account of the witchsign.' Marek cast his eyes across the room. 'It will be the same with this place.'

'Witchsign isn't contagious.'

'Isn't it?' Marek smiled.

'Well, no.' Kjellrunn frowned. 'Otherwise you and Steiner would have it too.'

'How do you know I don't?' He smiled again, but Kjellrunn could only find his poor attempt at humour in bad taste.

'I don't know that you don't have witchsign, but then you never told us anything about what you did before you came to Cinderfell.' She watched his expression harden and matched it with a stern one of her own. 'And you never spoke of our mother.'

'And for good reason,' said Marek. He stood up from the table and turned away from her.

'Even now, with Steiner gone, you still won't share your secrets?'

'The things I know, the things I've seen, they're not the type of stories you tell a sixteen-year-old child.'

'Childhood ended the moment they took Steiner.'

Marek's face was pained with regret and he held out his scarred and battered hands to the fire for comfort. 'That much is true. Just mind yourself around the Okhrana, Kjell. Of all of the Emperor's dogs they're the most wild, the most dangerous.'

Kjellrunn nodded and cleared the plates, then busied herself washing the bowls to hide her alarm.

'Goodnight, Kjell.' He stumbled to bed sober; the first time since Steiner had left.

Her anger faded after a time and her mind whirled with what tomorrow would bring. The few coins she'd hoarded under her pillow would come in useful, though she'd have to face a trip into town.

'It's nice to see you,' said Kristofine, though there was a tightness around her eyes and her words were clipped. 'I've not seen you since . . .' She offered a small smile to substitute the words omitted.

'Since the day they took him.' They stood outside the baker's shop, each with a shawl wrapped around slender shoulders, headscarves tied tight against a bitter north-westerly that keened over rooftops. Baskets hung from the crooks of their elbows and each regarded the other with a wary gaze. Kjellrunn shuffled her feet and struggled to look the girl in the face. Woman, she corrected herself. Kristofine had undergone that subtle transformation, leaving Kjellrunn feeling scarecrow-like by contrast.

'Has there been any word? From the island?' Kristofine cast a look over her shoulder, but the street was quiet.

'Nothing,' replied Kjellrunn. 'I didn't realize it was such an open secret,' she added.

'Only if you sit close to Verner when he's drunk and maudlin.'

'And all of those clichés about fishermen's wives—'

'Don't seem so bad when you've listened to the men,' said Kristofine. It was a well-known saying along the coast. They offered smiles of consolation to each other, feeling the silence between them, the wind more vocal by far.

'I should let you hurry on,' said Kristofine. 'Your father will be waiting on his lunch.'

Kjellrunn eyed the basket's contents and nodded. 'Yes, he will,' she lied. 'I'm sorry things were so strained between us when the Okhrana called at the tavern.'

'I've heard plenty of rumours about the Vigilants in Helwick,' said Kristofine quietly. 'I'd rather not know if you know something. And I'd rather pretend you don't know anything either.'

Kjellrunn nodded and didn't trust herself to say the right thing, yet she felt gratitude all the same.

'Well met and take care, Kjell.'

'And you,' she replied. Kristofine headed up the steep hill to the tavern and Kjellrunn wondered why the woman had taken a sudden interest in her brother. Certainly they'd never been friends while at school. She narrowed her eyes and bowed her head, feet quick and light on cobbles that would lead her from the town, climbing the incline to the woods of the northern headlands. Three times she encountered women-folk as she wound her way through the narrow streets. Three times they called out in reluctant greeting, her own wave and smile equally reluctant.

'Probably only waving out of pity,' she hissed to herself. 'Probably surprised that Steiner was taken and I was the one left behind.' She bit her lip and blinked away tears. 'They're not the only ones.'

The trees were no less bare than they had been a week ago. The woodland was a damp and muddy misery but for the occasional pine tree, remaining resolute and green despite the season. There was no hesitation, her stride was not broken.

'Better to do a thing than to stand and contemplate it.' That's what her father had always said. Though he said little these days.

The chalet looked much as it had when she'd fled. The thatch still needed changing, the stones remained thick with moss. A plume of smoke drifted from the chimney and lantern light gilded the windowsills.

'So, I didn't imagine it.' She smiled. 'Perhaps the fox will be there too.'

The chalet was quiet but for the snap and pop of fire devouring wood in the hearth. Kjellrunn knocked on the door and felt a terrible dread turn her guts to stone. What was she doing here? Why had she trekked back to the old chalet in the bleak weather?

'Who's there?' called a voice, accent heavy, most certainly from Solmindre. No way to know if it were angry or fearful.

'My name is Kjellrunn. I've brought food. Fresh fish and bread still warm from the oven.' This last was a lie, the autumn chill had sapped the warmth from everything, including her near-numb fingertips.

The door opened to reveal a serious face. She was old by Cinderfell standards, where people rarely lasted longer than sixty years. A grubby headscarf was tied over grey hair shorn close to her skull.

'I came to apologize for breaking in the other day,' said Kjellrunn, holding up the basket.

'Why should you apologize? I broke in myself,' replied the woman. She didn't trouble herself to look at the offering, intent on the girl shivering on the doorstep. Kjellrunn frowned and shuffled her feet. The introduction was not going how she had planned.

'No one has lived here for thirty years,' said Kjellrunn. 'I don't suppose you knew that, did you?'

The old woman broke into a slow smile, though Kjellrunn didn't care for it much. 'So, you have spirit.'

'Steiner says I look like a rusalka most of the time.'

'I said you *have* spirit, not you *are* spirit.' The old woman blinked, then chuckled. 'It is rare in these parts. People in Nordvlast have brains of dung and no soul.' The old woman glanced at the sky and the flurry of snowflakes descending. 'Best you come in out of the snow, before you end up frozen to death.'

Kjellrunn didn't move.

'I will not eat you, I'm not a witch. And you are too big for the cooking pot, even if I hacked off your arms and legs.'

'You are one strange old lady,' said Kjellrunn.

'And you are a strange girl,' said the old woman. Kjellrunn was suddenly aware that the old woman in the doorway didn't look frail or unsteady like the old folk she knew in town. There was steeliness here, in mind and posture and movement. Kjellrunn set down the basket on the doorstep.

'I must get home.' She was overtaken by the need to be back there, as even the cramped and dim kitchen seemed preferable to being on the steps of the woodcutter's chalet.

'Come back soon,' called the old woman as Kjellrunn picked her way across the snowy clearing.

'Come back?' Kjellrunn's eyes widened in surprise.

'So I can teach you.'

'What could you possibly teach me?' said Kjellrunn. She'd half a mind to take the basket with her.

'To use your powers of course.' The old woman crossed her arms and frowned. 'That is why you came. You want to use your powers to rescue your brother on Vladibogdan.'

'How do you know about my brother?' Kjellrunn frowned.

'I know so many things, Kjellrunn Vartiainen.' The old woman lifted the basket and cradled it like an infant. 'As you will soon find out.'

CHAPTER SIXTEEN

Steiner

Though few would dare to say so openly, Vladibogdan is the dark reflection of Arkiv Island in every way. Arkiv, with its many libraries, promises a wealth of knowledge and solitude between the stacks, whereas Vladibogdan is concerned with the physical. Arkiv enjoys a temperate climate, while Vladibogdan suffers bitterly cold winds or the searing heat of the furnaces. It is not only weapons that are forged on the cruel north-western island, but Vigilants, careers, and even destinies.

– From the field notes of Hierarch Khigir,
Vigilant of the Imperial Synod.

Steiner woke to the usual cacophony, a backdrop of sound he could not ignore. He'd taken to wadding up bundles of sackcloth and holding them to his ears so he might sleep. A candle flared to life in the cave, a tawny glow revealing the barren interior, but also a guest. Steiner sat up, blinked, and wiped the sleep from his eyes.

'Oh, it's you,' was all he managed. His shoulders and neck ached and his thighs were heavy.

'Morning,' said Tief, his voice gentle.

'Is it?' Steiner frowned. 'How do you tell without daylight?'

'I sneak up the steps first thing, to get a breath of fresh air.'

'This is a curious sort of prison,' replied Steiner, rolling his shoulders and yawning. 'No locks on the doors.'

'And no doors for the locks, just lots and lots of soldiers.' Tief pulled out his pipe, running his fingers over the cracked clay. 'The forge isn't the prison, the island is the prison.'

'And without a ship we've no way of getting away from here,' added Steiner.

'Don't think I haven't tried.' Tief sighed and looked back into the forges. 'Here comes Taiga, I need to start work. Don't be long with breakfast.'

'What breakfast?' asked Steiner. Tief slipped out through the fissure in the wall and Taiga replaced him a moment later, bearing a tray.

'There's porridge for you,' she said. 'You're getting thin. Eat.' She set both hands against the barrel of water in the corner and bowed her head.

'What are you doing?'

'I'm trying to concentrate.' A note of pique in her voice.

'Concentrate on what?'

'*Shhh.*'

Steiner leaned forward and picked up the rough wooden bowl and slender spoon from the floor. The porridge was almost cold but that didn't stop him devouring it. All the while Taiga kept her hands on the barrel and her head bowed. Steiner kept spooning the tepid porridge as quietly as he could and waited when it was gone. Finally Taiga turned to him and smiled. He could see her better in the candlelight, just a few feet from where he sat on his crude sackcloth bed. Her hair was a wavy bob of brown a few tones darker than her skin with ivy leaves woven into her tresses. The leaves remained a splendid green despite the ever-present soot of the furnaces. Her eyes featured the same cast as her brother, narrow at the corners yet delicate.

'You never saw a Spriggani before you came here.' Not a question.

'My sister . . .' Steiner felt his throat become thick, blocking words that would not come.

'She believed in Frøya and Frejna, didn't she? Told the old tales of Se and Venter.'

Steiner nodded, wiped his nose on his sleeve and cleared his throat.

'And you mocked her for it. Mocked her plenty.'

Taiga came close and pushed his hair back from his forehead with a tender hand. 'Tief tells me you're talking about escape, but I just can't see it.'

'I need to think of something, focus on something, I can't just stay here.'

'Sundra, Tief, Enkhtuya and myself have been here for some years now. We've never found a way off the island. But things could change.'

'How?'

'I don't know, I was hoping you might. You changed things just by sneaking up to the kitchens.'

She withdrew to the split in the rock, framed by the ragged stone, silhouetted by the orange red of the furnace glow. Steiner eyed the barrel of water in the corner.

'What did you do to the water?' asked Steiner.

'I made it clean, I made it pure. That is, Frøya did.'

'How?'

'Because I asked her to. You can drink it now. And you should wash. The soot will dry out you skin and become infected.' Taiga smiled and turned away, obscured by the gloom outside.

The following month settled into a routine. The furnaces had their own rhythms, replacing the rising and setting of the sun. Taiga would appear silently each morning, lighting a candle to rouse him and asking Frøya's blessing to purify the water. Porridge would appear, the bowl always too small, the portion the same. The day was an endless trudge, carrying sacks of coal from where they landed at the bottom of an angled chute. Steiner, and the many cinderwraiths on the same detail, would ferry the sacks to each workstation, starting at the outer edge and working across the whole cavern. Only when all of the workstations had been supplied would anyone dare to approach the dais and deliver coal to Enkhtuya.

'The cinderwraiths won't go near her since she nearly snuffed one of them out,' explained Tief. 'Seems you've got the duty. Don't say anything foolish. I'd rather avoid mopping you up off the floor.'

'That makes two of us.' Steiner shook his head and tried to ignore his aches and pains. His rib still troubled him with each jarring step, flaring into bright pain when he stooped to lift or drop one of the sacks.

Lunch fell in the gap between the delivery of coal and the afternoon's activity of taking finished weapons and carrying them to crates, where cinderwraiths packed them with old straw and canvas.

'Straw? In a cavern of thirty-odd furnaces?' Steiner grumbled. 'Whose idea was that?'

'We need it for packing,' replied Tief with a frown.

'I don't fancy our chances if any of this catches fire.'

'I don't fancy our chances at all,' said Tief, rubbing tired eyes with the back of one hand.

Northman and Spriggani sat on empty wooden crates and chewed on black bread, imagining butter or even a sliver of meat to liven the meagre fare. Taiga purified the water of the ever-present soot. Steiner closed his eyes and felt the grit beneath his lids. Wiping it away would do no good, just press more coal dust into his eyes.

'Have you had any more thoughts on escape?' he asked.

Tief tugged at one ear, then shook his head. 'Even if we could sneak out of here and across Academy Square, we'd still need to overpower the guards at the gatehouse. And once we'd done that we'd still be stuck with the basic problem.'

'No ship,' said Steiner. 'What about the crates?' He rapped his knuckles on the crate he was sitting on. 'We could smuggle ourselves out.'

'They inspect every shipment,' said Tief. 'Not a single crate of weapons leaves the island without being checked over.'

'Your sister told me things will change,' muttered Steiner.

'Taiga hopes you'll see a way out that we've missed.' Tief rubbed a hand over his stubble and sighed. 'But if we fail' – the Spriggani nodded at the cinderwraiths going about their endless work – 'we'll be joining them.'

Steiner lingered on the edge of sleep. A dull part of his mind knew that Taiga would appear shortly with her too-small bowl of half-warm porridge, but that didn't stop him dreaming of meat. He could almost taste it. He could smell it.

He lurched upright in bed, disorientated and blinking in the dark.

'I *can* smell it,' he croaked with a parched throat.

Steiner dressed quickly, the scent of roasting meat maddening. His fingers fumbled with laces and he'd barely pulled his smock over his head before stumbling through the ragged split in the rock to the cavern beyond.

'Where is everybody?' he whispered.

None of the cinderwraiths were at their stations, the constant percussion of hammers on metal was absent. Steiner cast his eye towards the centre where a great swirl of wraiths gathered like a raincloud, occluding whatever business was occurring on the dais. That business involved cooked meat, and it was a business he would be a part of.

Steiner broke into a run, slowing when he realized how

weak he was and how the motion jarred his rib. The last month had hardened his limbs, but also stripped him bare of any fat. His wrists were cruel knobs of bone, his fingers almost black where soot had stained his calluses.

'Excuse me,' he said, slipping between the insubstantial bodies of the dusty spirits. The crowd parted and Steiner realized why the cinderwraiths had downed tools.

'And that's how Steiner saved me from Shirinov, your highness,' said Maxim, performing a low bow.

'Is this true?' said Kimi, regarding the boy with a wry smile.

'Seems Shirinov is still spitting blood about it,' replied Romola. She was flipping slices of meat in wide pan in much the same way Steiner had a month ago. 'That's why Felgenhauer sent him down here; out of sight, out of mind.'

'You have to admit,' said Tief, 'the boy has some stones.' He was sitting cross-legged on the dais buttering thick slices of bread.

The Yamal princess shrugged and looked away. 'One Northman is much like another to me.'

'You can't judge all Northmen based on the deeds of the Solmindre Empire,' countered Romola.

'He is awake,' added Sundra in a flat voice. She was tossing the bones on the square of black velvet and regarding the results with a dispassionate eye. 'He comes now.'

Steiner blinked. There was a dreamlike quality to the scene, as if he was invisible while they spoke of him, concealed by the press of cindery spirits.

'Can I have some water?' he croaked in a parched voice. All the living creatures on the dais flinched as he emerged from the halo of dark bodies.

'There he is!' said Tief. Taiga smiled, while Sundra muttered under her breath. Maxim beamed and held up a hand of greeting.

'Hoy there, Steiner.'

'Hoy there. How did you get down here?'

Maxim puffed himself up. 'I have my orders. I was told to bring some food down.'

'By whom?' Steiner frowned, but Romola interrupted before Maxim could reply.

'Oh, Steiner,' said the pirate. 'What have they done to you?'

He looked down at his limbs and the scrawny expanse of his chest. His britches hung from his hips, on the verge of slipping down. Even his boots felt bigger, looser somehow.

'We've tried to feed him,' said Tief.

'But they send so little down to us,' added Sundra.

'What are you doing here?' Steiner asked Romola. 'You'll be killed if they find you.

'I'm delivering mail. I brought Kimi a letter from her father, and thought I'd check in on Maxim. He told me about your little adventure raiding the pantry. It seemed like such a good idea I thought I'd repeat it. And I bribed some of the guards, just to be sure.' Romola looked him over from head to toe. 'I'm glad I did. Eat this before you fade away.' She thrust a loaded plate towards him and he took it before slipping to his knees and spearing mackerel with a two-pronged fork. He chewed slowly, eyes closed with reverence.

Maxim slunk from Enkhtuya's side and knelt beside the boy, wrapping an arm around him.

'I thought you'd come back,' he whispered.

'I wanted to,' admitted Steiner, 'but I didn't want to get us both killed. Not when being dead isn't the worst thing that can happen.' He nodded to the cinderwraiths gathered around the dais, a shadowy choir with eyes burning bright.

Taiga appeared at his side with a wooden mug of water and Steiner drank half and released a sigh of relief. He eyed the scrunch of parchment in Enkhtuya's fist and looked to Romola with an awful pang in his chest.

'Is there anything for me? From my father?'

Romola looked away, turning her attention back to the sizzling fish. She took a deep breath and said, 'I didn't stop in at Cinderfell, Steiner. It's not on my usual route. Never has been. People might ask questions if I suddenly started dropping anchor there.' She looked up from the cooking. 'I'm sorry.'

Steiner acknowledged her with a curt nod, unable to shake the bitter pang of disappointment.

'What I will do is make sure you start getting more food,' said Romola.

Kimi stood and took a step towards Steiner, towering over him. Steiner frowned up at her, then staggered to his feet still clutching his food.

'Is this true?' asked Enkhtuya. 'That you raised your hammer against the Vigilant?'

'Yes, he was using the arcane on Maxim and I stopped him.'

'And you were brought here by mistake?' added Enkhtuya. 'You don't have witchsign?'

'No. My sister does. I was standing in front of her when the Vigilants noticed us. They assumed it was me, not her, who had witchsign.'

'And you let yourself be brought here, to suffer in her place.'

Steiner chewed his lip. It hadn't felt like he had much choice at the time, but he'd stayed silent, gone along with the lie.

Steiner nodded. 'I wanted her to be safe, I wanted to keep Kjellrunn away from here. They say the arcane burns you up and hollows you out. I didn't want that for her.'

'It must be difficult,' said Kimi, softly.

'I was angry with her at first. Angry that she never told me, and angry with my father too.' Steiner sighed; it was hard to speak of such things. 'But I've made my peace with it now.'

'And you gave blankets to the small ones on the ship?' said Kimi.

Steiner turned to Maxim. 'You really did tell her everything, didn't you?'

'You really started something when you took a swing at Shirinov,' said Maxim. 'There have been more punishments for disobedience in the last month than in the last year. That's what the older children say.'

Steiner couldn't keep the grin from his face as he imagined a small army of surly children making life difficult for the Vigilants.

Kimi regarded him with hard eyes beneath an equally hard frown.

'Listen,' said Steiner. 'Can you make it quick if you're going to start with the hitting again? My rib still aches from the last time and I don't want to go through all that again.'

The hand that Kimi offered him was not a fist, but the open palm of friendship. Steiner reached forward, swallowed in a dry throat, noticed how his hand shook as he offered it. She clasped his forearm and Steiner returned the gesture.

'Any enemy of the Empire is a friend of mine,' said Kimi. 'Even if you are a Northman.' She turned to Tief. 'We need to put some meat on his bones, and plenty of it.'

They sat and worked their way through the remaining food, carving apples and pears into thin slices, and dividing the segments of a rare fruit Romola called a satsuma. The taste left Steiner speechless and he watched the strange meal play out in front of him, not altogether convinced he wasn't dreaming.

'What just happened?' he whispered to Romola when she came to refill his mug with fresh water.

'The Yamal take family very seriously,' said the captain. 'And Kimi Enkhtuya is a younger sister too. I'd guess she'd give anything in the world for a brother like you, right?'

'It's good to see you again.'

'It's good to see you too,' said Romola with a smile. 'Taiga has high hopes.'

'High hopes for what?'

'Leaving this place, of course.'

'What about Sundra?'

Romola grimaced. 'Don't worry about her, she dances to her own tune.'

Steiner looked around the circle of his new friends, feeling as content as he'd ever been in the last dismal month, yet something in the pit of his stomach warned him it wouldn't last.

CHAPTER SEVENTEEN

Kjellrunn

*Each of the Scorched Republics has its own cultures and person-
alities. Nordvlast people are dirt poor and ever stoic though
somewhat sparse of humour. Vannerånd's many lakes are said to
be haunted by rusalka, which is why they are such a suspicious
lot. That Vannerånd's people produce so many children with
witchsign is also cause for wariness. The population of Drakefjord
pride themselves on being proud and upright citizens and loyal
fighters, while Svingettevei is a land dominated by hills and
winding roads, much like the minds of the people who live there.
Getting a straight answer or a fair deal in this part of the continent is near impossible.*

– From the field notes of Hierarch Khigir,
Vigilant of the Imperial Synod.

Kjellrunn had never liked the smithy's gloomy interior. She
preferred the bleak Nordvlast sunlight on the days clouds did
not obscure it completely. The sweltering heat generated by
the furnace never failed to make her thirsty, and as her temperature rose so did a nameless anxiety. This had always been a
place for her brother and father, sharing companionable silence

as they beat metal into new shapes. Her own company, while occasionally lonely, featured fewer questions, fewer awkward pauses.

'The place just isn't the same without you, Steiner.' She'd taken to speaking to him lately, entertaining the idea that the winds might spirit away her words and fetch them across the Spøkelsea. 'What would you make of an old crone living in the woodcutter's chalet?'

She opened the kitchen door and trudged outside, a jug tucked under one arm. Snow had gusted in from the north-west since her visit to the woods. It fell in a stately fashion, hiding Cinderfell beneath a covering of grey.

'Good morning,' said a voice without cheer, the two words loaded with wariness. Kristofine and her father, Bjørner, stood a dozen feet from the smithy, wrapped up warm against the chill.

'Good morning,' replied Kjellrunn, 'I was just taking my father some water.' She hefted the earthen jug, then glanced at the door.

'We're here to see him too.'

Kjellrunn nodded, not knowing what to say. She hurried to the doors, rapped her knuckles on the wood and lifted the latch.

'Hoy there,' said Marek, over one shoulder. 'You must have read my mind; it's been thirsty work this morning.'

Kjellrunn didn't reply, self-conscious in front of Kristofine and the tavern owner. The kindness on Marek's face faded as he caught sight of the visitors.

'Bjørner.' He gave a curt nod and set down the hammer with a clank, then tugged on his fingers until the knuckles popped.

'Marek.' The tavern owner cleared his throat and smiled, though Kjellrunn suspected there wouldn't be much smiling once he'd said his piece.

'Is it nails? A new skillet? A knife?' Marek's tone was pleasant, but he'd not stepped forward to shake hands, remaining by the anvil.

'No need for those today,' said Bjørner. 'Just a few words.'

'I'm sure I can spare a few of those,' said Marek, 'and fortunately for you, words are free.'

Kjellrunn crossed the smithy and passed the jug to her father, then waited, head bowed, curiosity burning. Bjørner looked from Marek to Kristofine and back to Kjellrunn, a brief frown crossing his face.

'Perhaps it would best if you started on lunch,' said Marek to his daughter. Kjellrunn opened her mouth to protest but Marek hugged her close and buried his face in her hair. 'Listen by the door if you must,' he said quietly.

'Of course,' replied Kjellrunn, then exited the smithy, noting how Bjørner and Kristofine retreated a step, staying beyond arm's reach as if she were sick with fever. The smithy door closed and Kjellrunn stomped on the snow, walking on the spot, making her footsteps quieter with each iteration.

'She's gone,' said Marek, voice loud despite the door's obstruction. 'Out with it then, Bjørner.'

Kjellrunn leaned close, pressing an ear against the door.

'It's like this, Marek.' Bjørner did not sound his confident self. This was a man on first-name terms with the whole town, a man who'd seen nearly everyone the worse for drink at some point. This was a pragmatic man who knew well the complexities of life. 'The night before Steiner left—'

'You mean the night before Steiner was taken,' countered Marek.

'Yes. Taken, of course. So, he stayed in the stables at the back of my tavern.'

'I had wondered where he fetched up that night.'

'I found him in there that morning, fairly reeking of mead and looking terrible.'

'I see,' said Marek. 'I wonder how that mead made its way out of your tavern and into my son?'

Kjellrunn strained to hear, trying to imagine the look on Kristofine's face.

'The thing is—' Bjørner cleared his throat. 'The thing is now people are saying Kristofine has witchsign, and that she should offer herself up for Invigilation when the Empire returns.'

'If she's not tainted then she's nothing to fear,' replied Marek. 'Witchsign isn't contagious. It's not a plague.'

'That's what I said, of course.'

Kjellrunn pressed her ear closer to the wood, thinking she had missed something. An ugly pause curdled between the two men.

'What do you want, Bjørner?' said Marek, and Kjellrunn knew the expression on his face would be flinty upon hearing the words.

'With everything that's happened,' said Bjørner, 'all the rumours about Kjellrunn, and now this business with Steiner . . .'

'Go on,' said Marek.

'Some of us think it best you moved on, set up shop in Helwick. I've a wagon and horse I could lend you for the trip.'

'That's kind of you,' said Marek, but Bjørner missed the hard edge to the blacksmith's voice, blundering on.

'Perhaps you'd want to go further. Steinwick is a busy town. People are always saying how pretty Vannerånd is—'

'Get out,' said Marek, so quietly Kjellrunn almost failed to hear through the stout wooden door. She did not have the same problem the second time. Marek's voice boomed, equal to the hammers he wielded.

Kjellrunn moved too slowly. She was only halfway back to the kitchen when Bjørner and Kristofine emerged from the smithy, he red-faced with embarrassment, she pale and tearful.

'And have a care not to return,' added Marek, as he stood in the open doorway, a hammer clutched in one fist to drive home his point. 'There'll be no welcome for you here. Warm or otherwise.'

'Just think on what I've said,' added Bjørner, the strength gone from his voice. He turned to leave with rounded shoulders.

Kristofine paused. 'I'm so sorry,' was all she whispered. Kjellrunn barely heard the words, but her intent was written across her pretty face for all to see.

'Sorry? We're all sorry,' said Kjellrunn, watching father and daughter walk away. 'Every last one of us.'

Two men in black waited on horseback at the end of the street.

'Just what we need,' grunted Marek. He flipped a salute to the horsemen.

'They're Okhrana, aren't they?' asked Kjellrunn, but Marek headed back into the smithy. The salute seemed to be all the men needed to urge their mounts into a trot, heading out of town.

Kjellrunn did not run to the woodcutter's chalet for fear of attracting attention but there was a purpose to her stride. Purpose and the knowledge that every step brought her closer to the old woman who had plucked her name from thin air. The snow continued to idle downward, covering the land in a shadowy grey. The woods offered some reprieve but she was glad of Steiner's old tunic all the same, worn over her own. She wasn't sure why she'd taken it, only knew that having something of his made venturing to the woods less terrible.

'Even now you're looking out for me, with your old cast-offs.'

She cast a wary glance about the clearing outside the chalet, then shrugged and shook her head.

'And who is looking out for you exactly?' The old woman

emerged from behind a pine tree with an axe in her hand. Kjellrunn threw up her hands and stepped back.

'Flighty today, are we?' Again, the thick Solska accent, making the words deadpan.

'I came back—'

'So it seems.

'To learn,' said Kjellrunn, feeling foolish, 'about the arcane.'

'I never doubted you would.'

'Do you have a name?'

The old woman considered this for a moment as if it were some complex riddle.

'You don't know your own name?' asked Kjellrunn.

'I'm not simple, not yet anyway.' The old woman looked away and narrowed her eyes, then stood straighter. 'You may call me Mistress Kamalov.'

'Kamalov.' Kjellrunn grimaced as she said it. It was every inch a Solmindre name and she didn't care for it much. 'How did you know my name? Before, when I came with the fish and bread.'

'It is just a tiny part of what we do. What I do. Your talents are different.'

'What talents?'

'You are a doubly gifted child, I suspect, so gifted I insist we go to the chalet. I'm too old to stay outside in this weather.' Snow had settled in the folds of her cloak and a few flakes had stuck to her wiry eyebrows. Mistress Kamalov stooped behind the tree and brought forth an armful of firewood.

'I can take that for you,' said Kjellrunn, suddenly aware of the woman's great age.

'Good. You have the makings of a good student. And you have motivation, yes?'

'Motivation?'

'Your brother. It's written all over your face.' Mistress Kamalov poked Kjellrunn in the chest with a bony finger.

'And over your heart,' she added, before walking back to the chalet. 'Tell me, how was he taken when you were left behind?'

Kjellrunn fought down a surge of disquiet, wanting to explain as best she could but the words would not come.

'Inside. I'll make *kompot*,' said Mistress Kamalov. 'I would prefer tea, but I cannot find a leaf of it in this wretched country.'

'We have tea.'

'Tea should come from Yamal. The tribes are good for two things.' She held up her bony fingers. 'Fighting and growing tea.'

'You've met someone from Yamal?' asked Kjellrunn as they entered the chalet. It was much changed since she'd seen it last. The leaves were all gone and the floor had been swept clean, a lantern burned with a steady light and the fire was banked up. A little of the bread and fish remained. Kjellrunn raised an eyebrow.

'I am trying to make it last,' explained Mistress Kamalov. 'I left quickly and left many things behind. Not least money, foolish old *kozel* that I am.'

'Left where?' Kjellrunn pulled out a chair and Mistress Kamalov held up one hand.

'You sit when I say sit. This is how the student learns. As for where, the Solmindre Empire, where else? As if there is anywhere in the world left to escape from.'

'Did you escape from the island?' Kjellrunn tugged at the hem of Steiner's tunic. 'Do you know it? Have you been there?'

'I can see it's always going to be questions with you,' said Mistress Kamalov. Her face became stern. 'Not so much with the listening.'

'I can listen,' said Kjellrunn.

'First, it's not simply called the Island, it's Vladibogdan. Merely knowing Vladibogdan exists is enough for the Empire to make you disappear.' She made a loud snap with her fingers. 'No questions. No one will see. You'll just be gone. Understand?'

Kjellrunn nodded. A violent energy lingered on Mistress Kamalov as she spoke of the Empire. Kjellrunn could see it in the grim line of her mouth, and her short choppy gestures.

'No one escapes Vladibogdan. Not unless they become a Vigilant, and even then . . .' The old woman looked away, tears at the corners of her eyes. She swallowed hard and grimaced. 'Do you understand?'

Kjellrunn nodded, wanting Mistress Kamalov to answer other questions but not daring to interrupt.

'Many wise men and women have studied the arcane over many decades. Ever since we cast down the dragons, over seventy years ago, children have begun to appear with gifts, talents.'

'Witchsign,' said Kjellrunn softly.

'Witchsign.' Mistress Kamalov's tone was all mocking. 'A pretty name for it, but the arcane is dangerous. Dangerous to other people, dangerous to the ones who use it. Understand?' Kjellrunn nodded again and Mistress Kamalov gave a curt nod that signalled her satisfaction. She took a knife to a few handfuls of berries and added them to a pan. After a while she settled into a rhythm and continued speaking.

'The arcane, the way dragons use it' – she shook her head – 'it's no good. The power of the air and the power of fire will make a person ill, over time it makes a body change, makes you older than you are. Even the powers of earth will corrupt you if you draw them from dark places.'

'My father told me not to use my powers,' said Kjellrunn.

'Your father is wise. Not so often you meet a blacksmith who knows much besides metal, not so often you meet a Nordvlast man who knows much at all.'

'I don't think he's from here,' said Kjellrunn, but Mistress Kamalov didn't catch the words, intent on her subject.

'Sometimes the arcane wreaks other changes.' Mistress Kamalov had turned her attention back to the berries. 'People who use these powers can lose their minds, become great fools or great monsters. Understand?'

Kjellrunn nodded. 'Will I be driven mad?'

'You are different.' Mistress Kamalov flashed a bitter smile. 'Very different.'

Kjellrunn opened her mouth to speak but Mistress Kamalov held the knife up, slick with the juice of red berries. The old woman looked far from sane by the flickering light of the fire.

Kjellrunn eyed the knife. 'I'll be quiet.'

'Quiet is good,' said Mistress Kamalov. 'So. You are different. I suspect you have two gifts, I am thinking one is the power of the earth and other is of water, the power of the ocean.'

'And this is what Steiner is learning on Vladibogdan,' said Kjellrunn.

'Always with questions.' Mistress Kamalov shook her head. 'Steiner? What power did he have?'

'Power? He . . . he didn't have any. The Vigilant made a mistake. Steiner went so I wouldn't have to.'

Mistress Kamalov set down the knife and gave Kjellrunn a long stare. 'Now you sit.'

Kjellrunn did as she was told and Mistress Kamalov did likewise. She leaned forward, lacing her fingers, a frown of deep thought on her lined face.

'Your brother was taken by mistake? Instead of you?'

Kjellrunn nodded, feeling the bright heat of tears. 'And I let him. I was too scared to go. I should have given myself up. I know that now. If I could just see him again I could—'

'There is nothing you can do.' Mistress Kamalov smoothed down her hair and sighed. 'How you sent a boy with no power is a mystery, but it's done now. There is no undoing this.'

'If I can learn the arcane. If I could be good, be strong,

maybe I could catch a ship and go to Vladibogdan. Maybe I could find him and—'

'He is already dead, Kjellrunn.'

Only the crackle of the fire dared disturb the silence between woman and girl. Kjellrunn heard the words. Each one entered her like a sliver of ice. She shook her head and opened her mouth to speak but her throat was tight and thick.

'Don't say that.' She dried her eyes on the back her hand and frowned. 'You don't know Steiner. He's clever, maybe not clever with books but he's hard-working and bright and never gives in. He has a heart like an auroch's . . .' Her words ran out as she realized the look in Mistress Kamalov's eyes was one of pity.

'The Empire does not tolerate little people knowing its secrets. And you, and your brother, this town, all of Nordvlast. You are little people. The Emperor cares nothing for you. The Emperor only cares that you submit to the will of the Empire. In time Nordvlast will become part of the Empire. Vannerånd, Drakefjord too. Even Svingettevei, though difficult to know why anyone would want that rabble of tricksters and liars.'

'I don't care about the Empire,' said Kjellrunn with gritted teeth. 'I care about my brother. Steiner's not dead. He can't be.'

'Do you think the Empire cares for the life of one boy? I promise you, it does not. I'm sorry, Kjellrunn, but he will need a miracle to stay alive in such a place.'

Mistress Kamalov picked up the knife and continued chopping.

'Go home now,' she said without looking up. 'Grieve for your brother and come to me three days from now. Yes?'

Kjellrunn stared at the woman and for a second she could hear the rushing of waves, as if all the Sommerende Ocean had crashed against the walls of the woodcutter's chalet and swept everything away.

'You're wrong,' she whispered, and though she had no way of knowing she begged Frøya and Frejna that it be true.

Kjellrunn left the chalet and the hush of snowfall followed her home, all through the dark woods and along Cinderfell's winding streets, like a sullen cur.

'Steiner's not dead. He can't be.' She repeated the words to herself, almost chanting them every few feet. She didn't weep until she was in bed, taking care to stifle her cries lest her father hear them.

CHAPTER EIGHTEEN

Steiner

Do not be fooled by the uniforms of the Holy Synod, nor the singular vision of the Emperor that guides it; a schism can be felt in every corridor, meeting room and antechamber. All of us must suffer the frustrations of bureaucracy from time to time, just as we must endure the bitter cold of winter. Rivalries drive individuals to make heated and rash decisions, but it is ideology that will tear the Empire apart, like a vast quake that shakes the world from horizon to horizon. Put simply, there are those who support the forthcoming war and those misguided fools who would prevent it.

– From the field notes of Hierarch Khigir,
Vigilant of the Imperial Synod.

Life in the forges would never be a happy one, but it was less wretched when one counted Kimi Enkhtuya among one's friends. She had said little, but favoured Steiner with a solemn nod of acknowledgement whenever he delivered coal to her workstation.

'I'm still not entirely sure she likes me,' grunted Steiner when Tief had appeared with two mugs of black tea one morning after the first set of deliveries. They were sitting near the entrance to the cavern, away from the worst of the heat.

'Has she punched you in the face lately?' said Tief.

'Well, no.'

'Then she likes you just fine.' Tief slurped at his tea. 'Perhaps you were expecting poems and flowers?'

Steiner smiled. 'I wasn't sure what to expect.'

'She's sizing you up is all,' said Tief, looking over Steiner as if he were a horse for market. 'Trying to get the measure of you.'

'I'm not that complicated. I'm a blacksmith's son from Cinderfell.'

'That's a small part of it, but there's never been anyone that fetched up on Vladibogdan because he was protecting someone else, and those who raise a hand in anger to the Vigilants and survive are few.'

'I only did that because Shirinov was attacking Maxim.'

'See, protection.' Tief smiled. 'Under different circumstances I'd say I'm glad that you're here, Steiner Vartiainen.' Tief looked over his shoulder and frowned. 'But don't you dare tell anyone or they'll think I've gone soft.'

'Good tea,' said Steiner.

'Of course it's good tea. It's Spriggani tea. None of that Nordvlast bilge water.'

'Nordvlast tea is just fine,' replied Steiner. 'But I miss the mead a good deal more. I'll buy you a pint when we get out of here.'

A dark look crossed Tief's face. 'We're not getting out of here, Steiner.'

'You can't give up hope. You mustn't give up hope.'

'Tea break is over,' said Tief, downing the reminder of his mug. 'Back to work.' He stomped off in the gloom.

Steiner had just hefted the sack of coal onto his shoulders when the voice called out in the darkness. 'Steiner?'

'Aurelian? What are you doing here?'

The blond-haired boy looked as miserable as a whipped dog. He shrugged and looked about the cavern with fearful eyes, almost flinching when cinderwraiths drew near. Steiner had felt sure the boy had witchsign, but here he was, cast down to the forges.

'Did Felgenhauer send you down here to work?' said Steiner. 'Was Shirinov wrong about you?'

All trace of moneyed arrogance had been scoured from the boy. He was a mean thing, dirty and round-shouldered, unable to even glance at Steiner.

Aurelian shook his head. 'I told them there had been a mistake. I just want to go home, just as you want to go home.' He paused a moment and Steiner caught a sly cast to the boy's eyes, though it was hard to tell in the angry red light of the forge. 'Just as you want to get back to your family, to your sister.'

Steiner set down the sack of coal slowly and fixed the boy with a look. Aurelian wiped his nose on a sleeve and forced a miserable grin.

'I never told you I had a sister,' replied Steiner.

'No,' admitted Aurelian. 'But Shirinov did.' And suddenly the old Aurelian was stood before him, shoulders pushed back, chin thrust out in challenge, favouring Steiner with a superior smile. 'Take him,' said the boy, addressing someone over Steiner's shoulder. It was only a small mistake, but Steiner seized on it all the same. His fist was raised before he'd turned to see his assailant. He was about the same age, neither boy nor man but somewhere in between, wider in the shoulder and well-fed. Steiner wondered what powers he was able to conjure. It didn't appear to help as Steiner's fist mashed the boy's nose and mouth and sent him sprawling on his arse.

Aurelian proved to be a different matter. The boy sucked in a great breath, fingers crooked like claws. A wicked smile crossed his face and his mouth yawned open, a terrible light emanating from within his throat. Steiner lunged away and the cavern was illuminated by a gout of fire. Steiner landed on his side hard enough to send the air from his lungs. His rib sang with pain and he winced.

'You can breathe fire like a dragon?' said Steiner in disbelief.

'You'd be amazed what they teach us at the academy,' replied Aurelian with a look of triumph. He opened his mouth once more and another fiery breath consumed two cinder-wraiths. The inferno blinked out leaving nothing of the ashen spirits.

'What did you do to them?' asked Steiner, voice hushed with shock. He scrabbled backwards before stumbling to his feet.

'They were in the way,' said Aurelian, sneering.

'They were the souls of dead children.'

Aurelian shrugged. 'Who cares? Better them than me.'

The larger boy had also risen to his feet, one hand pressed to his broken nose. This was not a battle Steiner would win alone. Where was Tief when he needed him?

Aurelian's chest rose and fell as if he'd run a mile, but he looked exhilarated rather than exhausted. Steiner didn't care to give him a chance to recover, running the few dozen feet towards the centre of the cavern. If Kimi were there he might stand a chance.

'And may Frejna's eye not find you,' he gasped between breaths. Cinderwraiths flitted from his path and the heat from the furnaces licked at his skin when he ran too close. Steiner arrived at the dais, the huge furnace towering over him like an iron god. Frantic eyes searched for the Yamal princess.

'Dammit, Kimi. Where are you?' Steiner clutched at the anvil to stop his hands shaking.

'Shirinov said you were trouble.' Aurelian had drawn close, not troubling himself to run. He idled, a touch of swagger to his steps. 'So I asked for help.'

The boy Steiner had struck emerged from the gloom, bleeding from his nose, yet not troubled by the injury. The boy closed his eyes and tensed, his skin becoming a mottled, rough grey. Clothes split and tore as he swelled, a grotesque living statue.

A flicker of movement drew Steiner's attention as another novice stepped forward. There was a flash of silver in the dark that might have been a sword but she remained a shadow for the most part. The novice gave a nod to Aurelian and Steiner feared something awful had happened to Tief, Taiga and Sundra.

'Shirinov said you wouldn't come willingly,' said Aurelian, stepping closer. 'And I've not forgotten your little display on the ship.' Aurelian's stony accomplice lumbered forward.

'We need him alive,' said Aurelian to the granite-skinned boy with a broad smile.

'You really shouldn't have destroyed those two cinder-wraiths,' grunted Steiner, his anger as hot as the furnace beside him.

'Friends of yours, were they?' gloated Aurelian. The smile slipped from his face as Steiner stepped away from Kimi's anvil, the anvil where Steiner's sledgehammer had lain waiting, waiting for him to heft and swing as he did now. The dull metal head of the sledgehammer was an ugly comet in the darkness. The strike reached its apex just as the granite-skinned boy crested the lip of the dais. His craggy head came apart in a shower of stone and grit. Everyone blinked in confusion. Huge stony hands reached for a face broken apart, stroking at space that should have contained a head. Awful moments slipped by and the hands fell away. The granite-skinned boy toppled with a deafening crash, sending up clouds of soot. One colossal arm fractured on the anvil and Steiner blinked in disbelief at the sledgehammer.

Who in Frejna's name was my great-grandfather? And how did he make this sledgehammer?

Aurelian's eyes widened in fury, his mouth opening in a silent howl. Steiner threw himself clear as more draconic fire scorched the air.

'You killed him!' shrieked the blond-haired boy as the fire guttered out.

'I didn't ask you to come here,' said Steiner, pulling himself to his feet, wincing at the graze along his arm, the skin red and raw. 'And I didn't ask him to attack me.' He looked down at the corpse, trying to reconcile the shattered creature with the boy he'd left bloody-nosed just moments earlier. Steiner gripped the sledgehammer tighter as his hands shook and the same thought repeated over and over. 'I didn't ask for any of this.'

You killed him! The words came to Steiner's mind, but the thought was not his own. Aurelian's second accomplice had drawn close, hair black and tangled, a cruel curving blade jutting from a white-knuckled fist, matching the twisted smile on her lips.

Come with us now. Set down the weapon. Her lips didn't move, each word appearing in Steiner's head like the chime of a distant bell. He was suddenly nauseous, as if on the *Watcher's Wait*, the sea doing its unkind work to his guts. Steiner spread his feet, grimaced and hefted the sledgehammer.

'There's plenty of this for everyone, lady. Get out of my head.'

He'd expected her to surge forward, expected her to slash with the cruel curving dagger, flaying the flesh from his bones. Instead she raised her hands to the ceiling and threw her head back. A high-pitched sound emerged from her mouth, almost painful to his ears, at the very limit of his hearing. Steiner stepped back and looked to Aurelian, who breathed another gout of fire. Steiner shrank down beside the anvil, which shielded him from the worst of the flames.

The witch's wordless shriek was answered by other shrieks and squeals and the sound of wings. The darkness of the cavern's roof became a roil of motion, a vast swarm of bodies wheeling about.

'Bats,' whispered Steiner. They swooped down and dozen of bodies buffeted him, claws swiping and scratching as they raced by almost too fast to see. Steiner flung up an arm to shield his face, turning away as more plummeted towards him. He scrambled away from the anvil and circled the furnace, hoping the heat would deter them, but still they came.

And then they were gone, rising up and circling around the cavern, voices crying out in wordless fury. Steiner cast a disbelieving glance over his arms, the flesh scored, blood forcing its way to the surface.

Aurelian grinned and held out a hand to the dark-haired girl. They circled the dais, drawing closer to Steiner. 'Set down the hammer and come with us. Shirinov wants you alive. He wants to talk to you. Something about a Troika in Helwick. This doesn't have to end in death.'

'But it already has,' said Steiner, nodding towards the corpse of the granite-skinned boy. He'd wanted to make the words a threat, but sounded regretful, even to himself.

'So be it,' grated Aurelian with gritted teeth. He gave a curt nod to the girl and bats wheeled about, coming closer. Steiner wanted to run to the safety of his cave, hoping the bats would struggle to gain access to his sanctuary. His mouth went dry, knowing he'd never make the winding route between furnaces and anvils. The cries of the bats grew louder until wings and dark bodies filled his vision before a terrible voice spoke aloud.

'It always ends in death.'

Sundra was standing atop Kimi's anvil, her body taut, all muscles tensed, hands balled into tiny fists. It was her face that unnerved Steiner the most; eyes set hard beneath a frown, mouth a sour line that spoke of her distaste for Aurelian and his accomplices.

'Have a care, Sundra,' said Steiner. 'He can breathe fire.'

A bat fell from the swarm and shattered on the dais, coming apart like a clay bowl. Then another. Steiner flicked a glance back to Sundra, but her eyes were the colour of stone, seemingly blind, awful in their unseeing. More bats fell from the air, now petrified. They fell about the dark-haired novice who summoned them, clipping a shoulder, glancing her elbow, smacking into the crown of her head. She threw up hands to ward off the stony projectiles and squeezed her eyes closed. Steiner saw blood on the girl's fingers, thought he heard an inhuman howl above the din of shattered rock.

'Sundra, let's run!' said Steiner. He fell back to where she stood atop the anvil, her gaze no less terrible. The bats wheeled about and swooped down once more, then fell from the air, exploding apart on the dais just as the first of their number reached Steiner. The last of the swarm broke apart, fleeing in all directions. Darkness swallowed them and all that remained of their passing was a high-pitched shriek. Aurelian retreated, holding up a hand that guttered with arcane flame. He lit the way for his injured accomplice and the cinderwraiths cowered at his passing. Steiner watched them go until a voice broke the stillness.

'You look like hammered shit.' Kimi Enkhtuya stood beside him.

'I feel like it too.'

'I was asleep.' Kimi nodded. 'I came as soon as I heard.'

She wasn't alone, the workforce of Spriggani had escorted her, fixing Steiner with enquiring stares and whispering among themselves. A few complained, bitter and loud, before Taiga hushed them.

'You'd best sit down before you fall down,' said Tief, rolling a barrel towards him before setting it on its end. Steiner couldn't summon the strength to perch on the makeshift seat and slumped to his knees, eyes still fixed on the fleeing form of Aurelian.

'Friends of yours?' said Tief. Taiga had fetched a bucket of clean water and was boiling strips of cloth. Sundra had not come down from her perch on the anvil, looking at the devastation of petrified bats with a curl of disapproval to her lips. Her eyes were no longer the impenetrable grey of stone.

'They're students of Shirinov. He knows about my sister.' Steiner released an exhausted breath. 'And he sent Aurelian to fetch me.'

'No doubt he has a few questions about your family,' added Tief, tamping down some leaf in his pipe. Steiner nodded. Family. He tried not to think about Verner heading off to Helwick to kill three Vigilants, tried not to think about how a simple fisherman would even attempt such a thing.

They remained in silence for some time. Taiga cleaned his wounds and Steiner grimaced and winced but said nothing. Tief smoked and cast sour looks towards the cavern entrance. Sundra remained atop the anvil, shoulders curved, head bowed, her animus spent. Only Kimi moved with purpose, sweeping up the many petrified bat wings and shattered bodies with a broom.

'Felgenhauer told me she can do that.' Steiner gestured towards the shards of stone that had once been bats.

'Of course she can,' replied Sundra. Kimi helped her down from the anvil and Sundra leaned close. 'It is a power of the earth, but it takes years of practise to master. The Vigilants think they know the nuances of it, but they are children compared to the power of the goddess.'

Steiner opened his mouth to ask more questions but Tief held up a hand. 'Don't speak to her when she's like this.' He blew out a plume of smoke and glanced over his shoulder. 'Besides, we've got other problems.' Tief nodded to where the corpse of the novice lay. The body was no longer stone and Steiner swallowed in a dry throat. Tief approached the body and Kimi shook her head and sighed.

You killed him. Aurelian's words echoed in Steiner's head and sickened him. He stared at the sledgehammer and drew in a shaky breath.

'Come on,' replied Tief. 'It's time I let you into another secret of Vladibogdan.'

'No good will come of this,' said Sundra to her brother. 'I don't need to cast the bones to tell you that.'

'What secret?' asked Steiner, at once curious and afraid.

'No good?' said Tief to Sundra. 'It's all you've been telling me since the boy arrived. Come on, Steiner.'

'I'll come too,' said Kimi, hefting the headless body over one shoulder as if it were no more than a sack of coal. Steiner struggled not to throw up as a slick of gore ran from the neck.

'Where are we going?' was all he managed.

'Somewhere even more wretched than this sad place,' said Tief, tugging at one ear. He cast a glance at the thin faces of the Spriggani standing by the dais and the cinderwraiths drifting behind them. 'As hard as that is to imagine.'

Steiner followed Kimi as she carried the corpse, feeling an icy sweat run down his back with each step.

CHAPTER NINETEEN

Steiner

Dragons are merely part of history to much of the populace. Those who can remember the days when vast reptiles darkened our skies are long in their graves. Only the Emperor recalls those times and he speaks of them rarely. What the peasants know is recorded in saga and song, and such tales are often embellished with each retelling.

– From the field notes of Hierarch Khigir,
Vigilant of the Imperial Synod.

Steiner's cave was on the opposite side of the cavern to his friends'. He knew Kimi and the Spriggani must have their own caves, but had never given it much thought.

'This is where I sleep,' said Kimi with a nod. The stone had been worked into an arch and the image of a mountain had been carved at the apex, so different to the ragged stone that led to his own cave.

'Did you do this?' said Steiner, tracing fingertips over circular motifs containing rows of angular lines. Kimi nodded and the ghost of a smile creased her lips.

'And this is where I live with my sisters,' grunted Tief. He gestured to a smaller, but no less elaborate, opening. The stone had been worked until it resembled entwined vines with broad pointed leaves decorating the arch. There were a dozen other arches for the other Spriggani, all lovingly crafted portals.

'You've been here a long time,' said Steiner, tracing callused fingertips over carved stone.

'Too long,' said Kimi.

'These carvings,' Tief ran his hand over some intertwined leaves near the top of the door, 'were carved by our elders, ones who have gone before us.'

Steiner bowed his head a moment, though he couldn't quite bring himself to draw his hand away from the carved doorway. He felt connected to the history of the brutal place by the simple means of contact.

'So who lives in this one?' he asked after a pause. He pointed at a wider arch, wide enough for men to enter three abreast.

'No one lives here.' Tief's voice had lost its usual edge, sounding despondent. 'It's a corridor. Come on.'

The passage was as wide as the arch that led to it, curving away into darkness. The ground tilted steeply, leading ever downward.

'I didn't think it was possible to go any lower,' said Steiner, his eye coming to rest on the corpse of the boy slung over Kimi's shoulder.

'This is low all right,' said Tief. 'This is as low as it gets.' He fetched a torch from the wall lest the darkness consume them entirely. Steiner followed, suddenly anxious.

'Are there more bats down here?'

'No.' Tief flashed an unhappy look over his shoulder. 'It's much worse than bats.'

'Where are you taking me, Tief?'

'To get rid of this body. You don't kill a novice without expecting someone to come looking. And Shirinov *will* come looking, you can bet your boots on that.'

The cavern they entered was lower and flatter than the vast cavern of furnaces above. The sickly sweet smell of dung mingled with a more acrid tang, forcing Steiner to hold a sleeve up to his nose.

'Ugh.'

'Brimstone. The vapours of Hel itself,' said Tief.

'What are these statues?' asked Steiner. Scattered across the room at intervals were slender columns, each of which appeared to have a monstrous form carved about it, indistinct in the gloom.

'They're not statues,' replied Tief. He approached the nearest of them and held up the torch, the tongue of flame small beside the creature that loomed above him.

'Frøya save me.' Steiner's mouth went dry. 'Is that . . . ?' The front legs had been chained to the top of the pillar, where bony claws like sickle blades curved. The stone was cross-hatched with marks of frustration. The long neck was held in place with a pitted rusting collar, also attached to the stone column. The wings were vast leathery expanses with old skin hanging in tatters, not quite sloughed off. The only movement was the swish of a tail, but even that was secured by chains. Steiner approached and craned his head back further and further until he was staring, open-mouthed, at the creature above him.

'They don't grow so big any more,' said Tief. 'They don't live so long either. Nothing could when kept like this.'

The reptiles were only a quarter of the size of the huge statue in Academy Square, and Steiner was unprepared for how broken and ragged they were.

'But the Empire told everyone the dragons were exterminated seventy-five years ago during the uprising.'

'The Emperor makes slaves of everyone,' said Tief. 'From Nordvlast to Yamal. Dragons are no different.'

'W-why are they here?' said Steiner in a reverent hush.

Tief pointed to a small aperture in the ceiling. It was blackened and scorched.

'They light the furnaces?' said Steiner.

Tief nodded and frowned, but there was no anger in it, just a pained sadness. Kimi wandered off, moving from column to column beyond the torchlight Tief held aloft. Steiner couldn't take his eyes from the creature before him.

'But why?'

'The fire they breathe,' Tief gestured to the huge reptile before them, 'has special qualities according to the Empire. They say the metal forged in such fire is more flexible, hardier, so they say. The wounds caused by such blades almost always become infected. I've heard it said the swords are luckier, though I daresay that's just wishful thinking.'

'How many?' asked Steiner, voice a shocked whisper.

'One for each of the thirty workstations above. A good breath of fire to light the furnace at the start of each shift, make the coals good and hot.' Tief tugged at one ear and glanced around the dismal chamber. 'We sent cinderwraiths to feed them before Kimi arrived. I'm quite attached to my fingers and they can be snappy.'

Steiner looked up at the long pointed head. The teeth were yellowed and a few were cracked, each the length of his finger. The eyelid slid open, the orb beneath discoloured with rheum. Wetness leaked across the scales and dripped onto the wings below.

'What happened to its eyes?' asked Steiner, trying to imagine being chained to a stone column, barely able to see.

'Infected,' said Tief. 'They're blind not long after they turn ten.' He cleared his throat and looked away. 'And usually dead by thirty.'

'Thirty?'

Tief nodded. 'The Empire uses them up like firewood. Keeps them weak and stunted. They need good fresh air and sunlight.' He folded his arms and sighed. 'They need forests and mountains. They need more food than we can give them.'

'I was always told dragons were wily and could speak.' Steiner looked at the chained and dying reptiles before him and felt sickened. 'Kjellrunn always said dragons were the cleverest of creatures.'

'It takes a dragon fifty years to reach maturity,' said Tief. 'These are just children really.'

'Like the children in the academy,' added Steiner.

Tief nodded. 'There is no callous act the Emperor will not stoop to in order to keep control of Nordvlast.'

'Do you breed them here?'

Tief shook his head, grimacing in disgust. 'No, they ship them in from Frøya knows where, and they get maybe twenty-five to thirty years shackled to a rock before they pass on. Difficult to believe these were the terrible predators during the Age of Wings.'

Kimi emerged from the gloom. 'Come on,' she said, 'we need to return. Shirinov will come calling. We'll need to be at work when he does or there'll be no rest.'

They spent the next few hours going about their tasks. The abject misery of the chamber below haunted Steiner's every thought. No one had much to say. Steiner and Tief gave in to despondence while Kimi vented her frustration on the anvil, hammer strikes ringing loud over the din of the cinder-wraiths' labour.

'Where is he?' grunted Steiner when they'd stopped for a mug of tea and a crust of bread. The wait for Shirinov was maddening and Steiner found his eyes drawn to where he'd struck the granite-skinned novice.

'He'll be worrying over his next move,' said Taiga. 'He'd hoped to snatch you when we weren't watching.'

'We are always watching,' said Sundra, turning a slender bone over and over in her fingers, her eyes distant and terrible.

'What did you do . . .' Steiner swallowed in a dry throat. He hadn't meant to kill someone. It had been an accident. 'What did you do with the body?' None missed the catch in his voice. Kimi shrugged her shoulders and looked away.

'What did you do?' asked Steiner. 'We took the body down to the . . .' His eyes widened. 'Kimi. What did you do with the corpse?'

But Kimi didn't answer and took a step back, refusing to meet his eye.

'She fed the body to the dragons,' said Sundra. She slunk up behind Steiner, close enough to touch. Steiner glanced down at the priestess of Frejna and didn't care too much for the look in her eye.

'It was always our intention to feed the dragons.'

Steiner shivered as she said the word again. People rarely spoke of them, and when they did it was of something long dead, creatures from a terrible past. Creatures from the Age of Wings and the Age of Tears.

'We hoped that if they regained their strength we might free them and escape,' continued Sundra.

'But the scraps from the kitchen are so few,' added Taiga.

'So they dine best when some foolish Northman comes here looking for trouble,' said Sundra, and the smile she gave Steiner made his blood run cold.

'This is isn't the first time, is it?' Steiner stared from Tief to Taiga and then to Kimi but none refuted the truth of it. 'I need to go,' was all he said. The walk to his cave at the side of the cavern was stifling and breathless in a way that had nothing to do with the forge. Steiner hunched into a corner and drew up the sack cloth, desperate for any comfort it might offer.

'What have I done?' he whispered, holding a hand to his aching brow.

*   *   *

Sleep would not come to him. Steiner turned this way and that on the stony floor, the sackcloth scratching his skin. He tried to forget smiting the rocky head from the granite-skinned novice, tried to ignore the idea of Kimi feeding the headless body to the dragons held captive below.

'Some folktale this turned out to be, Kjell.' He slunk from his bed, pausing to pull on his boots and wash the ever-present coal dust from his face. The cinderwraiths ignored him, going about their tasks, seemingly mindless. Kimi was not at her workstation, no doubt asleep or eating in her cave. The Spriggani were absent too, their voices a low murmur as Steiner crept past the entrances to their caves.

Down he went, descending the sloping corridor, casting furtive glances back over his shoulder. He'd stolen a torch along the way, the gutter and hiss of flame and pitch the only sound.

'Dragons,' he said, when he reached the chamber again. They were no less wretched or mean than before, scales dull, eyes closed or cloudy and unfocused. He wandered between them, wide-eyed with wonder and disbelief. Here were the very creatures the Empire declared exterminated. Here was the very darkest of the Solmindre Empire's lies.

One of the creatures appeared less diminished than the rest, a silvery sheen to the soot-slicked scales. Steiner reached out and held a hand to the dragon's chest, felt the steady industry of the heart beneath the ribs.

'She's one of the younger ones,' said Kimi, slipping out of the darkness with barely a sound. Steiner flinched so hard he almost dropped the torch.

'You move quietly.'

'Normally I have a herald to announce my arrival, but I gave him the night off.' Kimi approached and looked him over. 'Couldn't sleep?'

Steiner nodded, his throat thick with emotion, not trusting

himself to speak. He noticed the lines of tiredness etched into Kimi's face.

'Never killed anyone before?' she asked.

Steiner shook his head and looked away, eyes settling on the dragon before him.

'I was the same as you when I first came here.' She pressed the pad of one thumb to her lips thoughtfully, as if she might hold back the words. 'Three novices came down to have some fun. Heard a Yamal princess was down here and wanted to sate their curiosity about a few things. You know how men are.'

Steiner looked her in the eye and nodded slowly. 'Never had any trouble like that in Cinderfell, but I take your meaning.'

'Everyone assumes the Yamal are big and stupid, which is half true.' A slow smile crept across her face. 'Sometimes it's all true, depending on the Yamal you speak to.'

Steiner grinned in spite of himself. 'Nothing stupid about you.'

'And I have good hearing too,' said Kimi, 'which is how I came to hear you sneaking around tonight. You're not much of a sneak, Hammersmith.'

Steiner shrugged. 'Not much of anything, truth be told.' He swallowed in a dry throat and dared himself to ask the question. 'What happened to the three novices?'

'They weren't so good at sneaking either. I can't be sure how far they intended to take things but I do know I broke all three of them with a hammer and spear I'd just finished that day.' She lifted her tunic to show a deep crimson scar in her side. 'The thing you have to remember, Hammersmith,' she looked at the palms of her hands before making fists, 'is that it's them or it's you. This time it was them. Don't feel bad for defending yourself. They made their choice, and when they did they took your choice away. You simply did what you had to in order to survive, just as I did.'

The dragon beside Steiner made a clicking noise and opened one eye. Steiner was startled to see a huge amber orb, green at the edges, with a slash of black bisecting it.

'Like a cat's eye.'

'Don't go mistaking them for kittens,' said Kimi with a slow and weary smile.

Steiner held out a hand to the dragon once more, resting his palm against the cool scales, feeling a series of beats emanating from within.

'More than one heart,' explained Kimi. 'A creature that big needs all the help it can get to keep moving.'

'How old is this one?'

'Five, maybe six?' replied Kimi.

'I can't believe I'm stood here discussing dragons with a Yamal princess.'

'Do you like my gown?' said Kimi.

Steiner made a show of looking at the leather apron and the calluses on her hands. 'I've never seen such royalty,' he said with a grin.

'Come on,' said Kimi. 'You may want to stay up all night grieving for some idiot you didn't know, but I prefer my sleep.'

Steiner was just waking when the nimbus of candlelight entered his cave. The golden glow dappled Tief's olive skin and made his eyes twinkle in the gloom.

'Morning, Hammersmith. Did you sleep at all?'

'Some,' he grunted. Kimi's words had done much to soothe him. She'd escorted him back to his cave and he'd slunk to his sackcloth bed, sinking into exhaustion, mind quiet and numb.

'Kimi said she spoke to you. That's good. I don't want you moping around like some damn fool child today.'

'I feel like a damn fool child.'

'Well, you're eighteen.' Tief scowled. 'And you're on the

island of Vladibogdan. Childhood is over the moment the ship drops anchor.'

'I didn't mean it, Tief.' Steiner couldn't bring himself to say it. To kill him. 'I knocked his head clean off his shoulders. He could be a cinderwraith for all I know.'

'He most certainly is,' agreed Tief.

Steiner struggled to breathe and shook his head, but no matter how he fidgeted or where he looked the simple truth remained. He was a killer now.

Tief tugged at one ear. 'And if you hadn't fought back, where would you be? Up there in one of the academies, in the clutches of Shirinov and Corpsecandle. And he'd make you talk, it's what Shirinov does.'

'I wouldn't,' said Steiner, weakly.

'Not at first, not willingly,' said Tief. 'But he'd use all the ways and means at his disposal. In the end you'd give your sister up just to make the pain stop.'

'And when he tired,' said Steiner as an awful dread crept over him. 'He'd hand me over to Corpsecandle to continue the interrogation.'

'Shirinov will go back,' said Tief. 'Back to Cinderfell. Even a man in a mask has to save face. He can't let his reputation be soured by capturing you, a boy without witchsign.'

'I can't let him go back. All of this . . .' Steiner gestured to the cavern outside the cave. 'Me being here will be for nothing if Shirinov goes back for Kjell.'

'You'd best find a way to escape then. And soon,' replied Tief.

'But how? Even if we wander free of the cavern we still don't have a ship. You said yourself that we can't smuggle ourselves out of here in crates. And there's no wood of good quality to build a raft.'

Tief looked away and released a sigh. 'I've been trying to leave this island for longer than I care to remember.'

'Romola is our best hope to return to the mainland,' said Steiner.

'You think she'd risk her life for a handful of Spriggani, a princess and a boy from Cinderfell?'

'She has to, doesn't she?'

'Smuggling letters to the mainland is one thing,' said Tief. 'Helping people escape is another realm of trouble. You think I haven't asked her before?'

'Tief.' The word was a harsh whisper. Taiga's slender face appeared through the fissure in the rock. 'Shirinov is here and he's not alone.'

Steiner's eyes widened and the usual growl of hunger in his gut was replaced by one of fear. 'Shirinov? Here?'

'Come on. We knew this would happen.' Tief turned and stomped to the gap in the rock before glaring over his shoulder. 'And do me one favour, Hammersmith.'

'What's that?'

'Shut your mouth. Let an old Spriggani do the talking.'

CHAPTER TWENTY

Kjellrunn

It is a key doctrine of the Imperial Synod that we stoke the fires of fear and suspicion in the Solmindre Empire and the Scorched Republics. By convincing the peasantry that the arcane is both dangerous and sinfully aberrant the Synod reduces the chances of an uprising led by those with devastating powers. It is for this reason the self-same organisation cannot be seen to use arcane powers in public, and those seeing such displays must be silenced. Permanently.

— From the field notes of Hierarch Khigir,
Vigilant of the Imperial Synod.

'Have the Spriggani got your tongue?' said Marek, as they ate their morning porridge. 'You've barely said a word for the last week.'

Kjellrunn opened her mouth to speak, then settled for a shrug and continued eating. Her mind drifted from the horseman in black to Mistress Kamalov slicing up berries so her hands appeared to be covered in blood.

'And you've not been out to the woods lately.' Marek tapped his spoon against the bowl. 'Did you and your new friend have a disagreement?'

'We're not really friends,' said Kjellrunn, as she stirred her porridge and sighed. 'I barely know her.'

'A girl?' Kjellrunn thought she detected a note of quiet relief in her father's voice. 'One from the town?'

Kjellrunn shook her head. 'No. She's not from Cinderfell. She's not from Nordvlast either.'

'Is she . . .' Marek set down his spoon. 'Is she a Spriggani?'

'No!' Kjellrunn frowned and couldn't decide if her father was mocking her or not.

'Well, you go on about them enough.'

'You sound like Steiner.' For a second they stared at each other, but it was too painful and Kjellrunn fixed her eyes on the cold porridge.

'You should warm that up and finish it,' said Marek. 'It's not like we can waste food. I can't risk you becoming ill. I've not got the money for medicine and I need all the help I can get.'

Now that Steiner's gone, she wanted to add, but the words didn't need the luxury of being spoken. They both knew them by heart. *Now that Steiner's gone.* And never to return if Mistress Kamalov knew Vladibogdan as well as she pretended to.

'You should have never sent him,' said Kjellrunn.

'You don't know what you speak of, Kjell. You don't know what the arcane does to a person.'

'And I'm not likely to find out now, am I?'

'Used a little, there's barely a problem.' Marek frowned. 'But used a lot, and the way the Empire would have you use it . . .'

'And how is it you come to know so much about it?' Kjellrunn flicked her fringe from her face and glowered. 'Something so dangerous and forbidden? I thought you crafted pots and pans, not spells.'

'Mind your tone. I'm still your father. I put a roof over your head and money on the table.'

'When you're not drinking it.'

'I've stopped that now.' He stood, the chair jerking out behind him, falling over. 'I need to buy some things in town. I suggest you go for a walk, take yourself along the bay and find yourself some manners. Frøya knows I taught you better ones than these.'

Kjellrunn watched him leave, noted the way he gripped the door as if to slam it, then decided against it after he'd fixed her with a hard stare. Rare were the times Marek raised his voice, but his anger was not a stranger. His words had always taken a harsh sound when his mood darkened, but it was a harshness of accent as well as tone, much like Mistress Kamalov's.

'Losing Steiner was bad enough,' she muttered, clearing the bowls away. 'But to discover my own father is a stranger . . .'

Kjellrunn attended her chores, hands carrying out the same dull tasks, her mind drifting from one desolate thought to another. Before long she'd climbed into the loft. Long moments were lost kneeling in the darkness. Hands pawed through the nest of curios she guarded. A sliver of driftwood worn smooth, a dozen black feathers, and the sledgehammer brooch. She'd not intended to find it, and here it was, cradled in the rough skin of her palm, an ugly lump of metal amid the calluses.

'None of us would be in this situation if you'd just remained pinned to my shawl.' She sucked down a breath and closed her fingers around the metal. 'And Steiner would still be alive.'

'What am I to do?' Kjellrunn sat on an old crate lined with sea salt and watched the gulls hop about in the sand. They flapped their wings and crowed around as Verner gutted fish.

'You shouldn't give up hope,' said the fisherman. Difficult to tell if it were tiredness or just the weather that lined his face, he forced a smile. 'Steiner has a way about him, an

honest way, and people like that. Even the people on
Vladibogdan may like that.'

'But Mistress Kamalov said he was dead.'

Verner nodded. 'And who is Mistress Kamalov?' Strangers
were a rarity in Cinderfell, newcomers more rare still.

'A scary old peasant woman who's taken up staying in the
old woodcutter's chalet.'

Verner gave a grunt. 'And how would she know? Is she
on Vladibogdan this very moment? Did she receive a letter
telling her Steiner is dead? I think not.' Verner hacked the
head off a plaice and threw it at the gulls, scattering them.
'Getting letters into or out of that place is no mean feat,' he
muttered.

'So you think he could be alive?' Kjellrunn pulled her shawl
tighter. 'You think there's some way Steiner could be alive,
even without the arcane?'

'A good chance, if he wore those boots I sent for him.'
Verner frowned at the gulls, who were fighting over the fish
head. 'You know it's not just children with witchsign that
they send there. There was a time a lot Spriggani fetched up
on Vladibogdan too.'

'Why would the Empire send Spriggani?'

'It's a nice quiet place to keep people out of sight, and it's
also a good place to get rid of them. There may be some
Spriggani who live there now, but most of them fled south,
or to Yamal. The Empire forced them out of their homes in
the forest.'

'Why are you telling me about Spriggani?'

'What I'm trying to say,' Verner sighed, 'is the Spriggani
have never given up hope, and if you give up hope then
there's really very little to keep going for.'

'Steiner's alive. He has to be.'

'I don't know, I can't know. But this Mistress Kamalov
doesn't know he's dead either.'

'Neither living nor dead then,' complained Kjellrunn.

'That's the way of things. Life is all uncertainty, you may as well learn that now.'

Kjellrunn nodded. She knew in her bones that nothing had changed, but Verner's words had kindled something Mistress Kamalov had extinguished.

'And what do you propose I do now?' she asked, folding her hands beneath her armpits, trying to keep warm.

'What would Steiner want you to do?'

'He'd want me to learn how to protect myself. That and stay out of trouble with the Empire.'

'Perhaps it's good you spend time with this Mistress Kamalov,' said Verner. 'Go and spend time in the woods, it will keep you out from under the feet of the townsfolk. They barely let me in Bjørner's tavern these days.'

'I'm sorry,' replied Kjellrunn.

'It's not your fault, just a fearful and suspicious people who don't know even half of what they speak of. Go on now, run along, and keep an eye out for the Okhrana.'

'Haven't they moved on yet?'

'If only they had, I might sleep easier.' Verner looked out to sea and said nothing more.

Kjellrunn nodded. She felt lighter somehow. If Verner believed Steiner was still alive then she could too.

'Kjellrunn?'

She turned to see Verner cleaning the knife. 'Don't give up hope.'

'I won't.' She smiled.

Kjellrunn was reluctant to leave Verner's company but keen to be back in the warm. Her feet led her from the shore road and up Cinderfell's cobbled winding streets. Tonight they would have beef stew, she decided, with carrots, rutabaga, onion and potatoes. She'd make a meal to thaw Marek's frosty mood and there would be peace in the blacksmith's cottage. They'd eat a meal as father and daughter, not the hollow-eyed strangers they'd become.

She wasn't keen to enter the butcher's without Steiner at her shoulder, but there wasn't much choice.

'I don't have anything left for you today,' said Håkon, smoothing down his vast beard.

'But you have all this meat right in front of me.' Kjellrunn gestured to the cuts of beef on the slab before her.

'This is all for the Smouldering Standard. Big feast tonight, they need all of it. Best you buy your meat somewhere else.' The butcher wiped a greasy hand on his apron, the other gripped a cleaver.

'Is this something to do with Steiner?' she said. A glance over her shoulder confirmed they were alone. No customers could be seen by the door or waiting in the street.

'Best you buy your meat somewhere else,' repeated Håkon, and Kjellrunn realised he left the words *from now on* unsaid, but they rang loud all the same.

Kjellrunn looked at the money in her hand, the coins dull and always too few.

'I just want to make a stew for my father. He's been so . . .' She sighed. 'Since Steiner was taken, my father . . .' But the expression on the butcher's face told her there would be no appealing to his good nature, if indeed he had one.

'I would like to buy that beef, please,' said a confident voice from over Kjellrunn's shoulder. It was said in such a way that brooked no refusal, the accent making the words clipped and impatient. The butcher swallowed. For a moment his beady eyes wavered in their frowning steadfastness.

'Well, I . . .'

'Mistress Kamalov,' said Kjellrunn, nodding to her. The woman nodded back. She appeared larger than Kjellrunn remembered, her spine straight as an oar handle, eyes sharp

and hard like cut stones. She was well scrubbed and her wiry
hair was concealed beneath a headscarf; her clothes were
worn and tired but immaculate and clean.

'I would like to buy that beef. And I would like to buy it
before I grow old. Understand?'

'I, well . . .' Håkon fell silent, caught in his own lie. Kjellrunn
smiled bitterly at the butcher, enjoying his discomfort.

'Are you deaf or merely stupid?' continued Mistress
Kamalov. 'Would you have me write it down for you? Can
you even read?'

'I read just fine,' said the butcher, remembering himself
and resuming his usual frown.

'Good, you speak. And if you so much as entertain the
notion of overcharging me I will take my knife to you and
dine on your kidneys tonight, instead of this meagre offering.'
Of the Mistress Kamalov in the woods there was no sign.
Gone was the doddering stoop, the moments of introspection
and reverie, replaced by an imperious aspect that knew what
it was to be obeyed.

'There's no need to be rude, I was just—'

'There is every need to be rude. You were overcharging
this girl. Yes?'

The butcher opened his mouth to speak, flicked a guilty
glance at Kjellrunn, and closed his mouth.

'He was refusing to serve me,' said Kjellrunn, though it
pained her to admit it.

'I know too well Solmindre is mired in thieves and cowards.'
Kjellrunn's eyes widened as Mistress Kamalov scolded the
butcher. 'But I had hoped for better in Cinderfell, and from
a man of your position.'

'Take it.' The butcher thrust a heavy hand at her, laden
with meat wrapped in brown paper. 'Take it and leave my
shop with your noise and harangue.'

Mistress Kamalov laid a half-dozen coins on the counter,

took the meat and gave a curt nod. 'How dare you. I do not take charity. Do I look like a beggar? No. Do I look like a thief? No. I have my pride.'

Kjellrunn followed her into the street, stunned at seeing such a large man cut down to size.

'You can bet your boots there's going to be a few rumours going around after that.' She grinned, almost giddy with amusement.

'In a town this small?' Mistress Kamalov looked about her, eyeing a few folk further down the street hurrying home. 'There are always rumours. Best they speak of me for being a mean old crone than get ideas for themselves.' She looked at Kjellrunn and her expression softened. 'Here.' She took Kjellrunn's hand and gave her the beef. 'This is yours.'

'But—'

'You brought bread and fish to me when I was starving, so you'll take my kindness in turn.' She'd not raised her voice, but the note of command remained. 'I have my pride.' Kjellrunn nodded and thanked her.

'Besides, I caught a whole deer yesterday. Why eat beef when you can dine on venison?' She broke into a mischievous smile and Kjellrunn returned it.

They walked down the street, unhurried, neither feeling the need to fill the quiet with unneeded words. Kjellrunn snatched a glance from the corner of her eye and noticed Mistress Kamalov had resumed her stoop, becoming the old woman she had first met in the woods once more. The effect was like a change of clothes, ultimately the same person, but easy to mistake for someone else.

'There will be more of that to come,' said Mistress Kamalov, cocking her head at the butcher's shop. The owner stood in the doorway, hands on hips, glowering at them as they departed.

'Bjørner, the tavern owner, came to my father's smithy.'

Kjellrunn remembered the look of sadness on Kristofine's face. 'He told my father to think about moving on.' The pang of unhappiness was a physical thing as she said the words aloud, full of shame.

'It's often the way after an Invigilation,' said Mistress Kamalov. 'People fear what they do not understand.'

'Do you think I might come to your chalet tomorrow?' said Kjellrunn. 'To try some venison?'

'Venison. Yes. You will try venison. And you will also try using your gifts. You will need them in the years ahead. Do not waste any time, Kjellrunn. Already sixteen with no training and all this power.' Mistress Kamalov shook her head and tutted. 'It is unthinkable such a thing should happen.'

'Tomorrow then?' said Kjellrunn.

Mistress Kamalov gave a nod, then smiled. 'As early as you can. We have much work ahead of us. And more with the listening.'

'Not so much with the questions,' said Kjellrunn.

'Just so.'

CHAPTER TWENTY-ONE

Steiner

Artefacts are largely the domain of old tales: enchanted swords that whisper to the kings who wield them, enchanted rings granting immortality and so forth. In some rare cases artefacts do exist, but the greater ones are the creations of dragons, while charms and fetishes are almost always crafted by Spriggani. The latter should always be distrusted.

– From the field notes of Hierarch Khigir,
Vigilant of the Imperial Synod.

Shirinov stood on the central dais of the cavern, leaning on his cane. The gently smiling mask returned the steely stare of Enkhtuya. It was difficult to think of her as 'Kimi' when she stood like this, arms folded, frown set on her wide brow, eyes narrowed in suspicion. A sturdy hammer hung from her work belt, her leather apron more akin to armour. The air was loaded with accusation and violence was not far behind.

A heavy silence had descended over the furnaces. The cinderwraiths had vanished, perhaps hiding in the cavern's darker reaches. Matriarch-Commissar Felgenhauer was also present, along with Khigir, who Steiner couldn't help but think of as Corpsecandle. A score of soldiers escorted the Vigilants, more intimidating than usual in the gloom, armoured in black with the dull gleam of mail and spiked maces.

'This is much worse than I had hoped,' grumbled Tief, just low enough that the words reached Steiner and no further. 'The Matriarch-Commissar never set a foot down here before.'

'What do we do?' replied Steiner.

'Say nothing. The novices were never here. And you haven't seen anyone,' replied Tief.

Taiga took her place beside Sundra, the younger sister little more than shadows in black and green, the soldiers' lanterns illuminating the flat, unfriendly stares of the two women. The other Spriggani hid at their workstations, close enough to hear but beyond arm's reach.

Shirinov turned his gleaming mask to Steiner, leaning on his cane. The old Vigilant cocked his head to one side as if seeing Steiner anew. The effect of his gaze was chilling. Steiner wondered if a Vigilant could pluck the words from his mind as easily as the dark-haired novice had inserted them.

Tongues of fire performed a slow dance at Khigir's feet as he took his place beside Shirinov. The Vigilant looked especially unnatural, lit from below, pitted mask blank of everything but the frown crowding his eyes. The soldiers formed a loose circle around everyone, a deadly cordon.

'Why have you summoned us here?' said Shirinov, a note of complaint in his voice.

'One of our novices failed to report for lessons,' said Felgenhauer, her words measured and calm. She turned her stony, androgynous mask from Tief to Steiner and then Kimi. None flinched under the weight of her scrutiny, though Steiner wanted nothing more than to run back to his cave.

'Perhaps he swam the Spøkelsea and escaped?' said Tief with a bitter smile on his lips. 'Or hitched a ride in the mouth of whale.'

'The novice was a young man of considerable talent,' said Felgenhauer, ignoring Tief's insolence. 'You would know him, Shirinov, he was one of yours. Matthias Zhirov.'

The Vigilant spread one hand and gave a shrug. It was a curious gesture in his Vigilant's robes, made insincere by the mocking smile on his silver mask.

'Most strange,' said Khigir.

'Most strange,' agreed Shirinov. 'My novices are known for their utmost devotion to the Empire.'

'Runaways are not uncommon,' said Felgenhauer. 'If indeed he ran away.'

Steiner couldn't shake the feeling it was Shirinov who had earned the greater part of Felgenhauer's suspicion. The soldiers had split into two distinct factions; six of them bore axes and stood behind Felgenhauer, while the remaining six flanked Shirinov and Corpsecandle.

'I suggest we search the pirate's ship,' said Shirinov, his tone patronising, obviously pleased with himself. 'It is possible Zhirov found a way to bribe that odious pirate to give him passage.'

'She's here?' said Steiner, earning a dark look from Tief. Steiner reminded himself to be quiet.

'We must interrogate the pirate at once,' countered Khigir, the flames at his feet flickering as if excited by the prospect.

'No!' said Steiner, taking a step forward.

'Shut up, Steiner!' hissed Tief. For a moment he'd assumed his outburst would only make things worse, but the Matriarch-Commissar's quiet fury was reserved for the other Vigilants.

'The pirate's name is Captain Romola,' said Felgenhauer, stepping closer to Khigir. 'And she is a privateer in service to the Empire.'

'What in Frejna's name does this have to do with us?' said
Tief, and he flashed an angry glance at Steiner.

'Be quiet, Spriggani scum,' grunted Shirinov.

Steiner swallowed in a dry throat, edging the few steps to
Kimi's anvil where he had left his sledgehammer. He remembered the moment the granite-skinned boy's head had come
apart in a shower of stone.

'It's possible the runaway stumbled down here by accident,'
said Felgenhauer, her eyes on Steiner. 'Or perhaps he ventured
here for other reasons.' One by one each person turned to
him. Even Kimi ceased her baleful glaring at Shirinov to glance
at Steiner from the corner of her eye.

'I've not seen a soul,' said Steiner. The lie emerged from
his throat as a dusty croak. 'Busy carrying sacks of coal.'

'Then it must be the pirate who is responsible,' continued
Shirinov. 'Perhaps she thinks to steal our novices and smuggle
them to Shanisrond.'

'I agree,' said Corpsecandle, pulling himself up straight and
pushing back his shoulders.

'We can't trust her,' added Shirinov. 'Or any of her crew. A
full search of the ship will end this business once and for all.'

Steiner thought of the storyweaver and the small kindness
she'd shown him. He remembered the beautiful music and
imagined Shirinov entering the captain's cabin, the soldiers
smashing the domra. Anger kindled inside him and his fingers
curled around the sledgehammer handle. He eyed Felgenhauer
and Corpsecandle. Even if he managed to strike Shirinov
down he'd be killed a moment later. He forced his hand away
from the sledgehammer, felt it tremble. He couldn't protect
Romola by force of arms, but perhaps there was another way.

'Matthias Zhirov was here.'

There was a second of silence before Tief uttered 'Damn
fool boy', and covered his eyes with one hand. Taiga and
Sundra whispered to each other and Kimi let out a long sigh.

'What?' said the Matriarch-Commissar.

'Matthias Zhirov came here and attacked me. I fended him off and . . .'

'You?' Shirinov's voice was ripe with scorn. 'You fended off Matthias Zhirov? I think not.'

Steiner curled his lip. 'I fended you off in Academy Square, didn't I?'

'And you'd have us believe you fought off three novices?'

'I had help.'

The silver mask nodded and the Vigilant flexed his fingers. 'And here we are again, with a dozen soldiers at my command.'

'Shirinov.' Felgenhauer's voice was frosty. 'The boy didn't mention three novices. Curious that you know how many.'

'A lucky guess,' he replied. 'Vigilants frequently associate in threes, even the novices.'

Felgenhauer stepped closer. 'And that you've made no secret of the fact Zhirov is your favourite student. And these soldiers are under *my* command. Try to remember that.' She swept her gaze over all the soldiers. Clearly it wasn't just Shirinov that needed reminding. The androgynous mask turned back to Steiner. 'What else can you tell me about these three novices?'

'They fled,' said Tief, before Steiner could speak. 'They were aghast at the boy's terrible prowess with his sledgehammer, fleeing for their wretched lives before my sisters and I could intervene. Fled back to their damn fool masters, no doubt.' Tief glowered at Shirinov, who held one hand to the chin of his mask, mockingly pensive.

Felgenhauer approached Tief, towering over him. For a moment Steiner imagined she might grasp him by the throat and lift him from the ground.

'And that's how it happened, is it, Steiner?' said Felgenhauer.

Steiner cleared his throat. 'Yes, that's how it happened. With my hammer.'

'And your boots,' added Felgenhauer.

Steiner looked down at his feet and felt foolish. He wasn't much given to lying, and the untruths that had spilled before him, by him, had vast consequences he couldn't imagine. It was as he looked down that he noticed the grit and shards of stone. Was that a splinter of bone? Had Matthias Zhirov's skull transitioned back to the stuff it was born as? Did the evidence of Zhirov's death lie at Steiner's very feet? The cavern's heat was suddenly unbearable, intensified under the Matriarch-Commissar's gaze.

'You're very pale,' said Felgenhauer.

'Then send more food,' said Tief, earning himself an icy moment as Felgenhauer turned her attention back to him.

'I'm fine,' said Steiner with a weak smile. 'Just hungry.'

The Matriarch-Commissar turned, gesturing that the others should follow. Her stride was long, her step determined. Shirinov did his best to keep up, his cane counting out painful steps with a *clack-clack*. Corpsecandle spared a glance for Steiner before following Felgenhauer back to the surface. The soldiers jingled with each step. A few lingered behind to cast threatening stares at the many Spriggani who had witnessed the scene.

'Where are they going?' whispered Steiner.

'Who cares?' grunted Kimi. 'As long as they're out of my forge. They'd be dragon food right now if it was down to me.'

'Will they arrest Romola?' asked Steiner. 'Will they search the ship?'

'You did well.' Kimi wrapped a protective arm about his shoulders, a pleasant crush. 'Nothing like telling the truth to keep people off balance.'

'I was trying to keep Romola out of this,' mumbled Steiner. He thought of the domra and the beautiful yet haunting music.

'Let me do the talking, I said,' muttered Tief. 'Don't say a word, I said.' He stalked off. 'Damn fool child.' He scowled over his shoulder. 'What next?'

'Ignore him,' said Kimi. 'He's on edge is all.'

'He has a point. What *will* happen now?' said Steiner.

'Difficult to know for sure,' said Taiga. 'No knowing when Vigilants are involved.'

'I suppose we'd best get back to work,' rumbled Kimi, reaching beneath the stout leather apron.

'What are you doing?' asked Steiner.

'You'll see,' she said with a look of regret on her broad honest face. She fumbled at the throat of her tunic for an amulet the size of a child's fist, then pulled the chain over her head, casting a disapproving eye at the shard of worked stone. A wisp of faint yellow light writhed over the amulet, and particles of back ash danced in slow orbits.

'What's that?' asked Steiner, a terrible uneasiness over-taking him.

'This,' replied Kimi, her mouth twisting in disgust, 'is the Ashen Torment.' She held forth the amulet. 'A burden they gave me to carry. It doesn't look like much but it weighs on me all the same.'

Steiner reached for Kimi's hand with all the care of someone fetching a newborn. Kimi laid her palm flat and splayed her fingers. Nestled between the calluses was a cone of rock, like a stalagmite tip. A tiny dragon was wrapped around the stone, nose to tail. The carving was so fine Steiner wondered if it were real. The frail yellow light emanated from deep inside, fine lines glowing in the carving.

'What does it do?' said Steiner.

'Watch,' was all she said by way of reply, then held out the amulet at arm's length, closing her eyes. 'Wherever there is fire there is death,' intoned Kimi.

Steiner's eyes widened as the amulet was consumed by a writhing flame. Fire danced across its surface, a match for the dragon statue in Academy Square. Steiner was no less awed at the conjuration before him.

'Wherever there is fire there is death,' she said again, eyes still closed.

Steiner almost missed them, dark shadows against the gloom. Some emerged from cracks in the cavern floor, but most edged in from the walls. The cinderwraiths slunk and drifted back to their workstations, taking up tools in their indistinct hands, beginning the process of crafting weapons for the Empire that had killed them.

'The amulet controls them,' said Steiner.

Kimi nodded. 'When one says the right words, yes. This relic commands them, while another relic binds them to the island itself.'

'Who made such things?'

'Felgenhauer told me the Empire forced Bittervinge to craft the artefacts after they defeated him. Artefacts like this.'

'Bittervinge? The father of dragons? But he's just a folktale.' Steiner stopped talking as Kimi fixed him with a look that said he should know better.

'But Bittervinge was exterminated at the end of the war, along with all the other . . .' Steiner paused and thought of the dragons chained up in the chamber below. He looked across the vast cavern and saw each furnace, imagining the dragon beneath it. 'All the other dragons.'

Kimi looked across the the many workstations and released a slow breath. 'We don't worship Frejna where I come from, but if she came here, looking for all the souls that are rightfully hers, well, I'd hand her this amulet in a heartbeat.'

'Why don't you?'

Kimi looked at him, a weary slump to her broad shoulders. 'Are all Northmen so literal?'

Steiner smiled.

'And how do I hand the amulet over to Frejna?'

Steiner shook his head. 'I don't know. Hand it back to Felgenhauer. Refuse to carry it. Refuse to command the cinder-wraiths.'

Kimi smiled without warmth. 'I did that once. They stopped sending food. Taiga almost died. We were all so weak. In the end I put the amulet back on just to stop her and Tief starving to death. You don't disappoint the Matriarch-Commissar, Steiner. She has quotas to meet and the Empire will make her suffer if she's found wanting. And that means we suffer in turn.'

Kimi stoked the fire in her furnace, using a wooden pedal set in the floor to prod the dragon below. A jet of flame roared and the furnace door rattled on its hinges.

'I'm always gentle,' she said, noting Steiner's shocked expression. 'And I don't use it unless I have to. We're behind on swords and if things get much worse—'

'Then Felgenhauer will stop sending food down to us.'

Kimi nodded. Steiner frowned against the din of anvils, of swords being hammered into shape, more weapons for the Empire to prosecute the wars to come.

'Do you think they'll really invade Nordvlast and the Scorched Republics?' asked Steiner.

'Yes, in five years or so, after they've taken control of Shanisrond.'

Steiner nodded and stared into the flickering flames of the furnace.

'What are you thinking, Hammersmith?' said Kimi.

'I'm hoping Romola has set sail. I'm hoping she's far away from this awful place.' Most of all he hoped Shirinov hadn't found a way to hurt Romola in retaliation for Matthias Zhirov.

'I wouldn't hope for so much,' said Kimi. 'Hope is burned up all too quickly in a place like this.'

Steiner turned back to the cavern, to the scores of cinder-wraiths hard at work in eternal toil and the Spriggani tending to the furnaces. The smoke and ashes billowed above in a slow roil, lifted by the stifling heat. The ruddy light of dragon and coal fire was everywhere.

'I hope she gets away,' he said, as if the words alone were enough to make it happen.

Kimi nodded. 'So do I, Hammersmith. So do I.'

CHAPTER TWENTY-TWO

Steiner

The increase in patrols by the Imperial Navy in the Ashen Gulf has left large expanses of the Empire's coastline unguarded. It is for this reason that independent captains have been employed, despite the repeated recommendations of my colleague Shirinov and myself to avoid such outsiders. Trying to exert any influence over the Imperial Court at Khlystburg is almost impossible when one is consigned to Vladibogdan.

– From the field notes of Hierarch Khigir,
Vigilant of the Imperial Synod.

Steiner need not have worried for Romola, not least because she appeared the very next day wearing a crooked smile and a sling bag hung from her shoulder. Maxim trailed behind carrying an impressive burden in his arms.

'You stole an entire pig?' Steiner looked on aghast, worried it might suddenly jump down from Maxim's arms and start snuffling around.

'And there's a goat in the sack too, for Kimi,' added Maxim.

'"Stolen" is an unattractive word, right?' Romola paused

to look at Maxim. 'I'm merely redistributing resources in a meaningful manner that will benefit those most in need.'

Steiner frowned. 'What are you talking about?'

Romola smiled, then cackled, and Steiner wondered if she wasn't a little drunk or unhinged.

'You know Shirinov will have you arrested if you're found down here?'

'Best I don't get found then, right?' Romola's smile widened.

'He was here just yesterday and it was all I could do to stop him searching your ship.'

'He always wants to search my ship.' Romola sighed. 'The trick is to not have anything aboard that will get you into trouble.'

They picked their way across the cavern between the many furnaces and anvils, all attended by cinderwraiths and the odd Spriggani.

'If I didn't know so much about the arcane I'd assume I'd passed on to the other side,' said Romola. 'Eternal punishment for the wicked, right? Isn't that what the Holy Synod teach?'

Maxim and Steiner said nothing. Maxim eyed the apparitions fearfully and Steiner took the pig from him. 'They won't hurt you,' he whispered.

'Why do they look like that?' asked Maxim.

'I don't know,' admitted Steiner. 'And I don't know what the Synod teach either,' he said to Romola. 'Too busy working for a living to worry about all that old nonsense.'

'You don't believe in an afterlife?' pressed Romola.

'Mama says you have to live a good life,' said Maxim. 'Because if you don't you'll be re-incarcerated as a Spriggani.'

'I think you mean reincarnated,' replied Romola.

'That's what I said.' Maxim frowned.

'Well, I think your mama needs to learn a few things about the world. I wouldn't say that again down here. It won't make you any friends.'

'Ah, I didn't mean . . .'

'No, you didn't, but your words did. Think more carefully before opening your mouth.' Romola nodded at Steiner. 'And what about you?'

Steiner shrugged. 'My father says people pay lip service to the old gods in the Republics. I heard the Synod has made some converts in Svingettevei, worshipping the Emperor because of some divine right to rule. Father says it's always hard to know if a Sving is gaming with you or being straight. I'd rather go drown than kneel before the Emperor.'

'Straight-talking Svings do exist,' said Romola, leading them to the edge of the cavern. 'Though they're as rare as dragon's teeth. And there's nothing divine about the Emperor, you only have to look at how poor the people are in Solmindre to know that. Do you know what the Spriggani believe?'

'I feel like I'm speaking with my sister again,' said Steiner, and felt a pang of loss for Kjellrunn's ramblings.

'The Spriggani believe the truly wicked spend eternity clinging to a vast cliff above a fierce ocean. Frejna sends crows to peck at their eyes and fingers each day so they fall.'

'Small wonder people worship Frøya if that's the case,' Steiner said to Maxim.

'Once they fall into the sea they are dashed upon the rocks by the restless waves,' said Romola, leaning close to Maxim.

'That doesn't sound much like an eternity,' said Steiner.

'The following day it begins all over again,' explained Romola. 'Those souls who were less wicked have to watch their loved ones die over and over.'

'What happens to the good people?' asked Maxim.

'The good people?' Romola smiled again. 'Frøya sends the good people wily storyweavers who bring food and good cheer.'

'And how blessed we are.' Steiner shook his head. 'Where are we going, Romola?'

'Somewhere we can cook this meat.'

The fissure in the rock was not so very different to the entrance of Steiner's cave, but the passage beyond was tight and winding. Romola sang softly, holding up a lantern.

'Now there's a thing worth seeing,' muttered Steiner. The ceiling of the cave was studded with purpled quartz, like strange stars glittering in a stony sky. Still water occupied the end of the cave, reflecting more of the lantern light.

'Are we still underground?' asked Maxim.

'We are. Though you'd never know it.'

Steiner set down the pig and looked around in awe.

'Well, don't just stand there.' Romola removed the sling bag and threw it towards Steiner. He caught it, despite the weight.

'Have a care, won't you? What's this?'

'Firewood.' Romola grinned. 'You don't want to eat raw pork, right?'

The pig took forever to cook, even with the spit and fire pit that remained from an earlier meet. The fire burned more keenly after Steiner returned with a bucket of coal.

'You've been here before then?' said Steiner after the fire was fully ablaze.

'Of course. It's one of my favourite places.' Romola turned her face towards the roof. 'It's away from the listening ears at the academy. And you can lie back with a full belly and imagine you're gazing at the night sky.'

'I thought you said you'd never got any further onto the island than the gatehouse,' said Steiner.

'And I meant it.' Romola nodded. 'I didn't say anything about the island underneath the gatehouse.'

'Won't your crew miss you?' asked Steiner.

'My crew know better than to ask too many questions.'

'How are things up there?' Steiner turned to Maxim, who was peeling potatoes with deft motions, slicing them small and adding them to a pot of simmering water.

'At the academy?' Maxim released a weary sigh that belonged to someone twice his age. 'I learn more each day. Shirinov and Felgenhauer loathe each other, of course.'

'Anyone with eyes can see that,' replied Steiner. The boy frowned back at him.

'What you won't know,' said Maxim, 'is that Shirinov and Khigir weren't supposed to be in Cinderfell. They were investigating something in Helwick.'

'I've heard of it,' replied Steiner, thinking of Verner's deception. *Ah, it was nothing, nothing important. I just took some smoked fish to market.*

'They say Khigir's sister was murdered. The older children, I mean novices, they say she could control the air.'

'Just rumours, I expect,' said Steiner, though he couldn't be sure why he was so keen to pour cold water on the boy's tale.

'They're not rumours,' replied Maxim. 'The older novices heard it from Marozvolk. Silverdust said it too. And Cryptfrost lost her temper when she overheard some boys talking about it.'

'So what else did they say?' said Steiner, fearing that Verner might soon find himself hunted by the Synod, assuming he was still alive.

'Silverdust said Corpsecandle's sister sent a whisper with her dying breath and Khigir and Shirinov left at once to try and find the killer.'

The fire crackled and popped and Steiner rubbed the calluses on his fingers, thinking of his father and Verner the last time he'd seen them on the pier.

'They used to be part of a Troika, you see?' Maxim was still peeling potatoes, reeling off the tale as if he'd been doing this very thing all his life. 'One Vigilant specializes in fire.'

'Khigir,' said Steiner. Maxim nodded.

'One specializes in earth.'

'Shirinov.'

'And one specializes in air. The novices called her Sharpbreath, but she preferred Sister Khigir.'

Steiner glanced at Romola, who had said nothing, idly poking the fire with the tip of a long knife.

'But Sister Khigir went to Arkiv Island many years ago,' said Maxim. 'They say she wasn't the same after. She formed a new Troika and Corpsecandle never quite got over it.'

Pirate, blacksmith and boy worked at the meal, slicing carrots and leeks. Sometimes grumbling, sometimes dashing away tears brought on by diced onions. Steiner couldn't help but think of home, though this was far from the orderly kitchen he'd grown up in.

'The thing I don't understand,' he said, when the vegetables were all safely in a pot, 'is why a Troika consists of wind, fire and earth? Why does no one use the power of water?'

Romola had lain back with her head on a pack, eyes heavy-lidded, while Maxim was engaged in the time-honoured tradition of poking the fire's coals for no noticeably good reason.

'Water is the province of Frøya, and Frøya alone.' Romola stifled a yawn. 'The Vigilants say wind, fire and earth are powers derived from dragons. The Emperor has always seen the arcane as a challenge to his authority. And those powers he can't control he prohibits.'

'That doesn't make any sense,' grumbled Steiner. 'Why have an academy dedicated to water if the Emperor has forbidden such powers?'

'They hope to have some sort of breakthrough,' said Romola. 'If they can harness the powers of the ocean then the war in Shanisrond will be much easier. So far they've not been successful. Let's hope it stays that way.'

Steiner didn't have a chance to press her on the subject, as heavy footfalls echoed down the corridor.

'Soldiers,' breathed Steiner, remembering the score escorting the Vigilants down the day before.

'Soldiers?' Maxim looked around the cave, eyes frantic. He scrambled to his feet. 'They mustn't find me!'

'I knew I should have brought the sledge,' grunted Steiner.

'People will do anything for a free meal,' said Romola, sliding her sword from the scabbard.

The noise came closer, heavy footfalls that must surely belong to a man in armour. Steiner imagined the red star at the brow of the helm, spiked mace promising a painful death, chain mail glittering in the darkness.

'I can't believe you thought you could cook an entire pig without me,' said Kimi as she stepped into the light. Steiner and Maxim released a tense breath.

'I'm trying to feed the boy up is all,' replied Romola. 'And give him an education.'

'Education is good,' agreed Kimi, sitting cross-legged by the fire. 'But the whole pig?'

'Don't worry, I brought something for you too.' Maxim hefted the sack with both arms, struggling under the weight.

'I'm going to enjoy this,' said Kimi, pulling the goat free of the sack by its neck. 'How are you?'

Steiner eyed the spit and the fat that sizzled in the fire. 'Better than yesterday,' he said, though it was Matthias Zhirov's face he saw in the dancing flames.

The meal proved to be both long and glorious, with second and third helpings. Romola regaled them with stories of sailing the various seas and oceans surrounding Vinterkveld while Kimi ate half the goat, and tried to decide how to hide the rest.

It was almost perfect.

They had headed out into the cavern to say their goodbyes when the soldiers returned. At a distance they appeared as disembodied helms, their red stars bright in the glow of lanterns held high. Romola became very still, watching their approach.

'As final meals go, it will have to do,' she said to no one in particular.

'Steiner,' whispered Maxim. 'I'm scared. What will happen to us?'

'You'd best hope the Matriarch-Commissar can intervene,' said Steiner, 'or else we're all in for a long conversation with Shirinov.'

'One of these days I'm going to get even . . .' but anything else Romola said was drowned out by the stamp of booted feet and clatter of armour. The cinderwraiths paused as the procession of armoured men marched past. The dozen Spriggani on duty scurried away to safety. A trio of soldiers carried pikes, all levelled at Kimi who growled curse words in her mother tongue.

'Hoy there!' said Steiner, stepping forward. 'Tell us your business before pointing those things at my friend.'

'Have a care, Steiner,' said Romola, laying a gentle hand on his shoulder. 'This isn't about you.' She drew her sword from the scabbard slowly and surrendered the blade to the nearest of the soldiers. 'Let's do this quietly. No one needs to be hurt on my account, right? They're just children, after all.'

'The pirate,' said the nearest soldier. 'I should have guessed we'd find you here. Smuggling more novices off the island?'

'Just feeding my friends,' replied Romola.

The soldier dropped her sword on the ground. 'We're not here for you.'

'What?'

The soldier pushed past her, grabbing Steiner by the front of his tunic. 'Our orders are to fetch the boy.' The soldier wrenched Steiner forward and threw him to the mass of armoured bodies behind. 'No one said anything about the pirate or the princess.' There were a few chuckles at that.

'Hoy! What's this about?' Steiner grabbed the soldier's shoulder and was greeted with an elbow, slamming into his face. Pain erupted through his head, making his eyes water. He stumbled back, holding both hands to his nose.

'Shame,' said the soldier to Romola. 'Now we must arrest you too. I wanted this to be, how you say? Straightforward.'

'What foolishness is this?' shouted a familiar surly voice. The soldiers looked around and parted with reluctance. 'Out of my way, halfhead! What happened to you?' said Tief, pushing his way to the middle of the crowd.

'I think they broke my nose,' said Steiner. It was hard to see through his streaming eyes and his chin was slick with blood. He wasn't sure what was worse, the pain or the rising panic.

'Hands off the boy, you wretched bastards!' shouted Tief. And that's when it all went to Hel.

Kimi snatched one of the pikes from a soldier, using the end as a club to beat on his head, before turning the sharp end on her other opponents with a flourish.

Tief launched himself at the nearest soldier, slamming a flat palm under his chin, pushing the helm back until it crashed to the floor. The wiry Spriggani pulled the soldier's cloak up over his head and a knife flashed in the darkness.

Romola snatched up her sword, only to be separated from the main fight by two soldiers who pressed the attack with their maces. Steiner watched her trying to parry the savage blows, retreating further and further away.

Of Maxim there was no sign. Steiner glanced around to see if the boy had been pushed to the ground. Nothing. He grabbed a soldier and tried to ask but the soldier assumed he was under attack, cuffing Steiner across the face. He all but blacked out, the pain in his face excruciating, waking to find himself slung over an armoured shoulder when he regained his senses.

'Wait! We have to find Maxim!' he shouted, but the soldier

was already departing the melee, heading back to the many steps to Academy Square.

It wasn't until they reached the vast metal rungs that led to the gallery that Steiner was able see the centre of the cavern. The soldier set Steiner down and pointed upward.

'We climb, said the soldier.'

Steiner continued to stare after his friends. Kimi had been forced back, a pike protruding from her shoulder, pinned against a wooden crate. Her eyes were tightly shut and the pike she had liberated lay on the floor. Steiner called out to her but the sound was lost in the din of combat.

Romola was being carried by two soldiers, one at her shoulders, the other bearing her feet. Steiner gasped, unable to tell if she was dead or unconscious.

Tief stood on the dais, hands tied behind his back. A soldier slammed him to the ground before applying a boot to the guts.

Steiner started back toward the centre of the forge but the soldier grabbed him by the collar and swung him towards the metal rungs.

'Never mind that, just climb.'

'My friends!' *What have I done?*

Up they went, the sound of armoured men swearing in Solska following them with every step. Twice Steiner turned to see if Romola had survived and twice he was shoved so hard he should have fallen.

'My friends,' he whispered.

'Your friends should not have started a fight they could not finish,' said the soldier, and Steiner felt a crushing despair take hold of him.

Shirinov was not waiting for them in Academy Square as Steiner had expected, though every window of the four academies was lit. Novices of all ages peered from the windows.

The soldiers were conversing in Solska and those who brought up the rear joined their comrades. A few were missing a pauldron, another had lost his helmet. At least two had yet to return to the surface at all. Steiner looked around with growing dread. Maxim was nowhere to be seen and Romola had been dumped on the cobbles of Academy Square without care.

'What now?' mumbled Steiner, too scared to touch his face, his tunic spattered with red.

Another shove dictated his route, across the square to the gatehouse, then he was ushered up a spiral staircase. A boot to his backside was added incentive to enter the cell before him. The barred window was a narrow slot that let in the cold while the bed was narrow and filthy. Steiner wasn't sure what stained the blankets in the darkness.

'My friends . . .'

He grasped the bars of the cell and looked past the roiling flames of the dragon statue. One by one the many lights of the four academies were extinguished, each window a darkened eye. The novices called out to each other, and a few choice insults were slung across the square, meant for Steiner. The voices fell silent until one light remained, revealing a glint of silver peering from the window. A silver mask with a mocking smile. Shirinov. Steiner turned his back and slid down the wall, resting his head on his knees.

'And may Frøya keep me close,' he mumbled, before passing out.

CHAPTER TWENTY-THREE

Kjellrunn

Those who possess the powers of the air are often inscrutable, in thought and deed. Many students of Academy Vozdukha fail to finish their training, not because of incompetence or disobedience, but because they lose their minds. Telepathy and prescience are both born of the wind, and some things are best left unknown and unseen by young minds. Graduates of Academy Vozdukha learn to master hateful storms and freezing winds, and the most subtle can charm the birds from the trees.

– From the field notes of Hierarch Khigir,
Vigilant of the Imperial Synod.

Kjellrunn looked down at the chopping board and the dozen carrots, then dared a glance at Mistress Kamalov, who was perched on a rickety stool, skinning two hares on the other side of the kitchen table. It seemed that Kjellrunn hurried through her chores at home, only to find more waiting for her in the woodcutter's chalet. She longed for the day the real training began; her restlessness was like a strong tide and every day it pulled on her more keenly. She picked up the first carrot and struggled not to sigh. Surely the novices on Vladibogdan didn't have to endure such menial tedium?

'For the first year the students do little more than kitchen chores and sewing. If they are good they are taught meditations on calmness, but mostly the first year is obedience training. Like dogs.'

Kjellrunn picked up the knife and began slicing, fighting down the urge to say anything. Mistress Kamalov's gift for reading her mind, or merely guessing what she was thinking, had passed beyond being uncanny to inconvenient to deeply annoying.

'Peeling potatoes, gutting fish, sweeping corridors and polishing boots.'

'And you know this because you trained there,' replied Kjellrunn. She had no need to frame it as a question, the truth was self-evident. Mistress Kamalov didn't reply, trapped between her love of demonstrating her knowledge and a deep reticence of speaking about the past.

'This carrot chopping then,' said Kjellrunn, determined to get something meaningful from the day. 'What does it stand for? Do I just have to prove that I'll do as I'm told?'

Mistress Kamalov looked up with a skinned rabbit in one hand and a bloodied knife in the other.

'Do as you're told? By anyone else? No. But by me? Yes.'

'Obedience. Like dogs,' repeated Kjellrunn, as the last word brought a flush of anger to her cheeks.

'That's a small part of it. Obedience is important during training, important that you follow my directions, even when you are bored or scared. Or frustrated.'

'And when I'm angry?' Kjellrunn forced the knife through the top of the carrot and felt the metal bite against the chopping block.

'This is when obedience is most important. Anger can eclipse everything; it makes fools of us all if we pay no mind to it.'

'So when you say, "Like dogs", you're just trying to make me angry, you don't actually think I'm a dog.'

'Knowing when to obey and who to obey and why we do it is what separates us from dogs. This is why your training will be different from the training on Vladibogdan.'

Kjellrunn cleared her mind and took a few minutes to sharpen the knife by the fireside. Thoughts of Steiner came to her, memories of him lumbering about the smithy and other times where he watched their father intently, wanting to get every detail of their work together just so. She thought of his rough embraces and the fleeting moments when she'd basked in his kindness and protection. And underneath it all was the guilt for not telling him about her powers. She needed to get to Vladibogdan, and she needed to be powerful enough to overcome Shirinov and Khigir when she did.

When Kjellrunn returned to the chopping board she felt calmer, dicing the carrots and then two onions without pause or distraction. She headed to the well outside without being asked and returned with pails of water moments later without idling.

'What else is going into this soup, then?' she asked. 'What can I do next?'

Mistress Kamalov smiled a crooked smile and her eyes twinkled in delight. 'You are going to be a good student if you can just stay with what is happening right now, and not give rein to your impatience.'

Kjellrunn nodded, and again her thoughts drifted to her imaginings of Vladibogdan, a stony island shrouded in sea mist, and Steiner locked away in a dank cell.

'I can only promise to train you, Kjellrunn. I can't promise to help you get your brother back.'

Kjellrunn nodded and forced a tight smile. 'Tell me what I have to do.'

If Marek was curious or concerned about Kjellrunn's lengthy disappearances in the woods he didn't voice it. Often he'd venture into town to shop for food himself, sparing Kjellrunn the fearful glances and snatched whispers of the townsfolk.

'Time may be a great healer, but people have long memories in these parts,' he'd said to her more than once before heading to the butcher's.

'Come on, you old fool,' said Verner one morning, leaning against the doorframe like he owned the place. 'Come out in the boat today. The sea is nice and flat. Even your tender guts won't heave up your breakfast.'

'I've not had any breakfast yet. Perhaps you shouldn't come calling so damn early,' replied Marek.

Kjellrunn snorted a laugh. It was easy to forget the strangeness of the last month when they were like this.

'And I'm not coming out,' added Marek. 'I've got too much to do.'

'Lies,' said Verner. 'No one has bought anything from you in weeks.'

Kjellrunn eyed her father and saw that he didn't deny it, saw the tiny slump of his shoulders that spoke of his defeat and dismay.

'Come out and catch some fish with me,' said Verner, his voice softer now, not mocking or boorish, but imploring.

'Fine,' growled Marek, though he sounded anything but. 'Shut the door, won't you? You're letting the heat out and I'll be cold soon enough as it is.'

Kjellrunn nodded to Verner and fetched her broom, then headed for the smithy.

'And where are you off to?' he asked her, taking a seat at the table.

'Seems a good time to sweep the smithy without you men under my feet. Try not to lose my father overboard, won't you?'

The smithy was all darkness and a deep chill waited within. Kjellrunn guessed that Marek hadn't lit the furnace in days.

Ashes lay over the floor, white and grey, as cold to the touch as Nordvlast snow.

She began her work in earnest, thinking on Mistress Kamalov's words from the previous day and mulling over blind obedience and the willingness to learn. The knock at the door startled her so badly she almost dropped the broom.

'Who is it?'

No answer came and the latch rattled as it was lifted. A dark shadow filled the yawning gap as the door opened, the grey sky behind making a dire silhouette of the person who entered. Kjellrunn held up the broom like a spear and took a step forward.

'Get out of here! My father is in the kitchen, he'll beat you black and blue if you so much as—'

'It's me!' hissed Kristofine, slipping further into the smithy and shutting the door behind her. Kjellrunn lowered the broom and huffed, as much with chagrin as frustration.

'My father isn't here, he's gone fishing with Verner.'

Kristofine nodded and stood a little closer to the lantern light. Her hair had come loose from her headscarf and she looked unfinished somehow, as if she had left the house in a rush.

'I saw them head down to the bay. That's why I knocked. I don't want to speak to him, I wanted to speak with you.'

'After your father told my family to leave town?' Kjellrunn gripped the broom handle tighter.

'My father's opinions aren't mine, and I've no wish to see you leave town. He'd kill me if he knew I was here.'

'So why are you here?'

'I didn't have anywhere else to go.' Kristofine wrung her hands and looked down at the floor.

'Has Bjørner thrown you out?'

Kristofine shook her head and frowned a moment. 'Nothing like that, I meant that no one will talk to me. The townsfolk all cross the street when I pass by, and my father won't let me work in the tavern.'

'And you came to me for sympathy?' Kjellrunn couldn't keep the scowl from her face, already wondering how to get rid of the woman before her.

'I . . .' The words died on her pretty lips and Kristofine glanced at the door then back at the lantern. 'I spent the night with your brother in the stables behind the tavern.'

'Spent the night? What do you mean, spent the night? How did you spend it?' Kjellrunn had heard the expression used by adults on occasion but had never really grasped the meaning. Kristofine said nothing and tucked a stray hair behind her ear and forced an awkward smile.

'You spent *all* night in the stables with him,' said Kjellrunn, feeling the pieces coming together and not liking the image that was forming. 'You slept in the stables together?'

Kristofine gave a brittle nod. The smile remained frozen on her face but was pained.

'Oh. And . . .' Kjellrunn wrinkled her nose. 'And that's why these idiot townsfolk think you have witchsign.' She paused a moment. 'How did your father find out?'

'One of the draymen. He saw us slipping out the following morning as he was delivering the ale.'

'And do you have witchsign?' Kjellrunn couldn't resist. She'd been on the wrong side of those accusing stares for much too long.

'Do I what?'

'Do you have the witchsign?' Kjellrunn grinned. 'Can you breathe fire or fly? Did you make Steiner fall in love with you by wiggling your fingers?'

'He's not in love with me. I mean, I don't suppose he is. It was just one night and . . .' Kristofine looked more crest-fallen than Kjellrunn had ever seen her and she instinctively stepped forward and laid a hand on her arm.

'He was very excited that you two had started talking,' admitted Kjellrunn. 'He wasn't quite sure what to do about it; I don't think he'd ever spoken to a woman that wasn't serving him bread or bringing him ale.'

A small smile crept onto Kristofine's worried face.

'I know that he liked talking to you. And he liked you. A lot.'

'Did he say anything about me?'

'Well.' Kjellrunn struggled to remember. 'He said there wasn't a whole lot of nice in Cinderfell.'

Kristofine frowned. 'He said I was "nice".'

Kjellrunn shrugged. 'You know Steiner, he was never one for words. He's a blacksmith, not a poet.'

'Nice.' Kristofine smiled as tears tracked down her cheeks. 'I'm so scared, Kjell. I'm scared the Okhrana will take me away. I'm scared my father will let them take me. And I'm scared I'll never see Steiner again. I know it sounds stupid, but . . .'

'Come into the kitchen,' said Kjellrunn. 'We'll catch our deaths in this miserable old place.' Kjellrunn led Kristofine out of the smithy after checking the street was empty and there was no one to see them. It took a few moments to stoke up the fire and Kjellrunn flashed a smile over her shoulder.

'Strange to think it was you who took me in from the rain a few weeks ago.'

'Stranger that you've barely been seen since,' said Kristofine. 'Half the reason I came today was simply to see if you still lived in Cinderfell.'

Kjellrunn hefted the kettle over the fire and shrugged, feigning a casualness. 'I've got friends just outside of town.'

Kristofine blinked in surprise and seemed impressed.

'You're very precocious for a fifteen-year-old.'

'That's because I'm sixteen,' replied Kjellrunn. 'Did you

know they marry girls off in Svingettevei that have barely seen fourteen summers?'

'Fourteen?'

'Verner told me. Said it was younger still in Karelina Province.'

'This is the longest conversation I've had since we last spoke,' said Kristofine, slumping onto a chair. 'I thought I'd go mad.'

'A lot of people used to think I was mad,' said Kjellrunn. 'Now they worry I have witchsign.'

'What will we do?'

Kjellrunn frowned. 'We? What is this "we"?' She was suddenly aware she sounded like Mistress Kamalov and wasn't so sure she liked it. 'I'm sorry. Honestly, I don't know. I want to get Steiner back and I'm working on something with a . . .' Was she a teacher? Spy? Madwoman? 'With an old friend.'

'You're going to try and rescue him?'

'Well, yes.' Kjellrunn realized how ridiculous it sounded and frowned, then held up her chin a little higher. 'Yes, yes I am. I'm going to rescue my brother from the Empire, even it fucking kills me. And it probably will.'

Kristofine burst out laughing. 'Where did you learn such language?'

'You forget, Verner is my uncle.'

The two of them sat beside the fire, smiles on their faces, laughter fading to warm chuckles.

'Are you really going to rescue him?' said Kristofine after a pause.

'Yes, I really am. And I might need some help.'

Kristofine nodded and Kjellrunn saw it written in her eyes, as bright as polished steel. The woman before her had nothing to lose and a glimmer of something better if Steiner were freed.

CHAPTER TWENTY-FOUR

Steiner

Students from Academy Zemlya are often preferable to their fiery cousins in Academy Plamya; theirs is a more steadfast temperament. Students with the power of earth are rarely lost, even on the longest of marches. Zemlya is known for its strength or arms, for a warrior with a skin of stone is terrifying indeed. The very greatest graduates learn to slow living flesh with a gaze, petrifying their enemies with nothing more than a look.

– From the field notes of Hierarch Khigir,
Vigilant of the Imperial Synod.

The dull grunt of timber on stone woke Steiner as the cell door opened. He was still folded in on himself, forehead resting on his knees. Joints protested as he tried to stand, arse numb from a night on the floor, face a dull throb of pain. Weak sunlight filtered in through the barred window behind him, illuminating Matriarch-Commissar Felgenhauer as she stepped into the cramped room.

'I can't decide if you're wildly unlucky or intolerably stupid,' she said, one fist pressed into the palm of the other hand.

Steiner gave a slow nod. 'Why settle for one when I can be both?'

That might have earned him a round of laughter back in the tavern at Cinderfell, but Felgenhauer showed no sign of amusement.

'You look surprised to see me,' she said.

'I was expecting Shirinov.'

'I imagine you were,' replied Felgenhauer, crossing to the barred window and gazing out.

'Shirinov sent Matthias and Aurelian to bring me up here.' Steiner screwed up his face and winced in pain. 'And then soldiers arrived to . . .' He struggled to find the word. 'Escort me from the furnaces?'

The Matriarch-Commissar paused, then pressed her fingers to her forehead, a curiously human gesture at odds with the angular, androgynous mask. 'You thought Shirinov had sent the soldiers.' Not a question, she was merely putting pieces together. 'That's why your friends put up such resistance. They were trying to protect you.' Steiner hoped she understood, even if she couldn't approve. 'What the Hel happened to your face?' she asked.

'One of your soldiers. Don't ask me which one. They all look the same to me.'

'Five of them are in the infirmary as of this morning.'

'Wounded?' Steiner swallowed.

'One seriously,' intoned Felgenhauer. 'The other is dead.'

Steiner didn't speak for a moment. The consequences of what had happened were swirling all about him like a terrible storm.

'Is Kimi still alive?'

'For the moment.' Felgenhauer sighed. 'I've been up all night refusing requests from soldiers who want to execute her. It's a good thing she's a political prisoner. I ran out of excuses hours ago.'

'And Romola?'

'In the cell next to this one. You would not believe the lengths I went to ensuring Shirinov didn't come calling in the night.'

Steiner tried not think about Shirinov questioning Romola, tried not to think about the many sharp objects he'd use to retrieve the answers he wanted.

'Will the dead soldier become a cinderwraith?' asked Steiner.

Felgenhauer stiffened. 'Yes. I suppose he will, much like Matthias Zhirov I imagine. You killed him, didn't you?'

'I . . .' Steiner swallowed but couldn't bring himself to answer.

'You were defending yourself,' said Felgenhauer. 'And Shirinov should never have sent him.' She let the full import of her words linger on the cold air of the cell a moment, then snatched a glance along the corridor. 'Don't mention this conversation to anyone else. Anyone.'

Steiner nodded and turned to the barred window behind him. The dragon still glowered at Academy Square, the fire still roiled across the surface, just as it did on Kimi's amulet.

'Will I be executed?' said Steiner.

'It would make my life easier,' admitted Felgenhauer. 'And Shirinov would be delighted, but I have a better use for you.'

'Can I go back to the forges, with Tief and Kimi?'

'No. You'll work directly for me, answer directly to me, wait on me day and night.' She had stepped closer, impressive in her cream and crimson robes, the eyes beneath the mask calm despite the chaos. 'Come now, there is much to do and I won't have time to explain much of it.'

While Matriarch-Commissar Felgenhauer had made Steiner's future incarceration sound ominous, the reality was somewhat different. His room was located not far from hers on the sixth floor of Academy Voda. The bed was softer than anything he had slept on, while the windows were framed with curtains of dark, heavy fabric that kept the warmth in. The clatter and din of beaten metal had been replaced by the wind, howling around the island's jagged peaks. There was a stout dresser containing a change of clothes, which had the benefit of being warm and not liberally spattered with his blood. The clothes were not spattered with anyone's blood and Steiner was grateful for that too.

There was a thick sheepskin on the flagstones, just a few feet away from the hearth, where logs crackled to fend off the chilly climate. It was, Steiner decided, the finest place he had ever lived and yet a restlessness remained.

Felgenhauer did not spare him time to brood, setting him to work on a number of tasks that couldn't be more different to his work in the furnaces below. He boiled up water for the Matriarch-Commissar's baths; changed her bedding; brought her meals from the kitchen; swept and mopped the flagstones in her office, waiting room and the corridor beyond. He polished her boots and ferried her garments to the laundry in black canvas sacks. These many tasks revealed a truth Steiner could not have guessed at.

'You dine alone every night?' The question slipped free as he stacked the plates onto a tray, preparing to return to the kitchens. Felgenhauer was sitting at her desk, a huge pile of parchment and scrolls to one side, an inkwell and selection of quills on the other.

'Every night. Every morning. And at noon,' she replied. 'A Vigilant does not reveal their face to anyone else.'

'That sounds like a lonely business,' replied Steiner before giving thought to what he was saying or to whom he said it. A yearning for the rough kitchen table of home rose within him, and for meals shared with his father and Kjellrunn, of nights in the tavern with Verner.

'Are you just going to stand there for the rest of the night?'
said Felgenhauer with a note of annoyance.

'You don't even show your face to other Vigilants?' he said,
recovering from the pang of homesick reverie.

'Especially not the other Vigilants, and not to soldiers. That's
how problems start.'

'What problems?' pressed Steiner.

'Never mind. Take these things away. I have correspondence
I must attend to. Go to your room afterwards and read the
book I left on the dresser for you.'

'I, uh, I can't read . . .' said Steiner, feeling the familiar heat
of embarrassment in his cheeks. 'The words, they . . . uh.'

It was at this point adults would make a disparaging remark
about his brains, or insist he was lazy or idle. Not just adults
but a fair number of children too, especially the clever ones.
He'd heard all the variants of his supposed shortcomings.

'Is that so?' said the Matriarch-Commissar.

'The words. They, I don't know . . . they're hard to focus on.'

'That is unfortunate,' said Felgenhauer. 'I used to know
someone who had the same problem.'

'Really?'

'Yes, she was a notable Hierarch for a time.' Felgenhauer
rose from her desk and took a deep breath. 'I'll have to teach
you by word of mouth.'

'Teach me what?' said Steiner.

'How to speak Solska, of course. You won't be much use
if you only speak Nordspråk. Come back to me when your
chores are done.'

Steiner took the plates down the many stairs of Academy
Voda. He hoped to meet Maxim each time he ventured to
the kitchens, wanting to find the boy knee deep in buckets
of potatoes, or hefting bags of flour or firewood. None of the
novices would make eye contact with Steiner and his greet-
ings were met with stony silence. None answered his questions

regarding Maxim, and all were equally reticent when asking after Romola. The only words he heard were whispers.

Matthias.

Zhirov.

Murderer.

Shirinov.

Steiner ventured back to the Matriarch-Commissar's office and found it empty. He trudged the stairs to the floor above and the soldiers acknowledged him with curt nods. Steiner approached Felgenhauer's chamber but a soldier held out a hand, more gently than Steiner might have expected.

'Not tonight, boy. She's speaking with Marozvolk, said she didn't want to be disturbed. Best to leave her until dawn.'

Steiner nodded and slunk along the corridor, casting a glance over his shoulder. Strange times when the novices despised him and the soldiers offered free advice. He hurried on, passing his chamber door and heading to the stairs beyond, taking them ever upward, to the flat roof of Academy Voda.

The view down into the square was breathtaking; from eight floors up it resembled a deep crater, or a terrible abyss. The square itself was arranged around a natural depression in the rock. Hours of toil had exploited the stone and chipped away until a parade ground had been hewn out of the centre of the island. The four academies stood watch like vast sentries at the south side of the square. From this angle the dragon seemed to loom over the gatehouse on the opposite side. Arcane fire lit the scene, picking out windows, buttresses, and doorframes in golden light.

It took twenty years to build such a thing.

Steiner flinched at the words and panicked as he realized Silverdust must be close by. He turned slowly and saw the Vigilant gliding towards him, the familiar blank silver mask reflecting Steiner's clean scrubbed face and all the anxiety it held.

I will not tell anyone you have come here.

'Thanks,' mumbled Steiner. He took a moment to see past the specks of silver light that danced around the Vigilant in a nimbus. Silverdust's cream robes reached all the way to the ground, and the red leather surcoat was almost as long.

In truth, this is one of my favourite places on the island. Silverdust approached the edge of the roof, and reached out to the parapet to steady himself. *From up here the many trifles and concerns seem to belong to other people, smaller people.*

'And is Shirinov one of those smaller people?' Steiner swallowed, surprised at his own bold question.

There are many prisoners on this island, and not all of them are cinderwraiths or novices.

'What do you mean?'

The Emperor is capable of a broad spectrum of cruelty. He is not always the twisting knife or the torturer's whip, he knows the power of exile, of assigning people duties far from their families.

'Shirinov doesn't want to be here,' said Steiner, making sense of the phantom words that appeared in his mind. 'And Corpsecandle, uh, I mean Khigir?'

Khigir was broken the moment his sister departed their unhappy Troika. In truth he has always been broken, only complete when at his sister's side.

'You're talking about Sharpbreath, I don't know her real name.'

Silverdust's blank mask nodded slowly.

You have learned much.

For a time they stared down into Academy Square and watched the soldiers patrol in lazy circles. Steiner's eyes fell on the gatehouse and searched behind it for Temnet Cove. The *Watcher's Wait* remained at anchor, so close and yet denied to him.

This is why Khigir and Shirinov hate you so. Silverdust had drawn close, within arm's reach, and Steiner felt the heat from the aura of light all around him.

'What?'

Your sister, you seek to protect her. Just as Khigir once sought to protect his own. And Shirinov too, though his motives were very different.

'You can read my mind?'

I have been doing this a long time.

'So you know . . .'

I know about Kjellrunn and the Invigilation, about the brooch, about your sacrifice. I know you are from the Vartiainen line. I know all of these things.

Steiner's guts shrank and for a second he contemplated shoving the Vigilant over the parapet, shoving him down the eight storeys to the hard cobbles below. Silverdust raised one gloved finger and waved it from side to side, forbidding such a thing.

There is no need for such extreme measures; your secret, your sister's secret, is safe with me.

Steiner all but sighed with relief and stepped back from the parapet, looking away. 'But you're a Vigilant, Vigilants scour the land for witchsign, it's your duty. Why spare my sister?'

There are many prisoners on this island, and not all of them novices.

'You said that before,' grunted Steiner, his patience waning with each cryptic response. 'Can I trust you to keep this secret? You can't tell a soul, not Felgenhauer, not Marozvolk.'

A trade, then?

'What trade? I have nothing to give you.' Steiner immediately thought of his boots, his mother's boots, and how loath he was to give them up.

A secret for a secret of course, what else is there? Material items mean nothing to me.

'You already know my secret.' Steiner frowned at the Vigilant. 'You stole it from my mind. Theft isn't trade.'

For a moment Silverdust looked as if he might lace his gloved fingers in contemplation, but one hand reached for the other and began to tug the glove free. Steiner's eyes widened with the revelation. What he saw was not flesh, or even living stone. The hand was an insubstantial wisp of dark smoke.

'You're a cinderwraith.'

And now I have traded a secret for a secret.

'But you don't work in the furnaces? How?'

I have an unnaturally high resistance to such bidding. I forge my own path each day, rather than the Emperor's weapons.

Steiner could only stare in shocked silence as the Vigilant forced the glove back onto the ghostly hand.

So you see, some but not all prisoners on Vladibogdan are novices. I am here because I am bound to the Ashen Torment. Felgenhauer is here for misdeeds known only to her and the Emperor.

'And Shirinov?'

The sound of jingling armour seized Silverdust's attention before he could answer. A pair of soldiers clanked onto the roof.

'Is all well, Vigilant?'

The boy couldn't sleep, we were enjoying the view. Nothing more.

The soldiers snapped out salutes and returned downstairs, back into Academy Voda.

'Why did you tell me your secret?' whispered Steiner as they took one last look at Academy Square and the dragon statue at the centre.

Because like all prisoners I wish to escape. I have a feeling you may feature in that escape, Steiner. I am counting on it.

They headed back inside the academy and the Vigilant walked Steiner to his chamber. Silverdust nodded his head once and said nothing more, gliding on his way, to whichever part of the island he haunted through the long hours of the night.

Steiner pushed through the door into his room and set to stirring up the embers, holding out his hands to the warmth. His thoughts spun as he considered all that he'd learned. Vladibogdan was not just a secret island, but an island of secrets, mired in them, awash with them, on fire with them.

It was a long time before Steiner could settle down to sleep, the memory of Silverdust's insubstantial hand emerging from his glove playing over and over in his mind.

CHAPTER TWENTY-FIVE

Steiner

It is not for the sake of wordplay that the students of Academy Plamya are called hotheads. They are quick to find their fiery tempers and the heat of competition runs high between them. All too often they burn brightly but briefly.

A well-versed graduate of Academy Plamya can create flame with a click of their fingers, breathe fire like the dragons of old, send forth clouds of choking smoke, and heat metal with their fingertips. The most terrible to behold are those who become living flames, infernos given human form.

– From the field notes of Hierarch Khigir,
Vigilant of the Imperial Synod.

There were many things Steiner did not like about Solska. It was a guttural and coarse language to Steiner's ears, even when expressing joy. The language featured an abundance of 'V's and 'Z's and sounded as if the speaker were constantly trying to swallow their own words. And much worse than the speaking was the spelling of the words. Steiner hated every letter of the strange alphabet and squinted until his head ached from concentrating.

'Now spell the word "Vozdukha",' said Felgenhauer, sounding out the syllables behind her mask. She paced his room while he sat near the fire, comfortable on the sheepskin. She was always Felgenhauer in this place, never the Matriarch-Commissar. The mask stayed firmly in place yet there was a softening of tone, a lessening of command.

'This is making me feel sick,' replied Steiner, and took a deep breath, struggling to focus on the paper and not wanting to get anything wrong.

'Just a little longer,' replied Felgenhauer. 'You're doing well. Try and hold the quill how I showed you.'

Felgenhauer was just as concerned with the way he wrote as much as with what he wrote.

'Next, spell "Plamya".' Steiner couldn't be sure, but the words she chose to teach him were not for everyday conversation, at least no conversation that could be held anywhere but Vladibogdan. He worked the quill on the parchment and frowned hard.

'Now tell me what the previous word was,' said Felgenhauer. Steiner shook his head. 'I can't.' His grip on the quill turned into a clenched fist. 'I can't remember what the word was, even though I just wrote it down.' He sat back and stared at the parchment accusingly.

'That's what I thought,' replied Felgenhauer. 'It was the same for the Hierarch I knew. She would forget things very quickly when trying to write them down. The word you're trying to remember is "Vozdukha". It means simply means "air" in Solska.'

'Why do they make it so hard to spell if it's such a simple word?' Steiner jabbed the quill into the inkwell and crossed his arms.

Felgenhauer's shoulders shook and she raised a hand to her face, as if to cover her mouth. He realized she was laughing silently.

'The Sol make everything difficult,' she said after a moment.
'Not least their language.'

'You're not from there, are you? Not from Solmindre.'
Steiner looked at Felgenhauer, trying to see past the uniform
and the mask to the person beneath. 'I can't place your accent
though. Which of the Scorched Republics are you from?'

'Why, Nordvlast, of course. Though I don't speak of it. I've
not been there in many years and I don't intend to go back.'

'But your accent?' he replied.

'The Emperor has sent me to all corners of the continent,
Steiner. I've seen Arkiv Island and the stacks of old accounts
and accords. I've walked the Halls of Justice in Khlystburg
and seen traitors hung at dawn.' Something about the way
she pronounced the word 'traitors' gave Steiner pause. The
Matriarch-Commissar was steadfast in her loyalty to the
Empire, but the person who spoke to him here, in his chamber,
was someone very different. He suspected a certain disgust,
and wondered at conflict within.

'I've spied in the Republics and carried out Invigilations in
Novgoruske Province.' She sat down on the bed and her
shoulders curved slightly, as her parade ground posture had
given way to something weary. 'I've walked the Empire's
rutted tracks in winter and marched along bright avenues in
summer, sheltered in its forest from spring rains, and shivered
in the mountains at night.' Steiner felt the weight on her, the
exhaustion. Nothing else was said and Felgenhauer simply
sat, head bowed, hands on knees. Without knowing why
Steiner raised a hand and rested it upon Felgenhauer's. He
assumed she'd snatch it away, lurch to her feet and regain
her imperious aspect, but instead she sighed. After a moment
she turned her palm up and grasped Steiner's hand. They sat
there for long seconds, Steiner afraid to speak for fear he
break the spell of their fleeting union.

'What a pair we are, Steiner Vartiainen,' she said after a

moment. Her voice was soft and for the first time he heard the lilt of Nordspråk. She reached up with her other hand to wipe at her eyes, but the gesture was confounded by the mask that separated them. 'Even I, with the lofty title of Matriarch-Commissar, am as bound to this place as you are.'

She let go of his hand and smoothed down her robes, then stood and rolled her shoulders, as if shrugging on some cloak.

'Should we try more words?' he asked, reaching for the quill, keen that she not leave.

'No. It is late and you are tired.' She stood, and all traces of the Nordspråk accent had disappeared; her shoulders straightened, her chin came up and she was once more Matriarch-Commissar Felgenhauer, Flintgaze to those novices who dared to make fun of her. 'Sleep. There will be much to do tomorrow.'

The door closed quietly behind her and Steiner stared at his ink-stained fingers, trying to make sense of what had just happened.

Three weeks passed and all that was strange was made familiar by routine. A sharp knock on the door woke Steiner each morning and he'd hurry out of his nightshirt and slip on his clothes, keen to fetch the Matriarch-Commissar's breakfast. That's how he thought of her when he was at his tasks. She was only Felgenhauer during private conversations, all too infrequent for Steiner's liking. No one else in Academy Voda spoke to him at length.

Steiner slipped through his chamber door and nodded to the soldiers in the corridor. They nodded back, one offering a gesture part salute, part wave. It was easy to spot the Matriarch-Commissar's cadre for they carried axes instead of the customary mace. Their armour was always oiled and enamelled, their boots polished.

'Big storm today,' said one soldier as Steiner passed him.

'Good thing I've no cause to go out in it,' Steiner smiled. Felgenhauer had been true to her word, Steiner's tasks meant he was never far from her protective eye and he'd not left Academy Voda once in the whole three weeks.

'The storm could last all week,' said the soldier. 'No ships while the storm blows. No food.'

'And no vodka,' added his comrade.

'I'd best get going,' Steiner replied, heading along the corridor. Down he went, to the fifth floor where Felgenhauer kept her office, more soldiers standing guard here, more close-mouthed than their comrades on the sixth. The fourth floor provided barracks for the novices. Steiner was unnerved by the lack of noise. So many children together, yet no shouts or laughter, no taunts or chiding. The third floor consisted of classrooms, though Steiner had not seen them for himself and had no wish to. The stairs took him lower, to the second floor, where a vast refectory would feed the novices three times a day. Steiner guessed the portions were slim, judging by the gaunt frames of the children. Finally he arrived at his destination, the kitchens.

Three novices eyed him with a sullen disapproval. None had said a word to him for the duration he'd served here.

'The Matriarch-Commissar's breakfast?' he said, hoping he might goad some conversation from them. As one they pointed to a wooden tray but offered no greeting. All were younger than Kjellrunn, with pinched faces and ragged hair.

'Always a pleasure speaking with you,' said Steiner as he lifted the tray. He turned to leave and almost barged into Aurelian. A few seconds passed before either could think of anything to say.

'What in Frejna's name are you doing here?' asked Steiner. Aurelian of the fiery breath had to be a student in the Academy Plamya.

'Vigilant Shirinov asked me to escort him. It is a huge

honour.' Aurelian preened, standing a little taller. 'He has a meeting with the Matriarch-Commissar. I would have thought you'd know, seeing as you're her new pet.'

Steiner ignored the barb. 'Shirinov teaches at Academy Zemlya. Couldn't he get one of his own students to escort him?'

Aurelian shrugged. 'Usually Matthias would escort him. Now it's my turn.'

The novices in the kitchens hung on every word of the exchange, and Steiner felt the usual pang of regret upon hearing Matthias' name.

'Can't say I care too much for what Shirinov does, or who escorts him. Now you'd best get out of my way, the Matriarch-Commissar doesn't like to be kept waiting.'

Aurelian didn't move, his smile widening, a cruel cast to his eyes.

'Shame you don't have your sledgehammer with you,' he whispered. 'Going to kill me with a serving tray, are you? I suppose you peasants have to use whatever you can find.'

Steiner turned his shoulder to push past him, but Aurelian edged back and kicked out a foot. Steiner didn't fall but slammed into the wall, up-ending porridge and tea over himself. The tray clattered to the floor and Steiner spent a frantic moment shucking the tunic over his shoulders, skin scalded.

Aurelian let out a long mocking laugh and the novices in the kitchen scurried away, keen not to be involved. Steiner stared for a shocked second before pulling back a fist. The blond boy began to suck down a lungful of air, a terrible glow appearing at his throat as a Vigilant rounded the corner. Steiner recognized the Vigilant by the mask; it was the stylised wolf's face he'd seen in Academy Square. Steiner lowered his fist as the Vigilant delivered a sharp rap to the back of Aurelian's head. Aurelian stumbled forward, the fiery glow in his throat sputtering out. Tendrils of black smoke leaked

from the corners of his mouth and his nostrils; when he
looked up there were tears in the corners of his eyes.

'Incinerating the Matriarch-Commissar's aide is very bad
idea,' said the Vigilant, the wolf's snout pressed close to
Aurelian's pale face.

'I was just . . .' Aurelian rubbed the back of his head and
winced. The Vigilant looked down at the spilt porridge and
the shattered teapot.

'I can see perfectly well what you were doing.'

'What are your knuckles made out of? said Aurelian,
rubbing the back of his head. 'Granite?'

The wolf-masked Vigilant removed a glove revealing a
slender hand made of living stone. 'Why, yes, actually. Now
I suggest you cool off in the rain.'

'What?' Aurelian's face clouded with anger and disbelief.

The Vigilant grabbed the boy by the throat and slammed
him against the wall. 'Go and stand in the rain in Academy
Square until such a time as I say otherwise, or I will march
you to the Matriarch-Commissar's office this instant and make
you explain this.' The Vigilant gestured at the mess on the
floor.

Aurelian scuttled away, clutching his throat while the
Vigilant stared after him.

'Who are you?' asked Steiner, holding his tea-soaked tunic
in front of his chest.

'Ordinary Marozvolk,' she replied.

'You don't look very ordinary to me,' replied Steiner.

'It would mean "Frostwolf" in your somewhat limited
tongue,' she added, clearly not understanding him. 'Well,
don't just stand there, you fool. Fetch another breakfast. And
find some clothes.'

It was no surprise to see Shirinov in the waiting room outside
the Matriarch-Commissar's office but Steiner's heart stuttered

in his chest all the same. The soldiers in the antechamber did not stand to attention, but hefted their axes in readiness. The unspoken threat lay leaden on the room, and Steiner felt it press the air out of his lungs.

'She's barely out of bed,' said Steiner through gritted teeth.

'I can wait,' said Shirinov. 'I have all the time I could possibly need.'

Steiner glowered at the Vigilant. 'Why are you here?' whispered Steiner.

'I'm here to request we commandeer your pirate friend's ship.'

'Romola is still here?'

'Oh, yes. Incarcerated this whole time while you run errands for your mistress. We have searched the vessel most thoroughly and checked the logs.'

'And . . . ?' Steiner knew that not all of Romola's work was legal and wondered what trouble Shirinov might cause.

'Unfortunately they are all in order, but that doesn't get around the fact she was caught in the forges. Once I have that ship I'll sail for Cinderfell.'

'You'll do nothing of the sort,' said Felgenhauer from behind them. Steiner almost lost his grip on the tray, such was the volume. 'Where have you been?' said Matriarch-Commissar. Steiner opened his mouth to speak. 'This should have been here ten minutes ago!'

Steiner bowed his head rather than offer an excuse.

'Get out of my sight,' she said. 'It's bad enough I have to deal with the Vigilant at this time of day, to do it on an empty stomach is twice the insult.' And with that she swept past both of them into her office, slamming the door behind her. Steiner eyed Shirinov and realised how much he missed his sledgehammer.

'I will find a way back to Cinderfell,' whispered the Vigilant. 'Of that you can be assured. I have unfinished business there.'

A breathless panic took hold of Steiner, but he gritted his teeth and leaned in close to the Hierarch.

'The way I heard it, you were looking for Sharpbreath in Helwick. Lose an old friend, did you?'

'Sharpbreath is not dead,' replied Shirinov, and even with the mask Steiner could tell he was furious.

'First you lose Sharpbreath, then Matthias. You should be more careful, old man.'

'I think you're missing the point, boy. I could raze Helwick to the ground as retaliation for two murdered Vigilants. As for Sharpbreath, we will find her, be assured of that.'

'You wouldn't dare raze Helwick.' Though Steiner felt his certainty slipping away.

'We are the Imperial Synod. We dare to do things lesser men haven't the stomach for every day of the week. And I doubt anyone would care if we razed Cinderfell at the same time.'

Felgenhauer called out from her office and Steiner slunk away as Shirinov hobbled to his meeting. He'd come to Vladibogdan to protect Kjellrunn, but who was going to protect Helwick and Cinderfell from Shirinov's fury?

CHAPTER TWENTY-SIX

Kjellrunn

In truth, we must all get our hands dirty in service to the Empire. Even the Vigilants, who are the Emperor's political foot soldiers, find themselves with blood on their hands. The soldiers are expected to be killers; the faint-hearted among them are sent home to work the fields. And the Okhrana, they are the bloodiest of all, scouts, investigators, assassins.

– From the field notes of Hierarch Khigir,
Vigilant of the Imperial Synod.

'It's a shame you didn't arrive six months ago when it was warmer,' said Kjellrunn. Mistress Kamalov had led her deeper into the forest, away from the chalet. The trees reached into the pale skies, everything a vast slumbering stillness; only the snow made a sound, crunching beneath their boots, deep prints to mark their passing.

'I'm sure we could do this inside,' said Kjellrunn.

'And I am sure that when I woke this morning I was still the teacher and you were the whip. Yes? Or was it a dream?'

'A whip?'

'A whip is a young tree.' Mistress Kamalov shook her head. 'How can you live near a forest and not know this?'

In truth Kjellrunn was glad to be free of the woodcutter's chalet. She had spent a dutiful three weeks sweeping, polishing, and peeling a variety of vegetables. None of it had seemed very mysterious, and she'd been sure to mention it.

'Pay attention, yes. Close your eyes. Breathe.' Mistress Kamalov's voice was low and calm. 'Think of the forest all around you. Every tree. Every branch. Think of the roots reaching into the soul of the earth. Do not let your mind linger too long on any one thing, yes?'

Kjellrunn did as she was told, imagined reaching into the dark soil with long fingers, her breath mingling with the carpet of leaves. Sounds emerged from the silence, faint at first, gulls flying high along the coast, the wind ushering their mournful cries. Few animals were abroad at this time of year, tucked away in nooks and hollows, yet she imagined each one. Each squirrel and hedgehog, every fox and vole.

'What do you feel?' said Mistress Kamalov.

'Cold.'

'This is obvious, but the cold never killed anyone.'

Kjellrunn opened her eyes and raised an incredulous eyebrow.

'That wasn't the best turn of phrase,' admitted Mistress Kamalov. She shrugged and cleared her throat. 'Close your eyes, concentrate. What do you feel?'

'I don't feel anything. I imagined all the animals sleeping for the winter. I heard the gulls, probably fighting for scraps in the bay.'

'No feeling at all?'

Kjellrunn shook her head. 'No. Just cold. Can we go back to the chalet now? I can't feel my feet.'

Mistress Kamalov took her gently by the shoulders and began to turn her on the spot, like a wooden top.

'What are you—?'

'Hush, child. Turn, turn. Yes, like this. Like a spindle.'

The trees spun and Mistress Kamalov's face blurred past with each revolution. Faster and faster she went until suddenly the old woman's hands had collected her in a tight grip. The forest continued its lazy swirl, the branches reaching in every direction. Kjellrunn stumbled and wondered if this was how it felt to be drunk.

'Which way is north?'

'What?'

'Do not think about it, just tell me. Which way is north?'

Kjellrunn raised her arm and spread her feet in the snow, now trampled to slush beneath her turning steps. The forest continued to spin but her aim was resolute.

'Why?' asked Mistress Kamalov, expression stern.

'Why did you spin me?'

'No. Why is that way north?'

'Because, it's not south?' Kjellrunn shrugged. The forest was still moving at the edges of her vision, but the dizziness was easing.

'Very good. Very funny,' said Mistress Kamalov with a scowl. 'The smart girl has a smart answer for everything.'

'I don't know why it's north. It just . . .' Kjellrunn sighed. 'It feels like north. I can't explain it, I just know.'

'This is good, remember this feeling.' Mistress Kamalov clapped her hands and grinned with something approaching mania in her eyes. 'Ha! I knew it. I knew you had it.'

Kjellrunn took a step back, stunned by the look of delight from the stony-faced old woman.

'What does it mean that I know which direction north is?'

'It means you have the gift of earth, and the gift of earth will help you endure the times ahead.' Mistress Kamalov stroked her chin. 'Fire would better, but we must work with what we can.'

'Thanks,' said Kjellrunn bitterly.

'I mean no insult,' replied Mistress Kamalov, and had the good grace to look ashamed for a moment. 'The gift of earth means many things, but can be difficult to master. It requires the utmost discipline. Not like hotheads from the school of fire. Flame, flame is anger and instinct, but earth, earth is measure and concentration, yes?'

Kjellrunn nodded. They'd spent the morning finding north, something any damn fool woodsman could achieve.

'Yes. This is good.' Mistress Kamalov clapped her hands again.

But it didn't feel good to Kjellrunn. How would knowing true north help her rescue Steiner? How would she fight her way past soldiers, or sneak past them?

Mistress Kamalov detected some inkling of Kjellrunn's thoughts. 'The arcane starts with small gifts and blooms into other, powerful talents. Patience! There is more. Come!'

The old woman strode past her and Kjellrunn stumbled in the snow on numb feet before following.

'Are we going back to the chalet now? To warm up a little?'

'No. We're going to the cliffs now. We will see what else is hiding in here.' She prodded Kjellrunn's chest, just over her heart. 'And here.' She tapped her head, not hard, but Kjellrunn flinched all the same.

'I think I'd prefer to stay in the forest,' she said under her breath as the old woman hurried away.

The northern reach of the forest was thick with fir trees. Grey snow fluttered down and clung to branches laden with pine needles. All was silent save for the muted *crunch-crunch* of their boots.

'If we killed the dragons seventy-five years ago,' said Kjellrunn, 'why is our snow so dirty?'

'All lies,' said Mistress Kamalov. 'The snow falls white and pure further south, when it snows at all. Only here in Nordvlast is the snow tainted.'

'But why?' pressed Kjellrunn.

Mistress Kamalov gestured north-west. 'The fires of Vladibogdan run day and night, furnaces burning brightly. They forge weapons that will see the Empire victorious over the city states of Shanisrond.'

'A war?' asked Kjellrunn. Mistress Kamalov opened her mouth to say more but paused, interrupted. A low rumble followed with a slight pause, then again, rhythmic, growing louder with each iteration.

'Horsemen,' said Mistress Kamalov. The trees parted to afford a view of the Spøkelsea, rushing to meet the cliffs, the waves ecstatic against the rock.

Mistress Kamalov wrapped an arm about Kjellrunn's shoulders and pulled her into the nearest evergreen's embrace. Needles pressed and chafed, branches flexed and snow tumbled, the smell of earth and pine hung heavy in the air.

'What do you think you're—' but Kjellrunn's question was answered with a finger pressed to her lips and a furious glare.

The sound of hooves drumming along the coastal road intensified and Kjellrunn caught a glimpse of two men in black, high in the stirrups as the horses raced along the coastal path. The sound of hooves was swallowed by the roar and boom of the sea. They waited long moments until the horsemen were well on their way. Kjellrunn extricated herself from both the tree and Mistress Kamalov, who needed help to escape the grasp of the branches. The air was filled with her harsh words, but Kjellrunn understood none of them, guessing the old woman spoke in Solska. Mistress Kamalov gave the tree a venomous look and Kjellrunn struggled not to snigger.

'Come,' was all she said, and headed back into the forest.

'I thought you wanted to go to the cliffs.'

'Cliffs, yes. You will need to stand at the cliffs one day soon.'

'To see if I have power over water?'

'Exactly. Perhaps I'll spin you around more often, it seems to get your brain working.'

'Why aren't we going now?' Kjellrunn frowned. 'Is it the horsemen?

'Smart girl.' Mistress Kamalov followed the impressions their boots had made in the snow, stamping on her own footprints.

'I didn't have a chance to see them before you pulled me into that tree.'

'I saw them good enough for both of us. They were Okhrana.'

'How can you know something like that?'

Mistress Kamalov stopped walking and glanced over her shoulder. 'How many people in Cinderfell have a horse?'

'Probably a dozen.'

'Not a pony.' She held a finger up and frowned. 'A horse. Different, yes?'

'Yes.' Kjellrunn thought about the question. 'Three?'

'Good. How many people need to get home so fast they would run their horse through snow and bad weather?'

'Maybe they just want to get warm? That's what I'd do.'

Mistress Kamalov gave a grunt of exasperation and resumed walking. 'How many towns lie north of Cinderfell?'

'None,' replied Kjellrunn. 'It's the northernmost town in Nordvlast, perhaps even the whole continent. There are a few lone fishermen, and Steiner used to talk about smugglers, but . . .'

'So where did the horsemen come from?'

Kjellrunn shrugged, then raised her eyebrows. 'They didn't come from anywhere. They're on the road. Looking for someone.'

Mistress Kamalov stooped and picked up a few sticks of wood.

'What are you doing?' asked Kjellrunn.

'I am being an old woman collecting firewood in the forest.'

Kjellrunn thought about this for a moment before saying, 'Because whoever the horsemen are looking for . . .'

'Does not look like an old woman collecting firewood in the forest.' Mistress Kamalov stooped and affected a limp, the pile of wood in her arms growing from moment to moment.

'Are the Okhrana like Vigilants?' asked Kjellrunn, once she had gathered her own selection of firewood.

'No, often they're much worse.'

'And they have witchsign?'

Mistress Kamalov shook her head. 'No, this is what makes them special. Often they have a resistance to the arcane. It's why I couldn't read the thoughts of those two riders as they went by. Okhrana aren't fooled by illusions, neither are they swayed by enchantments. The most powerful of them can even resist petrification.'

'Petrification?' Kjellrunn shook her head.

'Never mind.' Mistress Kamalov grimaced. 'Now we go back to the chalet, get in warm and pretend you are my niece.'

Kjellrunn did as she was told, watching her teacher limp through the snow, deeper into the forest. Questions begged to be answered, but Kjellrunn could only follow the old woman, sparing fearful glances over her shoulder as she went, wondering how bad the Okhrana truly were.

Night had fallen as Kjellrunn emerged from the forest's darkness. The last remnant of evening light lay on the horizon, gossamer threads over the cobalt and black swells of the Spøkelsea. Head down, shoulders hunched against the cold, hands tucked away beneath her shawl, there was only one thought that burned in her mind.

Why couldn't I have the power of fire. I'd never be cold again.

The cottage was dark when she entered and long moments were spent coaxing flames from the embers. In time she raised a fitful blaze, using more firewood than Marek would have liked.

'I hope Steiner is warmer than we are this winter,' she muttered, holding out blue-tipped fingers to the heat. Boots slammed against the packed snow outside, crunching in the frost. Kjellrunn spun about, startled by the sound of running feet. She had forgotten to light a lantern in her haste to be warm. She snatched a knife from the sideboard in a heartbeat and held the blade low like her father had taught her, eyes hard in the dancing firelight.

'Who's there?'

The door rattled as the key fumbled at the lock.

'Kjell's home, you damn fool.' Verner's voice from the outside, then the door yawned open and he stumbled over the doorstep with Marek hanging from one shoulder. 'Kjell? Awful dark in here. No money for lantern oil?'

'I've not been in long myself. What in Frøya's name happened to you?'

'We ran into some trouble,' said Verner, hefting her father onto a chair.

Kjellrunn stepped forward, wrinkled her nose and frowned. 'Ran into trouble? Ran into a brewery, more like it.'

Verner held up his hands. 'I tried to tell him to come home, then just when he was too drunk to—'

'Stand?'

'I was going to say argue.' Verner sighed. 'Just as we were leaving, Bjørner said something about your brother and things went sour. We fought Bjørner and Håkon and then I dragged him out of there. Two men followed. I think we lost them on Hoar Frost Lane.'

The fishermen made to light a lantern but Kjellrunn stepped in front of him. 'No need to draw attention to ourselves,' she said.

'I suppose not,' admitted Verner.

'Is he hurt?'

'No. At least nothing that he'll notice until tomorrow.'

'You'd best take him up to the loft,' said Kjellrunn. 'He can't sleep down here. And neither can you.'

Verner slipped his hands under Marek's armpits and struggled and stumbled through the darkness.

'Be careful when you go to the woods, Kjell,' called Verner from the top of the stairs. 'Cinderfell isn't safe.'

'You think I didn't notice? Cinderfell hasn't been safe for me since Steiner left.' She ran her fingers over the hammer brooch that her father had given her and hoped it might keep her safe.

'This is different,' said Verner. 'The Okhrana are different.'

'One type of danger feels much like the rest to me,' replied Kjellrunn, but Verner didn't hear her, gone to bed down for the night and sleep off the drink.

The night was long and the kitchen chair hard, but she refused to slip upstairs and sleep. All night she waited, knife in hand, waiting for the *rap, rap, rap* on the door. Waiting for the Okhrana to come looking for her father and Verner.

CHAPTER TWENTY-SEVEN

Steiner

Academy Voda has long been the weakest of the four schools. The power manifests later than other powers. Only a thorough understanding of Frøya gives the students much chance of fully developing their talent, and such a thing is forbidden in the Empire. Why the Matriarch-Commissar makes her office there is a mystery and should be treated with suspicion.

— From the field notes of Hierarch Khigir,
Vigilant of the Imperial Synod.

The following day was a misery of terse silences from the Matriarch-Commissar. Steiner had wanted to ask after Romola but the right moment failed to present itself. He was clearing the bowl and plate from Felgenhauer's desk when she stood up and waved him away.

'Leave those. Come with me.' She passed through the circular door of her office at a brisk pace and growled something in a low voice as the slouching soldiers roused themselves. The soldiers stood to attention, but did not follow the Matriarch-Commissar. Steiner noticed the maces that hung from their belts; these were not Felgenhauer's axe-wielding cadre.

Steiner wondered where Felgenhauer might go unescorted. Twice he wanted to speak and twice he thought better of it. Felgenhauer dismissed another four soldiers from escorting her without breaking stride. Icy rain sheeted down in Academy Square as they emerged from Academy Voda.

'What's going on?' muttered Steiner as they passed the fiery statue. The rain hissed as it met the flames, turning to steam and shrouding the square in a haze.

'The guard changed at midnight last night,' replied Felgenhauer. 'The soldiers on duty in Academy Voda are loyal to Shirinov. I'm forced to live with thirty spies from the moment I wake to the moment I sleep.'

'Thirty?'

'Ten men to a section, each section works an eight-hour shift. Three sections form a troop.'

'And there are five troops on the island,' said Steiner, 'one for each academy and one for the gatehouse.'

'You've been paying attention.' Felgenhauer sounded impressed. 'All together the five troops form a company.'

'These thirty soldiers, the ones loyal to Shirinov.' Steiner wiped the rain out of his eyes. 'Can't you dismiss them?'

'Rotation is key within Imperial military dogma. Rotation reduces attachment.'

'It's not working very well, is it?' said Steiner, hair plastered to his scalp by the chilly rain. 'You've got your axemen and Shirinov has his loyalists.'

Felgenhauer rounded on him as they neared the gatehouse.

'No. It is not.' She took a step back and a low chuckle escaped the stony mask. 'You have a fearless way of speaking your mind.' She turned away and pushed through the door.

Steiner thought this a strange comment but his attention turned to Romola as they climbed the spiral staircase. Silverdust was waiting in the corridor with a ring of keys clasped in his hands. Steiner felt the regard of the blank reflective face and fought a shiver that had nothing to do with the rain trickling down his back. As ever, silvery light flared to life around the Vigilant, who remained statue still.

'She is unharmed?' said Felgenhauer.

Silverdust nodded once and turned to leave, motes of dust igniting with each step, like constellations dying.

'One of the soldiers in Academy Voda will have slipped away to Shirinov to tell him where I am by now,' said Felgenhauer. 'Mark my words.'

Steiner nodded. 'Is this cell . . . ?'

The Matriarch-Commissar opened the door and Steiner winced, not knowing what condition the captain would be in. She looked up from a neatly made bed, where she was tuning the domra and humming softly.

Steiner frowned. 'What's all this?'

There was a rug on the floor and a small brazier crackled and popped, shedding orange light and a pleasant heat. The window had been boarded up to ward off the chill.

'She's perfectly fine!' said Steiner.

'Perfectly bored would be closer to the truth,' replied Romola.

'I didn't get a cell like this,' grumbled Steiner.

'You were in for a single night,' replied Romola. 'I've been here for three weeks. And the novices in the kitchen can't cook to save their lives.' She nodded towards a half-full bowl of greasy broth.

'You locked her up here to keep her safe from Shirinov,' said Steiner to Felgenhauer. Romola slipped off the bed and pushed her head through the doorway, looking left and right. 'Why don't you announce it to the whole island, you half-wit?'

'We don't have time for this,' said Felgenhauer. 'Gather your things.' Romola nodded and retreated back to the bed. 'And you,' the Matriarch-Commissar prodded Steiner in the chest, 'keep your mouth closed.'

Romola didn't take long to fetch a thick travel cloak, a slender book, and small bag. 'Three weeks. Have you any idea how much it costs to feed an entire crew for three weeks while they sit around doing nothing?'

'They haven't been doing nothing,' said Felgenhauer. 'They've been loading on cargo and you'll be very well paid when you deliver it.'

'Three weeks.' Romola rolled her eyes. 'I could be in Svingettevei by now.'

'You could be dead now too,' mumbled Steiner, but neither woman heard him. Felgenhauer wasn't interested in Romola's complaints, striding along the corridor and down the spiralling steps.

'You could at least say thanks,' said Steiner, which produced some interesting words from Romola in a language he'd not heard before. Romola let slip a few more choice phrases when they reached Academy Square. Shirinov and Corpsecandle were waiting for them, flanked by half a dozen soldiers. Ordinary Marozvolk stood to one side in her snarling mask and six soldiers waited behind her, bearing brutal-looking two-handed axes. Behind all of them was Silverdust, who seemed untroubled by the rain, haloed by a strange shimmering. His blank mask was tipped back, as if he were staring into the sky on a fine day.

'Matriarch-Commissar,' said Shirinov, inclining his head in the semblance of a bow. 'I trust you are about to sentence the pirate to death?'

'She's not a pirate,' said Steiner.

'Thank you, boy,' said Felgenhauer, her tone excoriating. 'I was escorting Captain Romola to my office where I intended to terminate her contract with the Empire.' Shirinov attempted to speak but Felgenhauer continued more loudly. 'She will have two days to set sail from Vladibogdan and not return.'

Shirinov turned to Corpsecandle, the latter clearing his throat before Shirinov said, 'This is most unseemly.'

'Unseemly,' agreed Corpsecandle in his mournful tone.

'It seems fine to me,' said Romola. 'I'm sick of the sight of you.' She turned to Felgenhauer. 'All of you. I'll be taking my leave now.'

'As will I,' intoned Shirinov. Steiner's heart lurched in his chest.

'Something you wish to share?' said Felgenhauer.

'I intend to present myself to the Emperor at Khlystburg.' Shirinov stood up straighter. 'So that I might report the many irregularities that have occurred on the island in the last few months.'

The Matriarch-Commissar stepped forward until there was barely an arm's length separating the two Vigilants. 'You would go to Khlystburg and report *me* for *your* failure in Cinderfell?'

The soldiers behind Shirinov shifted and a few clutched at their maces. Steiner wished he had his sledgehammer to hand.

'I don't presume to know the full extent of what is occurring here.' Shirinov gestured towards Steiner and Romola. 'But it is clear to me our leadership is . . . troubled.'

Felgenhauer's loyalists took a step forward, axes glinting by the light of flickering sconces. The Matriarch-Commissar held out a hand to still them.

'Romola,' said Felgenhauer, taking a step back. 'How much to ferry Ordinary Shirinov and Hierarch Khigir to the mainland?'

Romola pressed a thumb to her lip and a frown of deliberation appeared over her narrowed eyes. She sucked down a low breath and winced. 'Well, now that I'm out of contract I'm afraid to say my prices have increased—'

'How much, you filthy pirate?' said Shirinov.

'Significantly.' Romola smiled without humour. 'You might even say exorbitantly.'

'I order you to take me to the coast! I order you as a citizen of the Solmindre Empire—'

Romola held out her hands in mock apology. 'But I'm not a citizen of the Empire. I wouldn't take your rotting carcass a single league across the Spøkelsea for all the coins in Dos Uykhur.'

'Perhaps it's best if you wait on your ship,' said Felgenhauer to Romola.

'I know I'd feel a lot safer down there . . .' Romola walked to the archway of the gatehouse, '. . . than up here.' And with that she flicked out a lazy salute and headed off. Steiner felt a pang of hopelessness as she went.

Shirinov made a strangled noise behind his mask as Felgenhauer departed for Academy Voda. She paused to spare a look over her shoulder.

'Marozvolk. Stay here with your soldiers. Ensure no one goes down to Temnet Cove.' The wolf-masked Vigilant nodded once and took up a position by the gatehouse, the soldiers with axes falling in beside her.

'I don't want anyone smuggling themselves off the island.' The angular mask turned to Steiner. 'Anyone.'

'I thought the soldiers were going to attack each other,' whispered Steiner when they had reached the Matriarch-Commissar's office. Silverdust had followed them to the doors of Academy Voda, a ghostly yet silent presence. He waited in the vestibule and dismissed the soldiers on duty with a nod.

'It's not the soldiers you have to worry about,' said Felgenhauer, closing the door to her office. 'Shirinov is very powerful, and Khigir is tricky. The outcome was anything but assured had Marozvolk and I tried to stop them.'

Steiner swallowed, trying to imagine the scale of arcane destruction as they climbed the stairs to the next floor.

'Would Silverdust have helped you?' he asked when they had reached Felgenhauer's office.

'Difficult to know,' replied Felgenhauer, after a pause. 'He's his own master in a lot of ways, never actively disobedient, just . . . he sees the world differently to you and I.'

'How old is Silverdust?'

'What?' Felgenhauer closed the door to her office. 'Why would you want to know that?'

'I was just curious,' said Steiner, thinking of Silverdust's secret.

'I have no idea. Vigilants rarely share much personal information with each other. He has been on Vladibogdan since before I arrived. That would make him fairly old, I suppose. Why is his age important?'

'Just idle curiosity,' said Steiner as they both dried themselves in front of the fire.

'I'm not going to have you being idly curious, or idle at all,' said Felgenhauer. 'And I don't intend to sit here until that crooked oaf comes whining.'

'Where are we going?' asked Steiner. For a moment he hoped they might leave with Romola, leave the island and all its tensions, but what would happen to Tief, Taiga, Sundra and Kimi?

'We're going to inspect the schools. At times like this the soldiers need to be reminded who is in charge.'

They set off down the stairs, Steiner hurrying behind the long strides of the Matriarch-Commissar.

'Where are we going first?'

'To Academy Zemlya, of course. It's where Shirinov teaches, and most of the Vigilants opposed to me reside there.'

The building was identical in every way to Academy Voda as far as Steiner could determine but the students were more stocky than their counterparts in the other schools.

'An element of the arcane manifests in the physical forms of the student as usage increases,' said the Matriarch-Commissar, as if reciting from a book.

'And what does that mean?' whispered Steiner as they exited one classroom and proceeded along the corridor to another.

'At first, nothing more than a darkening of the skin. Some suffer a deeper discolouration, becoming grey and rough.'

The next class consisted of older children who glowered at Steiner, sullen and sneering. Steiner looked past their expressions for traces of witchsign. All looked dirty, some were the pale brown of a field in drought, others bore an unhealthy hue, pale grey making them sickly. Steiner's mouth became dry as he remembered Matthias Zhirov.

'Matriarch-Commissar, you grace us with your presence,' said a novice, rising from his seat and performing a neat bow.

'And you grace the Empire with your learning, Konstantin,' replied the Matriarch-Commissar, before nodding to the teacher. The Vigilant wore a mask of pitted black metal bearing a grim expression, though the effect was undone by his rounded shoulders as he cowered in the corner.

'He's one of Shirinov's supporters?' said Steiner when they were in the corridor again.

'Ordinary Evtohov. And Konstantin too,' said Felgenhauer, each syllable dripping with scorn.

'What powers do the children have here?'

'A worthy question,' said Felgenhauer, as she stood outside another classroom, listening to the lesson being taught through the door. 'Those born with the power of earth are rarely lost, they always know true north. If trained correctly they can call on great strength and transmute themselves into living rock, as you already know.'

Steiner nodded and said nothing.

'A fully trained Vigilant can lift objects from the ground with their mind,' said the Matriarch-Commissar.

'As Shirinov did with Maxim.'

Felgenhauer nodded. 'The most powerful of us can petrify flesh with a look.'

Two soldiers stood guard at the end of the corridor and Felgenhauer appraised each in turn. The Matriarch-Commissar reeled off a string of words in Solska, the volume and tone indicating her displeasure.

'What was that about?' asked Steiner as they exited the academy.

'I told them to polish their boots, wash their cloaks, and bathe more frequently. If they can't be loyal to me they can at least look like soldiers.'

Academy Plamya was no different, providing one had no sense of smell.

'What is that?'

'Sulphur,' replied Felgenhauer. 'Children born with the power of fire often bear unfortunate odours. I once knew a man who smelled faintly of woodsmoke . . .' The Matriarch-Commissar tailed off and Steiner looked around.

'Are you unwell?'

'What?' asked Felgenhauer. 'No. Fine. As I was saying, unfortunate. Most smell of sulphur, I believe they call it brimstone in Khlystburg.'

Felgenhauer was less interested in the classes here, and her attention focused on the soldiers, delivering stern rebukes.

'What powers do these children have?' asked Steiner as they climbed another flight of stairs.

'See for yourself,' replied Felgenhauer, gesturing to a wide room bereft of furnishings. With good reason as it turned out. Three children of about fourteen stood side by side, breathing fire in unison, just as Aurelian had.

'I think we should leave,' said Steiner, mouth dry and pulse hammering in his veins.

'Not yet,' countered Felgenhauer. Another child in the corner of the room stood before the novices, naked yet oblivious to embarrassment.

'What in Frejna's name is going on—'

Felgenhauer held up a finger to the angular mask's mouth. 'Watch.'

The naked novice bloomed into a living tongue of fire, a swirl of orange and red flame.

'That's terrifying,' whispered Steiner.

'Fire is the greatest of the dragon's gifts. The ability to summon it and breathe it, to command choking clouds of smoke, to cast flame as if it were a javelin. And to be immune to it. When the Emperor orders these children to march on Shanisrond it will be as if the dragons themselves have returned.'

Felgenhauer turned away and descended the stairs, leaving Steiner to grow increasingly uncomfortable under the smouldering gazes of the novices.

'I suppose you heard about Zhirov too,' he muttered.

The Matriarch-Commissar was waiting outside Academy Vozdukha when Steiner caught up with her. She stood before the door, hands clasped in the small of her back, chin raised.

'You're not going in?'

'No point.' Felgenhauer regarded the natural rock far above Academy Square. 'The Vigilants take the novices up to the cliffs unless the rain is fierce. They say they can't teach the wind if they can't feel it on their faces. I say they're all far gone with drink and madness.'

'Is this where Silverdust lives?'

'Not exactly. Silverdust doesn't teach, and he channels the powers of both wind and fire. No one knows where Silverdust lives, he just exists.' Felgenhauer started off before Steiner had a chance to voice his questions.

'What does Voda mean?' he called out to her as she crossed the threshold of the last academy.

She turned slowly as he mounted the steps. 'It's the Solska word for water.'

'But the arcane power for the water school doesn't come from dragons.' Steiner felt strangely proud of this tiny fleck of knowledge.

'Quite the expert,' said Felgenhauer, her tone unimpressed. 'Knowing such things will get you killed in the Empire. Unless you're a Vigilant.'

'I, ah, I must have overheard that somewhere. Can't remember where.' Steiner forced a smile and shrugged.

'Academy Voda is where they send children born with the power of water,' said Felgenhauer in a quiet voice. 'The Empire's style of teaching does not suit the novices. We encourage them to use other powers, other disciplines.'

'It's not like we need Vigilants summoning rain, is it?' said Steiner, looking to the skies.

'Very few of the water novices graduate,' replied Felgenhauer.

'Why?'

'Because very few of the water novices survive the first year.'

Steiner rolled over in bed, kicking at sheets that clung to his legs.

Zhirov.

He slipped from the bed, hissing as the flagstones chilled his naked feet.

'I didn't ask him to come down to the furnaces,' mumbled Steiner, blinking awake in the darkened room. He stepped onto the sheepskin and fetched the poker to stir the fire. The door handle rattled and he straightened up slowly, grip tightening on the poker as if it were a sword.

'Who's there?' he whispered.

No answer, the handle rattled again but he'd locked the door and didn't care to open it. A sliver of parchment slid through the gap at the bottom. Steiner's heart beat loud in his chest but his curiosity outweighed his fear. He snatched up the note, knowing even as he raised it to his eyes the words would make no sense. The loops and whorls of ink performed a lazy dance on the parchment and Steiner growled in frustration.

'What in Frøya's name is this?'

Britches were pulled on, his boots left unlaced. He was still clutching the poker when he unlocked the door and emerged into the corridor.

'Hoy there,' muttered one of the soldiers from a few feet away.

'Hoy,' replied Steiner and set the poker down in his room lest his intentions be misunderstood. He didn't trust the soldier, but he didn't need to start a fight.

'Did you see who came by here?'

The soldier shook his head. 'We just changed shifts, though I saw Ordinary Marozvolk just a moment ago.' Steiner breathed with relief that the soldier knew Nordsspråk. He regarded the note and the swirls of script so unclear to him.

'What does it say?' pressed the soldier.

Steiner held it out to him. 'I can't . . .' said Steiner. 'I can't read.'

'It is from the Matriarch-Commissar,' said the soldier after a brief glance. 'It says you are to gather your things and go to Temnet Cove and depart with the privateer.'

'What? That's impossible.' Steiner frowned. All his hopes for escape had been answered in one simple note, stuffed under his door in the dead of night. 'When?'

'Tonight,' said the soldier.

'I should . . . I should say goodbye to Felgenhauer.'

'She is not here,' said the soldier. 'She had some business with Silverdust. I'd go this very minute if I were you. The pirate will not wait long.'

CHAPTER TWENTY-EIGHT

Steiner

While novices rarely form a bond with the Vigilants that train them, they do cultivate lifelong allies with novices of similar ages. This should not be mistaken for friendship. A Vigilant cannot enjoy such a luxury. There are only comrades in the eyes of the Empire. Even family comes second to the will of the Emperor.

– From the field notes of Hierarch Khigir,
Vigilant of the Imperial Synod.

Steiner felt no loss for Academy Voda as he exited the double doors, pausing only to pick up a lantern. He descended the steps to Academy Square, gaze drawn to the darkened alley leading to the furnaces. It would take many minutes to descend to where Kimi and Tief slumbered. He lost a moment in the gloom, breath steaming on the air, thinking of Taiga and Sundra and how badly he wanted to say goodbye to them. The roiling fire of the dragon statue set Steiner's shadow writhing across the cobbles, flickering uncertainly in one direction and then another. It would be just his luck for Romola to cast off without him while he said his farewells, he decided.

Soldiers appeared out of the gloom, startling him into action.

He bowed his head against the rain and trudged across the square to the gatehouse and the black steps beyond. Marozvolk had retired for the night. The soldiers on duty bore maces, not the axes he'd seen earlier.

'I have a letter from the Matriarch-Commissar,' he said, holding up the parchment that had wilted in the rain. The soldiers grunted at him in Solska. One of them nodded he should pass.

Steiner stared from one soldier to the other, expecting either of them to stop him. He couldn't believe he was headed for Cinderfell, couldn't believe he'd be home with his father and Kjellrunn.

The soldiers jerked a thumb over their shoulders towards the ship and Steiner slunk beneath the arch, picking his way down the many steps. The bleak rock of Temnet Cove was darker than the night itself. The *Watcher's Wait* nestled against the pier, the water around it dappled with a halo of gold lantern light.

Steiner took a deep breath. He was going home. Back to Kjellrunn and his father. Back to Verner. He'd embrace each of them, tell them that nothing mattered except being together. He'd tell them they'd been right to send him and not Kjell. He'd find a way of keeping his sister safe from Shirinov. They'd need to leave Cinderfell of course, that was a given. Not a soul in the drab grey town would speak to him after all that had happened. No one came back from an Invigilation; it would be as if he'd returned from the dead.

Steiner held the lantern higher and blinked into the darkness. Two statues flanked the bottom of the steps, sculptures of young men looking out to sea in heroic poses bearing spears. He thought briefly of Felgenhauer's ability to turn people to stone but an unknown dread stilled his furtive steps. The statues had not been here when he arrived, of that he was sure.

The pier had a selection of crates dotted here and there.

Steiner squinted past the limit of the light's reach. The rain pattered down as he wondered if it was hope or naivety that had led him here. Had he really trusted his escape to a scrap of parchment he couldn't read? Had Marozvolk delivered it as he'd hoped? Would Felgenhauer give him leave to escape the island, now that he knew all of the Empire's secrets?

Steiner held up the sodden parchment to the lantern light, watching the ink spread across the page in blurry stains. The words, always so hard to read, were being washed away with all his hopes. The note fluttered from his grasp as he realized something was dreadfully wrong.

'Shit,' he whispered. A chill wind blew hard into the cove and shrieked past the gatehouse, taking the note with it. He looked back to the source of the sound, knowing he had to climb the many worn and slippery steps, knowing he had to sneak back to bed.

'I should have known you'd be involved in this,' said Steiner. Aurelian was standing halfway down the black steps, a look of sneering victory curling his lip.

'I really thought I was going home, you little bastard,' said Steiner, hands balling into fists.

'No one goes home,' replied Aurelian. 'Not me, not you, not anyone.' He descended the steps, unhurried and confident.

'I'm not dying because of some jumped-up merchant's son from Helwick.'

Steiner dared a quick look over his shoulder and had his suspicions confirmed. The two statues turned to face him, brandishing their spears, while another figure on the pier emerged from beneath a tarpaulin.

'Can't fault your thinking,' said Steiner. 'If three novices won't work then best bring four.'

'Did you leave your precious hammer somewhere?' said Aurelian. Steiner cursed himself. The sledgehammer had been left by Kimi's workstation and he'd not had a chance to retrieve it. 'Such a shame,' added the blond-haired boy. 'Matthias Zhirov sends his regards.'

Aurelian spread his arms and splayed his fingers, breathing deep. Soon the glow of draconic fire would appear in his throat. Steiner ran down the steps and drew back his right arm, teeth gritted. The granite-skinned novice grinned, knowing he was impervious to flesh and bone; he had nothing to fear from Steiner's fist. It was strange to hear the fearsome boy yelp as Steiner smashed the lantern into his face, the oil dowsing his nose and chin, igniting in a burst of orange.

Steiner suffered a moment of sharp pain in his hand, broken glass from the lantern he guessed. He had no time to check, dodging aside to avoid the savage thrust from the other spear-wielding boy. Steiner had no idea if the fire would harm his attacker, but the boy stumbled around all the same, clawing at his face, spear discarded on the stone steps. Steiner snatched up the weapon and swung on instinct, as if clutching his sledgehammer. The wooden shaft snapped in two as it met the granite neck of the other boy.

'That was stupid,' grunted Steiner. He scrambled backwards up a few steps before remembering Aurelian, turning just in time to see the torrent of fire rolling towards him. Steiner threw himself off the step and time slowed. Several sensations vied for his attention at once. The way his heart kicked fitfully in his chest; the wash of singeing heat across his back; the burning novice stumbling into his comrade. There was a strange jolt as Steiner found himself standing at the base of the steps, smock smoking in the night air.

Aurelian stared at him in disbelief. How he hadn't broken an ankle was a mystery. Steiner threw up an obscene gesture and ran, tilting forward, arms pumping, eyes set on the *Watcher's Wait* at the pier's end, heedless of everything. Heedless of the cruel-eyed girl who stood between him and the ship, heedless of her high-pitched shriek.

The swarm of bats swept down from the cliffs and Steiner staggered as the leathery wings buffeted him, stalling his progress. He stumbled as furred bodies impacted on his arms, face, head and chest. The bright sting of ripping claws and sharp teeth made him cry out. He was engulfed in a cloud of them, unsure which way he was headed. And then he was in the water, the chill depths forcing the air from his lungs. The taste of brine invaded his mouth, his legs kicked and thrashed, not knowing which way was up in the darkness. The sea gave way to cold air as he breached the surface, gasping down breaths.

'Over here!' said a voice close by. Steiner blinked seawater out of his eyes as Aurelian reached the edge of the pier, an orange glow building at his throat. Steiner dived, forcing cold limbs against the dark water, feeling the swell and chop carry him towards the cliffs. The water became bright, forcing Steiner to redouble his efforts. There could be no going back now. Another burst of flame overhead, illuminating the waters and the rocks beneath. Steiner dared one more breath, snatched from the surface, then dived for his life, away from the novices sent to ambush him.

The darkness might have been total if not for the glittering stones of the quartz cave and the orange glow of the fire pit. Steiner squatted down and poked the coals, shivering violently, but the fire was spent and the cave's icy chill settled into his bones.

'Kimi,' was all he said from between chattering teeth.

The corridor was long, much longer than he remembered. He spent fearful minutes feeling his way along rough stone walls before a glow appeared in the unlit fastness.

'Kimi?' he croaked, stumbling towards the light. The heat of the furnaces brushed against him as he trudged on, eyes closed, shivering against clothes scorched yet soaking. On he went until the heat was all around, pressing against him, leeching his strength until he was on his knees. His eyes fluttered open to see Kimi, Tief and Taiga, expressions both stern and shocked.

'So many cuts,' breathed Taiga.

'Let's get him out of those clothes,' said Tief. 'Quick now. He's dying.'

Kimi said nothing, stepping forward to enfold him in her arms. Steiner closed his eyes.

'I was so foolish,' he whispered, thinking of the scrap of parchment. His eyelids fell closed and the motion of Kimi's long strides was all he knew.

Steiner woke to a silent forge. No din of hammers beating steel, no thump of crates being stacked and loaded, no hiss of metal quenched in water. He curled in a ball on his side, body a dirge of pain. For a time he tried to ignore it, but everything hurt and rolling onto his back only made it worse. He pushed himself up, eyes wide with disbelief, regarding arms swaddled in bandages. Spots of red had bled through, so dark they were almost black on the cream fabric. The light and heat of Kimi's giant furnace was like the dawn of a summer's day.

Tief, Taiga and Sundra were all adoze, slumped in a huddle beneath blankets. They sat with their backs to a large crate, arms folded or hands resting in their laps, heads nodding on their chests. Sundra snored quietly, which did much to undo her otherworldly imperiousness. A ghost of a smile crossed Steiner's lips before weakness insisted he lay down. It was the usual bed of sack cloth, far from the cotton sheets and mattress he had enjoyed in the academy.

'So, you've led us a merry dance,' said Kimi, her face suddenly very close to his.

'Do the Yamal dance?' asked Steiner.

'Not much,' admitted Kimi. 'But it's an expression I've heard Tief use and I've always liked it.'

'Was I any good?' said Steiner, wincing at the pain in his arms. 'At this merry dance?'

'There was plenty of blood, on account of all the cuts. Sundra guessed it for the work of bats. Was she right?'

Steiner nodded.

'Your back is burned and it will be a long time until your hair grows back. Your clothes are ruined, naturally.'

'What's all this? Is he awake?' Tief pushed himself to his feet with a grunt and took a moment to work the kinks out of his back. 'We don't see you for weeks and when you finally turn up you're half dead. Typical house guest. Never show up unless they need something.' Tief edged forward and broke into a broad smile. 'I wasn't sure we'd ever see you again. Better we see you half dead than not at all, I suppose.'

'I'm not sure I agree.'

The many cinderwraiths congregated at the edge of the dais in a vigil. Rank after rank of them formed an array of smoky silhouettes, all watching with gently glowing eyes.

'They've been very anxious,' said Kimi, nodding towards the mass of spirits. Steiner opened his mouth to speak as his eyes fell on Kimi's shoulder. She was not wearing her customary leather apron and her shoulder was bound up in bandages, much like his own.

'The soldiers . . .' he whispered, reaching out to her. She enfolded his hand in her palm, a gentle smile on her broad face. 'I'm so sorry.'

'Hush now. I started something I couldn't finish.' She rolled her eyes. 'No change there.'

'I should go,' said Steiner, 'before anyone else gets hurt. Shirinov may send more soldiers . . .' But the effort required to stand was beyond him. He closed his eyes and lost track of time. Felgenhauer and Maxim stood before him when he blinked awake.

'You look terrible,' said the Matriarch-Commissar.

'Really terrible,' agreed Maxim. 'Like dead terrible.'

'Either I'm dreaming,' said Steiner, 'or Sundra gave me a remedy with some vivid side effects.'

'You are not dreaming,' said Felgenhauer. 'Maxim snuck up to inform me of your whereabouts.'

'You've been down here the whole time?' said Steiner to the boy, aggrieved rather than incredulous.

'The Matriarch-Commissar said it would be useful to have a pair of eyes in the forge, to make sure no more soldiers came down making trouble.'

Steiner smiled. Of the whimpering boy he'd met in the hold of the *Watcher's Wait* there was no sign.

'You're a spy.'

'An observer,' countered Felgenhauer.

Kimi pressed a damp cloth to Steiner's forehead.

'Is Romola . . . ?'

'Still at anchor,' said the Matriarch-Commissar, 'despite Aurelian's fiery display. What happened?'

'There were two novices from Academy Zemlya. I think I may have set fire to one of them.'

'I doubt it,' said Felgenhauer. 'Rock does not burn.'

'And the girl who can summon bats, she was there. That's how I came by all these cuts.'

'Academy Vozdukha. Shirinov has been recruiting widely, and from the young and talented.' Felgenhauer sighed with irritation. 'Why were you in Temnet Cove? Did you think you could escape?'

'Can I get a hand here?' said Steiner, and Kimi helped him to his feet, propping him against the anvil.

'I received a letter,' said Steiner, clearing his throat. 'I had one of the soldiers read it and he said it came from you.'

Felgenhauer took a step closer. 'What letter?'

Tief shook his head and pressed a hand to his brow. 'Now you've started something.'

'A letter was pushed under my door. It said I could leave with Romola.'

'Who forged a letter in my name?' said Felgenhauer, and a terrible anger sounded in each word.

'I don't know,' admitted Steiner. 'But I didn't realize it was a trap until I'd almost sprung it. I'm the living proof of Shirinov's mistake. That's why he hates me, and that's why you've kept me so close the last three weeks.'

Felgenhauer had balled her gloved hands into fists. 'Yes, I admit it. I have been protecting you.'

'I have to get back to Cinderfell before he does,' said Steiner. 'If he can't kill me he'll kill my family.' It was a half a truth, but it hurt to tell a half-lie to Felgenhauer after everything she'd done for him.

'I am the Matriarch-Commissar of Vladibogdan, Steiner. You know things about the Empire that people have died for. I cannot send you on your way with my blessing. You must stay here.'

For a second he imagined she might say she was sorry, but the silence stretched out between them and everyone had a look of despondency. For a second they'd all hoped Felgenhauer might let him go.

Steiner grimaced and pushed himself off the anvil. 'You think I'm going to stand by and watch you let Shirinov hunt down my family. It won't be long until the next supply ship arrives and he'll leave.'

'I'll forbid him from setting sail.'

'He'll disobey you.' Steiner's vision swam with darkness, dizzy from losing so much blood, but he forced himself to stand all the same. 'He's already bragged about razing Helwick and Cinderfell. It's only a matter of time until he gets to me too, and then . . .' Steiner gestured to the throng of cinderwraiths, all still and ominous, hundreds of unblinking glowing eyes in the darkness. 'I'll be like these lost souls.'

'I can't allow it, Steiner.' All sternness was leached from the Matriarch-Commissar's tone, the words loaded with resignation. 'You have to stay on Vladibogdan.'

'Then I'm as a good as dead,' snarled Steiner.

'I forbid you from leaving this cavern,' said the Matriarch-Commissar. 'Shirinov thinks you're dead. Let's not disabuse him of that notion.' She stepped closer. 'Stay. Here.' She punctuated each word with one finger, prodding his chest.

'I have to get to my sister . . .' he said, but Felgenhauer didn't hear him, she'd already turned on her heel and gestured to Maxim. The boy snatched a worried glance at Steiner and ran to keep up with the Matriarch-Commissar.

'I have to get back back to Kjellrunn,' whispered Steiner to Kimi. 'You can understand that, can't you?'

Kimi nodded and wrapped an arm about his shoulders.

'I'd do anything to keep my family safe,' said Taiga.

'And what will you do when you reach Cinderfell?' asked Tief, full of scorn. 'You can barely stand. You can't fight the Empire, and they will never stop hunting you and your family.'

'I don't know what to do,' admitted Steiner, 'but my father will. I can't stay here while Shirinov plots his next move.

'Did you hear me?' said Tief. 'You can barely stand.'

'Wrong,' said Sundra. 'He can barely stand unaided. There's no telling what a person can do with the right help.' The priestess of Frejna approached and Steiner felt a chill of anxiety.

'Kneel,' said Sundra. 'We must invoke the goddess.'

'But I don't believe.'

'Not yet,' said Sundra. 'But you will.'

CHAPTER TWENTY-NINE

Steiner

The death priestesses of the Spriggani are by far the most unnerving people I have ever encountered in any province of Solmindre, almost a match for the horrors of Izhoria. Many are fakers and pretend to powers they do not possess, but some of them are the equal of the highest-ranking Vigilant.

– From the field notes of Hierarch Khigir,
Vigilant of the Imperial Synod.

Steiner slipped to his knees before Sundra and let out a long sigh.

'I'm dead on my feet after all.'

'You are not dead,' intoned Sundra as she drew closer.

'It's a figure of speech, not be taken . . .' Sundra pressed her forehead against his and clasped the sides of his head with both hands. '. . . Uh, literally.' He swallowed and tried to snatch a glance at Kimi, but his vision was filled with Sundra's face, from her small and pointed nose, to the delicate and narrow eyes, now closed. Her hands were icy against his ears and her scent teased at his recognition, a scent he'd not sampled in far too long. She smelled like woodlands, she smelled like Kjellrunn.

'What are we doing, Sundra?'

'We are shutting up and concentrating.'

Steiner waited, thinking how awkward he must look to
Kimi, Tief and Taiga.

'Yes, yes. You are uncomfortable and this is strange. Try to
let go of all these thoughts.' Her voice was low, the usual
note of scolding replaced by something warmer. 'Let go of
the cavern, let go of the island.' Her voice was barely more
than a whisper. 'Let go of all the tension within. Your shoulders, your neck.' She drew a deep breath and Steiner found
himself doing the same. 'Your heart.'

Steiner tried as best he could, despite aching knees and the
many cuts on his arms and face. Every muscle droned with
a dull pain. The image of a woodland in autumn came to
mind with a sky of pale blue, a sky the likes of which he had
rarely seen in all his years in Cinderfell. The trees reached
up with bare branches, imploring the spring to return while
a sliver of a stream reflected silver in the sunlight. Sundra's
fragrance was all these things. The gentle sweetness of leaves
decomposing, of rich earth churned by hooves, the first scent
of rain before it falls, the sharpness in the air before snowfall.

'I'm in a forest,' he whispered. And he was, kneeling before
Sundra in a nameless woodland beneath a sky he yearned
to see.

'Hush now,' urged the priestess. 'The bones whisper your
name. I see you. Your burdens are the greater wound, not
these trifles playing out across the flesh.'

'Burdens?' said Steiner in a whisper.

'The conflict you feel for your family.'

'But, there is no conflict,' replied Steiner. 'They're my family.
They're all I have. I'm here to protect Kjellrunn.'

'So why this heavy burden over your heart? I see it, like
a shadow in the morning, like woodsmoke, like darkness.'

'They sent me here.' The words were too difficult to say.

More vast than the trees standing over him, sharper than the thorns on the bushes, colder than the stream rippling past. 'My father. He chose Kjell to stay, but not me.'

'And you miss him?'

'Of course. I miss working with him, and the smithy, and dinner with Kjell. I miss . . . all of it.'

'How much do you miss it?'

'Bitterly.'

'This is your problem.' Sundra turned her back on him and paced some way into the clearing. 'Nothing flourishes in bitterness. He sent you here to do something Kjellrunn could not.'

'I don't understand,' said Steiner, heart heavy in his chest, face flushed with all he held back.

'Endure, Steiner. He sent you to endure. He sent you to survive that which Kjellrunn could not. Not once have you fallen to an enemy. You may slip and you may stumble but you do not fall. Steiner means stone in the old dialects; as it is so are you. Your father sent you here to endure because he trusted you to do so.'

Steiner drew a shaky breath and thought back to Kjellrunn, how she'd never shown any sign of the arcane, how he'd never witnessed anything untoward. Mainly he thought of how she'd never told him, never shared her secret with him.

'You are angry with her,' said Sundra. 'It is the way of siblings. We nurse grudges and resentments towards our kin while hoping all the while no evil befalls them.'

'If she were here then I'd still be in Cinderfell . . .' His words tailed off as the shame of his admission crushed him.

'She was not ready to come to the island,' said Sundra. 'She would have perished, just as Felgenhauer told you, just as your father told you.'

'I understand,' said Steiner. 'I've always understood. I just . . .'

'Felt bitter about it,' said Sundra quietly.

Steiner nodded and felt tears sting the corners of his eyes. He sucked down a breath and tried to stifle the deep well of unhappiness he felt.

A clutch of snowdrops emerged from the earth, bringing hints of green and white to the endless brown and gold of the woods.

'Good, Steiner, good,' said Sundra. 'Let go of your burdens.'

'She wasn't ready to come to the island.' He was so tired, even in this place, it was all he could do to stare at the flowers. 'My father never put me in danger, he always took the utmost care of me in the smithy, always made sure Kjellrunn and I had enough to eat when money was scarce.'

More snowdrops pushed their way through the earth, spears of green blooming white at their tips. All around, snowdrops pushed their way through the earth until the woodland was no longer a place of barren decay, but vibrant and lush with the promise of seasons to come.

'Even when I came to Vladibogdan he gave me a hammer to fight with and sturdy boots.'

Steiner raised his head to see the trees had transformed, splendid in their greenery, the leaves whispering in a susurrus of joy.

'Hammersmith!' Steiner opened his eyes, but it was not Sundra that stood before him but Tief. 'You've been kneeling here for half an hour with that damn fool stupid smile on your face. Are you going to come back to the land of the living?'

'I'd have preferred to stay in the woods.'

'On that we can agree,' replied Tief. 'You're going to need this.' He handed Steiner the sledgehammer and Steiner smiled as his fist closed upon the handle.

'My great-grandfather's hammer.'

Tief paused a moment and tugged at one ear. 'Sundra took

you to the woods then?' He looked at Steiner from the corner
of his eye.

'You've been there too?'

'Of course I've been there. It's an echo of where we grew
up, where we lived.'

Steiner blinked and looked at Kimi, who knelt beside him.

'How do you feel?' she said, taking one of his hands in
her own.

'Well, nothing hurts.' He began to unwrap the bandages
on his arms and found not cuts weeping blood, but faint
marks of scarlet.

'I'm covered in scars,' he whispered.

'Frejna is the goddess of death,' said Sundra from beside
Kimi's anvil, one hand resting on the metal to support herself.
Taiga stood close with a hand to her sister's back. 'Wounds
are one of her provinces, yet she will not take the memory
of pain. We all need reminders. You will need to remember
this moment if you are to endure as your father wishes.'

Steiner approached the priestess, bending to kiss her softly
on each cheek.

'Yes, yes, enough with that.' She waved him away. 'You
are chosen, it seems. The bones—'

'Whisper my name?' said Steiner with a smile.

'And now you must live up to their promise,' replied Sundra,
her usual stern demeanour firmly in place.

'But how?' asked Steiner.

'Only you can know that,' replied Sundra. 'The goddess
played her part, as did I, and Kimi and Taiga. What happens
now is up to you.'

Steiner slept for a good long time and woke from dreams of
forests and open blue skies. He paused to wash, marvelling
at the tracery of scars that crossed his skin. He spied his
reflection in the water and found himself near-unrecognizable.

His hair was no more than stubble and his face bore a motley of bruises.

Fresh clothes had been laid out for him, hardly new but clean at least. He slipped on his boots and took up his sledge-hammer.

No sooner had he grasped the stout wooden handle than a small stone rolled into the room and abruptly changed course, rolling in a tight circle, once, twice, three times.

'What in Hel?

And then the stone rolled back the way it had come. Steiner followed, frowning in disbelief. What strangeness was this? What minor miracle of the arcane? And why?

The stone sphere rolled between the furnaces, weaving and rolling ever onward. Steiner trailed after it, struggling to keep up as he dodged around cinderwraiths and stacks of crates.

'Ah, you're up then,' said Tief, who was sitting on the edge of the dais, fixing his pipe for a smoke.

'Yes, I . . .' Steiner squinted into the darkness. 'I have to go and . . .'

He marched on, almost running now. Tief grumbled something but Steiner paid no mind to it, following the rolling stone all the way along the wide corridor and down to the dragons.

'So it was you who sent the stone?'

Sundra stood beside the silvery dragon, one hand against the beast's chest, her eyes closed in deep concentration. They made quite the pair, Sundra all in black and adorned with bones, while the dragon appeared to be brighter and larger than before.

'Are you healing her wounds the same way you healed mine?' asked Steiner.

'As best I can,' said Sundra, dropping her hand.

Steiner knelt down and picked up the stone that had led him. It was black, he realized, and perfectly smooth.

'Obsidian,' said Sundra, holding out her hand. 'It was my mother's, before the Empire came and killed her.'

'I'm sorry,' said Steiner. 'My own mother left when I was very young.'

Sundra nodded and a moment of silent understanding passed between them.

'Why did you send your stone for me? Why not send Tief or Taiga?'

'Because what I have to say is for your ears alone.'

Sundra began a slow walk around the dank cavern, taking in the other dragons, sometimes running a hand over their limbs where a chain or manacle had chafed them. Steiner could feel only horror, not the horror he expected in the presence of dragons, but at the hideous cruelty the creatures were subjected to.

'And what is it that you want to say?' he asked almost reverently.

'Tief gave up looking for a way out a long time ago. He gave up looking for himself, and he gave up looking for all of us.' Sundra caught Steiner's eye and he struggled not to shiver despite the room's heat. There was an awful chill to the stern look on her face. 'Taiga is as dutiful as she is beautiful. It wouldn't occur to her to leave me to escape by herself, just as it wouldn't occur to her to look for a way in the first place.'

'Why are you telling me this?' said Steiner as the priestess stopped beside another dragon. She smoothed down its ragged wings and crooned something in a language Steiner hadn't heard before.

'I am telling you because I see you. I see how Kimi looks at you. I see how protective you are of the boy Maxim, and your loyalty to Felgenhauer, though goddess knows she doesn't deserve it.'

'But that's not a bad thing.' He hadn't noticed Kimi looking at him in any particular way, but he didn't mention it.

'It is a bad thing, Steiner. It is the worst thing.' Sundra grabbed him by the shoulders and scowled. 'All of this, all of Vladibogdan, is becoming normal to you. The academies are normal, the arcane is becoming normal—'

'The arcane will never be normal to me!'

'And yet I summoned you here with an obsidian marble.' Sundra rolled the smooth stone between thumb and fore-finger. 'And not once did you think it was something best avoided. You followed willingly.'

'Well, I mean, sure. But I never said it was normal.'

'Even this.' Sundra gestured to the captive dragons, chained against their pillars, sinuous necks held fast, mighty jaws pointed towards the ceiling. 'Even this is becoming normal to you.'

'Never,' whispered Steiner, eyeing the horror all about him.

'You have to be the one to escape, Steiner. No one else will do this thing. You must get back to the mainland and take your sister far to the south, away from Shirinov, away from Vladibogdan, away from us.'

'But you're my friends. I can't leave you. Look, we'll find a way to get onto Romola's ship and—'

Sundra placed her cold fingers on his lips and silenced him with a shake of her head. 'Loyalty is a fine, fine thing, and comes at a steep, steep cost. The bones whisper your name, they whisper you'll do something never seen before, they whisper to me in the dead of night when I am asleep. They speak to me dreams and they speak to me upon waking.'

'And what if they're wrong?'

Sundra gave a bleak smile. 'Then we are all of us dead, and to no good end. Your sister too in time, and your father and uncle.'

'I suppose the bones told you that too, did they?' said Steiner, flushed with anger.

Sundra nodded and pursed her lips. 'Hold on to that

anger, it will see you through hard times, but don't let it
consume you.'

Steiner headed back to the furnaces with a heavy heart,
gripping onto the sledgehammer handle, feeling the weight
of the weapon as if it were the very dilemma Sundra had just
put upon his shoulders.

Maxim appeared out of the gloom and Kimi stepped down
from the dais to greet him. She caught sight of Steiner and
flashed him a broad smile.

'Look who I found sneaking about.' She ruffled Maxim's
hair and he ducked away, looking affronted.

'I thought you'd gone back to the surface with Felgenhauer?'
said Steiner.

'I did,' said Maxim, 'but she sent me down here to tell you
that Romola cast off today.' Steiner felt as if the ground
beneath his feet shifted slightly.

'No.'

The boy nodded, a look of regret like sickness on his face.
'And another ship was seen on the horizon. An Imperial ship.'

'Coming here?'

Maxim nodded again. 'I'm afraid so.'

Kimi took Steiner's hand in her own. 'They'll be no stopping
Shirinov from leaving now.'

'Felgenhauer will stop him,' said Steiner, though he didn't
believe it.

Kimi shook her head. 'You'd better hope she does, or that
sister of yours will fetch up on Vladibogdan in no time at all.'

CHAPTER THIRTY

Kjellrunn

A soldier of the Solmindre Empire is more than just a blunt tool to bully the population into obedience. Soldiers see much and hear much of what is best left unknown by the peasantry. When a soldier joins the Imperial army he swears an oath of loyalty that lasts a lifetime. Should that loyalty diminish then the Empire ensures the corresponding soldier also diminishes. This is why one rarely sees retired soldiers.

– From the field notes of Hierarch Khigir,
Vigilant of the Imperial Synod.

'This is exactly what we need.' Mistress Kamalov stalked from window to hearth and back again. Kjellrunn had pressed herself up against the wall to give the woman, and her pacing, some much needed room.

'Your father gets drunk, flies into a rage at the tavern owner, then is chased home by Okhrana—'

'We don't know for sure that the horsemen are Okhrana,' said Kjellrunn, aware of how unconvincing she sounded.

'Did you think they would announce themselves? Always someone is spying, Kjellrunn,' Mistress Kamalov lectured with a wagging finger. 'Always the Empire is watching.' The old woman turned to the window once more and squinted through the dirty glass. 'Sometimes you can reason with a spy and sometimes . . .' Mistress Kamalov fixed her headscarf, threw open the door, and marched out into the clearing. 'You can come inside,' she shouted. 'I know you are here.'

Silence. Only the wind provided a reply, gusting through the trees like the voice of a frail old man moaning at the terrible cold.

Kjellrunn approached the door and gazed at each snow-laden tree and the many logs and branches littering the ground. She held her breath and waited for the horsemen to swagger from their hiding places. Would they bring cold steel or only dangerous words? Would they kill Mistress Kamalov or take Kjellrunn to Vladibogdan before she was ready?

'I have fire and I have tea from Yamal,' said Mistress Kamalov, adopting a friendlier tone. 'You may as well show yourself or you will have neither.'

No response expect for the distant call of crows.

'You must be very cold.'

A rustling in a nearby bush disclosed Kristofine, who pulled herself free of the branches and shook the snow off her shoulders with a scowl. Her feet became tangled in the scrub and she stumbled a moment before collecting herself, a look of chagrin on her face.

'You followed me?' said Kjellrunn.

'You wouldn't tell me who your mysterious friend is,' said Kristofine. 'And there's nothing for me to do in Cinderfell any more.'

'Nothing to do?' said Mistress Kamalov. 'Not a problem, I have many chores for you and Kjellrunn could use the help.' Kjellrunn blinked. Mistress Kamalov had become the tall and imperious woman she had witnessed at the butcher's shop. Kristofine eyed the older woman warily from the corner of her eye and said nothing. 'Now, do you want tea or not?'

'And who might you be?' said Kristofine. 'With your fancy tea from Yamal.'

Kjellrunn winced, waiting for the rebuke, but Mistress Kamalov grinned and clapped her hands.

'Pretty and spirited! Too spirited for a miserable town like this. Come!' Mistress Kamalov gestured. 'And close the door, I have no wish for any more unexpected visitors today.'

'This is Kristofine,' said Kjellrunn once they were inside the chalet. 'She and Steiner were courting. Briefly.'

'Very briefly,' added Kristofine, tucking her hair behind one ear as a slow blush crossed her face.

'And now you come to the old woman in the woods to get your boy back from the Empire.'

Kristofine looked at Kjellrunn, keen not to say the wrong thing. Kjellrunn didn't doubt that Mistress Kamalov still believed Steiner was dead, but she'd rather the old woman kept such thoughts to herself. Kjellrunn shook her head, warning Kristofine off the subject.

'I just wanted to make sure Kjellrunn was safe,' lied Kristofine.

Mistress Kamalov scowled and took Kristofine's head in her hands, angling her jaw this way and then that. 'You lie badly.' The old woman ran her fingertips over Kristofine's scalp and pulled on her earlobes gently. 'Open your mouth.' Kristofine paused and dared an anxious glance at Kjellrunn. 'I won't hurt you, foolish girl. Open your mouth!'

Kristofine did as she was told and Mistress Kamalov inspected her teeth and then took a step back, before giving a satisfied nod and a grunt.

'You do not have witchsign.'

'What?' Kristofine wrapped her arms around herself, a look of affront on her face. 'How can you tell?'

'You do not have witchsign,' repeated Mistress Kamalov. 'But this is why you have nothing to do, yes? The fine folk of Cinderfell think you have the taint, all because you tumbled with Steiner.'

Kristofine looked at Kjellrunn, annoyed and surprised.

'I didn't tell her,' protested Kjellrunn. 'She just knows things. You may as well get used to it if you're going to come sneaking after me each day.'

'Steiner doesn't have witchsign either,' continued Mistress Kamalov. 'But I can't give any guarantees for your babies.'

'Babies?' Kristofine was suddenly deathly pale. Her hands went to her stomach and Kjellrunn blinked in surprise. Mistress Kamalov frowned a moment, then let out a howl of laughter that made Kjellrunn jump. She took a few moments to compose herself.

'It was a joke. You are not pregnant, foolish girl. At least I don't think you are pregnant.' Mistress Kamalov shrugged. 'Are you pregnant?'

Kristofine gave the old woman a hard look and ignored the question. 'If Steiner doesn't have witchsign then why was he taken?'

'That I can't tell you,' said Mistress Kamalov, lifting the black iron kettle from the hearth. Kjellrunn noticed how the old woman didn't make eye contact, not daring even to look at Kjellrunn while witchsign was being discussed.

'But that doesn't make any sense. Why would the Empire take Steiner?' Kristofine looked from Mistress Kamalov to Kjellrunn and back again. The old woman set out the tea mugs but did not look up.

'It wasn't Steiner they should have taken,' said Kjellrunn after an awkward pause. She wanted to say more but the words wouldn't come.

'It was you,' breathed Kristofine. 'They were supposed to have taken you.'

'And that's why I have to go to the island. This is all my fault.'

'And you're helping her?' said Kristofine to the old woman.

'I am teaching her to use her powers, safely. What she does with them after that is up to her.'

Mistress Kamalov poured the tea. 'Very tired,' she murmured, sitting at the table. A look of sadness had etched itself upon her face, each line a minor grief, each wrinkle a regret. 'Many years I have seen what happens to people when witchsign comes. Friendships fray, lovers are torn apart.' She gestured at Kristofine. 'And families become strangers.'

Kjellrunn struggled to hold back the tears as Kristofine looked at her with disbelief and worry.

'Hush now,' said Mistress Kamalov.

'You're the reason the Okhrana visit my father's tavern, week after week.'

'I never wanted any of this,' said Kjellrunn, sadness replaced by a keen defiance.

'What will happen if they catch you?' asked Kristofine.

'It looks like we're about to find out,' said Mistress Kamalov. She rose from her seat and crossed to the window. 'They've just ridden into the clearing.' No one spoke for a moment, the steady *thump-thump* of hooves on earth the only sound. 'Just like we practised,' was all Mistress Kamalov said, taking off her headscarf and pulling the scrappy locks of her hair all about her face. A length of bandage appeared from a pocket and was tied over her eyes.

'Practice? What practice? What about me?' said Kristofine.

'Hop into the bed out the back,' said Kjellrunn. 'And be quick about it.'

The door rattled on its hinges, and Kjellrunn, far from being rattled herself, was deeply afraid. She took a moment to compose herself, then flung the door open and stared up into the face of the horseman, who had clearly kicked the door to summon her.

'I'm not deaf,' she blurted, hearing an echo of Steiner in

the words. She took comfort from it, even as the mounted man swung down from the black mare. She didn't care for the way he looked her over from head to toe, nor the black suede britches and jacket. He was big across the chest and in the thigh, sturdy riding boots sheathing his legs past the knee. There was no trace of a weapon, but Kjellrunn had the feeling he didn't need one. Certainly his eyes were dangerous enough, hard and watchful. His beard was dark and trimmed down, while his hair hung in dark curls about his face.

A long line of syllables rolled off his tongue, earning a savage grin from his companion. Kjellrunn guessed the language for Solska and struggled to stand her ground. How easy it would be to shrink back and slam the door; easy but short-sighted.

'Hoy there,' said the horseman. 'I meant no intrusion.'

'Then perhaps you'd like to wipe your boot mark off my door then,' said Kjellrunn. The smirk on the rider's face was insult enough without his words.

'My friend and I are looking for someone. An old acquaint-ance, one we fear has become lost in your beautiful country.' That smirk again, and the way he twisted the last two words, letting Kjellrunn know he'd rather be anywhere in Vinterkveld than Nordvlast.

'You're a long way from home to track down a mere acquaintance.' Kjellrunn crossed her arms, as if this were enough to bar the horseman's entrance into the chalet. 'He must be very dear to you.'

'I never said my acquaintance was a he.'

Another quiet comment in Solska, this time from the second rider. He was a blond man with bloodshot eyes that stared out of a pale face. The second rider took the reins of both horses and tied them to the bough of a nearby tree.

'Perhaps we could speak inside?' said the dark-haired horse-man. 'No good comes from an open door on a winter's day.'

Kjellrunn edged back into the room, not turning her back, not taking her eyes from them for a heartbeat.

Mistress Kamalov sat on a chair, head cocked on one side. One hand pawed at her cheek, while the other lay in her lap, twisted and useless. A song drifted from her lips, soft and dreamlike. The old woman rocked back and forth, keeping time with the song.

'What's wrong with her eyes?' said the dark-haired horseman, indicating the bandage. His smile slipped and he stopped at the door.

'She lost her sight,' said Kjellrunn. 'Sometimes she wanders. We couldn't afford the paint for a white stick, so a bandage will have to do.'

The second rider slipped into the room, bloodshot eyes moving from one corner to another, taking in every detail, every stick of furniture and the mugs of hot tea. Kjellrunn guessed the horsemen were the same age, younger than her father by a good ten years.

'Why is she singing that song?' said the dark-haired horseman. Mistress Kamalov kept keening, kept rocking back and forth, one hand pawing gently at her face over and over. Kjellrunn swallowed in a dry throat, felt the bravery drain out of her. The song was in Solska and she had no way of knowing the meaning.

'It's the song . . .' Both riders looked at her and she took a step back on instinct. The song had never been part of Mistress Kamalov's plans; now it might doom both of them. And Kristofine too.

'It's the song that the soldiers sang when they killed my uncle.' Kjellrunn blinked, unsure where the lie had sprung from.

'Your uncle must have been a very bad man,' said the dark-haired horseman, the smirk back in place.

'He was run down by a cart while carrying potatoes,' replied Kjellrunn.

'He should have paid more attention,' said the blond man, but a glimmer of shame crossed his face.

'He was deaf,' added Kjellrunn, suddenly angry for the fictional uncle.

'I'm sorry,' said the blond man, but the dark-haired horseman kept his mocking smile and glanced about the chalet.

'Is anyone in the back room?'

'My sister is sleeping.'

'A sister? Perhaps we should wake her?' The horseman grinned at his comrade. 'Perhaps she too has a song for us?'

'You don't want to go in there,' said Kjellrunn. Fear squeezed the air from her lungs and she took another step back, one hand going to her throat. She wasn't sure how many more lies she had in her.

'But I do want to go in there,' said the dark-haired horseman.

'She's been with fever for the last four days. It's very catching.'

The horseman stopped. 'Fever?'

'I wouldn't risk it unless you've coin to spare for medicine,' added Kjellrunn. 'And the blisters, they weep for days and scar if you scratch them.'

The horseman blinked at her, then turned to his friend. A few words were shunted back and forth, all harsh, all Solska. The blond man shrugged and the dark-haired horseman stepped away from the bedroom, his smirk faded to a grimace of disgust.

'I need to sweep the kitchen and get firewood, so if you've nothing else to ask . . .' Kjellrunn fell silent under the dark-haired horseman's withering gaze.

The second rider stepped forward and laid a coin on the table. 'For your sister's medicine,' was all he said, then turned and pulled open the door, leaving without a second glance.

The dark-haired horseman turned just as Kjellrunn released a quiet breath of relief. The man paused but Mistress Kamalov kept singing, kept rocking gently.

'You have tea from Yamal?'

Kjellrunn's eyes widened before she composed herself, then made a disgusted sound. 'As if we could afford such things. Besides, I'd never drink that filth. This is good Nordvlast tea.'

The horseman blinked, then sniffed the air, eyeing the steaming cups. 'My mistake,' he said, unimpressed, then slunk out of the door.

'How did you find us here?' called Kjellrunn as the two men mounted their black horses.

'The butcher in the town said an old crone with a nasty mouth lived in the woods.' The horseman shrugged. 'Seems he was wrong. Though you seem to be shaping up nicely.'

Kjellrunn slammed the door and pressed her back against it, trying to stop her hands shaking as the sound of hooves receded into the distance. The singing stopped and Mistress Kamalov pulled the bandage from her eyes. She fixed Kjellrunn with a hard stare, then snorted her amusement, a smile spreading across her face. 'You lie like a Shanisrond sea captain.'

'You saved us,' whispered Kristofine from the bedroom doorway. She approached Kjellrunn and squeezed her hand. 'You saved us.'

'Yes. She did.' Mistress Kamalov traced her lip with one finger. 'And if you are half as good with the arcane as you are at lying I will have a formidable student. Tomorrow we go to the cliffs.'

'Why?' Kjellrunn frowned. 'It snows every day and the cold . . .'

The expression on Mistress Kamalov's face silenced further objection.

'Because to defeat men like this,' she gestured to the

departed horsemen, 'sometimes you need more than just quick words. Sometimes you need powers, sometimes you need the arcane.'

Kjellrunn's mind drifted to Steiner, trying to imagine what the island must be like and what had happened to him.

'Know this,' said Mistress Kamalov, holding up a finger. 'The Vigilants on the island must know that Steiner does not have witchsign by now. And the deaths of those two Vigilants in Helwick will only keep them busy for so long before—'

'They come back here.'

Mistress Kamalov nodded and drank her tea while Kjellrunn struggled to comprehend just how much her life had changed in the short time Steiner had been gone.

'But I've barely started learning, how can I . . .' She gestured at the door, indicating the departed horsemen.

'Not how,' said Mistress Kamalov. 'Only that you must.'

CHAPTER THIRTY-ONE

Steiner

Not every child with witchsign has the raw ability to become a Vigilant. While most failures die there are some who persist in living. These failures have lived on Vladibogdan and know the secrets of the Synod and the Solmindre Empire. Rather than destroy these failures, the Emperor, in his wisdom, gave them a purpose. They are the Imperial Envoys.

> – From the field notes of Hierarch Khigir,
> Vigilant of the Imperial Synod.

The furnace cavern had never been a place of joy, yet the misery of Maxim's announcement weighed on all of them like manacles. Romola was gone and, worse yet, an Imperial ship had been sighted.

'I really thought I was going to escape the island,' said Steiner as he took a moment to catch his breath.

'I know,' said Kimi. She set down her tools and stepped down off the dais. 'The letter was cruel, but Romola's leaving seems crueller still.'

Steiner chewed his lip. 'It feels selfish to even consider escape, leaving the rest of you behind.'

'It's not selfish,' replied Kimi. 'Just natural.' She looked about the vast cavern. The cinderwraiths appeared from cracks in the rock like smoke while others went about their work, a procession of the lost, orange eyes shedding gentle light.

'Damn foolish to think Romola would help you,' said Tief from behind them. 'Or any of us. She's never bothered before. Always too busy looking out for herself.'

'I didn't have the chance to ask.' Steiner sighed and Kimi wrapped an arm about his shoulders.

'It was damn foolish to hope for such a thing,' continued Tief.

'And how many times have you tried to escape, Tief?' Steiner turned on the man and frowned. 'Once? Twice? My money is on never. You've never tried to escape because you don't have the stones for it.'

'Don't have the stones?' Tief shook his head. 'You expect me to leave my sisters, my people, in this forsaken place?'

'But you've never tried, not for yourself and not for anyone else. Even after all this time. All you've ever done is kept your head below ground and hope Felgenhauer forgets about you.'

'Better to stay out of her way than catch her attention.' Tief addressed a handful of Spriggani who had formed a circle around them. A few muttered unkind words and shared sullen looks.

'This argument serves no purpose,' said Sundra, appearing out of the darkness like a phantom. 'Steiner did that which we could not.' She placed herself before her brother and fixed him with a stern gaze.

'And what was that, dear sister?'

'He dared to hope,' said Sundra. 'And he dared to do something about it.' The Spriggani fell silent at the words of the priestess. 'And what is a life spent without hope?'

'Hope? Pah. Fine talk from a priestess of Frejna. So much for the bones whispering his name! Just another witless

Northman, as if Vinterkveld doesn't have enough of those already.'

'Be quiet,' said Kimi. All eyes turned to the Yamal princess as she squared up to Tief. 'Enough.'

Tief's anger subsided into a guilty glare, then that too faded and he turned away. The Spriggani trailed after him, a few shooting dark glances over their shoulders as they left.

'I can't believe Romola has gone,' said Steiner. 'After everything that's happened.'

'You can't blame her for taking her leave the first moment she was able,' replied Kimi.

Steiner's curiosity prickled along with the heat as the many smoking furnaces rumbled, whispering plumes of smoke into the darkness.

'I should be up there,' he grumbled, raising his eyes to the ceiling.

Kimi nodded. 'Shirinov might be surprised to see you, on account of you being dead and all.'

'I forgot I was dead.'

'It's easily done,' replied Kimi with a smile.

'Being dead should have certain advantages,' replied Steiner as they headed for the centre of the cavern and Kimi's workstation.

'Such as?'

'I don't know.' Steiner shrugged. 'I've not been dead that long. I'm still getting used to it.'

'Come on.' Kimi jutted her head towards the cave where she slept. 'I'm in no mood to work.' She strode off across the cavern and Steiner struggled to keep up.

'Where are we going?' asked Steiner.

'To feed the dragons. I don't like leaving them too long.'

They descended the sloping corridor to the chamber of dragons, still shackled to the stone columns, still as wretched as Steiner remembered. Kimi hefted a large bucket of raw beef. The meat was half rancid and no better than gristle on closer inspection.

'That *is* beef, isn't it?' said Steiner, sick and anxious.

'Cow. Straight from the kitchen,' Kimi growled. 'Small wonder they fade so quickly when given such slops.'

'You promise it's not a soldier, or a novice?'

Another chuckle from Kimi. 'I promise.'

They went from dragon to dragon, Kimi reaching high to push scraps between the ragged creatures' yellowed teeth. Finally they came to the silver dragon at the centre. Steiner suspected Kimi had kept the better portions of the meat back for this one. The eye nearest Steiner opened and twitched from woman to man.

'Probably hungry enough to eat both of us without blinking,' said Kimi, taking care not to lose a finger to the silvery dragon's bites.

'Why aren't you angry with me?' said Steiner when the beef was all gone. 'Tief's anger seems be born from me daring to hope, and looking like I might have had a chance, but you . . .'

Kimi shrugged. 'I'm never getting off this island, Steiner. I can't even daydream about it.'

'What do you mean?'

'If I leave this island there is no telling what Solmindre will do to the Yamal. And it won't stop there. Some Yamal live in the Empire among humans; they are merchants and labourers and soldiers. They would be rounded up in the night, falsely accused of anything and everything.'

'But . . .'

'I have to stay on Vladibogdan so others are safe. That's why I respect you so much. We have much in common. I'm here to safeguard my people, and you're here for your sister.' She smiled again.

'I came here so Kjell would be safe,' said Steiner as he ran a hand over the silvery scales. The dragon's tail swished as much as it could given the binding. 'But none of that will matter if Shirinov returns to the mainland. He'll raze Cinderfell and Helwick, and then he'll hunt down Kjellrunn. You understand why I wanted to get back so badly?'

'Of course.' Kimi nodded. 'Family always comes first. It's what I like best about you.'

'I just need a way to get up to Academy Square.' Steiner sighed. 'So I can see if Shirinov slips free of Felgenhauer on that Imperial ship.'

Kimi pressed a thumb to her lips, deep in thought. 'So.' She gave a half shrug. 'The soldier that stabbed me with his spear—'

'Ehh. You fed him to the dragons, didn't you?' Steiner eyed the bucket once more and shuddered.

Kimi gave another shrug of her shoulders. 'It's a shame to let good meat go to waste. And there was an unexpected benefit.' She glanced across the chamber and Steiner's eyes widened as he followed her gaze.

'Kimi!' Piled up at the far side of the chamber was a collection of armour. The quilted long coat had been doubled up, the mail slung in a heap on top. Two helmets and a few pauldrons were scuffed but not damaged.

'So, you need a way back to Academy Square, but have to remain unrecognizable.' She nodded thoughtfully. 'This we can do.'

Steiner lifted a helm from the pile and placed it atop his head.

'Kimi, this is excellent.' His voice sounded strange inside the helm.

'Let's get you strapped in. Time is slipping away and you'll need to get back up there quickly.'

'Right.'

'And you'll need to be careful.'

'I'm always careful.'

Kimi snorted a laugh. 'Of course you are, Hammersmith. Of course you are.'

Steiner had never worn armour before. His breath sounded overly loud in the confines of the helmet and his heart raced with the heavy load on his shoulders.

'How is anyone supposed to fight in armour this heavy?' he muttered, each step a chore under such a burden. 'No wonder the soldiers are so bad-tempered.'

Sneaking out of the cavern had been easy. The Spriggani had all retired, too despondent to work after the failed escape. Kimi escorted him to the battered rungs, intending to shield him from prying eyes, but only cinderwraiths remained, staring at the soldier and the princess with unblinking gazes.

'Maxim said the ship didn't look like the usual supply ship they send,' said Kimi. 'So keep your wits about you.'

She'd helped him up the first few rungs, then waited to pick him up should the mail and plate prove too heavy. Steiner's grip did not fail him. He arrived on the ledge above, breathless but excited. It was strange to look down on Kimi. She smiled up and he waved back.

'Go. Quick. Find out what is happening with the Imperial ship.'

Steiner nodded and regretted it immediately. Nodding was not a pleasant motion to undertake in the heavy helmet. A mace hung from his belt and slapped his leg with each lurching step. In the end he carried it, rubbing the back of his knee. The cloak, obviously a necessity for the island's frigid climes, only added to his encumbrance.

'I'm going to be a lot shorter when this is over,' he complained, pushing on through the darkness by guttering torchlight.

Steiner emerged from the alley and blinked in surprise. On the far side of Academy Square, beyond the vast draconic statue, were two rows of ten soldiers. Each wore a thick black cord across their breastplate that looped back on itself, ending in a tassel. Their cloaks, along with their boots and the star at their brow, were also black instead of the customary red.

The regular soldiers stood to attention in front of the gate-house, dotted around the square in threes. Novices stared from academy windows, eyes set on the black-clad soldiers. The air was taut with anticipation and Steiner wondered who would arrive next. A cry went up from the gatehouse, an announcement perhaps, or a warning.

Steiner edged into the square, the visibility poor through the narrow eye slot. Felgenhauer and Marozvolk waited on the steps before Academy Voda. Felgenhauer had strapped on a sword – it did not look ceremonial. Her loyalists stood behind, clutching their axes. A few soldiers at the back stood at ease and were looking over towards Academy Zemlya, where Shirinov and Khigir stood, along with two score of Vigilants.

A hand pressed down on Steiner's shoulder and an icy chill ran down his spine. How could he have been caught so soon, and before he'd seen anything of note?

You are supposed to be dead, are you not?

Silverdust's sightless gaze looked out over Academy Square, but he did not take his gloved hand from Steiner's shoulder. Steiner couldn't help but think of what he'd seen that night on the roof of Academy Voda.

'I just wanted to see what was going on,' whispered Steiner. 'I need to see if Felgenhauer prevents Shirinov from leaving the island.' The heat from Silverdust's arcane aura was making the armour hot.

It is best I do not remain here. Silverdust's ghostly words were still unsettling, perhaps more so now that Steiner knew the Vigilant's secret. *You would be better off heading back to the forges, but I can tell you have set your mind on this.*

'Who comes?' said Steiner, gripping the mace tightly.

*An Envoy. One of the Vigilants must have sent word to the main-
land, most likely at the behest of Shirinov.*

'What will happen to Felgenhauer?'

*That remains to be seen, and while I have great respect for the
Matriarch-Commissar, I am not ready to die for her just yet.*

Steiner opened his mouth to speak, but Silverdust was
already drifting away, drifting towards the long tunnel that
led to the forges.

'The forges and all the other cinderwraiths,' said Steiner
under his breath as he watched the Vigilant leave. For a second
Steiner considered following Silverdust back into the darkness,
but a loud voice called out in Solska. He'd been seen.

CHAPTER THIRTY-TWO

Steiner

Envoys are often charismatic bordering on arrogant. They have the deep conviction of being able to speak with the Emperor's authority. Such privilege does not easily foster humility, fairness or moderation. It is said the Emperor rarely gathers the Envoys together, as they are given to displays of hubris like competitive siblings. In this way they are the spoilt children of the Empire.

– From the field notes of Hierarch Khigir,
Vigilant of the Imperial Synod.

A harsh voice startled Steiner as a soldier approached from the side. The man uttered words in Solska and pointed at Felgenhauer. Steiner made to bow then remembered himself and saluted, struggling to raise his arm under the heavy pauldrons.

'I hope you asked me to stand beside her,' he muttered to himself as he crossed Academy Square. 'Or this will be the most short-lived disguise in the history of the Scorched Republics.' He sweated despite the cold and *clank-clanked* across the square. 'Frøya keep me close,' he whispered, taking a position a few feet behind the Matriarch-Commissar. He had no time to feel anxious, as the soldiers at the gatehouse snapped a crisp salute, closely followed by all the soldiers in the square. All except Steiner, who remembered a second too late. Only Marozvolk noticed, giving him a hard stare from the snarling wolf mask.

There was no question the black-clad soldiers had escorted someone and Steiner blinked when she appeared, stepping out from the shadow of the gatehouse with an easy confidence. This was the Envoy Silverdust had spoken of judging by her gown: a blue so vivid he'd never seen its like before. The fabric was not the familiar weight of wool, nor was it canvas or leather. There was a shimmer to it that drew the eye. The way it clung to the curves of her body brought heat to Steiner's already ruddy cheeks. A belt of delicate gold links hung low on broad hips, while a dagger lay in a filigreed sheath across her backside. It was the stole of winter fox that seized Steiner's attention above all else. That the stark white fur contrasted with the brilliant blue was cause enough, but the fox's head remained attached. The eyes staring from the vulpine face were glassy and unfocused. Steiner wrinkled his nose in disgust, glad the helm hid his revulsion.

Felgenhauer descended the steps from Academy Voda and bowed, one hand on the pommel of her sword. To Steiner's surprise the next words that graced the air were in Nordspråk.

'I do so hate coming so far north,' said the Envoy. 'Such a dour climate. And the sea! Have I expressed to you quite how much I dislike life aboard ship? So cramped, no privacy, no luxury. And the smell!'

'We all must play our parts, Envoy,' replied Felgenhauer, her voice steady, but Steiner thought he detected a note of wariness. 'The will of the Emperor must be obeyed,' continued the Matriarch-Commissar, 'even by those of us who enjoy a long leash.' Both of the women were speaking loud enough for all to hear. A duel then, not of blades or the arcane, but influence and wit.

'It is indeed the Emperor's will that I journey here,' replied the Envoy. 'And I come from him directly at Khlystburg.' Her accent was not one Steiner could place; perhaps she'd lived in Svingettevei once, or Vanneránd. There was no mistaking her tone. Arrogant. Bored. 'This is no simple errand, one does not simply despatch an Envoy on whim.'

'No,' agreed Felgenhauer, her grip tightening on the sword. 'I myself have never despatched anyone on a whim.'

Steiner couldn't miss the note of challenge in Felgenhauer's voice, nor the Envoy's response; a mocking smile and raised eyebrow.

'It has been some time since I walked Academy Square,' said the Envoy, looking up to the novices from where they looked down from their dormitory windows. She gave a broad smile and a slow wave. 'And what long and terrible years they were.'

Shirinov stepped forward from the shadow of Academy Zemlya, tottering down the steps. The cane clattered on the cobbles until he had interposed himself between the two women. Khigir followed, ever the faithful shadow, the tongues of fire flickering weakly at his boots.

'How fares the most beloved Emperor, Envoy de Vries?' said the hunched Vigilant.

'Shirinov,' purred the Envoy. 'There you are. And so formal. Please, you know better than that. Call me Femke. I, unlike you, have no need for masks and epithets.'

A moment of awkward silence pulled taut between Envoy and Vigilant, Shirinov's shoulder's hunching a little higher. Steiner imagined he was seething.

'We hunger for news of the Empire,' said Shirinov, the silver mask ever smiling. 'We are cut off from so many things on Vladibogdan.'

'Hungry?' said the Envoy. 'I daresay you are. And what do you hunger for the most from the Empire?'

Shirinov turned to one side, one hand gesturing. 'Why, its culture, its food, its influence.' A pause. 'Its discipline.'

'Yes.' Femke de Vries drifted around Academy Square as if conducting an inspection, stopping at soldiers every so often. She brushed snowy ash from a soldier's pauldron with a petulant tut. 'The Empire does not forget those who remain out of sight, even here, on Vladibogdan.' She moved from one soldier to another, moving closer to Steiner. 'The Emperor keeps those souls in mind, perhaps most keenly of all.' The Envoy raised her eyes to the fiery statue. 'And when the Emperor's mind is turned to something, when the Emperor hears a thing that rouses his curiosity . . .' She clasped her hands and shrugged, a girlish smile on her face. 'Well! The Emperor will not be denied.'

'What does the Emperor request?' said Shirinov, dropping to one knee. The cost of such a dramatic gesture made the old man grunt and Steiner smirked. Femke de Vries circled around behind Felgenhauer, up the steps of Academy Voda, drifting closer to Steiner. The dead eyes of the winter fox came closer and Steiner could do little but stare back in sick fascination.

'The Emperor has heard rumours of mistakes,' said the Envoy. 'Whispers reach us that all is not as it should be on the isle of Vladibogdan.' She stood directly before Steiner, glancing over his armour.

'The Emperor hears the truth of things,' said Felgenhauer. 'There was a mistake concerning a boy. A boy without witch-sign. But he's dead now and the matter is of no importance.'

'No importance?' said Shirinov. 'A soldier and a novice died. More were injured, and we're employing Shanisrond pirates to ferry our weapons.'

'Be quiet,' said Felgenhauer to no avail.

'And a Troika are dead and missing in Helwick,' continued Shirinov. 'If these are not matters of some import then what is?'

'Truly,' said Corpsecandle, nodding solemnly.

'These matters are under control, Envoy de Vries,' said the Matriarch-Commissar.

The Envoy continued to appraise Steiner, unconcerned by Shirinov behind her. Steiner clenched his arms at his sides, lest his shaking hands betray him.

'You forget yourself, Matriarch-Commissar,' said the Envoy, her tone gently chiding. 'It is for the Emperor to decide what is important and what is not. It is not for us to choose. We are merely instruments.'

'This is so,' added Corpsecandle, taking a step forward to beside Shirinov.

The Envoy smiled over her shoulder at Felgenhauer. 'Which is why you'll be delighted to learn that the Emperor has invited the Matriarch-Commissar to Khlystburg to explain these occurrences herself.' The Envoy leaned close to Steiner, so close the sweetness of her perfume made him cough. 'You really need to spend more time polishing this armour,' she whispered. 'You look as if you've been beaten to death in it.' He tried not to think about the dead man who had worn the armour.

'I would happily come to Khlystburg to make such a report,' said Shirinov, standing a little taller. Femke de Vries glanced over her shoulder with a malicious smile.

'No, no, no, my dear Shirinov.' She slunk down the steps like a cat. Steiner stared after her, transfixed by the dead fox, struggling to believe how close to discovery he had come.

'The Emperor was very clear,' continued the Envoy. 'It must be the Matriarch-Commissar.'

'But I insist!' grunted Shirinov.

'We insist,' intoned Corpsecandle.

'You will stay here,' said Felgenhauer, as she approached Shirinov and towered over the hunched old Vigilant.

'Indeed he will,' agreed Femke de Vries. 'Strange that you

and I should agree on something, Matriarch-Commissar.' The Envoy brought one hand to Shirinov's smiling mask, touching the chin lightly. 'The Emperor is keen that you oversee production of weapons in the Matriarch-Commissar's absence. Weapons made of steel . . .' The Envoy raised her eyes to where the novices stared down from the academy windows. 'And weapons made of flesh.'

Shirinov leaned on his staff, shoulders slumped. 'It will be as the Emperor wishes,' he replied wearily.

'Very good, Hierarch.'

'It's . . .' Shirinov cleared his throat. 'It's Ordinary now. Since the mistake with the boy.'

'I see,' said Femke de Vries, raising her eyebrows in surprise. 'How the mighty have fallen.' She extended a hand to the Matriarch-Commissar, and beckoned with one finger, a curiously coquettish gesture. 'Come, come. We sail immediately. I long to be back on the mainland, away from all *this*.' She gestured around the square, her eyes alighting on Steiner once more.

'It will be some time before you see the Matriarch-Commissar again, Shirinov,' said Femke de Vries. 'I do so hope the fates of Vladibogdan rest in safe hands.'

'We live to serve his will,' replied Corpsecandle. Shirinov said nothing, shaking his head slowly, clutching his cane. Felgenhauer barked a long string of words in Solska, followed by something else. Ten soldiers, all armed with heavy axes, marched off with purpose.

'Bringing an honour guard of your own, Felgenhauer?' Femke de Vries smiled. 'Quite a bold statement, rebellious even.'

'No more bold than bringing twenty Semyonovsky Guard to Vladibogdan,' replied Felgenhauer. 'I hope you asked the Emperor before you borrowed them.'

The Envoy leaned close, as if sharing a secret with a close

friend. 'I had no need to borrow them. The Emperor sent them willingly, Matriarch-Commissar.' She narrowed her eyes. 'Willingly.'

Felgenhauer departed without pause. The Envoy followed and twenty soldiers marched under the arch of the gatehouse. In a daze, Steiner followed, watching them descend the steps, hearing the heavy foot falls. They stood in neat rows for a time and Felgenhauer's soldiers joined them, bearing stout bags and two wooden chests for the journey ahead. One by one they boarded the ship. Steiner's heart sank a little lower in his chest as each ascended the gangplank. The relief that Shirinov remained was tempered with the misery that he himself would too. Losing Felgenhauer was merely salt in the wound.

Felgenhauer stood at the prow, looking out to sea, more forbidding than the masthead. Things would be very different without the Matriarch-Commissar on the island. Different for the novices and different for the prisoners. Steiner hoped that Marozvolk or Silverdust might lead in her absence, but it seemed unlikely.

'You there. What are you doing?' said a voice beside him. Steiner didn't need to see the man to know it was Shirinov. He bowed his head as the Vigilant raised his voice, saying something in Solska. Steiner didn't reply, ignorant of the words and the question the Vigilant had set before him.

'I asked you a question, soldier,' said Shirinov, reverting to Nordspråk once again. 'Did you struggle to understand it? Is it possible you're not from Solmindre?'

'I . . .' Steiner's mouth went dry and he dared one last look at the pier. Another ship setting off without him. Another missed opportunity to sail home to Kjellrunn and his father. If only there had been time to slip aboard and stow away among the supplies.

'Felgenhauer,' was all he said, a desolate dread filling his

chest. The ship cast off and the oars worked in unison to take
the Matriarch-Commissar out to sea and back to Khlystburg.

'And if you are not from Solmindre, then where are you
from?' continued Shirinov.

Steiner lifted the mace from his belt and swung back with
a snatched breath of desperation. Shirinov hobbled back and
lifted one hand, reminding Steiner of the day he'd first arrived
with Maxim, seeing the boy suspended above the cobbles,
being crushed to death.

'That didn't work so well last time, did it?' said Shirinov
as Steiner tried to swing. A soldier had slipped behind him
and grabbed his arm. Steiner turned and kicked the man in
the shin before another soldier seized him. The mace was
wrested from his grip and more soldiers crowded in. Shirinov
stepped forward and lifted the helmet from his head.

'And in the armour of the man you helped kill,' said
Shirinov. 'One of these days you will stay dead, Steiner
Vartiainen.' The Vigilant laughed behind the silver mask. 'And
I fear that day is almost upon you now that the Matriarch-
Commissar has gone.'

Steiner didn't need to understand Solska to know what
came next.

Take him away.

The soldiers dragged him across the square as the novices
jeered and gestured. Steiner caught a glimpse of Aurelian
before a soldier wrapped his cloak about his head. It took all
of his control not to panic at the crude blindfold as he was
led away.

CHAPTER THIRTY-THREE

Kjellrunn

The Emperor has a deep affinity for familial ties, and their undoing. He is keen to know a subject's background, education, and siblings. 'To know a person you must know their family,' he once said. 'In this way you can truly hurt someone. It is for this reason, I suspect, he recruits the majority of the Okhrana from orphanages. The Empire becomes their family, their career, their life.

– From the field notes of Hierarch Khigir,
Vigilant of the Imperial Synod.

Kjellrunn spent her days as a child of two worlds. The mornings were spent at her chores with brief visits into town, while the afternoons were spent at the woodcutter's chalet. The days were short this far north as the months drew on, the constant twilight brightening for a meagre handful of hours each day. This was when Kjellrunn hurried to the forest, glad to be free of Marek, who all but fawned over his infrequent customers, desperately grateful for any few coins that came their way.

The Spøkelsea was a dark and turbid green. Rarely at rest, the waves pounded at the pier like a surly drunk. There was much that was surly in the slow crawl of days following the horsemen's visit to the chalet. Mistress Kamalov most of all. The old woman's temper was barely concealed, though she was a good deal more talkative than Kjellrunn's father.

'Good. Close your eyes. Imagine going down to deep spaces in the earth, through the mud, between the rock, between the stones. Imagine the roots of the trees, so ancient, and all the bodies of the creatures who have died—'

'Bodies?' Kjellrunn wrinkled her nose. 'You're morbid today. I thought I was trying to turn my body to living stone, not become a shambling corpse.'

'Fine. No bodies.' Mistress Kamalov glared. 'Though I promise, one more interruption and I make a body out of you. A nice shallow grave, not warm but then you will be dead, so you will not care. Yes?'

'You could just tell me to be quiet.'

'I would and I have. It rarely works. Now close your eyes and mouth and think, think! Imagine I am coming at you with a knife. Your skin is all that stands in the way of being gutted like a fish. What do you do?'

Kjellrunn knew well she should be able to turn the blade aside by transmuting her pale and fragile flesh to granite, yet somehow the change refused to come. She looked down at her spare frame and found herself thinking of Kristofine. Was mastering the arcane akin to coming into womanhood? How much longer would she have to wait?

Kjellrunn opened her eyes a sliver and found Mistress Kamalov standing so close she flinched backwards.

'I did not say you could open your eyes!'

'I am trying.'

'Yes, trying. Very trying.'

'Has Kristofine called by today?' said Kjellrunn, keen to have a moment's reprieve from her unsuccessful attempts. 'Perhaps her father has started speaking to her again. Or she's spying on the Okhrana in the tavern?'

'Who knows?' The old woman stalked across the kitchen to where a shallow basket of vegetables waited. 'Do not think about her, think about stone!' A deft hand snatched up a carrot and threw it. Kjellrunn tensed, focused. Her hands clenched into fists but she made no move. The carrot impacted from an unseen barrier and flopped to the floor.

'Good. I was hoping for you to turn skin to stone, but ward is just as good. No matter if it is a carrot or a dagger or an arrow.'

Another carrot followed the first. Again Kjellrunn snatched a breath, forcing herself not to throw up an arm to shield herself. The carrot stopped a few inches from her chest, then fell to the floor.

'Good. Try to stop it before it reaches you. Nothing puts fear into an enemy like seeing an arrow snapped in air.'

Kjellrunn waited for Mistress Kamalov's next task.

'Now tidy them up.'

Kjellrunn dropped to one knee and reached for the projectiles.

'With your mind!' bellowed Mistress Kamalov. 'Not with your hands, with your mind! Like I teach you day in and day out.'

'Sorry,' mumbled Kjellrunn.

'If you think like a serving girl the world will treat you as a serving girl. Yes?'

Kjellrunn frowned.

'Do you want to be a serving girl your whole life? Doing your father's chores? Serving stew and washing dishes? Married off to a lazy pig? Do you want a lazy pig for a husband?'

Kjellrunn shook her head, took a breath and focused her mind. Mistress Kamalov paced the room, tutting her impatience or giving exasperated grunts every so often. Kjellrunn felt the prickly heat of sweat at her brow.

'Two carrots. I am not asking you to lift an entire galleon from the sea!'

Kjellrunn's frown deepened. There was a blur of orange

followed by a *thud-thud* and Mistress Kamalov blinked. The carrots had leapt up from the floor and sped across the room, hitting the wall just above the old woman's shoulder.

'I . . . probably shouldn't have done that,' said Kjellrunn. Mistress Kamalov stooped, gathering up one carrot in each hand.

'Our lessons have become more interesting.' She gave a chuckle and hefted a carrot. 'Again! And try and hit me this time, serving girl.'

Kjellrunn tensed and threw up a ward as Mistress Kamalov threw the carrot back at her. It was going to be a long afternoon.

'Hoy there, Kjell,' said Verner. He was sitting at the kitchen table cleaning under his nails with a folding knife. 'You're home late.'

'That's a disgusting habit. I wiped that table clean this morning.'

The fisherman swept the grit off the table with a careful hand and discarded it into the hearth amid dancing flames.

'Sorry, Kjell. Where have you been today?'

'Fetching carrots and firewood.' She crossed the room and deposited a heavy bundle beside the chimney breast. The carrots hung from her belt.

'Did you dig up the smallest ones you could find?'

'Better wizened and small than a growling stomach. I see you come laden with things for the pot, as ever.'

Verner cleared his throat, embarrassed, then reached into a pocket and slipped a few coins onto the table.

'We can't eat money. Would it kill you to stop at the shops occasionally? Or bring some fish? You *are* a fisherman, aren't you?'

Verner's eyes widened but he said nothing.

'How is he today?' said Kjellrunn, jutting her head towards the smithy.

Verner smiled and made to say something, but caught the look of warning in her eye and puffed out his cheeks. He raised his hand, palm down, and waggled it.

'No one has bought a thing from the smithy all week. As if losing Steiner isn't bad enough,' Kjellrunn tied on her apron, 'now we have to starve to death.'

'He did make some money today,' said Verner. 'We took some things to Helwick early this morning. Spent most of the day on the road, truth be told. The local smith wasn't so keen to see us, but life is full of disappointments.'

She wanted to agree with him, but the day had been anything but disappointing. Mistress Kamalov's look of pride as she'd said farewell was reward enough. Protecting oneself from flying carrots was hardly the stuff of legend but Kjellrunn enjoyed the warm surge of satisfaction all the same.

'Were they there?' she asked, fetching a knife and chopping board. Who 'they' were was not in question. The horsemen had not been seen since visiting Mistress Kamalov's chalet.

Verner shook his head. 'It's why we didn't go to Helwick sooner. They've searched every inch of that town. A lot of unhappy people there. People unhappy we were asking after the horsemen too.' They were only ever 'the horsemen', as if to say the word Okhrana might summon them like an evil spirit. 'I had to do some quick talking to avoid suspicion.'

'Avoiding suspicion is all we ever do,' said Kjellrunn. Her thoughts turned to her conversation with Mistress Kamalov and how the Okhrana hunted disobedient Vigilants.

Verner nodded and tucked away his knife, a look of weary sadness crossing his face. 'I don't like it any more than you do, Kjell.'

'Answer me straight, not as a child, not as the little girl you used to lift up on your shoulder. Tell me the truth or may Frejna strike you blind.'

Verner frowned. 'What truth?'

'Are you one them, the Okhrana? Were you one of them? Nothing makes sense. You promised my father that Cinderfell will be passed over for Invigilation, two Vigilants in a nearby town die and another goes missing. Now I learn the Empire uses Okhrana to hunt its own. How does this all fit together?'

Verner released a slow breath and sat back in his seat. 'That head has always been full of questions.'

'This head wants answers.'

'I'm not Okhrana. I swear to you, Kjellrunn. The horsemen, Okhrana, whatever they are, they are here looking for someone.'

'Looking for you. Because of what happened in Helwick.'

'No. Yes. Well, they're looking for the last Vigilant. If there's one thing the Empire hates more than a dead Vigilant, then it's a Vigilant who defects.'

'She's going to be in a lot of trouble when they find her,' said Kjellrunn, thinking of the wizened old woman in the woodcutter's chalet, the same old woman who could be icy and imperious in the blink of an eye.

'It's the same all over, Kjell. Most soldiers serve their whole life, no retirement. A Vigilant is as much a slave to the Empire as the Yamal to the south. And the Okhrana, they're little better than a gang of thugs. You're in the gang or you're in the ground. No exceptions.'

'And you?' Kjellrunn shook her head. 'Just like that you're off the hook?'

'To them it must seem that the last Vigilant killed her colleagues and fled into Nordvlast. No reason to suspect anyone else.'

'So you're not in danger?' she said.

'I don't think so. Or no more than anyone else, I'd think.'

He smiled a moment and looked down at hands that had gutted any number of fish and gods knew what else. Or who else. 'What I did in Helwick I did to protect you. I swear it by Frøya and Frejna, and by the north wind.'

Kjellrunn nodded but couldn't say she felt any satisfaction in his answer.

Verner rose from the table. 'I'm sorry.'

Kjellrunn set down the knife and sighed. 'No. It's I that should be sorry. You've always worked hard to keep us fed and looked out for us over the years. I don't know what we'd have done without you.'

'I didn't do such a great job of looking out for Steiner.'

Kjellrunn wanted to tell her uncle how she was going to get Steiner back, but just then the door latch rattled and Marek entered, tired and stooped.

'No, it didn't work out so well for Steiner,' said Marek. 'And I might suggest you speak of other things, I can hear you outside. Our friends are back in town.'

Kjellrunn snatched a glance through the window, but only darkness waited beyond the glass. Her mind conjured memories of the two horsemen at the chalet, how they'd leered at her, and the easy contempt they'd shown.

'You mean . . . the dark-haired horseman, is he back?'

Marek nodded. 'And there's no telling which doors they'll press their ears to, but this one will be high on the list, especially after the business with Steiner.'

'Did you see them?' asked Verner.

Marek shook his head and pointed a thumb back over his shoulder. Kristofine stood in the doorway.

'You need to be careful,' replied Kjellrunn. 'It's not only me that's under suspicion.'

'But I don't have witchsign,' Kristofine sighed. 'I came to warn you, I wanted to help.'

'And help you did,' said Verner. 'Now it's best you be on your way, and keep out of the tavern while they're in town.'

'The tavern?' Kristofine gave a bitter laugh. 'You think my father will let me work in the tavern since all this started? He barely speaks to me.'

Kjellrunn and Marek exchanged a guilty glance.

'You'd best pull up a chair then,' said Marek. 'We don't have much though.'

'So they're back,' said Kjellrunn as she prepared the dinner, but no one answered her. They dined by the light of the lantern, wooden spoons scraping their bowls all too soon as the meagre fare was eaten.

'Thank you,' said Kristofine when the meal was done.

'I have money to buy meat tomorrow,' said Marek, laying a tender hand atop of Kjellrunn's.

'And I'll go into town to fetch it,' said Verner. 'Spare you the trouble of dealing with that butcher.'

Kristofine rolled her eyes at the mention of Håkon.

'I take it he's no fan of yours, then?' said Verner to Kristofine. She sighed.

'He used to be very keen on me, too keen.' Kristofine shook her head. 'But that changed when everyone assumed I have witchsign.'

A knock on the door set them all rigid with nerves and all eyes turned to the source of the noise.

'It's late,' shouted Marek, as he pulled a kitchen knife from the counter and hefted it.

'It's cold too,' came the reply. 'And it's not getting any warmer, right.'

Verner and Marek exchanged a look of surprise and the blacksmith threw the door open. 'Get in, quickly. There's eyes everywhere.'

'What the Hel are you doing here?' whispered Verner.

Kjellrunn blinked as Romola entered.

'You've picked a bad time to come calling in the night,' said Marek.

'You think I want to be here? You think I had an easy time persuading my first mate we should drop in at Cinderfell under the cover of night like smugglers?'

'Solmindre has sent watchers,' said Verner.

'Solmindre has watchers everywhere.' replied Romola. 'I only just escaped Vladibogdan with my life.'

'Is Steiner with you?' The desperation on Marek's face was difficult to witness. The captain shook her head. A look of annoyance crossed her face, though if Kjellrunn had to guess she'd have said the woman was more annoyed with herself.

'He's so much like you it makes my head hurt,' said Romola to Marek.

'He's . . .' Marek's hands twisted together, as if clasping onto a shred of hope. 'Is he still . . .'

'Alive? You can bet your boots the boy lives. There's little that will slow that one down.'

The room became chaotic with the scraping of chairs. Verner hugged Marek, who in turn hugged Kjellrunn and Kristofine, somewhat awkwardly.

'I knew he'd survive,' said Verner after they'd retaken their seats and shared relieved smiles. 'What happened?' he pressed.

'What happened is that I've made an enemy of Shirinov. I've cut ties with the Empire and I'll be staying in southern waters for a good time to come.'

'But without you we've no way of contacting Steiner,' said Marek.

'I'm sorry,' said Romola, 'But things are difficult over there. All you can do is pray the boy makes it off that rock by himself.'

All the joy Kjellrunn had felt at receiving the news was washed away by that one simple statement.

'No one escapes Vladibogdan,' she said. 'Not without help from the outside.'

'I'm sorry,' replied Romola. 'Really I am, but there's nothing else I can do.'

'Will you stay in touch, at least?' said Verner.

Romola shrugged. 'I'm going far to the south and don't

intend to return. There's trouble brewing between the different factions, and it would be too easy to get caught up in it. I have my own problems.'

Kristofine looked up at the pirate but said nothing, though the frown on her face said she longed to. Verner shook his head with resignation.

'Thank you for bringing word of my son,' said Marek.

Moments later the pirate was gone, back into the frigid night, back to the frigate by the pier.

'Steiner is alive,' whispered Kjellrunn, through tears of joy. He was alive and she would rescue him.

CHAPTER THIRTY-FOUR

Steiner

A Troika of Vigilants is a distinct unit, each group as individual as the three Vigilants that form its number. A Troika is required to serve during times of war. The Vigilants are sanctioned to use their abilities in the open provided there are no witness to speak of their powers. Other Troika serve the Emperor in more discreet ways.

– From the field notes of Hierarch Khigir,
Vigilant of the Imperial Synod.

Things were easier when the Matriarch-Commissar had you locked up in the gatehouse.

At first Steiner thought he was dreaming, or succumbing to madness. His face ached down the left side where the soldiers had beaten him into submission. He was grateful they'd used fists and not maces.

The gatehouse is more secure than this old ruin. Something about the words made Steiner open his eyes, the way they drifted into his mind like a procession of ghosts.

'Silverdust?'

The Vigilant stood near the door, head bowed. The blank

mask showed Steiner a bloodied and warped reflection. The corridor beyond the dank cell was all darkness save for the dull gleam of mail and armour. Steiner coughed a bitter laugh, shocked that he could be important enough to warrant a guard.

'I didn't expect to see you again,' he croaked, his throat parched. His left wrist was raw where it remained held fast against the stone wall of the circular room. He'd not been able to see once they wrapped his cloak around his head, and hadn't been able to determine where he was being held. The cloak lay on the floor, a bloody reminder of the beating they'd meted out as revenge for their fallen comrade. 'Where I am?'

An old tower in Academy Zemlya. Silverdust regarded the empty cell and the rusty chain that circled Steiner's wrist. *No one has come to this place in a very long time.*

Steiner had spent the days lamenting Felgenhauer's departure and worrying at the fates of Kjellrunn and his father.

The soldier outside will not speak of my passing. We have an arrangement, but I cannot be too long.

Silverdust drew close, lowered himself to his knees and produced half a loaf, an apple, a waterskin and some cold chicken. He drifted back to his place by the door without a word.

Steiner gorged himself, forcing down scraps of food and closing his eyes.

When was the last time you ate? asked Silverdust, glancing over his shoulder to ensure they were undisturbed.

'How long have I been up here?' asked Steiner, trying to chew and speak, and chew some more.

Three days. It is why I came. Shirinov would have you half dead. I would prefer otherwise.

Steiner didn't interrupt his hurried feast to question the Vigilant's motives. Silverdust crossed the room to the narrow window that allowed a meagre light to enter. The cell existed

in a feverish state of permanent twilight. There was no feature
to inspect or anything of interest in the room, which made
the two orbs of orange light somewhat conspicuous.

'Why did you bring a cinderwraith with you?'

The shade blinked glowing eyes and drifted to a spot behind
the door, keen to remain unseen by the soldier outside.

It was Kimi's idea. Silverdust looked over his shoulder at the
apparition. *Keep your voice down. Things will not go well if Shirinov
discovers the Ashen Court has a spy in your jail cell.*

'What's the Ashen Court?'

*The cinderwraiths feel a kinship with you, Steiner, ever since you
first arrived on Vladibogdan. And I in turn have my own kinship
with the cinderwraiths, as you well know. We have decided that we
should make efforts to escape our enslavement and have named
ourselves the Ashen Court.*

'You're going to rebel against Shirinov?'

Silverdust nodded. *Kimi asked me to send the cinderwraith to
keep an eye on you. She worries Shirinov will have you executed.*

'And Kimi is in this Ashen Court, is she?' Steiner's heart
was beating loudly in his chest; his mouth was dry with
excitement.

*No, she is not welcome among our ranks. We have very specific
entry requirements.*

'Why *hasn't* Shirinov had me executed me yet?' Steiner felt
the familiar pang of panic in his gut and throat. 'I've been
here for three days, he could have had me killed at any time.'

He has plans that require you to draw breath. He told me as much.

'Why would Shirinov tell you anything? I thought you
were allied with Felgenhauer?'

*Now the Matriarch-Commissar has gone it serves my interests to
play along and ingratiate myself, though in truth I have always
thought Shirinov a thug and an ass.*

'I'd always assumed you, Felgenhauer and Marozvolk were
a Troika,' said Steiner.

Not officially a Troika as you know it, but we share a certain point of view. It pleases me to work together, for the moment.

Steiner leaned forward as much as the chain would allow. 'Why should I trust you?' he whispered. 'And what's Shirinov up to?'

Shirinov is keeping you alive because he intends to present you as proof to the Emperor.

'Proof? Of what?'

Khigir's sister has gone missing on the mainland, her colleagues are slain, and you have some connection to the deaths.

'Sharpbreath.'

Exactly. Khigir and Shirinov think Sharpbreath's disappearance is part of a larger conspiracy. Silverdust steepled his fingers. *A conspiracy of rebels trying to keep the children in Nordvlast safe.*

'Children like Kjellrunn,' said Steiner.

Specifically Kjellrunn is my guess, and Shirinov is keen to redress his mistake.

'So how is Sharpbreath caught up in this?'

Sharpbreath only just survived her training, and many of the Vigilants never trusted her. Now she is missing and the two Vigilants she served with were killed before they could carry out Invigilations. Shirinov is sure the roots of that conspiracy reach back to Vladibogdan.

'And that's why the Matriarch-Commissar was taken by the Envoy,' said Steiner. 'Shirinov thinks Felgenhauer hired the assassin in Helwick to protect Kjellrunn.' He glanced up at the curving mask. 'Did she?'

It is possible. While we agreed on many things, we also disagreed on many more. Felgenhauer may have been compelled to help if she knew of a family in Nordvlast that might fail an Invigilation.

Steiner chewed his lip, not trusting himself to say anything else, still unsure how much he could trust the Vigilant before him.

Did your family know Felgenhauer? Do they have ties to Matriarch-Commissar?

'No,' said Steiner. 'No, nothing.'

Though in truth there is much that you do not know. Your own
father is hardly trustworthy, is he?

'Stay out of my head,' growled Steiner. Silverdust drifted
across the cell and picked up Steiner's bloodied cloak.

Shirinov and Khigir will not stop until they have found Sharpbreath
and saved face, even if that means turning you over to the Emperor
himself.

Steiner felt an icy chill. He had no wish to be transferred
to Khlystburg and presented to the Emperor. The city of whips
would draw every truth and secret out of him. He'd shout
Verner's name to make the searing irons stop, he'd give
up Kjellrunn just to stall the razor-sharp blades from carving
his flesh.

'You have to get me out of here,' said Steiner. 'I can't to
go to Khlystburg. I'll do anything.' But Silverdust didn't reply;
the silence was just another discomfort in the drab cell.

Harsh words in Solska caused Steiner to flinch as the soldier
shouldered his way through the door. Silverdust exited the
chamber without pause or ceremony, leaving Steiner to agonise
over Shirinov's next move.

Hours passed by and light at the window dimmed. Steiner
shifted and cursed when his backside went numb on the cold
flagstones. Occasionally he stood in order to take the pressure
off his shackled arm, but no position was entirely comfortable.
The silence beyond the cell door was broken, and Steiner's
stomach clenched in fear; perhaps Shirinov had changed his
mind. The reality was rather different.

Vigilant Khigir stood in the doorway, tongues of flickering
fire dancing about the floor, making the room bright.

'Corpsecandle,' said Steiner from between gritted teeth. He
narrowed his eyes and blinked. The Vigilant's flames were
too bright for eyes that had known days of darkness. Khigir

dragged a chair with him, the wooden legs protesting on the flagstones, much too loud after the abundance of silence in the dim circular cell.

'Bastard boy of Cinderfell,' said Khigir in his maudlin tone. The chair was positioned in the centre of the room, and after a brief examination of the prisoner, the Vigilant sat down.

'Shirinov's shadow,' said Steiner. He turned his eyes away from the frowning, pitted mask, away from the Vigilant's scrutiny. His breathing was too loud and his heart raced.

'She was much like you,' said the Vigilant after a pause. 'Chained up in this very room. Shirinov chooses not to remember those times, but I do. Sometimes they would let me visit her.'

Steiner shook his arm but the chain held fast and his wrist bled from the effort. 'Shut up, I don't want to hear it.'

But Corpsecandle continued. 'I know her by another name. Sharpbreath was my sister, younger than me in much the same way Kjellrunn is younger than you.'

'Shut up. I don't want to hear about your sister.'

'I too felt protective.' Khigir nodded. 'Just as you do, but she was always a danger to herself. Much like your sister, I imagine.'

'Why was she was chained up?' Steiner eyed the shackle and his own red-raw wrist in disbelief.

'Every few years, perhaps once a decade, a child comes to Vladibogdan, a child with much power. These children have a nuance for the arcane far beyond their years. They can call on an element as if it were old friend, not the enigmatic power so many struggle to bend to their will. A tiny proportion of these children also have principles, fostering a hatred for the Empire that borders on insanity. A fanaticism, if you will.'

'Your sister . . . ?'

The Vigilant nodded thoughtfully. 'The Patriarch who ran

Vladibogdan chained her in this cell until she could be broken. Sharpbreath was starved for days at a time, or they made it so she could not sleep. Sometimes the methods were physical, other times they tortured her with the arcane.'

'Why are you telling me this?' said Steiner.

'I am telling you this because she did break in the end, Steiner Vartiainen. She became a talented Vigilant with fine mastery of wind. She also became loyal to the Solmindre Empire. She understood that witchsign left unchecked could be dangerous. She understood that without the purity of order there can be only chaos and ruin. She understood sacrifices have to be made along the way. Those too weak to bear the glorious burden of Empire will be snuffed out by its greatness.'

'Any great country that has to kill its own people to remain great is missing the point.' Steiner curled his lip and wished his sledgehammer was nearby.

'Sacrifices must be made,' said Khigir, leaning forward on the chair. The flames by his feet flickered in agitation. 'Kjellrunn will be tested for witchsign. The Matriarch-Commissar prevented Shirinov from doing it, but it will happen, Steiner. It is for the best. Can you not see it?'

'I can see twisted old Vigilants taking children from their families. I can see an Empire spreading lies. I can see a pathetic old man who didn't do enough to protect his sister.'

Corpsecandle lurched to his feet and the tongues of fire grew brighter, taller. His hands flexed and flames sprang into life around his fingers, roiling and twisting in orange and white.

'We will break you, Steiner. And we will break Kjellrunn too. All bravado fails before the might of the Solmindre Empire. You will swear loyalty or you will perish. It is too late for your father, but you might try to save yourself.'

'My father?'

'We know he was connected to the murder in Helwick. We

know he has been engaged in correspondence with the Matriarch-Commissar. We rifled her room two nights ago.'

'What correspondence?' asked Steiner. 'My father doesn't know who Felgenhauer is.' But Marek had always kept his secrets; this might yet be another one.

'She hid letters and locked them up well,' said Corpsecandle, 'but Shirinov was thorough. We found them in the end.'

'Shirinov,' Steiner sneered. 'He's more insane than you are.'

'Shirinov has been waiting years for this. His demotion at your hands only made him more determined, just as I am determined to find my sister and bring her back to the Empire.'

Steiner pressed himself against the wall as the Vigilant stepped forward, holding up hands consumed by flame. The heat made his skin prickle and the faint smell of singeing hair drifted on his senses.

'I don't know anything about that,' protested Steiner. 'I don't know anything. Just leave my sister alone!' But Khigir did not withdraw, holding out fiery palms to each side of Steiner's face. Sweat ran and hair singed, his breath quickened with panic, but there was no escape from the room, the shackle, or the Vigilant before him. Steiner stared into the frowning mask, watching the fire reflect from the pitted brow. The eye holes held only darkness, and Steiner imagined his ears, crisping, melting, burning.

'I don't know anything about Helwick,' shouted Steiner, 'I just worked in the smithy. I don't know anything about Sharpbreath.'

'You filthy Nordvlast swine took her from me. You vermin of the Scorched Republics. Why can you not see our desire for a unified Empire is just and proper? All countries must be joined in service to the Emperor.'

'Hierarch Khigir.' A voice from outside the cell. The Vigilant straightened and turned to the source of the interruption. A soldier stood in the doorway, helm removed and lodged under one arm. He looked from Steiner to the Vigilant and cleared his throat. He wasn't a Solmindre man, the sandy blonde hair and beard along with pale blue eyes marked him as one from Vannerånd or Drakefjord.

'The supply ship is here,' he said in Nordvlast. 'A few days early. It will dock in the next few hours. Ordinary Shirinov requests your presence at once.'

Steiner looked from soldier to Vigilant and felt sweat roll down his neck and cheeks. Khigir swept from the room, igniting the chair as went, leaving it to flame and smoke. The soldier remained, anxious eyes moving from burning chair to prisoner.

'How can you serve them when they do this to people?' said Steiner after a moment.

'You speak as if I had a choice,' said the soldier, shaking his head. The soldier left and Steiner wondered just how long it would take for Shirinov to depart for Cinderfell.

CHAPTER THIRTY-FIVE

Steiner

Many Vigilants cling to the hope that their remains are interred beneath the catacombs of the Imperial Palace in Khlystburg. In this way they pretend to some measure of immortality, hoping to be remembered in the ages to come. However, for every loyal comrade who takes his rest in the capital, there are three Vigilants lost to foreign battlefields or darker intrigues.

– From the field notes of Hierarch Khigir,
Vigilant of the Imperial Synod.

Steiner dragged himself upright. Sweat cooled on skin that had come painfully close to being burned just moments before. He dared to look through the narrow window and pressed his forehead against cool stone.

'Dammit.' He closed his eyes, confirming what he feared most. The sea was choppy but no impediment for the Imperial galley that crashed through wave after wave, white sails billowing in the high wind.

Steiner rattled his chain and inspected the lock but escape was impossible – he'd need tools, not chilled fingers, to slip free. The ship continued closing on the island and Steiner's

heart turned to stone. His hands curled about the chain and
he strained and yanked and swore as hard as he could. The
metal links held fast, refusing to surrender their purchase,
embedded in the tower wall.

A fiery glow startled him, turning his attention from narrow
window to gloomy cell. He'd expected to find Corpsecandle,
and was surprised to find a cinderwraith looming at his
shoulder, the orange coals of its eyes a steady light in the
half light.

'I'd forgotten you were here.' Steiner turned back to the
window and eyed the approaching ship. 'Shirinov is going to
use that ship to get to the mainland.' Steiner wondered if the
cinderwraith could understand him, but carried on talking
regardless. 'I have to get back to protect my family.'

The cinderwraith nodded and they looked out at a sea of
dark green and surging cobalt, the Imperial ship edging closer.

'And not just my family, but everyone in Cinderfell and
Helwick.' Steiner tugged at the chain. 'I'd stop the Vigilants
from taking any Nordvlast children if I could.' The cinderwraith was so close he could smell the ashes and the tang of
heated metal. So like the smells of his father's forge, the scent
calmed him and he began to think more clearly. He thought
of Kimi and the amulet she wore. 'I'd set the cinderwraiths
free too,' he whispered, 'and I think I know how.'

The cinderwraith retreated from him, drifting towards the
door, but did not take its eyes from Steiner.

'I'd even set the dragons free if I could.' The ship was close
now, so close he could see the crew on deck, all going about
their tasks in the fine rain, the same crew that would ferry
Shirinov back to Cinderfell. 'They're hardly the fierce monsters
of legend, are they?' But when he turned the cinderwraith
was no longer there, not lurking in the shadows or hiding
behind the door.

'You might have cared to say you were leaving.' Steiner

slumped down against the wall, surrendering to futility. 'It's not even a terribly well-made chain,' he said, noting the craftsmanship.

The door opened once more. The brief flicker of hope that Steiner dared to kindle was soon extinguished as Aurelian slouched into the room. His was a victorious smile, pale eyes full of gloating.

'You should try being imprisoned,' said Steiner. 'I've never had so many guests.'

'Guests?' Aurelian looked a touch less sure of himself.

'Mainly guests in masks,' said Steiner, trying not to think of Khigir's fiery interrogation. 'And now I have to look at your stupid face.'

'I thought it would be good manners to come and say my farewells.' Aurelian flashed another grin as the colour drained from Steiner's face.

'You're leaving?' He could hardly bring himself to say the words.

'Not leaving, Steiner.' Aurelian waggled a chiding a finger. 'No one leaves Vladibogdan. Surely you, of all people, know that by now.' He paced across the cell and turned back to Steiner. 'But Hierarch Shirinov—'

'You mean Ordinary Shirinov,' said Steiner. 'Felgenhauer demoted him.'

'Ah, Felgenhauer.' Aurelian smiled. 'She's not going to be around forever, Steiner. What am I saying? She's not even here right now, is she? And Shirinov has no intention of letting his demotion stand.'

Steiner nodded. He'd always known it would come to this. How those worries had gnawed at him, more than the meagre food and heavy work, more than missing his family and home.

'Don't hurt Kjellrunn, Aurelian. She's just—'

'A child? We're all children, Steiner.' Aurelian placed his hands on his hips and gave a wicked grin. 'And if I have to live on this hateful island then so can she. No exceptions, Steiner. The Empire doesn't allow it. The Emperor won't tolerate it, and neither will I.'

The door slammed shut before Steiner could respond. He shook his head and curled up against the wall, shivering and cursing silently. In time he settled into a doze but the sound of the waves and the rain entered his dreams, leaving him sick and wretched on waking. A soldier had dragged a brazier in while he'd been asleep and a blanket had been placed around his shoulders.

'Perhaps not everyone in the Empire is so terrible after all.' And for some reason this bothered him more than he could articulate. Steiner hobbled from his place beside the wall, his feet a bright pain of pins and needles, his fingers nearly numb with cold. He squatted closer to the brazier and held out a shaking hand. His imagination swept down the many staircases of House Zemlya and into Academy Square, further still to Temnet Cove where the Imperial galley would be tying up alongside the pier. He imagined the supplies brought ashore by the sailors; Shirinov insisting he speak with the captain immediately. At no point did Steiner imagine escaping; he could not guess how he might stop this flow of events, chained and alone as he was.

A dull thump from outside made Steiner jerk upright, almost tripping over the chain. There was a shout in Solska, then another dull thump, the sound of metal on stone.

'What in Frøya's name . . . ?'

It was then that the cell door rattled on its hinges from a heavy strike. The second blow split the door down the middle, showering splinters of wood everywhere. Steiner held up a hand to his face and blinked. Standing in the doorway, looming over the ruined timber, was Kimi, bearing his sledgehammer, and she was not alone.

'We could have used the keys, halfhead!' scolded Tief. 'You

just knocked the guard out. Look, here they are!' Tief clambered through the shattered door with the aforementioned keys clasped in his fist before scowling over his shoulder. Kimi kicked at the remaining wood, taking a certain pleasure in it if Steiner guessed right.

'Knock, knock,' she said, grinning, then stooped beneath the lintel and into the cell, followed by three cinderwraiths.

'Is it true?' said Tief.

'What?' Steiner looked at them with wide eyes. 'Is what true?'

'You told one of the cinderwraiths you could free them,' said Kimi, her eyes full of wariness.

'Yes.' Steiner shrugged. 'I think so.'

'You think so?' said Tief, his tone disbelieving.

'Why have you come here?' said Steiner.

'We came because some damn fool boy told one of the cinderwraiths he was going to free them from an eternity of toil and imprisonment.' Tief glowered at Steiner. 'All these lost souls have done nothing since you made your proclamation. No work means no weapons. No weapons means no food.'

'I didn't tell them to stop work.'

'What were you thinking?' Tief stamped his foot and shouted into Steiner's face. 'They're calling it a strike. And they've organized themselves, call themselves the Ashen Court.' More cinderwraiths crowded into the room, as if on cue.

'I know about the Ashen Court,' admitted Steiner.

'How do you know? You've been locked in a cell for four days.'

Steiner shrugged.

'They've been meeting for a while,' said Kimi, 'conversing among themselves.'

'How do you know all this?' Steiner regarded the many cinderwraiths crowding into the cell. 'They can't speak.'

'They've started writing in the coal dust,' said Kimi. 'Single words at first, then more and more until whole sentences appeared. I think Silverdust taught them.'

'You can't possibly know how to unmake the Ashen Torment,' said Tief, shaking his head. 'Why promise to release them?'

'Give me my hammer,' said Steiner, hand outstretched to Kimi as he glowered at Tief.

'There's no not doing this, once it's been done,' said Kimi softly.

'You just killed two soldiers and knocked the door off the hinges,' replied Steiner. 'I'd say we're long past the point of no return.' He hammered at the wall where the chain joined it, tugging and hammering until the chain rattled to the floor. He bound up his wrist in the metal links and when he turned back to the room, more cinderwraiths had slunk into the cell. They emerged from cracks in the stone or drifted through the door.

'Do you know how to do it, Hammersmith?' said Tief. 'Do you know how to set the wraiths free? Tell the truth of it.'

'Kimi, give me the amulet.'

The Yamal princess shook her head. 'This burden is mine, Steiner.'

'But it doesn't have to be. If we can free the cinderwraiths—'

'The Empire entrusted this to me,' said Kimi, one hand pressed to the front of her chest. 'If you free the wraiths my people will suffer.'

'We have to start somewhere,' said Steiner, 'and right now I need all the help I can get. I need an army of lost souls who want revenge on the Empire that killed them. And once we do this, who's to say what we'll do next? There's no reason we can't free the Yamal too.'

All eyes in the room turned to Kimi, dozens of glowing eyes, all waiting on what the princess would say next. Kimi shook her head.

'They'll order the execution of every Yamal that draws breath if I give this to you,' said Kimi. 'You don't know what they've done already, you don't know what they're capable of.'

'The Empire will exterminate every Spriggani and every Yamal they can find,' said Steiner. 'They're just preoccupied with Shanisrond right now. Once the war is over nowhere will be safe.'

'The boy speaks the truth of it.' Tief nodded, tugging one ear.

'He speaks your truth,' replied Kimi. 'This is what you believe, Tief. Who's to say what the Empire will do once they've unified Vinterkveld?'

The cinderwraiths shrank back, many bowing their heads. Tief looked through the door and released an irritable sigh.

'How many Spriggani and Yamal have you seen wearing an Imperial uniform?' said Steiner.

'None,' admitted Kimi.

'And do you think that will change any time soon? You think the Empire is going to become more tolerant after it wins the war in Shanisrond?'

'No.' Kimi rubbed her eyes. 'But not letting us become citizens of the Empire is different to exterminating us.'

'They'll be a lot of weapons after they defeat the south,' said Steiner.

'And a lot of veterans that know how to use them,' added Tief.

'This act of rebellion can be the clarion that unites the Scorched Republics and the Spriggani and the Yamal to rise up and attack the Empire.' Steiner took a step closer and looked into Kimi's broad face, saw the worry in the set of her brow, the conflict as she tensed her jaw. 'If we do this now things can change.'

'You promise?' said Kimi.

'I can't promise anything. I'm just a blacksmith's son who can't read, with nothing but my boots and a sledgehammer to my name. But it's better to try for a thing than not try at all.'

Kimi reached into her tunic and brought forth the shard of stone, the dragon etched in exquisite detail.

'I'm not just giving this artefact to you, Steiner. I'm handing over the fate of my people.'

Steiner nodded and held out his hand, trying to ignore how it shook. 'We can stop them, Kimi. I don't know how yet, but I intend to find out.'

Kimi lowered her eyes and handed over the amulet. Steiner opened his mouth to thank her but she turned and exited the room, ducking beneath the low doorway. Steiner started after her, only for Tief to block the way.

'You can bet your boots she needs some time alone after that. This is no small thing she's given up.'

Steiner looked around at the congregation of cinderwraiths crowding the room.

'If you do this for me, if you help me now, I'll make sure you're freed. You'll never work another day in the furnaces, never drag another sack of coal or hammer steel into weapons for the Empire that killed you.'

The wraiths dipped their heads, almost in unison, a wave of dark grey shadows signalling their agreement. Steiner smiled, feeling a thrill of danger course through his veins.

'Hunt down the soldiers.' Steiner hefted the sledgehammer, felt the reassuring weight of the metal head. 'I'm going to settle a score with Shirinov.'

The cinderwraiths fled from the room. They swept through Academy Zemlya, no longer lost souls toiling for the Empire, but avenging spirits come to haunt the living. Startled cries sounded through the building, high-pitched voices of scared novices mingling with the surprised grunts of soldiers.

'How will Kimi get back to the furnaces?' asked Steiner, unable to turn his full attention to the task at hand.

'The same way we arrived,' said Tief, a mischievous twinkle in his eyes. 'There is a secret way through the rock to this academy. You didn't think we'd be foolish enough to try and cross Academy Square in broad daylight, did you?'

Steiner smiled.

'Come on.' Tief drew a curved knife from under his jacket. 'Let's find this Vigilant of yours and finish this once and for all.'

CHAPTER THIRTY-SIX

Kjellrunn

A soldier has his discipline and a Vigilant his authority, but the motives of the Okhrana are less clear. Some are no better than feral dogs given a long leash. Others fancy themselves noble justiciars, meting out punishments to those who have displeased the Emperor. They are a ramshackle lot, unpredictable and all the more dangerous for it.

– From the field notes of Hierarch Khigir,
Vigilant of the Imperial Synod.

Kjellrunn emerged from the cottage door and settled the yoke across her shoulders, buckets dangling from fraying ropes. The day remained shrouded in darkness, no way of knowing what the time was, earlier than she'd like, that was for sure. It'd be a comfort to stay in bed an hour longer and curl up in the blankets. All her waking thoughts turned to riders in black and she couldn't remember her dreams; in truth she had no wish to. It was a fair bet her slumbering mind would conjure Okhrana and soldiers and Vigilants, all storming over the border and breaking across Nordvlast, an irresistible wave of violence.

Her breath steamed on the chilly air. Small rectangles of

golden light spilled across the cobbled streets from windows. In other places the light slashed the ground, escaping from gaps between shutters. The sky overhead was a vast canvas of darkness, only a faint aura of pale light betrayed the fading moon's place behind the cloud.

Kjellrunn's thoughts turned to the captain of the *Watcher's Wait*. That she'd brought word Steiner remained alive was a comfort, though the comfort was bitter; there would be no escape from Vladibogdan.

'One day soon I'll travel south,
to clearer skies and sunshine bright.
One day soon I'll travel south,
to stars that glitter through the night.'

The song had woken inside her, as if hibernating in a deep corner of memory, come to her lips unbidden. She had not sung loud but the words drifted on the morning air all same, finding an audience.

'A pretty song for a pretty girl,' said a voice in the dawn gloaming. Kjellrunn stumbled, stopped. The buckets swung on their ropes, buffeting an elbow.

'Who's there? Show yourself.'

Slivers of shadow moved in the dawn gloom, detaching from it, stepping closer to the light of a window.

'Apologies,' said the dark-haired horseman. He performed a mocking bow, never taking his eyes from her, thick curls tumbling across his forehead. Kjellrunn struggled to keep her face neutral. 'We were just on our way to see the blacksmith.'

'He's not awake yet,' lied Kjellrunn, hearing the edge in her voice.

'And how would you know that?' said the horseman. She was sure he was the very rider who'd left his boot print on Mistress Kamalov's door. Though indistinct in the darkness there was no mistaking the cruel twist to his words, nor the harsh Solska accent.

'I'm his daughter,' said Kjellrunn, fearing this small truth might be the snare that saw her trapped.

'You look much like another girl in this town, but as I say to Yuri here, you Nordvlast girls all look the same to me. Thin as a whip, with sour faces that don't remember to smile when a man passes by.'

'Perhaps if there was more food there'd be more to smile about.' Kjellrunn lifted her chin and her anger rose up like a wave. 'And I'm not here to smile for strangers, much less strange men. Now if you'll excuse me, I've water to fetch.'

The horsemen sniggered.

'Still no smile?' he called after her. For a moment she wanted to turn and issue another rebuke, but the yoke was an ungainly burden and she stomped to the well with gritted teeth.

It had never taken so long to fill two buckets. Her mind raced with each turn of the handle, hands burning with the deep cold of the winter morning.

'One day soon I'll travel south, simply to be spared this miserable climate.' Her anger built, a storm inside, the rise and swell of the ocean, a stinging rain of irritation. Beneath all of it was a quiet voice like a sinister whisper, speaking of all the things the horsemen would do to her father. What they might be doing to him this very moment. A smithy was not so very different to a torture chamber after all. Or might they simply snatch him away? That would be worse still, being left behind and not knowing where they had taken him.

Kjellrunn hurried back, short of breath and panicking, not caring that water slopped from the buckets, not caring that she'd have to make another trip later in the day. She only cared about returning to the smithy, and to Marek. He may well keep truths from her she couldn't guess at, but he and Verner were all she had left.

The furnace was lit, a glow beneath the stout wooden doors, falling as slivers of gilt on black cobbles. Kjellrunn divested herself of the buckets in the kitchen, then grasped the yoke in both hands. The wood was almost as wide as she was tall and had none of the balance required for a weapon. She strained to hear but the muffled sound of voices in the darkness gave no clue to what fate had befallen Marek.

In desperation she took the kitchen knife, knowing she wouldn't shirk from bloodletting should horsemen threaten her father. Silent feet spirited her outside, picking her way through slush and reaching the smithy doors, still ajar by a handspan. The voices were clearer now, strong voices yet not pitched in anger. Kjellrunn's eyes widened as she realized Marek was speaking in Solska. While the words remained unknown to her the voice was the bedrock of her life. Solska was the language of soldiers, the tongue of Invigilation, the command of a cruel Empire. To hear it spoken by Marek unsettled her in ways that hushed the roaring anger within, leaving a cold driving rain of dread.

Slowly, silently begging Frejna not to see her, entreating Frøya to keep her close, Kjellrunn retreated to the kitchen. With trembling hands she surrendered the knife, feeling foolish for even considering she could fight. Her father's evasions about the past were many, but surely he couldn't be connected to the Empire? Hadn't Verner said they were spying on the Empire, not for them?

Kjellrunn ran. Running through darkened streets deep with grey snow. Running past homes and families that knew each other, away from families that were as open books with all their tales for the telling. Each breath stung her lungs with freezing air, each step took her away from a father with secrets she dare not discover, away from a father that spoke in the tongue of their enemy.

*   *   *

'No lesson today,' said Mistress Kamalov. She poured tea and drummed her fingers on the table. Kjellrunn had forced her way into the chalet, just as the words had forced their way out of her mouth. 'We sit, we wait.'

'He was speaking in Solska,' whispered Kjellrunn, repeating herself for the fourth or fifth time. She lingered by the door, glancing through the window every few heartbeats.

'Lots of people speak Solska,' said Mistress Kamalov. 'It does not mean they are bad people any more than having witchsign does.'

'But my own father!' Kjellrunn glared at the old woman. How could she not see how important this was? 'He was speaking Solska, the language of the Empire.'

'The language of Solmindre,' said Mistress Kamalov, holding up a finger. 'The language of the Empire is fear. Which sounds entirely different.'

'But they're evil. And now my father is speaking Solska too.'

'I speak Solska,' said Mistress Kamalov. The stooped peasant woman was gone; she stood before Kjellrunn with a noble bearing, eyes hard, mouth set in a thin line of disapproval. 'Not everyone in the Empire loves the Emperor. Solska was spoken before the Empire was even an idea. Try to separate the language and the culture from the actions of a dangerous and power-hungry tyrant.'

'Sorry,' whispered Kjellrunn.

'How easy life would be if you could tell evil by language alone,' continued Mistress Kamalov. 'Or the colour of your skin.'

'I've not met anyone from Solmindre that was anything but evil though.'

Mistress Kamalov frowned. 'It is not the point! The point is people are people, some are good and some are bad. And every now and then some one you thought was bad does something kind, just to confuse you.'

'But why would my father be speaking in Solska to the Okhrana?'

'Why don't we ask him?' said Mistress Kamalov.

'What?'

The old woman pointed through the window. 'He's at the edge of the clearing now.'

Kjellrunn lunged for the counter and snatched up a knife. She flung open the door and gestured with the blade, an accusing finger of steel.

'Stay away. I want nothing from you. Nothing. You're a liar.'

Marek and Verner exchanged a glance and Marek held out his hands, palms uppermost.

'I just want to talk, Kjell,' said Marek. 'There's been too much not talking but that time is over.'

'We both do,' admitted Verner.

Mistress Kamalov wrapped an arm about Kjellrunn's shoulders and eased the knife from her grasp.

'Please. Come in. And stop shouting in my forest. You will wake up the animals. You may even wake the dead.'

It didn't take too long for the four of them to crowd into the kitchen.

'You have some truths to tell,' said Mistress Kamalov to Marek as she poured the tea. 'She is not a child any more. Not since they took her brother. She needs to know.'

'I know, but . . .' Marek shook his head.

'And I did not think I would see *you* again,' said Mistress Kamalov to Verner.

'How do you two know each other?' said Kjellrunn.

'I have a confession,' said Verner. He eyed Marek, regret writ large on his honest face. 'I went to Helwick to kill the Troika, just as you asked, so Kjell would be safe. I wanted to send a message to the Empire, truly I did. I wanted to let them know they couldn't come here and take our children.'

Verner looked into the dark mug of tea and sighed. 'The first two died easily, I caught them unawares and it was over before they knew it. But when the time came to kill the third Vigilant I couldn't do it. She was waiting for me, wide awake as if it were the most natural thing in the world for an assassin to have broken into her room in the dead of night.'

'Why didn't you tell me this?' asked Marek, stern and pale in equal measure.

'Seeing her there, without her mask, without her robes, she wasn't a Vigilant, she was just an old woman in bed, trying to sleep.'

Kjellrunn then looked to Mistress Kamalov. 'What?'

'I thought you knew?' Mistress Kamalov shrugged.

'I suspected you'd been a Vigilant at some time in your life,' muttered Kjellrunn. 'I didn't know you were the missing Vigilant from Helwick.'

'And why not?' said Mistress Kamalov.

'Well . . .' Kjellrunn wrinkled her nose. 'You're so old. I thought—'

Mistress Kamalov rolled her eyes. 'And I suppose Vigilants Khigir and Shirinov are spring chickens, yes?'

Marek stood up from the table and stared out of the window, into the clearing.

'I couldn't tell you I'd failed,' said Verner, not looking at Marek. 'Not after everything you've done for me.'

'What?' Kjellrunn looked from her uncle to her father. 'What did he do for you?'

Verner opened his mouth to speak but Marek cut him off. 'A long time ago, before your mother and I got together, I was an Imperial soldier. I found two soldiers beating a man, robbing him for the little money he had. It was late at night and the man was drunk, but he didn't deserve what he was getting. I tried to stop it. Things went . . . wrong.'

'He saved my life,' said Verner, looking up from his tea.

'For the cost of two soldiers who should have known better,' admitted Marek.

'You killed both of them?' asked Kjellrunn.

'I'm not Marek's brother,' explained Verner, 'I'm his brother-in-law.'

'So, you knew my mother?' said Kjellrunn, leaning close to Verner.

'You might say that.' The fisherman grinned and for a second he was his old self. The half-drunk, smiling fisherman of a hundred tall stories. 'Your mother was my older sister.'

'Was?' Kjellrunn felt the hot spike of tears at the corners of her eyes, burning with disappointment.

'I'm one of three, but the Empire took two of us.' Verner forced a bitter smile. 'I'm all that's left.'

'But you're still my uncle.'

'Very much so. But an uncle on your mother's side.'

Kjellrunn hugged Verner fiercely. 'And you were a soldier?' she asked her father, keeping her distance from him.

'I served with your mother and in time we fell in love, which is forbidden. Everything is forbidden in the Empire. Your mother came with me when I defected, but in time she went back. She didn't want to, but she knew they'd hunt her until the ends of Vinterkveld. That's how we came to be in Cinderfell, we were always on the move.'

'And she's . . . ?' Kjellrunn couldn't bring herself to say it.

'She was a Vigilant. A high-ranking one too. The Empire asked more and more of her.' Marek squeezed his eyes shut and pressed a fist to his mouth. When he spoke his voice was a faint rumble, every syllable loaded with pain. 'In the end the arcane used her up, hollowed her out until there was nothing left. That's why I couldn't let them take you to Vladibogdan, Kjell. I couldn't let what happened to your mother happen to you.'

'She did not rejoin the Empire because she was tired of

running,' said Mistress Kamalov. 'I met her once. She said the Empire needed moderate voices to speak up from within. Attacking the Empire from the outside only ever means death, but from inside, with her influence, with her rank, she hoped for something better.'

'I didn't say she was tired of running,' said Marek. 'She wanted to avoid the Okhrana turning up on our doorstep to kill our children.'

Kjellrunn rose from her chair and held Marek close, both wordless in their grief.

'And now we have a new Vigilant in our midst,' said Verner.

'Not a Vigilant, not any more.' Mistress Kamalov frowned. 'Had I known you lived in Cinderfell I would never have come here. I assumed you were from Helwick. Still, I am grateful you helped me defect. It is better than being dead, though almost as cold.'

'What happens now?' asked Kjellrunn.

'What happens now is that we find a way to get Steiner off that island,' said Marek.

'What happens now is we are arrested,' said Mistress Kamalov quietly. 'Your father came here not realizing he led the Okhrana to my door.'

'We weren't followed,' said Verner, though his eyes flitted to the window, uncertainty writ across his face.

'Perhaps I am imagining the dozen men sneaking through the trees? Perhaps I am imagining the thoughts of men, thoughts formed from words in Solska?'

Marek stood, face grim, hand straying to the long knife at his belt. Verner cursed softly and fisherman and blacksmith slunk to each side of the window.

'I think I'd like that knife back now,' said Kjellrunn.

'I think it would be best if you were unarmed,' Mistress Kamalov said. 'Less likely to kill you this way. Not much, but less.'

Kjellrunn opened the door, causing Marek to round on her. 'What are you doing?' he said, an outraged hiss.

'We know they're coming.'

'There's the small issue of numbers, Kjell,' said Verner. 'They have them, we don't.'

Kjellrunn didn't wait for their approval. The clearing had been home to countless lessons, fears and furies, questions and occasionally answers. It might also be the place she died.

'Better here among the trees than in that wretched town.'

A movement to her right confirmed Mistress Kamalov's warning.

'You don't seem surprised to see us,' said the dark-haired horseman. The smirk was firmly in place on his lips. 'One of the advantages of knowing someone who can read minds, I suppose.'

'Stay away,' said Kjellrunn, her voice a flat monotone. The sound of the Spøkelsea was rushing in her ears, her every sense alive to the forest and the winter chill. Crows called a warning to each other in the distance and the trees whispered feverishly.

'My dear child. I will not be staying away.' The horseman grinned. 'And neither will my many friends.'

Three more Okhrana emerged from the woods, a few more attired as peasants. Bjørner hid in the shadow of a tree, keen informer yet reluctant witness, Kjellrunn guessed. Marek stepped out and stood beside Kjellrunn, knife unsheathed.

'Hail, friend,' said the horseman.

'You're no friend of mine,' said Marek.

'And yet you are a legend to us.' Kjellrunn counted a dozen of them now, the knife in her hand too small for so many men. 'A legend among the Okhrana,' continued the horseman, turning to his comrades as if telling a tale by the fireside in a tavern. 'And to think, we came here seeking a missing

Vigilant, but here you are, the man who betrayed the Empire for love and seduced a Vigilant.'

'I left the Empire because I tired of killing.'

'Killing is all that we have, brother,' said the horseman.

'I don't believe that,' said Marek. 'There's more to life than killing, and you're no brother of mine.'

'A brother in arms surely? Too bad we have to kill you, Marek, legends are so hard to find these days.'

'You're not killing anyone,' said Kjellrunn.

'We're well trained at killing defecting Vigilants,' said the horseman. 'You won't pose too much of a problem, little girl.'

'Your hateful Empire took my brother, you won't take anyone else from me.' Her anger was the gale that tears along the coast and the waves that crash against unyielding cliffs. Her rage was the rain turned to hail, thundering from the heavens.

'Kjellrunn.' Marek's voice was a strangled whisper. 'Kjellrunn, you're levitating.'

The Okhrana advanced, blades bared in the gloom of the forest.

CHAPTER THIRTY-SEVEN

Steiner

Perhaps when I was younger I could believe that this meant some-thing, as Shirinov still does. I've seen too many people die, too many towns ruined and sacked, too many lives crippled by fear and misery. The Emperor takes all the glory for himself, there is none for anyone but him. All the medals and honours and titles are just set dressing in some grotesque play; we are all but spear carriers and minor roles to him. But what else is there? Defection always means death.

– From the field notes of Hierarch Khigir,
Vigilant of the Imperial Synod.

Steiner stepped over the shattered door of his cell and into the corridor beyond, noting the broken corpses of two soldiers.

'I thought I was going to die in that cell.'

'We thought you were going to die in that cell too,' said Tief. 'Kimi was very keen to break you out from the moment you were captured.'

Steiner thought of Kimi and how close they'd grown, and how he'd do anything for her. The Ashen Torment hung around his neck, a dire weight that carried not just the fate of the cinderwraiths, but of every Yamal across Vinterkveld.

'Come on,' said Steiner, 'We've work to do, and I need to stop Shirinov getting aboard that ship

The sight that greeted Steiner and Tief defied belief. Academy Zemlya was a surge and roil of conflict and fear. Cinderwraiths accosted soldiers in threes, forming shadowy Troikas of their own. The first victims died of suffocation, wheezing and coughing, the taste of ghostly ashes in mouths crying out for mercy. A soldier stumbled along a corridor and raised his mace to strike Steiner, only to find the shadows were alive with accusing orange glares. Spectral hands wrestled the weapon free of the soldier's grasp even as others were sending tendrils of smoke into the soldier's lungs. The man fell to his knees and clutched his throat with one hand, the other swiping the air.

'Are the cinderwraiths . . . impervious?'

'You can't kill something that's already dead,' said Tief, watching the soldier die. 'Though water will slow them down. And the arcane too, I expect.'

Their way ahead was not free of impediment. Steiner caught a crushing strike from a soldier's mace on the shaft of his hammer. Tief slipped around and jerked his knife under the soldier's arm, up into his lung. The soldier stumbled back, wheezing. Steiner's overhead swing smashed an armoured shoulder, denting metal and snapping bones, knocking the man to the floor. Tief darted in once more and jerked his knife across the man's throat.

'What did you kill him for?' said Steiner, incredulous.

'He was already dead, mostly likely. Especially after that great hammer of yours.'

'But why . . . ? Steiner gestured at his throat.

'Dead men tell no tales, Steiner. And he was no friend to you. He'd have captured your sister at Shirinov's command, just like any of them.'

Steiner nodded and tried to ignore the blood, pressing on through the academy and down the stairs to the double doors. Three novices awaited him, all granite-skinned with eyes of polished marble.

'Dammit. I won't be slashing their throats,' said Tief with a surly expression. The blade flashed bright in his hand, a smear of red along its edge. Steiner hefted the sledgehammer and looked from one novice to another. They were young, difficult to guess their ages under their stony skins, but the eldest wasn't older than fifteen by Steiner's reckoning.

'I don't want to fight you,' he said, 'I know you didn't ask to be brought to Vladibogdan. You didn't ask to have witch-sign either. You certainly didn't ask to serve an Empire you don't care for.'

One of the novices shivered. A faint white glow suffused her as the arcane left her skin. The novice resumed her normal form, head bowed, favouring Steiner with a sullen eye.

'They sent my brother here three years before I was taken, and when I arrived I couldn't find him. Do you know Dimitri? Have you seen him?'

Steiner shook his head, swallowing in a dry throat, unable to tell her the awful truth of the Ashen Torment and the many cinderwraiths bound to it.

'I'm trying to make sure the Empire stops taking children like you from their families,' said Steiner. 'But I need to get through those doors to stop Shirinov.'

The novices shared nervous glances at the mention of the Vigilant's name.

'If you let me past I'll do whatever I can to stop this.' Steiner gestured to the academy. 'All of this.'

The novices shared a wary look, then flinched as the sounds of fighting from Academy Square intensified.

'You'd best be on your way,' said the eldest, stepping aside. 'Tell no one you saw us.'

'Thanks,' said Steiner, moving past the novices.

'What happened to him?' asked the girl as Steiner and Tief tugged the doors open. 'Where is Dimitri?'

'I don't know.' Steiner looked into her eyes and saw an echo of Kjellrunn.

'Come on,' said Tief, tugging his tunic. 'I didn't think you'd talk them down.'

'They're only children. Killing Matthias was enough. I'll kill no more if I can help it.'

Tief fixed him with a look and laid a hand on the doors. 'Ready?'

They pushed past the great doors and ran down the steps of Academy Zemlya into the square.

'Frejna's teeth, this is bad,' said Tief, brandishing the curved knife.

'We've really started something,' said Steiner.

The square was a roaring confusion. Armoured bodies tried to impose order, shadowy forms flickered and drifted from one victim to the next. A small knot of novices from Academy Vozdukha were duelling with rival students from Academy Plamya. The grim-faced novices summoned unnatural gales to extinguish the arcane fire of their attackers.

'What the Hel's going on?' said Tief, dodging a wild swing from a soldier's mace.

'I think the Vozdukha novices are showing their true colours,' replied Steiner. 'And they aren't Imperial ones.'

Maxim crouched beside the Vozdukha students, casting fretful glances as fiery breath and the occasional half-formed fireball came dangerously close.

'Plamya students,' said Steiner, stalking towards the duel. His first strike took one of the fire novices at the knees. There was a crunch followed by a yelp. The novice curled up with both hands pressed to the shattered limb.

'Get out of my way!' snarled Steiner. His second swing took

the next fire novice in the chest, and he tottered back wheezing, then collapsed in a tangle of limbs.

The remaining novice stepped forward and grabbed Steiner by the throat. There'd be no chance to swing the sledge-hammer like this. The novice sucked down a great breath, the telltale glow of the arcane emanating from his throat.

'Look out,' shouted Tief, but the novice fell back under a well-timed headbutt. Tief was on the novice in a moment with his knife poised.

'Wait!' said Steiner, and punched the novice into uncon-sciousness.

'So he can burn you but I can't kill him?' said Tief. 'Some logic you have there.'

The Vozdukha novices crowded forward and gave their thanks, and Steiner urged them to keep fighting. Maxim pushed through the press of bodies, grasping Steiner by the arm.

'You need to stop Shirinov,' said the boy. 'He left before the cinderwraiths began their attack.'

'Kjell,' whispered Steiner, running as best he could through the jostling bodies. A lone soldier stood before the gatehouse, feet planted wide, weapon gripped in heavy gauntlets. Steiner ducked beneath a swing that would have shattered his skull. He staggered forward, turned and swung with a curse on his lips. The soldier lurched back in his heavy armour, away from the upward arc of the sledgehammer. Cobbles slick with blood and rain betrayed the soldier and his boots skidded from under him. Tief tried to slip clear but fared no better; the soldier collapsed onto him. The soldier jerked once and lay still, a dead weight.

'Get this halfhead off me!' shouted Tief.

Steiner struggled to shift the bulk of the armoured man. Tief pulled himself to his feet with a furious look.

'Is anything broken?' asked Steiner. Tief held up the curved knife, which had snapped halfway along the blade. The remainder was red to the hilt.

'I meant you,' said Steiner. 'Where's the other bit of the blade?'

Tief gestured to the soldier and grimaced. 'So much for dragon-forged blades being hardier.'

Startled shouts in Solska and Nordspråk filled the air. Steiner spotted several soldiers standing still amid the fighting. A second glance confirmed they had been turned to stone, red cloaks and black armour now the colour of slate.

'There's someone here, someone powerful.' Steiner looked about with growing panic. 'Powerful enough to petrify people.'

Tief pointed cheerfully to the alley between Academy Vozdukha and Academy Voda, where the black-clad priestess of Frejna turned a terrible gaze on any who ventured near. Taiga stood behind her, wielding a dagger and a wary expression.

'She'll make sure none of the soldiers reach the furnaces.'

Steiner nodded and entered the dim arch beneath the gatehouse, keen to prevent the Imperial galley from departing. The figure that ascended the steps to Temnet Cove was not Shirinov, as Steiner had hoped, but Hierarch Khigir. A knot of fear tied Steiner's insides tight as thoughts turned to the fiery interrogation in the circular cell.

'You should have stayed chained to the wall, boy,' said Corpsecandle in his mournful tone. 'Now I will finish what I began.'

Steiner snatched the dragon-carved amulet from his tunic and held it before him. 'Wherever there is fire there is death.' A flicker of flame rippled across the carved stone before the amulet burst into life, fire lapping and twisting about it.

'What is this?' Khigir paused on the steps. 'Another trinket for your arsenal?'

Two cinderwraiths rose from the corpses of nearby soldiers, heeding the call of the Ashen Torment.

'Take him,' said Steiner with a curl of his lip. The cinderwraiths surged forward, unable to deny the compulsion to obey.

Khigir was undeterred by his spectral attackers. The tongues of white flame that danced around his feet grew brighter as he uttered dark words behind the frowning mask. The Vigilant reached out with both hands, sending red motes from his palms. The smouldering lights struck each of the newly formed cinderwraiths. One moment the ashen spectres were drifting forward, the next they were orange and white outlines, so bright Steiner had to look away.

'He destroyed them,' breathed Tief, eyes wide in shock.

'I am a Hierarch,' said Khigir in a measured tone. 'Did you think I would merely breathe fire like some novice?' He brushed ashes from his robes, the attack no more than an inconvenience. 'And now for you, Vartiainen. It is clear to me you will not be turned to a higher calling. It is best we end this insurrection now.'

'Insurrection?' Steiner was already moving before the word had left his mouth. Whereas Shirinov could ward off physical attacks with a gesture, Khigir could not. The Vigilant stepped back and avoided Steiner's wild swing, almost toppling down the steps. His outstretched hand cast a bright arc of fire that washed close by, but Steiner had stepped within arm's reach of the Vigilant. The heat pressed against his back and the smell of singed hair came soon after. Tief gave a startled curse and dived away, landing on his side with grunt. The fire blinked out and Steiner grabbed the Vigilant's face with his free hand and mashed Khigir's head into the gatehouse wall.

'I'll show you' – Steiner jerked the Vigilant into the wall again – 'insurrection.' Steiner dragged the limp form of Khigir forward. 'Your time is over, old man.'

The strike that met the underside of Steiner's jaw was unexpected, all the more so because it came from the addled Vigilant. The coppery taste of blood infused Steiner's mouth, along with the dim awareness he'd bitten his tongue. He recoiled and made to swing the sledgehammer, but not before Corpsecandle reached forward with hands that burned white hot.

'I am not so easily bested, boy.'

Steiner stared in horror, imagining his flesh seared to the bone. He swung the sledge, more from panic than a will to do violence. Khigir jerked back and approached again, white-hot hands burning bright as steel from the furnace. The flames went out, dowsed in brackish water and the gatehouse tunnel was consumed with an acrid stench. Steiner stared around to discover Taiga and Tief clutching buckets. Khigir fell back, arcane fire extinguished, steam rising from his gnarled hands.

'You hateful Spriggani, you worthless vermin—'

But anything else he had to say was lost as Steiner's strike took him across the shoulder, spinning him towards the descent to Temnet Cove. Steiner didn't leave the Vigilant's fate to chance, and a solid kick to the arse sent the old man down the many stone steps. Tief and Taiga joined Steiner as they watched the Vigilant fall, tumbling and bouncing off the black stone, coming to rest in a shattered heap at the base of the pier. Steiner started down the steps when a hand touched his arm.

'It's too late,' said Tief.

'They've cast off,' added Taiga, eyes following the Imperial galley as it edged away from the pier, ropes and sails unfurling as it went.

'The crew cast off during the fight with Khigir,' said Tief.

The ship sailed beyond the dark, jagged confines of Temnet Cove. Soon it would be out in open water, traversing around the Nordscales before setting course for Cinderfell. And Kjellrunn.

Steiner let forth a series of curses and Taiga raised an eyebrow. Behind them the sounds of fighting had died down. Those students still loyal to the old ways had retreated to their academies, while those of a more rebellious nature waited in the square, all eyes on Steiner.

'It's the statue, isn't it?' said Tief. 'That's the source.'

'I don't know for sure,' said Steiner, hefting the sledge-hammer. 'But I'm keen to find out.'

A hushed anticipation fell across Academy Square as Steiner approached the dragon statue. He squared up with one of the statue's legs, as thick as an old pine trunk.

Silverdust appeared beside him and nodded, his hands clasped together expectantly.

'Do it, Steiner,' said Sundra.

The hammer swung up high and came around in a vicious arc. Steiner felt the shock all the way up his arms, felt it so badly it made his shoulders ache. He gritted his teeth and struck again, and was rewarded with a tracery of hairline cracks that thickened and spread.

Steiner let out a great roar as the next strike landed, higher up the leg of the statue. The novices in the square howled and yelled with him, a wordless excitement, a savage fury. The fire that roiled about the stone dragon guttered and died and the shouting and swearing died with it. The cracks raced across the surface of the stone; portions of wing shattered and came apart.

'Steiner, get away from there!' yelled Tief.

The dragon statue toppled forward to smash into the gate-house, so loud that Steiner clapped his hands to his ears. Dust and flecks of stone filled the air, followed by coughing and shocked silence. All around, cinderwraiths drifted across Academy Square, clasping insubstantial hands together. The Ashen Torment vibrated against his chest and Steiner reached into his tunic for it.

'What is it?' asked Sundra.

'They *were* linked.' Steiner eyed the destroyed masonry. 'I knew it. The statue and the artefact were linked.'

The statue was the binding part of the power, said Silverdust. *The part that binds dead souls on Vladibogdan. The part that bound me from speaking of it.*

'And now it's destroyed,' said Steiner. 'No more lost souls for the Empire.'

Yes. Silverdust nodded and laid a gloved hand on Steiner's shoulder. *You have my gratitude.*

'This is impressive,' said Taiga in a quiet voice. 'But it doesn't help your sister. What are we going to do now?'

'We need to find a way off the island.' Steiner eyed the fallen statue. 'And there's only one way left.'

CHAPTER THIRTY-EIGHT

Kjellrunn

Many more scholarly Vigilants wonder at the source of the arcane. Was it always the dragon's intent to pass on their powers to more lowly humans? And if the dragons were truly exterminated, might the arcane also be lost from the world? So it is that Vladibogdan is not just a prison for dragons, but a place where we might safeguard them for the future.

– Untainted Histories Volume 3: Serebryanyy Pyli

Kjellrunn's breathing was slow and steady; it was the rise and fall of someone asleep, surrendered to dreaming. There was much that was dreamlike in that moment: the way she drifted above the ground, the black-clad Okhrana moving slow through the dark forest, Bjørner's expression of horrified awe. It was difficult to believe such things were happening. Most of the Okhrana came with swords, but a handful carried nets and crossbows.

'Kjellrunn,' said Marek, his face pale and full of reverence. 'You're levitating.'

'Run back inside, Father, where it's safe.'

No sooner had she said the words than an Okhrana stood

and fired his crossbow. Kjellrunn turned, a dismissive frown on her young face, a slow wave from her right hand. The crossbow bolt ricocheted away from the chalet.

'Hoy!' shouted Verner, falling onto his arse in the mud.

Kjellrunn turned all her attention to the Okhrana with the crossbow, lifting him from the ground with a gesture. The man screamed as he ascended through the forest, hitting branches and speeding higher into the sky.

The distraction almost cost Kjellrunn her life.

'Kjell! Look out,' shouted Verner, pointing to the other side of the clearing. A second crossbowman sighted down his weapon, a curse frozen on his lips. Kjellrunn slammed a hand across her body, turning slightly in the air with the force of it. The bolt changed direction, splintering tree bark. The Okhrana dropped to one knee, reloading the weapon, eyes wide with panic.

The first shooter surrendered to gravity, bereft of Kjellrunn's power. His scream during the descent rang out across the forest, a shrill wail that chilled the blood of all present. The cry was cut short and many of the Okhrana looked over their shoulders.

Kjellrunn eyed the man she had killed, still lost to the dreamlike calm wrapped about her like mist. Two more Okhrana fired and Kjellrunn blinked, every muscle in her body clenched and taut. The first bolt exploded in mid-air, disintegrating silently. A stinging sensation followed, clipping her shoulder, spinning her round. The pain made her gasp and suddenly she was on the ground, hands slick with mud, head thundering with an angry heartbeat. The second bolt had not been so easily stopped. A glance at her shoulder confirmed the flimsy fabric of her tunic had ripped, the flesh beneath no different. A dark red halo soaked through her clothes.

'Concentrate, foolish girl,' said Kjellrunn in a daze.

Verner and Marek surged forward, roaring like berserkers of old. Marek barely bothered with the knife, stepping inside his opponent's reach, knocking aside the hasty thrust. The blacksmith slammed a shoulder into the man's sternum, knocking him flat.

'Father,' screamed Kjellrunn as another attacker approached, but Marek ducked beneath the sword stroke and lashed out. He gripped the knife, point down, raking wide across the Okhrana's vitals beneath the leather jack. The man fell back screaming, collapsed to his knees, eyes fixed with a dread certainty on the spreading stain at his guts.

Verner was no less fierce, jabbing and ducking, weaving through a tangle of limbs. A sword flashed forward and both fisherman and Okhrana found their momentum stalled, too close for an attack of consequence. Verner turned his shoulder and wrestled his attacker's sword from his grasp. A moment later and Verner had run the man through the chest, even as the Okhrana clutched at his face.

Kjellrunn lurched to her feet, one hand pressed to her shoulder. Marek glanced over and opened his mouth to shout. That was when the net fell on him. The Okhrana beat him into submission with the flats of their swords.

'Dammit, Marek!' said the dark-haired Okhrana. 'We're not here for you. Only the Vigilant. Where is she?'

Kjellrunn tried to marshal the icy resolve of her lessons, reached out for the the powers of earth and water, strained to hear the angry roar of the Spøkelsea. Nothing came, no sensation, no sound, just the awful dread of watching her father, knocked to his knees, face bloodied.

'Where is Sharpbreath?' shouted the Okhrana.

The remaining Okhrana were almost upon Kjellrunn when Mistress Kamalov emerged from the chalet. Gone was the stooped, cantankerous woman of the woods. Tall and imperious, with a grave expression full of indignation, Mistress

Kamalov reached out with one hand. Kjellrunn had failed to see the Okhrana with a net approaching but she saw him now. He fell to his knees screaming, clutching the sides of his head. The wind in the clearing whipped the bare trees and set the conifers to swaying.

'You do not come to my house and capture me,' said Mistress Kamalov. 'You do not capture my student. It is I who capture you. Yes?' She flung her arms above her head and let forth a birdlike shriek. The Okhrana, far from being unnerved by such a display, ignored all others and sped towards the old woman at a flat run.

Birds of all descriptions swooped down, blackbirds and crows, gulls and cormorants. Kjellrunn thought she sighted a hawk in the confusion of feathered bodies and surging wings.

The Okhrana dropped to the ground as one, scores of tiny cuts opening across their hands and faces, scalps left bloody by scoring talons. The birds drifted higher, above the reach of the trees, then circled about.

Kjellrunn wasted no time. She ran towards her father, breath hot and fast in her lungs, wrenching the net from his crumpled form. Marek looked at her, not with the eyes of her father, always so steadfast, but with the eyes of a man knowing they were lost.

'There are too many.'

'Mistress Kamalov will save us,' said Kjellrunn. 'Look.'

The rag-tag flock surged down through the trees, wings beating at the air in a fury. The Okhrana had barely recovered and cried out in dismay, all but one. The dark-haired horseman stood up, mocking smirk in place, as bright as the torch he carried in his hand. The birds descended and the horseman beat at them with the fire, singeing feathers. The air was filled with the smell of burning and angry calls of pain. Other Okhrana followed the horseman's example, wrestling flint and torches from their packs. The birds wheeled about and Marek stumbled to his feet, one hand grasping Kjellrunn's wrist.

'I'm taking you away from this.'

'Where?'

'Somewhere safe,' growled Marek.

'Father.' Marek stopped as if he'd been struck. 'They came to Cinderfell for her, but they won't stop until they have us too. Nowhere will ever be safe again.'

The horseman continued to flail at Mistress Kamalov's birds with the torch, buying time for his friends. Other torches were lit to help fend off Mistress Kamalov's flock.

'We have to help her,' said Kjellrunn, but Marek only glanced towards the edge of the clearing, back towards home and Cinderfell.

Mistress Kamalov remained at the chalet's doorway, reaching into the skies again to summon the birds, who were now scattered and shrieking as more flaming torches appeared in the hands of the Okhrana. The old woman bellowed words in Solska but the flock did not heed the call, cut short as it was.

Kjellrunn called out as a lone Okhrana emerged from the chalet behind Mistress Kamalov and clubbed her in the head with the pommel of his sword. The old woman crumpled, the birds above fled in all directions.

A cry went up from the Okhrana, short-lived as Verner appeared behind Mistress Kamalov's attacker. Two short blades flashed in the weak light and the Okhrana was on his knees. The blades flashed again and the man was clutching his neck, eyes wide with shock, face pale as the snow in the clearing.

The dark-haired Okhrana swore in Solska and threw down his torch before shouting at a comrade. Verner charged forward as a crossbow took him in the shoulder.

'Verner? No!' Kjellrunn screamed, feeling an awful chill that had nothing to do with the cruel wind.

Verner stumbled on, lashing out at the nearest Okhrana

and forcing back his weapon, slashing his opponent across the thigh. For a second the Okhrana stumbled and Verner shuddered, once, twice, as two more bolts took him in the chest and gut.

Verner, Uncle Verner, the half-drunk fisherman and teller of tall tales, collapsed to the forest floor and didn't move.

'Verner!' Marek's cry signalled the end of the fight. The blacksmith hobbled to his fallen friend and clutched his body close, but Verner didn't reply. Kjellrunn stared wordlessly from Verner to Mistress Kamalov, who lay still, dead or unconscious. The Okhrana circled the fallen, bright blades in eager hands.

Kjellrunn couldn't speak, shock stealing every word and every thought.

'You Nordvlast girls all look the same to me,' sneered the horseman, streaked with soot and bearing a trio of scratches. He had not lost his smirk during the fighting. 'All thin as whips, with sour faces that don't remember to smile when a man passes by.'

'You want me to smile?' whispered Kjellrunn, eyes burning with unshed tears. 'You want me to smile?' she said again, louder. The roar of the Spøkelsea was in her ears, in her veins, an irresistible susurrus. 'You want me to smile?' she was shouting, howling above the noise in her head. It was the sound of stone breaking and trees splintering, falling snapping.

'Frøya save us,' said Marek. He was not looking at the Okhrana, but Kjellrunn.

Stones wrenched themselves free of the forest floor along with the weapons of the fallen. Old timber and shards of bone from animals long dead floated above the ground. A few of the Okhrana began to run but were caught in the vortex of debris as it swirled about the clearing. Men were pelted and beaten, bludgeoned in a storm that lifted them from their feet. The screams of the Okhrana stopped one by one as the men were smashed head first into trees, or collided with swords. The air was filled with a blur of violence and Kjellrunn drifted at the eye of the storm, teeth gritted, fists clenched so hard her nails drew blood from her palms. On and on the vortex whirled, until the shrieks of the dying were silenced and only the terrible voice of the wind remained.

'Kjellrunn!' came Marek's voice amid the fury. 'Kjellrunn, they're all dead.'

They had killed Verner. She would not stop until every bone was broken. Her power would not be dismissed so quickly.

'Kjellrunn. Stop!' Marek stood beneath her, pleading. 'The chalet is coming apart!'

Kjellrunn regarded the little house. Watched the thatch come free of the roof, whipped up into the sky, watching the walls and shutters pelted by rocks and the corpses of the Okhrana.

'Kjellrunn, you have to stop or the whole forest will be destroyed.'

The storm raged on, irresistible. How had she never tapped into this before? Such power. Always cowering from other children, from the stares of the townsfolk. Never again.

'Kjell! You're going to kill Mistress Kamalov. We've already lost Verner.'

The clearing was filled with the sounds of debris crashing to ground. Kjellrunn floated down, feet alighting on bloodied snow. She closed her eyes and took a long steadying breath, trying to fight the feeling of sickness that grew within her.

'You did it, Kjell. You saved us.' Marek limped towards the shattered chalet, lifting a broken branch from where it had fallen on Mistress Kamalov. He slumped down by the chalet, sitting with his back to the wall, eyeing the devastation.

All was silent in the forest, no clash of swords, no thump of stone on timber, no roars of the brave or dying whimpers. All was silent but for the terrible sobs that wracked Marek, hands pressed to his face, wordless with grief but for one name.

'Verner.'

It began to snow, and yet Kjellrunn had no desire to move. She stood frozen at the centre of the clearing, afraid a single step might spell her collapse. Her hands shook but not with cold. A terrible emptiness had taken the place of the fury in her head. Bjørner looked out from behind a tree and stared at Kjellrunn, either too stupid or too terrified to run away.

'Kjell.' Marek gestured to the far side of the clearing. A bundle of black rags rolled over and began crawling through the mud, shuffling past rocks and corpses. The man made no sound, save for the soft wheeze of someone badly hurt.

Kjellrunn took a step forward, legs shaking beneath her as she went. The Okhrana stared over his shoulder, twisting onto his back and scrambling away on hands and feet, arse scuffing the ground. The storm of stone and wood had scoured the smirk from his face, leaving only disbelief and fear.

'Please,' said the dark-haired horseman.'Please.' Gone was the swagger of the Okhrana who had chiding her for not smiling.

Kjellrunn stepped forward, then took another step, feeling her strength return as the horseman's fear grew. Her foot nudged a short blade in the mud and she stooped to retrieve it.

'Please, I'm unarmed.'

'There is only killing.' Kjellrunn stalked over to the fallen Okhrana. 'That's what you said. And how many unarmed men and women have you killed?'

The horseman fell silent.

'How many in the name of your beloved Empire?'

'No, wait. Please.'

'You killed my uncle!'

Kjellrunn raised the curved blade above her head, and then the horseman spoke no more.

'Go home, Bjørner,' said Kjellrunn, without looking up from the Okhrana's corpse.

The tavern keeper emerged from behind a tree, guilt and fear filling eyes that had seen too much. 'Go home to your daughter.'

Bjørner nodded.

'And if you mistreat her . . .' Kjellrunn indicated the horseman.

Bjørner nodded again, and then he was gone, fleeing the devastated woodland. Kjellrunn's stony gaze followed every step of his departure.

CHAPTER THIRTY-NINE

Steiner

The darkest fear of any Imperial servant is a unification of a different kind. We would face a war on three fronts if the people of Shanisrond and the Scorched Republics were to enter into an alliance with the Yamal. But such an uprising would be hard-pressed to overcome the military might of the Emperor. I fear he must be taken down from within, and then the issue of succession hangs over the continent like a spectre.

– Untainted Histories Volume 3: Serebryanyy Pyli

'This is bad,' grumbled Tief. Academy Square was a strange tableau; some soldiers remained standing, petrified by Sundra's arcane gaze, while the bodies of others lay sprawled across the flagstones, suffocated by the cinderwraiths. The soldiers were not the only casualties. Charred corpses were among the dead, too small to be soldiers. Steiner guessed they were novices. Others had been bludgeoned to death.

'At least they won't become cinderwraiths now,' whispered Steiner.

'I meant Shirinov escaping. This is bad.' Tief gestured to

the destruction all around them. 'But the damage Shirinov could do with twenty soldiers and no oversight . . .'

'I know, don't think I've forgotten.' Steiner hefted his sledge-hammer and wiped the grit from his eyes.

Taiga supported her sister, who looked exhausted after petrifying so many soldiers. Silverdust remained at Steiner's shoulder, his uniform curiously pristine despite the desolation. *What will you do now?*

'Come on.' Steiner glanced over his shoulder and headed back along the alley between Academy Vozdukha and Academy Voda. 'I have an idea.'

The cinderwraiths followed, all trace of malevolence now faded. The Ashen Court drifted behind, silent and obedient with Silverdust leading. Steiner raised the flickering amulet a little higher. Arcane light danced along the walls of the sloping corridor.

You promised to free them. Silverdust loomed over Steiner, the aura of light and heat uncomfortable. Steiner frowned at the Vigilant.

'I will free you, I promise,' said Steiner, 'but our work isn't over yet.'

It is not as they they have a choice, is it? replied Silverdust.

'You've a remarkable talent for missing the boat,' said Tief, rubbing his forehead. He had the decency to look abashed when Steiner glowered at him.

'If I get this right I won't need a boat,' said Steiner as he ventured down the many steps to the forges.

'Get what right?' asked Tief as they descended yet deeper beneath the island.

'You hate surprises, don't you?' said Steiner.

'No good ever came of a surprise.' Tief screwed up his face.

'There is another way off Vladibogdan,' said Sundra, 'but it is no simple undertaking.'

Steiner snorted a bitter laugh. 'When is anything simple on Vladibogdan?'

It is the only way. Steiner couldn't be sure if Silverdust's words were heard by everyone or him alone.

'It stands to reason you'd know what I'm thinking,' he said, hearing his own frustration.

I have been doing this a long time. Decades in fact.

In time they reached the wide stone balcony, overlooking furnaces left to cool. The usual din of industry was silent without the army of cinderwraiths to work their stations. Only one hammer rose and fell, one hammer ringing out like a watchtower bell, a warning that all was not well. Kimi was still at work near her huge furnace, still atop her dais working at weapons.

'Tread softly here, Steiner. She's not going to be thrilled that you missed the boat after she gave up the amulet.'

'I'm not thrilled either. I'm less thrilled about what I have to do next.'

'Are you going to share this plan?' said Taiga. She had one arm around her sister and a look of wariness on her slender face.

'I'm going to ask to borrow a dragon,' said Steiner.

'A dragon?' said Tief. 'Couldn't think of anything more damn foolish to do, I suppose?'

'You know me,' said Steiner, glancing over the Ashen Court as they crowded about him. He held the flickering amulet a little higher. 'Come on.'

Kimi acknowledged their arrival with a grunt.

'Hoy there,' said Steiner, sounding a good deal more cheerful than he felt. Kimi continued her work. 'I didn't manage to get aboard the ship.'

'I have eyes.' Breathing hard, she hammered a piece of steel where it lay across the anvil.

'Shirinov sent Khigir to stall me. We defeated him.' Steiner spared a glance for Tief, Taiga and Sundra and felt a swell of gratitude. 'But by the time we defeated Khigir—'

'Shirinov had set sail,' said Kimi. Another clang as the hammer continued its brutal work shaping the metal. 'Leaving you in charge of the island, I suppose?'

'I don't want to be in charge—'

'Do you know how many cinderwraiths have found their way down here in the last hour?' Another deafening peal as Kimi's hammer fell. 'Newly created cinderwraiths?'

'I . . .' Steiner's eyes widened as he thought of the bodies sprawled across Academy Square, each one bearing a soul that had since been captured by the Ashen Torment. 'I didn't think—'

'No,' said Kimi, 'you didn't. You're like every other Northman I've met.' Hammer and anvil rang out again. 'Impulse first, consequence later.'

'That's hardly fair, Kimi,' said Taiga.

'Death is inevitable,' said Sundra.

'We had to fight,' added Tief. 'We couldn't just smuggle the lad aboard.'

'There won't be any more cinderwraiths now,' said Steiner. 'The dragon statue in Academy Square was the key. I destroyed it.'

'What?' Kimi paused from beating the steel and frowned.

'The Ashen Torment worked in tandem with the statue. One artefact to bind the souls to the island, one to command them.'

'And you know that for a fact, do you?' said Kimi.

It is as he says. Silverdust drifted up onto the dais and Kimi blinked in surprise.

'No more cinderwraiths,' added Steiner. 'I promise.'

'That may be, but I trusted you with that.' Kimi pointed at the amulet hanging from the chain, the dragon carving flickered with arcane flame. 'And you've made everything worse.'

Steiner didn't care for the way Kimi pointed at the amulet. He'd had his fill of people pointing at him over the years. Usually they pointed because of his strange sister, wrapped up in her daydreams of folklore and old gods. Other times they pointed and sniggered behind their hands, *'There goes the illiterate blacksmith's son. Too stupid to take over his father's business.'*

'I've made everything worse?' replied Steiner with an incredulous curl to his lip. 'Worse than being enslaved underground? Worse than being forced to make weapons that will kill people in Shanisrond?' He looked around at the cold furnaces. 'Worse than being starved if we don't fulfil the quotas for arms and armour?'

'Steiner, calm yourself. She's a right to be worried,' said Tief.

'Worse than working for an Empire that doesn't care if we live or die?' continued Steiner, feeling the heat of his anger and frustration.

'I gave you the amulet, didn't I?' said Kimi. 'And we're no better off than we were before we freed you.'

'Yes,' said Steiner quietly, 'and I'm grateful, but now I need something else. Now I need your dragon.'

'Själsstyrka?' Kimi frowned, incomprehension rather than anger.

'You named it?' said Tief.

'I thought we all agreed not to name them,' added Taiga. 'It's less upsetting when they die that way.'

'Death comes to us all, even dragons,' muttered Sundra. Steiner wondered if she wasn't a little delirious after the fight.

'She's called Själsstyrka?' asked Steiner.

'Who said it was a female?' said Tief. 'Suddenly the boy is an expert on dragons.'

'I always thought of the silver one as a girl, I suppose.' Steiner shrugged and felt a touch embarrassed.

'I always thought Själsstyrka was a girl too,' said Kimi, pressing her thumb to her lips, eyes lost to thought. 'So,' she said after a few moments, 'we'll need to feed her up first. She's weak and there's no telling how she'll feel about you wanting to ride her like a horse.'

'You'll be fortunate if she doesn't eat you alive,' said Tief.

'It is as the bones foretold,' said Sundra.

'We need to get moving.' Steiner jutted his head towards the wide corridor that led to the dragons. 'I don't want Shirinov to reach Cinderfell before I do.'

'I'm so glad we didn't bring everyone we know down here,' said Tief, passing an annoyed glance across Kimi, Silverdust, Taiga, Sundra and the host of cinderwraiths following in Steiner's wake. 'It's not like we're about to let this dragon slip free of her bonds for the first time. I mean, we wouldn't want to startle her.'

'It's not the first time,' said Kimi. 'I let her stretch her wings and her legs once a day.'

Tief stared at Kimi as if she had lost her mind. 'Once a day? When do you find the time?'

'I make time,' said Kimi as she unlocked the heavy padlocks with a ring of keys retrieved from a back pocket.

Maxim pushed his way to the front of the crowd, eyes wide with shock. 'Be careful, Steiner,' he whispered.

'You'll want to bring that bucket of beef over here,' she added. 'Being unchained means food, and there's no telling what will happen if there's no meat.'

Steiner fetched the bucket of gristle and stepped towards Själsstyrka. Tief's eyes were wide with anticipation, while Silverdust remained inscrutable behind his mask, a dozen feet away.

'Perhaps we should give her a little room,' admitted Steiner. Everyone shuffled back, the sense of excitement almost as bad as the feeling of dread. One by one the chains fell to the floor, rattling as they went, scraping on the flagstones. The other dragons stirred and tails swished with agitation or excitement. Steiner looked down at his own chain, still wrapped about his wrist like a bracer. He'd endured three days of such confinement, he couldn't imagine the dragons' misery.

'Själsstyrka,' said Kimi, tenderly.

'It's a good name,' admitted Steiner as the dragon slumped to the floor. It paused a moment before standing on all four legs and arching its back. Talons flexed and clawed at stone and Steiner offered a fistful of beef.

'They caught her in Drakefjord when she was young,' explained Kimi. 'It's rare when that happens. Most of them are born into captivity.'

Själsstyrka growled a moment, then snatched the beef from Steiner's hand. He felt the teeth brush his open palm and struggled not to flinch.

'There are still dragons in the wild?' asked Steiner.

'Not many,' admitted Kimi. 'They never make it to maturity. They know to stay close to Shanisrond and Svingettevei. Any further north is too cold for them. It seemed right I give her a name in Nordspråk, so I called her Själsstyrka.'

'I don't know that word,' admitted Maxim. 'What does it mean?'

'It's an old word, an antiquated word for "fortitude",' said Sundra. 'I had no idea you were so conversant in languages, Kimi.'

Steiner offered more meat to the snapping jaws of the silver dragon. Själsstyrka appeared to delight in cracking open the bones, causing Steiner to wince.

'I once hoped to travel and found trade routes with the Scorched Republics,' said Kimi. 'I wanted Yamal to enjoy riches again.' Another hunk of beef disappeared down the dragon's gullet. 'But the Empire will never let the Yamal be free, never let us choose our own way.'

Själsstyrka gave a low rumble, her slitted eyes blinked, then became heavy-lidded. Steiner had run out of beef and took a step back, suddenly afraid he might be next.

'That's good,' said Sundra. 'She's sated now.' The priestess approached the dragon and held out a hand, palm outstretched. 'Hush now, Själsstyrka. You are fed and sleepy, but you are not so strong that you do not need my help.'

Själsstyrka sniffed at the slender hand of the black-garbed priestess and eyed her with wariness.

'Hush now, close your eyes and kneel before me. My kin have never been allies of your kind, only prey. But let us not think of such things.'

To Steiner's surprise Själsstyrka folded her legs beneath her and lay on the flagstones. Her sinuous neck remained upright, and the wedge of her long skull pointed towards the priestess like a spearhead. Sundra stepped closer, resting her palm on the ridge of bone between Själsstyrka's eyes.

'You can bet your boots you'll never see the likes of this again,' said Tief, tugging at one ear. Sundra turned her head, beckoning to Steiner with her free hand.

'Come, kneel before me in the presence of the goddess. Let us see if we can join your will with Själsstyrka's.'

Steiner stepped forward, unnerved to his very bones. 'I have to kneel? Are you sure she's had enough to eat?'

'You must be joined,' said Sundra in a harsh whisper. 'Kneel.' Steiner did as he was told, closing his eyes and releasing a shaky breath.

'Remember what I told you,' said Sundra. 'Release yourself from thoughts of this island. Release all concerns for unfeeling stone and wretched suffering. Hush now.'

Though it took long moments to calm himself, Steiner was back in the echo of the forest, a memory of the woodlands Sundra carried within herself. The snowdrops had gone but the trees were lush and green; tall grasses swayed in a gentle wind. Ferns crowded together and the stream reflected silver in the sunlight, like steel, like Själsstyrka. Steiner breathed the gentle scent of the woodland, savouring the rich earth and pleasant warmth of summer. Two crows occupied a low branch and muttered to one another. Woodsmoke drifted on the air.

'Pay attention,' whispered Sundra. She stood before him in the clearing, just as she had done in the chamber of dragons. One hand rested on Själsstyrka's brow while the other was a cool presence on Steiner's forehead. Her black robes were more splendid here, the bird bones polished, tiny flecks of black glass sewn along the collar. Bangles of obsidian hung from her slender wrists.

'You look different,' whispered Steiner.

'I am here as I used to be,' said Sundra, wistful. 'I am here as I remember myself best. Free and young and beautiful.'

Själsstyrka released a long growl from deep in her chest and Steiner struggled not to panic and run behind the nearest tree.

'Tell her,' said Sundra.

'Tell her what?'

'That you need her help, of course.'

'Will she understand me?'

'Don't put it into words, merely think it, imagine it, picture it in your mind.'

Steiner thought of Cinderfell and riding Själsstyrka through the clouds.

'That's good,' whispered Sundra. 'What else?'

Steiner imagined the long skull jabbing forward at soldiers, splitting wide open to reveal rows of teeth. He imagined the great wings buffeting Shirinov and knocking him into the sea.

'Yes, that's it,' said Sundra.

Steiner breathed deeply and felt the strangest sensation: reaching his arms wide, stretching his limbs until they were held out at his sides, magnificent and strong. Not arms, he realized, wings. Själsstyrka's wings were opened, almost filling the clearing. The silver was more vibrant, iridescent and startling, hues of blue and purple shimmering beneath the surface. There was a moment taut with expectation, an undercurrent of anxiety. Steiner imagined being swept up in her claws and wrenched into the sky.

'She will smell your fear,' said Sundra. 'Clear your mind!'

The wings snapped down and a gust of air made the leaves and twigs dance in the clearing. Another beat of the vast silver wings forced Steiner backwards and he held up one hand to his eyes.

'Look,' said Sundra, her voice full of awe. Above the canopy of the trees, against a pale blue cloudless sky, Själsstyrka held herself aloft with great beats of scaled and powerful wings.

'Själsstyrka is ready to fly,' said Sundra with reverence. 'Are you?'

Steiner nodded. 'And Frøya keep me close,' he whispered.

CHAPTER FORTY

Kjellrunn

The people of Solmindre do not deal with loss well, and I write this as one of them. A Solmindre serf scowls at death, curses its name, and spits on the floor at barely a mention of the afterlife. They despise those taken for having the audacity to die. A great deal of blame is heaped upon the deceased until the vodka flows, and then finally, tears may be seen.

– Untainted Histories Volume 3: Serebryanyy Pyli

'It didn't take them long to arrive,' said Kjellrunn, taking a moment to catch her breath. She'd not dug a grave before and couldn't say she cared for it much. A murder of crows filled the trees above them, all muttering to one another, extending black wings and calling out every so often.

Marek raised eyes from the turned earth and looked across the clearing. The bodies of the Okhrana lay strewn across the ground, smashed trees watched over the scene of devastation. Snapped branches and upturned stones littered the ground.

'Crows,' said Mistress Kamalov. She sat outside the chalet, staring at the desolation as if in a trance. 'Lady Frejna's messengers and consorts all. They heed the call of death and bear witness to it.'

'Let's hope there's no more death to come,' said Kjellrunn, though she didn't feel much optimism.

'There's always more death to come,' said Mistress Kamalov. 'It's the only truth you can count on in life.'

'How deep should we make it?' asked Kjellrunn, flashing a glance at Marek, who was glowering at the old Vigilant.

'A good few feet,' said Marek after a pause. 'Or the scavengers will dig him up and that's no good. You might want to get in there and dig.'

Kjellrunn climbed into the shallow trench and thrust the spade into the earth, lifting and shovelling and lifting again. Long minutes passed by and the soil grew in a heap. Kjellrunn paused to catch her breath.

'I keep thinking he's at his cottage in town,' she said. 'Or he'll come to us tonight with empty pockets and that big, broad smile of his.' Kjellrunn eyed the bundle of old canvas. Not much of a shroud, but it was all they had. She hoped Verner would understand.

'I know,' said Marek with tears in his eyes. 'It's hard, and it will always be hard. Sometimes you'll find yourself thinking of him as if he were an old friend who moved to the next town. Then you'll remember, and all the pain and sadness will return.'

Kjellrunn wiped her tears with the back of a muddied hand. 'First my brother, now my uncle.'

'Verner died protecting you,' said Marek. 'A hero's death. He didn't drown in a squall, or get knifed in bar fight gone bad. He died a proper death, resisting the Empire, looking out for those he loved. And Steiner's not dead.'

'He may as well be if we can't get to the island.'

'He's not dead,' repeated Marek. 'Don't speak that way.'

A glimmer of light snared their attention. Mistress Kamalov

hobbled closer, holding up a lantern. 'It gets dark so quickly.' Her voice was tree bark and grit, eyes unfocused. 'Frejna only knows why you'd bring your family this far north.'

'I wanted to be close to the island,' said Marek. 'My wife was sent there for a time. After she died, well, I just didn't have it in me to start over somewhere else.'

Kjellrunn pulled herself out of the grave. 'She was a Vigilant, and you a lowly soldier. It doesn't make any sense.'

'An unlikely combination,' agreed Mistress Kamalov.

'Not that lowly as it turns out. I was a sergeant. I knew her for a long time, and things happen when you serve alongside someone. A trust develops, even for someone in a mask.' Marek looked up at the darkening sky and sighed. 'We always knew what the Empire was doing was wrong. We hoped things would change in time. We hoped the leaders would become less complacent, less intolerant, less vindictive.'

'You've been waiting a long time,' said Mistress Kamalov. 'We all have.'

'That's how it goes with power.' Marek looked away to the clearing and the many corpses, where the crows had begun their grisly feast. 'Given to someone great, power is a boon to all. Given to someone weak, it's a curse to everyone else.'

Kjellrunn remembered how the arcane had surged through her, lifting her from the ground, coursing through every fibre of her body, an irresistible storm. 'I don't want to use my power again,' she said. 'Not after today.'

Mistress Kamalov and Marek stared for a moment.

'I'll let you bury Verner,' she added. 'I can't be here to watch that. I won't . . .' Any other words were lost to the thick swell in her throat, washed away by the tears tracking down her cheeks. She stalked away, letting the shovel drop without a care.

Kjellrunn was on the floor of the chalet when Mistress Kamalov found her. She was staring into the flames hoping to forget the many corpses outside and what she had done. The old woman's breaths sounded gently in the silence, her eyes glimmering firelight.

'Too bad the roof has mostly gone,' said Mistress Kamalov. 'And too bad I have to move home so soon. I was just settling in.'

Kjellrunn bowed her head and wept. She wept for Verner in his canvas shroud. She wept for her father beaten and broken by the Okhrana. She wept for Steiner, alive on the island yet impossible to reach.

'It is perfectly natural,' said Mistress Kamalov, placing a gentle hand on her shoulder.

'I'd say it's pretty unnatural.' Kjellrunn pulled her knees to her chest and hugged her legs.

'The arcane and death are not so different.' The old woman sat at the kitchen table. 'Both are part of life, both are things we would prefer not to speak of, prefer not to think of. This is why the Spriggani are such a mystery to Northmen. They live each day with death as a companion, as a goddess.'

'Maybe they have the truth of it,' said Kjellrunn.

'Perhaps,' agreed Mistress Kamalov. 'Sleep now. Today has been unkind and there is nothing else to be done.'

Kjellrunn stood up and found herself face to face with the old woman. Without a word they fell into each other's arms and Kjellrunn sobbed some more.

'Sleep, clever girl, brave girl. Sleep.'

The silence in the chalet bore down on each of them, so heavy it might have been a wet cloak or a weighted net. Kjellrunn lingered by the door to the back room, watching Marek and Mistress Kamalov at the table, two strangers united by a common threat.

'It stands to reason he couldn't kill you,' said Marek. 'He always was a soft touch when it came to women. And not just the pretty ones. In his own way he was always looking out for his sisters.' Marek sighed. 'I should never have let him go to Helwick.'

'He was a good man,' said Mistress Kamalov. 'I would have liked to know him better.'

'And what will you do now?' said Marek. 'You can't stay here.'

'That much is true,' said Mistress Kamalov. 'I need a ship. I will go south, to Shanisrond. It is the only place left for people wanted by the Empire.' Mistress Kamalov turned in her seat and looked directly at Kjellrunn. 'And you must come too. Word will get out, it always does, and it will bring soldiers, Vigilants, more Okhrana.'

'I'm not going through that again.' Kjellrunn nodded outside. A glance out of the window revealed only darkness. None of the corpses could be seen but the sun would be up soon. Even the forest couldn't hide all the terrible things Kjellrunn's power had wrought.

'Someone comes,' said Mistress Kamalov, making a lazy gesture towards the door. 'Someone from town. Not Okhrana.'

Marek stood and drew his knife.

'I said they're not Okhrana,' repeated Mistress Kamalov.

'Just because they're not from the Empire doesn't mean they're not dangerous,' said Marek, though he looked unsteady on his feet and Kjellrunn wondered if he would be able to fight at all, given his injuries.

'Leave this to me, Father.' Kjellrunn opened the door. The darkness of the forest was near-absolute, the sky a shade lighter than the deep shadows between the trees. A light bobbed through the gloom.

'What time is it?' she asked.

'Who knows in this wretched country,' replied Mistress Kamalov. 'Even the sun refuses to come here.'

'A few hours before dawn, I think,' said Marek.

'Hoy there!' Kjellrunn shouted into the darkness, a good imitation of Steiner.

'Hoy there.' The response was quieter, a woman's voice.

'Kristofine?'

The lantern came closer and hesitated in the middle of the clearing. An anxious face appeared in the light. 'Yes.'

'You'd best come in,' said Kjellrunn. 'I assume your no-good father threw you out?'

'My no-good father has done no such thing. He sent me to warn you.' Kristofine slipped through the door, her eyes widening as they settled on Marek. Kjellrunn was glad it was still dark outside, the devastated woodlands and strewn corpses would take some explaining.

'The Okhrana came for us,' said Marek. 'Things didn't go so well.'

Kristofine blinked and looked to Kjellrunn. 'Things are about to become worse.'

'What do you mean?' asked Kjellrunn.

'They sent a ship,' said Mistress Kamalov.

Kristofine nodded and slumped into an empty chair.

'You will have tea?' said Mistress Kamalov.

Kristofine took Kjellrunn's hand. 'The fishermen saw a light when they set out this morning. They think a ship is coming, but the headwind is all wrong and it's making slow progress.'

'The wind will not be our ally for long. Wind changes. We must leave Cinderfell now.' Mistress Kamalov pointed at Kristofine. 'You will come too.'

'I can't. My father is here, my tavern is here.' Kristofine looked at Marek. 'There's the whole town to think of.'

'And when has the whole town ever thought about you?' asked Marek. 'Or me, or Kjellrunn? Never. They only spared us a thought when they suspected us of witchsign.'

'The ship is Imperial,' said Mistress Kamalov. 'Trust me. I feel it in my bones. We must leave now.'

'But everyone in the town will die,' said Kristofine.

'You need to decide what you want,' said Marek. 'You can come with us, or die with them.'

'Father!' Kjellrunn glared at Marek.

'The only one who knows anything is Bjørner,' said Marek.

'He won't say anything.' Kristofine glanced at Kjellrunn, then back to Marek. 'I promise he won't say anything.' But no matter where she looked none believed her.

'Your father may keep his mouth shut at first,' said Mistress Kamalov. 'But he'll speak of what he's seen. They always do.'

'The Synod will send for Kjellrunn,' said Marek, 'and the whole town will pay the price for the dead Vigilants, and all these dead Okhrana.'

'We leave now.' Mistress Kamalov stood up and crossed to the door. 'I'm not staying here to be butchered by the very madmen I am trying to escape.'

'I'm not leaving.' Kjellrunn had not raised her voice, but all eyes turned her, silhouetted by the fire.

'Kjell, we have to go . . .' Marek fell silent as his daughter looked up from the dancing flames in the hearth.

'I'm going to Vladibogdan to find Steiner. You can do as you please, but I'm staying in Cinderfell.'

'Kjell.' Marek held a hand to his forehead. 'It's bad enough we've lost Verner—'

'I am staying.'

'And what have you got in mind?' said Mistress Kamalov.

'Can't you tell?' said Kjellrunn. 'Can't you read my mind?'

A tense moment passed in the chalet. Marek and Kristofine waited for Mistress Kamalov to speak.

'It is not something you can do alone,' the old woman said. 'You will need my help. It is a good plan. More ambitious than sane but . . .' The old woman shrugged.

'You said you weren't going to use the arcane again,' said Marek.

'It's not as if there's another choice,' said Kjellrunn, 'not another good choice, anyway. And I want Steiner back.'

'What's this plan then?' asked Kristofine.

'Come on,' said Kjellrunn. 'I'll tell you on the way to the cliffs.'

'Why do we need to go to the cliffs?' said Marek.

'You'll see,' said Kjellrunn, hearing the hushed roar of the Spøkelsea in her mind.

CHAPTER FORTY-ONE

Steiner

Many within the Empire question how Vladibogdan can contain such dangerous beasts, yet there is more to dragons than merely fiery breath and gouging talons. Theirs is a singular intelligence, but it is an intelligence that is easily stunted. Starvation, cold, and a lack of freedom reduce even the most mighty dragons to little more than dumb beasts. Dragons are not so very different to humans in this regard.

– Untainted Histories Volume 3: Serebryanyy Pyli

Academy Square looked no better as a corpse-strewn battle-field. Bodies and weapons lay forgotten and discarded on cobbles slick with freezing rain. The dragon statue lay crumpled across the cobbles, the vast panes of stone wings shattered, like uneven flagstones. Steiner forced himself not to stare at the blank faces of the fallen. The novices had hurried back to their academies and Steiner hoped the smarter ones had barricaded themselves in.

'We made a real mess, didn't we?' said Steiner, looking around the square.

Tief rubbed his forehead. 'I've seen worse.' Steiner thought he was gaming, but the expression on Tief's face confirmed the contrary. 'Much worse.'

'When the Empire came for the Spriggani?'

Tief nodded and looked away, unwilling or unable to say anything else.

Silverdust watched silently as Sundra and Taiga bundled him up for the weather, using the clothes of fallen soldiers. Steiner shrugged on a padded coat but declined the mail armour on account of the weight. No one said anything, but all shared anxious looks. Would Själsstyrka be strong enough to carry him to Cinderfell, or would they plummet into the Spøkelsea and drown?

Själsstyrka emerged into Academy Square step by reluctant step. The wedge-shaped head cast about slowly, then she lifted the mighty jaw to look at the sky. Silvery wings shivered with anticipation or excitement, Steiner wasn't sure which, but knew he would find out soon enough.

Sundra fashioned a scarf out of a long scrap of fabric she'd scavenged and bade Steiner kneel down. 'Keep warm. You're no good to anyone if you arrive frozen to death.'

'But I'm chosen,' said Steiner, smiling sadly. 'The bones whisper my name, remember?'

'The bones don't feel the cold, but you do.' A glimmer of a smile crossed her slender face. 'Now go to your sister, and know that Frøya and Frejna's blessings fly with you.'

Steiner stood up and Kimi approached holding a Vigilant's red leather surcoat. 'Something for you. It might help keep the rain off.' She held out the surcoat and Steiner slipped his arms into the garment.

'I'll come back,' he said, mouth twisting with upset. 'I'll find a way to come back for you.'

'You owe me,' said Kimi, handling him the sledgehammer. 'Once you've done this you have to find a way to keep the Yamal safe, or I'll kill you myself.'

'It's not Shirinov I'm afraid of,' said Steiner, 'it's you.' He was surprised to find that he meant it. It was not a physical fear of Kimi, but the fear of letting her down. The Ashen Torment hung heavy around his neck and his hand strayed to the artefact and patted the bulge by his heart.

Maxim stepped forward and flung his arms around Steiner. The boy tried to say something, then wiped his eyes with his sleeve and ran off.

'He'll be fine,' said Kimi. 'I'll look out for him.'

Sundra held out a hand to the dragon and rested it on the ridge of bone that ran along the pointed head. 'Själsstyrka, we have freed you and you have dined. Now take our friend to the shore where he may avenge himself on his enemies.'

'Avenge myself?'

Sundra frowned. 'Dragons care nothing for rescues, but vengeance is quite a different matter.' Steiner nodded and Sundra continued her entreaty.

'Själsstyrka, do this thing and we will ask no more from you.'

The dragon lay down and lifted her wings until they were vertical.

'She can understand you?' said Steiner.

'Not language perhaps, but dragons perceive intent,' said Sundra. 'Don't ever lie to a dragon, Steiner. They have no patience for it.'

Steiner eyed the row of sharp spines that began at the nape of the neck.

'This could be uncomfortable.' He edged towards the dragon, noting that the spikes were shorter where they ran between the dragon's wings, flat at the section of spine that came after.

'Not much good if you pierce a wing on your own back-bone,' said Tief, urging Steiner to climb on. 'And a useful spot to cling on.'

'There's not much to hold on to,' said Steiner, anxious he would be thrown off the moment they launched into the air.

'Then lie low, best to get out of the way of the—'

And with one great beat the wings flared out, like silver sails in a headwind.

'Maybe we could find a saddle?' Steiner grasped a great spike of bone where it emerged before him, lying flat along Själsstyrka's spine to do so.

'Hold on tight, Hammersmith!' shouted Tief.

The dragon lurched upward before Steiner could reply. The rocky chasm of Academy Square raced by to one side while Steiner gazed down at his friends as they spun beneath him. Själsstyrka was circling Academy Square, flying so close to the sides she must surely smash her wings. Steiner clung on with hands and legs, his boots pressed tight to Själsstyrka's flanks. Round they went in a dizzying arc, banking sharply until they were flying in a tight circle over Academy Square.

'Shit, shit, shit.' Steiner looked down to see his friends made small by distance. The rock on all sides dropped away and Själsstyrka opened her wings even wider.

'I'd thought we might try hovering above the ground a bit first,' shouted Steiner. Själsstyrka answered with a plume of smoke that emerged from her nostrils and raced along her back, into Steiner's face.

'It's going to be like that is it?'

The wings snapped out and beat no more, held out wide above the island that had kept them prisoner for so long. The only sound was the keening wind.

'I really hope you're strong enough to carry me back to land,' muttered Steiner, eyes fixed on the green and choppy swell of the ocean below. To his surprise Själsstyrka gave a dismissive snort and wheeled about once more, climbing ever higher.

'Much more of this and we'll reach the clouds.' His teeth were already starting to chatter and he was glad of the leather gloves Taiga had forced onto his hands. A quick glance over his shoulder confirmed the sledgehammer was still in place, the shaft forced under a thick leather belt that circled his waist twice. Själsstyrka tensed and beat her wings just once, her body moving sinuously.

'I can't tell if we're moving or not this far up,' said Steiner. Again she beat her wings and Steiner dared himself to look down, past boots clamped to the dragon's silvery sides. Vladibogdan and the shattered rock of the Nordscale Islands were far behind.

'You're doing it,' said Steiner. 'You're taking me home.'

Själsstyrka gave a snort and beat her vast silvery wings, iridescence dancing in the meagre light of the winter's day, flying so high they must surely graze the clouds with their passing.

Steiner's heart leapt when he sighted Cinderfell. It was not a pretty town, but it was all he had ever known. The ashen pall, so much a part of life in Nordvlast, was fortified by dark clouds that promised icy rain. Far below, sailing an oblique towards the shore, was the Imperial galley.

'Shirinov!' Steiner's hand strayed to the sledgehammer and he felt his anger and impatience as keenly as the wind. Själsstyrka seemed to understand and began to descend. The wind, their constant companion during the flight, was now roaring in his ears. For the first time Själsstyrka struggled, the headwind a match for her powerful wings. For a time they simply hung in the air. The ship fared little better, edging towards the pier, lashed by angry waves.

Steiner blinked. 'This can't be right.' Despite the darkness, despite the rain, his gaze fell on three figures who stood on the headland to the north of Cinderfell. Two of the people held arms raised to the skies, as if reaching out to the wind itself, the third held a torch.

'Vigilants from Academy Vozdukha?' said Steiner, hoping the dragon understood him. 'What are they doing here?'

Själsstyrka lurched downward, head dipping lower and lower, wings held along her body, barely extended at all. Steiner clung to her sides with both hands as the wind tore at his clothes, threatening to unseat him. Anxiety rose in his gut as he pitched further forward, sure he would tumble along Själsstyrka's spine, spinning away, past her angular skull to fall to the waves below. Steiner closed his eyes, blinded by wind-whipped tears. He imagined hitting the Spøkelsea so hard it would be no different to crashing into rock.

A sudden lurch forced him to look. Själsstyrka had plummeted until she was gliding above the violent waves, trailing the Imperial vessel like a silver shadow. A sailor at the back of the ship started so violently he slipped and fell. A host of cries and shouts issued from the length and breadth of the vessel. They were flying so close that Steiner could see each of the crew clearly, the pained look of panic, the disbelieving wrench of fear that crossed every face. The shouts became louder, more shrill. Själsstyrka lunged forward with a beat of her silver wings. The bleak day was sundered as a plume of flame in pale blue erupted from Själsstyrka's jaws. The main mast responded, catching fire where the sail had been stowed away.

Steiner eyed the ship with shock. He was very warm, the insides of his legs uncomfortably so. Själsstyrka dived forward again, coming up over the handrail at the stern of the ship and banking hard. There was a tortured heartbeat as Steiner realised she'd drawn her wings in tight, and then the dragon slammed down on the deck, a sailor pinioned by her talons. Steiner was flung from her back and found himself in a dazed tangle, head resting against the ship's wheel.

'That was a landing?'

Själsstyrka snorted black smoke, followed by a guttural snarl.

The captain of the ship stared in sickened fury, then drew his cutlass and and lunged for Steiner, still sprawled at his feet. Steiner fumbled for the sledgehammer but it was held fast in his belt. The cutlass hacked into the deck as Steiner rolled to one side, then the captain made to strike again, but Själsstyrka reared up, lunging down with an open mouth, revealing rows of serrated teeth. The captain was consumed to the waist, screaming as the teeth impaled his soft flesh. Själsstyrka whipped her neck back and the captain continued screaming, his legs running on empty air. The dragon shook her head to one side, breaking the captain's spine with a terrible snap.

Steiner struggled to his feet, watching as Själsstyrka savaged the corpse on the deck. 'Thanks,' he breathed, pulling the sledgehammer from his belt. The main deck had surrendered to chaos, sailors torn between defending themselves from the winged terror or extinguishing the fire raging on the sails and rigging. Only one person on deck moved towards Steiner with any surety, clad in the red leather surcoat of the Vigilants. He did not pause or rush, but one step followed another up the wooden steps to the stern, accompanied by the *clack-clack* of his walking staff.

Steiner backed off a few paces, hefting the sledgehammer, aware of the silver shadow at his back, still gnawing on the hapless captain.

'You are beginning to annoy me, boy,' said Shirinov.

Steiner scowled. 'You've been annoying the shit out of me since I met you.'

'The dragon was an audacious move,' said Shirinov, leaning on his staff, 'but they're fickle creatures.'

'We'll see.'

Shirinov stepped forward and Steiner pointed. 'Take him, Själsstyrka.'

It was at that moment the dragon finished dining, flared her wings, and launched into the skies. Steiner and the Vigilant watched her go with quiet reverence. She did not turn sharply and descend in a fury of talons, nor did she incinerate the hated Vigilant with a fiery breath as Steiner had hoped.

'Fuck.' Steiner looked at Shirinov and thought the old man might be laughing beneath the silver mask. 'I guess we do this the old-fashioned way then?'

'You have your hammer, while I wield the arcane,' replied the Vigilant, the silver mask mocking.

Steiner hefted the sledgehammer past his shoulder, swinging as the ship's sails came free of their masts in sheets of flame. Shirinov raised a hand, deflecting the main force of Steiner's attack but the ship chose that moment to pitch forward, a wash of spray exploding over the prow. Shirinov's feet slipped as the sledgehammer impacted on his arcane ward, flinging the old man backwards, over the lip of the steps. The Vigilant landed on his side, shuddering in pain.

'Old fashioned is good.' Steiner descended the steps.

'Get away from me!' wheezed Shirinov as he raised one trembling hand. The main mast was a great pillar of flame, plumes of ruddy orange and vibrant red running the length of the wood.

'You'll never reach Kjellrunn.' said Steiner, teeth gritted in determination, and lifted the sledgehammer above his head.

CHAPTER FORTY-TWO

Kjellrunn

Perhaps the most unnerving aspect of Frøya and Frejna is that they bestow their adherents with powers denied most Vigilants. While it is not seemly to mention this at the academy, the subject is raised on occasion and always the fear is the same. 'We know not what they are capable of.'

The ability to cast fiery spears and turn one's self to stone pales next to the fury of the ocean.

– Untainted Histories Volume 3: Serebryanyy Pyli

'It is not working,' said Mistress Kamalov. The wind whipped about the headland, the pines swayed and complained in hushed voices.

'But you've been trying for hours,' said Kristofine from behind them, a flaming torch held aloft. 'What can I do to help?'

The skies were pale grey to the south and south-west, but overhead was oppressive with dark clouds, a tumult of wind and rain with the low rumble of thunder in the distance.

'Now would be a good time to reveal you do have witch-sign after all,' said Kjellrunn. She was bathed in sweat from trying to drag the ship north; hours had gone by, spent stirring up the tides, urging the Spøkelsea to rise up against the Imperial ship.

'Let's head into town,' said Kristofine. 'If we can't stop them here . . .'

Kjellrunn shook her head. Her entreaty to the tide had left her weak, but she remained standing on the headland. Mistress Kamalov had marshalled the wind, struggling to turn the vessel. Instead the crew had stowed the sails and relied on oars alone.

'They will run aground on the beach,' said Mistress Kamalov. 'No more than that. This task is too big for an old woman and young girl. We need four, five, six Vigilants.'

'If we could just crash the ship into the pier.' Kjellrunn felt the ebb and flow of the Spøkelsea, it pulled at every muscle and strained every tendon. She was bruised with it, unable to bear such an immense force.

'We must make it sink,' said Mistress Kamalov, 'leave no evidence for the Empire. Bad enough we have scores of graves to dig for the Okhrana.'

Kjellrunn stumbled, buffeted by the wind. Kristofine caught her and shared a concerned look with Mistress Kamalov.

'You can't keep this up much longer,' said Kristofine. 'Your hands are like ice and you must be shattered.'

Kjellrunn nodded with a heavy heart.

'Things are worse.' Mistress Kamalov shook her head, shoulders slumping with exhaustion.

'What's worse?' said Kjellrunn, squinting through the rain and darkness.

'Look!' A finger pointed to the sea. 'They have brought a dragon. Soldiers are bad, but a dragon . . . There will be no fighting a dragon.'

'There are no dragons—' But anything else Kjellrunn wanted to say was lost to the wind as a vast plume of blue fire illuminated the ship and the creature who breathed it.

Vast wings the colour of steel stretched wide, the serpentine body writhing with unnatural grace. 'Frøya save us.'

'An actual dragon,' whispered Kristofine, her grasp tightening on Kjellrunn's hand.

'Wait! It is attacking the ship.' Mistress Kamalov frowned.

'What does that mean?' asked Kristofine. They watched in disbelief as the dragon landed on the deck, then a struggle followed and men's screams could be heard. The storm abated as Kjellrunn's and Mistress Kamalov's attention dwindled.

'It means that we're not the only ones trying to stop that ship from reaching Cinderfell,' said Kjellrunn.

'This is a more direct way of sinking a ship,' said Mistress Kamalov, nodding her head, obviously impressed. 'Your brother's work perhaps?'

'Steiner?' Kjellrunn shook her head, such a thing was impossible.

'He is the only person who wants to stop that ship as much as we do,' said Mistress Kamalov. 'Even if it means flying a dragon from Vladibogdan.'

'Steiner?' Kjellrunn could barely dare to hope Steiner could be so close.

'He must be crazy,' said Mistress Kamalov, 'or a berserker. Perhaps both.'

'Steiner's come back?' There was a note of hope in Kristofine's voice that felt irresistible to Kjellrunn, irresistible and yet terrible. If it wasn't him, if he hadn't ridden a dragon from Vladibogdan . . . Kjellrunn clasped Kristofine's hand and stared out to sea, hoping for a glimpse of her missing brother.

'I was wrong,' said Mistress Kamalov.

'About what?' said Kristofine.

'About my brother,' said Kjellrunn. 'She said he'd be killed the moment they discovered he doesn't have witchsign.'

'I am sorry, Kjellrunn. I was wrong.' Mistress Kamalov shook her head. 'In my experience, so many have died . . .'

But Kjellrunn wasn't interested. She headed along the cliffs, almost running back to town.

'Where are you going?' called Kristofine.

'I'm going to see if Steiner survives drowning in the storm I raised,' she shouted over her shoulder.

Kjellrunn knew they would follow but did not slow her pace for the old woman. Cinderfell's bay was illuminated by the burning masts of the Imperial ship. Somewhere amid all the burning timber and briny spume was her brother, somewhere amid the chaos and terror was the boy who had gone to Vladibogdan so she might be spared.

'Steiner?' Her pace quickened, eyes fixed on the ship, caught in the cruel swell of the Spøkelsea. 'Steiner!' The dragon ascended from the deck, rising into the sky, leaving the ship to burn. Kjellrunn's heart grew cold and heavy. Was he leaving so soon?

CHAPTER FORTY-THREE

Steiner

Above all, a Vigilant is encouraged to use their powers in subtle ways that do not arouse suspicion. Keeping the arcane secret is the most important task any servant of the Empire can attend to. It would not do to call down a mighty storm and howling winds, such things are conspicuous, even to serfs riddled with superstitions.

– Untainted Histories Volume 3: Serebryanyy Pyli

Steiner ran forward and raised the sledgehammer in both hands, poised for the blow that would end Shirinov's persecution. Aurelian emerged out of the press of bodies, elbowing and shoving at men much larger than himself. A bitter smile crossed his face as he cradled one hand inside the other then flung them forward. Steiner had not been struck by a fireball before. The force of the strike was surprising, knocking him back, sending the sledgehammer tumbling from his grip. Flames reached all around him and guttered to nothing in the rain. His padded coat caught fire at the sleeve as he covered his face with an arm. The leather surcoat was charred black.

Steiner stumbled away, whipping his arm back and forth, but the flames remained. A sailor ran past with a bucket and

Steiner snatched it from him, upending the water over the
spreading flames.

'Thanks,' said Steiner, but the sailor was unimpressed,
reaching for his knife. Steiner lashed out with the bucket,
hitting the man in face, sending him sprawling against the
rail as the ship listed to one side. A sudden shout was followed
by a splash and Steiner stared from the man overboard to the
battered bucket.

'Of course there would be storm. Just my luck,' he said,
clinging on to the handrail to avoid the same fate as the
sailor. A moment later Steiner had retrieved his sledgehammer and glanced across the deck. Aurelian had helped
Shirinov to his feet while Steiner had fought the sailor.
Vigilant and novice approached, only to be barged aside as
soldiers fled the hold. There was a lot of shouting and Steiner
understood none of it.

'We have you now,' said Aurelian, grinning beside his master.

Steiner looked around for some advantage but found nothing.
He was outnumbered twenty to one, but the soldiers had no
mind to attack, fleeing for the lifeboats being lowered to the
waves below. The ships's masts burned fitfully above them in
the rain, the flames on the sailcloth stubbornly refusing to die.

'Armoured men have no business at sea,' said Steiner as he
retreated up the steps to the stern. A shocked silence smothered
the ship as the crow's nest fell, a flaming comet that smashed
into the forecastle, ending a dozen lives in a heartbeat.

'Aurelian! Wait!' Shirinov's voice was desperate above the
din. Steiner spent long moments casting his gaze across the
deck, thick with rushing men and burning wood. Shirinov's
novice was lost in the throng. Steiner fell back as the ship
lurched under violent waves. The deck rose up before him
and he stumbled backwards, colliding with a sailor. Not a
sailor. Aurelian. The blond-haired boy had snuck across the
main deck and circled around behind.

'You always seem to be under my feet,' said Steiner, raising one arm in anticipation of the flames to come. He set his head down and charged into the boy. There was dull smacking sound as Steiner's elbow connected with something. He hoped for Aurelian's nose, but any part of his face would do. Aurelian was undoubtedly more powerful, with fireballs and fiery breath at his disposal, but Steiner pushed him across the deck, shoving him with an elbow mashed into his face. The novice fell back against the rail, unable to concentrate enough to focus on the arcane. A glance over Aurelian's shoulder revealed roaring waves surging about the ship's hull, forbidding blue, and the stark white of storm spray. Aurelian snatched a look behind and Steiner didn't waste the moment of distraction. Too close to swing the hammer, the punch was sufficient to send the boy overboard, catching Aurelian under his chin. There was a moment of flailing limbs, hands reaching for the handrail, followed by a wordless cry.

Steiner scowled as Aurelian thrashed in the water. A high wave smashed down on the boy, dragging him inland. 'Try breathing fire now.' But his joy was a short-lived thing.

Själsstyrka's fiery breath had spread to all parts of the ship. The mizzenmast toppled like a felled tree, meeting the sea with a boom and splash. Everywhere the crackle of flames and groaning wood sounded loudly. The shouts of men were few, a handful of fishermen's boats had come to rescue those aboard during the fighting. Steiner held a hand to his mouth and coughed as smoke seared his lungs.

'Where are you, Shirinov?'

Rigging and sails lay across the deck, burning bright. Everywhere was shattered timber and the bodies of men who hadn't reached the lifeboats. The sailors had taken their chances with the Spøkelsea, tiny figures casting about in the waves, swept this way and that by furious waters.

Steiner had neared the prow when he caught sight of the

Vigilant. Shirinov raised his hands and a selection of burning debris rose into the air at his command.

'It's a shame about Aurelian,' said the Vigilant, staring at the cloud of blazing debris overhead. 'He showed such promise.'

Steiner didn't have a chance to reply, diving to one side, curling around the base of a barrel. Wood and fire rained down and several impacts beat against his ribs and shoulder. He'd barely pulled himself from the drift of shattered wood when Shirinov loomed out of the smoke, grabbing him by the throat. Steiner thought of Marozvolk and the way she had turned her hand to stone. 'Off. Me,' was the only sound he had time to make, throwing up an arm, too weak and too late to fend off the old man. The blow caught him across the temple. For a heartbeat the inferno around him became glaring white, the ship itself indistinct. Shirinov released him and Steiner sprawled across the barrels, dazed and unfocused.

'Stay away from my sister,' growled Steiner, swinging the sledgehammer blindly with every muscle and sinew.

Shirinov was already moving, hobbling to one side of the strike. But the swing described a wider arc than the old man had anticipated; the sledgehammer caught him across the shoulder with a dull clang of metal on stone. Shirinov stumbled back, clutching his arm with his free hand. The other arm lay limp at his side. Steiner was reminded of Matthias Zhirov, the way his head had shattered like masonry.

'That's quite the hammer you have, boy,' said the Vigilant.

'It was my great-grandfather's,' replied Steiner, glancing at the weapon with reverence, though who his great-grandfather had been was yet another of Marek's secrets.

'It is unfortunate that the hammer will go down with the ship.'

The vessel listed to one side and Steiner caught sight of Cinderfell, a large crowd on the pier, cowed by soldiers disembarking from their small boats.

'Then we'll both drown,' said Steiner as the ship lurched again, an icy wave splashing down over the deck. Some of the fires hissed to wet ashes, but the damage was done. That which had not burned would surely sink.

'Both of us?' Shirinov's tone was gloating. 'I think not. An inglorious end for one such as I. Hardly befitting a Vigilant of the Holy Synod.'

Steiner looked about as the sea splashed over the sides of the vessel a little more with each panicked breath. With no plan and nothing left to lose, Steiner sprang forward, the sledgehammer held over his head.

Shirinov made a flicking gesture with both hands, as if shaking off water. He ascended into the air, higher than the sledgehammer, out of reach and drifting higher.

'Enjoy the ship, boy. Such a shame it's your last voyage.'

Steiner could only watch as Shirinov ascended higher and higher into the air. The wind whipped at the Vigilant's robes, bringing snatches of hateful laughter. The ship groaned its last beneath Steiner's boots, slipping beneath the waves as the snapped masts continued burning.

CHAPTER FORTY-FOUR

Steiner

Not every problem in life can be solved with the arcane, any more than every conflict can be won with strength of arms alone. The Emperor learned this during the war with the dragons and remembered it well. Used in concert, the arcane and strength at arms are fierce indeed, greater than the sum of their parts. This is why I fear for the Scorched Republics and the people of Shanisrond.

– Untainted Histories Volume 3: Serebryanyy Pyli

'Coward!' bellowed Steiner. 'Come back here and fight!'

The Vigilant drifted through the air, alighting on the end of the pier as if he'd just stepped off a gangplank. The townsfolk of Cinderfell cried out in alarm, awed by the arcane power. Several fled back to the town itself.

Steiner ran to the edge of the deck, steeling himself to dive off and swim to shore. Only then did he realize that the burning vessel had not slowed during the fight. The sails were long gone but the onrushing waves ushered the ship towards the shore. To jump in would risk being run down by the very ship he sought to escape.

'Frøya, if you exist, if you can hear me,' – Steiner crouched at the prow by the figurehead, an eagle, yellow paint peeling and salt-bleached – 'keep me close!'

The wood groaned and shuddered beneath his boots as the hull slid against the shingle. Barrels and crates and corpses jolted along the deck as the vessel slewed into the beach. The ship turned, waves battering the hull, forcing it against the shore. Wood exploded, a shower of spikes and splinters, and then the stony beach was racing towards Steiner. A glance confirmed he'd been thrown clear of the prow, as legs stumbled on nothing, one hand clawing the empty air, while his other hand gripped at the sledgehammer. And then stone, slamming into face, ribs, knees. For long seconds his lungs would not work and when they did his ears were filled with a pitiful wheezing.

Is there anything left that isn't bruised or burned?

The sea ran up the beach in a blue surge, splashing over his boots and up his legs. The freezing brine shocked him out of the daze and Steiner staggered to his feet with gritted teeth. A weary look over his shoulder confirmed the ship was a shattered hulk; the flames flickered despite the rain and smoke twisted above the broken wreck. So much smoke.

A loose semicircle of soldiers waited further up the beach. All had maces ready, their black cloaks fluttering in the chill breeze. Steiner guessed there were nearly twenty.

Where are you, Själsstyrka? But of the silver shadow in the sky there was no sign.

Shirinov walked the length of the pier as if he owned Cinderfell itself.

'It ends now, Steiner. You're outnumbered.' Steiner thought he could hear laughter on the wind and wanted to hammer the mocking smile of Shirinov's mask into scrap.

The soldiers advanced a step, wary.

'I can't fight all of you,' admitted Steiner. 'But perhaps I don't have to.' He reached into his tunic and brought forth the dragon-carved rock, then set his sights on the burning ship.

'Wherever there is fire there is death,' bellowed Steiner.

Nothing. Rain pattered from his face as the soldier's boots crunched on the shingle beach as they came closer. Steiner could taste blood.

'Dammit.'

'Now we put you down, as we should have when you first arrived on Vladibogdan,' said one of the soldiers.

'Wherever there is fire there is death.' Quieter now, the words heavy with desperation. The jag of stone remained just that, a hunk of rock with a carving, nothing more. Was it too wet? Had the shattering of the dragon statue leached the power from the artefact? Steiner shook the chain and stumbled backwards, away from the line of soldiers who inched forward, step by careful step. 'Please, I need you.' A glimmer was followed by a spark, and then another. The flames sprang into life along the stone and the soldiers jerked back.

Dark figures emerged from the roaring fire of the burning hulk. In twos and threes they came, living wisps of smoke with unblinking eyes of smouldering orange. The artefact hung on the chain before Steiner, flickering and roaring with flame. More and more cinderwraiths emerged from the broken ship, like infernal stowaways. At first a dozen of the phantoms emerged from the wrecked ship, and then twice that again.

'Take them!' yelled Steiner.

The cinderwraiths advanced up the beach. Fleet and dark they closed with the soldiers and Steiner charged with them, swinging with fury, rewarded with the dull clang of metal and grunts of pain. The fight was a jarring, stumbling confusion. Soldiers fell about, assailed by dark shadows, coughing on fumes and strangled by phantoms. They fell to their knees one by one until only two living souls remained on the beach. Steiner stared at the man in the mocking silver mask.

'Not so much to smile about now, is there?' said Steiner. The Vigilant still clutched his shoulder where Steiner had struck him before.

'This day will be mine,' said Shirinov. 'I have been demoted, I have been disgraced, I have been derided!' The old man hobbled forward. 'Felgenhauer isn't here to save you this time.'

A large stone sprang up from the beach at Shirinov's command, as if shot from a catapult. Steiner tried to duck out of the way, but a cinderwraith shot forward and wrapped its ghostly form about the stone, absorbing the force. Again Shirinov lifted a rock from the beach, then launched the hunk of stone at Steiner with flick of his hand. Again a cinderwraith charged forward to deflect the projectile. And all the while Steiner closed with the Vigilant, the Ashen Torment held up in one hand, the sledgehammer held low in the other.

'You will not best me, boy!' howled Shirinov. More and more stones jumped up from the beach to pelt Steiner, each met by the fleet form of a cinderwraith.

'Who's outnumbered now, halfhead?' Steiner swung the sledgehammer up, but feinted and changed direction, swinging towards Shirinov's knees. The old man couldn't move in time, but summoned a ward of force with the flat of one hand, knocking the blow aside. Steiner's arms hurt as the sledgehammer strike met resistance.

Steiner stepped in close and shoulder-barged the Vigilant before he could retaliate, sending Shirinov staggering along the shingle. Somehow the old man remained standing, but Steiner had lined up his strike and swung with every bruised muscle and aching tendon. Shirinov raised a hand to ward the hammer from his chest, but Steiner had set his sights higher. The dull metal head of the hammer hit the smiling mask by the left eye and a peal of sound rolled over the beach like bells.

'What have you done?' raged the Vigilant, as a shock of

red gore dripped from the mask's left eye hole. 'I'll kill you.'
Stones sprang up from the beach around him, hovering all
around. 'I'll kill your sister and your father and—'

'Enough!' said Steiner through gritted teeth. He surged
forward as the first of the stones raced towards him. The
hammer swept through the air, a dull blur of metal. Shirinov
struggled to raise an arm, seeking to ward off the blow, but
his wounded shoulder refused to obey. The hammer strike
took the Vigilant straight on the chest. There was no snapping
of bones, no wheezing shout of pain, just the crack of splitting
stone.

Shirinov trembled. 'What have you done?'

The Vigilant fell to pieces, each shattered arm sliding from
a sleeve. His legs went out from under him, torso crumbling.

'All this time you tried to break me,' said Steiner, breathing
heavily. He rested on the shaft of the sledgehammer for
support, so tired he wanted to drop to his knees. 'You don't
break me. I break you.'

The roar of the sea grew louder and the many cinderwraiths
turned and fled up the beach, dark shadows racing over
shingle. Steiner looked over his shoulder. The wave that
approached the shore was twice his height, a wall of moving
midnight blue, too close to escape from. White spray ran along
the apex of the swell, towering over him. All was icy cold as
the wave crashed down. His ears were filled with the dull
roar of the angry ocean as the Spøkelsea claimed him, dragging him out to the depths.

CHAPTER FORTY-FIVE

Steiner

Vladibogdan began as a prison for dragons and a place to exile political prisoners, but in time the Emperor became wise to the many possibilities of the island. Small wonder then that novices were trained on the bleak isle, or that Vigilants would find themselves posted there as a punishment.

– Untainted Histories Volume 3: Serebryanyy Pyli

The frenzied waves of the Spøkelsea took Steiner down into their depths. Only frenzied kicks and desperate paddling saw him breach the surface. He was swept high and low as the frigid waters continued to thrash the shore.

'It's fine,' he reassured himself, 'I'll just wait until the tide throws me up on the beach. Like the ship.' The ship lay on its side, still burning and smoking, but the wreck grew more distant with each passing moment. Steiner kicked, growing tired with each heartbeat, paddling one-handed, determined not to release the sledgehammer.

Apparently this is your great-grandfather's. Romola's words drifted through his mind as the rain hissed on the dark green waves. The tide dragged him away to a place of icy cold and slow drowning. His teeth chattered fitfully and no matter how high the wave or how violent the swell he refused to take his eyes from Cinderfell.

'I did it, Kjell. I stopped him. I killed the Vigilant. You'll be safe now, for a little while at least.' He knew she couldn't hear him, but it felt important to speak the words out loud; he had a feeling they might be his last.

It seemed appropriate that his story should end here, within sight of the pier, not so very far from the school up on the hill. He marvelled at the things he'd done since departing from home: meeting Spriggani; befriending a Yamal princess; seeing the power of the arcane displayed openly; witnessing an Imperial Envoy with full honour guard. And who in Cinderfell could claim to have ridden a dragon in flight? Who in Nordvlast?

'Not bad,' he said as the shore grew more distant. He'd never be able to tell his father or Kjellrunn how sorry he was that he'd never said goodbye, but he'd seen enough to know that fate rarely played fair.

Steiner's vision grew dark and a tightness about the chest forced the air from his lungs. Would these be his final thoughts? Was this when he would pass over into Frejna's realm? His eyes were heavy and began to close.

A lurch, and suddenly he was in the air again. His eyes widened as he looked up. Själsstyrka had wrapped her tail about him, constricting tight to be sure she didn't lose him to the Spøkelsea.

'I can't breathe!' he hissed.

The dragon flew on and the tail relaxed. Steiner blinked away the dark spots that blurred before his eyes. Her wings were vast expanses of silver, beating at the winds and speeding them onward. Själsstyrka flew straight for the shore, swooping low over the pier and circling around. She released him into the arms of his father, strangely tender for all her size and ferocity. Steiner looked up, dazed and shivering. Själsstyrka snorted a plume of smoke, then launched into the air once more.

'Thank you,' was all he said, and then passed out.

Steiner woke in the tavern, bundled up in the cloak of an Imperial soldier. The fire in the hearth roared and popped. Someone had hung his clothes up to dry above the mantel, though they were blackened with soot and the sleeve of his padded coat was all but burned away.

'Is this one of those dreams where I'm naked in front of my friends?'

That earned him a few chuckles. Everyone he knew from Cinderfell had gathered, crowding around the tables, standing at the bar, leaning against the walls. All eyes were turned towards him and none spoke, save one.

'My son.' Marek Vartiainen had long given up trying to stifle his sobs. 'My beautiful son.' Kristofine peeked over Marek's shoulder. 'He's fine, Marek. Takes more than a dip in the Spøkelsea to take Steiner away from us.'

'I-I'm sorry,' said Steiner.

'Whatever for?' replied Marek.

'For not saying farewell when I left. I've regretted it every day.'

His father nodded and buried his face in Steiner's neck, his beard tickling soft skin. 'My boy, what have they done to you?'

'Burned and beaten me in the main,' said Steiner with a grimace. 'How long have I been asleep?'

'About a day and a half,' said Marek. 'Once we brought you here I didn't want to move you. It's spiteful cold out there.'

'That's quite the pet you've got for yourself,' said Kristofine with a raised eyebrow.

'What pet?'

'The dragon that's currently sat on the roof of this very

tavern. It's got its belly against the chimney. We dare not let the fire go out.'

'*It* is a *she*,' said Steiner, smiling at the tavern-keeper's daughter.

'Well, you've had quite an effect on her.' Kristofine shook her head and grinned. 'She followed you all the way here like a wolfhound. Wanted to make sure we did right by you.'

'She's called Själsstyrka. A Yamal princess I know gave her the name.'

'You'll be telling us you're friends with a tribe of Spriggani next,' said Marek.

'They don't live in tribes,' said Steiner. 'They have families, just like us, get tired, just like us, and are scared of the Empire.'

'Just like us,' added Kristofine. That caused some muttering to break out around the tavern as the townsfolk reflected on what had been said.

'Where's Bjørner?' asked Steiner, looking for the grubby tavern owner.

'He's out the back.' Kristofine leaned close to Steiner. 'He drinks neat vodka when he drinks at all, won't touch any food and refuses to speak. It's an improvement if I'm honest, he's been awful to me since you left.'

'I missed you,' said Steiner, glad that he'd said the words and embarrassed all at the same time. They'd had such a short time together, and yet she was just as enchanting as he'd remembered.

'We missed you too,' she replied, and Steiner felt his heart sink for a moment before she said, 'I missed you, I'm glad you're back.'

Steaming hot broth was provided with bread still warm from the oven; neither lasted very long. The questions began the moment he laid down his spoon.

How had he mastered flying a dragon?

What happened to children with witchsign?

Could he cast spells and did he have witchsign?

'And now that you know these things,' Steiner stood up, though his body ached, 'now that you've seen a Vigilant use his powers, and seen a dragon in flight, the Empire will hunt you and they will kill you. Just knowing these things puts you in danger.'

The tavern fell silent at that and a few people scowled and stormed out. Others glanced anxiously at each other, not knowing what to do or say.

'They can't kill all of us, just because we've seen one of their dragons,' said one of the younger fishermen.

'They'll raze the whole town,' said Steiner. 'The Vigilant I killed on the beach,' he gestured out of the window to the Spøkelsea, 'that's what he was coming here to do. Kill every single one of you. And there's no reason to think it will be any different when the next Troika of Vigilants arrive.'

The townsfolk made their way out into the cold day and Steiner could already see that some of them knew what it meant. They would have to leave Cinderfell and start again in some other place.

'Where is Kjell?' he whispered to his father as the boots scuffed the floor and the grumbling of the townsfolk filled the tavern.

Marek looked guilty for a moment, running a hand over his beard. 'She's not the young girl you left behind, Steiner.'

'Where is she?'

His father gestured to the door. 'You'd best get dressed.' Steiner hurried into his clothes, using the cloak as best he could to save his dignity.

'So many scars and burns,' said Kristofine, running a hand across his shoulders, and Steiner winced.

'The island will do that to you,' replied Steiner, thinking of the friends he'd left behind.

'Come on,' said Marek, 'time's getting short.'

Some of the townsfolk followed, more interested in their newfound hero than attending to the business of packing up their gear. The storm assailing the coastline had abated like a common squall. The waters were smooth blue glass and Romola's red frigate rested at anchor near the pier.

'The *Watcher's Wait*?'

'Romola is an old acquaintance of mine,' said his father. 'We pass secrets to one another.'

'So I hear. Corpsecandle, I mean Vigilant Khigir, and Shirinov found the letters from Felgenhauer.'

Marek looked concerned. 'I wondered if you'd meet Felgenhauer. The fact they found the letters means trouble.'

'We're in trouble anyway,' replied Steiner. 'Felgenhauer was summoned to Khlystburg before the letters were discovered. Hopefully that secret will die with Shirinov.'

'And Khigir?' asked Marek.

'Dead too.'

'But how can you be so sure?' asked Marek.

'The same way I'm sure that Shirinov is dead. Because I killed him.'

They walked down to the pier in awkward silence as Marek reflected on what he'd been told.

'You're going to have to tell me about Romola at some point,' said Steiner.

'She said she wouldn't come back,' replied Marek, 'but it seems her curiosity got the better of her.'

'I'm not sure I've got much to say to Romola,' said Steiner. 'She had a few chances to get me off Vladibogdan and not once did she try. She's only out for herself.'

'Most people are,' said his father with a smile edged in sadness. 'But if you don't come to the pier you won't be able to say your farewells.'

'Farewell? To Romola?' Steiner snorted a derisive laugh. 'I'd rather be in the tavern with my arms around Kristofine.'

'Steiner, Kjellrunn is leaving. Today.'

'What?' Steiner stumbled and became still. Marek nodded and his eyes glittered at the corners, unable to meet Steiner's look of incomprehension.

'What do you mean?'

'I'll let her explain. Come now. Romola won't stop long, we'd best be quick.'

CHAPTER FORTY-SIX

Kjellrunn

The punishment for killing a Vigilant is death. The punishment for learning of Vladibogdan was death. The punishment for avoiding Invigilation was also death. This would be impressive if not for the fact that most crimes in the Solmindre Empire are punishable by death. The Emperor was never terribly imaginative in that regard.

– Untainted Histories Volume 3: Serebryanyy Pyli

Kjellrunn stood on the pier, watching the crew of the *Watcher's Wait* stocking up with supplies for the long voyage south. She'd stocked up on a few supplies of her own, new boots and a sheepskin jerkin, a good leather skirt and a few blouses; all paid for with the coins of dead Okhrana. No one in town had dared inflate their prices; she was the sister of the dragon rider, and witchsign or no, that meant something.

Håkon had arrived on the pier with a handcart, selling up all the meat he owned by the look of it.

'Have a care not to overcharge the good captain, won't you?' said Kjellrunn, a dangerous edge to her tone.

Håkon stared at her a moment, then nodded meekly.

'I take it Bjørner told you what he saw in the forest.'

Håkon nodded again, barely able to make eye contact.

'You were right about me, I do have the witchsign, I aways have.' She stepped closer and the butcher struggled to stand his ground, clearly wanting to be away from the pier as quickly as possible.

'Strange, isn't it?' said Kjellrunn. 'You spent all that time doing your best to make me feel uncomfortable, and you're nothing. Just an ugly man who needs to trim his beard and mind his manners.'

And still the butcher remained silent.

'What will you do now?' she said. 'Now that all this death and chaos has come to Cinderfell?'

'Move on, of course.' Håkon's voice was a whisper, no sign of the leer on his face as he replied. 'I don't want to be here when the Empire arrives. They'll ask a lot of questions, and they're not fussy about how they get their answers. I've seen it before. I've no wish to see it again.'

Kjellrunn nodded. 'I'm sorry.'

'Sorry?' Håkon stared at her, then barked a bitter laugh. 'You should be. The whole town will have to move away. If they have any sense,' – he glowered accusingly at the drab grey cottages – 'and I'm not sure they do, but if they have any sense they'll flee all the way to Svingettevei.'

'Do you think I meant for this to happen?' said Kjellrunn. 'I never asked for the Empire to tear my family apart, just as I never asked for these powers.'

'You're not the only one who has lost family to witchsign and the hated Empire,' said the butcher, tears in his bloodshot eyes. 'I moved here to get away from all that shit, and now it's happened again.'

Håkon spat at the sea and dragged his handcart with him, the wheels skidding on the cobbles. Kjellrunn had never thought she'd feel much of anything for Håkon except hate.

She watched the bald slab of a man retreat into the town with a pity that surprised her.

Her eye was drawn to the smoking hulk, beached and ruined on the shingle. A whale had washed up in Cinderfell during her seventh summer, drawing the townsfolk down to the bay much as the wrecked ship had yesterday. They had all marvelled at the size of the creature. Kjellrunn had cried for a full day when the whale died, and Verner had told her tales of voyages south and the Spriggani and Shanisrond to soothe her. The pain of remembering was immediate, rising beneath her breast unbidden.

'I'm so sorry, Verner,' she whispered, but none heard the words, which were lost in the commotion on the pier, forgotten in the preparation to sail.

'There he is!' came a cry from the stern of the ship.

Romola stepped off the gangplank and fixed Kjellrunn with a hard stare.

'You're sure about this? He's not going to be happy.'

'What choice do I have?' Kjellrunn sighed. 'I can't stay here. None of us can.'

Kjellrunn looked to the gentle slope of the road leading to the pier. Steiner walked, trying his best not to hobble, though gods knew he had a right to walk however he wished. Marek lingered beside him, trying at once to hold him up with a protective arm while proudly declaring his son to the world. Torn between the two tasks, Marek opted for the former, a fierce grin crossing his face all the same. A clutch of locals from the tavern trailed after him, all chatting in a fever of excitement.

'And now he's a hero, right?' said Romola.

'Not to Håkon, perhaps,' said Kjellrunn. 'But he's everything to me.'

So much had changed in such a short time. There was a leanness to him, a hard edge to the look in his eye. His nose was crooked, broken she suspected, and his hair was burned down to stubble with more of the same along his jaw. He was etched in soot and marked by scars and suffering, and yet unbowed.

Mistress Kamalov appeared on deck, squinting at the new arrivals. 'So this is the madman who escaped Vladibogdan on a dragon?'

Steiner looked from rogue Vigilant to pirate to sister and gave a curt nod. 'And you'd be Sharpbreath, sister to Khigir.'

Mistress Kamalov smiled. 'I do not use that name any more.'

'You never told me you were Khigir's sister,' said Kjellrunn.

'No time.' Mistress Kamalov shrugged. 'I was busy teaching you how to use the arcane. Besides, I can not answer if you do not ask.'

'Perhaps it would be better to continue this conversation in my cabin,' said Romola, glancing at her crew. 'They've only just got around to the idea of having a woman aboard. A rogue Vigilant might push them to mutiny.'

Romola's cabin was just large enough for the five of them; Mistress Kamalov and Marek took the two chairs, while everyone else stood. The pirate fetched five wooden tumblers and poured a rough vodka for each of them. Kjellrunn winced as she drank it and tried not to cough, while Mistress Kamalov and Marek knocked theirs back in one motion.

'And how is my brother?' asked Mistress Kamalov, picking up the thread of the conversation they had broken on the pier.

Steiner hesitated a moment, his face serious. 'Still on the island as far as I know.'

'He is dead, yes?' Mistress Kamalov said the words so matter-of-factly that Kjellrunn almost missed their import. Steiner didn't reply. 'He has been dead to me a long time,' said the old woman. 'But now I suppose I shall never have the chance to say goodbye to him.'

'You're not sad?' said Steiner, a frown of confusion on his face.

'Sad?' Mistress Kamalov scowled. 'It was he that told the Empire I had witchsign. It was he that tried again and again to convince me of the righteousness of the Emperor. It was he, my own brother, who demanded I join his Troika so he could keep a watch on me. Sad? I am furious. Furious I did not kill him myself. I hope he rots in Hel.'

Steiner exchanged a surprised look with Kjellrunn and a tense silence followed. Marek cleared his throat and Romola poured more vodka.

'I'm sorry,' said Steiner, and the howl of the wind outside made Kjellrunn shiver as he said it, the look in his eye full of regret.

'And I'm sorry too,' said Romola as she poured Steiner another shot of vodka. 'I should have tried harder to get you off the island, but it was impossible with Shirinov breathing down my neck.'

'I think I know a way you can make it up to me.' Steiner squinted at the map hanging on the wall of the cabin. He stood up and inspected the north-western corner of the parchment, where the Nordscale islands lay. 'I think I know a way you can make it up to a lot of people.'

Romola shrugged. 'I promised my crew I'd never go back there, Steiner. If you're thinking what I think you're thinking, well, you may be in for a disappointment.' Romola knocked back her vodka and poured another.

'Things have changed,' said Steiner. 'The Matriarch-Commissar was summoned by the Emperor to Khlystburg to explain herself. Vladibogdan is in chaos and Shirinov is dead.'

Romola let out a low whistle. 'You certainly know how to upset the apple cart.'

'I'm just getting started,' replied Steiner, clenching his fists.

Romola looked at the map on the wall and sighed. 'Whatever we choose to do, we need to leave Cinderfell, and fast.'

The truth of those simple words silenced all of them for a moment and Steiner looked from Mistress Kamalov to Kjellrunn and back again. 'It was you, on the headland, summoning the storm.'

Kjellrunn nodded. 'Mistress Kamalov brought the wind, I stirred up the Spøkelsea, as best I could. We would never have started had we known you were coming on the dragon. You, on a dragon.' Kjellrunn shook her head. 'After all the times you scolded me for speaking of such things.'

Kjellrunn stepped forward and took Steiner's hand. The calluses were nothing new, but the scars that criss-crossed his skin shocked her.

'Thank you. For going. For buying me time. I would never have met Mistress Kamalov if it hadn't been for you.'

Steiner slipped his arms around his sister and squeezed her close. 'You don't have to thank me. I would have gone if you'd asked. I just didn't care to be told I had no choice.'

'That was my fault,' said Marek. 'I'm too used to giving orders and not thinking about how they sound.'

'We need to go soon,' said Romola. 'The tide waits for no man, or woman, regardless of whether she's pirate or witch.'

'So you are a pirate then?' asked Steiner.

'When the mood takes me. A woman can be whatever she chooses.' Romola cocked her head to one side. 'Won't you come with us? I might make a good sailor out of you. Anything has to be an improvement on the furnaces of Vladibogdan, right?'

Steiner looked out of the window to the sea, past the end of the pier to the horizon, where the flat line of blue met the ever-present grey. 'One way or another I have to get the Spriggani and Kimi away from that island. And I made a promise to Silverdust.'

'I want help you, Steiner, but I made a promise too. My crew are likely to mutiny if I suggest sailing north.'

Steiner and the pirate exchanged a long look and Kjellrunn felt deeply uncomfortable.

A knock at the door broke the stalemate and Romola opened it to reveal Kristofine. She had a sack slung over her shoulder and wore a new travel cloak. By the look of her red-rimmed eyes Kjellrunn guessed she'd had another conversation with Bjørner, probably the last one.

'I need to speak to the captain about booking passage to Shanisrond. That's where you're heading, right?'

Romola eyed the woman a moment and exchanged smiles with Kjellrunn.

'It's unlucky to have a woman aboard, apparently.' She looked around the cabin. 'But with this much bad luck I'm sure a little more won't hurt.'

Kristofine stepped into the cabin and Mistress Kamalov went to her wordlessly, taking the woman in her arms.

Marek stood up and made to leave.

'And what will you do, blacksmith?' said Romola, holding the door.

'I'm getting my tools and everything I own. Don't cast off without me. I'll be back in an hour.'

Romola raised an eyebrow. 'Going to be a crowded voyage at this rate.'

Kjellrunn watched all these events swirl about her, watched the irresistible tide of onrushing consequences. The only one who appeared unmoved was Steiner, still staring at the map, still mulling over the promise he'd made on Vladibogdan.

CHAPTER FORTY-SEVEN

Kimi

The Spriggani found themselves confined by stricter and stricter controls. First the western borders of the Solmindre Empire were sealed off so Spriggani coming from the Scorched Republics were turned away. Within months the Spriggani within the Solmindre Empire were rounded up and taken. They took the men first. Many of the women fled and those who survived ended up in Yamal, forging an unlikely alliance deep in the south.

– Untainted Histories Volume 3: Serebryanyy Pyli

The everyday routine of Vladibogdan, much like the statue that had stood at its centre, had been shattered, shaken to the foundations. Kimi had taken advantage of the chaos and set herself up in the gatehouse. The Spriggani hadn't needed much encouragement to join her away from the forges. She directed them to arm and armour themselves as best they could. The first day was spent looting the dead for armour and cloaks, or washing the blood out of clothes. Tief disappeared for a time only to return with Corpsecandle's frowning mask, though it was dented and scratched.

'I pushed him in the cove,' said Tief to no one in particular.

'He might as well be fish food than stink the place up as he rots.'

'We should move the corpses from Academy Square,' said Taiga, 'or disease will be on us before we know it.'

'She's right,' said Kimi, and though the idea of dragging the dead down the steps to Temnet Cove filled her with revulsion she was the first to volunteer for the duty.

Silverdust was always on hand, though the Vigilant said little, his blank mask always turned towards the dark waters of Temnet Cove and the many steps that led to it. It was never difficult to find him, the aura of gentle light following him always.

'You can take your mask off now if you like,' said Kimi. 'I've not seen any other Vigilants, perhaps they're all hiding. Or dead, killed by their own students.' She wondered what might be revealed when the Exarch discarded his uniform, wondered where he came from and what he'd lost. Silverdust nodded thoughtfully, but didn't remove the reflective surface that made him such a mystery. Kimi shrugged and moved on, checking in with the Spriggani in the gatehouse, checking people were keeping watch and that they had enough to eat.

Maxim had taken up with some Academy Vozdukha novices in the kitchen, all badly shaken by the open battle in the square. They sat in silence, huddling about the fireplace and whispering to each other. Always the same words would reach Kimi's ears over and over.

When is Steiner coming back?

Sundra had laid out her square of black velvet cloth and consulted the bones a number of times, but her dark muttering had given way to the odd frustrated sigh, and even boredom. The priestess had no answers for them and time crawled by.

Tief, Taiga and Sundra sat around a brazier in a guardroom, having pulled the beds into a semicircle. Kimi sat down beside Taiga and took some tea, feeling the weight of her tiredness keenly. It was all she could do sit up.

Sundra stared out of the window, watching the snow float down between the buildings and alight on the rubble and ruin in Academy Square.

'Fuck this,' said the priestess as darkness fell on the second night. 'I'm having a bath.' Even Tief blinked to hear his sister using such profanity. Sundra swept out of the room with a deep frown on her face, her lips pursed.

'She really likes that boy,' said Taiga, when her sister had left the room.

'We all really like that boy,' said Kimi.

'I don't,' said Tief, then chuckled at his own joke, though no one else did.

'She keeps casting the bones,' said Taiga, 'looking for some reading or interpretation that Steiner is safe, but she never gets a casting that pleases her.'

'He'll come back,' said Tief after a pause, as he fussed with Corpsecandle's mask. 'He has a good heart, and he knows to do right. No brains, mind, but you can't have it all is what I always say.'

Taiga began to laugh but caught the look on Kimi's face.

'And if he doesn't?' said the princess. 'Maybe we starve, or maybe the Empire arrives and kills all of us. I don't know. I don't know what will happen to me or my people.'

No one had much to say after that, and they settled down to sleep, or whatever thoughts that gnawed on their nerves through the chilly night.

It was still snowing when they woke the next day and Kimi couldn't get warm or find any cheer. She made her rounds and stepped out of a side door to cast an eye over the square. Dark figures made their way through the falling snow and Kimi was put in mind of the cinderwraiths, stalking the soldiers and suffocating them with ashes and smoke. If the cinderwraiths had returned then perhaps Steiner was close by.

Vigilant Marozvolk appeared out of the gloom and Kimi pulled the mace from her belt and held it before her.

'I come with empty hands,' said the Vigilant, though the snarling wolf mask made her as fearsome as ever. 'I want no trouble.'

'What do you want?' said Kimi, noticing other people following Marozvolk in the gloom.

'Just that these novices be given a chance to escape.'

Kimi nodded. She lowered the mace and the tension drained out of her. 'Of course, but we have no plan and we have no ship. We're hoping Steiner returns with one, but so far nothing.'

The novices from Academy Voda bustled past Kimi, glad to be inside and in the warm. They joined Maxim and the Vozdukha novices in the kitchen and began talking about the battle and the dragon and how Steiner had toppled the statue.

'How are you?' asked Kimi, though it felt strange to ask a Vigilant such a question.

Marozvolk nodded, then took off her mask, looking down at the metal wolf's face.

'I am very tired,' she replied in Yamali. 'It has been a long time since I could take this off in public and speak my mother tongue.'

Kimi smiled and took the woman's hand.

'We are all very tired, sister,' Kimi replied in Yamali. 'And it is good to hear Yamali after so many years.'

'I'm so sorry,' said Marozvolk. 'All this time and I did nothing.'

'Why don't you come up to the guardroom? It's a touch crowded in here with all of these children. Maybe you can get some sleep?'

But the guardroom was not the haven of quiet that Kimi had been hoping for.

'Maybe he didn't make it,' said Tief, who was making up his pipe with the last of his weed. 'There was an awful gale coming from inland and that dragon hadn't flown in quite some time.'

No one answered.

'And who the Hel is this?' muttered Tief as Kimi led the maskless Vigilant into the room.

'You knew me as Marozvolk, and there may come a time that I need to be Marozvolk again, so that name will suffice.'

Sundra and Taiga exchanged an unimpressed look and said nothing.

'Why have you come here?' said Tief. 'Don't you have novices to abuse in one of those awful academies?'

Kimi cleared her throat, but it sounded more like a growl of impatience even to herself. 'She brought her novices to us, so we could smuggle them off the island, halfhead.'

'Oh.' Tief smoked his pipe. 'Well, I still don't trust you, even if you have taken your mask off.'

The corridor grew bright and Silverdust appeared in the doorway, hands clasped together, head bowed in thought.

A ship approaches.

Everyone in the room sat up a little straighter and Kimi struggled to breathe. A ship full of Imperial soldiers could be headed towards Vladibogdan. There was no telling how long the ragtag band of survivors could defend the gatehouse, even with Sundra and two Vigilants on their side, if Silverdust was on anyone's side.

'Is it an Imperial ship?' asked Tief.

Impossible to tell with the snow. Silverdust glided down the corridor silently.

Sundra cast her bones and pouted a moment. 'All is confusion, many that oppressed us stand with us, that which was hidden has been revealed, and those who were slaves remain slaves.'

'You got all that from one toss of the bones?' said Kimi, raising an eyebrow.

'Sometimes the goddess is not so forthcoming with her portents,' admitted Sundra. 'So it helps to state what has gone before.'

'Get everyone ready,' said Kimi, taking up a stout pickaxe. 'And I mean everyone. Vigilants, novices, anyone that can swing a mace. I'm not giving up this gatehouse without a fight.'

Tief choked on his pipe smoke, then recovered and bowed to Kimi.

'It will be as you say.'

CHAPTER FORTY-EIGHT

Steiner

The Emperor was ever mercurial with smaller matters of court, and ever more so as he grew older. More serious matters brought out his fondness for scheming; intrigues could play out over weeks, months, or even years. To the outsider, it must have appeared as if orders were given seemingly on a whim, impulsive and violent. Life at court was never boring.

> – Untainted Histories Volume 3: Serebryanyy Pyli

Steiner stepped off the deck of the *Watcher's Wait* and looked up the rocky stairs of Temnet Cove and the black rock that towered above him. Vladibogdan was no more welcoming, and there was no way of knowing what had happened since Själsstyrka had spirited him away on her silver wings.

'Steiner?' A voice bellowed from the gatehouse. 'Is that you?'

Steiner waved and saw arms and hands waving back from the top of the steps. Marek came down the gangplank behind him and rested a hand on his shoulder.

'Looks like you've made a few friends.'

'Reckon I did that,' Steiner grinned. 'Come on, I'll introduce you to them. I'll introduce you to everyone.'

They spent an hour all meeting and hugging. For all the laughter there were just as many tears, some of relief and some of sadness. Tief took it upon himself to tell Marek about all the stupid things Steiner had done when he had first arrived, before regaling him with how Steiner had never given up or lost hope. Steiner drifted away from the two men, surprised to see Marozvolk without her mask, and more surprised that she hailed from Yamal.

'You have your sister?' said Marozvolk.

Steiner nodded.

'When the Empire discovers what happened in Cinderfell—' said Marozvolk.

'The whole town will be destroyed,' said Kimi, who stood beside the Vigilant, almost protectively Steiner thought. Taiga lingered close by, drinking up every word.

'It was always going to be so,' said Steiner. 'Shirinov was determined to raze the place as an act of revenge for his demotion. Anyone with any sense will leave. I told them as much.'

'It's a hollow victory is all,' said Taiga, looking away and taking an uneasy breath. 'But I'm glad you're safe.'

'The victory wasn't as hollow as you might think,' said Steiner.

'You killed Shirinov?' said Taiga.

'The bones are silent for the Vigilant.' Sundra appeared out of the crowd, inspecting a handful of bone tokens and scraps of debris. 'His time is no more.'

'How did it end?' asked Taiga.

'It ended with a beached and burning ship,' said Steiner. 'It ended in a fierce storm called up by my sister and Sharpbreath. It ended when I finally landed a blow on him, just as it did for Matthias Zhirov.'

'Seems that hammer isn't just for show,' said Kimi.

'Seems that way,' replied Steiner. 'But I couldn't have done it without the help you gave me.'

'Do you still have the Ashen Torment?' said Kimi.

'Yes, of course.' Steiner saw the way she looked at him, as if giving back the artefact could guarantee the safety of all the Yamal people.

The revellers swirled about Steiner and someone pressed a mug of ale into his hand. Sundra and Taiga entered into a hushed conversation with Kjellrunn, obviously keen to meet her, while Kristofine regarded Kimi with less enthusiasm.

'You didn't tell me your Yamal princess was quite so beautiful,' said the tavern-keeper's daughter quietly.

'I . . .' Steiner had no answer for her. He supposed Kimi was attractive, but he'd never had much time to give it any thought, much less pursue her.

'Did anything happen between you two?'

Steiner shook his head and found himself glad to be on the right side of the truth. 'No, too busy staying alive for anything like that.'

'But if you hadn't been busy then perhaps something might have happened?' said Kristofine.

'What? No, I didn't mean anything by it, I just . . .' But Kristofine had headed off into the crowd. Steiner started after her but found his way blocked by Silverdust, who loomed over him. The Vigilant made a beckoning gesture and Steiner nodded, resigned to what must come next.

For a moment, he thought they might slip free of the mass of bodies in Academy Square, but Steiner found himself joined by Kimi, Sundra, Tief and Taiga. It seemed fitting, given these were the people he'd lived with in the very forges Silverdust led them to.

'What happened to Själsstyrka?' said Kimi, as they descended the stairs into the bowels of the island for what Steiner hoped would be the last time.

'I left her on the roof of a tavern in Cinderfell. She was wrapped around the chimney warming herself last I looked.'

'Aren't you afraid she'll eat the townsfolk?' replied Kimi.

'I hadn't thought of that,' admitted Steiner with a grimace.

'How the Hel did you persuade Romola to sail back here?' said Tief. 'I never thought we'd see her again.'

'I didn't speak with Romola, I spoke with her crew,' said Steiner. 'I told them there was an entire island that they could ransack if they provided passage for Kimi and the Spriggani.'

'Never underestimate a pirate's greed,' said Kimi.

'It's going to be a little crowded,' said Steiner, 'but it's the best I could do.'

'You did just fine,' said Taiga.

They were almost at the main cavern now, and stood on the balcony looking over the many furnaces, now cold and dark. The Vigilant was radiant in the darkness, the aura warm and safe. Silverdust turned to them and Steiner felt the expectation weigh upon him.

You made a promise. Steiner shivered as the phantom words appeared in his head.

'I know, and I intend to see it through.'

Orange eyes appeared in the gloom below, from one side of the furnace chamber to the other. The cinderwraiths were invisible in the darkness but for their eyes.

'There are so many of them,' breathed Steiner.

'A lot more since the battle in Academy Square,' said Kimi, and Steiner felt the twist of disapproval in her words. She'd found a lantern from somewhere and stood close, eyeing him with a look of worry on her face.

'They came without summons,' said Sundra.

'Might as well get on with it,' said Steiner. 'They stood by me when I fought Shirinov and his soldiers, and now I have to keep my side of the bargain.'

'The Ashen Torment,' whispered Sundra with reverence as

Steiner lifted the artefact from his tunic. He slipped the chain over his head and regarded the artefact, the finely carved dragon, the exquisite detail.

'We could defeat the whole Empire with such a thing,' said Tief, a wistful note in his voice.

'Wherever there is fire there is death,' intoned Kimi, eyeing the jag of rock as it hung from the chain. 'You could give that back to me and my people would be safe.'

'It won't make any difference, Kimi.' Steiner looked out over the Ashen Court, a sea of ghosts, a black and grey tide of lost souls that gathered at the base of the balcony, illuminated by Silverdust's aura and Kimi's lantern. 'The Empire will send someone to Cinderfell soon enough, and someone will tell them what they know.'

'Think about it, Steiner.' Tief edged closer, his eyes transfixed on the artefact. 'An army of ghosts to command, an entire Empire to defeat, unlimited power. You could be Emperor yourself. Think of all the good you could do!'

'No. I won't forge a new way of life with the souls of dead children.' Steiner placed the artefact at the edge of the balcony, then pulled his sledgehammer from where it rested in a loop on his belt. 'They helped me stop Shirinov, I owe them a debt of gratitude.'

'You'll never have this sort of power again,' said Tief, shaking his head.

'It's not too late to give it back,' said Kimi.

'I'm sorry,' was all Steiner said, raising the sledgehammer high. When the hammer fell a nimbus of light shone, brighter than any day they had seen. The Ashen Torment split in three, dissolving into sand after a stunned and breathless moment. The nimbus faded from yellow to white, turning blue before fading to darkness. A chorus of sighs sounded from below them and the dark shapes of cinderwraiths dropped away like cloaks discarded. A stark white light took the place of every phantom, glittering stars in the gloom. A handful ascended, slowly at first, the others trailing after.

'What are those?' asked Tief.

'Corpsecandles,' said Steiner.

'They are souls,' said Sundra, 'souls released from obligation.'

The lights drifted higher, a constellation of stars beneath the iron-grey and soot-stained rock.

'Where are they going?' said Steiner.

'They are finally going to Frejna. Some she will send back, born into new bodies.' One by one they blinked out, melting into the cavern roof above. The priestess sighed. 'I have never seen such a thing in all my six decades. You have done a great thing.'

Steiner was surprised to find himself smiling, smiling with joy and smiling with relief. He was suddenly exhausted and leaned on the sledgehammer like a crutch.

Silverdust had not moved from his place on the balcony. He had not moved at all.

'I thought you might go with them?' said Steiner, after the last of the souls had drifted into the rock above.

Realization dawned on the faces of Kimi, Tief, Taiga and Sundra. Silverdust nodded mournfully, and clenched his hands before his chest as if he wore manacles.

I am deeply conflicted. For over forty years I have haunted this place, and yet I desire nothing else but to see the Emperor brought low. Now, for the first time, I can admit that the Emperor's destruction might be possible.

'If only that were true,' said Steiner.

You have given me hope, Steiner. I think perhaps I will stay here on Vladibogdan. When the Vigilants come, as Vigilants will, I will lie to them. I will lie to protect you.

'That's going to have to be some lie,' said Tief.

I will tell them that you escaped by ship, but the ship sank and all lives were lost. It may not help for long, but it may give you some time to begin again.

'It may be the lie to save my people,' said Kimi.

Silverdust knelt down and picked up the chain that the Ashen Torment had hung from. A sliver of rock remained attached, and this he handed to the princess.

I will do whatever I can to make it so. Now go, it is time you were finally away from here. Head south with all the four winds at your back, and begin new lives in sunnier lands.

Steiner hugged the Vigilant, worried the cinderwraith within the uniform might crumple, but Silverdust hugged him back.

Thank you, Steiner. Keep fighting. Keep fighting no matter what the Emperor sends after you.

Steiner left the forges in darkness. The only illumination was the aura of silver light that danced around the Vigilant, sparks of grit sparking and dying in the heat of his arcane power.

'I can't believe it,' said Tief. 'We're really leaving.'

'Yes,' said Steiner. 'We really are.'

CHAPTER FORTY-NINE

Kjellrunn

The Wreck of Vladibogdan, as it became known, was an incident that sent terrible fear through the Empire. All Vigilants felt the loss keenly, no matter how conflicted they may have felt about their old teaching institution. Soldiers worried at the escape of the dragons and Envoys and Okhrana were left wondering what had transpired on that bleak island, and who was responsible.

– Untainted Histories Volume 3: Serebryanyy Pyli

Kjellrunn stood at the stern of the *Watcher's Wait* and watched the ripples of green and blue the ship left in its wake. They were many miles from the Nordscales now. The island's forges were cold and silent, and the smudge of grey smoke that had haunted the skies these long decades had lessened. In time it would dissipate entirely, but not today.

'Cinderfell on your port side,' shouted Romola over her shoulder. The captain stood at the ship's wheel with her feet planted wide, wrapped up in thick woollens to ward off the spiteful cold. 'Best say your final goodbyes, right. Or pay your respects.'

It was easy to see the truth of Romola's words. Cinderfell

was a dead town and anyone who stayed there would soon be dead too. Kjellrunn found herself thinking of Håkon and where the ugly stub of a man might fetch up next.

Steiner approached and leaned on the handrail. He'd borrowed Kristofine's travel cloak and stolen a Vigilant's leather long coat. His sledgehammer hung from a loop on his hip. She'd never seen such a mismatched person, all burned and broken and fierce. He was almost a stranger to her, and he looked out to sea at their old home.

'We're really leaving,' said Kjellrunn, though it barely needed saying.

'We are,' said Steiner, though his voice was a broken whisper. There was a redness to his eyes and he was dreadfully pale.

'Father told you about Verner then,' said Kjellrunn, and she placed a hand on her brother's shoulder. His head dipped and she could feel him holding on to all the pain of their uncle's passing. She felt her own pain rise in response and gripped her brother a little tighter.

For a long time they said nothing; Kjellrunn wrapped an arm about her brother's shoulders and felt the *Watcher's Wait* move across the Spøkelsea, wave by wave, league by league, heading south.

'I'm going to kill all of them,' said Steiner, straightening. His hands gripped the handrail as if he might snap it apart like kindling. 'And I'm going to enjoy killing the Okhrana most of all.'

His eyes were set on the grey horizon and Kjellrunn pulled him round to look her in the eye.

'There's no need to avenge Verner. I took care of that. I killed a score of them.'

'It doesn't feel enough,' said Steiner, his face twisting in grief.

'No, it doesn't,' agreed Kjellrunn. 'And I don't suppose it

ever will, but Verner gave his life trying to protect us. He wouldn't want us to choose the lives of killers, of assassins.'

'Then what?' said Steiner, and she could feel the heat of his anger.

'You wanted to be a blacksmith once, didn't you?'

'You think I can go back to that after all I've seen?'

'That's for you to decide, but I know Verner wouldn't want us to go picking a fight we can't finish.'

Steiner shrugged her off and rubbed his forehead with a scarred hand. He grunted with frustration. 'And if we don't pick a fight, then who will? Not the Spriggani, what few are left of them.'

'Not the peoples of Shanisrond,' called Romola over her shoulder. 'They live in separate cities, all bickering and feuding, they're barely a country at all.'

'Have you been listening to us this whole time?' asked Steiner, his tone gruff.

'There are no secrets on ships, Steiner,' replied Romola. 'Best you get used to it.'

'What about Kimi?' said Kjellrunn. 'There's no telling what Yamal will do once they have their princess back.'

Steiner let out a long sigh and shivered in the wind. 'I don't know what will happen next, but I can't let the Empire go unchecked and unchallenged. They're calling me "Unbroken" below deck. I have a name, the Unbroken.'

Kjellrunn frowned and shook her head.

'Because the Vigilants tried to break me and I never gave up hope, though Frøya knows it was hard sometimes.'

'So you're a folk hero. Fine.' Kjellrunn glowered at him. 'Well, if you must go to war you can damn well promise me two things.'

'Of course,' he replied.

'Don't get yourself killed, and stop wearing your girlfriend's cloak. Be a man and buy your own.'

Steiner grinned, but Kjellrunn stalked off. She'd hidden her fear and her anger in the joke, but it remained all the same. She'd just got her brother back, and here he was desperate to get himself killed again.

Mistress Kamalov stood at the prow, not in her guise as the bent and stooped widow of the woods, but the imperious and watchful rogue Vigilant that Kjellrunn liked best.

'Give him time,' was all she said before Kjellrunn could even put her thoughts in order.

'What do you mean?'

'Steiner. He has been through a lot, and none of us acts wisely when we're in the throes of grief. It's easier to be angry than let ourselves be touched by pain, and Steiner has a lot of anger against the Empire.'

Kjellrunn nodded, seeing the sense of it.

'And you have been through a lot too, Kjellrunn. You have learned a lot in a very short space of time, a dangerous amount even. You have killed and lost loved ones. You have given up your home. All these things need time, just like any other wound.'

'I need something to hold on to,' said Kjellrunn after listening to the sea wash against the prow.

'Something I can give you, perhaps?'

'Certainty.'

Mistress Kamalov barked a coarse laugh. 'There is precious little of that in this cruel world.'

'What will we do next?' She toyed with the hammer brooch Marek had given her. 'Where will we go?'

Mistress Kamalov shrugged and turned to look across the main deck and the quarterdeck. Kjellrunn followed her gaze. Tief was telling tales to a crowd of novices, while Kristofine chatted to Sundra and Taiga. Kimi and Marozvolk were nowhere to be seen, huddled up below decks if Kjellrunn had to guess. Maxim had taken to following Marek around the ship wherever he went, and the blacksmith didn't seem to mind.

'They will all want to go to different places,' said Mistress Kamalov. 'And Steiner may have rescued them, but he isn't responsible for them, though he may think otherwise right now.' The old woman turned to Kjellrunn, her eyes bright and gaze firm. 'Where do you want to go?'

'Away from the Empire,' said Kjellrunn. 'Somewhere I can learn to use my powers. I nearly lost control in the forest and it . . .' She chewed her lip.

'And it scared you.'

Kjellrunn nodded, remembering the vortex of earth and broken branches, the way the men had been flung around the clearing, mashed into bloody pulp.

'We will go south and I will teach you, Kjellrunn. Of that I am certain.' Mistress Kamalov gave a crooked smiled and sighed contentedly. 'And now I am going below to sleep for as long as I can.'

Kjellrunn nodded and watched the rogue Vigilant go. Kristofine appeared by her side with a smile.

'Come with me,' was all she said.

'If it's something to do with Steiner then I'd rather not. I'm not best pleased with him, to tell the truth.'

Kristofine paused. 'It's not about Steiner. Are you jealous of him? What with his new-found fame and all.'

'Not jealous. I just don't want him getting himself killed.'

'Well, that makes two of us,' said Kristofine, and took her hand, leading her back to the stern of the ship.

Before too long they were in the captain's cabin, where Kimi and Marozvolk were standing by the window with a long tube of leather.

'What's that?' asked Kjellrunn, glad to be inside.

'It lets you see things that are far away,' said Kimi. 'It's called a telescope. Here, come and try for yourself.'

Kjellrunn approached the window and looked out to sea, squinting through the lenses.

'Do you see them?' said Kristofine.

Kjellrunn scanned the horizon and then tilted the tube upward. They looked like birds, dark birds in the pale grey sky.

'You brought me all this way to see a few rangy gulls.'

Marozvolk and Kimi started laughing and Kjellrunn felt herself blush.

'They're dragons,' said Kimi. 'Silverdust freed the dragons, just as I asked him to.'

'I didn't hear you ask him,' replied Kjellrunn.

'I didn't have to. Silverdust has a way of knowing what's on your mind.'

'Where will they go?' Kjellrunn was suddenly very afraid. 'Won't they attack the towns of the Scorched Republics?'

Kimi cocked her head to one side. 'I don't think so. They've been following us south for the last hour now.'

'Dragons,' said Kjellrunn. 'As if two witches and a Yamal princess weren't enough.'

'And a folk hero,' added Kristofine.

Kjellrunn looked through the telescope and regarded the dragons again. Steiner was right. There was no way he could go back to being a blacksmith after this, any more than Kjellrunn could go back to chopping firewood and preparing fish stew each day.

'What will we do?' asked Kjellrunn.

'Hope they don't get too hungry,' replied Marozvolk.

'And that your brother knows how to keep them under control,' added Kimi. 'Though I'm sure he'll have help from Sundra.'

'We're free, Kjell. We're free.' Kristofine smiled. 'Free of Cinderfell and Vladibogdan, free of the Empire.'

Kjellrunn nodded and tried to smile back, but it seemed

there were a lot of responsibilities that came with being free, and each of them would take some getting used to.

Kristofine wrapped an arm about Kjellrunn and they both looked out at the Spøkelsea where the dragons glided over the waves. Free.

Acknowledgements

Steiner and gang have taken a long and winding road to reach publication. It would not have been possible without the following people. First and foremost, Juliet, who always championed both the book and myself, even when I was a massive grouch, which was often. Julie Crisp has been everything you could ask for from an agent; steady and wise. Thanks to Jen Williams, Emma Trevayne and Tom Pollock, who have been there for advice on writing and publishing in general. Much gratitude to Lily, Jack and Tash at Harper Voyager for all their suggestions, support, and belief. And also all the people who are forgotten such as the art department, publicity, and copy editor.

And thanks to you, the reader. Welcome to Vinterkveld.

KU-673-285

THE GREAT BIG
BAKING BOOK

THE GREAT BIG
BAKING BOOK

CAROLE CLEMENTS

PREMIER

This edition published in 1998 by Lorenz Books

© Anness Publishing Limited 1994

Lorenz Books is an imprint of
Anness Publishing Limited
Hermes House
88-89 Blackfriars Road
London SE1 8HA

All rights reserved. No part of this publication may be reproduced, stored
in a retrieval system, or transmitted in any way or by any means,
electronic, mechanical, photocopying, recording or otherwise,
without the prior written permission of the copyright holder.

ISBN 1 85967 846 7

A CIP catalogue record is available from the British Library

Publisher: Joanna Lorenz
Project Editor: Carole Clements
Designer: Sheila Volpe
Photography, styling: Amanda Heywood
Food Styling: Elizabeth Wolf-Cohen, Carla Capalbo,
steps by Cara Hobday, Teresa Goldfinch, Nicola Fowler

Printed and bound in Hong Kong

1 3 5 7 9 10 8 6 4 2

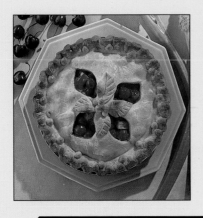

CONTENTS

~

INTRODUCTION

~

Nothing equals the satisfaction of home baking. No commercial cake mix or shop-bought biscuit can match one that is made from the best fresh ingredients with all the added enjoyment that baking at home provides – the enticing aromas that fill the house and stimulate appetites, the delicious straight-from-the-oven flavour, as well as the pride of having created such wonderful goodies yourself.

The Great Big Baking Book is filled with familiar favourites as well as many other lesser known recipes. Explore the wealth of biscuits, buns, tea breads, yeast breads, pies, tarts, and cakes within these pages. Even if you are a novice baker, the easy-to-follow and clear step-by-step photographs will help you achieve good results. For the more experienced home baker, this book will provide some new recipes to add to your repertoire.

Baking is an exact science and needs to be approached in an ordered way. First read through the recipe from beginning to end. Set out all the required ingredients before you begin. Size 3 eggs are assumed unless specified otherwise, and they should be at room temperature for best results. Sift the flour after you have measured it, and incorporate other dry ingredients as specified in the individual recipes. If you sift the flour from a fair height, it will have more chance to aerate and lighten.

When a recipe calls for folding one ingredient into another, it should be done in a way that incorporates as much air as possible into the mixture. Use either a large metal spoon or a long rubber or plastic scraper. Gently plunge the spoon or scraper deep into the centre of the mixture and, scooping up a large amount of the mixture, fold it over. Turn the bowl slightly so each scoop folds over another part of the mixture.

No two ovens are alike. Buy a reliable oven thermometer and test the temperature of your oven. When possible bake in the centre of the oven where the heat is more likely to be constant. If using a fan-assisted oven, follow the manufacturer's guidelines for baking. Good quality baking tins can improve your results, as they conduct heat more efficiently.

Practice, patience and enthusiasm are the keys to confident and successful baking. *The Great Big Baking Book* will inspire you to start sifting flour, breaking eggs and stirring up all sorts of delectable homemade treats – all guaranteed to bring great satisfaction to both the baker and those lucky enough to enjoy the results.

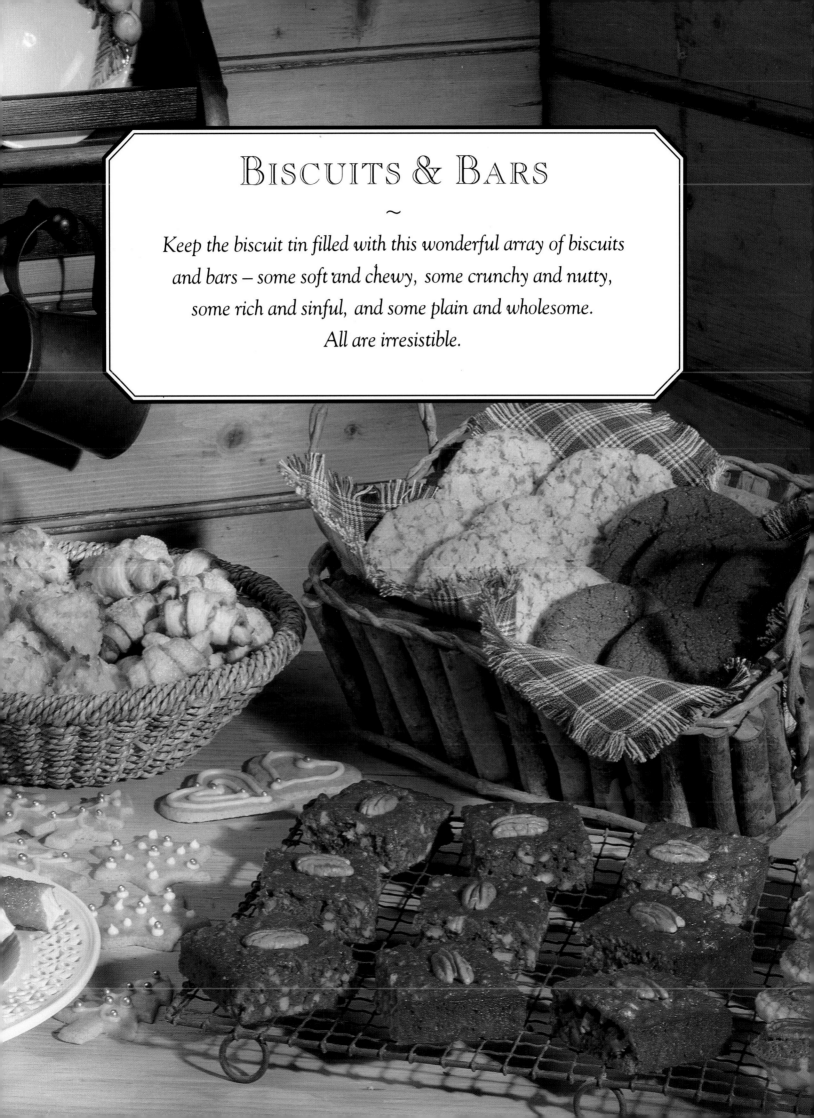

BISCUITS & BARS

~

Keep the biscuit tin filled with this wonderful array of biscuits
and bars – some soft and chewy, some crunchy and nutty,
some rich and sinful, and some plain and wholesome.
All are irresistible.

Farmhouse Biscuits

MAKES 18

4 oz (115 g) butter or margarine, at room temperature

3½ oz (100 g) light brown sugar

2½ oz (70 g) crunchy peanut butter

1 egg

2 oz (55 g) plain flour

½ tsp baking powder

½ tsp ground cinnamon

⅛ tsp salt

6 oz (170 g) muesli

2 oz (55 g) raisins

2 oz (55 g) chopped walnuts

1 Preheat a 350°F/180°C/Gas 4 oven. Grease a baking sheet.

2 With an electric mixer, cream the butter or margarine and sugar until light and fluffy. Beat in the peanut butter. Beat in the egg.

3 ▲ Sift the flour, baking powder, cinnamon and salt over the peanut butter mixture and stir to blend. Stir in the muesli, raisins and walnuts. Taste the mixture to see if it needs more sugar, as muesli varies.

4 ▲ Drop rounded tablespoonfuls of the mixture onto the prepared baking sheet about 1 in (2.5 cm) apart. Press gently with the back of a spoon to spread each mound into a circle.

5 Bake until lightly coloured, about 15 minutes. With a metal spatula, transfer to a rack to cool. Store in an airtight container.

Crunchy Oatmeal Biscuits

MAKES 14

6 oz (170 g) butter or margarine, at room temperature

6 oz (170 g) caster sugar

1 egg yolk

6 oz (170 g) plain flour

1 tsp bicarbonate of soda

½ tsp salt

2 oz (55 g) rolled oats

2 oz (55 g) small crunchy nugget cereal

~ **VARIATION** ~

For Nutty Oatmeal Biscuits, substitute an equal quantity of chopped walnuts or pecans for the cereal, and prepare as described.

1 ▲ With an electric mixer, cream the butter or margarine and sugar together until light and fluffy. Mix in the egg yolk.

2 Sift over the flour, bicarbonate of soda and salt, then stir into the butter mixture. Add the oats and cereal and stir to blend. Refrigerate for at least 20 minutes.

3 Preheat a 375°F/190°C/Gas 5 oven. Grease a baking sheet.

4 ▲ Roll the mixture into balls. Place them on the sheet and flatten with the bottom of a floured glass.

5 Bake until golden, 10–12 minutes. With a metal spatula, transfer to a rack to cool completely. Store in an airtight container.

Farmhouse Biscuits (top), Crunchy Oatmeal Biscuits

Oaty Coconut Biscuits

MAKES 48

6 oz (170 g) quick-cooking oats

3 oz (85 g) desiccated coconut

8 oz (225 g) butter or margarine, at room temperature

4 oz (115 g) caster sugar + 2 tbsp

2 oz (55 g) dark brown sugar

2 eggs

4 tbsp milk

1½ tsp vanilla essence

4 oz (115 g) plain flour

½ tsp bicarbonate of soda

½ tsp salt

1 tsp ground cinnamon

1 Preheat a 400°F/200°C/Gas 6 oven. Lightly grease 2 baking sheets.

2 ▲ Spread the oats and coconut on an ungreased baking sheet. Bake until golden brown, 8–10 minutes, stirring occasionally.

3 With an electric mixer, cream the butter or margarine and both sugars until light and fluffy. Beat in the eggs, 1 at a time, then the milk and vanilla. Sift over the dry ingredients and fold in. Stir in the oats and coconut.

4 ▼ Drop spoonfuls of the mixture 1–2 in (2.5–5 cm) apart on the prepared sheets and flatten with the bottom of a greased glass dipped in sugar. Bake until golden, 8–10 minutes. Transfer to a rack to cool.

Crunchy Jumbles

MAKES 36

4 oz (115 g) butter or margarine, at room temperature

8 oz (225 g) caster sugar

1 egg

1 tsp vanilla essence

5 oz (140 g) plain flour

½ tsp bicarbonate of soda

⅛ tsp salt

2 oz (55 g) crisped rice cereal

6 oz (170 g) chocolate chips

~ VARIATION ~

For even crunchier biscuits, add 2 oz (55 g) walnuts, coarsely chopped, with the cereal and chocolate chips.

1 Preheat a 350°F/180°C/Gas 4 oven. Lightly grease 2 baking sheets.

2 ▲ With an electric mixer, cream the butter or margarine and sugar until light and fluffy. Beat in the egg and vanilla. Sift over the flour, bicarbonate of soda and salt and fold in carefully.

3 ▼ Add the cereal and chocolate chips. Stir to mix thoroughly.

4 Drop spoonfuls of the mixture 1–2 in (2.5–5 cm) apart on the sheets. Bake until golden, 10–12 minutes. Transfer to a rack to cool.

Oaty Coconut Biscuits (top), Crunchy Jumbles

Ginger Biscuits

MAKES 36

8 oz (225 g) caster sugar
3½ oz (100 g) light brown sugar
4 oz (115 g) butter, at room temperature
4 oz (115 g) margarine, at room temperature
1 egg
3 fl oz (85 ml) black treacle
9 oz (250 g) plain flour
2 tsp ground ginger
½ tsp grated nutmeg
1 tsp ground cinnamon
2 tsp bicarbonate of soda
½ tsp salt

1 Preheat a 325°F/170°F/Gas 3 oven. Line 2–3 baking sheets with greaseproof paper and grease lightly.

2 ▲ With an electric mixer, cream half of the caster sugar, the brown sugar, butter and margarine until light and fluffy. Add the egg and continue beating to blend well. Add the treacle.

3 ▲ Sift the dry ingredients 3 times, then stir into the butter mixture. Refrigerate for 30 minutes.

4 ▲ Place the remaining sugar in a shallow dish. Roll tablespoonfuls of the biscuit mixture into balls, then roll the balls in the sugar to coat.

5 Place the balls 2 in (5 cm) apart on the prepared sheets and flatten slightly. Bake until golden around the edges but soft in the middle, 12–15 minutes. Let stand for 5 minutes before transferring to a rack to cool.

~ VARIATION ~

To make Gingerbread Men, increase the amount of flour by 1 oz (30g). Roll out the mixture and cut out shapes with a special cutter. Decorate with icing, if wished.

Orange Biscuits

MAKES 30

4 oz (115 g) butter, at room temperature
7 oz (200 g) sugar
2 egg yolks
1 tablespoon fresh orange juice
grated rind of 1 large orange
7 oz (200 g) plain flour
1 tablespoon cornflour
½ teaspoon salt
1 teaspoon baking powder

1 ▲ With an electric mixer, cream the butter and sugar until light and fluffy. Add the yolks, orange juice and rind, and continue beating to blend. Set aside.

2 In another bowl, sift together the flour, cornflour, salt and baking powder. Add to the butter mixture and stir until it forms a dough.

3 ▲ Wrap the dough in greaseproof paper and refrigerate for 2 hours.

4 Preheat the oven to 375°F/190°C/ Gas 5. Grease 2 baking sheets.

5 ▲ Roll spoonfuls of the dough into balls and place 1–2 in (2.5–5 cm) apart on the prepared sheets.

6 ▼ Press down with a fork to flatten. Bake until golden brown, 8–10 minutes. With a metal palette knife transfer to a rack to cool.

Cinnamon-Coated Cookies

MAKES 30

4 oz (115 g) butter, at room temperature

12 oz (350 g) caster sugar

1 tsp vanilla essence

2 eggs

2 fl oz (65 ml) milk

14 oz (400 g) plain flour

1 tsp bicarbonate of soda

2 oz (55 g) finely chopped walnuts

FOR THE COATING

5 tbsp sugar

2 tbsp ground cinnamon

1 Preheat a 375°F/190°C/Gas 5 oven. Grease 2 baking sheets.

2 With an electric mixer, cream the butter until light. Add the sugar and vanilla and continue mixing until fluffy. Beat in the eggs, then the milk.

3 ▲ Sift the flour and bicarbonate of soda over the butter mixture and stir to blend. Stir in the nuts. Refrigerate for 15 minutes.

4 ▲ For the coating, mix the sugar and cinnamon. Roll tablespoonfuls of the mixture into walnut-size balls. Roll the balls in the sugar mixture. You may need to work in batches.

5 Place 2 in (5 cm) apart on the prepared sheets and flatten slightly. Bake until golden, about 10 minutes. Transfer to a rack to cool.

Chewy Chocolate Biscuits

MAKES 18

4 egg whites

10 oz (285 g) icing sugar

4 oz (115 g) cocoa powder

2 tbsp plain flour

1 tsp instant coffee

1 tbsp water

4 oz (115 g) finely chopped walnuts

1 Preheat a 350°F/180°C/Gas 4 oven. Line 2 baking sheets with greaseproof paper and grease the paper.

~ **VARIATION** ~

If wished, add 3 oz (85 g) chocolate chips to the mixture with the nuts.

2 With an electric mixer, beat the egg whites until frothy.

3 ▼ Sift the sugar, cocoa, flour and coffee into the whites. Add the water and continue beating on low speed to blend, then on high for a few minutes until the mixture thickens. With a rubber spatula, fold in the walnuts.

4 ▲ Place generous spoonfuls of the mixture 1 in (2.5 cm) apart on the prepared sheets. Bake until firm and cracked on top but soft on the inside, 12–15 minutes. With a metal spatula, transfer to a rack to cool.

Cinnamon-Coated Cookies (top), Chewy Chocolate Biscuits

Chocolate Pretzels

MAKES 28

5 oz (140 g) plain flour

⅛ teaspoon salt

¾ oz (25 g) unsweetened cocoa powder

4 oz (115 g) butter, at room temperature

4½ oz (125 g) sugar

1 egg

1 egg white, lightly beaten, for glazing

sugar crystals, for sprinkling

1 Sift together the flour, salt and cocoa powder. Set aside. Grease 2 baking sheets.

2 ▲ With an electric mixer, cream the butter until light. Add the sugar and continue beating until light and fluffy. Beat in the egg. Add the dry ingredients and stir to blend. Gather the dough into a ball, wrap in clear film, and refrigerate for 1 hour or freeze for 30 minutes.

3 ▲ Roll the dough into 28 small balls. Refrigerate the balls until needed. Preheat the oven to 375°F/190°C/Gas 5.

4 ▲ Roll each ball into a rope about 10 in (25 cm) long. With each rope, form a loop with the two ends facing you. Twist the ends and fold back on to the circle, pressing in to make a pretzel shape. Place on the sheets.

5 ▲ Brush the pretzels with the egg white. Sprinkle sugar crystals over the tops and bake until firm, 10–12 minutes. Transfer to a rack to cool.

Cream Cheese Spirals

MAKES 32

8 oz (225 g) butter, at room temperature

8 oz (225 g) cream cheese

2 tsp caster sugar

8 oz (225 g) plain flour

1 egg white beaten with 1 tbsp water, for glazing

caster sugar, for sprinkling

FOR THE FILLING

4 oz (115 g) finely chopped walnuts

4 oz (115 g) light brown sugar

1 tsp ground cinnamon

1 With an electric mixer, cream the butter, cream cheese and sugar until soft. Sift over the flour and mix until combined. Gather into a ball and divide in half. Flatten each half, wrap in greaseproof paper and refrigerate for at least 30 minutes.

2 Meanwhile, make the filling. Mix together the chopped walnuts, the brown sugar and the cinnamon. Set aside.

3 Preheat a 375°F/190°F/Gas 5 oven. Grease 2 baking sheets.

4 ▲ Working with one half of the mixture at a time, roll out thinly into a circle about 11 in (28 cm) in diameter. Trim the edges with a knife, using a dinner plate as a guide.

5 ▼ Brush the surface with the egg white glaze and then sprinkle evenly with half the filling.

6 Cut the circle into quarters, and each quarter into 4 sections, to form 16 triangles.

7 ▲ Starting from the base of the triangles, roll up to form spirals.

8 Place on the sheets and brush with the remaining glaze. Sprinkle with caster sugar. Bake until golden, 15–20 minutes. Cool on a rack.

Vanilla Crescents

MAKES 36

6 oz (175 g) unblanched almonds

4 oz (115 g) plain flour

pinch of salt

8 oz (225 g) unsalted butter

4 oz (115 g) granulated sugar

1 teaspoon vanilla essence

icing sugar for dusting

1 Grind the almonds with a few tablespoons of the flour in a food processor, blender or nut grinder.

2 Sift the remaining flour with the salt into a bowl. Set aside.

3 With an electric mixer, cream together the butter and sugar until light and fluffy.

4 ▼ Add the almonds, vanilla essence and the flour mixture. Stir to mix well. Gather the dough into a ball, wrap in greaseproof paper, and chill for at least 30 minutes.

5 Preheat the oven to 325°F/170°C/ Gas 3. Lightly grease two baking sheets.

6 ▲ Break off walnut-size pieces of dough and roll into small cylinders about ½ in (1 cm) in diameter. Bend into small crescents and place on the prepared baking sheets.

7 Bake for about 20 minutes until dry but not brown. Transfer to a wire rack to cool only slightly. Set the rack over a baking sheet and dust with an even layer of icing sugar. Leave to cool completely.

Walnut Crescents

MAKES 72

4 oz (115 g) walnuts

8 oz (225 g) unsalted butter

4 oz (115 g) granulated sugar

½ teaspoon vanilla extract

8 oz (225 g) flour

¼ teaspoon salt

confectioners' sugar for dusting

1 Preheat the oven to 350°F/ 180°C/Gas 4.

2 Grind the walnuts in a food processor, blender or nut grinder until they are almost a paste. Transfer to a bowl.

3 Add the butter to the walnuts and mix with a wooden spoon until blended. Add the granulated sugar and vanilla and stir to blend.

4 ▼ Sift the flour and salt into the walnut mixture. Work into a dough.

5 Shape the dough into small cylinders about 1½ in (4 cm) long. Bend into crescents and place evenly spaced on an ungreased baking sheet.

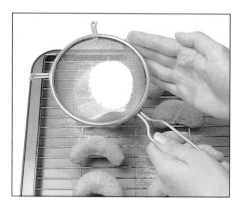

6 ▲ Bake until lightly browned, about 15 minutes. Transfer to a rack to cool only slightly. Set the rack over a baking sheet and dust lightly with confectioners' sugar.

Vanilla Crescents (top), Walnut Crescents

Pecan Puffs

MAKES 24

4 oz (115 g) unsalted butter
2 tablespoons granulated sugar
pinch of salt
1 teaspoon vanilla essence
4 oz (115 g) pecans
4 oz (115 g) plain flour, sifted
icing sugar for dusting

1 Preheat the oven to 300°F/150°C/ Gas 2. Grease two baking sheets.

2 ▲ Cream the butter and sugar until light and fluffy. Stir in the salt and vanilla essence.

3 Grind the nuts in a food processor, blender or nut grinder. Stir several times to prevent nuts becoming oily. If necessary, grind in batches.

4 ▲ Push the ground nuts through a sieve set over a bowl to aerate them. Pieces too large to go through the sieve can be ground again.

5 ▲ Stir the nuts and flour into the butter mixture to make a firm, springy dough.

6 Roll the dough into marble-size balls between the palms of your hands. Place on the prepared baking sheets and bake for 45 minutes.

7 ▲ While the puffs are still hot, roll them in icing sugar. Leave to cool completely, then roll once more in icing sugar.

Pecan Tassies

MAKES 24

4 oz (115 g) cream cheese
4 oz (115 g) butter
4 oz (115 g) plain flour
FOR THE FILLING
2 eggs
4 oz (115 g) dark brown sugar
1 teaspoon vanilla essence
pinch of salt
2 tablespoons butter, melted
4 oz (115 g) pecans

1 Place a baking sheet in the oven and preheat to 350°F/180°C/Gas 4. Grease 24 mini-muffin tins.

2 Chop the cream cheese and butter into cubes. Put them in a mixing bowl. Sift over half the flour and mix. Add the remaining flour and continue mixing to form a dough.

3 ▲ Roll out the dough thinly. With a floured fluted pastry cutter, stamp out 24 2½ in/7cm rounds. Line the tins with the rounds and chill.

4 To make the filling, lightly whisk the eggs in a bowl. Gradually whisk in the brown sugar, and add the vanilla essence, salt and butter. Set aside until required.

5 ▼ Reserve 24 undamaged pecan halves and chop the rest coarsely with a sharp knife.

~ VARIATION ~

To make Jam Tassies, fill the cream cheese pastry shells with raspberry or blackberry jam, or other fruit jams. Bake as described.

6 ▲ Place a spoonful of chopped nuts in each muffin tin and cover with the filling. Set a pecan half on the top of each.

7 Bake on the hot baking sheet for about 20 minutes, until puffed and set. Transfer to a wire rack to cool. Serve at room temperature.

Lady Fingers

MAKES 18

3½ oz (90 g) plain flour

pinch of salt

4 eggs, separated

4 oz (115 g) granulated sugar

½ teaspoon vanilla essence

icing sugar for sprinkling

1 Preheat the oven to 300°F/150°C/ Gas 2. Grease 2 baking sheets, then coat lightly with flour, and shake off the excess.

2 Sift the flour and salt together twice in a bowl.

~ **COOK'S TIP** ~

To make the biscuits all the same length, mark parallel lines 4 in (10 cm) apart on the greased baking sheets.

3 With an electric mixer beat the egg yolks with half of the sugar until thick enough to leave a ribbon trail when the beaters are lifted.

4 ▲ In another bowl, beat the egg whites until stiff. Beat in the remaining sugar until glossy.

5 Sift the flour over the yolks and spoon a large dollop of egg whites over the flour. Carefully fold in with a large metal spoon, adding the vanilla essence. Gently fold in the remaining whites.

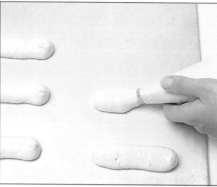

6 ▲ Spoon the mixture into a piping bag fitted with a large plain nozzle. Pipe 4 in (10 cm) long lines on the prepared baking sheets about 1 in (2.5 cm) apart. Sift over a layer of icing sugar. Turn the sheet upside down to dislodge any excess sugar.

7 Bake for about 20 minutes until crusty on the outside but soft in the centre. Cool slightly on the baking sheets before transferring to a wire rack to cool completely.

Walnut Cookies

MAKES 60

4 oz (115 g) butter or margarine

6 oz (175 g) caster sugar

4 oz (115 g) plain flour

2 teaspoons vanilla essence

4 oz (115 g) walnuts, finely chopped

~ **VARIATION** ~

To make Almond Cookies, use an equal amount of finely chopped unblanched almonds instead of walnuts. Replace half the vanilla with ½ teaspoon almond essence.

1 Preheat the oven to 300°F/150°C/ Gas 2. Grease 2 baking sheets.

2 ▲ With an electric mixer, cream the butter or margarine until soft. Add 2 oz (50 g) of the sugar and continue beating until light and fluffy. Stir in the flour, vanilla essence and walnuts.

3 Drop teaspoonfuls of the batter 1–2 in (2.5–5 cm) apart on the prepared baking sheets and flatten slightly. Bake for about 25 minutes.

4 ▼ Transfer to a wire rack set over a baking sheet and sprinkle with the remaining sugar.

Lady Fingers (top), Walnut Cookies

Italian Almond Biscotti

MAKES 48

7 oz (200 g) whole unblanched almonds
7½ oz (215 g) plain flour
3½ oz (100 g) sugar
⅛ teaspoon salt
⅛ teaspoon saffron powder
½ teaspoon bicarbonate of soda
2 eggs
1 egg white, lightly beaten

~ COOK'S TIP ~

Serve biscotti after a meal, for dunking in glasses of sweet white wine, such as an Italian *Vin Santo* or a French *Muscat de Beaumes-de-Venise*.

1 Preheat a 375°F/190°C/Gas 5 oven. Grease and flour 2 baking sheets.

2 ▲ Spread the almonds in a baking tray and bake until lightly browned, about 15 minutes. When cool, grind 2 oz (55 g) of the almonds in a food processor, blender, or coffee grinder until pulverized. Coarsely chop the remaining almonds in 2 or 3 pieces each. Set aside.

3 ▲ Combine the flour, sugar, salt, saffron, bicarbonate of soda and ground almonds in a bowl and mix to blend. Make a well in the centre and add the eggs. Stir to form a rough dough. Transfer to a floured surface and knead until well blended. Knead in the chopped almonds.

4 ▲ Divide the dough into 3 equal parts. Roll into logs about 1 in (2.5 cm) in diameter. Place on one of the prepared sheets, brush with the egg white and bake for 20 minutes. Remove from the oven.

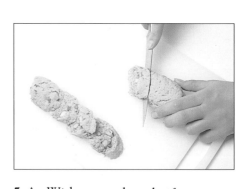

5 ▲ With a very sharp knife, cut into each log at an angle making ½ in (1 cm) slices. Return the slices on the baking sheets to a 275°F/140°C/Gas 1 oven and bake for 25 minutes more. Transfer to a rack to cool.

Christmas Cookies

MAKES 30

6 oz (170 g) unsalted butter, at room temperature
10 oz (285 g) caster sugar
1 egg
1 egg yolk
1 tsp vanilla essence
grated rind of 1 lemon
¼ tsp salt
10 oz (285 g) plain flour
FOR DECORATING (OPTIONAL)
coloured icing and small decorations

1 Preheat a 350°F/180°C/Gas 4 oven.

2 ▲ With an electric mixer, cream the butter until soft. Add the sugar gradually and continue beating until light and fluffy.

3 ▲ Using a wooden spoon, slowly mix in the whole egg and the egg yolk. Add the vanilla, lemon rind and salt. Stir to mix well.

4 Add the flour and stir until blended. Gather the mixture into a ball, wrap in greaseproof paper, and refrigerate for at least 30 minutes.

5 ▼ On a floured surface, roll out the mixture about ⅛ in (3 mm) thick.

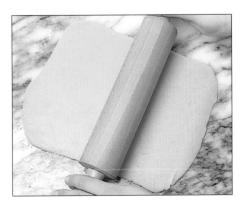

6 ▲ Stamp out shapes or rounds with biscuit cutters.

7 Bake until lightly coloured, about 8 minutes. Transfer to a rack and let cool completely before icing and decorating, if wished.

Toasted Oat Meringues

MAKES 12

2 oz (55 g) rolled oats
2 egg whites
⅛ tsp salt
1½ tsp cornflour
6 oz (170 g) caster sugar

1 Preheat a 275°F/140°C/Gas 1 oven. Spread the oats on a baking sheet and toast in the oven until golden, about 10 minutes. Lower the heat to 250°F/130°C/Gas ½. Grease and flour a baking sheet.

~ **VARIATION** ~

Add ½ teaspoon ground cinnamon with the oats, and fold in gently.

2 ▼ With an electric mixer, beat the egg whites and salt until they start to form soft peaks.

3 Sift over the cornflour and continue beating until the whites hold stiff peaks. Add half the sugar and whisk until glossy.

4 ▲ Add the remaining sugar and fold in, then fold in the oats.

5 Gently spoon the mixture onto the prepared sheet and bake for 2 hours.

6 When done, turn off the oven. Lift the meringues from the sheet, turn over, and set in another place on the sheet to prevent sticking. Leave in the oven as it cools down.

Meringues

MAKES 24

4 egg whites
⅛ tsp salt
10 oz (285 g) caster sugar
½ tsp vanilla or almond essence (optional)
8 fl oz (250 ml) whipped cream (optional)

1 Preheat a 225°F/110°C/Gas ¼ oven. Grease and flour 2 large baking sheets.

2 With an electric mixer, beat the egg whites and salt in a very clean metal bowl on low speed. When they start to form soft peaks, add half the sugar and continue beating until the mixture holds stiff peaks.

3 ▲ With a large metal spoon, fold in the remaining sugar and vanilla or almond essence, if using.

4 ▼ Pipe the meringue mixture or gently spoon it on the prepared sheet.

5 Bake for 2 hours. Turn off the oven. Loosen the meringues, invert, and set in another place on the sheets to prevent sticking. Leave in the oven as it cools. Serve sandwiched with whipped cream, if wished.

Toasted Oat Meringues (top), Meringues

Chocolate Macaroons

MAKES 24

2 oz (55 g) plain chocolate

6 oz (170 g) blanched almonds

8 oz (225 g) caster sugar

3 egg whites

½ tsp vanilla essence

¼ tsp almond essence

icing sugar, for dusting

1 Preheat a 325°F/170°C/Gas 3 oven. Line 2 baking sheets with greaseproof paper and grease the paper.

2 ▼ Melt the chocolate in the top of a double boiler, or in a heatproof bowl set over a pan of hot water.

3 ▲ Grind the almonds finely in a food processor, blender or grinder. Transfer to a mixing bowl.

4 ▲ Add the sugar, egg whites, vanilla, and almond essence and stir to blend. Stir in the chocolate. The mixture should just hold its shape. If it is too soft, refrigerate for 15 minutes.

5 ▲ Use a teaspoon and your hands to shape the mixture into walnut-size balls. Place on the sheets and flatten slightly. Brush each ball with a little water and sift over a thin layer of icing sugar. Bake until just firm, 10–12 minutes. With a metal spatula, transfer to a rack to cool.

~ VARIATION ~

For Chocolate Pine Nut Macaroons, spread 3 oz (85 g) pine nuts in a shallow dish. Press the chocolate macaroon balls into the nuts to cover one side and bake as described, nut-side up.

Coconut Macaroons

MAKES 24

1½ oz (45 g) plain flour

⅛ tsp salt

8 oz (225 g) desiccated coconut

5½ fl oz (170 ml) sweetened condensed milk

1 tsp vanilla essence

1 Preheat a 350°F/180°C/Gas 4 oven. Grease 2 baking sheets.

2 Sift the flour and salt into a bowl. Stir in the coconut.

3 ▲ Pour in the milk. Add the vanilla and stir from the centre to make a very thick mixture.

4 ▼ Drop heaped tablespoonfuls of mixture 1 in (2.5 cm) apart on the sheets. Bake until golden brown, about 20 minutes. Cool on a rack.

Chocolate Macaroons (top), Coconut Macaroons

Almond Tiles

MAKES 40

2 oz (55 g) blanched almonds
4 oz (115 g) sugar
1¼ oz (50 g) unsalted butter
2 egg whites
1½ oz (45 g) plain flour
½ teaspoon vanilla essence
4 oz (115 g) slivered almonds

1 Grind the blanched almonds with 2 tablespoons of the sugar in a food processor, blender or nut grinder. If necessary, grind in batches.

2 Preheat the oven to 425°F/220°C/ Gas 7. Grease 2 baking sheets.

3 ▲ Put the butter in a large bowl and mix in the remaining sugar, using a metal spoon. With an electric mixer, cream them together until light and fluffy.

4 Add the egg whites and stir until blended. Sift over the flour and fold in with a metal spoon. Fold in the ground almonds and vanilla essence.

5 ▲ Working in small batches, drop tablespoonfuls of the mixture 3 in (7.5 cm) apart on one of the prepared sheets. With the back of a spoon, spread out into thin, almost transparent circles about 6 cm (2½ in) in diameter. Sprinkle each circle with some of the slivered almonds.

6 Bake until the outer edges have browned slightly, about 4 minutes.

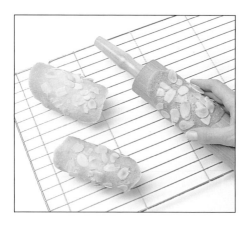

7 ▲ Remove from the oven. With a metal spatula, quickly drape the biscuits over a rolling pin to form a curved shape. Transfer to a rack when firm. If the biscuits harden too quickly to shape, reheat briefly. Repeat the baking and shaping process until the mixture is used up. Store in an airtight container.

Florentines

MAKES 36

1½ oz (45 g) butter
4 fl oz (125 ml) whipping cream
4½ oz (125 g) sugar
4½ oz (125 g) flaked almonds
2 oz (55 g) orange or mixed peel, finely chopped
1½ oz (45 g) glacé cherries, chopped
2½ oz (70 g) plain flour, sifted
8 oz (225 g) plain chocolate
1 teaspoon vegetable oil

1 Preheat the oven to 350°F/180°C/ Gas 4. Grease 2 baking sheets.

2 ▲ Melt the butter, cream and sugar together and slowly bring to the boil. Take off the heat and stir in the almonds, orange or mixed peel, cherries and flour until blended.

3 Drop teaspoonfuls of the batter 1–2 in (2.5–5 cm) apart on the prepared sheets and flatten with a fork.

4 Bake until the cookies brown at the edges, about 10 minutes. Remove from the oven and correct the shape by quickly pushing in any thin uneven edges with a knife or a round biscuit cutter. Work fast or they will cool and harden while still on the sheets. If necessary, return to the oven for a few moments to soften. While still hot, use a metal palette knife to transfer the florentines to a clean, flat surface.

5 Melt the chocolate in the top of a double boiler or in a heatproof bowl set over a pan of hot water. Add the oil and stir to blend.

6 ▲ With a metal palette knife, spread the smooth underside of the cooled florentines with a thin coating of the melted chocolate.

7 ▼ When the chocolate is about to set, draw a serrated knife across the surface with a slight sawing motion to make wavy lines. Store in an airtight container in a cool place.

Nut Lace Wafers

MAKES 18

2½ oz (70 g) whole blanched almonds
2 oz (55 g) butter
1½ oz (45 g) plain flour
3½ oz (100 g) sugar
1 fl oz (30 ml) double cream
½ teaspoon vanilla essence

1 Preheat the oven to 375°F/190°C/ Gas 5. Grease 1–2 baking sheets.

2 With a sharp knife, chop the almonds as fine as possible. Alternatively, use a food processor, blender, or coffee grinder to chop the nuts very fine.

3 ▼ Melt the butter in a saucepan over low heat. Remove from the heat and stir in the remaining ingredients and the almonds.

4 Drop teaspoonfuls 2½ in (6 cm) apart on the prepared sheets. Bake until golden, about 5 minutes. Cool on the baking sheets briefly, just until the wafers are stiff enough to remove.

5 ▲ With a metal palette knife, transfer to a rack to cool completely.

> **~ VARIATION ~**
>
> Add 2 oz (55 g) finely chopped orange peel to the mixture.

Oatmeal Lace Rounds

MAKES 36

5½ oz (150 g) butter or margarine
4½ oz (125 g) quick-cooking porridge oats
5¾ oz (165 g) dark brown sugar
5¼ oz (150 g) caster sugar
1½ oz (45 g) plain flour
¼ teaspoon salt
1 egg, lightly beaten
1 teaspoon vanilla essence
2½ oz (70 g) pecans or walnuts, finely chopped

1 Preheat the oven to 350°F/180°C/ Gas 4. Grease 2 baking sheets.

2 Melt the butter in a saucepan over low heat. Set aside.

3 In a mixing bowl, combine the oats, brown sugar, caster sugar, flour and salt.

4 ▲ Make a well in the centre and add the butter or margarine, egg and vanilla.

5 ▼ Mix until blended, then stir in the chopped nuts.

6 Drop rounded teaspoonfuls of the mixture about 2 in (5 cm) apart on the prepared sheets. Bake until lightly browned on the edges and bubbling, 5–8 minutes. Let cool on the sheet for 2 minutes, then transfer to a rack to cool completely.

Nut Lace Wafers (top), Oatmeal Lace Rounds

Raspberry Sandwich Biscuits

MAKES 32

6 oz (170 g) blanched almonds
6 oz (170 g) plain flour
6 oz (170 g) butter, at room temperature
4 oz (115 g) caster sugar
grated rind of 1 lemon
1 tsp vanilla essence
1 egg white
⅛ tsp salt
1 oz (30 g) flaked almonds
8 fl oz (250 ml) raspberry jam
1 tbsp fresh lemon juice

1 Place the blanched almonds and 3 tablespoons of the flour in a food processor, blender or grinder and process until finely ground. Set aside.

2 With an electric mixer, cream the butter and sugar together until light and fluffy. Stir in the lemon rind and vanilla. Add the ground almonds and remaining flour and mix well until combined. Gather into a ball, wrap in greaseproof paper, and refrigerate for at least 1 hour.

3 Preheat a 325°F/170°C/Gas 3 oven. Line 2 baking sheets with greaseproof paper.

4 Divide the biscuit mixture into 4 equal parts. Working with one section at a time, roll out to a thickness of ⅛ in (3 mm) on a lightly floured surface. With a 2½ in (6 cm) fluted pastry cutter, stamp out circles. Gather the scraps, roll out and stamp out more circles. Repeat with the remaining sections.

5 ▲ Using a ¾ in (2 cm) piping nozzle or pastry cutter, stamp out the centres from half the circles. Place the rings and circles 1 in (2.5 cm) apart on the prepared sheets.

6 ▲ Whisk the egg white with the salt until just frothy. Chop the flaked almonds. Brush only the biscuit rings with the egg white, then sprinkle over the almonds. Bake until very lightly browned, 12–15 minutes. Let cool for a few minutes on the sheets before transferring to a rack.

7 ▲ In a saucepan, melt the jam with the lemon juice until it comes to a simmer. Brush the jam over the biscuit circles and sandwich together with the rings. Store in an airtight container with sheets of greaseproof paper between the layers.

Brandysnaps

MAKES 18

2 oz (55 g) butter, at room temperature

5 oz (140 g) caster sugar

1 rounded tbsp golden syrup

1½ oz (45 g) plain flour

½ tsp ground ginger

FOR THE FILLING

8 fl oz (250 ml) whipping cream

2 tbsp brandy

1 With an electric mixer, cream together the butter and sugar until light and fluffy, then beat in the golden syrup. Sift over the flour and ginger and mix together.

2 ▲ Transfer the mixture to a work surface and knead until smooth. Cover and refrigerate for 30 minutes.

3 Preheat a 375°F/190°C/Gas 5 oven. Grease a baking sheet.

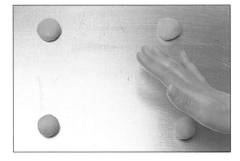

4 ▲ Working in batches of 4, form the mixture into walnut-size balls. Place far apart on the sheet and flatten slightly. Bake until golden and bubbling, about 10 minutes.

5 ▼ Remove from the oven and let cool a few moments. Working quickly, slide a metal spatula under each one, turn over, and wrap around the handle of a wooden spoon (have 4 spoons ready). If they firm up too quickly, reheat for a few seconds to soften. When firm, slide the snaps off and place on a rack to cool.

6 ▲ When all the brandy snaps are cool, prepare the filling. Whip the cream and brandy until soft peaks form. Fill a piping bag with the brandy cream. Pipe into each end of the brandy snaps just before serving.

Shortbread

MAKES 8

5½ oz (150 g) unsalted butter, at room temperature

3½ oz (100 g) caster sugar

6¼ oz (180 g) plain flour

2 oz (55 g) rice flour

¼ teaspoon baking powder

⅛ teaspoon salt

1 Preheat the oven to 325°F/170°C/Gas 3. Grease a shallow 8 in (20 cm) cake tin, preferably with a removable bottom.

2 With an electric mixer, cream the butter and sugar together until light and fluffy. Sift over the flours, baking powder and salt and mix well.

3 ▲ Press the dough neatly into the prepared tin, smoothing the surface with the back of a spoon.

4 Prick all over with a fork, then score into 8 equal wedges.

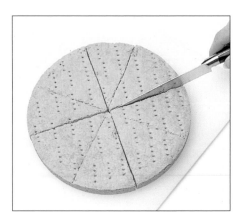

5 ▲ Bake until golden, 40–45 minutes. Leave in the tin until cool enough to handle, then turn out and recut the wedges while still hot. Store in an airtight container.

Flapjacks

MAKES 8

2 oz (55 g) butter

1 rounded tablespoon golden syrup

2¾ oz (80 g) dark brown sugar

3½ oz (100 g) quick-cooking porridge oats

⅛ teaspoon salt

1 ▲ Preheat a 350°F/180°C/Gas 4 oven. Line an 8 in (20 cm) cake tin with greaseproof paper and grease.

2 ▼ Place the butter, golden syrup and sugar in a saucepan over a low heat. Cook, stirring, until melted and combined.

~ **VARIATION** ~

If wished, add 1 teaspoon ground ginger to the melted butter.

3 ▲ Remove from the heat and add the oats and salt. Stir to blend.

4 Spoon into the prepared tin and smooth the surface. Place in the centre of the oven and bake until golden brown, 20–25 minutes. Leave in the tin until cool enough to handle, then turn out and cut into wedges while still hot.

Shortbread (top), Flapjacks

Chocolate Delights

MAKES 50

1 oz (30 g) plain chocolate
1 oz (30 g) bitter cooking chocolate
8 oz (225 g) plain flour
½ tsp salt
8 oz (225 g) unsalted butter, at room temperature
8 oz (225 g) caster sugar
2 eggs
1 tsp vanilla essence
4 oz (115 g) finely chopped walnuts

1 Melt the chocolates in the top of a double boiler, or in a heatproof bowl set over a pan of gently simmering water. Set aside.

2 ▼ In a small bowl, sift together the flour and salt. Set aside.

3 With an electric mixer, cream the butter until soft. Add the sugar and continue beating until the mixture is light and fluffy.

4 Mix the eggs and vanilla, then gradually stir into the butter mixture.

5 ▲ Stir in the chocolate, then the flour. Stir in the nuts.

6 ▲ Divide the mixture into 4 equal parts, and roll each into 2 in (5 cm) diameter logs. Wrap tightly in foil and refrigerate or freeze until firm.

7 Preheat a 375°F/190°C/Gas 5 oven. Grease 2 baking sheets.

8 With a sharp knife, cut the logs into ¼ in (5 mm) slices. Place the rounds on the prepared sheets and bake until lightly coloured, about 10 minutes. Transfer to a rack to cool.

~ **VARIATION** ~

For two-tone biscuits, melt only half the chocolate. Combine all the ingredients, except the chocolate, as above. Divide the mixture in half. Add the chocolate to one half. Roll out the plain mixture to a flat sheet. Roll out the chocolate mixture, place on top of the plain one and roll up. Wrap, slice and bake as described.

Cinnamon Treats

MAKES 50

9 oz (250 g) plain flour

½ tsp salt

2 tsp ground cinnamon

8 oz (225 g) unsalted butter, at room temperature

8 oz (225 g) caster sugar

2 eggs

1 tsp vanilla essence

1 In a bowl, sift together the flour, salt and cinnamon. Set aside.

2 ▲ With an electric mixer, cream the butter until soft. Add the sugar and continue beating until the mixture is light and fluffy.

3 Beat the eggs and vanilla, then gradually stir into the butter mixture.

4 ▲ Stir in the dry ingredients.

5 ▲ Divide the mixture into 4 equal parts, then roll each into 2 in (5 cm) diameter logs. Wrap tightly in foil and refrigerate or freeze until firm.

6 Preheat a 375°F/190°C/Gas 5 oven. Grease 2 baking sheets.

7 ▼ With a sharp knife, cut the logs into ¼ in (5 mm) slices. Place the rounds on the prepared sheets and bake until lightly coloured, about 10 minutes. With a metal spatula, transfer to a rack to cool.

Peanut Butter Biscuits

MAKES 24

5 oz (140 g) plain flour

½ teaspoon bicarbonate of soda

½ teaspoon salt

4 oz (115 g) butter, at room temperature

5¾ oz (165 g) light brown sugar

1 egg

1 teaspoon vanilla essence

9½ oz (265 g) crunchy peanut butter

1 Sift together the flour, bicarbonate of soda and salt and set aside.

2 With an electric mixer, cream the butter and sugar together until light and fluffy.

3 In another bowl, mix the egg and vanilla, then gradually beat into the butter mixture.

4 ▲ Stir in the peanut butter and blend thoroughly. Stir in the dry ingredients. Refrigerate for at least 30 minutes, or until firm.

5 Preheat the oven to 350°F/180°C/ Gas 4. Grease 2 baking sheets.

6 Spoon out rounded teaspoonfuls of the dough and roll into balls.

7 ▲ Place the balls on the prepared sheets and press flat with a fork into circles about 2½ in (6 cm) in diameter, making a criss-cross pattern. Bake until lightly coloured, 12–15 minutes. Transfer to a rack to cool.

~ **VARIATION** ~

Add 3 oz (85 g) peanuts, coarsely chopped, with the peanut butter.

Chocolate Chip Cookies

MAKES 24

4 oz (115 g) butter or margarine, at room temperature

1¾ oz (50 g) caster sugar

3¾ oz (110 g) dark brown sugar

1 egg

½ teaspoon vanilla essence

6 oz (170 g) plain flour

½ teaspoon bicarbonate of soda

⅛ teaspoon salt

6 oz (170 g) chocolate chips

2 oz (55 g) walnuts, chopped

1 Preheat the oven to 350°F/180°C/ Gas 4. Grease 2 large baking sheets.

2 ▼ With an electric mixer, cream the butter or margarine and two sugars together until light and fluffy.

3 In another bowl, mix the egg and vanilla, then gradually beat into the butter mixture. Sift over the flour, bicarbonate of soda and salt and stir.

4 ▲ Add the chocolate chips and walnuts, and mix to combine well.

5 Place heaped teaspoonfuls of the dough 2 in (5 cm) apart on the prepared sheets. Bake until lightly coloured, 10–15 minutes. Transfer to a rack to cool.

Peanut Butter Biscuits (top), Chocolate Chip Cookies

Salted Peanut Cookies

MAKES 70

12 oz (350 g) plain flour
½ teaspoon bicarbonate of soda
4 oz (115 g) butter
4 oz (115 g) margarine
9 oz (250 g) light brown sugar
2 eggs
2 teaspoons vanilla essence
8 oz (225 g) salted peanuts

1 Preheat the oven to 375°F/190°C/ Gas 5. Lightly grease 2 baking sheets. Grease the bottom of a glass and dip in sugar.

2 Sift together the flour and bicarbonate of soda. Set aside.

3 ▲ Cream the butter, margarine and sugar. Beat in the eggs and vanilla essence. Fold in the flour mixture.

4 ▲ Stir the peanuts into the butter mixture until evenly combined.

5 ▲ Drop teaspoonfuls 2 in (5 cm) apart on the prepared sheets. Flatten with the prepared glass.

6 Bake for about 10 minutes, until lightly coloured. With a metal spatula, transfer to a wire rack to cool.

~ **VARIATION** ~

To make Cashew Cookies, substitute an equal amount of salted cashews for the peanuts, and add as above.

Cheddar Pennies

MAKES 20

2 oz (50 g) butter
4 oz (115 g) Cheddar cheese, grated
1½ oz (40 g) plain flour
pinch of salt
pinch of chilli powder

1 Put the butter in a large bowl and cut into 1 in (2.5 cm) cubes. With an electric mixer, cream the butter until soft and fluffy.

2 ▲ Stir in the cheese, flour, salt and chilli. Gather to form a dough.

3 Transfer to a lightly floured surface. Shape into a cylinder about 1¼ in (3 cm) in diameter. Wrap in greaseproof paper and chill for 1–2 hours.

4 Preheat the oven to 350°F/180°C/ Gas 4. Grease 1–2 baking sheets.

5 ▲ Cut the dough into ¼ in (5 mm) thick slices and place on the prepared baking sheets. Bake for about 15 minutes, until golden. Transfer to a wire rack to cool.

Salted Peanut Cookies (top), Cheddar Pennies

Chocolate Chip Brownies

MAKES 24

4 oz (115 g) plain chocolate
4 oz (115 g) butter
3 eggs
7 oz (200 g) sugar
½ teaspoon vanilla essence
pinch of salt
5 oz (140 g) plain flour
6 oz (170 g) chocolate chips

1 ▼ Preheat a 350°F/180°C/Gas 4 oven. Line a 13 × 9 in (33 × 23 cm) tin with greaseproof paper and grease.

2 ▲ Melt the chocolate and butter in the top of a double boiler, or in a heatproof bowl set over a pan of gently simmering water.

3 ▲ Beat together the eggs, sugar, vanilla and salt. Stir in the chocolate mixture. Sift over the flour and fold in. Add the chocolate chips.

4 ▲ Pour the mixture into the prepared tin and spread evenly. Bake until just set, about 30 minutes. Do not overbake; the brownies should be slightly moist inside. Cool in the pan.

5 To turn out, run a knife all around the edge and invert onto a baking sheet. Remove the paper. Place another sheet on top and invert again so the brownies are right-side up. Cut into squares for serving.

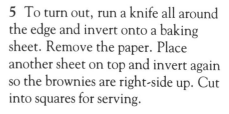

Marbled Brownies

MAKES 24

8 oz (225 g) plain chocolate
3 oz (85 g) butter
4 eggs
10½ oz (300 g) sugar
5 oz (140 g) plain flour
½ teaspoon salt
1 teaspoon baking powder
2 teaspoons vanilla essence
4 oz (115 g) walnuts, chopped

FOR THE PLAIN MIXTURE

2 oz (55 g) butter, at room temperature
6 oz (170 g) cream cheese
3½ oz (100 g) sugar
2 eggs
1 oz (30 g) plain flour
1 teaspoon vanilla essence

1 Preheat a 350°F/180°C/Gas 4 oven. Line a 13 × 9 in (33 × 23 cm) tin with greaseproof paper and grease.

2 Melt the chocolate and butter over very low heat, stirring constantly. Set aside to cool.

3 Meanwhile, beat the eggs until light and fluffy. Gradually add the sugar and continue beating until blended. Sift over the flour, salt and baking powder and fold to combine.

4 ▲ Stir in the cooled chocolate mixture. Add the vanilla and walnuts. Measure and set aside 16 fl oz (450 ml) of the chocolate mixture.

5 ▲ For the plain mixture, cream the butter and cream cheese with an electric mixer.

6 Add the sugar and continue beating until blended. Beat in the eggs, flour and vanilla.

7 Spread the unmeasured chocolate mixture in the tin. Pour over the plain mixture. Drop spoonfuls of the reserved chocolate mixture on top.

8 ▲ With a metal palette knife, swirl the mixtures to marble. Do not blend completely. Bake until just set, 35–40 minutes. Turn out when cool and cut into squares for serving.

Nutty Chocolate Squares

MAKES 16

2 eggs

2 tsp vanilla essence

⅛ tsp salt

6 oz (170 g) pecan nuts, coarsely chopped

2 oz (55 g) plain flour

2 oz (55 g) caster sugar

4 fl oz (125 ml) golden syrup

3 oz (85 g) plain chocolate, finely chopped

1½ oz (45 g) butter

16 pecan halves, for decorating

1 Preheat a 325°F/170°C/Gas 3 oven. Line the bottom and sides of an 8 in (20 cm) square baking tin with greaseproof paper and grease lightly.

2 ▼ Whisk together the eggs, vanilla and salt. In another bowl, mix together the pecans and flour. Set both aside.

3 In a saucepan, bring the sugar and golden syrup to a boil. Remove from the heat and stir in the chocolate and butter and blend thoroughly with a wooden spoon.

4 ▲ Mix in the beaten eggs, then fold in the pecan mixture.

5 Pour the mixture into the prepared tin and bake until set, about 35 minutes. Cool in the tin for 10 minutes before unmoulding. Cut into 2 in (5 cm) squares and press pecan halves into the tops while warm. Cool completely on a rack.

Raisin Brownies

MAKES 16

4 oz (115 g) butter or margarine

2 oz (55 g) cocoa powder

2 eggs

8 oz (225 g) caster sugar

1 tsp vanilla essence

1½ oz (45 g) plain flour

3 oz (85 g) chopped walnuts

3 oz (85 g) raisins

1 Preheat a 350°F/180°C/Gas 4 oven. Line the bottom and sides of an 8 in (20 cm) square baking tin with greaseproof paper and grease the paper.

2 ▼ Gently melt the butter or margarine in a small saucepan. Remove from the heat and stir in the cocoa powder.

3 With an electric mixer, beat the eggs, sugar and vanilla together until light. Add the cocoa mixture and stir to blend.

4 ▲ Sift the flour over the cocoa mixture and gently fold in. Add the walnuts and raisins and scrape the mixture into the prepared tin.

5 Bake in the centre of the oven for 30 minutes. Do not overbake. Leave in the tin to cool before cutting into 2 in (5 cm) squares and removing. The brownies should be soft and moist.

Nutty Chocolate Squares (top), Raisin Brownies

Chocolate Walnut Bars

MAKES 24

2 oz (55 g) walnuts

2¼ oz (60 g) caster sugar

3¾ oz (110 g) plain flour, sifted

3 oz (85 g) cold unsalted butter, cut into pieces

FOR THE TOPPING

1 oz (30 g) unsalted butter

3 fl oz (85 ml) water

1 oz (30 g) unsweetened cocoa powder

3½ oz (100 g) caster sugar

1 teaspoon vanilla essence

⅛ teaspoon salt

2 eggs

icing sugar, for dusting

1 Preheat a 350°F/180°C/Gas 4 oven. Grease the bottom and sides of an 8 in (20 cm) square baking tin.

2 ▼ Grind the walnuts with a few tablespoons of the sugar in a food processor, blender or coffee grinder.

3 In a bowl, combine the ground walnuts, remaining sugar and flour. With your fingertips, rub in the butter until the mixture resembles coarse breadcrumbs. Alternatively, process all the ingredients in a food processor until the mixture resembles coarse breadcrumbs.

4 ▲ Pat the walnut mixture into the bottom of the prepared tin in an even layer. Bake for 25 minutes.

5 ▲ Meanwhile, for the topping, melt the butter with the water. Whisk in the cocoa and sugar. Remove from the heat, stir in the vanilla and salt and let cool for 5 minutes. Whisk in the eggs until blended.

6 ▲ Pour the topping over the crust when baked.

7 Return to the oven and bake until set, about 20 minutes. Set the tin on a rack to cool. Cut into 2½ × 1 in (6 × 2.5 cm) bars and dust with icing sugar. Store in the refrigerator.

Pecan Squares

MAKES 36

8 oz (225 g) plain flour
pinch of salt
4 oz (115 g) granulated sugar
8 oz (225 g) cold butter or margarine, chopped
1 egg
finely grated rind of 1 lemon
FOR THE TOPPING
6 oz (175 g) butter
3 oz (75 g) honey
2 oz (50 g) granulated sugar
4 oz (115 g) dark brown sugar
5 tablespoons whipping cream
1 lb (450 g) pecan halves

1 Preheat the oven to 375°F/190°C/ Gas 5. Lightly grease a 15½ x 10½ x 1 in (37 x 27 x 2.5 cm) Swiss roll tin.

2 ▲ Sift the flour and salt into a mixing bowl. Stir in the sugar. Cut and rub in the butter or margarine until the mixture resembles coarse crumbs. Add the egg and lemon rind and blend with a fork until the mixture just holds together.

3 ▼ Spoon the mixture into the prepared tin. With floured fingertips, press into an even layer. Prick the pastry all over with a fork and chill for 10 minutes.

4 Bake the pastry crust for 15 minutes. Remove the tin from the oven, but keep the oven on while making the topping.

5 ▲ To make the topping, melt the butter, honey and both sugars. Bring to the boil. Boil, without stirring, for 2 minutes. Off the heat, stir in the cream and pecans. Pour over the crust, return to the oven and bake for 25 minutes. Leave to cool.

6 When cool, run a knife around the edge. Invert on to a baking sheet, place another sheet on top and invert again. Dip a sharp knife into very hot water and cut into squares for serving.

Figgy Bars

MAKES 48

12 oz (350 g) dried figs

3 eggs

6 oz (170 g) caster sugar

3 oz (85 g) plain flour

1 tsp baking powder

½ tsp ground cinnamon

¼ tsp ground cloves

¼ tsp grated nutmeg

¼ tsp salt

3 oz (85 g) finely chopped walnuts

2 tbsp brandy or cognac

icing sugar, for dusting

1 Preheat a 325°F/170°C/Gas 3 oven.

2 Line a 12 × 8 × 1½ in (30 × 20 × 3 cm) tin with greaseproof paper and grease the paper.

3 ▲ With a sharp knife, chop the figs roughly. Set aside.

4 In a bowl, whisk the eggs and sugar until well blended. In another bowl, sift together the dry ingredients, then fold into the egg mixture in several batches.

5 ▼ Stir in the figs, walnuts and brandy or cognac.

6 Scrape the mixture into the prepared tin and bake until the top is firm and brown, 35–40 minutes. It should still be soft underneath.

7 Let cool in the tin for 5 minutes, then unmould and transfer to a sheet of greaseproof paper lightly sprinkled with icing sugar. Cut into bars.

Lemon Bars

MAKES 36

2 oz (55 g) icing sugar

6 oz (170 g) plain flour

½ tsp salt

6 oz (170 g) butter, cut in small pieces

FOR THE TOPPING

4 eggs

12 oz (350 g) caster sugar

grated rind of 1 lemon

4 fl oz (125 ml) fresh lemon juice

6 fl oz (175 ml) whipping cream

icing sugar, for dusting

1 Preheat a 325°F/170°C/Gas 3 oven.

2 Grease a 13 × 9 in (33 × 23 cm) baking tin.

3 Sift the sugar, flour and salt into a bowl. With a pastry blender, cut in the butter until the mixture resembles coarse breadcrumbs.

4 ▲ Press the mixture into the bottom of the prepared tin. Bake until golden brown, about 20 minutes.

5 Meanwhile, for the topping, whisk the eggs and sugar together until blended. Add the lemon rind and juice and mix well.

6 ▲ Lightly whip the cream and fold into the egg mixture. Pour over the still warm base, return to the oven, and bake until set, about 40 minutes.

7 Cool completely before cutting into bars. Dust with icing sugar.

Figgy Bars (top), Lemon Bars

Apricot Specials

MAKES 12

3½ oz (100 g) light brown sugar

3 oz (85 g) plain flour

3 oz (85 g) cold unsalted butter, cut in pieces

FOR THE TOPPING

5 oz (140 g) dried apricots

8 fl oz (250 ml) water

grated rind of 1 lemon

2½ oz (75 g) caster sugar

2 tsp cornflour

2 oz (55 g) chopped walnuts

1 Preheat a 350°F/180°C/Gas 4 oven.

2 ▲ In a bowl, combine the brown sugar and flour. With a pastry blender, cut in the butter until the mixture resembles coarse breadcrumbs.

3 ▲ Transfer to an 8 in (20 cm) square baking tin and press level. Bake for 15 minutes. Remove from the oven but leave the oven on.

4 Meanwhile, for the topping, combine the apricots and water in a saucepan and simmer until soft, about 10 minutes. Strain the liquid and reserve. Chop the apricots.

5 ▲ Return the apricots to the saucepan and add the lemon rind, caster sugar, cornflour, and 4 tablespoons of the soaking liquid. Cook for 1 minute.

6 ▲ Cool slightly before spreading the topping over the base. Sprinkle over the walnuts and continue baking for 20 minutes more. Let cool in the tin before cutting into bars.

Almond-Topped Squares

MAKES 18

3 oz (75 g) butter

2 oz (50 g) granulated sugar

1 egg yolk

grated rind and juice of ½ lemon

½ teaspoon vanilla essence

2 tablespoons whipping cream

4 oz (115 g) plain flour

FOR THE TOPPING

8 oz (225 g) granulated sugar

3 oz (75 g) sliced almonds

4 egg whites

½ teaspoon ground ginger

½ teaspoon ground cinnamon

4 With lightly floured fingers, press the dough into the prepared tin. Bake for 15 minutes. Remove from the oven but leave the oven on.

5 ▲ To make the topping, combine all the ingredients in a heavy saucepan. Cook, stirring until the mixture comes to the boil.

6 Continue boiling until just golden, about 1 minute. Pour over the dough, spreading evenly.

7 ▲ Return to the oven and bake for about 45 minutes. Remove and score into bars or squares. Cool completely before cutting into squares and serving.

1 ▲ Preheat the oven to 375°F/190°C/Gas 5. Line a 13 x 9 in (33 x 23 cm) Swiss roll tin with greaseproof paper and grease the paper.

2 Cream the butter and sugar. Beat in the egg yolk, lemon rind and juice, vanilla essence and cream.

3 ▲ Gradually stir in the flour. Gather into a ball of dough.

Spiced Raisin Bars

MAKES 30

3¾ oz (110 g) plain flour

1½ teaspoons baking powder

1 teaspoon ground cinnamon

½ teaspoon grated nutmeg

¼ teaspoon ground cloves

¼ teaspoon ground allspsice

7½ oz (215 g) raisins

4 oz (115 g) butter or margarine, at room
    temperature

3½ oz (100 g) sugar

2 eggs

5¾ oz (165 g) molasses

2 oz (55 g) walnuts, chopped

1 Preheat a 350°F/180°C/Gas 4 oven. Line a 13 × 9 in (33 × 23 cm) tin with greaseproof paper and grease.

2 Sift together the flour, baking powder and spices.

3 ▲ Place the raisins in another bowl and toss with a few tablespoons of the flour mixture.

4 ▲ With an electric mixer, cream the butter or margarine and sugar together until light and fluffy. Beat in the eggs, 1 at a time, then the molasses. Stir in the flour mixture, raisins and walnuts.

5 Spread evenly in the tin. Bake until just set, 15–18 minutes. Let cool in the tin before cutting into bars.

Toffee Meringue Bars

MAKES 12

2 oz (55 g) butter

7½ oz (215 g) dark brown sugar

1 egg

½ teaspoon vanilla essence

2½ oz (70 g) plain flour

½ teaspoon salt

¼ teaspoon grated nutmeg

FOR THE TOPPING

1 egg white

⅛ teaspoon salt

1 tablespoon golden syrup

3½ oz (100 g) caster sugar

2 oz (55 g) walnuts, finely chopped

1 ▲ Combine the butter and brown sugar in a saucepan and heat until bubbling. Set aside to cool.

2 Preheat the oven to 350°F/180°C/ Gas 4. Line the bottom and sides of an 8 in (20 cm) square cake tin with greaseproof paper and grease.

3 Beat the egg and vanilla into cooled sugar mixture. Sift over the flour, salt and nutmeg and fold in. Spread in the bottom of the tin.

4 ▲ For the topping, beat the egg white with the salt until it holds soft peaks. Beat in the golden syrup, then the sugar and continue beating until the mixture holds stiff peaks. Fold in the nuts and spread on top. Bake for 30 minutes. Cut into bars when cool.

Spiced Raisin Bars (top), Toffee Meringue Bars

BUNS & TEA BREADS

~

*Easy to make and satisfying to eat, these buns and tea breads
will fill the house with mouthwatering scents and lure your
family and friends to linger over breakfast, coffee or tea –
and they are great for snacks or lunch.*

Blueberry Muffins

MAKES 12

6¼ oz (180 g) plain flour

2¼ oz (60 g) sugar

2 teaspoons baking powder

¼ teaspoon salt

2 eggs

2 oz (55 g) butter, melted

6 fl oz (175 ml) milk

1 teaspoon vanilla essence

1 teaspoon grated lemon rind

6 oz (170 g) fresh blueberries

1 Preheat a 400°F/200°C/Gas 6 oven.

2 ▼ Grease a 12-cup muffin tin or use paper cases.

3 ▲ Sift the flour, sugar, baking powder and salt into a bowl.

4 In another bowl, whisk the eggs until blended. Add the melted butter, milk, vanilla and lemon rind and stir to combine.

5 Make a well in the dry ingredients and pour in the egg mixture. With a large metal spoon, stir just until the flour is moistened, not until smooth.

6 ▲ Fold in the blueberries.

7 ▲ Spoon the batter into the cups, leaving room for the muffins to rise.

8 Bake until the tops spring back when touched lightly, 20–25 minutes. Let cool in the pan for 5 minutes before turning out.

Apple and Cranberry Muffins

MAKES 12

2 oz (55 g) butter or margarine
1 egg
3½ oz (100 g) sugar
grated rind of 1 large orange
4 fl oz (125 ml) freshly squeezed orange juice
5 oz (140 g) plain flour
1 teaspoon baking powder
½ teaspoon bicarbonate of soda
1 teaspoon ground cinnamon
½ teaspoon grated nutmeg
½ teaspoon ground allspice
¼ teaspoon ground ginger
¼ teaspoon salt
1–2 dessert apples
6 oz (170 g) cranberries
2 oz (55 g) walnuts, chopped
icing sugar, for dusting (optional)

1 Preheat the oven to 350°F/180°C/ Gas 4. Grease a 12-cup muffin tin or use paper cases.

2 Melt the butter or margarine over gentle heat. Set aside to cool.

3 ▲ Place the egg in a mixing bowl and whisk lightly. Add the melted butter or margarine and whisk to combine.

4 Add the sugar, orange rind and juice. Whisk to blend, then set aside.

5 In a large bowl, sift together the flour, baking powder, bicarbonate of soda, cinnamon, nutmeg, allspice, ginger and salt. Set aside.

6 ▲ Quarter, core and peel the apples. With a sharp knife, chop coarsely.

7 Make a well in the dry ingredients and pour in the egg mixture. With a spoon, stir until just blended.

8 ▲ Add the apples, cranberries and walnuts and stir to blend.

9 Fill the cups three-quarters full and bake until the tops spring back when touched lightly, 25–30 minutes. Transfer to a rack to cool. Dust with icing sugar, if desired.

Chocolate Chip Muffins

MAKES 10

4 oz (115 g) butter or margarine, at room
temperature

2½ oz (70 g) caster sugar

1 oz (30 g) dark brown sugar

2 eggs, at room temperature

7½ oz (215 g) plain flour

1 teaspoon baking powder

4 fl oz (125 ml) milk

6 oz (170 g) plain chocolate chips

1 Preheat the oven to 375°F/190°C/
Gas 5. Grease 10 muffin cups or use
paper cases.

2 ▼ With an electric mixer, cream
the butter until soft. Add both sugars
and beat until light and fluffy. Beat in
the eggs, 1 at a time.

3 Sift together the flour and baking
powder, twice. Fold into the butter
mixture, alternating with the milk.

4 ▲ Divide half the mixture between
the muffin cups. Sprinkle several
chocolate chips on top, then cover
with a spoonful of the batter. To
ensure even baking, half-fill any
empty cups with water.

5 Bake until lightly coloured, about
25 minutes. Let stand 5 minutes
before turning out.

Chocolate Walnut Muffins

MAKES 12

6 oz (170 g) unsalted butter

5 oz (140 g) plain chocolate

7 oz (200 g) caster sugar

2 oz (55 g) dark brown sugar

4 eggs

1 teaspoon vanilla essence

¼ teaspoon almond essence

3¾ oz (110 g) plain flour

1 tablespoon unsweetened cocoa powder

4 oz (115 g) walnuts, chopped

1 Preheat the oven to 350°F/180°C/
Gas 4. Grease a 12-cup muffin pan or
use paper cases.

2 ▼ Melt the butter with the
chocolate in the top of a double boiler
or in a heatproof bowl set over a pan
of hot water. Transfer to a large
mixing bowl.

3 Stir both the sugars into the
chocolate mixture. Mix in the eggs,
1 at a time, then add the vanilla and
almond essences.

4 Sift over the flour and cocoa.

5 ▲ Fold in and stir in the walnuts.

6 Fill the prepared cups almost to the
top and bake until a skewer inserted in
the centre barely comes out clean,
30–35 minutes. Let stand 5 minutes
before turning out onto a rack to cool
completely.

Chocolate Chip Muffins (top), Chocolate Walnut Muffins

Raisin Bran Buns

MAKES 15

2 oz (55 g) butter or margarine

1½ oz (45 g) plain flour

2 oz (55 g) wholewheat flour

1½ tsp bicarbonate of soda

⅛ tsp salt

1 tsp ground cinnamon

1 oz (30 g) bran

3 oz (85 g) raisins

2½ oz (65 g) dark brown sugar

2 oz (55 g) caster sugar

1 egg

8 fl oz (250 ml) buttermilk

juice of ½ lemon

1 Preheat a 400°F/200°C/Gas 6 oven. Grease 15 bun-tray cups.

2 ▲ Place the butter or margarine in a saucepan and melt over gentle heat. Set aside.

3 In a mixing bowl, sift together the flours, bicarbonate of soda, salt and cinnamon.

4 ▲ Add the bran, raisins and sugars and stir until blended.

5 In another bowl, mix together the egg, buttermilk, lemon juice and melted butter.

6 ▲ Add the buttermilk mixture to the dry ingredients and stir lightly and quickly just until moistened; do not mix until smooth.

7 ▲ Spoon the mixture into the prepared bun tray, filling the cups almost to the top. Half-fill any empty cups with water.

8 Bake until golden, 15–20 minutes. Serve warm or at room temperature.

Raspberry Crumble Buns

MAKES 12

6 oz (170 g) plain flour

2 oz (55 g) caster sugar

1¾ oz (50 g) light brown sugar

2 tsp baking powder

⅛ tsp salt

1 tsp ground cinnamon

4 oz (115 g) butter, melted

1 egg

4 fl oz (125 ml) milk

5 oz (140 g) fresh raspberries

grated rind of 1 lemon

FOR THE CRUMBLE TOPPING

1 oz (30 g) finely chopped pecan nuts or walnuts

2 oz (55 g) dark brown sugar

3 tbsp plain flour

1 tsp ground cinnamon

3 tbsp butter, melted

1 Preheat a 350°F/180°C/Gas 4 oven. Grease a 12-cup bun tray or use paper cases.

2 Sift the flour into a bowl. Add the sugars, baking powder, salt and cinnamon and stir to blend.

3 ▲ Make a well in the centre. Place the butter, egg and milk in the well and mix until just combined. Stir in the raspberries and lemon rind. Spoon the mixture into the prepared bun tray, filling the cups almost to the top.

4 ▼ For the crumble topping, mix the nuts, dark brown sugar, flour and cinnamon in a bowl. Add the melted butter and stir to blend.

5 ▲ Spoon some of the crumble over each bun. Bake until browned, about 25 minutes. Transfer to a rack to cool slightly. Serve warm.

Carrot Buns

MAKES 12

6 oz (170 g) margarine, at room temperature

3½ oz (100 g) dark brown sugar

1 egg, at room temperature

1 tbsp water

8 oz (225 g) carrots, grated

5 oz (140 g) plain flour

1 tsp baking powder

½ tsp bicarbonate of soda

1 tsp ground cinnamon

¼ tsp grated nutmeg

½ tsp salt

1 Preheat a 350°F/180°C/Gas 4 oven. Grease a 12-cup bun tray or use paper cases.

2 With an electric mixer, cream the margarine and sugar until light and fluffy. Beat in the egg and water.

3 ▲ Stir in the carrots.

4 Sift over the flour, baking powder, bicarbonate of soda, cinnamon, nutmeg and salt. Stir to blend.

5 ▼ Spoon the mixture into the prepared bun tray, filling the cups almost to the top. Bake until the tops spring back when touched lightly, about 35 minutes. Let stand 10 minutes before transferring to a rack.

Dried Cherry Buns

MAKES 16

8 fl oz (250 ml) plain yoghurt

6 oz (170 g) dried cherries

4 oz (115 g) butter, at room temperature

6 oz (170 g) caster sugar

2 eggs, at room temperature

1 tsp vanilla essence

7 oz (200 g) plain flour

2 tsp baking powder

1 tsp bicarbonate of soda

⅛ tsp salt

1 In a mixing bowl, combine the yoghurt and cherries. Cover and let stand for 30 minutes.

2 Preheat a 350°F/180°C/Gas 4 oven. Grease 16 bun-tray cups or use paper cases.

3 With an electric mixer, cream the butter and sugar together until light and fluffy.

4 ▼ Add the eggs, 1 at a time, beating well after each addition. Add the vanilla and the cherry mixture and stir to blend. Set aside.

5 ▲ In another bowl, sift together the flour, baking powder, bicarbonate soda and salt. Fold into the cherry mixture in 3 batches.

6 Fill the prepared cups two-thirds full. For even baking, half-fill any empty cups with water. Bake until the tops spring back when touched lightly, about 20 minutes. Transfer to a rack to cool.

Carrot Buns (top), Dried Cherry Buns

Oat and Raisin Muffins

MAKES 12

3 oz (85 g) rolled oats

8 fl oz (250 ml) buttermilk

4 oz (120 g) butter, at room temperature

3½ oz (100 g) dark brown sugar

1 egg, at room temperature

4 oz (120 g) flour

1 teaspoon baking powder

½ teaspoon bicarbonate of soda

¼ teaspoon salt

1 oz (30 g) raisins

~ **COOK'S TIP** ~

If buttermilk is not available, add 1 teaspoon lemon juice or vinegar to milk. Let the mixture stand for a few minutes to curdle.

1 ▲ In a bowl, combine the oats and buttermilk and let soak for 1 hour.

2 ▲ Lightly grease a 12-cup muffin tin or use paper cases.

3 ▲ Preheat the oven to 400°F/ 200°C/Gas 6. With an electric mixer, cream the butter and sugar until light and fluffy. Beat in the egg.

4 In another bowl, sift the flour, baking powder, bicarbonate of soda and salt. Stir into the butter mixture, alternating with the oat mixture. Fold in the raisins. Do not overmix.

5 Fill the prepared cups two-thirds full. Bake until a skewer inserted in the centre comes out clean, 20–25 minutes. Transfer to a rack to cool.

Pumpkin Muffins

MAKES 14

4 oz (120 g) butter or margarine, at room temperature

5 oz (150 g) dark brown sugar

4 tablespoons molasses

1 egg, at room temperature, beaten

8 oz (225 g) cooked or canned pumpkin

8 oz (225 g) flour

¼ teaspoon salt

1 teaspoon bicarbonate of soda

1½ teaspoons ground cinnamon

1 teaspoon grated nutmeg

1 oz (30 g) currants or raisins

1 Preheat the oven to 400°F/200°C/ Gas 6. Grease 14 muffin cups or use paper cases.

2 With an electric mixer, cream the butter or margarine until soft. Add the sugar and molasses and beat until light and fluffy.

3 ▲ Add the egg and pumpkin and stir until well blended.

4 Sift over the flour, salt, bicarbonate of soda, cinnamon and nutmeg. Fold just enough to blend; do not overmix.

5 ▼ Fold in the currants or raisins.

6 Spoon the mixture into the prepared muffin cups, filling them three-quarters full.

7 Bake until the tops spring back when touched lightly, 12–15 minutes. Serve warm or cold.

Prune Muffins

MAKES 12

1 egg

8 fl oz (250 ml) milk

4 fl oz (125 ml) vegetable oil

1¾ oz (50 g) caster sugar

1 oz (30 g) dark brown sugar

10 oz (285 g) plain flour

2 teaspoons baking powder

½ teaspoon salt

¼ teaspoon grated nutmeg

4 oz (115 g) cooked stoned prunes, chopped

1 Preheat a 400°F/200°C/Gas 6 oven. Grease a 12-cup muffin tin.

2 Break the egg into a mixing bowl and beat with a fork. Beat in the milk and oil.

3 ▼ Stir in the sugars. Set aside.

4 Sift the flour, baking powder, salt and nutmeg into a mixing bowl. Make a well in the centre, pour in the egg mixture and stir until moistened. Do not overmix; the batter should be slightly lumpy.

5 ▲ Fold in the prunes.

6 Fill the prepared cups two-thirds full. Bake until golden brown, about 20 minutes. Let stand 10 minutes before turning out. Serve warm or at room temperature.

Yogurt and Honey Muffins

MAKES 12

2 oz (55 g) butter

5 tablespoons clear honey

8 fl oz (250 ml) plain yogurt

1 large egg, at room temperature

grated rind of 1 lemon

2 fl oz (65 ml) lemon juice

5 oz (140 g) plain flour

6 oz (170 g) wholemeal flour

1½ teaspoons bicarbonate of soda

⅛ teaspoon grated nutmeg

~ **VARIATION** ~

For Walnut Yogurt Honey Muffins, add 2 oz (55 g) chopped walnuts, folded in with the flour. This makes a more substantial muffin.

1 Preheat a 375°F/190°C/Gas 5 oven. Grease a 12-cup muffin tin or use paper cases.

2 In a saucepan, melt the butter and honey. Remove from the heat and set aside to cool slightly.

3 ▲ In a bowl, whisk together the yogurt, egg, lemon rind and juice. Add the butter and honey mixture. Set aside.

4 ▲ In another bowl, sift together the dry ingredients.

5 Fold the dry ingredients into the yogurt mixture to blend.

6 Fill the prepared cups two-thirds full. Bake until the tops spring back when touched lightly, 20–25 minutes. Let cool in the tin for 5 minutes before turning out. Serve warm or at room temperature.

Prune Muffins (top), Yogurt and Honey Muffins

Banana Muffins

MAKES 10

9 oz (250 g) plain flour

1 teaspoon baking powder

1 teaspoon bicarbonate of soda

¼ teaspoon salt

½ teaspoon ground cinnamon

¼ teaspoon grated nutmeg

3 large ripe bananas

1 egg

2½ oz (70 g) dark brown sugar

2 fl oz (50 ml) vegetable oil

1 oz (30 g) raisins

1 ▼ Preheat the oven to 375°F/ 190°C/Gas 5. Lightly grease or line 10 deep muffin tins with paper cases.

2 Sift together the flour, baking powder, bicarbonate of soda, salt, cinnamon and nutmeg. Set aside.

3 ▲ With an electric mixer, beat the peeled bananas at moderate speed until mashed.

4 ▲ Beat in the egg, sugar and oil.

5 Add the dry ingredients and beat in gradually, on low speed. Mix just until blended. With a wooden spoon, stir in the raisins.

6 Fill the prepared cups two-thirds full. For even baking, half-fill any empty cups with water.

7 ▲ Bake until the tops spring back when touched lightly, 20–25 minutes. Transfer to a rack to cool.

Maple Pecan Muffins

MAKES 20

6 oz (170 g) pecans
12 oz (340 g) flour
1 teaspoon baking powder
1 teaspoon bicarbonate of soda
¼ teaspoon salt
¼ teaspoon ground cinnamon
3½ oz (100 g) caster sugar
2½ oz (70 g) light brown sugar
3 tablespoons maple syrup
5 oz (150 g) butter, at room temperature
3 eggs, at room temperature
½ pint (300 ml) buttermilk
60 pecan halves, for decorating

1 Preheat the oven to 350°F/180°C/ Gas 4. Lightly grease 24 deep muffin tins or use paper cases.

2 ▲ Spread the pecans on a baking sheet and toast in the oven for 5 minutes. When cool, chop coarsely and set aside.

<hr>

~ VARIATION ~

For Pecan Spice Muffins, substitute an equal quantity of golden syrup for the maple syrup. Increase the cinnamon to ½ teaspoon, and add 1 teaspoon ground ginger and ½ teaspoon grated nutmeg, sifted with the dry ingredients.

3 In a bowl, sift together the flour, baking powder, bicarbonate of soda, salt and cinnamon. Set aside.

4 ▲ In a large mixing bowl, combine the caster sugar, light brown sugar, maple syrup and butter. Beat with an electric mixer until light and fluffy.

5 Add the eggs, 1 at a time, beating to incorporate thoroughly after each addition.

6 ▲ Pour half the buttermilk and half the dry ingredients into the butter mixture, then stir until blended. Repeat with the remaining buttermilk and dry ingredients.

7 Fold in the chopped pecans. Fill the prepared cups two-thirds full. Top with the pecan halves. For even baking, half-fill any empty cups with water.

8 Bake until puffed up and golden, 20–25 minutes. Let stand 5 minutes before unmoulding.

Cheese Muffins

Makes 9

2 oz (55 g) butter

7 oz (200 g) plain flour

2 teaspoons baking powder

2 tablespoons sugar

¼ teaspoon salt

1 teaspoon paprika

2 eggs

4 fl oz (125 ml) milk

1 teaspoon dried thyme

2 oz (55 g) mature Cheddar cheese, cut
into ½ in (1 cm) dice

1 Preheat the oven to 375°F/190°C/
Gas 5. Thickly grease 9 deep muffin
tins or use paper cases.

2 Melt the butter and set aside.

3 ▼ In a mixing bowl, sift together
the flour, baking powder, sugar, salt
and paprika.

4 ▲ In another bowl, combine the
eggs, milk, melted butter and thyme,
and whisk to blend.

5 Add the milk mixture to the dry
ingredients and stir just until
moistened; do not mix until smooth.

6 ▲ Place a heaped spoonful of
batter into the prepared cups. Drop a
few pieces of cheese over each, then
top with another spoonful of batter.
For even baking, half-fill any empty
muffin cups with water.

7 ▲ Bake until puffed and golden,
about 25 minutes. Let stand 5 minutes
before unmoulding on to a rack. Serve
warm or at room temperature.

Bacon and Cornmeal Muffins

MAKES 14

8 bacon rashers

2 oz (55 g) butter

2 oz (55 g) margarine

4 oz (120 g) plain flour

1 tablespoon baking powder

1 teaspoon sugar

¼ teaspoon salt

8 oz (225 g) cornmeal

4 fl oz (125 ml) milk

2 eggs

1 Preheat the oven to 400°F/200°C/ Gas 6. Lightly grease 14 deep muffin tins or use paper cases.

2 ▲ Fry the bacon until crisp. Drain on kitchen paper, then chop into small pieces. Set aside.

3 Gently melt the butter and margarine and set aside.

4 ▲ Sift the flour, baking powder, sugar, and salt into a large mixing bowl. Stir in the cornmeal, then make a well in the centre.

5 In a saucepan, heat the milk to lukewarm. In a small bowl, lightly whisk the eggs, then add to the milk. Stir in the melted fats.

6 ▼ Pour the milk mixture into the centre of the well and stir until smooth and well blended.

7 ▲ Stir the bacon into the mixture, then spoon the mixture into the prepared cups, filling them half-full. Bake until risen and lightly coloured, about 20 minutes. Serve hot or warm.

Corn Bread

MAKES 1 LOAF

4 oz (115 g) plain flour
2½ oz (75 g) caster sugar
1 tsp salt
1 tbsp baking powder
6 oz (170 g) cornmeal, or polenta
12 fl oz (350 ml) milk
2 eggs
3 oz (85 g) butter, melted
4 oz (115 g) margarine, melted

1 Preheat a 400°F/200°C/Gas 6 oven. Line a 9 × 5 in (23 × 13 cm) loaf tin with greaseproof paper and grease.

2 Sift the flour, sugar, salt and baking powder into a mixing bowl.

3 ▼ Add the cornmeal and stir to blend. Make a well in the centre.

4 ▲ Whisk together the milk, eggs, butter and margarine. Pour the mixture into the well. Stir until just blended; do not overmix.

5 Pour into the tin and bake until a skewer inserted in the centre comes out clean, about 45 minutes. Serve hot or at room temperature.

Spicy Sweetcorn Bread

MAKES 9 SQUARES

3–4 whole canned chilli peppers, drained
2 eggs
16 fl oz (450 ml) buttermilk
2 oz (55 g) butter, melted
2 oz (55 g) plain flour
1 tsp bicarbonate of soda
2 tsp salt
6 oz (170 g) cornmeal, or polenta
12 oz (350 g) canned sweetcorn or frozen sweetcorn, thawed

1 Preheat a 400°F/200°C/Gas 6 oven. Line the bottom and sides of a 9 in (23 cm) square cake tin with greaseproof paper and grease lightly.

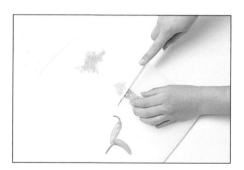

2 ▲ With a sharp knife, finely chop the chillis and set aside.

3 ▲ In a large bowl, whisk the eggs until frothy, then whisk in the buttermilk. Add the melted butter.

4 In another large bowl, sift together the flour, bicarbonate of soda and salt. Fold into the buttermilk mixture in 3 batches, then fold in the cornmeal in 3 batches.

5 ▲ Fold in the chillis and sweetcorn.

6 Pour the mixture into the prepared tin and bake until a skewer inserted in the middle comes out clean, 25–30 minutes. Let stand for 2–3 minutes before unmoulding. Cut into squares and serve warm.

Corn Bread (top), Spicy Sweetcorn Bread

Fruity Tea Bread

MAKES 1 LOAF

8 oz (225 g) plain flour

4 oz (115 g) caster sugar

1 tbsp baking powder

½ tsp salt

grated rind of 1 large orange

5½ fl oz (170 ml) fresh orange juice

2 eggs, lightly beaten

3 oz (85 g) butter or margarine, melted

4 oz (115 g) fresh cranberries, or bilberries

2 oz (55 g) chopped walnuts

1 Preheat a 350°F/180°C/Gas 4 oven. Line a 9 × 5 in (23 × 13 cm) loaf tin with greaseproof paper and grease.

2 Sift the flour, sugar, baking powder and salt into a mixing bowl.

3 ▼ Stir in the orange rind.

4 ▲ Make a well in the centre and add the orange juice, eggs and melted butter or margarine. Stir from the centre until the ingredients are blended; do not overmix.

5 ▲ Add the berries and walnuts and stir until blended.

6 Transfer the mixture to the prepared tin and bake until a skewer inserted in the centre comes out clean, 45–50 minutes.

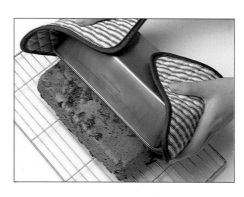

7 ▲ Let cool in the tin for 10 minutes before transferring to a rack to cool completely. Serve thinly sliced, toasted or plain, with butter or cream cheese and jam.

Date and Pecan Loaf

MAKES 1 LOAF

6 oz (170 g) stoned dates, chopped

6 fl oz (175 ml) boiling water

2 oz (55 g) unsalted butter, at room temperature

2 oz (55 g) dark brown sugar

2 oz (55 g) caster sugar

1 egg, at room temperature

2 tbsp brandy

5½ oz (165 g) plain flour

2 tsp baking powder

½ tsp salt

¾ tsp freshly grated nutmeg

3 oz (85 g) coarsely chopped pecans or walnuts

1 ▲ Place the dates in a bowl and pour over the boiling water. Set aside to cool.

2 Preheat a 350°F/180°C/Gas 4 oven. Line a 9 × 5 in (23 × 13 cm) loaf tin with greaseproof paper and grease.

3 ▲ With an electric mixer, cream the butter and sugars until light and fluffy. Beat in the egg and brandy, then set aside.

4 Sift the flour, baking powder, salt and nutmeg together, 3 times.

5 ▼ Fold the dry ingredients into the sugar mixture in 3 batches, alternating with the dates and water.

6 ▲ Fold in the nuts.

7 Pour the mixture into the prepared tin and bake until a skewer inserted in the centre comes out clean, 45–50 minutes. Let cool in the tin for 10 minutes before transferring to a rack to cool completely.

Orange and Honey Tea Bread

MAKES 1 LOAF

13½ oz (385 g) plain flour

2½ teaspoons baking powder

½ teaspoon bicarbonate of soda

½ teaspoon salt

1 oz (30 g) margarine

8 fl oz (250 ml) clear honey

1 egg, at room temperature, lightly beaten

1½ tablespoons grated orange rind

6 fl oz (175 ml) freshly squeezed orange juice

4 oz (115 g) walnuts, chopped

1 Preheat a 325°F/170°C/Gas 3 oven.

2 Sift together the flour, baking powder, bicarbonate of soda and salt.

3 Line the bottom and sides of a 9 × 5 in (23 × 13 cm) loaf tin with greaseproof paper and grease.

4 ▲ With an electric mixer, cream the margarine until soft. Stir in the honey until blended, then stir in the egg. Add the orange rind and stir to combine thoroughly.

5 ▲ Fold the flour mixture into the honey and egg mixture in 3 batches, alternating with the orange juice. Stir in the walnuts.

6 Pour into the tin and bake until a skewer inserted in the centre comes out clean, 60–70 minutes. Let stand 10 minutes before turning out onto a rack to cool.

Apple Loaf

MAKES 1 LOAF

1 egg

8 fl oz (250 ml) bottled or homemade apple sauce

2 oz (55 g) butter or margarine, melted

3¾ oz (110 g) dark brown sugar

1¾ oz (50 g) caster sugar

10 oz (285 g) plain flour

2 teaspoons baking powder

½ teaspoon bicarbonate of soda

½ teaspoon salt

1 teaspoon ground cinnamon

½ teaspoon grated nutmeg

2½ oz (70 g) currants or raisins

2 oz (55 g) pecans or walnuts, chopped

1 Preheat a 350°F/180°C/Gas 4 oven. Line a 9 × 5 in (23 × 13 cm) loaf tin with greaseproof paper and grease.

2 ▲ Break the egg into a bowl and beat lightly. Stir in the apple sauce, butter or margarine and both sugars. Set aside.

3 In another bowl, sift together the flour, baking powder, bicarbonate of soda, salt, cinnamon and nutmeg. Fold dry ingredients into the apple sauce mixture in 3 batches.

4 ▼ Stir in the currants or raisins, and nuts.

5 Pour into the prepared tin and bake until a skewer inserted in the centre comes out clean, about 1 hour. Let stand 10 minutes. Turn out onto a rack and cool completely.

Orange and Honey Tea Bread (top), Apple Loaf

Lemon and Walnut Tea Bread

MAKES 1 LOAF

4 oz (115 g) butter or margarine, at room temperature

3½ oz (100 g) sugar

2 eggs, at room temperature, separated

grated rind of 2 lemons

2 tablespoons lemon juice

7½ oz (215 g) plain flour

2 teaspoons baking powder

4 fl oz (125 ml) milk

2 oz (55 g) walnuts, chopped

⅛ teaspoon salt

1 Preheat a 350°F/180°C/Gas 4 oven. Line a 9 × 5 in (23 × 13 cm) loaf tin with greaseproof paper and grease.

2 With an electric mixer, cream the butter or margarine with the sugar until light and fluffy.

3 ▲ Beat in the egg yolks.

4 Add the lemon rind and juice and stir until blended. Set aside.

5 ▲ In another bowl, sift together the flour and baking powder, 3 times. Fold into the butter mixture in 3 batches, alternating with the milk. Fold in the walnuts. Set aside.

6 ▲ Beat the egg whites and salt until stiff peaks form. Fold a large dollop of the egg whites into the walnut mixture to lighten it. Fold in the remaining egg whites carefully until just blended.

7 ▲ Pour the batter into the prepared tin and bake until a skewer inserted in the centre of the loaf comes out clean, 45–50 minutes. Let stand 5 minutes before turning out onto a rack to cool completely.

Apricot Nut Loaf

MAKES 1 LOAF

4 oz (115 g) dried apricots
1 large orange
3 oz (85 g) raisins
5 oz (140 g) caster sugar
3 fl oz (85 ml) oil
2 eggs, lightly beaten
9 oz (250 g) plain flour
2 tsp baking powder
½ tsp salt
1 tsp bicarbonate of soda
2 oz (55 g) chopped walnuts

1 Preheat a 350°F/180°C/Gas 4 oven. Line a 9 × 5 in (23 × 13 cm) loaf tin with greaseproof paper and grease.

2 Place the apricots in a bowl, cover with lukewarm water and leave to stand for 30 minutes.

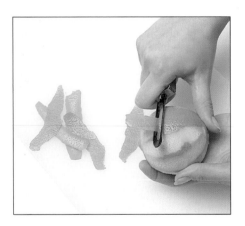

3 ▲ With a vegetable peeler, remove the orange rind, leaving the pith.

4 With a sharp knife, finely chop the orange rind strips.

5 Drain the apricots and chop coarsely. Place in a bowl with the orange rind and raisins. Set aside.

6 Squeeze the peeled orange. Measure the juice and add enough hot water to obtain 6 fl oz (175 ml) liquid.

7 ▼ Pour the orange juice mixture over the apricot mixture. Stir in the sugar, oil and eggs. Set aside.

8 In another bowl, sift together the flour, baking powder, salt and bicarbonate of soda. Fold the flour mixture into the apricot mixture in 3 batches.

9 ▲ Stir in the walnuts.

10 Spoon the mixture into the prepared tin and bake until a skewer inserted in the centre comes out clean, 55–60 minutes. If the loaf browns too quickly, protect the top with a sheet of foil. Let cool in the pan for 10 minutes before transferring to a rack to cool completely.

Mango Tea Bread

MAKES 2 LOAVES

10 oz (285 g) plain flour

2 teaspoons bicarbonate of soda

2 teaspoons ground cinnamon

½ teaspoon salt

4 oz (115 g) margarine, at room temperature

3 eggs, at room temperature

10½ oz (300 g) sugar

4 fl oz (125 ml) vegetable oil

1 large ripe mango, peeled and chopped

3¼ oz (90 g) desiccated coconut

2½ oz (70 g) raisins

1 Preheat the oven to 350°F/180°C/ Gas 4. Line the bottom and sides of 2 9 × 5 in (23 × 13 cm) loaf tins with greaseproof paper and grease.

2 Sift together the flour, bicarbonate of soda, cinnamon and salt. Set aside.

3 With an electric mixer, cream the margarine until soft.

4 ▼ Beat in the eggs and sugar until light and fluffy. Beat in the oil.

5 Fold the dry ingredients into the creamed ingredients in 3 batches.

6 Fold in the mangoes, two-thirds of the coconut and the raisins.

7 ▲ Spoon the batter into the pans.

8 Sprinkle over the remaining coconut. Bake until a skewer inserted in the centre comes out clean, 50–60 minutes. Let stand for 10 minutes before turning out onto a rack to cool completely.

Courgette Tea Bread

MAKES 1 LOAF

2 oz (55 g) butter

3 eggs

8 fl oz (250 ml) vegetable oil

10½ oz (300 g) sugar

2 medium unpeeled courgettes, grated

10 oz (285 g) plain flour

2 teaspoons bicarbonate of soda

1 teaspoon baking powder

1 teaspoon salt

1 teaspoon ground cinnamon

1 teaspoon grated nutmeg

¼ teaspoon ground cloves

4 oz (115 g) walnuts, chopped

1 Preheat the oven to 350°F/180°C/ Gas 4.

2 Line the bottom and sides of a 9 × 5 in (23 × 13 cm) loaf tin with greaseproof paper and grease.

3 ▲ In a saucepan, melt the butter over low heat. Set aside.

4 With an electric mixer, beat the eggs and oil together until thick. Beat in the sugar. Stir in the melted butter and courgettes. Set aside.

5 ▲ In another bowl, sift all the dry ingredients together 3 times. Carefully fold into the courgette mixture. Fold in the walnuts.

6 Pour into the tin and bake until a skewer inserted in the centre comes out clean, 60–70 minutes. Let stand 10 minutes before turning out onto wire rack to cool completely.

Mango Tea Bread (top), Courgette Tea Bread

Wholewheat Banana Nut Loaf

MAKES 1 LOAF

4 oz (115 g) butter, at room temperature

4 oz (115 g) caster sugar

2 eggs, at room temperature

4 oz (115 g) plain flour

1 tsp bicarbonate of soda

¼ tsp salt

1 tsp ground cinnamon

2 oz (55 g) wholewheat flour

3 large ripe bananas

1 tsp vanilla essence

2 oz (55 g) chopped walnuts

1 Preheat a 350°F/180°C/Gas 4 oven. Line the bottom and sides of a 9 × 5 in (23 × 13 cm) loaf tin with greaseproof paper and grease the paper.

2 With an electric mixer, cream the butter and sugar together until light and fluffy.

3 ▲ Add the eggs, 1 at a time, beating well after each addition.

4 Sift the plain flour, bicarbonate of soda, salt and cinnamon over the butter mixture and stir to blend.

5 ▲ Stir in the wholewheat flour.

6 ▲ With a fork, mash the bananas to a purée, then stir into the mixture. Stir in the vanilla and nuts.

7 ▲ Pour the mixture into the prepared tin and spread level.

8 Bake until a skewer inserted in the centre comes out clean, 50–60 minutes. Let stand 10 minutes before transferring to a rack.

Dried Fruit Loaf

MAKES 1 LOAF

1 lb (450 g) mixed dried fruit, such as currants, raisins, chopped dried apricots and dried cherries
10 fl oz (300 ml) cold strong tea
7 oz (200 g) dark brown sugar
grated rind and juice of 1 small orange
grated rind and juice of 1 lemon
1 egg, lightly beaten
7 oz (200 g) plain flour
1 tbsp baking powder
⅛ tsp salt

1 ▲ In a bowl, mix the dried fruit with the tea and soak overnight.

2 Preheat a 350°F/180°C/Gas 4 oven. Line the bottom and sides of a 9 × 5 in (23 × 13 cm) loaf tin with greaseproof paper and grease the paper.

3 ▲ Strain the fruit, reserving the liquid. In a bowl, combine the sugar, orange and lemon rind, and fruit.

4 ▼ Pour the orange and lemon juice into a measuring jug; if the quantity is less than 8 fl oz (250 ml), top up with the soaking liquid.

5 Stir the citrus juices and egg into the dried fruit mixture.

6 In another bowl, sift together the flour, baking powder and salt. Stir into the fruit mixture until blended.

7 Transfer to the prepared tin and bake until a skewer inserted in the centre comes out clean, about 1¼ hours. Let stand 10 minutes before unmoulding.

Bilberry Tea Bread

Makes 8 pieces

2 oz (55 g) butter or margarine, at room temperature

6 oz (170 g) caster sugar

1 egg, at room temperature

4 fl oz (125 ml) milk

8 oz (225 g) plain flour

2 tsp baking powder

½ tsp salt

10 oz (285 g) fresh bilberries, or blueberries

For the topping

4 oz (115 g) sugar

1½ oz (45 g) plain flour

½ tsp ground cinnamon

2 oz (55 g) butter, cut in pieces

1 Preheat a 375°F/190°C/Gas 5 oven. Grease a 9 in (23 cm) baking dish.

2 With an electric mixer, cream the butter or margarine with the sugar until light and fluffy. Add the egg, beat to combine, then mix in the milk until blended.

3 ▼ Sift over the flour, baking powder and salt and stir just enough to blend the ingredients.

4 ▲ Add the berries and stir.

5 Transfer to the baking dish.

6 ▲ For the topping, place the sugar, flour, cinnamon and butter in a mixing bowl. Cut in with a pastry blender until the mixture resembles coarse breadcrumbs.

7 ▲ Sprinkle the topping over the mixture in the baking dish.

8 Bake until a skewer inserted in the centre comes out clean, about 45 minutes. Serve warm or cold.

Chocolate Chip Walnut Loaf

MAKES 1 LOAF

3½ oz (100 g) caster sugar
3½ oz (100 g) flour
1 teaspoon baking powder
4 tablespoons cornflour
4½ oz (130 g) butter, at room temperature
2 eggs, at room temperature
1 teaspoon vanilla extract
2 tablespoons currants or raisins
1 oz (30 g) walnuts, finely chopped
grated rind of ½ lemon
3 tablespoons plain chocolate chips
icing sugar, for dusting

1 Preheat the oven to 350°F/180°C/ Gas 4. Grease and line an 8½ × 4½ in (22 × 12 cm) loaf tin.

2 ▲ Sprinkle 1½ tablespoons of the caster sugar into the pan and tilt to distribute the sugar in an even layer over the bottom and sides. Shake out any excess.

3 ▼ Sift together the flour, baking powder and cornflour into a mixing bowl, 3 times. Set aside.

4 With an electric mixer, cream the butter until soft. Add the remaining sugar and continue beating until light and fluffy. Add the eggs, 1 at a time, beating to incorporate thoroughly after each addition.

5 Gently fold the dry ingredients into the butter mixture, in 3 batches; do not overmix.

6 ▲ Fold in the vanilla, currants or raisins, walnuts, lemon rind, and chocolate chips until just blended.

7 Pour the mixture into the prepared tin and bake until a cake tester inserted in the centre comes out clean, 45–50 minutes. Let cool in the tin for 5 minutes before transferring to a rack to cool completely. Dust over an even layer of icing sugar before serving.

Glazed Banana Spice Loaf

MAKES 1 LOAF

1 large ripe banana

4 oz (115 g) butter, at room temperature

5½ oz (150 g) caster sugar

2 eggs, at room temperature

7½ oz (215 g) plain flour

1 teaspoon salt

1 teaspoon bicarbonate of soda

½ teaspoon grated nutmeg

¼ teaspoon ground allspice

¼ teaspoon ground cloves

6 fl oz (175 ml) soured cream

1 teaspoon vanilla essence

FOR THE GLAZE

4 oz (115 g) icing sugar

1–2 tablespoons lemon juice

1 Preheat a 350°F/180°C/Gas 4 oven. Line an 8½ × 4½ in (21.5 × 11.5 cm) loaf tin with greaseproof and grease.

2 ▼ With a fork, mash the banana in a bowl. Set aside.

3 With an electric mixer, cream the butter and sugar until light and fluffy. Add the eggs, 1 at a time, beating to blend well after each addition.

4 Sift together the flour, salt, bicarbonate of soda, nutmeg, allspice and cloves. Add to the butter mixture and stir to combine well.

5 ▲ Add the soured cream, banana, and vanilla and mix just enough to blend. Pour into the prepared tin.

6 ▲ Bake until the top springs back when touched lightly, 45–50 minutes. Let cool in the pan for 10 minutes. Turn out onto wire rack to cool.

7 ▲ For the glaze, combine the icing sugar and lemon juice, then stir until smooth.

8 To glaze, place the cooled loaf on a rack set over a baking sheet. Pour the glaze over the top of the loaf and allow to set.

Sweet Sesame Loaf

MAKES 1 OR 2 LOAVES

3 oz (85 g) sesame seeds

10 oz (285 g) plain flour

2½ teaspoons baking powder

1 teaspoon salt

2 oz (55 g) butter or margarine, at room temperature

4½ oz (125 g) sugar

2 eggs, at room temperature

grated rind of 1 lemon

12 fl oz (350 ml) milk

1 Preheat a 350°F/180°C/Gas 4 oven. Line a 9 × 5 in (23 × 13 cm) loaf tin with greaseproof paper and grease.

2 ▲ Reserve 2 tablespoons of the sesame seeds. Spread the rest on a baking sheet and bake until lightly toasted, about 10 minutes.

3 Sift the flour, salt and baking powder into a bowl.

4 ▲ Stir in the toasted sesame seeds and set aside.

5 With an electric mixer, cream the butter or margarine and sugar together until light and fluffy. Beat in the eggs, then stir in the lemon rind and milk.

6 ▼ Pour the milk mixture over the dry ingredients and fold in with a large metal spoon until just blended.

7 ▲ Pour into the tin and sprinkle over the reserved sesame seeds.

8 Bake until a skewer inserted in the centre comes out clean, about 1 hour. Let cool in the tin for 10 minutes. Turn out onto wire rack to cool completely.

Wholemeal Scones

MAKES 16

6 oz (170 g) cold butter
12 oz (350 g) wholemeal flour
5 oz (140 g) plain flour
2 tablespoons sugar
½ teaspoon salt
2½ teaspoons bicarbonate of soda
2 eggs
6 fl oz (175 ml) buttermilk
1¼ oz (35 g) raisins

1 Preheat the oven to 400°F/200°C/ Gas 6. Grease and flour a large baking sheet.

2 ▲ Cut the butter into small pieces.

3 Combine the dry ingredients in a bowl. Add the butter and rub in with your fingertips until the mixture resembles coarse breadcrumbs. Set aside.

4 In another bowl, whisk together the eggs and buttermilk. Set aside 2 tablespoons for glazing.

5 Stir the remaining egg mixture into the dry ingredients until it just holds together. Stir in the raisins.

6 Roll out the dough about ¾ in (2 cm) thick. Stamp out circles with a biscuit cutter. Place on the prepared sheet and brush with the glaze.

7 Bake until golden, 12–15 minutes. Allow to cool slightly before serving. Split in two with a fork while still warm and spread with butter and jam, if wished.

Orange and Raisin Scones

MAKES 16

10 oz (285 g) plain flour
1½ tablespoons baking powder
2¼ oz (60 g) sugar
½ teaspoon salt
2½ g (70 g) butter, diced
2½ g (70 g) margarine, diced
grated rind of 1 large orange
2 oz (55 g) raisins
4 fl oz (125 ml) buttermilk
milk, for glazing

1 Preheat the oven to 425°F/220°C/ Gas 7. Grease and flour a large baking sheet.

2 Combine the dry ingredients in a large bowl. Add the butter and margarine and rub in with your fingertips until the mixture resembles coarse breadcrumbs.

3 ▲ Add the orange rind and raisins.

4 Gradually stir in the buttermilk to form a soft dough.

5 ▲ Roll out the dough about ¾ in (2 cm) thick. Stamp out circles with a biscuit cutter.

6 ▲ Place on the prepared sheet and brush the tops with milk.

7 Bake until golden, 12–15 minutes. Serve hot or warm, with butter, or whipped or clotted cream, and jam.

~ COOK'S TIP ~

For light tender scones, handle the dough as little as possible. If you wish, split the scones when cool and toast them under a preheated grill. Butter them while still hot.

Wholemeal Scones (top), Orange and Raisin Scones

Buttermilk Scones

MAKES 15

7 oz (200 g) plain flour

1 teaspoon salt

1 teaspoon baking powder

½ teaspoon bicarbonate of soda

4 tablespoons cold butter or margarine

6 fl oz (175 ml) buttermilk

1 Preheat the oven to 425°F/220°C/ Gas 7. Grease a baking sheet.

2 Sift the dry ingredients into a bowl. Rub in the butter or margarine with your fingertips until the mixture resembles breadcrumbs.

3 ▼ Gradually pour in the buttermilk, stirring with a fork to form a soft dough.

4 ▲ Roll out the dough until about ½ in (1 cm) thick. Stamp out rounds with a 2-inch (5 cm) biscuit cutter.

5 Place on the prepared baking sheet and bake until golden, 12–15 minutes. Serve warm or at room temperature.

Traditional Sweet Scones

MAKES 8

6 oz (170 g) flour

2 tablespoons sugar

3 teaspoons baking powder

⅛ teaspoon salt

5 tablespoons cold butter, cut in pieces

4 fl oz (125 ml) milk

1 Preheat the oven to 425°F/220°C/ Gas 7. Grease a baking sheet.

2 ▲ Sift the flour, sugar, baking powder, and salt into a bowl.

3 Cut in the butter with a pastry blender until the mixture resembles coarse crumbs.

4 Pour in the milk and stir with a fork to form a soft dough.

5 ▲ Roll out the dough about ¼ in (½ cm) thick. Stamp out rounds using a 2½ in (6 cm) biscuit cutter.

6 Place on the prepared sheet and bake until golden, about 12 minutes. Serve hot or warm, with butter and jam, to accompany tea or coffee.

~ VARIATION ~

To make a delicious and speedy dessert, split the scones in half while still warm. Butter one half, top with lightly sugared fresh strawberries, raspberries or blueberries, and sandwich with the other half. Serve at once with dollops of whipped cream.

Herb Popovers

MAKES 12

3 eggs

8 fl oz (250 ml) milk

1 oz (30 g) butter, melted

3 oz (85 g) plain flour

⅛ tsp salt

1 small sprig each mixed fresh herbs, such as chives, tarragon, dill and parsley

1 Preheat a 425°F/220°C/Gas 7 oven. Grease 12 small ramekins or individual baking cups.

2 With an electric mixer, beat the eggs until blended. Beat in the milk and melted butter.

3 Sift together the flour and salt, then beat into the egg mixture to combine thoroughly.

4 ▼ Strip the herb leaves from the stems and chop finely. Mix together and measure out 2 tablespoons. Stir the herbs into the batter.

5 ▲ Fill the prepared cups half-full.

6 Bake until golden, 25–30 minutes. Do not open the oven door during baking time or the popovers may collapse. For drier popovers, pierce each one with a knife after the 30 minute baking time and bake for 5 minutes more. Serve hot.

Cheese Popovers

MAKES 12

3 eggs

8 fl oz (250 ml) milk

1 oz (30 g) butter, melted

3 oz (85 g) plain flour

¼ tsp salt

¼ tsp paprika

1 oz (30 g) freshly grated Parmesan cheese

~ **VARIATION** ~

For traditional Yorkshire Pudding, omit the cheese and paprika, and use 4–6 tablespoons of beef dripping to replace the butter. Put them into the oven in time to serve warm as an accompaniment for roast beef.

1 Preheat a 425°F/220°C/Gas 7 oven. Grease 12 small ramekins.

2 ▲ With an electric mixer, beat the eggs until blended. Beat in the milk and melted butter.

3 ▲ Sift together the flour, salt and paprika, then beat into the egg mixture. Add the cheese and stir.

4 Fill the prepared cups half-full and bake until golden, 25–30 minutes. Do not open the oven door or the popovers may collapse. For drier popovers, pierce each one with a knife after the 30 minute baking time and bake for 5 minutes more. Serve hot.

Herb Popovers (top), Cheese Popovers

YEAST BREADS

~

Though the pace of today's life leaves little time for baking,
breadmaking can be very therapeutic. The process is simple
yet infinitely variable, as the loaves that follow prove.
Roll up your sleeves and create a tradition.

White Bread

MAKES 2 LOAVES

2 fl oz (65 ml) lukewarm water
1 tablespoon active dried yeast
2 tablespoons sugar
16 fl oz (450 ml) lukewarm milk
1 oz (30 g) butter or margarine, at room temperature
2 teaspoons salt
1 lb 14 oz–2 lbs (850–900 g) strong flour

1 Combine the water, yeast and 1 tablespoon of sugar in a measuring jug and let stand for 15 minutes until the mixture is frothy.

2 ▼ Pour the milk into a large bowl. Add the remaining sugar, the butter or margarine, and salt. Stir in the yeast mixture.

3 Stir in the flour, 5 oz (140 g) at a time, until a stiff dough is obtained. Alternatively, use a food processor.

4 ▲ Transfer the dough to a floured surface. To knead, push the dough away from you with the palm of your hand, then fold it towards you, and push it away again. Repeat until the dough is smooth and elastic.

5 Place the dough in a large greased bowl, cover with a plastic bag, and leave to rise in a warm place until doubled in volume, 2–3 hours.

6 Grease 2 9 × 5 in (23 × 13 cm) tins.

7 ▲ Punch down the risen dough with your fist and divide in half. Form into a loaf shape and place in the tins, seam-side down. Cover and let rise in a warm place until almost doubled in volume, about 45 minutes.

8 Preheat a 375°F/190°C/Gas 5 oven.

9 Bake until firm and brown, 45–50 minutes. Turn out and tap the bottom of a loaf: if it sounds hollow the loaf is done. If necessary, return to the oven and bake a few minutes more.

10 Let cool on a rack.

Country Bread

MAKES 2 LOAVES

12 oz (350 g) wholewheat flour
12 oz (350 g) plain flour
5 oz (140 g) strong plain flour
4 tsp salt
2 oz (55 g) butter, at room temperature
16 fl oz (450 ml) lukewarm milk
FOR THE STARTER
1 tbsp active dry yeast
8 fl oz (250 ml) lukewarm water
5 oz (140 g) plain flour
¼ tsp caster sugar

1 ▲ For the starter, combine the yeast, water, flour and sugar in a bowl and stir with a fork. Cover and leave in a warm place for 2–3 hours, or leave overnight in a cool place.

2 Place the flours, salt and butter in a food processor and process just until blended, 1–2 minutes.

3 Stir together the milk and starter, then slowly pour into the processor, with the motor running, until the mixture forms a dough. If necessary, add more water. Alternatively, the dough can be mixed by hand. Transfer to a floured surface and knead until smooth and elastic.

4 Place in an ungreased bowl, cover with a plastic bag, and leave to rise in a warm place until doubled in volume, about 1½ hours.

5 Transfer to a floured surface and knead briefly. Return to the bowl and leave to rise until tripled in volume, about 1½ hours.

6 ▲ Divide the dough in half. Cut off one-third of the dough from each half and shape into balls. Shape the larger remaining portion of each half into balls. Grease a baking sheet.

7 ▲ For each loaf, top the large ball with the small ball and press the centre with the handle of a wooden spoon to secure. Cover with a plastic bag, slash the top, and leave to rise.

8 Preheat a 400°F/200°C/Gas 6 oven. Dust the dough with flour and bake until the top is browned and the bottom sounds hollow when tapped, 45–50 minutes. Cool on a rack.

Plaited Loaf

MAKES 1 LOAF

1 tablespoon active dried yeast
1 teaspoon honey
8 fl oz (250 ml) lukewarm milk
2 oz (55 g) butter, melted
15 oz (420 g) strong flour
1 teaspoon salt
1 egg, lightly beaten
1 egg yolk beaten with 1 teaspoon milk, for glazing

1 ▼ Combine the yeast, honey, milk and butter. Stir and leave for 15 minutes to dissolve.

2 In a large bowl, mix together the flour and salt. Make a well in the centre and add the yeast mixture and egg. With a wooden spoon, stir from the centre, incorporating flour with each turn, to obtain a rough dough.

3 Transfer to a floured surface and knead until smooth and elastic. Place in a clean bowl, cover and leave to rise in a warm place until doubled in volume, about 1½ hours.

4 Grease a baking sheet. Punch down the dough and divide into three equal pieces. Roll to shape each piece into a long thin strip.

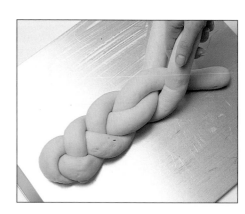

5 ▲ Begin plaiting with the centre strip, tucking in the ends. Cover loosely and leave to rise in a warm place for 30 minutes.

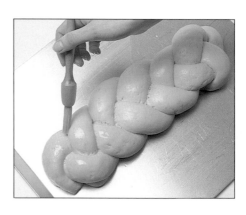

6 ▲ Preheat a 375°F/190°C/Gas 5 oven. Place the bread in a cool place while the oven heats. Brush with the glaze and bake until golden, 40–45 minutes. Turn out onto a rack to cool.

Sesame Seed Bread

MAKES 1 LOAF

2 tsp active dry yeast

10 fl oz (300 ml) lukewarm water

7 oz (200 g) plain flour

7 oz (200 g) wholewheat flour

2 tsp salt

2½ oz (70 g) toasted sesame seeds

milk, for glazing

2 tbsp sesame seeds, for sprinkling

1 Combine the yeast and 5 tbsp of the water and leave to dissolve. Mix the flours and salt in a large bowl. Make a well in the centre and pour in the yeast and water.

2 ▲ With a wooden spoon, stir from the centre, incorporating flour with each turn, to obtain a rough dough.

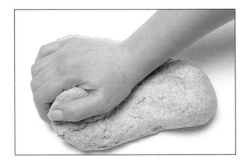

3 ▲ Transfer to a floured surface. To knead, push the dough away from you with the palm of your hand, then fold it towards you and push away again. Repeat until smooth and elastic, then return to the bowl and cover with a plastic bag. Leave in a warm place until doubled in volume, 1½–2 hours.

4 ▲ Grease a 9 in (23 cm) cake tin. Punch down the dough and knead in the sesame seeds. Divide the dough into 16 balls and place in the pan. Cover with a plastic bag and leave in a warm place until risen above the rim of the tin.

5 ▼ Preheat a 425°F/220°C/Gas 7 oven. Brush the loaf with milk and sprinkle with the sesame seeds. Bake for 15 minutes. Lower the heat to 375°F/190°C/Gas 5 and bake until the bottom sounds hollow when tapped, about 30 minutes more. Cool on a rack.

Wholewheat Bread

MAKES 1 LOAF

1 lb 5 oz (600 g) wholewheat flour
2 tsp salt
4 tsp active dry yeast
15 fl oz (425 ml) lukewarm water
2 tbsp honey
3 tbsp oil
1½ oz (45 g) wheatgerm
milk, for glazing

1 Combine the flour and salt in a bowl and place in the oven at its lowest setting until warmed, 8–10 minutes.

2 Meanwhile, combine the yeast with half of the water in a small bowl and leave to dissolve.

3 ▼ Make a well in the centre of the flour. Pour in the yeast mixture, the remaining water, honey, oil and wheatgerm. With a wooden spoon, stir from the centre until smooth.

4 Transfer the dough to a lightly floured surface and knead just enough to shape into a loaf.

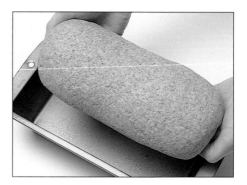

5 ▲ Grease a 9 × 5 in (23 × 13 cm) loaf tin, place the dough in it and cover with a plastic bag. Leave in a warm place until the dough is about 1 in (2.5 cm) higher than the tin rim, about 1 hour.

6 Preheat a 400°F/200°C/Gas 6 oven. Bake until the bottom sounds hollow when tapped, 35–40 minutes. Cool.

Rye Bread

MAKES 1 LOAF

7 oz (200 g) rye flour
16 fl oz (450 ml) boiling water
4 fl oz (125 ml) black treacle
2½ oz (70 g) butter, cut in pieces
1 tbsp salt
2 tbsp caraway seeds
1 tbsp active dry yeast
4 fl oz (125 ml) lukewarm water
about 1 lb 14 oz (850 g) plain flour
semolina or flour, for dusting

~ COOK'S TIP ~

To bring out the flavour of the caraway seeds, toast them lightly. Spread the seeds on a baking tray and place in a preheated 325°F/170°C/ Gas 3 oven for about 7 minutes.

1 ▲ Mix the rye flour, boiling water, treacle, butter, salt and caraway seeds in a large bowl. Leave to cool.

2 In another bowl, mix the yeast and lukewarm water and leave to dissolve. Stir into the rye flour mixture. Stir in just enough plain flour to obtain a stiff dough. If it becomes too stiff, stir with your hands.

3 Transfer to a floured surface and knead until the dough is no longer sticky and is smooth and shiny.

4 Place in a greased bowl, cover with a plastic bag, and leave in a warm place until doubled in volume. Punch down the dough, cover, and let rise again for 30 minutes.

5 Preheat a 350°F/180°C/Gas 4 oven. Dust a baking sheet with semolina.

6 ▼ Shape the dough into a ball. Place on the sheet and score several times across the top. Bake until the bottom sounds hollow when tapped, about 40 minutes. Cool on a rack.

Wholewheat Bread (top), Rye Bread

Buttermilk Graham Bread

SERVES 8

2 teaspoons active dried yeast

4 fl oz (120 ml) lukewarm water

8 oz (225 g) graham or wholewheat
flour

12 oz (350 g) plain flour

4½ oz (130 g) cornmeal

2 teaspoons salt

2 tablespoons sugar

4 tablespoons butter, at room
temperature

16 fl oz (475 ml) lukewarm
buttermilk

1 beaten egg, for glazing

sesame seeds, for sprinkling

1 Combine the yeast and water, stir, and leave for 15 minutes to dissolve.

2 ▲ Mix together the two flours, cornmeal, salt and sugar in a large bowl. Make a well in the centre and pour in the yeast mixture, then add the butter and the buttermilk.

3 ▲ Stir from the centre, mixing in the flour until a rough dough is formed. If too stiff, use your hands.

4 ▲ Transfer to a floured surface and knead until smooth. Place in a clean bowl, cover, and leave in a warm place for 2–3 hours.

5 ▲ Grease 2 8 in (20 cm) square baking tins. Punch down the dough. Divide into eight pieces and roll them into balls. Place four in each tin. Cover and leave in a warm place for about 1 hour.

6 Preheat the oven to 375°F/190°C/ Gas 5. Brush with the glaze, then sprinkle over the sesame seeds. Bake for about 50 minutes, or until the bottoms sound hollow when tapped. Cool on a wire rack.

Multi-Grain Bread

MAKES 2 LOAVES

1 tablespoon active dried yeast
2 fl oz (65 ml) lukewarm water
2½ oz (70 g) rolled oats (not quick cooking)
16 fl oz (450 ml) milk
2 teaspoons salt
2 fl oz (65 ml) oil
2 oz (55 g) light brown sugar
2 tablespoons honey
2 eggs, lightly beaten
1 oz (30 g) wheat germ
6 oz (170 g) soya flour
12 oz (350 g) wholemeal flour
15 oz–1 lb 1½ oz (420–490 g) strong flour

1 Combine the yeast and water, stir, and leave for 15 minutes to dissolve.

2 ▲ Place the oats in a large bowl. Scald the milk, then pour over the rolled oats.

3 Stir in the salt, oil, sugar and honey. Leave until lukewarm.

~ **VARIATION** ~

Different flours may be used in this recipe, such as rye, barley, buckwheat or cornmeal. Try replacing the wheat germ and the soya flour with one or two of these, using the same total amount.

4 ▲ Stir in the yeast mixture, eggs, wheat germ, soya and wholemeal flours. Gradually stir in enough strong flour to obtain a rough dough.

5 Transfer the dough to a floured surface and knead, adding flour if necessary, until smooth and elastic. Return to a clean bowl, cover and leave to rise in a warm place until doubled in volume, about 2½ hours.

6 Grease 2 8½ × 4½ in (21.5 × 11.5 cm) bread tins. Punch down the risen dough and knead briefly.

7 Divide the dough into quarters. Roll each quarter into a cylinder 1½ in (3 cm) thick. Twist together 2 cylinders and place in a tin; repeat for remaining cylinders.

8 Cover and leave to rise until doubled in size, about 1 hour.

9 Preheat a 375°F/190°C/Gas 5 oven.

10 ▲ Bake until the bottoms sound hollow when tapped lightly, 45–50 minutes. Cool on a rack.

Potato Bread

MAKES 2 LOAVES

4 tsp active dry yeast

8 fl oz (250 ml) lukewarm milk

8 oz (225 g) potatoes, boiled (reserve 8 fl oz (250 ml) of potato cooking liquid)

2 tbsp oil

4 tsp salt

1 lb 14 oz–2 lb (850–900 g) plain flour

1 Combine the yeast and milk in a large bowl and leave to dissolve, about 15 minutes.

2 Meanwhile, mash the potatoes.

3 ▲ Add the potatoes, oil and salt to the yeast mixture and mix well. Stir in the reserved cooking water, then stir in the flour, in 6 separate batches, to form a stiff dough.

4 Transfer to a floured surface and knead until smooth and elastic. Return to the bowl, cover, and leave in a warm place until doubled in size, 1–1½ hours. Punch down, then leave to rise for another 40 minutes.

5 Grease 2 9 × 5 in (23 × 13 cm) loaf tins. Roll the dough into 20 small balls. Place 2 rows of balls in each tin. Leave until the dough has risen above the rim of the tins.

6 Preheat a 400°F/200°C/Gas 6 oven. Bake for 10 minutes, then lower the heat to 375°F/190°C/Gas 5. Bake until the bottoms sound hollow when tapped, 40 minutes. Cool on a rack.

Irish Soda Bread

MAKES 1 LOAF

10 oz (285 g) plain flour

5 oz (140 g) wholewheat flour

1 tsp bicarbonate of soda

1 tsp salt

1 oz (30 g) butter or margarine, at room temperature

10 fl oz (300 ml) buttermilk

1 tbsp plain flour, for dusting

1 Preheat a 400°F/200°C/Gas 6 oven. Grease a baking sheet.

2 Sift the flours, bicarbonate of soda and salt together into a bowl. Make a well in the centre and add the butter or margarine and buttermilk. Working outwards from the centre, stir with a fork until a soft dough is formed.

3 ▲ With floured hands, gather the dough into a ball.

4 ▲ Transfer to a floured surface and knead for 3 minutes. Shape the dough into a large round.

5 ▲ Place on the baking sheet. Cut a cross in the top with a sharp knife.

6 ▲ Dust with flour. Bake until brown, 40–50 minutes. Transfer to a rack to cool.

Potato Bread (top), Irish Soda Bread

Anadama Bread

MAKES 2 LOAVES

2 teaspoons active dried yeast

4 tablespoons lukewarm water

2 oz (50 g) cornmeal

3 tablespoons butter or margarine

4 tablespoons molasses

6 fl oz (175 ml) boiling water

1 egg

12 oz (350 g) flour

2 tablespoons salt

1 Combine the yeast and lukewarm water, stir well, and leave for 15 minutes to dissolve.

2 ▼ Meanwhile, combine the cornmeal, butter or margarine, molasses and boiling water in a large bowl. Add the yeast, egg, and half of the flour. Stir together to blend.

3 ▲ Stir in the remaining flour and salt. When the dough becomes too stiff, stir with your hands until it comes away from the sides of the bowl. If it is too sticky, add more flour; if too stiff, add a little water.

4 ▲ Transfer to a floured surface and knead until smooth and elastic. Place in a bowl, cover with a plastic bag, and leave in a warm place until doubled in size, for 2–3 hours.

5 Grease 2 7 x 3 in (18 x 7.5 cm) bread tins. Punch down the dough. Shape into two loaves and place in the tins, seam-side down. Cover and leave in a warm place for 1–2 hours.

6 ▲ Preheat the oven to 375°F/ 190°C/Gas 6. Bake for 50 minutes. Remove and cool on a wire rack.

Oatmeal Bread

MAKES 2 LOAVES

16 fl oz (450 ml) milk
1 oz (30 g) butter
2 oz (55 g) dark brown sugar
2 teaspoons salt
1 tablespoon active dried yeast
2 fl oz (65 ml) lukewarm water
13¾ oz (390 g) rolled oats (not quick-cooking)
1 lb 8 oz–1 lb 14 oz (700–850 g) strong flour

1 ▲ Scald the milk. Remove from the heat and stir in the butter, brown sugar and salt. Leave until lukewarm.

2 Combine the yeast and warm water in a large bowl and leave until the yeast is dissolved and the mixture is frothy. Stir in the milk mixture.

3 ▲ Add 10 oz (285 g) of the oats and enough flour to obtain a soft dough.

4 Transfer to a floured surface and knead until smooth and elastic.

5 ▲ Place in a greased bowl, cover with a plastic bag, and leave until doubled in volume, 2–3 hours.

6 Grease a large baking sheet. Transfer the dough to a lightly floured surface and divide in half.

7 ▼ Shape into rounds. Place on the baking sheet, cover with a tea towel and leave to rise until doubled in volume, about 1 hour.

8 Preheat a 400°F/200°C/Gas 6 oven. Score the tops and sprinkle with the remaining oats. Bake until the bottoms sound hollow when tapped, 45–50 minutes. Cool on racks.

Sourdough Bread

MAKES 1 LOAF

12 oz (350 g) flour
1 tablespoon salt
8 fl oz (250 ml) Sourdough Starter
4 fl oz (120 ml) lukewarm water

1 ▲ Combine the flour and salt in a large bowl. Make a well in the centre and add the starter and water. With a wooden spoon, stir from the centre, incorporating more flour with each turn, to obtain a rough dough.

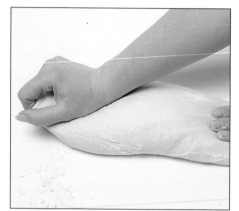

2 ▲ Transfer the dough to a floured surface. To knead, push the dough away from you with the palm of your hand, then fold it towards you, and push it away again. Repeat the process until the dough has become smooth and elastic.

3 Place in a clean bowl, cover, and leave to rise in a warm place until doubled in volume, for about 2 hours.

4 Lightly grease an 8 x 4 in (20 x 10 cm) bread tin.

5 ▼ Punch down the dough with your fist. Knead briefly, then form into a loaf shape and place in the tin, seam-side down. Cover with a plastic bag, and leave to rise in a warm place, for about 1½ hours.

6 Preheat the oven to 425°F/220°C/ Gas 7. Dust the top of the loaf with flour, then score lengthways. Bake for 15 minutes. Lower the heat to 375°F/190°C/Gas 5 and bake for about 30 minutes more, or until the bottom sounds hollow when tapped.

Sourdough Starter

MAKES 1¼ PINTS (750 ML)

1 teaspoon active dried yeast
6 fl oz (175 ml) lukewarm water
2 oz (50 g) flour

~ COOK'S TIP ~

After using, feed the starter with a handful of flour and enough water to restore it to a thick batter. The starter can be refrigerated for up to 1 week, but must be brought back to room temperature before using.

1 ▲ For the starter, combine the yeast and water, stir and leave for 15 minutes to dissolve.

2 ▼ Sprinkle over the flour and whisk until it forms a batter. Cover and leave to rise in a warm place for at least 24 hours or preferably 2–4 days, before using.

Sourdough French Loaves

MAKES 2 LOAVES

2 teaspoons active dried yeast
12 fl oz (350 ml) lukewarm water
8 fl oz (250 ml) Sourdough Starter
1 lb 8 oz (700 g) plain flour
1 tablespoon salt
1 teaspoon sugar
cornmeal, for sprinkling
1 teaspoon cornflour
4 fl oz (125 ml) water

1 In a large bowl, combine the yeast and lukewarm water, stir and leave for 15 minutes to dissolve.

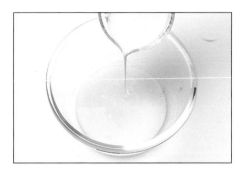

2 ▲ Pour in the sourdough starter. Add 1 lb (450 g) of the flour, the salt and the sugar. Stir until smooth. Cover the bowl with a plastic bag and leave the dough to rise in a warm place until doubled in volume, about 1½ hours.

3 Stir in just enough flour to obtain a rough dough. Transfer to a floured surface and knead until the dough is smooth and elastic. Divide in half, then shape each half into a 14 in (35 cm) cylinder with rounded ends.

4 ▲ Place loaves on a wooden board or tray sprinkled with cornmeal. Cover loosely with a dish towel or greaseproof paper and leave to rise in a warm place until nearly doubled in volume.

5 Preheat the oven to 425°F/220°C/ Gas 7. Place a 15 x 12 in (38 x 30 cm) baking sheet in the oven. Half-fill a shallow baking dish with hot water and put it on the bottom of the oven.

6 Mix the cornflour and water in a small saucepan. Bring to the boil.

7 ▲ With a sharp knife, make several diagonal slashes across the loaves. Slide on to the hot baking sheet and brush over the cornflour mixture. Bake until the tops are golden and the bottoms sound hollow when tapped, about 25 minutes. Cool on a wire rack.

Sourdough Rye Bread

MAKES 2 LOAVES

2 teaspoons active dried yeast
4 fl oz (125 ml) lukewarm water
1 oz (30 g) butter, melted
1 tablespoon salt
4 oz (115 g) wholemeal flour
14–16 oz (400–450 g) plain flour
1 egg mixed with 1 tablespoon water, for glazing
FOR THE STARTER
1 tablespoon active dried yeast
12 fl oz (350 ml) lukewarm water
3 tablespoons black treacle
2 tablespoons caraway seeds
9 oz (250 g) rye flour

1 For the starter, combine the yeast and water, stir and leave for 15 minutes to dissolve.

2 ▲ Stir in the black treacle, caraway seeds and rye flour. Cover and leave in a warm place for 2–3 days.

3 In a large bowl, combine the yeast and water, stir and leave for 10 minutes. Stir in the melted butter, salt, wholemeal flour and 14 oz (400 g) of the plain flour.

4 ▲ Make a well in the centre and pour in the starter.

5 Stir to obtain a rough dough, then transfer to a floured surface and knead until smooth and elastic. Return to the bowl, cover and leave to rise in a warm place until doubled in volume, about 2 hours.

6 Grease a large baking sheet. Knock back the dough and knead briefly. Cut the dough in half and form each half into log-shaped loaves.

7 ▼ Place the loaves on the baking sheet and score the tops with a sharp knife. Cover and leave to rise in a warm place until almost doubled, about 50 minutes.

8 Preheat the oven to 375°F/190°C/ Gas 5. Brush the loaves with the egg wash to glaze them, then bake until the bottoms sound hollow when tapped, about 50–55 minutes. If the tops brown too quickly, place a sheet of foil over the tops to protect them. Cool on a wire rack.

Wholewheat Rolls

MAKES 12

2 tsp active dry yeast
2 fl oz (65 ml) lukewarm water
1 tsp caster sugar
6 fl oz (175 ml) lukewarm buttermilk
¼ tsp bicarbonate of soda
1 tsp salt
1½ oz (45 g) butter, at room temperature
7 oz (200 g) wholewheat flour
5 oz (140 g) plain flour
1 beaten egg, for glazing

1 In a large bowl, combine the yeast, water and sugar. Stir, and leave for 15 minutes to dissolve.

2 ▲ Add the buttermilk, bicarbonate of soda, salt and butter and stir to blend. Stir in the wholewheat flour.

3 Add just enough of the plain flour to obtain a rough dough.

4 Transfer to a floured surface and knead until smooth and elastic. Divide into 3 equal parts. Roll each into a cylinder, then cut in 4.

5 ▼ Form the pieces into torpedo shapes. Place on a greased baking sheet, cover and leave in a warm place until doubled in volume.

6 Preheat a 400°F/200°C/Gas 6 oven. Brush the rolls with the glaze. Bake until firm, 15–20 minutes. Cool on a rack.

French Bread

MAKES 2 LOAVES

1 tbsp active dry yeast
16 fl oz (450 ml) lukewarm water
1 tbsp salt
1 lb 14 oz–2 lb 8 oz (850 g–1.2 kg) plain flour
semolina or flour, for sprinkling

1 Combine the yeast and water, stir, and leave for 15 minutes to dissolve. Stir in the salt.

2 Add the flour, 5 oz (140 g) at a time. Beat in with a wooden spoon, adding just enough flour to obtain a smooth dough. Alternatively, use an electric mixer with a dough hook.

3 Transfer to a floured surface and knead until smooth and elastic.

4 Shape into a ball, place in a greased bowl and cover with a plastic bag. Leave to rise in a warm place until doubled in volume, 2–4 hours.

5 ▲ Transfer to a lightly floured board and shape into 2 long loaves. Place on a baking sheet sprinkled with semolina or flour and let rise for 5 minutes.

6 ▲ Score the tops in several places with a very sharp knife. Brush with water and place in a cold oven. Set a pan of boiling water on the bottom of the oven and set the oven to 400°F/200°C/Gas 6. Bake until crusty and golden, about 40 minutes. Cool on a rack.

Wholewheat Rolls (top), French Bread

Pleated Rolls

MAKES 48 ROLLS

1 tablespoon active dried yeast
16 fl oz (450 ml) lukewarm milk
4 oz (115 g) margarine
5 tablespoons sugar
2 teaspoons salt
2 eggs
2 lb 3 oz–2 lb 8 oz (985 g–1.2 kg) strong flour
2 oz (55 g) butter

1 Combine the yeast and 4 fl oz (125 ml) milk in a large bowl. Stir and leave for 15 minutes to dissolve.

2 Scald the remaining milk, cool for 5 minutes, then beat in the margarine, sugar, salt and eggs. Let cool to lukewarm.

3 ▲ Pour the milk mixture into the yeast mixture. Stir in half the flour with a wooden spoon. Add the remaining flour, 5 oz (190 g) at a time, until a rough dough is obtained.

4 Transfer the dough to a lightly floured surface and knead until smooth and elastic. Place in a clean bowl, cover with a plastic bag and leave to rise in a warm place until doubled in volume, about 2 hours.

5 In a saucepan, melt the butter and set aside. Grease 2 baking sheets.

6 Punch down the dough and divide into 4 equal pieces. Roll each piece into a 12 × 8 in (30 × 20 cm) rectangle, about ¼ in (5 mm) thick.

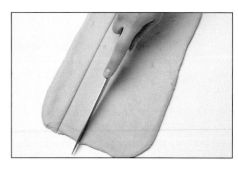

7 ▲ Cut each of the rectangles into 4 long strips. Cut each strip into 3 4 × 2 in (10 × 5 cm) rectangles.

8 ▲ Brush each rectangle with melted butter, then fold the rectangles in half, so that the top extends about ½ in (1 cm) over the bottom.

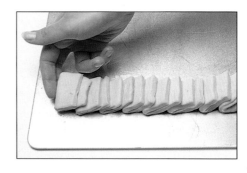

9 ▲ Place the rectangles slightly overlapping on the baking sheet, with the longer side facing up.

10 Cover and refrigerate for 30 minutes. Preheat a 350°F/180°C/Gas 4 oven. Bake until golden, 18–20 minutes. Cool slightly before serving.

Clover Leaf Rolls

MAKES 24

10 fl oz (300 ml) milk

2 tbsp caster sugar

2 oz (55 g) butter, at room temperature,

2 tsp active dry yeast

1 egg

2 tsp salt

1 lb 2 oz–1 lb 4 oz (500–575 g) plain flour

melted butter, for glazing

4 Grease 2 12-cup bun trays.

5 ▼ Punch down the dough. Cut into 4 equal pieces. Roll each piece into a rope 14 in (35 cm) long. Cut each rope into 18 pieces, then roll each into a ball.

6 ▲ Place 3 balls, side by side, in each bun cup. Cover loosely and leave to rise in a warm place until doubled in volume, about 1½ hours.

7 Preheat a 400°F/200°C/Gas 6 oven.

8 Brush the rolls with glaze. Bake until lightly browned, about 20 minutes. Cool slightly before serving.

1 ▲ Heat the milk until lukewarm; test the temperature with your knuckle. Pour into a large bowl and stir in the sugar, butter and yeast. Leave for 15 minutes to dissolve.

2 Stir the egg and salt into the yeast mixture. Gradually stir in 1 lb 2 oz (500 g) of the flour. Add just enough extra flour to obtain a rough dough.

3 ▲ Transfer to a floured surface and knead until smooth and elastic. Place in a greased bowl, cover and leave in a warm place until doubled in volume, about 1½ hours.

Poppyseed Knots

MAKES 12

10 fl oz (300 ml) lukewarm milk

2 oz (55 g) butter, at room temperature

1 tsp caster sugar

2 tsp active dry yeast

1 egg yolk

2 tsp salt

1 lb 2 oz–1 lb 4 oz (500–575 g) plain flour

1 egg beaten with 2 tsp of water, for glazing

poppyseeds, for sprinkling

1 In a large bowl, stir together the milk, butter, sugar and yeast. Leave for 15 minutes to dissolve.

2 Stir in the egg yolk, salt and 10 oz (285 g) flour. Add half the remaining flour and stir to obtain a soft dough.

3 Transfer to a floured surface and knead, adding flour if necessary, until smooth and elastic. Place in a bowl, cover and leave in a warm place until doubled in volume, 1½–2 hours.

4 ▲ Grease a baking sheet. Punch down the dough with your fist and cut into 12 pieces the size of golf balls.

5 ▲ Roll each piece to a rope, twist to form a knot and place 1 in (2.5 cm) apart on the sheet. Cover loosely and leave to rise in a warm place until doubled in volume, 1–1½ hours.

6 Preheat a 350°F/180°C/Gas 4 oven.

7 ▲ Brush the knots with the egg glaze and sprinkle over the poppyseeds. Bake until the tops are lightly browned, 25–30 minutes. Cool slightly on a rack before serving.

Bread Sticks

MAKES 18–20

1 tbsp active dry yeast
10 fl oz (300 ml) lukewarm water
15 oz (420 g) plain flour
2 tsp salt
1 tsp caster sugar
2 tbsp olive oil
5 oz (140 g) sesame seeds
1 beaten egg, for glazing
coarse salt, for sprinkling

1 Combine the yeast and water, stir and leave for 15 minutes to dissolve.

2 ▲ Place the flour, salt, sugar and olive oil in a food processor. With the motor running, slowly pour in the yeast mixture and process until the dough forms a ball. If sticky, add more flour; if dry, add more water.

3 Transfer to a floured surface and knead until smooth and elastic. Place in a bowl, cover and leave to rise in a warm place for 45 minutes.

4 ▲ Lightly toast the sesame seeds in a frying pan. Grease 2 baking sheets.

5 ▼ Roll small handfuls of dough into cylinders, about 12 in (30 cm) long. Place on the baking sheets.

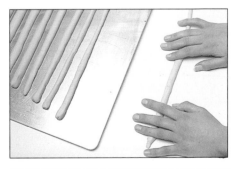

~ **VARIATION** ~

If preferred, use other seeds, such as poppy or caraway, or for plain bread sticks, omit the seeds and salt.

6 ▲ Brush with egg glaze, sprinkle with the sesame seeds, then sprinkle over some coarse salt. Leave to rise, uncovered, until almost doubled in volume, about 20 minutes.

7 Preheat a 400°F/200°C/Gas 6 oven. Bake until golden, about 15 minutes. Turn off the heat but leave the bread sticks in the oven for 5 minutes more. Serve warm or cool.

Croissants

MAKES 18

1 tbsp active dry yeast
11 fl oz (335 ml) lukewarm milk
2 tsp caster sugar
1½ tsp salt
15 oz–1 lb 2 oz (420–500 g) plain flour
8 oz (225 g) cold unsalted butter
1 egg beaten with 2 tsp water, for glazing

1 In the large bowl of an electric mixer, stir together the yeast and warm milk. Leave for 15 minutes to dissolve. Stir in the sugar, salt and 5 oz (140 g) of the flour.

2 Using a dough hook, on low speed, gradually add the remaining flour. Beat on high until the dough pulls away from the sides of the bowl. Cover and let rise in a warm place until doubled, about 1½ hours.

3 On a floured surface, knead the dough until smooth. Wrap in greaseproof paper and refrigerate for 15 minutes.

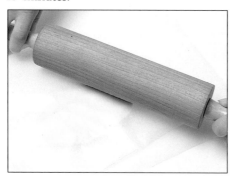

4 ▲ Divide the butter into 2 halves and place each between 2 sheets of greaseproof paper. With a rolling pin, flatten each to form a 6 × 4 in (15 × 10 cm) rectangle. Set aside.

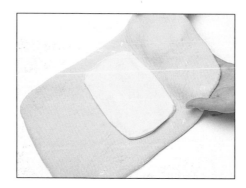

5 ▲ On a floured surface, roll out the dough to 12 × 8 in (30 × 20 cm). Place a butter rectangle in the centre. Fold the bottom third of dough over the butter and press gently to seal. Top with the other butter rectangle, then fold over the top dough third.

6 ▲ Turn the dough so that the short side is facing you, with the long folded edge on the left and the long open edge on the right, like a book.

7 Roll the dough gently into a 12 × 8 in (30 × 20 cm) rectangle; do not press the butter out. Fold in thirds again and mark one corner with your fingertip to indicate the first turn. Wrap and refrigerate for 30 minutes.

8 Repeat twice more: again position the dough like a book, roll, fold in thirds, mark, wrap, and chill. After the third fold, refrigerate at least 2 hours (or overnight).

9 Roll out the dough about ⅛ in (3 mm) thick to a rectangle about 13 in (33 cm) wide. Trim the sides to neaten.

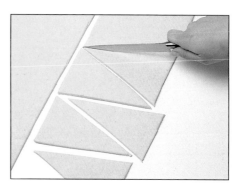

10 ▲ Cut the dough in half lengthwise, then cut into triangles 6 in (15 cm) high with a 4 in (10 cm) base.

11 ▲ Gently go over the triangles lengthwise with a rolling pin to stretch slightly. Roll up from base to point. Place point-down on baking sheets and curve to form a crescent. Cover and let rise in a warm place until more than doubled in volume, 1–1½ hours. (Or, refrigerate overnight and bake the next day.)

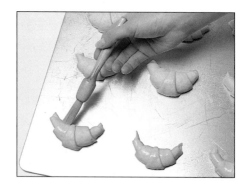

12 ▲ Preheat a 475°F/240°C/Gas 9 oven. Brush with the glaze. Bake for 2 minutes. Lower the heat to 375°F/190°C/Gas 5 and bake until golden, 10–12 more minutes. Serve warm.

Dill Bread

MAKES 2 LOAVES

4 teaspoons active dried yeast

16 fl oz (450 ml) lukewarm water

2 tablespoons sugar

2 lb 5½ oz (1.05 kg) strong flour

½ onion, chopped

4 tablespoons oil

l large bunch of dill, finely chopped

2 eggs, lightly beaten

5½ oz (150 g) cottage cheese

4 teaspoons salt

milk, for glazing

1 Mix together the yeast, water and sugar in a large bowl and leave for 15 minutes to dissolve.

2 ▼ Stir in about half of the flour. Cover and leave to rise in a warm place for 45 minutes.

3 ▲ In a frying pan, cook the onion in 1 tablespoon of the oil until soft. Set aside to cool, then stir into the yeast mixture. Stir the dill, eggs, cottage cheese, salt and remaining oil into the yeast. Gradually add the remaining flour until too stiff to stir.

4 ▲ Transfer to a floured surface and knead until smooth and elastic. Place in a bowl, cover and leave to rise until doubled in volume, 1–1½ hours.

5 ▲ Grease a large baking sheet. Cut the dough in half and shape into 2 rounds. Leave to rise in a warm place for 30 minutes.

6 Preheat a 375°F/190°C/Gas 5 oven. Score the tops, brush with the milk and bake until browned, about 50 minutes. Cool on a rack.

Spiral Herb Bread

MAKES 2 LOAVES

2 tablespoons active dried yeast
1 pt (600 ml) lukewarm water
15 oz (420 g) strong flour
1 lb 2 oz (505 g) wholemeal flour
3 teaspoons salt
1 oz (30 g) butter
1 large bunch of parsley, finely chopped
1 bunch of spring onions, chopped
1 garlic clove, finely chopped
salt and freshly ground black pepper
1 egg, lightly beaten
milk, for glazing

1 Combine the yeast and 2 fl oz (65 ml) of the water, stir and leave for 15 minutes to dissolve.

2 Combine the flours and salt in a large bowl. Make a well in the centre and pour in the yeast mixture and the remaining water. With a wooden spoon, stir from the centre, working outwards to obtain a rough dough.

3 Transfer the dough to a floured surface and knead until smooth and elastic. Return to the bowl, cover with a plastic bag, and leave until doubled in volume, about 2 hours.

4 ▲ Meanwhile, combine the butter, parsley, spring onions and garlic in a large frying pan. Cook over low heat, stirring, until softened. Season and set aside.

5 Grease 2 9 × 5 in (23 × 13 cm) tins. When the dough has risen, cut in half and roll each half into a rectangle about 14 × 9 in (35 × 23 cm).

6 ▼ Brush both with the beaten egg. Divide the herb mixture between the two, spreading just up to the edges.

7 ▲ Roll up to enclose the filling and pinch the short ends to seal. Place in the tins, seam-side down. Cover, and leave in a warm place until the dough rises above the rim of the tins.

8 Preheat a 375°F/190°C/Gas 5 oven. Brush with milk and bake until the bottoms sound hollow when tapped, about 55 minutes. Cool on a rack.

Pizza

MAKES 2

1 lb 2 oz (500 g) plain flour
1 tsp salt
2 tsp active dry yeast
10 fl oz (300 ml) lukewarm water
2–4 fl oz (65–125 ml) extra-virgin olive oil
tomato sauce, grated cheese, olives and herbs, for topping

1 Combine the flour and salt in a large mixing bowl. Make a well in the centre and add the yeast, water and 2 tablespoons of the olive oil. Leave for 15 minutes to dissolve the yeast.

2 With your hands, stir until the dough just holds together. Transfer to a floured surface and knead until smooth and elastic. Avoid adding too much flour while kneading.

3 ▲ Brush the inside of a clean bowl with 1 tablespoon of the oil. Place the dough in the bowl and roll around to coat with the oil. Cover with a plastic bag and leave to rise in a warm place until more than doubled in volume, about 45 minutes.

4 Divide the dough into 2 balls. Preheat a 400°F/200°C/Gas 6 oven.

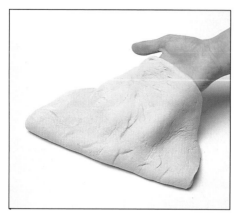

5 ▲ Roll each ball into a 10 in (25 cm) circle. Flip the circles over and onto your palm. Set each circle on the work surface and rotate, stretching the dough as you turn, until it is about 12 in (30 cm) in diameter.

6 ▲ Brush 2 pizza pans with oil. Place the dough circles in the pans and neaten the edges. Brush with oil.

7 ▲ Cover with the toppings and bake until golden, 10–12 minutes.

Cheese Bread

MAKES 1 LOAF

1 tablespoon active dried yeast
8 fl oz (250 ml) lukewarm milk
1 oz (30 g) butter
15 oz (420 g) strong flour
2 teaspoons salt
3½ oz (100 g) mature cheddar cheese, grated

1 Combine the yeast and milk. Stir and leave for 15 minutes to dissolve.

2 Melt the butter, let cool, and add to the yeast mixture.

3 Mix the flour and salt together in a large bowl. Make a well in the centre and pour in the yeast mixture.

4 With a wooden spoon, stir from the centre, incorporating flour with each turn, to obtain a rough dough. If the dough seems too dry, add 2–3 tablespoons water.

5 Transfer to a floured surface and knead until smooth and elastic. Return to the bowl, cover and leave to rise in a warm place until doubled in volume, 2–3 hours.

6 ▲ Grease a 9 × 5 in (23 × 13 cm) bread tin. Punch down the dough with your fist. Knead in the cheese, distributing it as evenly as possible.

7 ▼ Twist the dough, form into a loaf shape and place in the tin, tucking the ends under. Leave in a warm place until the dough rises above the rim of the tin.

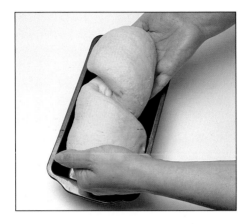

8 ▲ Preheat a 400°F/200°C/Gas 6 oven. Bake for 15 minutes, then lower to 375°F/190°C/Gas 5 and bake until the bottom sounds hollow when tapped, about 30 minutes more.

Italian Flat Bread With Sage

MAKES 1 LOAF

2 teaspoons active dried yeast
8 fl oz (250 ml) lukewarm water
12 oz (375 g) plain flour
2 teaspoons salt
5 tablespoons extra virgin olive oil
12 fresh sage leaves, chopped

1 Combine the yeast and water, stir and leave for 15 minutes until the yeast has completely dissolved.

2 Mix the flour and salt in a large bowl, and make a well in the centre.

3 Stir in the yeast mixture and 4 tablespoons of the oil. Stir from the centre, incorporating flour with each turn, to obtain a rough dough.

4 ▲ Transfer the dough to a lightly floured surface and knead until it is smooth and elastic. Shape into a ball and place in a lightly oiled bowl. Cover and leave to rise in a warm place until doubled in volume, for about 2 hours.

5 Preheat the oven to 400°F/200°C/ Gas 6 and place a baking sheet in the centre of the oven.

6 Punch down the dough. Knead in the sage leaves, then roll into a 12 in (30 cm) round. Leave to rise slightly.

7 ▼ Dimple the surface all over with your finger. Drizzle the remaining oil on top. Slide a floured board under the bread, carry to the oven, and slide off on the hot baking sheet. Bake for about 35 minutes, or until golden brown. Cool on a rack.

Courgette Yeast Bread

SERVES 10

1 lb (450 g) courgettes, grated
2 tablespoons salt
2 teaspoons active dried yeast
½ pint (300 ml) lukewarm water
14 oz (400 g) plain flour
olive oil, for brushing

1 In a colander, alternate the layers of grated courgettes and salt. Leave for 30 minutes, then squeeze out the moisture with your hands.

2 Combine the yeast with 2 fl oz (50 ml) warm water. Leave for 15 minutes.

3 ▲ Place the courgettes, yeast and flour in a bowl. Stir together and add just enough of the remaining water to obtain a rough dough.

4 Transfer to a floured surface and knead until smooth and elastic. Return the dough to the bowl, cover with a plastic bag, and leave to rise in a warm place until doubled in volume, for about 1½ hours.

5 Punch down the risen dough with your fist and knead into a tapered cylinder. Place on a greased baking sheet, cover and leave to rise in a warm place until doubled in volume.

6 ▼ Preheat the oven to 425°F/ 220°C/Gas 7. Brush the bread with olive oil and bake for 40–45 minutes, or until the loaf is a golden colour.

Italian Flat Bread with Sage (top), Courgette Yeast Bread

Olive Bread

MAKES 2 LOAVES

4 teaspoons active dried yeast
16 fl oz (450 ml) warm water
14 oz (400 g) plain flour
6 oz (170 g) wholemeal flour
2½ oz (70 g) cornmeal
2 teaspoons salt
2 tablespoons olive oil
4 oz (115 g) mixed stoned green and black olives, cut in half
cornmeal, for sprinkling

1 Combine the yeast and water, stir and leave for 5 minutes to dissolve.

2 Stir in 8 oz (225 g) of the plain flour, cover and leave in a warm place for 1 hour.

3 In a large mixing bowl, combine the remaining plain flour, the wholemeal flour, cornmeal and salt. Make a well in the centre; pour in the olive oil and yeast mixture.

4 ▼ With a wooden spoon, stir from the centre, incorporating flour with each turn. When the dough becomes stiff, stir with your hands until a rough dough is obtained.

5 Transfer to a floured surface and knead until smooth and elastic. Return to the bowl, cover and leave to rise in a warm place until doubled in volume, about 1½ hours.

6 ▲ Knock back the dough with your fist. Add the olives and knead.

7 Cut the dough in half and shape each half into a round. Sprinkle a baking sheet with cornmeal. Place the rounds on the sheet, seam-side down. Cover and leave to rise until nearly doubled in volume.

8 Place a baking tin in the bottom of the oven and half fill it with hot water. Preheat the oven to 425°F/ 220°C/Gas 7.

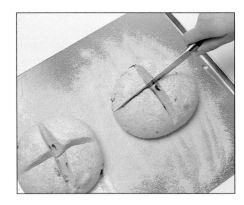

9 ▲ With a sharp knife, score the tops of the loaves. Bake for 20 minutes. Lower the heat to 375°F/ 190°C/Gas 5 and bake for 25–30 minutes more, or until the bottoms sound hollow when tapped. Cool on a wire rack.

Pumpkin Spice Bread

MAKES 1 LOAF

2 tablespoons active dried yeast
8 fl oz (250 ml) lukewarm water
2 teaspoons ground cinnamon
1 teaspoon ground ginger
1 teaspoon ground allspice
¼ teaspoon ground cloves
1 teaspoon salt
3 oz (85 g) dried skimmed milk
6 oz (170 g) cooked or canned pumpkin
12 oz (350 g) sugar
4 oz (115 g) butter, melted
1 lb 6 oz (625 g) plain flour
2 oz (55 g) pecans, finely chopped

1 Using an electric mixer, combine the yeast and water, stir and leave for 15 minutes to dissolve. In another bowl, mix the spices together.

2 To the yeast, add the salt, milk, pumpkin, 115 g (4 oz) of the sugar, 3 tablespoons of the melted butter, 2 teaspoons of the spice mixture and 8 oz (225 g) of the flour.

3 ▲ With the dough hook, mix on low speed until blended. Gradually add the remaining flour and mix on medium speed until a rough dough is formed. Alternatively, mix by hand.

4 Transfer to a floured surface and knead until smooth. Place in a bowl, cover and leave to rise in a warm place until doubled, 1–1½ hours.

5 ▼ Knock back and knead briefly. Divide the dough into thirds. Roll each third into an 18 in (46 cm) rope. Cut each rope into 18 equal pieces, then roll into balls.

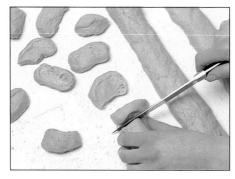

6 Grease a 10 in (25 cm) tube tin. Stir the remaining sugar into the remaining spice mixture. Roll the balls in the remaining melted butter, then in the sugar and spice mixture.

7 ▲ Place 18 balls in the tin and sprinkle over half the pecans. Add the remaining balls, then sprinkle over the remaining pecans. Cover and leave to rise in a warm place until almost doubled, about 45 minutes.

8 Preheat the oven to 350°F/180°C/Gas 4. Bake for 55 minutes. Cool in the tin for 20 minutes, then turn out on a rack. Serve warm.

Walnut Bread

MAKES 1 LOAF

15 oz (420 g) wholemeal flour
5 oz (140 g) strong flour
2½ teaspoons salt
18 fl oz (525 ml) lukewarm water
1 tablespoon honey
1 tablespoon active dried yeast
5 oz (140 g) walnut pieces, plus more for decorating
1 beaten egg, for glazing

1 Combine the flours and salt in a large bowl. Make a well in the centre and add 8 fl oz (250 ml) of the water, the honey and the yeast.

2 Set aside until the yeast dissolves and the mixture is frothy.

3 Add the remaining water. With a wooden spoon, stir from the centre, incorporating flour with each turn, to obtain a smooth dough. Add more flour if the dough is too sticky and use your hands if the dough becomes too stiff to stir.

4 Transfer to a floured board and knead, adding flour if necessary, until the dough is smooth and elastic. Place in a greased bowl and roll the dough around in the bowl to coat thoroughly on all sides.

5 ▲ Cover with a plastic bag and leave in a warm place until doubled in volume, about 1½ hours.

6 ▲ Punch down the dough and knead in the walnuts evenly.

7 Grease a baking sheet. Shape into a round loaf and place on the baking sheet. Press in walnut pieces to decorate the top. Cover loosely with a damp cloth and leave to rise in a warm place until doubled, 25–30 minutes.

8 Preheat a 425°F/220°C/Gas 7 oven.

9 ▲ With a sharp knife, score the top. Brush with the glaze. Bake for 15 minutes. Lower the heat to 375°F/ 190°C/Gas 5 and bake until the bottom sounds hollow when tapped, about 40 minutes. Cool on a rack.

Pecan Rye Bread

MAKES 2 LOAVES

1½ tablespoons active dried yeast
24 fl oz (700 ml) lukewarm water
1 lb 8 oz (700 g) strong flour
1 lb 2 oz (500 g) rye flour
2 tablespoons salt
1 tablespoon honey
2 teaspoons caraway seeds, (optional)
4 oz (115 g) butter, at room temperature
8 oz (225 g) pecans, chopped

1 Combine the yeast and 4 fl oz (125 ml) of the water. Stir and leave for 15 minutes to dissolve.

2 In the bowl of an electric mixer, combine the flours, salt, honey, caraway seeds and butter. With the dough hook, mix on low speed until well blended.

3 Add the yeast mixture and the remaining water and mix on medium speed until the dough forms a ball.

4 ▲ Transfer to a floured surface and knead in the pecans.

5 Return the dough to a bowl, cover with a plastic bag and leave in a warm place until doubled, about 2 hours.

6 Grease 2 8½ × 4½ in (21.5 × 11.5 cm) bread tins.

7 ▲ Punch down the risen dough.

8 Divide the dough in half and form into loaves. Place in the tins, seam-side down. Dust the tops with flour.

9 Cover with plastic bags and leave to rise in a warm place until doubled in volume, about 1 hour.

10 Preheat a 375°F/190°C/Gas 5 oven.

11 ▼ Bake until the bottoms sound hollow when tapped, 45–50 minutes. Cool on racks.

Sticky Buns

MAKES 18

5½ fl oz (170 ml) milk

1 tablespoon active dried yeast

2 tablespoons caster sugar

15 oz–1 lb (420–450 g) strong flour

1 teaspoon salt

4 oz (115 g) cold butter, cut into pieces

2 eggs, lightly beaten

grated rind of 1 lemon

FOR THE TOPPING AND FILLING

10 oz (285 g) dark brown sugar

2½ oz (70 g) butter

4 fl oz (125 ml) water

3 oz (85 g) pecans or walnuts, chopped

3 tablespoons caster sugar

2 teaspoons ground cinnamon

5½ oz (150 g) raisins

1 Heat the milk to lukewarm. Add the yeast and sugar and leave until frothy, about 15 minutes.

2 Combine the flour and salt in a large mixing bowl. Add the butter and rub in with your fingertips until the mixture resembles coarse breadcrumbs.

3 ▲ Make a well in the centre and add the yeast mixture, eggs and lemon rind. With a wooden spoon, stir from the centre, incorporating flour with each turn. When it becomes too stiff, stir by hand to obtain a rough dough.

4 Transfer to a floured surface and knead until smooth and elastic. Return to the bowl, cover with a plastic bag and leave to rise in a warm place until doubled in volume, about 2 hours.

5 Meanwhile, for the topping, make the syrup. Combine the brown sugar, butter and water in a heavy saucepan. Bring to the boil and boil gently until thick and syrupy, about 10 minutes.

6 ▲ Place 1 tablespoon of the syrup in the bottom of each of 18 1½ in (4 cm) muffin cups. Sprinkle in a thin layer of chopped nuts, reserving the rest for the filling.

7 Punch down the dough and transfer to a floured surface. Roll out to an 18 × 12 in (45 × 30 cm) rectangle.

8 ▲ For the filling, combine the caster sugar, cinnamon, raisins and reserved nuts. Sprinkle over the dough in an even layer.

9 ▲ Roll up tightly, from the long side, to form a cylinder.

10 ▲ Cut the cylinder into 1 in (2.5 cm) rounds. Place each in a prepared muffin cup, cut-side up. Leave to rise in a warm place until increased by half, about 30 minutes.

11 Preheat a 350°F/180°C/Gas 4 oven. Place foil under the tins to catch any syrup that bubbles over. Bake until golden, about 25 minutes.

12 Remove from the oven and invert the tins onto a baking sheet. Leave for 3–5 minutes, then remove buns from the tins. Transfer to a rack to cool. Serve sticky-side up.

~ COOK'S TIP ~

To save time and energy, make double the recipe and freeze half for another occasion.

Raisin Bread

MAKES 2 LOAVES

1 tablespoon active dried yeast
16 fl oz (450 ml) lukewarm milk
5 oz (140 g) raisins
2½ oz (70 g) currants
1 tablespoon sherry or brandy
½ teaspoon grated nutmeg
grated rind of 1 large orange
2¼ oz (60 g) sugar
1 tablespoon salt
4 oz (115 g) butter, melted
1 lb 8 oz–1 lb 14 oz (700–850 g) strong flour
1 egg beaten with 1 tablespoon cream, for glazing

1 Stir together the yeast and 4 fl oz (125 ml) of the milk and let stand for 15 minutes to dissolve.

2 ▲ Mix the raisins, currants, sherry or brandy, nutmeg and orange rind together and set aside.

3 In another bowl, mix the remaining milk, sugar, salt and half the butter. Add the yeast mixture. With a wooden spoon, stir in half the flour, 5 oz (140 g) at a time, until blended. Add the remaining flour as needed for a stiff dough.

4 Transfer to a floured surface and knead until smooth and elastic. Place in a greased bowl, cover and leave to rise in a warm place until doubled in volume, about 2½ hours.

5 Punch down the dough, return to the bowl, cover and leave to rise in a warm place for 30 minutes.

6 Grease 2 8½ × 4½ in (21.5 × 11.5 cm) bread tins. Divide the dough in half and roll each half into a 20 × 7 in (50 × 18 cm) rectangle.

7 ▲ Brush the rectangles with the remaining melted butter. Sprinkle over the raisin mixture, then roll up tightly, tucking in the ends slightly as you roll. Place in the prepared tins, cover, and leave to rise until almost doubled in volume.

8 ▲ Preheat a 400°F/200°C/Gas 6 oven. Brush the loaves with the glaze. Bake for 20 minutes. Lower to 350°F/180°C/Gas 4 and bake until golden, 25–30 minutes more. Cool on racks.

Prune Bread

MAKES 1 LOAF

8 oz (225 g) dried prunes
1 tablespoon active dried yeast
3 oz (85 g) wholemeal flour
13½–15 oz (385–420 g) strong flour
½ teaspoon bicarbonate of soda
1 teaspoon salt
1 teaspoon pepper
1 oz (30 g) butter, at room temperature
6 fl oz (175 ml) buttermilk
2 oz (55 g) walnuts, chopped
milk, for glazing

1 Simmer the prunes in water to cover until soft, or soak overnight. Drain, reserving 2 fl oz (65 ml) of the soaking liquid. Stone and chop the prunes.

2 Combine the yeast and the reserved prune liquid, stir and leave for 15 minutes to dissolve.

3 In a large bowl, stir together the flours, bicarbonate of soda, salt and pepper. Make a well in the centre.

4 ▲ Add the chopped prunes, butter, and buttermilk. Pour in the yeast mixture. With a wooden spoon, stir from the centre, incorporating more flour with each turn, to obtain a rough dough.

5 Transfer to a floured surface and knead until smooth and elastic. Return to the bowl, cover with a plastic bag and leave to rise in a warm place until doubled in volume, about 1½ hours.

6 Grease a baking sheet.

7 ▲ Punch down the dough with your fist, then knead in the walnuts.

8 Shape the dough into a long, cylindrical loaf. Place on the baking sheet, cover loosely, and leave to rise in a warm place for 45 minutes.

9 Preheat a 425°F/220°C/Gas 7 oven.

10 ▼ With a sharp knife, score the top deeply. Brush with milk and bake for 15 minutes. Lower to 375°F/190°C/Gas 5 and bake until the bottom sounds hollow when tapped, about 35 minutes more. Cool.

Plaited Prune Bread

MAKES 1 LOAF

1 tbsp active dry yeast
2 fl oz (65 ml) lukewarm water
2 fl oz (65 ml) lukewarm milk
2 oz (55 g) caster sugar
½ tsp salt
1 egg
2 oz (55 g) butter, at room temperature
15 oz–1 lb 2 oz (420–500 g) plain flour
1 egg beaten with 2 tsp water, for glazing
FOR THE FILLING
7 oz (200 g) cooked prunes
2 tsp grated lemon rind
1 tsp grated orange rind
¼ tsp freshly grated nutmeg
1½ oz (45 g) butter, melted
2 oz (55 g) very finely chopped walnuts
2 tbsp caster sugar

1 In a large bowl, combine the yeast and water, stir and leave for 15 minutes to dissolve.

2 Stir in the milk, sugar, salt, egg and butter. Gradually stir in 12 oz (350 g) of the flour to obtain a soft dough.

3 Transfer to a floured surface and knead in just enough flour to obtain a dough that is smooth and elastic. Put into a clean bowl, cover and leave to rise in a warm place until doubled in volume, about 1½ hours.

~ VARIATION ~

For Plaited Apricot Bread, replace the prunes with the same amount of dried apricots. It is not necessary to cook them, but to soften, soak them in hot tea and discard the liquid before using.

4 ▲ Meanwhile, for the filling, combine the prunes, lemon and orange rinds, nutmeg, butter, walnuts and sugar and stir together to blend. Set aside.

5 Grease a large baking sheet. Punch down the dough and transfer to a lightly floured surface. Knead briefly, then roll out into a 15 × 10 in (38 × 25 cm) rectangle. Carefully transfer to the baking sheet.

6 ▲ Spread the filling in the centre.

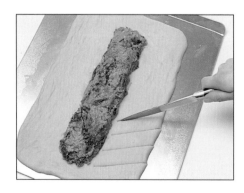

7 ▲ With a sharp knife, cut 10 strips at an angle on either side of the filling, cutting just to the filling.

8 ▲ For a plaited pattern, fold up one end neatly, then fold over the strips from alternating sides until all the strips are folded over. Tuck excess dough underneath at the ends.

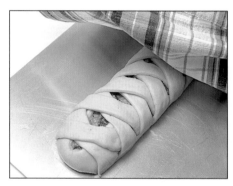

9 ▲ Cover loosely with a tea towel and leave to rise in a warm place until almost doubled in volume.

10 ▲ Preheat a 375°F/190°C/Gas 5 oven. Brush with the glaze. Bake until browned, about 30 minutes. Transfer to a rack to cool.

Kugelhopf

MAKES 1 LOAF

3¾ oz (110 g) raisins

1 tablespoon kirsch or brandy

1 tablespoon active dried yeast

4 fl oz (125 ml) lukewarm water

4 oz (115 g) unsalted butter, at room temperature

3½ oz (100 g) sugar

3 eggs, at room temperature

grated rind of 1 lemon

1 teaspoon salt

½ teaspoon vanilla essence

15 oz (420 g) strong flour

4 fl oz (125 ml) milk

1 oz (30 g) flaked almonds

3¼ oz (90 g) whole blanched almonds, chopped

icing sugar, for dusting

1 ▼ In a bowl, combine the raisins and kirsch or brandy. Set aside.

2 Combine the yeast and water, stir and leave for 15 minutes to dissolve.

3 With an electric mixer, cream the butter and sugar until thick and fluffy. Beat in the eggs, one at a time. Add the lemon rind, salt and vanilla. Stir in the yeast mixture.

4 ▲ Add the flour, alternating with the milk, until the mixture is well blended. Cover and leave to rise in a warm place until doubled in volume, about 2 hours.

5 ▲ Grease a 4½ pt kugelhopf mould, then sprinkle the flaked almonds evenly over the bottom.

6 Work the raisins and almonds into the dough, then spoon into the mould. Cover with a plastic bag, and leave to rise in a warm place until the dough almost reaches the top of the tin, about 1 hour.

7 Preheat a 350°F/180°C/Gas 4 oven.

8 Bake until golden brown, about 45 minutes. If the top browns too quickly, protect with a sheet of foil. Let cool in the tin for 15 minutes, then turn out onto a rack. Dust the top lightly with icing sugar before serving.

Panettone

MAKES 1 LOAF

5 fl oz (150 ml) lukewarm milk
1 tablespoon active dried yeast
12–14 oz (350–400 g) plain flour
2½ oz (70 g) sugar
2 teaspoons salt
2 eggs
5 egg yolks
6 oz (170 g) unsalted butter, at room temperature
4½ oz (125 g) raisins
grated rind of 1 lemon
3 oz (85 g) mixed peel

1 Combine the milk and yeast in a large warmed bowl and leave for 10 minutes to dissolve.

2 Stir in 4 oz (115 g) of the flour, cover loosely and leave in a warm place for 30 minutes.

3 Sift over the remaining flour and stir into the dough mixture. Make a well in the centre and add the sugar, salt, eggs and egg yolks.

4 ▲ Stir with a wooden spoon until stiff, then stir with your hands to obtain a very elastic and sticky dough. Add a little more flour if necessary, but keep the dough as soft as possible.

5 ▲ To incorporate the butter, smear it over the dough, then work it in with your hands. When the butter is evenly distributed, cover and leave to rise in a warm place until doubled in volume, 3–4 hours.

6 Grease a 3½ pint (2 litre) charlotte tin or a 2 lb 4 oz (1 kg) coffee tin and line the bottom with greaseproof paper. Grease the paper.

7 Knock back the dough and transfer to a floured surface. Knead in the raisins, lemon rind and mixed peel.

8 ▲ Put the dough in the tin. Cover and leave to rise in a warm place until it is well above the top of the tin, about 2 hours.

9 Preheat the oven to 400°F/200°C/Gas 6. Bake for 15 minutes, cover the top with foil and lower the heat to 350°F/180°C/Gas 4. Bake for 30 minutes more. Cool in the tin for 5 minutes, then transfer to a rack.

Danish Wreath

¼ oz (7 g) active dried yeast
6 fl oz (175 ml) lukewarm milk
2 oz (55 g) caster sugar
1 lb (450 g) strong flour
½ teaspoon salt
½ teaspoon vanilla essence
1 egg, beaten
2 × 4 oz (115 g) blocks unsalted butter
1 egg yolk beaten with 2 teaspoons water, for glazing
4 oz (115 g) icing sugar
1–2 tablespoons water
chopped pecans or walnuts, for sprinkling

FOR THE FILLING

7 oz (200 g) dark brown sugar
1 teaspoon ground cinnamon
2 oz (55 g) pecans or walnuts, toasted and chopped

1 Combine the yeast, milk and ½ teaspoon of the sugar. Stir and leave for 15 minutes to dissolve.

2 Combine the flour, sugar and salt. Make a well in the centre and add the yeast mixture, vanilla and egg. Stir until a rough dough is formed.

3 Transfer to a floured surface and knead until smooth and elastic. Wrap and refrigerate for 15 minutes.

~ **VARIATION** ~

For a different filling, substitute
3 tart apples, peeled and grated,
the grated rind of 1 lemon,
1 tablespoon lemon juice,
½ teaspoon ground cinnamon,
3 tablespoons sugar, 1¼ oz
(35 g) currants, and 1 oz (30 g)
chopped walnuts. Combine well
and use as described.

4 ▲ Meanwhile, place the butter between two sheets of greaseproof paper. With a rolling pin, flatten to form 2 6 × 4 in (15 × 10 cm) rectangles. Set aside.

5 ▲ Roll out the dough to a 12 × 8 in (30 × 20 cm) rectangle. Place one butter rectangle in the centre. Fold the bottom third of dough over the butter and seal the edge. Place the other butter rectangle on top and cover with the top third of the dough.

6 Turn the dough so the shorter side faces you. Roll into an 12 × 8 in (30 × 20 cm) rectangle. Fold into thirds, and indent one edge with your finger to indicate the first turn. Wrap in clear film and refrigerate for 30 minutes.

7 Repeat two more times; rolling, folding, marking and chilling between each turn. After the third fold refrigerate for 1–2 hours, or longer.

8 Grease a large baking sheet. In a bowl, stir together all the filling ingredients until blended.

9 ▲ Roll out the dough to a 25 × 6 in (3 × 15 cm) strip. Spread over the filling, leaving a ½ in (1 cm) border.

10 Roll up the dough lengthways into a cylinder. Place on the baking sheet and form into a circle, pinching the edges together to seal. Cover with an inverted bowl and leave in a warm place to rise for 45 minutes.

11 ▲ Preheat the oven to 400°F/ 200°C/Gas 6. Slash the top every 2 in (5 cm), cutting about ½ in (1 cm) deep. Brush with the egg glaze. Bake until golden, 35–40 minutes. Cool on a rack. To serve, mix the icing sugar and water, then drizzle over the wreath. Sprinkle with the pecans or walnuts.

PIES & TARTS

~

Here is every sort of filling – from orchard fruits to
autumn nuts, tangy citrus to luscious chocolate – for the
most memorable pies and tarts. Some are plain and
some are fancy, but all are delicious.

Plum Pie

SERVES 8

2 lb (900 g) red or purple plums

grated rind of 1 lemon

1 tbsp fresh lemon juice

4–6 oz (115–170 g) caster sugar

3 tbsp quick-cooking tapioca

⅛ tsp salt

½ tsp ground cinnamon

¼ tsp grated nutmeg

FOR THE PASTRY

10 oz (285 g) plain flour

1 tsp salt

3 oz (85 g) cold butter, cut in pieces

2 oz (55 g) cold vegetable fat or lard, cut in pieces

2–4 fl oz (65–125 ml) iced water

milk, for glazing

1 ▼ For the pastry, sift the flour and salt into a bowl. Add the butter and fat and cut in with a pastry blender until the mixture resembles coarse breadcrumbs.

2 Stir in just enough water to bind the pastry. Gather into 2 balls, 1 slightly larger than the other. Wrap and refrigerate for 20 minutes.

3 Preheat a baking sheet in the centre of a 425°F/220°C/Gas 7 oven.

4 On a lightly floured surface, roll out the larger pastry ball to about ⅛ in (3 mm) thick. Transfer to a 9 in (23 cm) pie dish and trim the edge.

5 ▲ Halve the plums, discard the stones, and cut in large pieces. Mix all the filling ingredients together (if the plums are very tart, use extra sugar). Transfer to the pastry case.

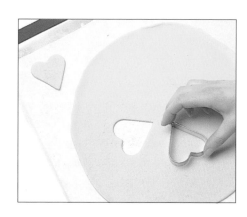

6 ▲ Roll out the remaining pastry and place on a baking tray lined with greaseproof paper. With a cutter, stamp out 4 hearts. Transfer the pastry lid to the pie using the paper.

7 Trim to leave a ¾ in (2 cm) overhang. Fold the top edge under the bottom and pinch to seal. Arrange the hearts on top. Brush with the milk. Bake for 15 minutes. Reduce the heat to 350°F/180°C/Gas 4 and bake 30–35 minutes more. If the crust browns too quickly, protect with a sheet of foil.

Lattice Berry Pie

SERVES 8

1 lb (450 g) berries, such as bilberries, blueberries, blackcurrants etc
4 oz (115 g) caster sugar
3 tbsp cornflour
2 tbsp fresh lemon juice
1 oz (30 g) butter, diced
FOR THE PASTRY
10 oz (285 g) plain flour
¾ tsp salt
4 oz (115 g) cold butter, cut in pieces
1½ oz (45 g) cold vegetable fat or lard, cut in pieces
5–6 tbsp iced water
1 egg beaten with 1 tbsp water, for glazing

1 For the pastry, sift the flour and salt into a bowl. Add the butter and fat and cut in with a pastry blender until the mixture resembles coarse breadcrumbs. With a fork, stir in just enough water to bind the pastry. Form into 2 balls, wrap in greaseproof paper, and refrigerate for 20 minutes.

2 On a lightly floured surface, roll out one ball about ⅛ in (3 mm) thick. Transfer to a 9 in (23 cm) pie dish and trim to leave a ½ in (1 cm) overhang. Brush the bottom with egg glaze.

3 ▲ Mix all the filling ingredients together, except the butter (reserve a few berries for decoration). Spoon into the pastry case and dot with the butter. Brush the egg glaze around the rim of the pastry case.

4 Preheat a baking sheet in the centre of a 425°F/220°C/Gas 7 oven.

5 ▼ Roll out the remaining pastry on a baking tray lined with greaseproof paper. With a serrated pastry wheel, cut out 24 thin pastry strips. Roll out the scraps and cut out leaf shapes. Mark veins in the leaves with the point of a knife.

6 ▲ Weave the strips in a close lattice, then transfer to the pie using the paper. Press the edges to seal and trim. Arrange the pastry leaves around the rim. Brush with egg glaze.

7 Bake for 10 minutes. Reduce the heat to 350°F/180°C/Gas 4 and bake until the pastry is golden, 40–45 minutes more. Decorate with berries.

Raspberry Tart

SERVES 8

4 egg yolks
2½ oz (70 g) caster sugar
3 tbsp plain flour
10 fl oz (300 ml) milk
⅛ tsp salt
½ tsp vanilla essence
1 lb (450 g) fresh raspberries
5 tbsp red currant jelly
1 tbsp fresh orange juice
FOR THE PASTRY
6½ oz (190 g) plain flour
½ tsp baking powder
¼ tsp salt
1 tbsp sugar
grated rind of ½ orange
3 oz (85 g) cold butter, cut in pieces
1 egg yolk
3–4 tbsp whipping cream

1 For the pastry, sift the flour, baking powder and salt into a bowl. Stir in the sugar and orange rind. Add the butter and cut in with a pastry blender until the mixture resembles coarse breadcrumbs. Stir in the egg yolk and just enough cream to bind the dough. Gather into a ball, wrap in greaseproof paper and refrigerate.

2 For the custard filling, beat the egg yolks and sugar until thick and lemon-coloured. Gradually stir in the flour.

3 In a saucepan, bring the milk and salt just to the boil, then remove from the heat. Whisk into the egg yolk mixture, return to the pan and continue whisking over moderately high heat until just bubbling. Cook for 3 minutes to thicken. Transfer immediately to a bowl. Add the vanilla and stir to blend.

4 ▲ Cover with greaseproof paper to prevent a skin from forming.

5 ▲ Preheat a 400°F/200°C/Gas 6 oven. On a floured surface, roll out the pastry ⅛ in (3 mm) thick, transfer to a 10 in (25 cm) pie dish and trim. Prick the bottom with a fork and line with crumpled greaseproof. Fill with baking beans and bake for 15 minutes. Remove the paper and beans. Continue baking until golden, 6–8 minutes more. Let cool.

6 ▲ Spread an even layer of the pastry cream filling in the pastry case and arrange the raspberries on top. Melt the jelly and orange juice in a pan and brush on top to glaze.

Rhubarb and Cherry Pie

1 lb (450 g) rhubarb, cut into 1 in (2.5 cm) pieces

1 lb (450 g) canned stoned tart red or black cherries, drained

10 oz (285 g) caster sugar

1 oz (30 g) quick-cooking tapioca

FOR THE PASTRY

10 oz (285 g) plain flour

1 tsp salt

3 oz (85 g) cold butter, cut in pieces

2 oz (55 g) cold vegetable fat or lard, cut in pieces

2–4 fl oz (65–125 ml) iced water

milk, for glazing

1 ▲ For the pastry, sift the flour and salt into a bowl. Add the butter and fat to the dry ingredients and cut in with a pastry blender until the mixture resembles coarse breadcrumbs.

2 With a fork, stir in just enough water to bind the pastry. Gather into 2 balls, 1 slightly larger than the other. Wrap the pastry in greaseproof paper and refrigerate for at least 20 minutes.

3 Preheat a baking sheet in the centre of a 400°F/200°C/Gas 6 oven.

4 On a lightly floured surface, roll out the larger pastry ball to a thickness of about ⅛ in (3 mm).

5 ▼ Roll the pastry around the rolling pin and transfer to a 9 in (23 cm) pie dish. Trim the edge to leave a ½ in (1 cm) overhang.

6 Refrigerate the pastry case while making the filling.

7 In a mixing bowl, combine the rhubarb, cherries, sugar and tapioca and spoon into the pie shell.

8 ▲ Roll out the remaining pastry and cut out leaf shapes.

9 Transfer the pastry lid to the pie and trim to leave a ¾ in (2 cm) overhang. Fold the top edge under the bottom and flute. Roll small balls from the scraps. Mark veins in the pastry leaves and place on top with the balls.

10 Glaze the top and bake until golden, 40–50 minutes.

Peach Leaf Pie

SERVES 8

2 lb 8 oz (1.2 kg) ripe peaches
juice of 1 lemon
3½ oz (100 g) sugar
3 tablespoons cornflour
¼ teaspoon grated nutmeg
½ teaspoon ground cinnamon
1 oz (30 g) butter, diced

FOR THE CRUST

10 oz (285 g) plain flour
¾ teaspoon salt
4 oz (115 g) cold butter, cut into pieces
2¼ oz (60 g) cold vegetable fat or lard, cut into pieces
5–6 tablespoons iced water
1 egg beaten with 1 tablespoon water, for glazing

1 For the pastry, sift the flour and salt into a bowl. Add the butter and fat and rub in with your fingertips until the mixture resembles coarse breadcrumbs.

2 ▲ With a fork, stir in just enough water to bind the dough. Gather into 2 balls, one slightly larger than the other. Wrap in clear film and refrigerate for at least 20 minutes.

3 Place a baking sheet in the oven and preheat to 425°F/220°C/Gas 7.

4 ▲ Drop a few peaches at a time into boiling water for 20 seconds, then transfer to a bowl of cold water. When cool, peel off the skins.

5 Slice the peaches and combine with the lemon juice, sugar, cornstarch and spices. Set aside.

6 ▲ On a lightly floured surface, roll out the larger dough ball about ⅛ in (3 mm) thick. Transfer to a 9 in (23 cm) pie tin and trim. Refrigerate.

7 ▲ Roll out the remaining dough ¼ in (5 mm) thick. Cut out leaf shapes 3 in (8 cm) long, using a template if needed. Mark veins with a knife. With the scraps, roll a few balls.

8 ▲ Brush the bottom of the pastry shell with egg glaze. Add the peaches, piling them higher in the centre. Dot with the butter.

9 ▲ To assemble, start from the outside edge and cover the peaches with a ring of leaves. Place a second ring of leaves above, staggering the positions. Continue with rows of leaves until covered. Place the balls in the centre. Brush with glaze.

10 Bake for 10 minutes. Lower the heat to 350°F/180°C/Gas 4 and bake for 35–40 minutes more.

~ COOK'S TIP ~

Baking the pie on a preheated baking sheet helps to make the bottom crust crisp. The moisture from the filling keeps the bottom crust more humid than the top, but this baking method helps to compensate for the top crust being better exposed to the heat source.

Peach Tart with Almond Cream

SERVES 8–10

4 large ripe peaches
4 oz (115 g) blanched almonds
2 tbsp plain flour
3½ oz (100 g) unsalted butter, at room temperature
4 oz (115 g) plus 2 tbsp caster sugar
1 egg
1 egg yolk
½ tsp vanilla essence, or 2 tsp rum
FOR THE PASTRY
6½ oz (190 g) plain flour
¾ tsp salt
3½ oz (100 g) cold unsalted butter, cut in pieces
1 egg yolk
2½–3 tbsp iced water

1 ▲ For the pastry, sift the flour and salt into a bowl.

2 Add the butter and cut in with a pastry blender until the mixture resembles coarse breadcrumbs. Stir in the egg yolk and just enough water to bind the pastry. Gather into a ball, wrap in greaseproof paper, and refrigerate for at least 20 minutes.

3 Preheat a baking sheet in the centre of a 400°F/200°C/Gas 6 oven.

4 ▲ On a floured surface, roll out the pastry ⅛ in (3 mm) thick. Transfer to a 10 in (25 cm) pie dish. Trim the edge, prick the bottom and refrigerate.

5 ▲ Score the bottoms of the peaches. Drop the peaches, 1 at a time, into boiling water. Boil for 20 seconds, then dip in cold water. Peel off the skins using a sharp knife.

6 ▲ Grind the almonds finely with the flour in a food processor, blender or grinder. With an electric mixer, cream the butter and 4 oz (115 g) of the sugar until light and fluffy. Gradually beat in the egg and yolk. Stir in the almonds and vanilla or rum. Spread in the pastry case.

7 ▲ Halve the peaches and remove the stones. Cut crosswise in thin slices and arrange on top of the almond cream like the spokes of a wheel; keep the slices of each peach-half together. Fan out by pressing down gently at a slight angle.

8 ▲ Bake until the pastry begins to brown, 10–15 minutes. Lower the heat to 350°F/180°C/Gas 4 and continue baking until the almond cream sets, about 15 minutes more. Ten minutes before the end of the cooking time, sprinkle with the remaining 2 tablespoons of sugar.

~ **VARIATION** ~

For a Nectarine and Apricot Tart with Almond Cream, replace the peaches with nectarines, prepared and arranged the same way. Peel and chop 3 fresh apricots. Fill the spaces between the fanned-out nectarines with 1 tablespoon of chopped apricots. Bake as above.

Apple and Cranberry Lattice Pie

SERVES 8

grated rind of 1 orange
3 tablespoons fresh orange juice
2 large, tart cooking apples
6 oz (170 g) cranberries
2½ oz (70 g) raisins
1 oz (30 g) walnuts, chopped
7½ oz (215 g) caster sugar
4 oz (115 g) dark brown sugar
2 tablespoons plain flour
FOR THE CRUST
10 oz (285 g) plain flour
½ teaspoon salt
3 oz (85 g) cold butter, cut into pieces
3 oz (85 g) cold vegetable fat or lard, cut into pieces
2–4 fl oz (65–125 ml) iced water

1 ▼ For the crust, sift the flour and salt into a bowl. Add the butter and fat and rub in with your fingertips until the mixture resembles coarse breadcrumbs. With a fork, stir in just enough water to bind the dough. Gather into 2 equal balls, wrap in cling film, and refrigerate for at least 20 minutes.

2 ▲ Put the orange rind and juice into a mixing bowl. Peel and core the apples and grate into the bowl. Stir in the cranberries, raisins, walnuts, all except 1 tablespoon of the caster sugar, the brown sugar and flour.

3 Place a baking sheet in the oven and preheat to 400°F/200°C/Gas 6.

4 On a lightly floured surface, roll out 1 ball of dough about ⅛ in (3 mm) thick. Transfer to a 9 in (23 cm) pie plate and trim. Spoon the cranberry and apple mixture into the shell.

5 ▲ Roll out the remaining dough to a circle about 11 in (28 cm) in diameter. With a serrated pastry wheel, cut the dough into 10 strips, ¾ in (2 cm) wide. Place 5 strips horizontally across the top of the tart at 1 in (2.5 cm) intervals. Weave in 5 vertical strips and trim. Sprinkle the top with the remaining sugar.

6 Bake for 20 minutes. Reduce the heat to 350°F/180°C/Gas 4 and bake until the crust is golden and the filling is bubbling, about 15 minutes more.

Open Apple Pie

SERVES 8

3 lb (1.4 kg) sweet-tart firm eating or cooking apples

1¾ oz (50 g) sugar

2 teaspoons ground cinnamon

grated rind and juice of 1 lemon

1 oz (30 g) butter, diced

2–3 tablespoons honey

FOR THE CRUST

10 oz (285 g) plain flour

½ teaspoon salt

4 oz (115 g) cold butter, cut into pieces

2¼ oz (60 g) cold vegetable fat or lard, cut into pieces

5–6 tablespoons iced water

1 For the crust, sift the flour and salt into a bowl. Add the butter and fat and rub in with your fingertips until the mixture resembles coarse breadcrumbs.

2 ▲ With a fork, stir in just enough water to bind the dough. Gather into a ball, wrap in clear film, and refrigerate for at least 20 minutes.

3 Place a baking sheet in the centre of the oven and preheat to 400°F/200°C/Gas 6.

4 ▼ Peel, core, and slice the apples. Combine the sugar and cinnamon in a bowl. Add the apples, lemon rind and juice and stir.

5 On a lightly floured surface, roll out the dough to a circle about 12 in (30 cm) in diameter. Transfer to a 9 in (23 cm) diameter deep pie dish; leave the dough hanging over the edge. Fill with the apple slices.

6 ▲ Fold in the edges and crimp loosely for a decorative border. Dot the apples with diced butter.

7 Bake on the hot sheet until the pastry is golden and the apples are tender, about 45 minutes.

8 Melt the honey in a saucepan and brush over the apples to glaze. Serve warm or at room temperature.

Apple Pie

SERVES 8

2 lb (900 g) tart cooking apples
2 tbsp plain flour
4 oz (115 g) caster sugar
1½ tbsp fresh lemon juice
½ tsp ground cinnamon
½ tsp ground allspice
¼ tsp ground ginger
¼ tsp grated nutmeg
¼ tsp salt
2 oz (55 g) butter, diced

FOR THE PASTRY

10 oz (285 g) plain flour
1 tsp salt
3 oz (85 g) cold butter, cut in pieces
2 oz (55 g) cold vegetable fat or lard, cut in pieces
2–4 fl oz (65–125 ml) iced water

1 ▲ For the crust, sift the flour and salt into a bowl.

2 Add the butter and fat and cut in with a pastry blender or rub between your fingertips until the mixture resembles coarse breadcrumbs. With a fork, stir in just enough water to bind the pastry.

3 ▲ Form 2 balls, wrap in greaseproof paper and refrigerate for 20 minutes.

4 ▲ On a lightly floured surface, roll out 1 ball ⅛ in (3 mm) thick. Transfer to a 9 in (23 cm) pie dish and trim the edge. Preheat a baking sheet in the centre of a 425°F/220°C/Gas 7 oven.

5 ▲ Peel, core and slice the apples into a bowl. Toss with the flour, sugar, lemon juice, spices and salt. Spoon into pie shell; dot with butter.

6 ▲ Roll out the remaining pastry. Place on top of the pie and trim to leave a ¾ in (2 cm) overhang. Fold the overhang under the pastry base and press to seal. Crimp the edge.

7 ▲ Roll out the scraps and cut out leaf shapes and roll balls. Arrange on top of the pie. Cut steam vents.

8 Bake for 10 minutes. Reduce the heat to 350°F/180°C/Gas 4 and bake until golden, 40–45 minutes more. If the pie browns too quickly, protect with foil.

~ COOK'S TIP ~

Instead of using cooking apples, choose crisp eaters such as Granny Smith, that will not soften too much during cooking.

Pear and Apple Crumble Pie

SERVES 8

3 firm pears

4 cooking apples

6 oz (170 g) caster sugar

2 tbsp cornflour

⅛ tsp salt

grated rind of 1 lemon

2 tbsp fresh lemon juice

3 oz (85 g) raisins

3 oz (85 g) plain flour

1 tsp ground cinnamon

3 oz (85 g) cold butter, cut in pieces

FOR THE PASTRY

5 oz (140 g) plain flour

½ tsp salt

2½ oz (70 g) cold vegetable fat or lard,
    cut in pieces

2 tbsp iced water

1 For the pastry, combine the flour and salt in a bowl. Add the fat and cut in with a pastry blender until the mixture resembles coarse breadcrumbs. Stir in just enough water to bind the pastry. Gather into a ball and transfer to a lightly floured surface. Roll out ⅛ in (3 mm) thick.

2 ▲ Transfer to a shallow 9 in (23 cm) pie dish and trim to leave a ½ in (1 cm) overhang. Fold the overhang under for double thickness. Flute the edge. Refrigerate.

3 Preheat a baking sheet in the centre of a 450°F/230°C/Gas 8 oven.

4 ▲ Peel and core the pears. Slice them into a bowl. Peel, core and slice the apples. Add to the pears. Stir in one-third of the sugar, the cornflour, salt and lemon rind. Add the lemon juice and raisins and stir to blend.

5 For the crumble topping, combine the remaining sugar, flour, cinnamon, and butter in a bowl. Blend with your fingertips until the mixture resembles coarse breadcrumbs. Set aside.

6 ▲ Spoon the fruit filling into the pastry case. Sprinkle the crumbs lightly and evenly over the top.

7 Bake for 10 minutes, then reduce the heat to 350°F/180°C/Gas 4. Cover the top of the pie loosely with a sheet of foil and continue baking until browned, 35–40 minutes more.

Chocolate Pear Tart

SERVES 8

4 oz (115 g) plain chocolate, grated

3 large firm, ripe pears

1 egg

1 egg yolk

4 fl oz (125 ml) single cream

½ tsp vanilla essence

3 tbsp caster sugar

FOR THE PASTRY

5 oz (140 g) plain flour

⅛ tsp salt

2 tbsp sugar

4 oz (115 g) cold unsalted butter, cut into pieces

1 egg yolk

1 tbsp fresh lemon juice

1 For the pastry, sift the flour and salt into a bowl. Add the sugar and butter. Cut in with a pastry blender until the mixture resembles coarse breadcrumbs. Stir in the egg yolk and lemon juice until the mixture forms a ball. Wrap in greaseproof paper, and refrigerate for at least 20 minutes.

2 Preheat a baking sheet in the centre of a 400°F/200°C/Gas 6 oven.

3 On a lightly floured surface, roll out the pastry ⅛ in (3 mm) thick. Transfer to a 10 in (25 cm) tart dish and trim.

4 ▲ Sprinkle the bottom of the case with the grated chocolate.

5 ▲ Peel, halve and core the pears. Cut in thin slices crosswise, then fan them out slightly.

6 Transfer the pear halves to the tart with the help of a metal spatula and arrange on top of the chocolate like the spokes of a wheel.

7 ▼ Whisk together the egg and egg yolk, cream and vanilla. Ladle over the pears, then sprinkle with sugar.

8 Bake for 10 minutes. Reduce the heat to 350°F/180°C/Gas 4 and cook until the custard is set and the pears begin to caramelize, about 20 minutes more. Serve warm.

Caramelized Upside-Down Pear Pie

SERVES 8

5–6 firm, ripe pears
6 oz (170 g) sugar
4 oz (115 g) unsalted butter
whipped cream, for serving
FOR THE PASTRY
4 oz (115 g) plain flour
¼ teaspoon salt
4½ oz (125 g) cold butter, cut into pieces
1½ oz (45 g) cold vegetable fat, cut into pieces
4 tablespoons iced water

1 ▲ For the pastry, combine the flour and salt in a bowl. Add the butter and vegetable fat and cut in with a pastry blender until the mixture resembles coarse crumbs. With a fork, stir in enough iced water to bind the dough. Gather into a ball, wrap in clear film and refrigerate for at least 20 minutes. Preheat the oven to 400°F/200°C/Gas 6.

~ VARIATION ~

For Caramelized Upside-Down Apple Pie, replace the pears with 8–9 firm, tart apples. There may seem to be too many apples, but they shrink slightly as they cook.

2 ▲ Quarter, peel and core the pears. Place in a bowl and toss with a few tablespoons of the sugar.

3 ▲ In a 10½ in (27 cm) ovenproof frying pan, melt the butter over moderately high heat. Add the remaining sugar. When it starts to colour, arrange the pears evenly around the edge and in the centre.

4 ▲ Continue cooking, uncovered, until caramelized, about 20 minutes.

5 ▲ Let the fruit cool. Roll out a circle of dough slightly larger than the diameter of the pan. Place the dough on top of the pears, tucking it around the edges. Transfer the pan to the oven and bake for 15 minutes, then reduce the heat to 350°F/180°C/Gas 4. Bake until golden, about 15 minutes more.

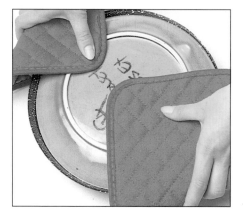

6 ▲ Let the pie cool in the pan for about 3–4 minutes. Run a knife around the edge of the pan to loosen the pie, ensuring that the knife reaches down to the bottom of the pan. Invert a plate on top and, protecting your hands with oven gloves, hold plate and pan firmly, and turn them both over quickly.

7 Lift off the pan. If any pears stick to the pan, remove them gently with a metal spatula and replace them carefully on the pie. Serve warm, with the whipped cream passed separately.

Lime Tart

SERVES 8

3 large egg yolks

1 × 14 oz (400 g) can sweetened condensed milk

1 tbsp grated lime rind

4 fl oz (125 ml) fresh lime juice

green food colouring (optional)

4 fl oz (125 ml) whipping cream

FOR THE BASE

4 oz (115 g) digestive biscuits, crushed

2½ oz (70 g) butter or margarine, melted

1   Preheat a 350°F/180°C/Gas 4 oven.

2 ▲ For the base, place the crushed biscuits in a bowl and add the butter or margarine. Mix to combine.

~ **VARIATION** ~

Use lemons instead of limes, with yellow food colouring.

3   Press the mixture evenly over the bottom and sides of a 9 in (23 cm) pie dish. Bake for 8 minutes. Let cool.

4 ▲ Beat the yolks until thick. Beat in the milk, lime rind and juice and colouring, if using. Pour into the pastry case and refrigerate until set, about 4 hours. To serve, whip the cream. Pipe a lattice pattern on top, or spoon dollops around the edge.

Fruit Tartlets

MAKES 8

6 fl oz (175 ml) red currant jelly

1 tbsp fresh lemon juice

6 fl oz (175 ml) whipping cream

1½ lb (700 g) fresh fruit, such as strawberries, raspberries, kiwi fruit, peaches, grapes or currants, peeled and sliced as necessary

FOR THE PASTRY

5 oz (140 g) cold butter, cut in pieces

2½ oz (65 g) dark brown sugar

3 tbsp cocoa powder

7 oz (200 g) plain flour

1 egg white

1   For the pastry, combine the butter, brown sugar and cocoa over low heat. When the butter is melted, remove from the heat and sift over the flour. Stir, then add just enough egg white to bind the mixture. Gather into a ball, wrap in greaseproof paper, and refrigerate for 30 minutes.

2 ▲ Grease 8 3 in (8 cm) tartlet tins. Roll out the pastry between 2 sheets of greaseproof paper. Stamp out 8 4 in (10 cm) rounds with a fluted cutter.

3   Line the tartlet tins. Prick the bottoms. Refrigerate for 15 minutes. Preheat a 350°F/180°C/Gas 4 oven.

4   Bake until firm, 20–25 minutes. Cool, then remove from the tins.

5 ▲ Melt the jelly with the lemon juice. Brush a thin layer in the bottom of the tartlets. Whip the cream and spread a thin layer in the tartlet cases. Arrange the fruit on top. Brush with the glaze and serve.

Lime Tart (top), Fruit Tartlets

Chocolate Lemon Tart

SERVES 8–10

8¾oz (240g) caster sugar

6 eggs

grated rind of 2 lemons

5½floz (170ml) fresh lemon juice

5½floz (170ml) whipping cream

chocolate curls, for decorating

FOR THE CRUST

6¼oz (180g) plain flour

2 tablespoons unsweetened cocoa powder

1oz (30g) icing sugar

½ teaspoon salt

4oz (115g) butter or margarine

1 tablespoon water

1 ▲ Grease a 10in (25cm) tart tin.

2 For the crust, sift the flour, cocoa powder, icing sugar and salt into a bowl. Set aside.

3 ▲ Melt the butter and water over a low heat. Pour over the flour mixture and stir with a wooden spoon until the dough is smooth and the flour has absorbed all the liquid.

4 Press the dough evenly over the base and side of the prepared tart tin. Refrigerate the tart shell while preparing the filling.

5 Preheat a baking sheet in a 375°F/190°C/Gas 5 oven.

6 ▲ Whisk the sugar and eggs until the sugar is dissolved. Add the lemon rind and juice and mix well. Add the cream. Taste the mixture and add more lemon juice or sugar if needed. It should taste tart but also sweet.

7 Pour the filling into the tart shell and bake on the hot sheet until the filling is set, 20–25 minutes. Cool on a rack. When cool, decorate with the chocolate curls.

Lemon Almond Tart

SERVES 8

5½ oz (150 g) whole blanched almonds

3½ oz (100 g) sugar

2 eggs

grated rind and juice of 1½ lemons

4 oz (115 g) butter, melted

strips of lemon rind, for decorating

FOR THE CRUST

6¼ oz (180 g) plain flour

1 tablespoon sugar

½ teaspoon salt

½ teaspoon baking powder

3 oz (85 g) cold unsalted butter, cut into pieces

3–4 tablespoons whipping cream

1 For the crust, sift the flour, sugar, salt and baking powder into a bowl. Add the butter and rub in with your fingertips until the mixture resembles coarse breadcrumbs.

2 ▲ With a fork, stir in just enough cream to bind the dough.

3 Gather into a ball and transfer to a lightly floured surface. Roll out the dough about ⅛ in (3 mm) thick and transfer to a 9 in (23 cm) tart tin. Trim and prick the base all over with a fork. Refrigerate for at least 20 minutes.

4 Preheat a baking sheet in a 400°F/ 200°C/Gas 6 oven.

5 Line the tart shell with crumpled greaseproof paper and fill with dried beans. Bake for 12 minutes. Remove the paper and beans and continue baking until golden, 6–8 minutes more. Reduce the oven temperature to 350°F/180°C/Gas 4.

6 ▲ Grind the almonds finely with 1 tablespoon of the sugar in a food processor, blender, or coffee grinder.

7 ▲ Set a mixing bowl over a pan of hot water. Add the eggs and the remaining sugar, and beat with an electric mixer until the mixture is thick enough to leave a ribbon trail when the beaters are lifted.

8 Stir in the lemon rind and juice, butter and ground almonds.

9 Pour into the prebaked shell. Bake until the filling is golden and set, about 35 minutes. Decorate with lemon rind.

Lemon Meringue Pie

SERVES 8

grated rind and juice of 1 large lemon
8 fl oz (250 ml) plus 1 tbsp cold water
4 oz (115 g) plus 6 tbsp caster sugar
1 oz (30 g) butter
3 tbsp cornflour
3 eggs, separated
⅛ tsp salt
⅛ tsp cream of tartar
FOR THE PASTRY
5 oz (140 g) plain flour
½ tsp salt
2½ oz (70 g) cold vegetable fat or lard, cut in pieces
2 tbsp iced water

1 For the pastry, sift the flour and salt into a bowl. Add the fat and cut in with a pastry blender until the mixture resembles coarse breadcrumbs. With a fork, stir in just enough water to bind the mixture. Gather the pastry into a ball.

2 ▲ On a lightly floured surface, roll out the pastry about ⅛ in (3 mm) thick. Transfer to a 9 in (23 cm) pie dish and trim the edge to leave a ½ in (2 cm) overhang.

3 ▲ Fold the overhang under and crimp the edge. Refrigerate the pastry case for at least 20 minutes.

4 Preheat a 400°F/200°C/Gas 6 oven.

5 ▲ Prick the case all over with a fork. Line with crumpled greaseproof paper and fill with baking beans. Bake for 12 minutes. Remove the paper and beans and continue baking until golden, 6–8 minutes more.

6 In a saucepan, combine the lemon rind and juice, 8 fl oz (250 ml) of the water, 4 oz (115 g) of the sugar, and butter. Bring the mixture to a boil.

7 Meanwhile, in a mixing bowl, dissolve the cornflour in the remaining water. Add the egg yolks.

~ **VARIATION** ~

For Lime Meringue Pie, substitute the grated rind and juice of 2 medium-sized limes for the lemon.

8 ▲ Add the egg yolks to the lemon mixture and return to the boil, whisking continuously until the mixture thickens, about 5 minutes.

9 Cover the surface with greaseproof paper and let cool.

10 ▲ For the meringue, using an electric mixer beat the egg whites with the salt and cream of tartar until they hold stiff peaks. Add the remaining sugar and beat until glossy.

11 ▲ Spoon the lemon mixture into the pastry case and level. Spoon the meringue on top, smoothing it up to the pastry rim to seal. Bake until golden, 12–15 minutes.

Orange Tart

SERVES 8

7 oz (200 g) sugar

8 fl oz (250 ml) fresh orange juice, strained

2 large navel oranges

5½ oz (150 g) whole blanched almonds

2 oz (55 g) butter

1 egg

1 tablespoon plain flour

3 tablespoons apricot jam

FOR THE CRUST

7½ oz (215 g) plain flour

½ teaspoon salt

2 oz (55 g) cold butter, cut into pieces

1½ oz (45 g) cold margarine, cut into pieces

3–4 tablespoons iced water

1 For the crust, sift the flour and salt into a bowl. Add the butter and margarine and rub in with your fingertips until the mixture resembles coarse breadcrumbs. Stir in just enough water to bind the dough. Gather into a ball, wrap in clear film, and refrigerate for at least 20 minutes.

2 On a lightly floured surface, roll out the dough ¼ in (5 mm) thick and transfer to an 8 in (20 cm) tart tin. Trim off the overhang. Refrigerate until needed.

3 In a saucepan, combine 5½ oz (150 g) of the sugar and the orange juice and boil until thick and syrupy, about 10 minutes.

4 ▲ Cut the oranges into ¼ in (5 mm) slices. Do not peel. Add to the syrup. Simmer gently for 10 minutes, or until glazed. Transfer to a rack to dry. When cool, cut in half. Reserve the syrup. Place a baking sheet in the oven and heat to 400°F/200°C/Gas 6.

5 Grind the almonds finely in a food processor, blender or coffee grinder. With an electric mixer, cream the butter and remaining sugar until light and fluffy. Beat in the egg and 2 tablespoons of the orange syrup. Stir in the almonds and flour.

6 Melt the jam over low heat, then brush over the tart shell. Pour in the almond mixture. Bake until set, about 20 minutes. Let cool.

7 ▲ Arrange overlapping orange slices on top. Boil the remaining syrup until thick. Brush on top to glaze.

Pumpkin Pie

SERVES 8

1 lb (450 g) cooked or canned
pumpkin

8 fl oz (250 ml) whipping cream

2 eggs

4 oz (115 g) dark brown sugar

4 tablespoons golden syrup

1½ teaspoons ground cinnamon

1 teaspoon ground ginger

¼ teaspoon ground cloves

½ teaspoon salt

FOR THE PASTRY

6 oz (170 g) plain flour

½ teaspoon salt

3 oz (85 g) cold butter, cut into
pieces

1½ oz (45 g) cold vegetable fat, cut
into pieces

3–4 tablespoons iced water

1 For the pastry, sift the flour and salt into a bowl. Cut in the butter and fat until it resembles coarse crumbs. Bind with iced water. Wrap in clear film and refrigerate for 20 minutes.

2 Roll out the dough and line a 9 in (23 cm) pie tin. Trim off the overhang. Roll out the trimmings and cut out leaf shapes. Wet the rim of the pastry case with a brush dipped in water.

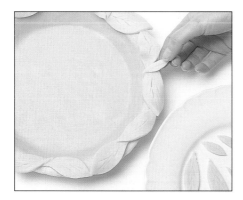

3 ▲ Place the dough leaves around the rim. Chill for 20 minutes. Preheat the oven to 400°F/200°C/Gas 6.

4 ▲ Line the pastry case with greaseproof paper. Fill with baking beans and bake for 12 minutes. Remove paper and beans and bake until golden, 6–8 minutes more. Reduce the heat to 375°F/ 190°C/Gas 5.

5 ▼ Beat together the pumpkin, cream, eggs, sugar, golden syrup, spices and salt. Pour into the pastry case and bake until set, 40 minutes.

Maple Walnut Tart

SERVES 8

3 eggs

⅛ tsp salt

2 oz (55 g) caster sugar

2 oz (55 g) butter or margarine, melted

8 fl oz (250 ml) pure maple syrup

4 oz (115 g) chopped walnuts

whipped cream, for decorating

FOR THE PASTRY

2½ oz (70 g) plain flour

2½ oz (70 g) wholewheat flour

⅛ tsp salt

2 oz (55 g) cold butter, cut in pieces

1½ oz (45 g) cold vegetable fat or lard, cut in pieces

1 egg yolk

2–3 tbsp iced water

1 ▼ For the pastry, mix the flours and salt in a bowl. Add the butter and fat and cut in with a pastry blender until the mixture resembles coarse breadcrumbs. With a fork, stir in the egg yolk and just enough water to bind the pastry. Form into a ball.

2 Wrap in greaseproof paper and refrigerate for 20 minutes.

3 Preheat a 425°F/220°C/Gas 7 oven.

4 On a lightly floured surface, roll out the pastry about ⅛ in (3 mm) thick and transfer to a 9 in (23 cm) pie dish. Trim the edge. To decorate, roll out the trimmings. With a small heart-shaped cutter, stamp out enough hearts to go around the rim of the pie. Brush the edge with water, then arrange the pastry hearts all around.

5 ▲ Prick the bottom with a fork. Line with crumpled greaseproof paper and fill with baking beans. Bake for 10 minutes. Remove the paper and beans and continue baking until golden brown, 3–6 minutes more.

6 In a bowl, whisk the eggs, salt and sugar together. Stir in the butter and maple syrup.

7 ▲ Set the pastry case on a baking sheet. Pour in the filling, then sprinkle the nuts over the top.

8 Bake until just set, about 35 minutes. Cool on a rack. Decorate with whipped cream, if wished.

Pecan Tart

SERVES 8

3 eggs
⅛ tsp salt
7 oz (200 g) dark brown sugar
4 fl oz (125 ml) golden syrup
2 tbsp fresh lemon juice
3 oz (85 g) butter, melted
5 oz (140 g) chopped pecan nuts
2 oz (55 g) pecan halves
FOR THE PASTRY
6 oz (170 g) plain flour
1 tbsp caster sugar
1 tsp baking powder
½ tsp salt
3 oz (85 g) cold unsalted butter, cut in pieces
1 egg yolk
3–4 tbsp whipping cream

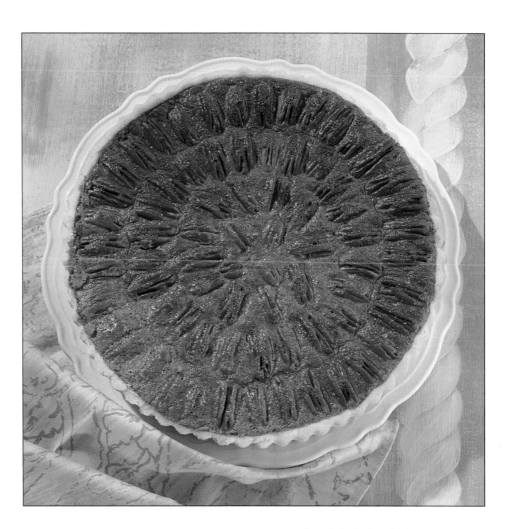

1 For the pastry, sift the flour, sugar, baking powder and salt into a bowl. Add the butter and cut in with a pastry blender until the mixture resembles coarse breadcrumbs.

2 ▼ In a bowl, beat together the egg yolk and cream until blended.

~ **COOK'S TIP** ~

Serve this tart warm, accompanied by ice cream or whipped cream, if wished.

3 ▲ Pour the cream mixture into the flour mixture and stir with a fork.

4 Gather the pastry into a ball. On a lightly floured surface, roll out ⅛ in (3 mm) thick and transfer to a 9 in (23 cm) pie dish. Trim the overhang and flute the edge with your fingers. Refrigerate for at least 20 minutes.

5 Preheat a baking sheet in the middle of a 400°F/200°C/Gas 6 oven.

6 In a bowl, lightly whisk the eggs and salt. Add the sugar, syrup, lemon juice and butter. Mix well and stir in the chopped nuts.

7 ▲ Pour into the pastry case and arrange the pecan halves in concentric circles on top.

8 Bake for 10 minutes. Reduce the heat to 325°F/170°C/Gas 3; continue baking 25 minutes more.

Mince Pies

MAKES 36

6 oz (170 g) finely chopped blanched almonds

5 oz (140 g) dried apricots, finely chopped

6 oz (170 g) raisins

5 oz (140 g) currants

5 oz (140 g) glacé cherries, chopped

5 oz (140 g) cut mixed peel, chopped

4 oz (115 g) finely chopped beef suet

grated rind and juice of 2 lemons

grated rind and juice of 1 orange

7 oz (200 g) dark brown sugar

4 cooking apples, peeled, cored and chopped

2 tsp ground cinnamon

1 tsp grated nutmeg

½ tsp ground cloves

8 fl oz (250 ml) brandy

8 oz (225 g) cream cheese

2 tbsp caster sugar

icing sugar, for dusting (optional)

FOR THE PASTRY

15 oz (420 g) plain flour

5 oz (140 g) icing sugar

12 oz (350 g) cold butter, cut in pieces

grated rind and juice of 1 orange

milk, for glazing

1 Mix the nuts, dried and preserved fruit, suet, citrus rind and juice, brown sugar, apples and spices.

2 ▲ Stir in the brandy. Cover and leave in a cool place for 2 days.

3 For the pastry, sift the flour and icing sugar into a bowl. Cut in the butter until the mixture resembles coarse breadcrumbs.

4 ▲ Add the orange rind. Stir in just enough orange juice to bind. Gather into a ball, wrap in greaseproof paper, and refrigerate for at least 20 minutes.

5 Preheat a 425°F/220°C/Gas 7 oven. Grease 2–3 bun trays. Beat together the cream cheese and sugar.

6 ▲ Roll out the pastry ¼ in (5 mm) thick. With a fluted pastry cutter, stamp out 36 3 in (8 cm) rounds.

~ COOK'S TIP ~

The mincemeat mixture may be packed into sterilized jars and sealed. It will keep refrigerated for several months. Add a few tablespoonfuls to give apple pies a lift, or make small mincemeat-filled parcels using filo pastry.

7 ▲ Transfer the rounds to the bun tray. Fill halfway with mincemeat. Top with a teaspoonful of the cream cheese mixture.

8 ▲ Roll out the remaining pastry and stamp out 36 2 in (5 cm) rounds with a fluted cutter. Brush the edges of the pies with milk, then set the rounds on top. Cut a small steam vent in the top of each pie.

9 ▲ Brush lightly with milk. Bake until golden, 15–20 minutes. Let cool for 10 minutes before unmoulding. Dust with icing sugar, if wished.

Shoofly Pie

SERVES 8

4 oz (115 g) plain flour
4 oz (115 g) dark brown sugar
¼ teaspoon each salt, ground ginger, cinnamon, mace and grated nutmeg
3 oz (85 g) cold butter, cut into pieces
2 eggs
4 fl oz (125 ml) molasses
4 fl oz (125 ml) boiling water
½ teaspoon bicarbonate of soda

FOR THE PASTRY

4 oz (115 g) cream cheese, at room temperature, cut into pieces
4 oz (115 g) cold butter, at room temperature, cut into pieces
4 oz (115 g) plain flour

1 For the pastry, put the cream cheese and butter in a mixing bowl. Sift over the flour.

2 ▲ Cut in with a pastry blender until the dough just holds together. Wrap in clear film and refrigerate for at least 30 minutes.

3 Put a baking sheet in the centre of the oven and preheat the oven to 375°F/190°C/Gas 5.

4 In a bowl, mix the flour, sugar, salt and spices. Rub in the butter with your fingertips until the mixture resembles coarse crumbs. Set aside.

5 On a lightly floured surface, roll out the dough and line a 9 in (23 cm) pie tin. Trim the overhanging pastry and flute the rim.

6 ▲ Spoon a third of the crumbed mixture into the pastry case.

7 ▲ To complete the filling, whisk the eggs with the molasses in a large bowl until combined.

8 Pour the boiling water into a small bowl. Stir in the bicarbonate of soda; the mixture will foam. Immediately whisk into the egg mixture. Pour carefully into the pastry case and sprinkle the remaining crumbed mixture evenly over the top.

9 Stand on the hot baking sheet and bake until browned, about 35 minutes. Leave to cool to room temperature, then serve.

Treacle Tart

SERVES 4–6

6 fl oz (175 ml) golden syrup

3 oz (85 g) fresh white breadcrumbs

grated rind of 1 lemon

2 tbsp fresh lemon juice

FOR THE PASTRY

6 oz (170 g) plain flour

½ tsp salt

3 oz (85 g) cold butter, cut in pieces

1½ oz (45 g) cold margarine, cut in pieces

3–4 tbsp iced water

1 For the pastry, combine the flour and salt in a bowl. Add the butter and margarine and cut in with a pastry blender until the mixture resembles coarse breadcrumbs.

2 ▲ With a fork, stir in just enough water to bind the pastry. Gather into a ball, wrap in greaseproof paper, and refrigerate for at least 20 minutes.

3 On a lightly floured surface, roll out the pastry ⅛ in (3 mm) thick. Transfer to an 8 in (20 cm) pie dish and trim off the overhang. Refrigerate for at least 20 minutes. Reserve the trimmings for the lattice top.

4 Preheat a baking sheet at the top of a 400°F/200°C/Gas 6 oven.

5 In a saucepan, warm the syrup until thin and runny.

6 ▲ Remove from the heat and stir in the breadcrumbs and lemon rind. Let sit for 10 minutes so the bread can absorb the syrup. Add more breadcrumbs if the mixture is thin. Stir in the lemon juice and spread evenly in the pastry case.

7 Roll out the pastry trimmings and cut into 10–12 thin strips.

8 ▼ Lay half the strips on the filling, then lay the remaining strips at an angle over them to form a lattice.

9 Place on the hot sheet and bake for 10 minutes. Lower the heat to 375°F/190°C/Gas 5. Bake until golden, about 15 minutes more. Serve warm or cold.

Chess Pie

SERVES 8

2 eggs

3 tablespoons whipping cream

4 oz (115 g) dark brown sugar

2 tablespoons granulated sugar

2 tablespoons plain flour

1 tablespoon whisky

1½ oz (45 g) butter, melted

2 oz (55 g) chopped walnuts

3 oz (85 g) stoned dates

whipped cream, for serving

FOR THE PASTRY

3 oz (85 g) cold butter

1½ oz (45 g) cold vegetable fat

6 oz (170 g) plain flour

½ teaspoon salt

3–4 tablespoons iced water

1 ▲ For the pastry, cut the butter and fat into small pieces.

2 Sift the flour and salt into a bowl. With a pastry blender, cut in the butter and fat until the mixture resembles coarse crumbs. Stir in just enough water to bind. Gather into a ball, wrap in greaseproof paper and refrigerate for at least 20 minutes.

3 Place a baking sheet in the oven and preheat it to 375°F/190°C/Gas 5.

4 Roll out the dough thinly and line a 9 in (23 cm) pie tin. Trim the edge. Roll out the trimmings, cut thin strips and plait them. Brush the edge of the pastry case with water and fit the pastry plaits around the rim.

5 ▲ In a mixing bowl, whisk together the eggs and cream.

6 Add both sugars and beat until well combined. Sift over 1 tablespoon of the flour and stir in. Add the whisky, the melted butter and the walnuts. Stir to combine.

7 ▲ Mix the dates with the remaining tablespoon of flour and stir into the walnut mixture.

8 Pour into the pastry case and bake until the pastry is golden and the filling puffed up, about 35 minutes. Serve at room temperature, with whipped cream, if liked.

Coconut Cream Tart

SERVES 8

5 oz (140 g) desiccated coconut

5 oz (140 g) caster sugar

4 tbsp cornflour

⅛ tsp salt

1 pt (625 ml) milk

2 fl oz (65 ml) whipping cream

2 egg yolks

1 oz (30 g) unsalted butter

2 tsp vanilla essence

FOR THE PASTRY

5 oz (140 g) plain flour

¼ tsp salt

1½ oz (45 g) cold butter, cut in pieces

1 oz (30 g) cold vegetable fat or lard

2–3 tbsp iced water

1 For the pastry, sift the flour and salt into a bowl. Add the butter and fat and cut in with a pastry blender until the mixture resembles coarse breadcrumbs.

2 ▲ With a fork, stir in just enough water to bind the pastry. Gather into a ball, wrap in greaseproof paper and refrigerate for 20 minutes.

3 Preheat a 425°F/220°C/Gas 7 oven. Roll out the pastry ⅛ in (3 mm) thick. Line a 9 in (23 cm) pie dish. Trim and flute the edges. Prick the bottom. Line with crumpled greaseproof and fill with baking beans. Bake 10–12 minutes. Remove paper and beans, reduce heat to 350°F/180°C/Gas 4 and bake until brown, 10–15 minutes.

4 ▲ Spread 2 oz (55 g) of the coconut on a baking sheet and toast in the oven until golden, 6–8 minutes, stirring often. Set aside for decorating.

5 Put the sugar, cornflour and salt in a saucepan. In a bowl, whisk the milk, cream and egg yolks. Add the egg mixture to the saucepan.

6 ▼ Cook over a low heat, stirring, until the mixture comes to the boil. Boil for 1 minute, then remove from the heat. Add the butter, vanilla and remaining coconut.

7 Pour into the prebaked pastry case. When cool, sprinkle toasted coconut in a ring in the centre.

Black Bottom Pie

SERVES 8

2 teaspoons gelatin

3 tablespoons cold water

2 eggs, separated

5 oz (140 g) caster sugar

½ oz (15 g) cornflour

½ teaspoon salt

16 fl oz (450 ml) milk

2 oz (55 g) plain chocolate, finely
    chopped

2 tablespoons rum

¼ teaspoon cream of tartar

chocolate curls, for decorating

FOR THE CRUST

6 oz (170 g) gingersnaps, crushed

2½ oz (70 g) butter, melted

1 Preheat a 350°F/180°C/Gas 4 oven.

2 For the crust, mix the crushed gingersnaps and melted butter.

3 ▲ Press the mixture evenly over the bottom and side of a 9 in (23 cm) pie plate. Bake for 6 minutes.

4 Sprinkle the gelatin over the water and let stand to soften.

5 Beat the egg yolks in a large mixing bowl and set aside.

6 In a saucepan, combine half the sugar, the cornflour and salt. Gradually stir in the milk. Boil for 1 minute, stirring constantly.

7 ▲ Whisk the hot milk mixture into the yolks, then pour all back into the saucepan and return to the boil, whisking. Cook for 1 minute, still whisking. Remove from the heat.

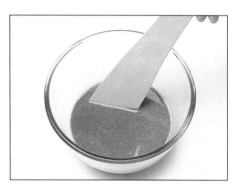

8 ▲ Measure out 8 oz (225 g) of the hot custard mixture and pour into a bowl. Add the chopped chocolate to the custard mixture, and stir until melted. Stir in half the rum and pour into the pie shell.

9 ▲ Whisk the softened gelatin into the plain custard until it has dissolved, then stir in the remaining rum. Set the pan in cold water until it reaches room temperature.

10 ▲ With an electric mixer, beat the egg whites and cream of tartar until they hold stiff peaks. Add the remaining sugar gradually, beating or whisking thoroughly at each addition.

11 ▲ Fold the custard into the egg whites, then spoon over the chocolate mixture in the pie shell. Refrigerate until set, about 2 hours.

12 Decorate the top with chocolate curls. Keep the pie refrigerated until ready to serve.

~ **COOK'S TIP** ~

To make chocolate curls, melt 8 oz (225 g) plain chocolate over hot water, stir in 1 tablespoon of vegetable fat and mould in a small foil-lined loaf tin. For large curls, soften the bar between your hands and scrape off curls from the wide side with a vegetable peeler; for small curls, grate from the narrow side using a box grater.

Velvety Mocha Tart

SERVES 8

2 tsp instant espresso coffee

2 tbsp hot water

12 fl oz (350 ml) whipping cream

6 oz (170 g) plain chocolate

1 oz (30 g) bitter cooking chocolate

4 fl oz (125 ml) whipped cream, for decorating

chocolate-covered coffee beans, for decorating

FOR THE BASE

5 oz (140 g) chocolate wafers, crushed

2 tbsp caster sugar

2½ oz (70 g) butter, melted

1 ▲ For the base, mix the crushed chocolate wafers and sugar together, then stir in the melted butter.

2 Press the mixture evenly over the bottom and sides of a 9 in (23 cm) pie dish. Refrigerate until firm.

3 In a bowl, dissolve the coffee in the water and set aside.

4 Pour the cream into a mixing bowl. Set the bowl in hot water to warm the cream, bringing it closer to the temperature of the chocolate.

5 Melt both the chocolates in the top of a double boiler, or in a heatproof bowl set over a pan of hot water. Remove from the heat when nearly melted and stir to continue melting. Set the bottom of the pan in cool water to reduce the temperature. Be careful not to splash any water on the chocolate or it will become grainy.

6 ▲ With an electric mixer, whip the cream until it is lightly fluffy. Add the dissolved coffee and whip until the cream just holds its shape.

7 ▲ When the chocolate is at room temperature, fold it gently into the cream with a large metal spoon.

8 Pour into the chilled biscuit base and refrigerate until firm. To serve, pipe a ring of whipped cream rosettes around the edge, then place a chocolate-covered coffee bean in the centre of each rosette.

Brandy Alexander Tart

SERVES 8

4 fl oz (125 ml) cold water
1 tablespoon powdered gelatine
4 oz (115 g) sugar
3 eggs, separated
4 tablespoons brandy
4 tablespoons crème de cacao
pinch of salt
10 fl oz (300 ml) whipping cream
chocolate curls, for decorating
FOR THE BISCUIT CRUST
8 oz (225 g) digestive biscuits, crumbed
2½ oz (70 g) butter, melted
1 tablespoon sugar

1 Preheat the oven to 375°F/190°C/Gas 5.

2 For the crust, mix the biscuit crumbs with the butter and sugar in a bowl.

3 ▲ Press the crumbs evenly on to the bottom and sides of a 9 in (23 cm) tart tin. Bake until just brown, about 10 minutes. Cool on a rack.

4 Place the water in the top of a double boiler set over hot water. Sprinkle over the gelatine and leave to stand for 5 minutes to soften. Add half the sugar and the egg yolks. Whisk constantly over very low heat until the gelatine dissolves and the mixture thickens slightly. Do not allow the mixture to boil.

5 ▲ Remove from the heat and stir in the brandy and crème de cacao.

6 Set the pan over iced water and stir occasionally until it cools and thickens; it should not set firmly.

7 With an electric mixer, beat the egg whites and salt until they hold stiff peaks. Beat in the remaining sugar. Spoon a dollop of whites into the yolk mixture and fold in to lighten.

8 ▼ Pour the egg yolk mixture over the remaining whites and fold together.

9 Whip the cream until soft peaks form, then gently fold into the filling. Spoon into the baked biscuit case and chill until set, 3–4 hours. Decorate the top with chocolate curls before serving.

Glacé Fruit Pie

SERVES 10

1 tablespoon rum
2 oz (55 g) mixed glacé fruit, chopped
16 fl oz (450 ml) milk
4 teaspoons gelatin
3½ oz (100 g) sugar
½ teaspoon salt
3 eggs, separated
8 fl oz (250 ml) whipping cream
chocolate curls, for decorating
FOR THE CRUST
6 oz (170 g) digestive biscuits, crushed
2½ oz (70 g) butter, melted
1 tablespoon sugar

1 For the crust, mix the crushed digestive biscuits, butter and sugar. Press evenly and firmly over the bottom and side of a 9 in (23 cm) pie plate. Refrigerate until firm.

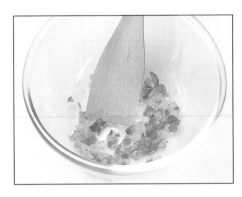

2 ▲ In a bowl, stir together the rum and glacé fruit. Set aside.

3 Pour 4 fl oz (125 ml) of the milk into a small bowl. Sprinkle over the gelatin and let stand 5 minutes to soften.

4 ▲ In the top of a double boiler, combine 1¾ oz (50 g) of the sugar, the remaining milk and salt. Stir in the gelatin mixture. Cook over hot water, stirring, until gelatin dissolves.

5 Whisk in the egg yolks and cook, stirring, until thick enough to coat a spoon. Do not boil. Pour the custard over the glacé fruit mixture. Set in a bowl of ice water to cool.

6 Whip the cream lightly. Set aside.

7 With an electric mixer, beat the egg whites until they hold soft peaks. Add the remaining sugar and beat just enough to blend. Fold in a large dollop of the egg whites into the cooled gelatin mixture. Pour into the remaining egg whites and carefully fold together. Fold in the cream.

8 ▲ Pour into the pie shell and chill until firm. Decorate the top with chocolate curls.

Chocolate Chiffon Pie

SERVES 8

7 oz (200 g) plain chocolate	
8 fl oz (250 ml) milk	
1 tablespoon gelatin	
3½ oz (100 g) sugar	
2 extra-large eggs, separated	
1 teaspoon vanilla essence	
12 fl oz (350 ml) whipping cream	
⅛ teaspoon salt	
whipped cream and chocolate curls, for decorating	

FOR THE CRUST

7 oz (200 g) digestive biscuits, crushed	
3 oz (85 g) butter, melted	

1 Place a baking sheet in the oven and preheat to 350°F/180°C/ Gas 4.

2 For the crust, mix the crushed digestive biscuits and butter in a bowl. Press evenly over the bottom and side of a 9 in (23 cm) pie plate. Bake for 8 minutes. Let cool.

3 Chop the chocolate, then grate in a food processor or blender. Set aside.

4 Place the milk in the top of a double boiler. Sprinkle over the gelatin. Let stand 5 minutes to soften.

5 ▲ Set the top of a double boiler over hot water. Add 1½ oz (45 g) sugar, the chocolate and egg yolks. Stir until dissolved. Add the vanilla.

6 ▲ Set the top of the double boiler in a bowl of ice and stir until the mixture reaches room temperature. Remove from the ice and set aside.

7 Whip the cream lightly. Set aside. With an electric mixer, beat the egg whites and salt until they hold soft peaks. Add the remaining sugar and beat only enough to blend.

8 Fold a dollop of egg whites into the chocolate mixture, then pour back into the whites and fold in.

9 ▲ Fold in the whipped cream and pour into the pie shell. Put in the freezer until just set, about 5 minutes. If the centre sinks, fill with any remaining mixture. Refrigerate for 3–4 hours. Decorate with whipped cream and chocolate curls. Serve cold.

Chocolate Cheesecake Tart

SERVES 8

12 oz (350 g) cream cheese

4 tbsp whipping cream

8 oz (225 g) caster sugar

2 oz (55 g) cocoa powder

½ tsp ground cinnamon

3 eggs

whipped cream, for decorating

chocolate curls, for decorating

FOR THE BASE

3 oz (85 g) digestive biscuits, crushed

1½ oz (45 g) crushed amaretti biscuits (if unavailable, use extra crushed digestive biscuits)

3 oz (85 g) butter, melted

1 Preheat a baking sheet in the centre of a 350°F/180°C/Gas 4 oven.

2 For the base, mix the crushed biscuits and butter in a bowl.

3 ▲ With a spoon, press the mixture over the bottom and sides of a 9 in (23 cm) pie dish. Bake for 8 minutes. Let cool. Keep the oven on.

4 With an electric mixer, beat the cheese and cream together until smooth. Beat in the sugar, cocoa and cinnamon until blended.

5 ▼ Add the eggs, 1 at a time, beating just enough to blend.

6 Pour into the biscuit base and bake on the hot sheet for 25–30 minutes. The filling will sink down as it cools. Decorate with whipped cream and chocolate curls.

Frozen Strawberry Tart

SERVES 8

8 oz (225 g) cream cheese

8 fl oz (250 ml) soured cream

1 lb 4 oz (575 g) frozen strawberries, thawed and sliced

FOR THE BASE

4 oz (115 g) digestive biscuits, crushed

1 tbsp caster sugar

2½ oz (70 g) butter, melted

~ **VARIATION** ~

For Frozen Raspberry Tart, use raspberries in place of the strawberries and prepare the same way, or try other frozen fruit.

1 ▲ For the base, mix together the biscuits, sugar and butter.

2 Press the mixture evenly and firmly over the bottom and sides of a 9 in (23 cm) pie dish. Freeze until firm.

3 ▼ Blend together the cream cheese and soured cream. Reserve 6 tablespoons of the strawberries. Add the rest to the cream cheese mixture.

4 Pour the filling into the biscuit base and freeze 6–8 hours until firm. To serve, spoon some of the reserved berries and juice on top.

Chocolate Cheesecake Pie (top), Frozen Strawberry Tart

Kiwi Ricotta Cheese Tart

SERVES 8

3 oz (75 g) blanched almonds, ground

3½ oz (130 g) sugar

2 lb (900 g) ricotta cheese

8 fl oz (250 ml) whipping cream

1 egg and 3 egg yolks

1 tablespoon plain flour

pinch of salt

2 tablespoons rum

grated rind of 1 lemon

2½ tablespoons lemon juice

2 tablespoons honey

5 kiwi fruit

FOR THE PASTRY

5 oz (150 g) plain flour

1 tablespoon sugar

½ teaspoon salt

½ teaspoon baking powder

6 tablespoons butter

1 egg yolk

3–4 tablespoons whipping cream

1 For the pastry, mix together the flour, sugar, salt and baking powder in a large bowl. Cut the butter into cubes and gradually rub it into the pastry mixture. Mix in the egg yolk and cream. Stir in just enough to bind the pastry.

2 ▲ Transfer to a lightly floured surface, flatten slightly, wrap and refrigerate for 30 minutes. Preheat the oven to 425°F/220°C/Gas 7.

3 ▲ On a lightly floured surface, roll out the dough to a ⅛ in (3 mm) thickness. Transfer to a 9 in (23 cm) springform tin. Crimp the edge.

4 ▲ Prick the pastry with a fork. Line with greaseproof paper and fill with dried beans. Bake for 10 minutes. Remove the paper and beans and bake for 6–8 minutes more until golden. Leave to cool. Reduce the temperature to 350°F/180°C/Gas 4.

5 ▲ Mix the almonds with 1 tablespoon of the sugar in a food processor or blender.

6 Beat the ricotta until creamy. Add the cream, egg, yolks, remaining sugar, flour, salt, rum, lemon rind and 2 tablespoons of lemon juice. Combine.

7 ▲ Stir in the ground almonds until well blended.

8 Pour into a pastry case and bake for 1 hour. Chill, loosely covered for 2–3 hours. Unmould and put on a plate.

9 Combine the honey and remaining lemon juice for the glaze.

10 ▲ Peel the kiwis. Halve them lengthwise, then slice. Arrange the slices in rows across the top of the tart. Just before serving, brush with the honey glaze.

Apple Strudel

SERVES 10–12

3 oz (85 g) raisins
2 tbsp brandy
5 eating apples, such as Granny Smith or Cox's
3 large cooking apples
3½ oz (100 g) dark brown sugar
1 tsp ground cinnamon
grated rind and juice of 1 lemon
1 oz (30 g) dry breadcrumbs
2 oz (55 g) chopped pecans or walnuts
12 sheets frozen filo pastry, thawed
6 oz (170 g) butter, melted
icing sugar, for dusting

1 Soak the raisins in the brandy for at least 15 minutes.

2 ▼ Peel, core and thinly slice the apples. In a bowl, combine the sugar, cinnamon and lemon rind. Stir in the apples and half the breadcrumbs.

3 Add the raisins, nuts and lemon juice and stir until blended.

4 Preheat a 375°F/190°C/Gas 5 oven. Grease 2 baking sheets.

5 ▲ Carefully unfold the filo sheets. Keep the unused sheets covered with greaseproof paper. Lift off 1 sheet, place on a clean surface and brush with melted butter. Lay a second sheet on top and brush with butter. Continue until you have a stack of 6 buttered sheets.

6 Sprinkle a few tablespoons of breadcrumbs over the last sheet and spoon half the apple mixture at the bottom edge of the strip.

7 ▲ Starting at the apple-filled end, roll up the pastry, as for a Swiss roll. Place on a baking sheet, seam-side down, and carefully fold under the ends to seal. Repeat the procedure to make a second strudel. Brush both with butter.

8 Bake the strudels for 45 minutes. Let cool slightly. Using a small sieve, dust with a fine layer of icing sugar. Serve warm.

Cherry Strudel

SERVES 8

2½ oz (70 g) fresh breadcrumbs
6 oz (170 g) butter, melted
7 oz (200 g) sugar
1 tablespoon ground cinnamon
1 teaspoon grated lemon rind
1 lb (450 g) sour cherries, stoned
8 sheets filo pastry
icing sugar, for dusting

1 In a frying pan, lightly fry the fresh breadcrumbs in 2½ oz (70 g) of the melted butter until golden. Set aside to cool.

2 ▲ In a large mixing bowl, toss together the sugar, cinnamon and lemon rind.

3 Stir in the cherries.

4 Preheat the oven to 375°F/190°C/ Gas 5. Grease a baking sheet.

5 Carefully unfold the filo sheets. Keep the unused sheets covered with damp kitchen paper. Lift off one sheet, place on a flat surface lined with parchment paper. Brush the pastry with melted butter. Sprinkle about an eighth of the breadcrumbs evenly over the surface.

6 ▲ Lay a second sheet of filo on top, brush with butter and sprinkle with crumbs. Continue until you have a stack of 8 buttered, crumbed sheets.

7 Spoon the cherry mixture at the bottom edge of the strip. Starting at the cherry-filled end, roll up the dough as for a Swiss roll. Use the paper to help flip the strudel onto the baking sheet, seam-side down.

8 ▼ Carefully fold under the ends to seal in the fruit. Brush the top with any remaining butter.

9 Bake the strudel for 45 minutes. Let cool slightly. Using a small sieve, dust with a fine layer of icing sugar.

Mushroom Quiche

SERVES 8

1 lb (450 g) mushrooms

2 tablespoons olive oil

1 tablespoon butter

1 clove garlic, finely chopped

1 tablespoon lemon juice

salt and pepper

2 tablespoons finely chopped parsley

3 eggs

12 fl oz (300 ml) whipping cream

2¼ oz (60 g) Parmesan cheese, grated

FOR THE CRUST

6¼ oz (180 g) plain flour

½ teaspoon salt

3 oz (85 g) cold butter, cut into pieces

1½ oz (45 g) cold margarine, cut into pieces

3–4 tablespoons iced water

1 For the crust, sift the flour and salt into a bowl. Rub in the butter and margarine until the mixture resembles coarse breadcrumbs. Stir in just enough water to bind.

2 Gather into a ball, wrap in clear film and refrigerate for 20 minutes.

3 Preheat a baking sheet in a 375°F/190°C/Gas 5 oven.

4 Roll out the dough ⅛ in (3 mm) thick. Transfer to a 9 in (23 cm) tart tin and trim. Prick the base all over with a fork. Line with greaseproof paper and fill with dried beans. Bake for 12 minutes. Remove the paper and beans and continue baking until golden, about 5 minutes more.

5 ▲ Wipe the mushrooms with damp kitchen paper to remove any dirt. Trim the ends of the stalks, place on a cutting board, and slice thinly.

6 Heat the oil and butter in a frying pan. Stir in the mushrooms, garlic and lemon juice. Season with salt and pepper. Cook until the mushrooms render their liquid, then raise the heat and cook until dry.

7 ▼ Stir in the parsley and add more salt and pepper if necessary.

8 Whisk the eggs and cream together, then stir in the mushrooms. Sprinkle the cheese over the bottom of the prebaked shell and pour the mushroom filling over the top.

9 Bake until puffed and brown, about 30 minutes. Serve the quiche warm.

Bacon and Cheese Quiche

SERVES 8

4 oz (115 g) medium-thick bacon slices

3 eggs

12 fl oz (350 ml) whipping cream

3½ oz (100 g) Gruyère cheese, grated

⅛ teaspoon grated nutmeg

salt and pepper

FOR THE CRUST

6¼ oz (180 g) plain flour

½ teaspoon salt

3 oz (85 g) cold butter, cut into pieces

1½ oz (45 g) cold margarine, cut into pieces

3–4 tablespoons iced water

1 Make the crust as directed in steps 1–4 above. Maintain the oven temperature at 375°F/190°C/Gas 5.

2 ▲ Fry the bacon until crisp. Drain, then crumble into small pieces. Sprinkle in the pastry shell.

3 ▲ Beat together the eggs, cream, cheese, nutmeg, salt and pepper. Pour over the bacon and bake until puffed and brown, about 30 minutes. Serve the quiche warm.

Mushroom Quiche (top), Bacon and Cheese Quiche

Cheesy Tomato Quiche

SERVES 6–8

10 medium tomatoes

1 × 2 oz (55 g) can anchovy fillets, drained and finely chopped

4 fl oz (125 ml) whipping cream

7 oz (200 g) mature Cheddar cheese, grated

1 oz (30 g) wholemeal breadcrumbs

½ teaspoon dried thyme

salt and pepper

FOR THE CRUST

7½ oz (215 g) plain flour

4 oz (115 g) cold butter, cut into pieces

1 egg yolk

2–3 tablespoons iced water

1 Preheat the oven to 400°F/200°C/ Gas 6.

2 For the crust, sift the flour into a bowl. Rub in the butter with your fingertips until the mixture resembles coarse breadcrumbs.

3 ▲ With a fork, stir in the egg yolk and enough water to bind the dough.

4 Roll out the dough about ⅛ in (3 mm) thick and transfer to a 9 in (23 cm) tart tin. Refrigerate until needed.

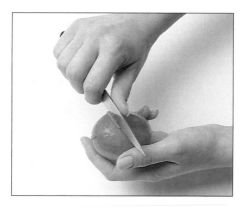

5 ▲ Score the bottoms of the tomatoes. Plunge in boiling water for 1 minute. Remove and peel off the skin with a knife. Cut in quarters and remove the seeds with a spoon.

6 ▲ In a bowl, mix the anchovies and cream. Stir in the cheese.

7 Sprinkle the breadcrumbs in the tart. Arrange the tomatoes on top. Season with thyme, salt and pepper.

8 ▲ Spoon the cheese mixture on top. Bake until golden, 25–30 minutes. Serve warm.

Onion and Anchovy Tart

SERVES 8

4 tablespoons olive oil

2 lb (900 g) onions, sliced

1 teaspoon dried thyme

salt and pepper

2–3 tomatoes, sliced

24 small black olives, stoned

1 × 2 oz (55 g) can anchovy fillets,
   drained and sliced

6 sun-dried tomatoes, cut into slivers

FOR THE CRUST

6¼ oz (180 g) plain flour

½ teaspoon salt

4 oz (115 g) cold butter, cut into pieces

1 egg yolk

2–3 tablespoons iced water

3 ▲ Heat the oil in a frying pan. Add the onions, thyme and seasoning. Cook over low heat, covered, for 25 minutes. Uncover and continue cooking until soft. Let cool. Preheat the oven to 400°F/200°C/Gas 6.

4 ▼ Spoon the onions into the tart shell and top with the tomato slices. Arrange the olives in rows. Make a lattice pattern, alternating lines of anchovies and sun-dried tomatoes. Bake until golden, 20–25 minutes.

1 ▲ For the crust, sift the flour and salt into a bowl. Rub in the butter with your fingertips until the mixture resembles coarse breadcrumbs. Stir in the yolk and enough water to bind.

2 ▲ Roll out the dough about ⅛ in (3 mm) thick. Transfer to a 9 in (23 cm) tart tin and trim the edge. Refrigerate until needed.

Ricotta and Basil Tart

SERVES 8–10

2 oz (55 g) basil leaves
1 oz (30 g) flat-leaf parsley
4 fl oz (125 ml) extra-virgin olive oil
salt and pepper
2 eggs
1 egg yolk
1 lb 12 oz (800 g) ricotta cheese
3½ oz (100 g) black olives, stoned
2¼ oz (60 g) Parmesan cheese, freshly grated
FOR THE CRUST
6½ oz (180 g) plain flour
½ teaspoon salt
3 oz (85 g) cold butter, cut into pieces
1½ oz (45 g) cold margarine, cut into pieces
3–4 tablespoons iced water

1 ▲ For the crust, combine the flour and salt in a bowl. Add the butter and margarine.

2 Rub in with your fingertips until the mixture resembles coarse breadcrumbs. With a fork, stir in just enough water to bind the dough. Gather into a ball, wrap in clear film, and refrigerate for at least 20 minutes.

3 Preheat a baking sheet in a 375°F/190°C/Gas 5 oven.

4 Roll out the dough ⅛ in (3 mm) thick and transfer to a 10 in (25 cm) tart tin. Prick the base with a fork and line with greaseproof. Fill with dried beans and bake for 12 minutes. Remove the paper and beans and bake until golden, 3–5 minutes more. Lower the heat to 350°F/180°C/Gas 4.

5 ▲ In a food processor, combine the basil, parsley and olive oil. Season well with salt and pepper and process until finely chopped.

6 In a bowl, whisk the eggs and yolk to blend. Gently fold in the ricotta.

7 ▲ Fold in the basil mixture and olives until well combined. Stir in the Parmesan and adjust the seasoning.

8 Pour into the prebaked shell and bake until set, 30–35 minutes.

Pennsylvania Dutch Ham and Apple Pie

SERVES 6–8

5 tart cooking apples
4 tablespoons light brown sugar
1 tablespoon plain flour
pinch of ground cloves
pinch of ground black pepper
6 oz (170 g) sliced cooked ham
1 oz (30 g) butter or margarine
4 tablespoons whipping cream
1 egg yolk
FOR THE PASTRY
8 oz (225 g) plain flour
½ teaspoon salt
3 oz (85 g) cold butter, cut into pieces
2 oz (55 g) cold margarine, cut into pieces
4–8 tablespoons iced water

1 For the pastry, sift the flour and salt into a large bowl. Rub in the butter and margarine until the mixture resembles coarse crumbs. Stir in enough water to bind together, gather into 2 balls, and wrap in clear film. Refrigerate for about 20 minutes. Preheat the oven to 425°F/220°C/Gas 7.

2 ▲ Quarter, core, peel and thinly slice the apples. Place in a bowl and toss with the sugar, flour, cloves and pepper to coat evenly. Set aside.

3 Roll out one dough ball thinly and line a 10 in (25 cm) pie tin, letting the excess pastry hang over the edge.

4 Arrange half the ham slices in the bottom of the pastry case. Top with a ring of spiced apple slices, then dot with half the butter or margarine.

5 ▲ Repeat the layers, finishing with apples. Dot with butter or margarine. Pour over 3 tablespoons of the cream.

6 Roll out the remaining pastry to make a lid. Place it on top, fold the top edge under the bottom and press.

7 ▲ Roll out the pastry scraps and cut out decorative shapes. Arrange on top of the pie. Scallop the edge, using your fingers and a fork. Cut steam vents. Mix the egg yolk and remaining cream and brush on top to glaze.

8 Bake for 10 minutes. Reduce the heat to 350°F/180°C/Gas 4 and bake until golden, 30–35 minutes more. Serve hot.

CAKES & GATEAUX

~

As delicious as they are beautiful, these cakes and gâteaux are perfect to serve at teatime or for dessert. Some delightful party cakes make special occasions memorable.

Angel Cake

SERVES 12–14

4½ oz (125 g) sifted plain flour
2 tablespoons cornflour
10½ oz (300 g) caster sugar
10–11 oz (285–310 g) egg whites (about 10–11 eggs)
1¼ teaspoons cream of tartar
¼ teaspoon salt
1 teaspoon vanilla essence
¼ teaspoon almond essence
icing sugar, for dusting

1 Preheat the oven to 325°F/170°C/Gas 3.

2 ▼ Sift the flours before measuring, then sift them 4 times with 3½ oz (100 g) of the sugar.

3 With an electric mixer, beat the egg whites until foamy. Sift over the cream of tartar and salt and continue to beat until the whites hold soft peaks when the beaters are lifted.

4 ▲ Add the remaining sugar in 3 batches, beating well after each addition. Stir in the vanilla and almond essences.

5 ▲ Add the flour mixture, in 2 batches, and fold in with a large metal spoon after each addition.

6 Transfer to an ungreased 10 in (25 cm) tube tin and bake until just browned on top, about 1 hour.

7 ▲ Turn the tin upside down onto a cake rack and let cool for 1 hour. If the cake does not turn out, run a knife around the edge to loosen it. Invert on a serving plate.

8 When cool, lay a star-shaped template on top of the cake, sift over icing sugar and remove template.

Marbled Ring Cake

SERVES 16

4 oz (115 g) plain chocolate
12 oz (350 g) plain flour
1 tsp baking powder
1 lb (450 g) butter, at room temperature
1 lb 10 oz (740 g) caster sugar
1 tbsp vanilla essence
10 eggs, at room temperature
icing sugar, for dusting

1 ▲ Preheat a 350°F/180°C/Gas 4 oven. Line a 10 × 4 in (25 × 10 cm) ring mould with greaseproof paper and grease the paper. Dust with flour.

2 ▲ Melt the chocolate in the top of a double boiler, or in a heatproof bowl set over a pan of hot water. Stir occasionally. Set aside.

3 In a bowl, sift together the flour and baking powder. In another bowl, cream the butter, sugar and vanilla with an electric mixer until light and fluffy. Add the eggs, 2 at a time, then gradually incorporate the flour mixture on low speed.

4 ▲ Spoon half of the mixture into the prepared tin.

5 ▲ Stir the chocolate into the remaining mixture, then spoon into the tin. With a metal spatula, swirl the mixtures for a marbled effect.

6 Bake until a skewer inserted in the centre comes out clean, about 1 hour 45 minutes. Cover with foil halfway through baking. Let stand 15 minutes, then unmould and transfer to a cooling rack. To serve, dust with icing sugar.

Coffee-Iced Ring

SERVES 16

10 oz (285 g) plain flour

1 tbsp baking powder

1 tsp salt

12 oz (350 g) caster sugar

4 fl oz (125 ml) vegetable oil

7 eggs, at room temperature, separated

6 fl oz (175 ml) cold water

2 tsp vanilla essence

2 tsp grated lemon rind

½ tsp cream of tartar

FOR THE ICING

5½ oz (165 g) unsalted butter, at room temperature

1 lb 4 oz (575 g) icing sugar

4 tsp instant coffee dissolved in 4 tbsp hot water

1 Preheat a 325°F/170°C/Gas 3 oven.

2 ▼ Sift the flour, baking powder and salt into a bowl. Stir in 8 oz (225 g) of the sugar. Make a well in the centre and add in the following order: oil, egg yolks, water, vanilla and lemon rind. Beat with a whisk or metal spoon until smooth.

3 With an electric mixer, beat the egg whites with the cream of tartar until they hold soft peaks. Add the remaining 4 oz (115 g) of sugar and beat until they hold stiff peaks.

4 ▲ Pour the flour mixture over the whites in 3 batches, folding well after each addition.

5 Transfer the mixture to a 10 × 4 in (25 × 10 cm) ring mould and bake until the top springs back when touched lightly, about 1 hour.

6 ▲ When baked, remove from the oven and immediately hang the cake upside-down over the neck of a funnel or a narrow bottle. Let cool. To remove the cake, run a knife around the inside to loosen, then turn the tin over and tap the sides sharply. Invert the cake onto a serving plate.

7 For the icing, beat together the butter and icing sugar with an electric mixer until smooth. Add the coffee and beat until fluffy. With a metal spatula, spread over the sides and top of the cake.

Spice Cake with Cream Cheese Frosting

SERVES 10–12

10 fl oz (300 ml) milk

2 tablespoons golden syrup

2 teaspoons vanilla essence

3 oz (85 g) walnuts, chopped

6 oz (170 g) butter, at room temperature

10½ oz (300 g) sugar

1 egg, at room temperature

3 egg yolks, at room temperature

10 oz (285 g) plain flour

1 tablespoon baking powder

1 teaspoon grated nutmeg

1 teaspoon ground cinnamon

½ teaspoon ground cloves

¼ teaspoon ground ginger

¼ teaspoon ground allspice

FOR THE FROSTING

6 oz (170 g) cream cheese

1 oz (30 g) unsalted butter

70 oz (200 g) icing sugar

2 tablespoons finely chopped stem ginger

2 tablespoons syrup from stem ginger

stem ginger pieces, for decorating

1 Preheat a 350°F/180°C/Gas 4 oven. Line 3 8 in (20 cm) cake tins with greaseproof paper and grease. In a bowl, combine the milk, golden syrup, vanilla and walnuts.

2 ▼ With an electric mixer, cream the butter and sugar until light and fluffy. Beat in the egg and egg yolks. Add the milk mixture and stir well.

3 Sift together the flour, baking powder and spices 3 times.

4 ▲ Add the flour mixture in 4 batches, and fold in carefully after each addition.

5 Divide the cake mixture between the tins. Bake until the cakes spring back when touched lightly, about 25 minutes. Let stand 5 minutes, then turn out and cool on a rack.

6 ▼ For the frosting, combine all the ingredients and beat with an electric mixer. Spread the frosting between the layers and over the top. Decorate with pieces of stem ginger.

Caramel Layer Cake

SERVES 8–10

10oz (285g) plain flour

| 1½ teaspoons baking powder |

| 6oz (170g) butter, at room temperature |

| 5½oz (150g) caster sugar |

| 4 eggs, at room temperature, beaten |

| 1 teaspoon vanilla essence |

| 8 tablespoons milk |

| whipped cream, for decorating |

| caramel threads, for decorating (optional, see below) |

FOR THE FROSTING

| 10½oz (300g) dark brown sugar |

| 8fl oz (250ml) milk |

| 1oz (30g) unsalted butter |

| 3–5 tablespoons whipping cream |

1 Preheat a 350°F/180°C/Gas 4 oven. Line 2 8in (20cm) cake tins with greaseproof paper and grease lightly.

2 ▲ Sift the flour and baking powder together 3 times. Set aside.

~ **COOK'S TIP** ~

To make caramel threads, combine 2½oz (70g) sugar and 2fl oz (65ml) water in a heavy saucepan. Boil until light brown. Dip the pan in cold water to halt cooking. Trail from a spoon on an oiled baking sheet.

3 With an electric mixer, cream the butter and caster sugar until light and fluffy.

4 ▲ Slowly mix in the beaten eggs. Add the vanilla. Fold in the flour mixture, alternating with the milk.

5 ▲ Divide the batter between the prepared tins and spread evenly, hollowing out the centres slightly.

6 Bake until the cakes pull away from the sides of the tin, about 30 minutes. Let stand 5 minutes, then turn out and cool on a rack.

7 ▲ For the frosting, combine the brown sugar and milk in a saucepan.

8 Bring to the boil, cover and cook for 3 minutes. Remove lid and continue to boil, without stirring, until the mixture reaches 238°F/119°C (soft ball stage) on a sugar thermometer.

9 ▲ Immediately remove the pan from the heat and add the butter, but do not stir it in. Let cool until lukewarm, then beat until the mixture is smooth and creamy.

10 Stir in enough cream to obtain a spreadable consistency. If necessary, refrigerate to thicken more.

11 ▲ Spread a layer of frosting on top of one cake. Sandwich with the second cake, then spread the top and sides with the rest of the frosting and smooth the surface.

12 To decorate, pipe whipped cream rosettes around the edge. If using, place a mound of caramel threads in the centre before serving.

Lady Baltimore Cake

SERVES 8–10

10 oz (285 g) plain flour

2½ teaspoons baking powder

½ teaspoon salt

4 eggs

12 oz (350 g) sugar

grated rind of 1 large orange

8 fl oz (250 ml) fresh orange juice

8 fl oz (250 ml) vegetable oil

18 pecan halves, for decorating

FOR THE FROSTING

2 egg whites

12 oz (350 g) sugar

5 tablespoons cold water

¼ teaspoon cream of tartar

1 teaspoon vanilla essence

2 oz (55 g) pecans, finely chopped

3 oz (85 g) raisins, chopped

3 dried figs, finely chopped

1 Preheat the oven to 350°F/180°C/ Gas 4. Grease 2 9 in (23 cm) round cake tins and line with greaseproof paper. Grease the paper. In a bowl, sift together the flour, baking powder and salt. Set aside.

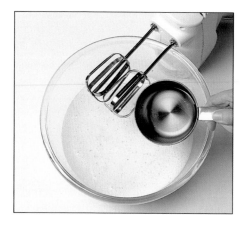

2 ▲ With an electric mixer, beat the eggs and sugar until thick and lemon-coloured. Beat in the orange rind and juice, then the oil.

3 On low speed, beat in the flour mixture in 3 batches. Divide the cake mixture between the tins.

4 ▲ Bake until a skewer inserted in the centre comes out clean, about 30 minutes. Leave to stand for 15 minutes, then run a knife around the inside of the cakes and transfer them to racks to cool completely.

5 ▲ For the frosting, combine the egg whites, sugar, water and cream of tartar in the top of a double boiler, or in a heatproof bowl set over boiling water. With an electric mixer, beat until glossy and thick. Off the heat, add the vanilla essence and continue beating until thick. Fold in the pecans, raisins and figs.

6 Spread a layer of frosting on top of one cake. Sandwich with the second cake, then spread the top and sides with the rest of the frosting. Arrange the pecan halves on top.

Carrot Cake

SERVES 12

1 lb (450 g) carrots, peeled

6 oz (170 g) plain flour

2 tsp baking powder

½ tsp bicarbonate of soda

1 tsp salt

2 tsp ground cinnamon

4 eggs

2 tsp vanilla essence

4 oz (115 g) dark brown sugar

2 oz (55 g) caster sugar

10 fl oz (300 ml) sunflower oil

4 oz (115 g) finely chopped walnuts

3 oz (85 g) raisins

walnut halves, for decorating (optional)

FOR THE ICING

3 oz (85 g) unsalted butter, at room
  temperature

12 oz (350 g) icing sugar

2 fl oz (65 ml) maple syrup

1 Preheat a 350°F/180°C/Gas 4 oven.
Line an 11 × 8 in (28 × 20 cm) tin
with greaseproof paper and grease.

2 ▲ Grate the carrots and set aside.

3 Sift the flour, baking powder,
bicarbonate of soda, salt and
cinnamon into a bowl. Set aside.

4 With an electric mixer, beat the
eggs until blended. Add the vanilla,
sugars and oil; beat to incorporate.
Add the dry ingredients, in 3 batches,
folding in well after each addition.

5 ▲ Add the carrots, walnuts and
raisins and fold in thoroughly.

6 Pour the mixture into the prepared
tin and bake until the cake springs
back when touched lightly, 40–45
minutes. Let stand 10 minutes, then
unmould and transfer to a rack.

7 ▼ For the icing, cream the butter
with half the icing sugar until soft.
Add the syrup, then beat in the
remaining sugar until blended.

8 Spread the icing over the top of the
cake. Using the tip of a palette knife,
make decorative ridges in the icing.
Cut into squares. Decorate with
walnut halves, if wished.

Cranberry Upside-Down Cake

SERVES 8

12–14 oz (350–400 g) fresh
cranberries

2 oz (55 g) butter

5 oz (140 g) sugar

FOR THE CAKE MIXTURE

2½ oz (70 g) plain flour

1 teaspoon baking powder

3 eggs

4 oz (115 g) sugar

grated rind of 1 orange

1½ oz (45 g) butter, melted

1 Preheat the oven to 350°F/180°C/
Gas 4. Place a baking sheet on the
middle shelf of the oven.

2 Wash the cranberries and pat dry.
Thickly smear the butter on the
bottom and sides of a 9 x 2 in
(23 x 5 cm) round cake tin. Add the
sugar and swirl the tin to coat evenly.

3 ▲ Add the cranberries and spread
in an even layer over the bottom of
the tin.

4 For the cake mixture, sift the flour
and baking powder twice. Set aside.

5 ▲ Combine the eggs, sugar and
orange rind in a heatproof bowl set
over a pan of hot but not boiling
water. With an electric mixer, beat
until the eggs leave a ribbon trail
when the beaters are lifted.

6 Add the flour mixture in
3 batches, folding in well after each
addition. Gently fold in the melted
butter, then pour over the cranberries.

7 Bake for 40 minutes. Leave to cool
for 5 minutes, then run a knife
around the inside edge to loosen.

8 ▲ While the cake is still warm,
invert a plate on top of the tin.
Protecting your hands with oven
gloves, hold plate and tin firmly and
turn them both over quickly. Lift off
the tin carefully.

Pineapple Upside-Down Cake

SERVES 8

4 oz (115 g) butter

7 oz (200 g) dark brown sugar

16 oz (450 g) canned pineapple slices, drained

4 eggs, separated

grated rind of 1 lemon

⅛ tsp salt

4 oz (115 g) caster sugar

3 oz (85 g) plain flour

1 tsp baking powder

1 Preheat a 350°F/180°C/Gas 4 oven.

2 Melt the butter in a 10 in (25 cm) ovenproof cast-iron frying pan. Remove 1 tablespoon of the melted butter and set aside.

3 ▲ Add the brown sugar to the pan and stir until blended. Place the drained pineapple slices on top in one layer. Set aside.

~ **VARIATION** ~

For Dried Apricot Upside-Down Cake, replace the pineapple slices with 8 oz (225 g) of dried apricots. If they need softening, simmer the apricots in about 4 fl oz (125 ml) orange juice until plump and soft. Drain the apricots and discard any remaining cooking liquid.

4 In a bowl, whisk together the egg yolks, reserved butter and lemon rind until well blended. Set aside.

5 ▼ With an electric mixer, beat the egg whites with the salt until stiff. Fold in the caster sugar, 2 tablespoons at a time. Fold in the egg yolk mixture.

6 Sift the flour and baking powder together. Carefully fold into the egg mixture in 3 batches.

7 ▲ Pour the mixture over the pineapple and smooth level.

8 Bake until a skewer inserted in the centre comes out clean, about 30 minutes.

9 While still hot, place a serving plate on top of the pan, bottom-side up. Holding them tightly together with oven gloves, quickly flip over. Serve hot or cold.

Lemon Coconut Layer Cake

SERVES 8–10

5 oz (140 g) plain flour
⅛ teaspoon salt
8 eggs
12¾ oz (375 g) caster sugar
1 tablespoon grated orange rind
grated rind of 2 lemons
juice of 1 lemon
2½ oz (70 g) sweetened, shredded coconut
2 tablespoons cornflour
8 fl oz (250 ml) water
3 oz (85 g) butter
FOR THE FROSTING
4 oz (115 g) unsalted butter
4 oz (115 g) icing sugar
grated rind of 1 lemon
6–8 tablespoons lemon juice
4 oz (115 g) sweetened shredded coconut

1 Preheat a 350°F/180°C/Gas 4 oven. Line 3 8 in (20 cm) cake tins with greaseproof paper and grease. In a bowl, sift together the flour and salt and set aside.

2 ▲ Place 6 of the eggs in a large heatproof bowl set over hot water. With an electric mixer, beat until frothy. Gradually beat in 5½ oz (150 g) caster sugar until the mixture doubles in volume and leaves a ribbon trail when the beaters are lifted, about 10 minutes.

3 ▲ Remove the bowl from the hot water. Fold in the orange rind, half the grated lemon rind and 1 tablespoon of the lemon juice until blended. Fold in the coconut.

4 Sift over the flour mixture in 3 batches, folding in thoroughly after each addition.

5 ▲ Divide the mixture between the prepared tins.

6 Bake until the cakes pull away from the sides of the tins, 25–30 minutes. Let stand 3–5 minutes, then turn out to cool on a rack.

7 In a bowl, blend the cornflour with a little cold water to dissolve. Whisk in the remaining eggs just until blended. Set aside.

8 ▲ In a saucepan, combine the remaining lemon rind and juice, the water, remaining sugar and butter.

9 Over a moderate heat, bring the mixture to the boil. Whisk in the eggs and cornstarch mixture, and return to the boil. Whisk continuously until thick, about 5 minutes. Remove from the heat. Cover with clear film to stop a skin forming and set aside.

10 ▲ For the frosting, cream the butter and icing sugar until smooth. Stir in the lemon rind and enough lemon juice to obtain a thick, spreadable consistency.

11 Sandwich the 3 cake layers with the lemon custard mixture. Spread the frosting over the top and sides. Cover the cake with the coconut, pressing it in gently.

Lemon Yogurt Ring

SERVES 12

8 oz (225 g) butter, at room temperature

10½ oz (300 g) caster sugar

4 eggs, at room temperature, separated

2 teaspoons grated lemon rind

3 fl oz (85 ml) lemon juice

8 fl oz (250 ml) plain yogurt

10 oz (285 g) plain flour

2 teaspoons baking powder

1 teaspoon bicarbonate of soda

½ teaspoon salt

FOR THE GLAZE

4 oz (115 g) icing sugar

2 tablespoons lemon juice

3–4 tablespoons plain yogurt

1 Preheat a 350°F/180°C/Gas 4 oven. Grease a 4⅔ pt (3 litre) bundt or fluted tube tin and dust with flour.

2 With an electric mixer, cream the butter and caster sugar until light and fluffy. Add the egg yolks, 1 at a time, beating well after each addition.

3 ▲ Add the lemon rind, juice and yogurt and stir to blend.

4 Sift together the flour, baking powder and bicarbonate of soda. In another bowl, beat the egg whites and salt until they hold stiff peaks.

5 ▲ Fold the dry ingredients into the butter mixture, then fold in a dollop of egg whites. Fold in the remaining whites until blended.

6 Pour into the tin and bake until a skewer inserted in the centre comes out clean, about 50 minutes. Let stand 15 minutes, then turn out and cool on a rack.

7 For the glaze, sift the icing sugar into a bowl. Stir in the lemon juice and just enough yogurt to make a smooth glaze.

8 ▲ Set the cooled cake on the rack over a sheet of greaseproof paper or a baking sheet. Pour over the glaze and let it drip down the sides. Allow the glaze to set before serving.

Soured Cream Crumble Cake

SERVES 12–14

4 oz (115 g) butter, at room temperature
4½ oz (125 g) caster sugar
3 eggs, at room temperature
7½ oz (215 g) plain flour
1 teaspoon bicarbonate of soda
1 teaspoon baking powder
8 fl oz (250 ml) soured cream
FOR THE TOPPING
8 oz (225 g) dark brown sugar
2 teaspoons ground cinnamon
4 oz (115 g) walnuts, finely chopped
2 oz (55 g) cold butter, cut into pieces

1 Preheat a 350°F/180°C/Gas 4 oven. Line the bottom of a 9 in (23 cm) square cake tin with greaseproof paper and grease.

2 ▲ For the topping, place the brown sugar, cinnamon and walnuts in a bowl. Mix with your fingertips, then add the butter and continue working with your fingertips until the mixture resembles breadcrumbs.

3 To make the cake, cream the butter with an electric mixer until soft. Add the sugar and continue beating until the mixture is light and fluffy.

4 Add the eggs, 1 at a time, beating well after each addition.

5 In another bowl, sift the flour, bicarbonate of soda and baking powder together 3 times.

6 ▲ Fold the dry ingredients into the butter mixture in 3 batches, alternating with the soured cream. Fold until blended after each addition.

7 ▲ Pour half of the batter into the prepared tin and sprinkle over half of the walnut crumb topping mixture.

8 Pour the remaining batter on top and sprinkle over the remaining walnut crumb mixture.

9 Bake until browned, 60–70 minutes. Let stand 5 minutes, then turn out and cool on a rack.

Plum Crumble Cake

SERVES 8–10

5 oz (140 g) butter or margarine, at room temperature
5 oz (140 g) caster sugar
4 eggs, at room temperature
1½ tsp vanilla essence
5 oz (140 g) plain flour
1 tsp baking powder
1½ lb (700 g) red plums, halved and stoned

FOR THE TOPPING

4 oz (115 g) plain flour
4½ oz (130 g) light brown sugar
1½ tsp ground cinnamon
3 oz (85 g) butter, cut in pieces

1 Preheat a 350°F/180°C/Gas 4 oven.

2 For the topping, combine the flour, light brown sugar and cinnamon in a bowl. Add the butter and work the mixture lightly with your fingertips until it resembles coarse breadcrumbs. Set aside.

3 ▲ Line a 10 × 2 in (25 × 5 cm) tin with greaseproof paper and grease.

4 Cream the butter and sugar until light and fluffy.

5 ▲ Beat in the eggs, 1 at a time. Stir in the vanilla.

6 In a bowl, sift together the flour and baking powder, then fold into the butter mixture in 3 batches.

7 ▲ Pour the mixture into the tin. Arrange the plums on top.

8 ▲ Sprinkle the topping over the plums in an even layer.

9 Bake until a skewer inserted in the centre comes out clean, about 45 minutes. Let cool in the tin.

10 To serve, run a knife around the inside edge and invert onto a plate. Invert again onto a serving plate so the topping is right-side up.

~ **VARIATION** ~

This cake can also be made with the same quantity of apricots, peeled if preferred, or stoned cherries, or use a mixture of fruit, such as red or yellow plums, greengages and apricots.

Peach Torte

SERVES 8

4 oz (115 g) plain flour

1 teaspoon baking powder

pinch of salt

4 oz (115 g) unsalted butter, at room
  temperature

6 oz (170 g) sugar

2 eggs, at room temperature

6–7 peaches

sugar and lemon juice, for sprinkling

whipped cream, for serving
  (optional)

1 Preheat the oven to 350°F/180°C/
Gas 4. Grease a 10 in (25 cm)
springform tin.

2 ▲ Sift together the flour, baking
powder and salt. Set aside.

3 With an electric mixer, cream the
butter and sugar until light and fluffy.
Beat in the eggs, then fold in the dry
ingredients until blended.

4 ▲ Spoon the mixture into the tin
and smooth it to make an even layer
over the bottom.

5 ▼ To skin the peaches, drop
several at a time into a pan of gently
boiling water. Boil for 10 seconds,
then remove with a slotted spoon.
Peel off the skin with the aid of a
sharp knife. Cut the peaches in half
and discard the stones.

6 ▲ Arrange the peach halves on
top of the mixture. Sprinkle lightly
with sugar and lemon juice.

7 Bake until golden brown and set,
50–60 minutes. Serve warm, with
whipped cream, if liked.

Apple Ring Cake

SERVES 12

7 eating apples, such as Cox's or Granny Smith
12 fl oz (350 ml) vegetable oil
1 lb (450 g) caster sugar
3 eggs
15 oz (420 g) plain flour
1 tsp salt
1 tsp bicarbonate of soda
1 tsp ground cinnamon
1 tsp vanilla essence
4 oz (115 g) chopped walnuts
6 oz (170 g) raisins
icing sugar, for dusting

1 Preheat a 350°F/180°C/Gas 4 oven. Grease a 9 in (23 cm) ring mould.

2 ▲ Quarter, peel, core and slice the apples into a bowl. Set aside.

3 With an electric mixer, beat the oil and sugar together until blended. Add the eggs and continue beating until the mixture is creamy.

4 Sift together the flour, salt, bicarbonate of soda and cinnamon.

5 ▼ Fold the flour mixture into the egg mixture with the vanilla. Stir in the apples, walnuts and raisins.

6 Pour into the tin and bake until the cake springs back when touched lightly, about 1¼ hours. Let stand 15 minutes, then unmould and transfer to a cooling rack. Dust with a layer of icing sugar before serving.

Orange Cake

SERVES 6

6 oz (170 g) plain flour
1½ tsp baking powder
⅛ tsp salt
4 oz (115 g) butter or margarine
4 oz (115 g) caster sugar
grated rind of 1 large orange
2 eggs, at room temperature
2 tbsp milk
FOR THE SYRUP AND DECORATION
4 oz (115 g) caster sugar
8 fl oz (250 ml) fresh orange juice, strained
3 orange slices, for decorating

1 Preheat a 350°F/180°C/Gas 4 oven. Line an 8 in (20 cm) cake tin with greaseproof paper and grease the paper.

2 ▲ Sift the flour, salt and baking powder onto greaseproof paper.

3 With an electric mixer, cream the butter or margarine until soft. Add the sugar and orange rind and continue beating until light and fluffy. Beat in the eggs, 1 at a time. Fold in the flour in 3 batches, then add the milk.

4 Spoon into the tin and bake until the cake pulls away from the sides, about 30 minutes. Remove from the oven but leave in the tin.

5 Meanwhile, for the syrup, dissolve the sugar in the orange juice over a low heat. Add the orange slices and simmer for 10 minutes. Remove and drain. Let the syrup cool.

6 ▲ Prick the cake all over with a fine skewer. Pour the syrup over the hot cake. It may seem at first that there is too much syrup for the cake to absorb, but it will soak it all up. Unmould when completely cooled and decorate with small triangles of the orange slices arranged on top.

Apple Ring Cake (top), Orange Cake

Orange and Walnut Swiss Roll

SERVES 8

4 eggs, separated

4 oz (115 g) caster sugar

4 oz (115 g) very finely chopped walnuts

⅛ tsp cream of tartar

⅛ tsp salt

icing sugar, for dusting

FOR THE FILLING

10 fl oz (300 ml) whipping cream

1 tbsp caster sugar

grated rind of 1 orange

1 tbsp orange liqueur, such as Grand
   Marnier

1 Preheat a 350°F/180°C/Gas 4 oven.
Line a 12 × 9½ in (30 × 24 cm) Swiss
roll tin with greaseproof paper and
grease the paper.

2 With an electric mixer, beat the
egg yolks and sugar until thick.

3 ▲ Stir in the walnuts.

4 In another bowl, beat the egg
whites with the cream of tartar and
salt until they hold stiff peaks. Fold
gently but thoroughly into the
walnut mixture.

5 Pour the mixture into the prepared
tin and spread level with a spatula.
Bake for 15 minutes.

6 Run a knife along the inside edge to
loosen, then invert the cake onto a
sheet of greaseproof paper dusted with
icing sugar.

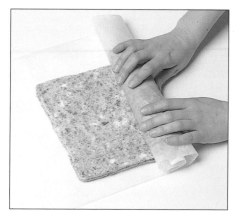

7 ▲ Peel off the baking paper. Roll
up the cake while it is still warm with
the help of the sugared paper. Set
aside to cool.

8 For the filling, whip the cream
until it holds soft peaks. Stir together
the caster sugar and orange rind, then
fold into the whipped cream. Add the
liqueur.

9 ▲ Gently unroll the cake. Spread
the inside with a layer of orange
whipped cream, then re-roll. Keep
refrigerated until ready to serve. Dust
the top with icing sugar just before
serving.

Chocolate Swiss Roll

SERVES 10

8 oz (225 g) plain chocolate

3 tbsp water

2 tbsp rum, brandy or strong coffee

7 eggs, separated

6 oz (170 g) caster sugar

⅛ tsp salt

12 fl oz (350 ml) whipping cream

icing sugar, for dusting

1 Preheat a 350°F/180°C/Gas 4 oven. Line a 15 × 13 in (38 × 33 cm) Swiss roll tin with greaseproof paper and grease the paper.

2 ▲ Combine the chocolate, water and rum or other flavouring in the top of a double boiler, or in a heatproof bowl set over hot water. Heat until melted. Set aside.

3 With an electric mixer, beat the egg yolks and sugar until thick.

4 ▲ Stir in the melted chocolate.

5 In another bowl, beat the egg whites and salt until they hold stiff peaks. Fold a large dollop of egg whites into the yolk mixture to lighten it, then carefully fold in the rest of the whites.

6 ▼ Pour the mixture into the pan; smooth evenly with a metal spatula.

7 Bake for 15 minutes. Remove from the oven, cover with greaseproof paper and a damp cloth. Let stand for 1–2 hours.

8 With an electric mixer, whip the cream until stiff. Set aside.

9 Run a knife along the inside edge to loosen, then invert the cake onto a sheet of greaseproof paper that has been dusted with icing sugar.

10 Peel off the baking paper. Spread with an even layer of whipped cream, then roll up the cake with the help of the sugared paper.

11 Refrigerate for several hours. Before serving, dust with an even layer of icing sugar.

Chocolate Frosted Layer Cake

SERVES 8

8 oz (225 g) butter or margarine, at room temperature

10½ oz (300 g) sugar

4 eggs, at room temperature, separated

2 teaspoons vanilla essence

13½ oz (385 g) plain flour

2 teaspoons baking powder

⅛ teaspoon salt

8 fl oz (250 ml) milk

FOR THE FROSTING

5 oz (140 g) plain chocolate

4 fl oz (125 ml) soured cream

⅛ teaspoon salt

1 Preheat a 350°F/180°C/Gas 4 oven. Line 2 8 in (20 cm) round cake tins with greaseproof and grease. Dust the tins with flour and shake to distribute evenly. Tap to dislodge excess flour.

2 With an electric mixer, cream the butter or margarine until soft. Gradually add the sugar and continue beating until light and fluffy.

3 ▲ Lightly beat the egg yolks, then mix into the creamed butter and sugar with the vanilla.

4 Sift the flour with the baking powder 3 times. Set aside.

5 In another bowl, beat the egg whites with the salt until they hold stiff peaks. Set aside.

6 ▲ Gently fold the dry ingredients into the butter mixture in 3 batches, alternating with the milk.

7 Add a large dollop of the whites and fold in to lighten the mixture. Carefully fold in the remaining whites until just blended.

8 Divide the batter between the tins and bake until the cakes pull away from the sides of the tins, about 30 minutes. Let stand 5 minutes. Turn out and cool on a rack.

9 ▲ For the frosting, melt the chocolate in the top of a double boiler or a bowl set over hot water. When cool, stir in the soured cream and salt.

10 Sandwich the layers with frosting, then spread on the top and side.

Devil's Food Cake with Orange Frosting

SERVES 8–10

2 oz (55 g) unsweetened cocoa powder

6 fl oz (175 ml) boiling water

6 oz (170 g) butter, at room
temperature

12 oz (350 g) dark brown sugar

3 eggs, at room temperature

10 oz (285 g) plain flour

1½ teaspoons bicarbonate of soda

¼ teaspoon baking powder

4 fl oz (125 ml) soured cream

orange rind strips, for decoration

FOR THE FROSTING

10½ oz (300 g) caster sugar

2 egg whites

4 tablespoons frozen orange juice
concentrate

1 tablespoon lemon juice

grated rind of 1 orange

1 Preheat a 350°F/180°C/Gas 4 oven.
Line 2 9 in (23 cm) cake tins with
greaseproof paper and grease. In a
bowl, mix the cocoa and water until
smooth. Set aside.

2 With an electric mixer, cream the
butter and sugar until light and fluffy.
Add the eggs, 1 at a time, beating well
after each addition.

3 ▲ When the cocoa mixture is
lukewarm, add to the butter mixture.

4 ▼ Sift together the flour, soda and
baking powder twice. Fold into the
cocoa mixture in 3 batches,
alternating with the soured cream.

5 Pour into the tins and bake until
the cakes pull away from the sides of
the tins, 30–35 minutes. Let stand 15
minutes. Turn out onto a rack.

6 Thinly slice the orange rind strips.
Blanch in boiling water for 1 minute.

7 ▲ For the frosting, place all the
ingredients in the top of a double
boiler or in a bowl set over hot water.
With an electric mixer, beat until the
mixture holds soft peaks. Continue
beating off the heat until thick
enough to spread.

8 Sandwich the cake layers with
frosting, then spread over the top and
side. Arrange the blanched orange
rind strips on top of the cake.

Best-Ever Chocolate Sandwich

SERVES 12–14

4oz (115g) unsalted butter
4oz (115g) plain flour
2oz (55g) cocoa powder
1 tsp baking powder
⅛ tsp salt
6 eggs
8oz (225g) caster sugar
2 tsp vanilla essence
FOR THE ICING
8oz (225g) plain chocolate, chopped
3oz (85g) unsalted butter
3 eggs, separated
8 floz (250ml) whipping cream
3 tbsp caster sugar

1 Preheat a 350°F/180°C/Gas 4 oven. Line 3 8 × 1½ in (20 × 3 cm) round tins with greaseproof paper and grease.

2 ▲ Dust evenly with flour and spread with a brush. Set aside.

~ **VARIATION** ~

For a simpler icing, combine 8 floz (250ml) whipping cream with 8oz (225g) finely chopped plain chocolate in a saucepan. Stir over a low heat until the chocolate has melted. Cool and whisk to spreading consistency.

3 ▲ Melt the butter over a low heat. With a spoon, skim off any foam that rises to the surface. Set aside.

4 ▲ Sift the flour, cocoa, baking powder and salt together 3 times and set aside.

5 Place the eggs and sugar in a large heatproof bowl set over a pan of hot water. With an electric mixer, beat until the mixture doubles in volume and is thick enough to leave a ribbon trail when the beaters are lifted, about 10 minutes. Add the vanilla.

6 ▲ Sift over the dry ingredients in 3 batches, folding in carefully after each addition. Fold in the butter.

7 Divide the mixture between the tins and bake until the cakes pull away from the sides of the tin, about 25 minutes. Transfer to a rack.

8 For the icing, melt the chopped chocolate in the top of a double boiler, or in a heatproof bowl set over hot water.

9 ▲ Off the heat, stir in the butter and egg yolks. Return to a low heat and stir until thick. Remove from the heat and set aside.

10 Whip the cream until firm; set aside. In another bowl, beat the egg whites until stiff. Add the sugar and beat until glossy.

11 Fold the cream into the chocolate mixture, then carefully fold in the egg whites. Refrigerate for 20 minutes to thicken the icing.

12 ▲ Sandwich the cake layers with icing, stacking them carefully. Spread the remaining icing evenly over the top and sides of the cake.

Rich Chocolate Nut Cake

SERVES 10

8 oz (225 g) butter
8 oz (225 g) plain chocolate
4 oz (115 g) cocoa powder
12 oz (350 g) caster sugar
6 eggs
3 fl oz (85 ml) brandy or cognac
8 oz (225 g) finely chopped hazelnuts
FOR THE GLAZE
2 oz (55 g) butter
5 oz (140 g) bitter cooking chocolate
2 tbsp milk
1 tsp vanilla essence

1 Preheat a 350°F/180°C/Gas 4 oven. Line a 9 × 2 in (23 × 5 cm) round tin with greaseproof paper and grease.

2 Melt the butter and chocolate together in the top of a double boiler, or in a heatproof bowl set over hot water. Set aside to cool.

3 ▼ Sift the cocoa into a bowl. Add the sugar and eggs and stir until just combined. Pour in the melted chocolate mixture and brandy.

4 Fold in three-quarters of the nuts, then pour the mixture into the prepared tin.

5 ▲ Set the tin inside a large tin and pour 1 in (2.5 cm) of hot water into the outer tin. Bake until the cake is firm to the touch, about 45 minutes. Let stand 15 minutes, then unmould and transfer to a cooling rack.

6 Wrap the cake in greaseproof paper and refrigerate for 6 hours.

7 For the glaze, combine the butter, chocolate, milk and vanilla in the top of a double boiler or in a heatproof bowl set over hot water, until melted.

8 Place a piece of greaseproof paper under the cake, then drizzle spoonfuls of glaze along the edge to drip down and coat the sides. Pour the remaining glaze on top of the cake.

9 ▲ Cover the sides of the cake with the remaining nuts, gently pressing them on with the palm of your hand.

Chocolate Layer Cake

SERVES 8–10

4 oz (115 g) plain chocolate
6 oz (170 g) butter
1 lb (450 g) caster sugar
3 eggs
1 tsp vanilla essence
6 oz (170 g) plain flour
1 tsp baking powder
4 oz (115 g) chopped walnuts
FOR THE TOPPING
12 fl oz (350 ml) whipping cream
8 oz (225 g) plain chocolate
1 tbsp vegetable oil

1 Preheat a 350°F/180°C/Gas 4 oven. Line 2 8 in (20 cm) cake tins with greaseproof paper and grease.

2 Melt the chocolate and butter together in the top of a double boiler, or in a heatproof bowl set over a saucepan of hot water.

3 ▲ Transfer to a mixing bowl and stir in the sugar. Add the eggs and vanilla and mix until well blended.

~ **VARIATION** ~

To make Chocolate Ice Cream Layer Cake, sandwich the cake layers with softened vanilla ice cream. Freeze before serving.

4 ▲ Sift over the flour and baking powder. Stir in the walnuts.

5 Divide the mixture between the prepared tins and spread level.

6 Bake until a skewer inserted in the centre comes out clean, about 30 minutes. Let stand 10 minutes, then unmould and transfer to a rack.

7 When the cakes are cool, whip the cream until firm. With a long serrated knife, carefully slice each cake in half horizontally.

8 Sandwich the layers with some of the whipped cream and spread the remainder over the top and sides of the cake. Refrigerate until needed.

9 ▼ For the chocolate curls, melt the chocolate and oil in the top of a double boiler or a bowl set over hot water. Transfer to a non-porous surface. Spread to a ⅜ in (1 cm) thick rectangle. Just before the chocolate sets, hold the blade of a straight knife at an angle to the chocolate and scrape across the surface to make curls. Place on top of the cake.

Sachertorte

SERVES 8–10

4 oz (115 g) plain chocolate
3 oz (85 g) unsalted butter, at room temperature
2 oz (55 g) sugar
4 eggs, separated
1 extra egg white
¼ teaspoon salt
2½ oz (70 g) plain flour, sifted
FOR THE TOPPING
5 tablespoons apricot jam
8 fl oz (250 ml) plus 1 tablespoon water
½ oz (15 g) unsalted butter
6 oz (170 g) plain chocolate
3 oz (85 g) sugar
ready-made chocolate decorating icing (optional)

1 Preheat the oven to 325°F/170°C/ Gas 3. Line a 9 × 2 in (23 × 5 cm) cake tin with greaseproof paper and grease.

2 ▲ Melt the chocolate in the top of a double boiler, or in a heatproof bowl set over hot water. Set aside.

3 With an electric mixer, cream the butter and sugar until light and fluffy. Stir in the chocolate.

4 ▲ Beat in the yolks, 1 at a time.

5 In another bowl, beat the egg whites with the salt until stiff.

6 ▲ Fold a dollop of whites into the chocolate mixture to lighten it. Fold in the remaining whites in 3 batches, alternating with the sifted flour.

7 ▲ Pour into the tin and bake until a cake tester comes out clean, about 45 minutes. Turn out onto a rack.

8 ▲ Meanwhile, melt the jam with 1 tablespoon of the water over low heat, then strain for a smooth consistency.

9 For the frosting, melt the butter and chocolate in the top of a double boiler or a bowl set over hot water.

10 ▲ In a heavy saucepan, dissolve the sugar in the remaining water over low heat. Raise the heat and boil until it reaches 225°F/107°C (thread stage) on a sugar thermometer. Immediately plunge the bottom of the pan into cold water for 1 minute. Pour into the chocolate mixture and stir to blend. Let cool for a few minutes.

11 To assemble, brush the warm jam over the cake. Starting in the centre, pour over the frosting and work outward in a circular movement. Tilt the rack to spread; use a palette knife to smooth the side of the cake. Leave to set overnight. If wished, decorate with chocolate icing.

Raspberry-Hazelnut Meringue Cake

SERVES 8

5 oz (140 g) hazelnuts
4 egg whites
⅛ teaspoon salt
7 oz (200 g) sugar
½ teaspoon vanilla essence
FOR THE FILLING
10 fl oz (300 ml) whipping cream
1 lb 8 oz (700 g) raspberries

1 Preheat a 350°F/180°C/Gas 4 oven. Line the bottom of 2 8 in (20 cm) cake tins with greaseproof paper and grease.

2 Spread the hazelnuts on a baking sheet and bake until lightly toasted, about 8 minutes. Let cool slightly.

3 ▲ Rub the hazelnuts vigorously in a clean tea towel to remove most of the skins.

4 Grind the nuts in a food processor, blender, or coffee grinder until they are the consistency of coarse sand.

5 Reduce oven to 300°F/150°C/Gas 2.

6 With an electric mixer, beat the egg whites and salt until they hold stiff peaks. Beat in 2 tablespoons of the sugar, then fold in the remaining sugar, a few tablespoons at a time, with a rubber scraper. Fold in the vanilla and the hazelnuts.

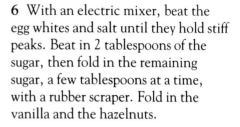

7 ▲ Divide the batter between the prepared tins and spread level.

8 Bake for 1¼ hours. If the meringues brown too quickly, protect with a sheet of foil. Let stand 5 minutes, then carefully run a knife around the inside edge of the tins to loosen. Turn out onto a rack to cool.

9 For the filling, whip the cream just until firm.

10 ▲ Spread half the cream in an even layer on one meringue round and top with half the raspberries.

11 Top with the other meringue round. Spread the remaining cream on top and arrange the remaining raspberries over the cream. Refrigerate for 1 hour to facilitate cutting.

Forgotten Gâteau

SERVES 6

6 egg whites, at room temperature

½ teaspoon cream of tartar

⅛ teaspoon salt

10½ oz (300 g) caster sugar

1 teaspoon vanilla essence

6 fl oz (175 ml) whipping cream

FOR THE SAUCE

12 oz (350 g) fresh or thawed frozen
raspberries

2–3 tablespoons icing sugar

1 Preheat a 450°F/230°C/Gas 8 oven.
Grease a 2⅓ pt (1.5 litre) ring mould.

2 ▲ With an electric mixer, beat the
egg whites, cream of tartar and salt
until they hold soft peaks. Gradually
add the sugar and beat until glossy and
stiff. Fold in the vanilla.

3 ▲ Spoon into the prepared mould
and smooth the top level.

4 Place in the oven, then turn the
oven off. Leave overnight; do not
open the oven door at any time.

5 ▼ To serve, gently loosen the edge
with a sharp knife and turn out onto a
serving plate. Whip the cream until
firm. Spread it over the top and upper
sides of the meringue and decorate
with any meringue crumbs.

6 ▲ For the sauce, purée the fruit,
then strain. Sweeten to taste.

~ COOK'S TIP ~

This recipe is not suitable for fan-
assisted and solid fuel ovens.

Nut and Apple Gâteau

SERVES 8

4 oz (115 g) pecan nuts or walnuts

2 oz (55 g) plain flour

2 tsp baking powder

¼ tsp salt

2 large cooking apples

3 eggs

8 oz (225 g) caster sugar

1 tsp vanilla essence

6 fl oz (175 ml) whipping cream

1 Preheat a 325°F/170°C/Gas 3 oven. Line 2 9 in (23 cm) cake tins with greaseproof paper and grease the paper. Spread the nuts on a baking sheet and bake for 10 minutes.

2 Finely chop the nuts. Reserve 1½ tablespoons and place the rest in a mixing bowl. Sift over the flour, baking powder and salt and stir.

3 ▲ Quarter, core and peel the apples. Cut into ⅛ in (3 mm) dice, then stir into the nut-flour mixture.

4 ▲ With an electric mixer, beat the eggs until frothy. Gradually add the sugar and vanilla and beat until a ribbon forms, about 8 minutes. Gently fold in the flour mixture.

5 Pour into the tins and level the tops. Bake until a skewer inserted in the centre comes out clean, about 35 minutes. Let stand 10 minutes.

6 ▲ To loosen, run a knife around the inside edge of each layer. Let cool.

7 ▲ Whip the cream until firm. Spread half over the cake. Top with the second cake. Pipe whipped cream rosettes on top and sprinkle over the reserved nuts before serving.

Almond Cake

SERVES 4–6

8 oz (225 g) blanched whole almonds, plus more for decorating
1 oz (30 g) butter
3 oz (85 g) icing sugar
3 eggs
½ tsp almond essence
1 oz (30 g) plain flour
3 egg whites
1 tbsp caster sugar

1 ▲ Preheat a 325°F/170°C/Gas 3 oven. Line a 9 in (23 cm) round cake tin with greaseproof paper and grease.

2 ▲ Spread the almonds in a baking tray and toast for 10 minutes. Cool, then coarsely chop 8 oz (225 g).

3 Melt the butter and set aside.

4 Preheat a 400°F/200°C/Gas 6 oven.

5 Grind the chopped almonds with half the icing sugar in a food processor, blender or grinder. Transfer to a mixing bowl.

6 ▲ Add the whole eggs and remaining icing sugar. With an electric mixer, beat until the mixture forms a ribbon when the beaters are lifted. Mix in the butter and almond essence. Sift over the flour and fold in gently.

7 With an electric mixer, beat the egg whites until they hold soft peaks. Add the caster sugar and beat until stiff and glossy.

8 ▲ Fold the whites into the almond mixture in 4 batches.

9 Spoon the mixture into the prepared tin and bake in the centre of the oven until golden brown, about 15–20 minutes. Decorate the top with the remaining toasted whole almonds. Serve warm.

Walnut Coffee Gâteau

SERVES 8–10

5 oz (140 g) walnuts
5½ oz (150 g) sugar
5 eggs, separated
2 oz (55 g) dry breadcrumbs
1 tablespoon unsweetened cocoa powder
1 tablespoon instant coffee
2 tablespoons rum or lemon juice
⅛ teaspoon salt
6 tablespoons redcurrant jelly
chopped walnuts, for decorating
FOR THE FROSTING
8 oz (225 g) plain chocolate
1¼ pt (750 ml) whipping cream

3 ▲ Grind the nuts with 3 tablespoons of the sugar in a food processor, blender, or coffee grinder.

4 With an electric mixer, beat the egg yolks and remaining sugar until thick and lemon-coloured.

5 ▲ Fold in the walnuts. Stir in the breadcrumbs, cocoa, coffee and rum or lemon juice.

6 ▲ In another bowl, beat the egg whites with the salt until they hold stiff peaks. Fold carefully into the walnut mixture with a rubber scraper.

7 Pour the meringue batter into the prepared tin and bake until the top of the cake springs back when touched lightly, about 45 minutes. Let the cake stand for 5 minutes, then turn out and cool on a rack.

8 ▲ When cool, slice the cake in half horizontally.

9 With an electric mixer, beat the chocolate frosting mixture on low speed until it becomes lighter, about 30 seconds. Do not overbeat or it may become grainy.

10 ▲ Warm the jelly in a saucepan until melted, then brush over the cut cake layer. Spread with some of the chocolate frosting, then sandwich with the remaining cake layer. Brush the top of the cake with jelly, then cover the side and top with the remaining chocolate frosting. Make a starburst pattern by pressing gently with a table knife in lines radiating from the centre. Sprinkle the chopped walnuts around the edge.

1 ▲ For the frosting, combine the chocolate and cream in the top of a double boiler, or in a heatproof bowl set over simmering water. Stir until the chocolate melts. Let cool, then cover and refrigerate overnight or until the mixture is firm.

2 Preheat the oven to 350°F/180°C/ Gas 4. Line a 9 × 2 in (23 × 5 cm) cake tin with greaseproof paper and grease.

Light Fruit Cake

MAKES 2 LOAVES

8 oz (225 g) prunes
8 oz (225 g) dates
8 oz (225 g) currants
8 oz (225 g) sultanas
8 fl oz (250 ml) dry white wine
8 fl oz (250 ml) rum
12 oz (350 g) plain flour
2 tsp baking powder
1 tsp ground cinnamon
½ tsp grated nutmeg
8 oz (225 g) butter, at room temperature
8 oz (225 g) caster sugar
4 eggs, at room temperature, lightly beaten
1 tsp vanilla essence

1 Stone the prunes and dates and chop finely. Place in a bowl with the currants and sultanas.

2 ▲ Stir in the wine and rum and let stand, covered, for 48 hours. Stir occasionally.

3 Preheat a 300°F/150°C/Gas 2 oven with a tray of hot water in the bottom. Line 2 9 × 5 in (23 × 13 cm) tins with greaseproof paper and grease.

4 Sift together the flour, baking powder, cinnamon, and nutmeg.

5 ▲ With an electric mixer, cream the butter and sugar together until light and fluffy.

6 Gradually add the eggs and vanilla. Fold in the flour mixture in 3 batches. Fold in the dried fruit mixture and its soaking liquid.

7 ▲ Divide the mixture between the tins and bake until a skewer inserted in the centre comes out clean, about 1½ hours.

8 Let stand 20 minutes, then unmould and transfer to a cooling rack. Wrap in foil and store in an airtight container. If possible, leave for at least 1 week before serving to allow the flavours to mellow.

Rich Fruit Cake

SERVES 12

5 oz (140 g) currants

6 oz (170 g) raisins

2 oz (55 g) sultanas

2 oz (55 g) glacé cherries, halved

3 tbsp sweet sherry

6 oz (170 g) butter

7 oz (200 g) dark brown sugar

2 size 1 eggs, at room temperature

7 oz (200 g) plain flour

2 tsp baking powder

2 tsp each ground ginger, allspice, and
   cinnamon

1 tbsp golden syrup

1 tbsp milk

2 oz (55 g) cut mixed peel

4 oz (115 g) chopped walnuts

FOR THE DECORATION

8 oz (225 g) caster sugar

4 fl oz (125 ml) water

1 lemon, thinly sliced

½ orange, thinly sliced

4 fl oz (125 ml) orange marmalade

glacé cherries

1 One day before preparing, combine the currants, raisins, sultanas and cherries in a bowl. Stir in the sherry. Cover and let stand overnight to soak.

2 Preheat a 300°F/150°C/Gas 2 oven. Line a 9 × 3 in (23 × 8 cm) springform tin with greaseproof paper and grease. Place a tray of hot water on the bottom of the oven.

3 With an electric mixer, cream the butter and sugar until light and fluffy. Beat in the eggs, 1 at a time.

4 ▲ Sift the flour, baking powder and spices together 3 times. Fold into the butter mixture in 3 batches. Fold in the syrup, milk, dried fruit and liquid, mixed peel and nuts.

5 ▲ Spoon into the tin, spreading out so there is a slight depression in the centre of the mixture.

6 Bake until a skewer inserted in the centre comes out clean, 2½–3 hours. Cover with foil when the top is golden to prevent over-browning. Cool in the tin on a rack.

7 ▲ For the decoration, combine the sugar and water in a saucepan and bring to the boil. Add the lemon and orange slices and cook until crystallized, about 20 minutes. Work in batches, if necessary. Remove the fruit with a slotted spoon. Pour the remaining syrup over the cake and let cool. Melt the marmalade over low heat, then brush over the top of the cake. Decorate with the crystallized citrus slices and cherries.

Whiskey Cake

MAKES 1 LOAF

6 oz (170 g) chopped walnuts

3 oz (85 g) raisins, chopped

3 oz (85 g) currants

4 oz (115 g) plain flour

1 tsp baking powder

¼ tsp salt

4 oz (115 g) butter

8 oz (225 g) caster sugar

3 eggs, at room temperature, separated

1 tsp grated nutmeg

½ tsp ground cinnamon

3 fl oz (85 ml) Irish whiskey or bourbon

icing sugar, for dusting

1 ▼ Preheat a 325°F/170°C/Gas 3 oven. Line a 9 × 5 in (23 × 13 cm) loaf tin with greaseproof paper. Grease the paper and sides of the pan.

2 ▲ Place the walnuts, raisins, and currants in a bowl. Sprinkle over 2 tablespoons of the flour, mix and set aside. Sift together the remaining flour, baking powder and salt.

3 ▲ Cream the butter and sugar until light and fluffy. Beat in the egg yolks.

4 Mix the nutmeg, cinnamon and whiskey. Fold into the butter mixture, alternating with the flour mixture.

5 ▲ In another bowl, beat the egg whites until stiff. Fold into the whiskey mixture until just blended. Fold in the walnut mixture.

6 Bake until a skewer inserted in the centre comes out clean, about 1 hour. Let cool in the pan. Dust with icing sugar over a template.

Gingerbread

SERVES 8–10

1 tbsp vinegar
6 fl oz (175 ml) milk
6 oz (170 g) plain flour
2 tsp baking powder
¼ tsp bicarbonate of soda
½ tsp salt
2 tsp ground ginger
1 tsp ground cinnamon
¼ tsp ground cloves
4 oz (115 g) butter, at room temperature
4 oz (115 g) caster sugar
1 egg, at room temperature
6 fl oz (175 ml) black treacle
whipped cream, for serving
chopped stem ginger, for decorating

1 ▲ Preheat a 350°F/180°C/Gas 4 oven. Line an 8 in (20 cm) square cake tin with greaseproof paper and grease the paper and the sides of the pan.

2 ▲ Add the vinegar to the milk and set aside. It will curdle.

3 In another mixing bowl, sift all the dry ingredients together 3 times and set aside.

4 With an electric mixer, cream the butter and sugar until light and fluffy. Beat in the egg until well combined.

5 ▼ Stir in the black treacle.

6 ▲ Fold in the dry ingredients in 4 batches, alternating with the curdled milk. Mix only enough to blend.

7 Pour into the prepared tin and bake until firm, 45–50 minutes. Cut into squares and serve warm, with whipped cream. Decorate with the stem ginger.

Classic Cheesecake

SERVES 8

2 oz (55 g) digestive biscuits, crushed

2 lb (900 g) cream cheese, at room temperature

8¾ oz (240 g) sugar

grated rind of 1 lemon

3 tablespoons lemon juice

1 teapoon vanilla essence

4 eggs, at room temperature

1 Preheat the oven to 325°F/170°C/ Gas 3. Grease an 8 in (20 cm) springform tin. Place on a round of foil 4–5 in (10–12.5 cm) larger than the diameter of the tin. Press it up the sides to seal tightly.

2 Sprinkle the crushed biscuits in the base of the tin. Press to form an even layer.

3 With an electric mixer, beat the cream cheese until smooth. Add the sugar, lemon rind and juice, and vanilla, and beat until blended. Beat in the eggs, 1 at a time. Beat just enough to blend thoroughly.

4 ▲ Pour into the prepared tin. Set the tin in a larger baking tray and place in the oven. Pour enough hot water in the outer tray to come 1 in (2.5 cm) up the side of the tin.

5 Bake until the top of the cake is golden brown, about 1½ hours. Let cool in the tin.

6 ▼ Run a knife around the edge to loosen, then remove the rim of the tin. Refrigerate for at least 4 hours before serving.

Chocolate Cheesecake

SERVES 10–12

10 oz (285 g) plain chocolate

2 lb 8 oz (1.2 kg) cream cheese, at room temperature

7 oz (200 g) sugar

2 teaspoons vanilla essence

4 eggs, at room temperature

6 fl oz (175 ml) soured cream

1 tablespoon cocoa powder

FOR THE BASE

7 oz (200 g) chocolate biscuits, crushed

3 oz (85 g) butter, melted

½ teaspoon ground cinnamon

1 Preheat a 350°F/180°C/Gas 4 oven. Grease the bottom and sides of a 9 × 3 in (23 × 7.5 cm) springform tin.

2 ▲ For the base, mix the crushed biscuits with the butter and cinnamon. Press evenly onto the bottom of the tin.

3 Melt the chocolate in the top of a double boiler, or in a heatproof bowl set over hot water. Set aside.

4 Beat the cream cheese until smooth, then beat in the sugar and vanilla. Add the eggs, 1 at a time.

5 Stir the soured cream into the cocoa powder to form a paste. Add to the cream cheese mixture. Stir in the melted chocolate.

6 ▼ Pour into the crust. Bake for 1 hour. Let cool in the tin; remove rim. Refrigerate before serving.

Classic Cheesecake (top), Chocolate Cheesecake

Lemon Mousse Cheesecake

SERVES 10–12

2½ lb (1.2 kg) cream cheese, at room temperature

12 oz (350 g) caster sugar

1½ oz (45 g) plain flour

4 eggs, at room temperature, separated

4 fl oz (125 ml) fresh lemon juice

grated rind of 2 lemons

4 oz (115 g) digestive biscuits, crushed

1 Preheat a 325°F/170°C/Gas 3 oven. Line a 10 × 2 in (25 × 5 cm) round cake tin with greaseproof paper and grease the paper.

2 With an electric mixer, beat the cream cheese until smooth. Gradually add 10 oz (285 g) of the sugar, and beat until light. Beat in the flour.

3 ▲ Add the egg yolks, and lemon juice and rind, and beat until smooth and well blended.

4 In another bowl, beat the egg whites until they hold soft peaks. Add the remaining sugar and beat until stiff and glossy.

5 ▲ Add the egg whites to the cheese mixture and gently fold in.

6 Pour the mixture into the prepared tin, then place the tin in a larger baking tin. Place in the oven and pour hot water in the outer tin to come 1 in (2.5 cm) up the side.

7 Bake until golden, 60–65 minutes. Let cool in the pan on a rack. Cover and refrigerate for at least 4 hours.

8 To unmould, run a knife around the inside edge. Place a flat plate, bottom-side up, over the pan and invert onto the plate. Smooth the top with a metal spatula.

9 ▲ Sprinkle the biscuits over the top in an even layer, pressing down slightly to make a top crust.

10 To serve, cut slices with a sharp knife dipped in hot water.

Marbled Cheesecake

SERVES 10

2 oz (55 g) unsweetened cocoa powder

5 tablespoons hot water

2 lb (900 g) cream cheese, at room
  temperature

7 oz (200 g) sugar

4 eggs

1 teaspoon vanilla essence

2½ oz (70 g) digestive biscuits, crushed

1 Preheat a 350°F/180°C/Gas 4 oven.
Line an 8 × 3 in (20 × 8 cm) cake tin
with greaseproof paper and grease.

2 Sift the cocoa powder into a bowl.
Pour over the hot water and stir to
dissolve. Set aside.

3 With an electric mixer, beat the
cheese until smooth and creamy. Add
the sugar and beat to incorporate.
Beat in the eggs, one at a time. Do not
overmix.

4 Divide the mixture evenly between
2 bowls. Stir the chocolate mixture
into one, then add the vanilla to the
remaining mixture.

5 ▲ Pour a cupful of the plain
mixture into the centre of the tin; it
will spread out into an even layer.
Slowly pour over a cupful of chocolate
mixture in the centre.

6 ▲ Repeat alternating cupfuls of the
batters in a circular pattern until both
are used up.

7 Set the tin in a larger baking tray
and pour in hot water to come 1½ in
(3 cm) up the sides of the cake tin.

8 Bake until the top of the cake is
golden, about 1½ hours. It will rise
during baking but will sink later. Let
cool in the tin on a rack.

9 To turn out, run a knife around the
inside edge. Place a flat plate, bottom-
side up, over the tin and invert onto
the plate.

10 ▼ Sprinkle the crushed biscuits
evenly over the base, gently place
another plate over them, and invert
again. Cover and refrigerate for at
least 3 hours, or overnight. To serve,
cut slices with a sharp knife dipped in
hot water.

Heart Cake

MAKES 1 CAKE

8 oz (225 g) butter or margarine, at room temperature

8 oz (225 g) caster sugar

4 eggs, at room temperature

6 oz (170 g) plain flour

1 tsp baking powder

½ tsp bicarbonate of soda

2 tbsp milk

1 tsp vanilla essence

FOR ICING AND DECORATING

3 egg whites

12 oz (350 g) caster sugar

2 tbsp cold water

2 tbsp fresh lemon juice

¼ tsp cream of tartar

pink food colouring

3–4 oz (85–115 g) icing sugar

1 Preheat a 350°F/180°C/Gas 4 oven. Line an 8 in (20 cm) heart-shaped tin with greaseproof paper and grease.

2 ▲ With an electric mixer, cream the butter or margarine and sugar until light and fluffy. Add the eggs, 1 at a time, beating thoroughly after each addition.

3 Sift the flour, baking powder and baking soda together. Fold the dry ingredients into the butter mixture in 3 batches, alternating with the milk. Stir in the vanilla.

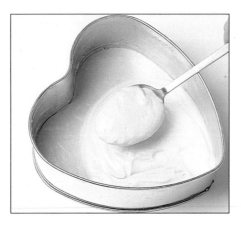

4 ▲ Spoon the mixture into the prepared tin and bake until a skewer inserted in the centre comes out clean, 35–40 minutes. Let the cake stand in the tin for 5 minutes, then unmould and transfer to a rack to cool completely.

5 For the icing, combine 2 of the egg whites, the caster sugar, water, lemon juice and cream of tartar in the top of a double boiler or in a bowl set over simmering water. With an electric mixer, beat until thick and holding soft peaks, about 7 minutes. Remove from the heat and continue beating until the mixture is thick enough to spread. Tint the icing with the pink food colouring.

6 ▲ Put the cake on a board, about 12 in (30 cm) square, covered in foil or in paper suitable for contact with food. Spread the icing evenly on the cake. Smooth the top and sides. Leave to set for 3–4 hours, or overnight.

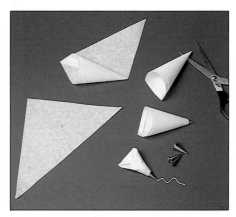

7 ▲ For the paper piping bags, fold an 11 × 8 in (28 × 20 cm) sheet of greaseproof paper in half diagonally, then cut into 2 pieces along the fold mark. Roll over the short side, so that it meets the right-angled corner and forms a cone. To form the piping bag, hold the cone in place with one hand, wrap the point of the long side of the triangle around the cone, and tuck inside, folding over twice to secure. Snip a hole in the pointed end and slip in a small metal piping nozzle to extend about ¼ in (5 mm).

8 For the piped decorations, place 1 tablespoon of the remaining egg white in a bowl and whisk until frothy. Gradually beat in enough icing sugar to make a stiff mixture suitable for piping.

9 ▲ Spoon into a paper piping bag to half-fill. Fold over the top and squeeze to pipe decorations on the top and sides of the cake.

Iced Fancies

MAKES 16

4 oz (115 g) butter, at room temperature
8 oz (225 g) caster sugar
2 eggs, at room temperature
6 oz (170 g) plain flour
¼ tsp salt
1½ tsp baking powder
4 fl oz (125 ml) plus 1 tbsp milk
1 tsp vanilla essence
FOR ICING AND DECORATING
2 large egg whites
14 oz (400 g) sifted icing sugar
1–2 drops glycerine
juice of 1 lemon
food colourings
hundreds and thousands, for decorating
crystallized lemon and orange slices, for decorating

1 Preheat a 375°F/190°C/Gas 5 oven.

2 ▲ Line 16 bun-tray cups with fluted paper baking cases, or grease.

~ COOK'S TIP ~

Ready-made cake decorating products are widely available, and may be used, if preferred, instead of the recipes given for icing and decorating. Coloured icing in ready-to-pipe tubes is useful.

3 With an electric mixer, cream the butter and sugar until light and fluffy. Add the eggs, 1 at a time, beating well after each addition.

4 Sift together the flour, salt and baking powder. Stir into the butter mixture, alternating with the milk. Stir in the vanilla.

5 ▲ Fill the cups half-full and bake until the tops spring back when touched lightly, about 20 minutes. Let the cakes stand in the tray for 5 minutes, then unmould and transfer to a rack to cool completely.

6 For the icing, beat the egg whites until stiff but not dry. Gradually add the sugar, glycerine and lemon juice, and continue beating for 1 minute. The consistency should be spreadable. If necessary, thin with a little water or add more sifted icing sugar.

7 ▲ Divide the icing between several bowls and tint with food colourings. Spread different coloured icings over the cooled cakes.

8 ▲ Decorate the cakes as wished, with sugar decorations such as hundreds and thousands.

9 ▲ Other decorations include crystallized orange and lemon slices. Cut into small pieces and arrange on top of the cakes. Alternatively, use other suitable sweets.

10 ▲ To make freehand iced decorations, fill paper piping bags with different colour icings. Pipe on faces, or make other designs.

Snake Cake

SERVES 10–12

8 oz (225 g) butter or margarine, at room temperature

grated rind and juice of 1 small orange

8 oz (225 g) sugar

4 eggs, at room temperature, separated

6 oz (170 g) plain flour

1 teaspoon baking powder

pinch of salt

FOR THE ICING AND DECORATING

1 oz (30 g) butter, at room temperature

12 oz (350 g) icing sugar

5 oz (140 g) plain chocolate

pinch of salt

4 fl oz (125 ml) soured cream

1 egg white

green and blue food colourings

1 Preheat the oven to 375°F/190°C/ Gas 5. Grease 2 8½ oz (22 cm) ring tins and dust them with flour.

2 Cream the butter or margarine, orange rind and sugar until light. Beat in the egg yolks, 1 at a time.

3 Sift the flour and baking powder. Fold into the butter mixture, alternating with the orange juice.

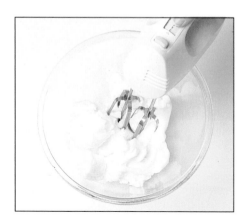

4 ▲ In another bowl, beat the egg whites and salt until stiff.

5 Fold a large dollop of the egg whites into the creamed butter mixture to lighten it, then gently fold in the remaining whites.

6 Divide the mixture between the prepared tins and bake until a skewer inserted in the centre comes out clean, about 25 minutes. Leave to stand for 5 minutes, then turn out on to a wire rack to cool.

7 Prepare a board, 24 x 8 in (60 x 20 cm), covered in paper suitable for contact with food, or in foil.

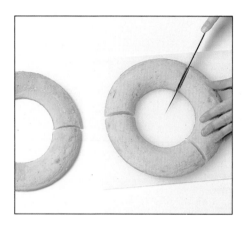

8 ▲ Cut the cakes into 3 even pieces. Trim to level the flat side, if necessary, and shape the head by cutting off wedges from the front. Shape the tail in the same way.

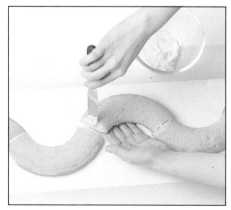

9 ▲ For the buttercream, mix the butter with 1½ oz (45 g) of the icing sugar. Use to join the cake sections and arrange on the board.

10 ▲ For the chocolate icing, melt the chocolate. Stir in the salt and soured cream. When cool, spread over the cake and smooth the surface.

11 ▲ For the decoration, beat the egg white until frothy. Add enough of the remaining icing sugar to obtain a thick mixture. Divide among several bowls and add food colourings.

12 ▲ Fill paper piping bags with icing and pipe decorations along the top of the cake.

Sun Cake

SERVES 10–12

4 oz (115 g) unsalted butter
6 eggs
8 oz (225 g) caster sugar
4 oz (115 g) plain flour
½ tsp salt
1 tsp vanilla essence

FOR ICING AND DECORATING

1 oz (30 g) unsalted butter, at room temperature
1 lb (450 g) sifted icing sugar
4 fl oz (125 ml) apricot jam
2 tbsp water
2 large egg whites
1–2 drops glycerine
juice of 1 lemon
yellow and orange food colourings

1 Preheat a 350°F/180°C/Gas 4 oven. Line 2 8 × 2 in (20 × 5 cm) round cake tins, then grease and flour.

2 In a saucepan, melt the butter over very low heat. Skim off any foam that rises to the surface, then set aside.

3 ▲ Place a heatproof bowl over a saucepan of hot water. Add the eggs and sugar. Beat with an electric mixer until the mixture doubles in volume and is thick enough to leave a ribbon trail when the beaters are lifted, 8–10 minutes.

4 Sift the flour and salt together 3 times. Sift over the egg mixture in 3 batches, folding in well after each addition. Fold in the melted butter and vanilla.

5 Divide the mixture between the tins. Level the surfaces and bake until the cakes shrink slightly from the sides of the tins, 25–30 minutes. Let stand 5 minutes, then unmould and transfer to a cooling rack.

6 Prepare a board, 16 in (40 cm) square, covered in paper suitable for contact with food, or in foil.

7 ▲ For the sunbeams, cut one of the cakes into 8 equal wedges. Cut away a rounded piece from the base of each so that they fit neatly up against the sides of the whole cake.

8 ▲ For the butter icing, mix the butter and 1 oz (30 g) of the icing sugar. Use to attach the sunbeams.

9 ▲ Melt the jam with the water and brush over the cake. Place on the board and straighten, if necessary.

10 ▲ For the icing, beat the egg whites until stiff but not dry. Gradually add 14 oz (400 g) icing sugar, the glycerine and lemon juice, and continue beating for 1 minute. If necessary, thin with water or add a little more sugar. Tint with yellow food colouring and spread over the cake.

11 ▲ Divide the remaining icing in half and tint with more food colouring to obtain bright yellow and orange. Pipe decorative zigzags on the sunbeams and a face in the middle.

Jack-O'-Lantern Cake

SERVES 8–10

6 oz (170 g) plain flour

2½ teaspoons baking powder

pinch of salt

4 oz (115 g) butter, at room
   temperature

8 oz (225 g) sugar

3 egg yolks, at room temperature,
   well beaten

1 teaspoon grated lemon rind

6 fl oz (175 ml) milk

FOR THE CAKE COVERING

1 lb 4 oz–1 lb 8 oz (565–700 g) icing
   sugar

2 egg whites

2 tablespoons liquid glucose

orange and black food colourings

1 Preheat the oven to 375°F/190°C/
Gas 5. Line an 8 in (20 cm) round
cake tin with greaseproof paper
and grease.

2 Sift together the flour, baking
powder and salt. Set aside.

3 With an electric mixer, cream the
butter and sugar until light and fluffy.
Gradually beat in the egg yolks, then
add the lemon rind. Fold in the flour
mixture in 3 batches, alternating
with the milk.

4 Spoon the mixture into the
prepared tin. Bake until a skewer
inserted in the centre comes out
clean, about 35 minutes. Leave to
stand, then turn out on to a rack.

> **~ COOK'S TIP ~**
>
> If preferred, use ready-made
> roll-out cake covering,
> available at cake decorating
> supply shops. Knead in food
> colouring, if required.

5 For the icing, sift 1 lb 4 oz (565 g)
of the icing sugar into a bowl. Make a
well in the centre, add 1 egg white,
the glucose and orange food
colouring. Stir until a dough forms.

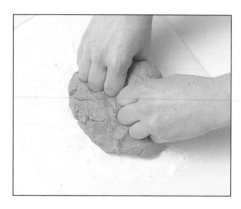

6 ▲ Transfer to a clean work
surface dusted with icing sugar and
knead briefly.

7 ▲ Carefully roll out the orange
cake covering to a thin sheet.

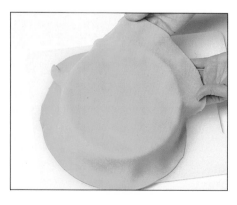

8 ▲ Place the sheet on top of the
cooled cake and smooth the sides.
Trim the excess icing and reserve.

9 ▲ From the trimmings, cut shapes
for the top. Tint the remaining cake
covering trimmings with black food
colouring. Roll out thinly and cut
shapes for the face.

10 ▲ Brush the undersides with
water and arrange the face on top of
the cake.

11 ▲ Place 1 tablespoon of the
remaining egg white in a bowl and
stir in enough icing sugar to make a
thick icing. Tint with black food
colouring, fill a paper piping bag and
complete the decoration.

Stars and Stripes Cake

SERVES 20

8 oz (225 g) butter or margarine, at
  room temperature

8 oz (225 g) dark brown sugar

8 oz (225 g) granulated sugar

5 eggs, at room temperature

10 oz (285 g) plain flour

2 teaspoons baking powder

1 teaspoon bicarbonate of soda

1 teaspoon ground cinnamon

1 teaspoon ground ginger

½ teaspoon ground allspice

¼ teaspoon ground cloves

¼ teaspoon salt

12 fl oz (350 ml) buttermilk

3 oz (85 g) raisins

FOR THE CAKE COVERING

1 oz (30 g) butter

2 lb 4 oz–2 lb 10 oz (1–1.3 kg) icing
  sugar

3 egg whites

4 tablespoons liquid glucose

red and blue food colourings

1 Preheat the oven to 350°F/180°C/
Gas 4. Line a 12 x 9 in (30 x 23 cm)
baking tin with greaseproof paper and
lightly grease.

2 With an electric mixer, cream the
butter or margarine and sugars until
light and fluffy. Gradually beat in the
eggs, 1 at a time, beating well after
each addition.

3 Sift together the flour, baking
powder, bicarbonate of soda, spices
and salt. Fold into the butter mixture
in 3 batches, alternating with the
buttermilk. Stir in the raisins.

4 Pour the mixture into the prepared
tin and bake until the cake springs
back when touched lightly, about
35 minutes. Leave to stand for
10 minutes, then turn out on to a
wire rack.

5 Make buttercream for assembling
the cake by mixing the butter with
1½ oz (45 g) of the icing sugar.

6 ▲ When the cake is cool, cut a
curved shape from the top.

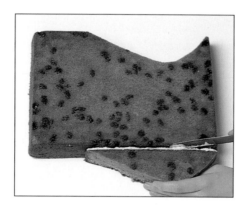

7 ▲ Attach it to the bottom of the
cake with the buttercream.

8 Prepare a board, about 16 x 12 in
(40 x 30 cm), covered in paper
suitable for contact with food, or in
foil. Transfer the cake to the board.

9 For the cake covering, sift 2 lb 4 oz
(1 kg) of the icing sugar into a bowl.
Add 2 of the egg whites and the
liquid glucose. Stir until the mixture
forms a dough.

10 Cover and set aside half of the
covering. On a clean work surface
lightly dusted with icing sugar, roll
out the remaining covering to a
sheet. Carefully transfer to the cake.
Smooth the sides and trim any excess
from the bottom edges.

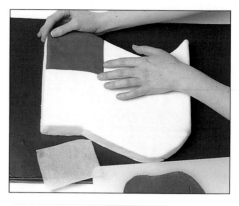

11 ▲ Tint one quarter of the
remaining covering blue and tint the
rest red. Roll out the blue to a thin
sheet and cut out the background for
the stars. Place on the cake.

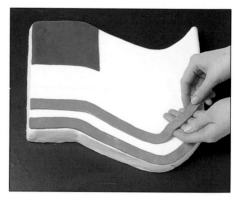

12 ▲ Roll out the red covering, cut
out stripes and place on the cake.

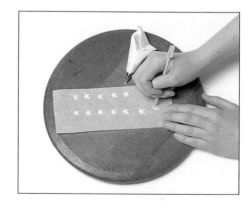

13 ▲ For the stars, mix
1 tablespoon of the egg white with
just enough icing sugar to thicken.
Pipe small stars on to a sheet of
greaseproof paper and leave to set.
When dry, peel them off and place on
the blue background.

INDEX

~